3xT

Baen Books by HARRY TURTLEDOVE

The War Between the Provinces series:
Sentry Peak
Marching Through Peachtree
Advance and Retreat

The Fox novels:
Wisdom of the Fox
Tale of the Fox

3 x T
Thessalonica
Alternate Generals, editor
Alternate Generals II, editor
Down in the Bottomlands (with L. Sprague de Camp)

3 X T

HARRY TURTLEDOVE

WEST BEND LIBRARY

3 x T

This is a work of fiction. All the characters and events portrayed in this book are fictional, and any resemblance to real people or incidents is purely coincidental.

Noninterference copyright © 1985, 1986, 1987; *Kaleidoscope* copyright © 1984, 1985, 1986, 1987, 1988, 1990; *Earthgrip*, copyright © 1987, 1989, 1991; all by Harry Turtledove.

All rights reserved, including the right to reproduce this book or portions thereof in any form.

A Baen Books Megabook

Baen Publishing Enterprises
P.O. Box 1403
Riverdale, NY 10471
www.baen.com

ISBN: 0-7434-8835-0

Cover art by Kurt Miller

First printing, July 2004

Library of Congress Cataloging-in-Publication Data

Turtledove, Harry.
3 x T / by Harry Turtledove.
p. cm.
ISBN 0-7434-8835-0 (hc)
1. Science fiction, American. 2. Life on other planets--Fiction. 3. Human-alien encounters--Fiction. 4. Space flight--Fiction. I. Title: Three times T. II. Turtledove, Harry. Earthgrip. III. Turtledove, Harry. Noninterference. IV. Turtledove, Harry. Kaleidoscope. V. Title: Earthgrip. VI. Title: Noninterference. VII. Title: Kaleidoscope. VIII. Title.

PS3570.U76A6123 2004
813′.54--dc22

2004007044

Distributed by Simon & Schuster
1230 Avenue of the Americas
New York, NY 10020

Production by Windhaven Press, Auburn, NH
Typeset by Bell Road Press, Sherwood, OR
Printed in the United States of America

10 9 8 7 6 5 4 3 2 1

CONTENTS

Noninterference 1

Kaleidoscope:
And So to Bed 203
Bluff 219
A Difficult Undertaking 247
The Weather's Fine 269
Crybaby 283
Hindsight 301
Gentlemen of the Shade 333
The Boring Beast *(with Kevin R. Sandes)* *363*
The Road Not Taken 377
The Castle of the Sparrowhawk 401
The Summer Garden 411
The Last Article 421
The Girl Who Took Lessons 453

Earthgrip 459

Noninterference

For the people who helped me make it
happen and make it better:
Stan and Russ and Owen and Shelly
and Shelley and Tina

FEDERACY
STANDARD
YEAR 1186

I

Sun, stench, racket: market day at Helmand.

The sun was a G-0 star, not much different from Sol. Asked to generate a name for it, the computer called it Bilbeis. It blazed from the blue cloisonne dome of the sky. Beyond the Margush river and the canals that drew its waters for the croplands of Helmand and the other river valley towns, the land was a desert, baked brown and bare.

The stench went with city life. The twelve or fifteen thousand inhabitants of Helmand had no better notion of sanitation than throwing their rubbish, chamber pots and all, into the narrow, winding streets. After a few years, the floors of their dwellings would be thirty or forty centimeters below street level. Then it was time to knock down the whole house and build a new mud-brick structure on the rubble. Helmand perched on a hill of its own making, a good fifteen meters above the Margush.

As for the racket, expect nothing else when large numbers of people gather to trade, as the folk of Helmand did once a nineday. And they *were* people. Only by such details as hair and skin color, beard pattern, and shape of features could they be told at a glance from Terrans. There were more subtle internal differences, but David Ware and Julian Crouzet had no trouble passing as foreigners from a distant land.

The two Survey Service anthropologists strolled through the marketplace. They paused gratefully in the long shadow of a temple for the time it took to drink a cup of thin, sour wine.

In their boots, denim coveralls, and caps, they attracted some attention from the people swarming around them, but not much. The city dwellers were already typical urban sophisticates, though

Helmand and the other towns of the Margush valley represented the first civilization on Bilbeis IV.

Most of the stares came from peasants, in from the fields with produce or livestock to trade for the things they could not make themselves. Here a farmer weighed out grain to pay for a new bronze sickle blade, there another quarreled with a potter over how much dried fruit he would have to give for a large storage jar. The latter man finally threw up his arms in disgust and stomped off to find a better deal.

David Ware had been taping the argument with a camera set in a heavy silver ring. "You think that one's unhappy," Crouzet murmured, "look at the trader over there."

The fellow at whom he nodded was from the Raidan foothills west of the Margush. He let his gray-green mustachios grow barbarously long and wore a knee-length tunic of gaudy green and saffron stripes. "You try to cheat me, you son of a pimp!" he shouted in nasally accented Helmandi, shaking his fist at the fat stonecutter who sat cross-legged in front of his stall.

"I do not," the stonecutter said calmly. "Seventy *diktats* of grain is all your obsidian is worth—more than you would get from some."

The hillman was frantic with frustration. "You lie! See here—I have three beastloads of prime stone. In my grandfather's day, my animals would have killed themselves hauling back to my village the grain that stone brought. Seventy *diktats*—faugh! I could carry that myself."

"In your grandfather's day, we would have used the obsidian for sickles and scythes at harvest time, and for edging war swords. Bronze was hard to come by then, and even dearer than stone. Now that we have plenty, we find it more useful. So what good is your obsidian? Oh, I can make some of it into trinkets, I suppose, but it is no precious stone like turquoise or emerald. The jewelry would be cheap and move slowly."

Ware turned away with a half-amused, half-cynical snort. "Even in a Bronze Age society, changing technology throws people out of work."

"That's true at any level of culture," Crouzet said. "I will admit, though, the pace has picked up in Helmand under Queen Sabium."

"I should say so." Ware's craggy face, normally rather dour, was lit now with enthusiasm. "She's one in a million."

His companion nodded. As if summoned by the mention of their ruler, a platoon of musicians marched into the square down the one real thoroughfare Helmand boasted: the road from the palace. They raised seashell trumpets to their lips and blew a discordant blast. The two Terrans winced. The market-day hubbub died away.

"Bow your heads!" a herald cried. "Forth comes Sabium, vicegerent of Illil the goddess of the moons and queen of Helmand." Actually, the word the herald used literally meant "lady king"; Helmandi had no exact equivalent for "queen," as Sabium was the only female ruler the town had ever known.

Fifteen years before, she had been principal wife of the last king. When he died, his firstborn son was a babe in arms, and Sabium administered affairs as regent. The town prospered as never before under her leadership. A few years later, the child-king died, too. Sabium ruled on, now in her own right, and did so well that no one thought to challenge her.

"I wonder what brings her out," Crouzet said, his eyes on the dirt. "She's missed the last couple of market days."

Ware nodded. "I didn't think she looked well, either, when she was here."

The royal bodyguard preceded the queen into the square. The troopers carried bronze-headed spears and maces with wicked spikes. They used their big leather shields to push people out of the way and clear a path to the raised brick platform in the center of the marketplace.

A retinue of Helmand's nobles followed. The hems of their long woolen robes dragged in the dust; their wide sleeves flapped languidly as they walked. Not for them the bright colors that delighted the semisavage obsidian seller: like the bodyguards and most Helmandis, they preferred white or sober shades of brown, gray, and blue. But gold and silver gleamed on their arms, around their necks, and in ear and nose rings.

A sedan chair borne by twelve husky servants brought up the rear of the procession. David Ware whistled softly when he saw it from the corner of his eye. "I'll bet she is sick, then!" he exclaimed. "She always walked here before."

"We'll know soon enough," Crouzet said calmly. He was a big moon-faced man; his phlegmatic nature made him a good foil for Ware, who sometimes went off half-cocked.

Skillfully keeping the sedan chair level, the porters carried it to the top of the platform, set it down, and scurried down the stairs. The white-robed priest of Illil who had accompanied them stayed behind. The shell-trumpets blared again. The priest drew back the silk curtain that screened the interior of the sedan chair from view.

"Behold the queen!" the herald shouted.

The crowd in the marketplace raised their heads. Ware lifted his arm as if to scratch, so he could record Sabium's emergence.

When he saw her, he tried to suppress his involuntary gasp of surprise and dismay but could not. It hardly mattered. The same sound came from Crouzet beside him and from the throats of everyone close enough to Sabium to see how ill she truly was.

A month before, Ware thought, she had been a handsome woman, even without making allowances for the differences between Terran and Helmandi standards of good looks. Her grayish-pink skin, light blue hair that receded at the temples, and downy cheeks seemed no more strange, after one was used to them, than Crouzet's blackness or his own knobby-kneed, gangly build. Even the false mustache she wore to appear more fully a king somehow lent her face dignity instead of making her ridiculous.

Her strength of character was responsible for that, of course. It shone through her violet eyes like sun through stained glass, animating her aquiline features. One could hear it in her clear contralto, see it in the brisk pace with which her stocky body moved. No wonder the whole city loved her.

Now she got out of the sedan chair with infinite care, as if every motion hurt. She had to lean on the priest's arm for a moment. Her body seemed shrunken within the heavy, elaborately fringed robe of state, shot all through with golden thread. She held the royal crown—a massy silver circlet encrusted with river pearls and other stones that glowed softly, like moonlight—in her hands instead of wearing it. Her face was more gray than pink.

"My God, she's dying!" Ware blurted.

"Yes, and heaven help Helmand after she goes," Crouzet agreed. The one thing Sabium had not done was provide for a successor. Probably, Ware thought, she was too proud to admit to herself that her body had betrayed her.

She could still force it to obey her for a time, though, and she carried on with the ceremony as if nothing were wrong. Her voice rang through the square: "Shumukin, son of Galzu, ascend to join me!"

A small, lithe man climbed the steps and went on his knees in front of the queen. Sabium declared, "For the beauty of your new hymn to Illil, I reward you with half a *diktat* of refined gold and the title of *ludlul*." The rank was of the lesser nobility; Shumukin went down on his belly in gratitude. The trumpeters at the edge of the square struck up a new tune, presumably Shumukin's hymn. The crowd applauded. Shumukin rose, smiling shyly, and stepped to one side.

There was a visible pause while Sabium gathered herself. The priest spoke to her, too softly for the Terrans to hear. She waved him aside and called out, "M'gishen, son of Nadin, ascend and join me!"

This time the Helmandi was old and stout. He leaned on a stick going up the stairs. The priest held the cane as he clumsily got to his knees. Sabium said, "For sharing with all of Helmand what you have learned, I reward you with three *diktats* of refined gold and the rank of *shaushludlul.*" That was a higher title than the one Shumukin had earned. M'gishen prostrated himself before the queen.

Sabium bent to bid him rise and could not hide a wince of pain. "Tell the people of what you found."

Shifting from foot to foot like a nervous schoolboy, M'gishen obeyed. His thin, reedy voice did not carry well. He had to start over two or three times before the calls of "Louder!" stopped coming from the back of the marketplace.

"Everybody knows what a taper is, of course," he said. "You take a wick and dip it in hot tallow. Well, if you dip it again and again and again, more and more tallow clings, y' see. When you light it then, it gives off a real glow like an oil lamp, not just a tiny little flame. Lasts as long as a lamp, too, maybe longer. Eh, well, that's what my new thing is." He reclaimed his stick and limped down the steps.

"Rewards await anyone who learns something new and useful and passes on his knowledge or who shows himself a worthy poet or sculptor or painter," Sabium said. "I set aside the first morning of every nineday to judge such things, and hope to see many of you then."

"Amazingly sophisticated attitude to find in such a primitive society," Crouzet remarked.

"I'm sorry, what was that?" David Ware had been watching the priest of Illil help Sabium back into the sedan chair. The process was slow and agonizing; he saw her bite down hard on her lower lip to distract herself from the other, greater torment. It was a relief when the silk draperies gave her back her privacy.

Crouzet repeated himself. "Oh, yes, absolutely," Ware agreed. "For this sort of culture it's better than a patent system; the bureaucracy to run anything like that won't exist here for hundreds of years. But the up-front reward encourages people to put ideas into the public domain instead of hanging on to them as family secrets."

"To say nothing of spurring invention." Crouzet's eyes followed the servitors bearing Sabium back to the palace. "What do you think the odds are of whoever comes after her keeping up what she's started?"

Ware laughed without humor. "What's the old saying? Two chances—slim and none."

"I'm afraid you're right. Sometimes the rule of noninterference is a shame." Survey Service personnel on worlds without spaceflight were observers only, doing nothing to meddle in local affairs.

When Ware did not reply at once, Crouzet turned to look at him. His colleague's face was a mask of furious concentration. Crouzet was no telepath, but he did not need to be to know what the other Terran was thinking. Alarm replaced the black man's usual amused detachment. "For God's sake, David! There's never justification for breaking the noninterference rule!"

"The hell there isn't," David Ware said.

Lucrezia Spini played the tape of Queen Sabium in the marketplace for the fourth time. "Yes, it might be a malignancy," the biologist said. "If I had to make a guess just from seeing this and from the speed of the illness's advance, I'd say it could well be. But making a real diagnosis on this kind of evidence is pure guesswork. There are so many ways to fall sick, and on a world like this we'll only learn a tiny fraction of them."

"What can you do to pin it down more closely?" Ware asked. A flier had brought him and Crouzet back to the *Leeuwenhoek* the night before. They had summoned the machine to a field several kilometers outside Helmand. It was silent; the local fear of demons who dwelt in darkness made the chance of being observed vanishingly small. The *Leeuwenhoek* itself had landed in the northern desert, safe from detection.

Spini rubbed her chin as she thought; had she been a man, she would have been the type to grow a beard for the sake of plucking at it. At last she said, "I suppose I could sneak a small infrared sensor onto the roof of the queen's bedchamber and do a body scan. If there are tumors, they'll show up warmer than the surrounding normal body areas."

"Would you?" Ware tried to hold the eagerness from his voice. He had kept quiet about his gut reaction back in the marketplace.

If Sabium was suffering from some exotic local disease, she would die, and that was all there was to it. If, on the other hand, she had cancer . . . Time enough to worry about that when he knew.

"Why not? Either way, I'll learn something." When the anthropologist kept hovering over her, she laughed at him. "I don't have the answers yet, you know. I have to program the sensor, camouflage it, and send it out. Come back in three days and I may be able to give you something."

Ware had plenty to keep him busy while he waited but could not help fretting. What if Sabium died while they were investigating? She had seemed so feeble. Ware also noticed Julian Crouzet giving him suspicious looks every so often. He pretended not to.

When the appointed day came, he fairly pounced on Lucrezia Spini, barking, "Well?"

She put a hand on his arm. "Easy, David, easy. Anyone would think you were in love with her."

He blinked. That had not occurred to him. He was honest enough with himself to take a long look at the idea. After a few seconds he said, "You know, I might be, if she came from a civilization comparable to ours. As is, I admire her tremendously. She's kindly but firm enough to rule, she boosts this culture in ways it couldn't expect for centuries yet, she's three times as smart as any of the local kings—and she carries on like a trouper in spite of what she's got. Whatever it is, she deserves better."

"No need to preach. I'm convinced." Spini laughed, but Ware could tell his earnestness had impressed her. She fed a cassette into the monitor in front of her. "This will interest you."

The screen lit in an abstract pattern of greens, blues, reds, and yellows: an infrared portrait of Sabium's boudoir. "Ignore these," Spini said, pointing to several brilliant spots of light. "They're lamps, so of course they show up brightly. Here, now—"

Yes, the pattern at the bottom might have been a reclining figure. "Lucky the Helmandis sleep nude," the biologist remarked. "In this climate it's no wonder, I suppose. Clothes would have confused the picture, though. Look here, and here, and especially here—" Her finger moved to one area after another that glowed yellow or even orange. "Hot spots."

"That's her belly?" Ware asked harshly.

Spini nodded. "Full of tumor. A classical diagnosis. Too bad, if what you say about her is true. If she were a Terran, I wouldn't give her more than another month, tops, with that much metastatic cancer in there."

"Just how different biologically are the locals, Lucrezia?" Ware hoped he sounded casual.

He must have, for she answered readily. "Not very. When you were in Helmand, you ate the food, drank the beer. Some of the desert herbs here synthesize chemicals that look promising as pharmaceuticals."

"How interesting," the anthropologist said.

"No," Senior Coordinator Chunder Sen said flatly. With his round brown face and fringe of white hair, he usually reminded David Ware of a kindly grandfather. Now he sounded downright stern—something Ware would not have imagined possible—as he declared, "The rule of noninterference must be inviolable."

Heads nodded in agreement all around the table in the *Leeuwenhoek*'s mess, which doubled as the assembly chamber. It was the only compartment that could hold the ship's twenty-person complement at once. Julian Crouzet had taken pains to sit as far from Ware as he could, as if to avoid any association with what his colleague was proposing.

"So this is what you were leading up to," Lucrezia Spini exclaimed. It sounded like an accusation.

The anthropologist nodded impatiently. "Of course it is. We ought to cure Queen Sabium, as I said when I asked for this meeting. It could be done, couldn't it?"

"Technically speaking, I don't see why not. I already told you that the natives' metabolism isn't much different from ours. With the interferons and other immunological amplifiers we have, we could stimulate her body to throw off the malignancy. But I don't think we should. Noninterference has been Federacy policy from the word go, and rightly. Where would we be if more advanced races had tinkered with Terra when we were just a single primitive world?"

"Maybe better off; who knows?" Ware saw at once he had been too flip. He backed off. "What's the reasoning behind the rule of noninterference, anyway?"

"Oh, really now, David," Jemala Gürsel snorted. The meteorologist went on: "There's no point to treating us like so many children. Everyone knows that." She shook a finger at Ware in annoyance.

"Let's get it out in the open and look at it," he persisted.

"Very well." That was Chunder Sen, sounding resigned. As a bureaucrat, he was vulnerable to proper procedure. "Julian, do the honors, will you?"

"Gladly," the other anthropologist said, "since a chance comment of mine seems to have touched David off in the first place. There are many sound reasons behind noninterference, but the most telling one is the one Lucrezia gave—less advanced cultures deserve to develop in their own ways. We have no right to meddle with them."

"That's exactly what I thought you'd say," Ware told him, "and it sounds very noble, but it doesn't bear much relation to reality. Truth is, we interfere every time we come into contact with a local."

"Nonsense!" Crouzet snapped, and that was one of the milder reactions. Coordinator Chunder Sen, a devout Hindu, could not have looked more pained if he had suddenly discovered he'd been eating beef the last six weeks.

Ware did not mind. He felt filled with a sudden crazy confidence, like a gambler who knows the next card will make his straight, the next roll will be a seven. "It isn't nonsense," he insisted. "The physicists have known for a couple of thousand years that the act of observation affects what's being observed."

"Don't throw old Heisenberg at us out of context," said Moshe Sharett, the chief engineer. "He's only relevant at the atomic level. For large-scale phenomena, the observer effect is negligible."

"Who says Helmand's a large-scale phenomenon? Fifteen thousand people or so strikes me as being awfully different from the sextillions of atoms chemists and physicists play with."

Sharett scratched at an ear. Several other people frowned thoughtfully. Julian Crouzet, though, said, "I defy you to show me how walking through the streets of Helmand could twist the culture out of shape."

"Even that might. Suppose we bumped into someone and made him late for an important meeting, so a decision was taken that he would have changed if he'd been there. But walking about isn't all we do, you know. Remember that scrawny vendor we bought wine from? The grain we gave him could well have kept him and his whole family from starving. We might have changed a thousand years of bloodlines if a child that would have died grows up to breed."

"Oh, come now," Courzet said. "If we hadn't bought from him, someone else would."

"Would they? Not many people did, or his ribs wouldn't have shown so clearly. Julian, I'm afraid we did him a good turn, whether we wanted to or not. Let's give ourselves up."

Crouzet threw his hands in the air. "Spare me your sarcasm.

What if we did? It's a long way from going in and healing Queen Sabium."

"Of course it is," Ware said at once, "but the difference is one of degree, not of kind—that's the point I'm trying to make. It's interference either way. For once, let it have a purpose. Here; I'm going to show two tapes and then I'm done."

He walked over to the big vision screen that took up most of one wall. The first tape was the one he and Crouzet had made of Sabium in the marketplace. "Give us a running translation for those who don't know Helmandi, will you, Jorge?" he said. "You're smoother than I am."

Jorge Morales, the ship's linguist, was a self-important little man. He jumped a bit but did as Ware asked him. The anthropologist nodded to himself. After two minutes of translating, Morales would think any attack on the tape was an attack on him personally.

But there were no attacks. Sabium's courage impressed the company of the *Leeuwenhoek* even more than her wisdom. In the dead silence that filled the mess hall, Ware inserted the other tape. "This has two parts," he said. "The first one is from a spy camera I had planted in the palace bedroom the other day."

Seen from above, attendants bustled around Sabium. One offered food and drink, most of which she declined. Others helped her take off the stifling royal robes; she accepted that attention with relief, as she did the cloth soaked in cool water that a serving maid pressed to her forehead.

Some of the water ran down her face and got into her false mustaches, which began to come off. She said something that made her attendants laugh. "What was that?" Moshe Sharett asked.

"Something to the effect that that was one thing her husband hadn't had to put up with," Morales replied. Several of the people watching the screen grinned; not all of them were those Ware expected to back him.

After a while the servants bowed their way out, leaving Sabium alone in the chamber, a small, tired woman wearing only a thin shift that covered her to midthigh. Much of the flesh had melted from her legs and arms, but the fabric of the shift stretched tight across her swollen belly, as if she were pregnant.

If she had not known how ill she was that day in the marketplace, she did now. She pressed herself here and there and flinched more than once in the self-examination. When she was done, she shrugged and spoke, though she did not think anyone was there to hear her. This time, Ware did the translating himself: "'Another day gone. Now to do the best I can with the ones I have left.'"

Sabium rose, stripped off the shift with an involuntary grunt of pain, and blew out the lamps. The leather thongs supporting the mattress creaked as the bedchamber went dark.

The second piece of tape was the infrared sequence Lucrezia Spini had taken: a death sentence in bright, cheerful false colors.

"Which is the greater distortion?" Ware asked softly. "To let such a queen as that die before her time, knowing that nothing she had worked for would survive her, or for her to live out her natural span? That's the choice before us now." He sat down.

Had Coordinator Chunder Sen been a military man instead of an administrator, he would never have let it come to a vote. But he was confident of the outcome. The rule of interference was as much an article of faith to him as his belief in Brahma, Shiva, and Vishnu. He could not imagine anyone else having a different opinion.

To his amazement, he lost, twelve votes to eight.

Ware turned curiously to Julian Crouzet as they walked through the streets of Helmand toward the palace. "Just why are you coming along if you disagree so strongly with what I'm doing?"

"Frankly, to keep an eye on you."

"I'm not going to give Sabium the secret of the stardrive, Julian. For one thing, I don't know it myself."

"Thank God for small favors."

Ware glared at him but let it go; they were coming up to the entrance of the palace.

The arched doorway was twice the height of a man. Most of the palace was built of the same sun-dried mud brick as the rest of Helmand, but in the wall that held the doorway expensive fired bricks had been used lavishly for show. Their fronts were enameled in bright colors, like giant mosaic tesserae. Here a predator was shown leaping on a herd animal, there a hunter's arrow brought down a flying creature. The entrance itself was flanked by a pair of apotropaic gods.

A steward—a low-ranking one, from his unadorned robe and plain white conical hat—approached the two Terrans, asking, "What do you foreigners wish?"

With Crouzet standing by in silent disapproval, Ware launched into the cover story that had been hammered out aboard the *Leeuwenhoek*: "As you can see, we are from a far country. We have done well for ourselves here in Helmand, and we would like to give your splendid city a gift in return. Forgive me if I speak now of intimate matters, but is it not true that your queen is unwell?"

The steward's eyes narrowed. "What if it is?"

"We saw her on her last trip to the marketplace, I and my friend," Ware said, including Crouzet whether he liked it or not. "If her illness is as it appears, it is one for which our people have a cure."

"As what charlatan does not?" the steward said scornfully. "And for your so-called cure, no doubt, you will want all the silver and half the grain in the city—payable in advance."

The Helmandis were very human indeed, Ware thought. He said, "No, it is a gift, as I told you. We will heal your queen if we can, and ask nothing for it. Indeed, we will refuse whatever you may offer."

The toplofty steward clearly was taken aback. "Come with me," he said after a few seconds, and led the Terrans into the palace. Away from the entrance, only torches lit the rush-strewn narrow halls, which smelled of burning fat, stale sweat, and ordure.

Several functionaries, each more important than the one before, grilled the anthropologists. The last barrier before Sabium was the priest of Illil who had helped her on the platform. "Do you swear by all your gods that your remedy will cure?" he demanded.

"No," Ware said at once. The natives' metabolism was almost identical to Terrans', but not quite—and there were always individual idiosyncrasies. "If it fails, it will not harm her," he added.

"Well, what is there to lose?" the priest muttered under his breath. Ware did not think he was supposed to hear. Then the local did speak directly to him. "Stay here. I shall take your words to the queen, to let her decide." Spearmen stood aside to let the priest pass but never stopped watching the Terrans.

The wait could not have been more than ten minutes, but it stretched till it seemed like hours. At last the priest of Illil returned. "This way," he said brusquely. Ware gave a sigh of relief and followed, Crouzet at his side.

Something small and nasty buzzed down onto Ware's neck, bit him, and flew away before he could swat it. Lucrezia Spini said the local pests weren't exactly insects. Close enough for government work, though, Ware thought, rubbing.

Braziers of incense smoked in the small chamber where Sabium received the Terrans, but the sweet, resinous smoke could not quite cover the sickroom odor of the place. The queen reclined on a low couch with a headrest; a rug embroidered with river flowers covered her legs. The walls of the chamber were whitewashed to help reflect torchlight.

Sabium had grown even thinner, Ware thought as he and Crouzet went on their knees before her. Only her eyes, smudged below with great dark circles, showed life. They glowed, enormous, in a face now skeletally lean.

"Rise," Sabium said. She studied the Terrans with an interest still undimmed by illness, commenting, "I remember noticing the two of you in the marketplace once or twice. What distant land do you come from that grows men of your colors?"

"It is near the great western ocean, Your Majesty," Ware replied. The Helmandis knew nothing about that part of the continent.

Sabium asked more questions; a scribe took down the answers the anthropologists gave. Only when a spasm of pain wracked her so that her hands twisted and her lips went white beneath her false mustache did she say, "Tupsharru"—she nodded toward the priest of Illil—"tells me your city is skilled in medicine." For all the emotion that showed in her voice, she might have been speaking of the weather.

"Yes, Your Majesty," Ware said eagerly. He drew a stout syringe from the pouch he wore on his belt. He showed her the point, warning, "I will have to prick your arm to give you the medicine. It may hurt you some."

She astonished him by laughing. "What is the sting of a needle against the beast of fire in my middle? Come forward, and fear not; if I were to harm the physicians who failed to cure me, none would be left in Helmand."

She did not flinch when he made the injection, and held her arm motionless until the entire dose had been administered. As she watched the medicine enter her, he could see her grasping the principle of the syringe. "Ah, the needle is hollow, like the sting of the *gurash,*" she murmured. "That idea might prove valuable in other ways as well."

Ware could feel the weight of Crouzet's sardonic glance on his back but did not turn around.

"That's all?" Sabium asked when he put away the hypodermic. He knew what was puzzling her: in Helmand, witchcraft and medicine were hard to tell apart, and drugs and elaborate charms went hand in hand.

He shrugged. "Yes, Your Majesty. To us, that our remedies work is more important than the spectacle involved in using them." She dipped her head thoughtfully, then returned to her questions about the Terrans' fictive homeland.

Before long, yawns began punctuating the interrogation. Lucrezia Spini had warned that drowsiness was a common side effect of the drugs, and so Ware was more encouraged than not to see Sabium sleepy—it was a first sign she was reacting as Terrans did. Tupsharru, though, started up in alarm when his queen dozed off in the middle of a sentence.

The priest searched Ware with his eyes as the anthropologist explained that there was no danger. "Then no doubt you will not object to staying here in the palace until Her Majesty returns to herself," Tupsharru said coldly.

"No doubt," Ware replied, and hoped he meant it.

Although it only had a slit window and was therefore very stuffy, the room in which the Terrans were confined was well appointed, and their evening meal fit for a noble: bread, salt fish, boiled leguminous plants, candied fruit, and a wine hardly less sweet. The squad of soldiers outside the barred door, however, did nothing to improve the appetite.

Most of a day went by before the door opened again; Crouzet beat Ware out of a week's pay at dice. They were still crouched over the plastic cubes when Tupsharru burst into the chamber, half a dozen spearmen at his back.

Ware grabbed for the stunner by his belt pouch, but there was no need. The priest of Illil went to one knee before him, as if in salute to a great lord. "She wakes without torment, for the first time in the gods know how many ninedays!" he said exultantly. "And she is hungry, as she has not been for even longer!"

"Well, David, you seem to have pulled it off," Julian Crouzet said, his voice sober. "I hope you're pleased."

Ware hardly heard him; he was too busy trying to be polite declining the gifts Tupsharru wanted to shower on him. At last he did take a couple of fine small bronzes, one a statuette of Illil with a moon in either hand, the other a portrait bust of Sabium that managed to capture something of her character in spite of being almost as rigidly formulaic as the image of the god.

"It would have been out of character for traders to turn down everything," he told Crouzet a little defensively as the two Terrans made their way back to the city gate. They had had to argue Tupsharru out of an honor guard.

"No doubt you're right," Crouzet said, and lapsed back into silence.

"You still think I was wrong, don't you?"

"Yes," Crouzet answered promptly. Ware thought he was going to leave it at that, but he went on with a sigh, "For better or worse, it's over, and there's nothing I can do about it anymore. Maybe it will all turn out for the best in the long run; who knows?"

"Julian, listen to me: in the long run, it won't matter at all. No matter what we say, noninterference just isn't that important on a preindustrial world, except as a policy to prevent exploitation. The same discoveries always get made, if not now, then in a few centuries."

"That's not what you were claiming back at the ship," Crouzet remarked.

"You're right, but I wouldn't have got anywhere taking that tack. Think about it, though. By the time the next survey ship comes to Bilbeis IV, in fifteen hundred years or so, who'll remember anything about Queen Sabium? The crew will, sure, because they'll have copies of the tapes we made here, but what about the locals? Maybe a priest or two will know of her name, if the Margush valley civilization survives—maybe not, too. So what, either way?"

Crouzet looked him in the eye. "You, my friend, are talking through your hat. What's more, you know it. You don't have the slightest idea what the effect of this interference is going to be, any more than anyone else does."

"Don't I?" Ware snapped. He sounded very tired. "Whatever it is, it won't be much. This society is as tradition-bound as any other early civilization. If Sabium gets too far out in front of her people, they won't follow her any more, and that'll be that. Or the priests will say her changes offend the gods, and overthrow her. That'll solve your problem, too. You tell me, damn it—am I right or not?"

Crouzet considered. "Maybe," was all he would let himself say.

To Ware, it was like a concession. "There, you see? What I set out to do was to save a good woman from a lot of anguish and a nasty death, and that's what I did—that's *all* I did. Where's the evil in it? That's what I want to know."

They walked on a while in silence, but it was not an angry silence anymore. Then Crouzet sadly said, "Oh, David, David, David," and put his arm around the other anthropologist's shoulder. "Justify it any way you like. When we get home, the review board will crucify you all the same, not least for playing on everyone's emotions so shamelessly."

"Let them," Ware said. "For my money, it's worth it." The walls of Helmand loomed ahead, close now. He began to whistle.

"You'll think I was [illegible]."

[illegible]

[illegible] when [illegible] in the [illegible]. No matter what [illegible] a [illegible] as [illegible].

"Don't care what you [illegible] back of the [illegible]."

[illegible] hundred years or so [illegible] about Queen [illegible]. The new will [illegible] [illegible].

[illegible] more than anyone else does.

[illegible]

[illegible] was like a [illegible] what I want to know."

[illegible]

[illegible]

FEDERACY STANDARD YEAR 2686

II

Bilbeis IV hung in the stereo tank: a blue globe, streaked with the white and gray of clouds. Like any terrestrial world seen from space, it was heart-stoppingly beautiful. The crew of the Survey Service ship *Jêng Ho* eyed it with the same affection they would have given a nest of scorpions at a picnic grounds.

"Why did it have to be us?" Atanasio Pedroza said to no one in particular. In spite of his name, the biologist was big and blond; long ago, his home planet had been settled by Guatemalans and by Afrikaner refugees fleeing the fall of South Africa.

"There's a technical term for the reason," Magda Kodaly said. Despite the anthropologist's cynical turn of mind, Pedroza looked at her expectantly. "It's called the short straw," she amplified.

"Oh, come now," Irfan Kawar said. His specialty was geology, so he was able to take a more dispassionate view of Bilbeis IV. "Odds are, David Ware's interference made no difference at all in the planet's cultural development, just as he said it wouldn't."

"Interference?" Magda snorted. Her green eyes glinted dangerously. "There's a technical term for that, too: fuckup, I think it is. Ware got less than he deserved, if you ask me." The Survey Service had cashiered David Ware, of course, as soon as Central learned what he had done. Now every new class of recruits had his folly drilled into it as the worst of bad examples.

Magda rose from her chair and stretched, deliberately turning her back on the image of Bilbeis IV. She was conscious of Pedroza's eyes following her, and suppressed a sigh. The *Jêng Ho* was cramped enough to make politeness essential, but he wanted her and she did not want him.

Maybe, she thought hopefully, he would be too busy to pester her anymore once they landed.

Hideko Narahara punched a button. The engineering officer said, "Observation satellites away,"

"Good," Kawar said. "I for one won't be sorry to have new data to work with."

"How much can a planet change in fifteen hundred years?" Pedroza asked rhetorically.

Kawar answered him. "A good deal. For one thing, there was a fair amount of glaciation when the last survey ship was here. They didn't stay long enough to find whether the ice was advancing or retreating. The answer will mean something to your biology, Atanasio, and also to Magda's area: changes in climate and sea level have to affect the locals' culture."

"I suppose so." Pedroza did not sound as though he meant it. He really wanted to believe every discipline had its own cubby-hole and operated in isolation from all the others. That struck Magda as intellectual apartheid; it was one reason she did not find the biologist appealing in spite of his blond good looks.

She started out of the control room. "Where are you going?" Pedroza asked. "Would you care for company?"

"No, thank you, Atanasio," she said, swallowing that sigh again. "I'm heading north back to my cabin to review Margushi irregular verbs."

Pedroza's clear, fair skin showed his flush. All he said, though, was, "It seems a waste of time, when odds are no one speaks the language anymore."

"They may still write it," she said, "or use tongues descended from it. Anyway, until we have some fresh information, it's the best I can do." She left quickly, before he came up with a different suggestion.

Magda was glad she liked working with Irfan Kawar. Over the next several days, she and the geologist from New Palestine spent a lot of time together, using the satellite photos to remap Bilbeis IV.

He made another comparison between the old coastline and the new. "Not much change, I'm afraid," he said, running his hand over the balding crown of his head. He smiled. "One always hopes for drama."

"Of course, if you want anyone to read your data card."

He cocked an eyebrow at her. "This once, I think you would be just as happy with obscurity."

"Between you and me, I won't say you're wrong."

"Be careful, my dear. Such sentiments could get you burned at the stake in the quad of any university in the Federacy."

Magda snorted. "God deliver me from that kind of academic. I delivered myself, by getting into fieldwork as fast as I could once I had my degree."

She bent over the photomosaic map of Bilbeis IV's main continent. The settlement pattern was peculiar. Not surprisingly, the Margush valley was still the most densely populated area. Several other river systems also had good-sized cities, which they hadn't before. And it was reasonable for towns to have arisen along the eastern coast, where only a narrow sea separated the main continent from a lesser neighbor.

But the western coastline also boasted some large towns. That was strange. High, rugged mountains separated it from the rest of the continent, and the ocean to the west stretched for several thousand empty kilometers. The data they had showed no minerals to draw settlers.

"Puzzling." Magda must have said that aloud, for Irfan Kawar gave a questioning grunt. She explained.

"Maybe it is an independent civilization," the geologist suggested.

Magda brushed auburn curls back from her face. "I hope so. Comparing it to the one that diffused out of the Margush would tell us a lot." She scribbled a note to herself. "I have to talk to Hideko. I need high-resolution photos of a western town to compare to some east of the mountains."

"I hate interrupting the mapping program I've set up," the engineering officer said when Magda called, "but I'll see what I can do." Coming from Hideko, that was better than Pedroza's solemn vow of aid.

All the same, the picture series was not done till late afternoon, ship's time. Magda popped a shot of a west-coast town, one from the Margush valley, and one from another valley into a viewer.

She whistled softly. That all three cities were built around large central squares was not surprising. The neat grid pattern of the surrounding streets was. And it was stretching the odds to find the same sort of hexagonal building in a prominent place in each square.

"Coincidence?" Pedroza asked in the galley when she mentioned what she'd found.

"Anything is possible," Magda shrugged, "but that's not very likely. Six-sided buildings aren't common anywhere. It's easier to imagine, say, a common cult than to think them separate developments. The other parts of the towns seem similar, too, and they shouldn't. What would attract people from the Margush valley culture out to that godforsaken coast?"

"Special timber, maybe, or some kind of fur or flavoring or drug?" Pedroza was not a fool—unfortunately, Magda thought. He would have been easier to dislike if he was. The suggestions were all plausible.

She gestured in frustration. "I wish there were more variation."

"Variety is the life of spice," Pedroza agreed with a look that was not quite a leer, and Magda decided he was not so hard to dislike after all.

Her distaste plainly showed. There were several seconds of uncomfortable silence before Norma Anderssen said, "We'll find all the variety we need, I'm sure, when we land." The linguist was pretty, fair as Pedroza, and even-tempered enough to put up with his machismo. Why hadn't he settled on her to bother? Magda thought unhappily.

She supposed that would have been too easy. Sighing, she took a long pull at the vodka and soda in front of her. It did not help much.

After a good deal of wrangling, the *Jêng Ho* made planetfall west of the mountain chain. To Magda's surprise—and to her annoyance—the person who agreed most vociferously with her was Pedroza. She was eager to investigate those anomalous western cities, he to see how much difference there was between the plants and animals east and west of the range.

Norma, on the other hand, complained. "So far from the site of the last survey, any linguistic work I do is going to be worthless."

Irfan Kawar echoed her. "The most detailed information I have is on the Margush valley and the desert to the north. I could really get a good picture of how they've changed over time—and here we are, six thousand kilometers away. Not that new data aren't welcome, you understand, but comparing new and old would yield more."

"I expect we'll get to the Margush eventually—" Magda began.

"Meanwhile, though, half the research staff might as well be twiddling their thumbs, for all they'll accomplish," Norma said. That she interrupted proved how upset she was.

"I don't think Captain Brusilov wants to get near the Margush any sooner than he has to," Magda said quietly.

"Ah," Kawar said with a slow nod. "That makes sense." Norma's eyes widened—she was too straightforward for that kind of explanation to have occurred to her.

Pedroza's specialty was the first to come in handy, disguising probes and sensors to look like local flying pests so the natives would not notice them. The resulting pictures and sound tapes made the world vividly real in a way the old records could not.

Had the locals not been so human, Magda thought, the immunological amplifier would not have worked on the long-ago Queen Sabium in the first place. That would have saved everyone a lot of trouble—except, the anthropologist had to admit, Sabium herself.

Magda voraciously studied the incoming data: it gave her the basis for whatever fieldwork she would be able to do. She saw to her relief that Bilbeis IV—or at least this little chunk of it—was not as male-dominated as most pretechnological cultures. That so often hampered women in the field. Sometimes the only role available for them was courtesan, and Magda knew she lacked the clinical detachment necessary for that.

Hereabouts, though, the sensors showed women going freely through the streets, buying and selling, working at looms and potters' wheels and in jewelers' and bakers' shops on much the same terms as men. And when Magda saw a recording of a man handing over square silver coins to a woman and receiving in turn a scrawled receipt, the likeliest interpretation she could put on the scene was that it involved paying rent—which seemed to mean women could own property.

"Unusual," Norma Anderssen said when Magda remarked on that: now she rather than Kawar worked most closely with the anthropologist. The same tapes interested them both.

"Certainly a change from the last visit," Magda agreed. "Then women hardly showed themselves in public. I daresay it's the influence of this new cult the locals have."

As Magda had expected, the big hexagonal building in the center of town was a temple. Fifteen hundred years ago, the natives had worshiped a typical pantheon, with gods and goddesses in charge of the various aspects of nature. Now, though, the dominant local religion centered on a mother goddess. Judging from the identical structures Magda had seen in the orbital pictures, it was the dominant religion all over the continent.

"Unusual," Norma said again. "Normally, from what I understand, mother-worshiping cultures aren't progressive technically. They tend to accept things as they are, don't they, instead of seeking change?"

"Yes, usually," Magda said. That bothered her, too. The natives used iron as well as bronze; their carts and wagons had pivoted front axles; they used waterwheels to grind their grain. They had come a long way in a relatively short time.

Magda pushed aside the thought of interference. She said, "My best guess would be that the religion is fairly new and that the technology we're seeing predates it."

"Maybe so. But why would a dynamic society shift to belief in a mother goddess?"

"I can think of several possibilities off the top of my head: internal strife might have made the locals look away from this world toward the next, for instance, or this cult might have grown up in a land annexed by the dominant culture and then spread through the big, politically unified area. That's what happened with Christianity, after all. Maybe we'll find out. What really interests me here is that everyone seems to belong."

The town had no temples but the central shrine. That was not so strange—state-supported faiths, as this one plainly was, tended to drive their rivals underground. But Magda had not been able to find any rivals, any signs that other religions existed at all. It puzzled her. Such perfect unity should have been impossible on a world with no better mass communication methods than signboard and megaphone.

Yet it was there. Every household into which Pedroza's disguised sensors had buzzed or crawled had an image of the local goddess prominently displayed. All were copies, good or bad, of the cult portrait in the hexagonal temple.

At first she suspected the ubiquitous images were in place only as an outward show of conformity. But no one ever came snooping to see if some house might not have a portrait on the wall. Not only that, the locals plainly believed in their goddess. It was not always showy, and so doubly convincing. A casual, friendly nod to an image as someone walked past said more than the rites at the temple.

Magda worked hard with Norma to pick up the local language. As she'd hoped, it was descended from the one the first Survey Service ship had learned. That helped a lot. These days, too, the natives wrote with a straightforward thirty-eight-character alphabet instead of the hodgepodge of syllabic signs, ideograms, and pictograms they'd used before. That helped even more.

Seeing the work she'd done on the way to Bilbeis IV paying off made it hard for Magda not to gloat at Pedroza. He had just started fighting with the language and was still a long way from the fluency he'd need for fieldwork in town. Magda wanted out of the *Jêng Ho* so badly she could taste it.

The sea breeze blew the stench from the city into the faces of Irfan Kawar and Magda as they hiked down from their hidden ship. The geologist coughed. "Plumbing often gets invented surprisingly late," Magda murmured.

"I knew I should have worn nose filters," Kawar said. "If I'd really wanted to experience the primitive at first hand, I'd've gone into anthropology the way you did."

She made a face at him. Their hiking boots scrunched over gravel. They were on their own, linked to their crewmates only by the little transceivers implanted behind their ears. Both wore khaki denim coveralls, standard Service issue. Traders in a variety of costumes plied their wares in the town's marketplace; one more drab style of clothing should not seem too out of place there.

The first native to spot them was a woman picking berries by the side of the path. She looked up warily, as if wondering whether to flee into the bushes. Magda and Irfan Kawar slowly approached, their hands clasped in front of them in the local greeting gesture.

"The peace of the eternal goddess on you," Magda said, hoping her accent was not too foul to understand.

She must have made herself clear, for the woman's eyes lit. "And on you," the woman replied. She stared at them with frank curiosity. Magda's red-brown curls and smooth cheeks, Kawar's swarthy skin and bald head, were unlike anything she knew. "What distant land are you from?" she asked.

"The far northwest," Kawar replied. The dominant culture had not reached that part of the continent, so the answer seemed safe enough.

The woman accepted it without blinking. Her next question, though, made the two Terrans look at each other in confusion for a moment. It sounded like, "What will you be doing in search?"

Magda was trying to twist the grammar to make the sentence mean "What are you searching for?" when she remembered that the literal meaning of Hotofras—the name of the town ahead—was "Search." She said, "We have jewels to sell or trade. Here, would you like to see?"

She unzipped a pocket and took out a handful of red, blue, and green stones: synthetic rubies, star sapphires, and emeralds from the ship's lab. "Our gems are very fine," she said cajolingly.

The woman's hand came out until she touched a sapphire with the tip of one finger. Then she jerked it away, as if scalded. "No matter how fair your stones, I must make do with beads and colored glass, I fear. My husband is but a candlemaker; we will never be rich."

Kawar chose a much smaller sapphire from Magda's palm and gave it to the woman. Her face was a study in confusion. "Do you seek to buy my body? This is the fee, many times over, did I wish to sell myself to you; but I do not."

"No," he assured her, smiling wryly—he was gay. "But surely you will tell many people of the foreigners who gave a jewel away. They will come to us without the wariness buyers should have, and we will make up the price of this stone many times over." His sly smile invited her to share in the scheme.

"Truly the goddess smiles on me today!" the woman exclaimed. She tucked the sapphire into a pouch that hung from her belt.

"Tell me of this goddess you people follow," Magda said. "When we use your language, we greet the folk we meet in her name, but in our far country we do not worship her ourselves."

The woman shook her head in disbelief. "How could anyone not worship the goddess? She lives forever and knows everything. I am only the poor wife of a candlemaker, and live far from her glory, but one day perhaps even I shall see her." Her face filled with awe at the thought.

"So say the priests of many goddesses," Kawar observed; the local tongue seemed to lack a masculine word for the divine. "How does anyone in this world know which goddess we shall meet in the next?"

"Careful," Magda warned in English-based Federacy Standard. "That might be heresy."

The woman gaped at them, but not for that reason. "The next world!" she burst out. "Who speaks of the next world? If I sold this stone you gave me, I might make enough silver for the journey to the goddess's own home, far though it is."

"Selling a sapphire will not take you to heaven." Magda frowned, again wondering how well she was understanding the local language.

The woman set hands on hips, exasperated with these ignorant strangers. "Your talk makes no sense! I do not need to die to see the goddess, only to travel to the Holy City where she dwells."

"The Holy City?" Kawar echoed.

The woman pointed westward, toward Hotofras. "If you seek

to learn more of these things than I can tell you, you have only to speak to one of the upper priests or to the chief magistrate. They have seen the goddess with their own eyes—how I envy them!"

"Perhaps we will do that," Magda said. She and Kawar were making ready to go when she remembered the roles they were playing. "And you, do not forget to speak of us and of the excellent gems we sell."

"I will not forget," the woman promised. "The peace of the eternal goddess on you." That served for good-bye as well as hello. The two Terrans returned it and walked on.

Magda snorted. "Nice setup they have here—the bigwigs talk directly to the goddess and tell everyone under them what to do. Who's going to argue?"

"Don't let your jaundiced point of view make you misread the facts," Kawar reproved. "From what the woman said, she could hope to visit the goddess herself. That would be the cult image the one in the temple here is based on, I suppose. Probably gorgeous, of gold and ivory—do they have ivory here?—and precious stones. That would be worth a long journey to see."

"So it would. I can't quite see, though, why she would refer to an image 'dwelling' in this Holy City of theirs. Maybe there's a line of high priestesses who assume the role of the goddess one after the other. Maybe—hell, what's the point in guessing before we know enough?"

A twinkle showed for a moment in Kawar's dark, liquid eyes. "Because it's fun, of course."

She grabbed his hand, liking him very much. Too damn bad he preferred men, she thought—no wonder he'd been amused at what the woman thought he wanted. But he certainly would be more enjoyable than the implacably serious Atanasio Pedroza. No, that didn't say enough of Irfan, Magda decided—almost anyone was more enjoyable than Pedroza. She sighed. If she'd wanted things to be simple, she should have stayed in her father's pastry shop.

The path from the mountain valley where the *Jêng Ho* lay hidden descended to meet the main road into Hotofras. The road was rammed earth, heavily graveled to make it of some use even in the rain. Coaches, carts, and wagons rattled along, drawn by the local draft animals, which looked something like zebras and something like camels. "Ugly, with stripes," Kawar put it.

Magda paid more attention to the coaches. Instead of subjecting their passengers to bone-crushing jounces, they had an arrangement of leather straps that cushioned riders from the worst jolts. "It's the first step toward springs," the anthropologist said.

"I think they have a good many more steps to go," Kawar said judiciously, watching a native flung against the side of the coach by the swaying motion the straps imparted. "That still looks bloody uncomfortable."

"Yes, yes, of course," Magda said. "But on Terra people took three times as long to come up with even this rotten a system."

Kawar groaned and put a hand to his kidneys.

Chuckling, Magda went on. "Yes, exactly. They've nipped a lot of aches and pains in the bud here."

"In the butt, you mean."

"That too." Magda made a face at the geologist.

The walls of Hotofras had been tall and strong once. Now they were ramshackle, as if often used to furnish building stone. Half the town lay outside their protection. To Magda that spoke of long years of peace, not what she would have expected from such an obviously energetic culture: that energy should have boiled over, and frequently.

Small boys in ragged smocks gaped at the Terrans. Adults ostentatiously ignored them, except for those who eyed Magda's exotic good looks. Even they were circumspect. Hotofras was a port that attracted all kinds of people—why get excited about one more set of strangers?

The innkeeper into whose establishment they walked found a reason—seeing a pair of foreigners, she tried to rent them a room at double the going rate. But Magda had viewed enough transactions of that sort to have a good idea of what she ought to pay, and her pungent sarcasm brought the woman back to reality with a bump.

"Was that really necessary?" Kawar asked as the chastened innkeeper led them upstairs to their room.

"It wouldn't be in character not to drive a sharp bargain." Magda shrugged. "Besides, everybody here enjoys haggling. If I'd've accepted that first outrageous price, she would have been almost disappointed to take my money . . . almost, but not quite."

The room was all right—cleaner, in fact, than Magda had expected. The cloth-covered mattress was supported by crisscrossing leather straps attached to a wooden bed frame.

Magda had noticed that arrangement before without thinking anything of it. But seen so soon after the coaches, it caught her eye. When she remarked on the similarity, the innkeeper said proudly, "Yes, it was a cousin of my father's who first thought to suspend coaches that way, and who earned the reward of the goddess for it."

"What is that?" Irfan Kawar asked. "The certainty of a happy life in the next world?"

The innkeeper stared at him. "You *are* from a far country, stranger, not to know of the goddess and her ways; I thought everyone did. No, Rumeli was summoned to the Holy City and rewarded with gold from the hands of the goddess herself."

"Might we speak to such an illustrious personage?" Kawar asked. "Could you introduce us to him?"

"Er, no," the innkeeper said, suddenly less proud. "I fear he squandered the goddess's gift on wine and loose women and died three years ago of an apoplexy." Someone shouted for her from the taproom below; she left with embarrassed haste.

Amused, Kawar turned to Magda, but his grin faded before her grim expression. "What's wrong?"

"The reward-for-invention scheme, that's what. It should have died with Sabium; it was far ahead of its time. But here it is, still. And if that's not cultural contamination, I don't know what is. Damn, damn, damn! Won't the Purists love that?"

She felt like kicking something. Noninterference was the rule the Survey Service lived by. Humanity had learned from painful experience that ramming one culture's answers down another's throat was the wrong way to go about things. Given time and freedom from meddling, intelligent beings usually worked out what they needed—and if they didn't, whose business was it but their own?

The Purists, though, thought any contact with pretechnological worlds was contamination. They were very well meaning . . . especially if you asked one of them. Magda knew a know-nothing when she heard one, even when the talk, as it all too often was these days, was couched in terms of budget cutting instead of ideology.

"We're a good many hundred years too late to do anything about it now," Kawar said practically. He yawned, then patted his ample belly. "As for me, I'm going down to see what the food and beer are like, then coming back up here to sack out."

"Sensible," Magda had to admit; Irfan usually was. Now that she wasn't on the go anymore, she felt unfamiliar muscles starting to ache; exercise in the *Jêng Ho*'s little gym wasn't the same as hiking over ground sometimes rough. She looked around and started to laugh. "With only one bed, I'd sooner share it with you, Irfan, than with a lot of people I could think of; you'll just use it for sleeping."

He reached out and swatted her on the bottom. She leaped in the air in surprise. "Who knows what strange perversions spending the night with you might tempt me into?"

She thought about it. "Maybe we'll find out."

Rather to her regret, the night passed uneventfully—except that Irfan snored. The sleepy man running the taproom grumbled when they asked him for hot porridge for breakfast the next morning; the locals ate at noon, sunset, and just before they went to sleep.

Action at the central bazaar was brisk by the time the Terrans arrived. Hucksters cried a hundred wares, from furs to roasted nuts to sailcloth. Almost as loudly, customers sneered at the quality of what they were offered. Magda and Kawar somehow managed to stake out a few square meters and took up a chant: "Rare jewels! Fine gems! Rare jewels! Fine gems!"

They quickly sold some sapphires and emeralds; those went well with the natives' coloring. The rubies proved harder to move. The locals would admire them in Magda's hands, then put them against their own skins and wince at the effect. The repeated failures annoyed her, even though she and Kawar were just using their role for concealment. Whatever she did, she wanted to do well.

The Terrans' location let them watch the main temple entrance. Those huge metal doors, splendid with cloisonnéwork, were open day and night. Locals went in and out, both layfolk and priests. The latter were easy to recognize by their sober robes of white or light blue; most of the rest of the people preferred tunics, vests, and baggy trousers dyed in a rainbow of gaudy colors. There seemed to be about as many female priests as men.

As the morning wore on, Magda began to feel she and Kawar were being studied in turn by the priests. She expected curiosity from the locals, but these long, measuring stares were something else again. So were the conversations the priests started having behind their hands.

"Be ready to disappear in a hurry," Magda muttered to Kawar. "I have a feeling we're attracting undue attention somehow."

"Very well," he said gravely, interrupting his call for customers. "At your signal I shall grow a thick head of blue hair and turn pinkish gray all over."

She snorted. "You're incorrigible." Of itself, her hand patted the stunner in a front pocket of her coveralls. That, of course, was nonlethal and for emergencies only. There were stories of Survey Service personnel who let dreadful things happen to them rather than use an offplanet weapon. Magda admired that kind of altruism but did not intend to imitate it.

But when the priests made their approach, it proved peaceable enough. One white-robed woman threaded her way through the crowded bazaar toward the two Terrans. She waited until Magda was done haggling with a magnate in a particularly repulsive purple cloak, then bowed politely. "The peace of the eternal goddess on you, strangers."

"And on you, mistress," Magda and Kawar replied together.

"May we interest you in some stones, mistress, for yourself or for the goddess's temple?" Magda continued.

The priestess blinked, as if that had not occurred to her. "Perhaps you may, at that. But I have seen precious stones before, and I have never seen any folk with your aspect." She smiled; it made her look much younger and gave her an individuality she had lacked before. "Therefore, I am more interested in you. Will you tell me where you come from?"

The Terrans looked at each other. Finding no harm in the question, Kawar answered with the story they had prepared. "From the far northwest. Not many of our people travel as far south as your lands."

"Yes, I can believe that," the priestess said. Magda wondered if the woman's tone really was as dry as it seemed. But when the priestess went on, her questions were of the sort any newcomers might get, on how they had reached Hotofras, what they thought of it, what their homeland was like. She listened gravely to their answers.

At last the priestess said, "I thank the both of you for your patience. We always search out new knowledge of strangers who come to Hotofras."

The use of the verb reminded Magda of the place's unusual name. "If I may ask a question in return," she said, "why is this town called 'Search'?"

"Because it was founded to search out knowledge of strangers, of course," the priestess replied, smiling ever so slightly. She bowed to the Terrans and made her way back to the temple. Pausing outside the entrance, she spoke with a priest in a blue robe. He looked toward Magda and Kawar, scratched his head, and followed the priestess into the shrine.

"I wonder what all that's in aid of," Kawar said. "If we were going to get such a thorough grilling, it should have been at the gate coming in so we wouldn't have the chance to lose ourselves if we were ne'er-do-wells."

Magda shrugged. "I think that was a purely religious interrogation, not a security check. Maybe they have some sort of obligation toward strangers. That would fit a mother-goddess cult: shelter the homeless because in a way they're orphans, and so on."

"Makes sense," Kawar said. "But then, it should, you being the anthropologist and all." Ignoring the face Magda made at him, he went back to extolling the virtues of their jewels.

By evening, they had sold several more stones, two to buyers who had heard of them from the candlemaker's wife. Both ended up paying more than their other customers. "What do you know?" Kawar said, bemused. "I wasn't even lying."

"That's no way to advertise," Magda said. "Enough for one day. Let's go back to the inn. My feet are getting numb from standing in one place so long."

After a dinner of broiled many-legged river creatures with spicy gravy, the two Terrans went up to their rooms to transmit the data they had gathered and to plan what to do next. The latter did not take long: visiting the temple was the obvious next step.

They were walking toward the central square the next morning when they met a delegation of priests heading toward their lodging. Before Magda and Kawar quite grasped what was happening, the priests were all around them. One gave a hand signal. Suddenly the Terrans were grasped and held.

With a curse, Magda kicked out backward. The blow should have caught a male captor where it would do the most good—but the priest was not there when her foot lashed out. Whatever other arcane secrets the clergy of the mother goddess owned, they knew hand-to-hand combat.

Irfan Kawar did not try to break away. Instead he protested angrily. "By what right do you do this to us? We are but harmless traders!"

"If that is so, you will have our apology and a handsome reward," said the priest who had signaled. He turned to his companions. "Search them."

Magda tried again to break free, to no avail; the priests gripping her were strong and alert. She snarled as the locals' hands explored her body, though the examiners took no more liberties than the task required. A priest extracted the pouch of jewels from her hip pocket.

"Are you robbers, then, in holy robes?" she demanded. Tears of fear and fury ran unheeded down her cheeks.

The priest opened the pouch, let bright stones cascade into his palm, and peered into the leather sack. When satisfied it was empty, he returned the gems to it. "By no means," he said quietly. "These lovelies are yours, and we shall give them back to you."

"What is the meaning of this outrage, then?" Kawar asked. "Do you always greet foreigners so? If you do, I wonder that you have so many ships tied up at your docks."

The priest in charge of the rest smiled thinly. "Foreigners of a certain sort interest us more than the rest: those who say they come from lands we know nothing of, and whose appearance bears them out. They interest us even more if they carry devices we cannot fathom." He hefted Magda's stunner.

"I will show you the use of that one, if you like," she said eagerly.

"Thank you, no," he replied with cool amusement. "It may be a weapon."

"Irfan! Magda! What's going on? Are you all right?" Norma Anderssen's voice sounded in their transceivers. All Norma and the people back at the *Jêng Ho* could do was listen and worry.

"What will you do with us?" Magda asked, as much to pass on information as for her own sake.

"Why, send you to the goddess, of course," the priest said.

Magda could not remember a ritual phrase of that sort in the local language. She wondered if it was a euphemism for human sacrifice. "To the next world?" she asked tensely.

The priest stared at her with the same puzzlement the candlemaker's wife had shown. "No, no," he said. "Do you think us barbarians? I meant only that you will be taken—under guard, lest you try to flee, but otherwise in comfort—to the Holy City, where the goddess dwells."

III

The leather straps that supported the body of the coach gave it a rolling motion like that of a small boat on the open sea. After four months of such travel, it had long since stopped bothering Magda or Kawar. Indeed, the solid ground seemed unstable when they got out to relieve themselves or to stop for the evening.

The Margush valley knew only two seasons: hot and hotter. Magda wiped sweat from her face. "This weather makes me wish we'd told the gang from the *Jêng Ho* to rescue us, after all."

"And miss a slow guided tour across the continent? You must be mad. The comparative planetologists will be playing with our data for the next five hundred years." Kawar twisted his wrist so the video unit hidden in his bracelet scanned a tributary joining the main current of the Margush.

"I suppose so," Magda said. "Still, do you want to know the real reason I turned down any try at spiriting us away?"

"Probably because you didn't want the fair Atanasio coming after you with stunner blazing."

"You've come to know me entirely too well."

"No wonder." Kawar patted her hand, then looked around at their escorts and shrugged. Thrown together on the long journey, it was not surprising they had turned to each other. In spite of Kawar's usual orientation, the background they shared made Magda a more attractive partner for him than the local priests.

She smiled back at him. She had known better lovers—though she did not say so—but also worse. He was gentle and tried hard to please her, which counted for a good deal. She did her best to return the favor; some of the variations he liked were interesting.

She stuck her head out the window of the coach. A city lay ahead.

Its walls were visible for a long distance across the floodplain of the Margush—like the other towns in the valley, it stood on a hill composed of a couple of thousand years of its own rubbish. "What's the name of that place?" she called up to the driver.

"That is Mawsil," the woman replied.

"We're getting to know where we are," Kawar said. He confidently spoke to the driver. "Helmand is the next city ahead?"

But her answer caught him by surprise. "No," she said, "the next city eastward is the Holy City, where the two of you, fortunate as you are, will meet the goddess."

Kawar scratched his head. "That has to be Helmand."

"So it does," Magda said grimly.

"More interference, you think?"

"I wish you'd convince me otherwise."

"Thankfully, the problem is not really mine—it's hard for geologists to interfere in a planet's life."

"Yes, but what happens when the Purists in the Assembly start yapping about terrible Terran cultural imperialism and cut the Survey Service budget in half? You'll find it even harder to interfere when you never get near another non-Federacy planet again."

"The Chairman can tell the Finance Committee that even if there was interference here, it turned out well," Kawar said. "This world argues for interference, not against it."

"Does not blowing your brains out at Russian roulette argue for playing it?" Magda retorted. "This is just as much fool luck as the other—once you spin the cylinder, you don't know what's going to happen till it's over. And when things go wrong, that's too bloody late, and somebody else has to clean up the mess. Us, in this case."

Magda also had a picture of the Survey Service Chairman going against doctrine in front of an Assembly committee. She kept it with her other fantasies, like guitar-playing woodpeckers and tap-dancing trees. The Chairman, a career bureaucrat named Paulina Koch, habitually wore gray only because there was no blander color.

They spent the night in a fine hostel in Mawsil, then pressed on to the Holy City with a fresh driver and a new set of priestly "escorts." As Magda had since entering the Margush valley, she questioned the newcomers about their faith. "How is a new goddess chosen when the old one dies?"

The leader of the escort was so startled, he almost fell off his mount. "The goddess does not die. If she died, how could she be a goddess?"

"Forgive me, please; I am only an ignorant foreigner," Magda said for the hundredth time. She tried another tack. "Does the earthly vessel holding the goddess's divinity die? If so, how is a new vessel chosen?"

"The goddess is the goddess," the priest said. Magda spread her hands and gave up. She'd gotten similar answers from others she'd questioned, but kept hoping that as she drew close to the Holy City she could penetrate the mummery surrounding the locals' deity. That she kept failing deterred her only a little.

Peasants labored in the lush green fields. They turned Archimedean screws to bring water from the Margush into the irrigation canals. Windmills also helped in that effort; Magda saw a crew repairing one. She pointed to them and asked the driver, "How long have your people known that device?"

The driver obviously had never thought in those terms. At last she said, "As long as anyone can remember."

"Not what one would call precise, but expressive," Kawar observed. Magda's agreement was strained.

The road, which paralleled the Margush, bent slightly south. Magda saw what had to be the Holy City ahead. "That's Helmand," she said flatly.

Irfan Kawar leaned out the window. "It's certainly in the same spot, isn't it?"

Traffic was heavy. Most of the travelers were pilgrims, seeking a glimpse of the goddess. But there were others. A woman propelled herself past the Terrans' coach on a contraption halfway between a scooter and a pedalless bicycle.

"I've never seen anything like that before," Magda said to one of the priests in the band of escorts.

"Nor have I," he said. "Doubtless she plans to present the invention to the goddess in hope of being rewarded for it."

"Doubtless," Magda agreed sourly. She was starting to wish none of the locals would ever have any more new thoughts; her reports would be a lot easier to write.

The Holy City was packed with people, beasts, and wagons. Because of the crush, the party took almost as long to find its hostel as they had traveling from Mawsil. Magda and Kawar gulped sour wine while one of their escorts went back out into the heat and crowd to report their arrival. "Poor devil," Kawar said, putting down his mug with a sigh of relief.

Magda leaned back in her chair. "Now that we're here, I expect we'll be able to relax a while. It'll take days for the word to pass up through the hierarchy—and more days, it looks like, for anyone to get through the jam to do anything about it."

"Good," Kawar said. "That will let me take a bath. I itch everywhere."

"Me too. God, I'd kill for a good cold shower."

"Don't speak of such things. I've been trying to forget they exist."

The tub was made of caulked wood. Servants hauled bucket after bucket of blood-warm river water to fill it; whatever else it boasted, the Holy City did not have much of a drainage system. The locals also knew nothing of soap—hard scrubbing and perfume made up some for the lack.

The Terrans flipped a coin to see who would get the tub first. Kawar won. The bathwater, already slightly turbid from the Margush, was even murkier after Magda unbelted the robe that had long since replaced her coveralls and started fighting the grime that coated her.

There was some sort of commotion down the hall. Magda was doing a good job of ignoring it until a squad of iron-corseleted troops burst into the bathroom. She yelped and grabbed at herself. The locals had no strong modesty taboos, but she did not care to be on display for them, either.

She shook her head to get the wet hair out of her face and glowered at the soldiers, as well as one can glower from a tub. "What are you armored louts doing here?" Her voice held thirty degrees of frost.

The squad leader did not leer at her; on the other hand, her hauteur failed to impress him. He said. "Dry and dress yourself as quickly as you may. The eternal goddess requires your presence."

He folded his arms and waited. Magda did not think he was trying to humiliate her, only to see she did not run. Nevertheless, it rankled. To make him fidget, she dallied as long as she could, until Irfan Kawar called anxiously from the hallway to make sure she was all right. She reassured him and moved faster.

Outside the hostel, a musician blew a harsh blast on a trumpet made from a seashell. "Clear a path!" she shouted. "Clear a path for the servants of the goddess!" *Taa-raaa!* "Clear a path!"

As nothing else had done, the discordant music melted the crowds. "The goddess *can* work miracles," Kawar said, nodding toward the empty roadway ahead. Despite his flip tone, he sounded worried; the summons was alarmingly abrupt.

Magda laughed, as much to keep up his spirits as for her own. She had her own reasons for concern, which she did not share with Kawar. The horn call was eerily like the royal flourish the *Leeuwenhoek* had recorded so long ago. The culture had changed so much in other ways that she wondered at such a strange piece of conservatism.

She had studied the *Leeuwenhoek*'s map of Helmand until she could have found her way around the town blindfolded. The Holy City's streets, though, were laid out in the same grid pattern that served most towns. It was nothing like the old maze. Nor was the building toward which the squad led the Terrans at all similar to the ancient royal palace. But Magda would have sworn it was in the same part of the city.

The soldiers hustled their charges along, so they had little chance to admire the goddess's residence. Magda kept her wrist camera busy, and made such notes as she could of the numerous artworks in their niches. A few were in the stiff, ornate style that had prevailed at the time of the first Survey Service visit. Others, newer, had a self-conscious, restrained excellence that reminded her of the work of Greece and Rome. The most recent sculpture and paintings were also fine work, but more lively and vibrant with motion.

While she was trying to examine the splendor of the palace, Kawar asked the guards, "What ceremony must we observe when we come before your goddess?"

"Why, everyone knows—" one of them began; then he paused, inspecting his charges. "No, I take it back; you may be from so far away, you do not. A bow before her will suffice. She is no mere king or chieftain, as I hear of in foreign lands, in need of being made great by ceremony. She is the goddess, and great by virtue of what she is."

The trumpeter blasted the fanfare one last time. The squad leader murmured to an official who stood in the doorway of a large, brightly lit chamber. That worthy dipped his head, turned, and called, "Mistress, the strangers you summoned!"

A moment later, a priestess escorted out a plump, prosperous matron. The woman glared at these funny-looking foreigners as she passed. Magda felt a twinge of sympathy for her. Who knew how long she had waited for her audience, only to have it cut short?

At the doorman's nod, the guardsmen led the Terrans into the goddess's chamber. Despite what the trooper had said about her not needing to stand on ceremony, the room was richly furnished. And the throne on which the goddess sat gleamed with gold and precious stones.

As for the goddess herself, she wore a plain white robe like those of her higher-ranking priests, but a gold circlet rested on her forehead and confined her hair. Rather to Magda's surprise, she closely resembled the countless portraits of her. As in the better images, her eyes were arresting; Magda had the odd feeling she was completely transparent to her. It was a relief to bow.

"Rise; let me look at you," the goddess said. Her voice was a smooth contralto.

Irfan Kawar obediently straightened. Magda stayed bowed, rigid with shock. She had not recognized the face; a false mustache worn long ago to counterfeit those of kings was now gone. But she had heard that voice on endless hours of tape, and knew it again at once.

The goddess was Queen Sabium.

Magda must have said the name out loud, though afterward she did not remember doing so. Kawar did not understand yet; his eyes were questioning but not full of amazement—or horror.

Queen Sabium . . . the goddess . . . whoever she was . . . gasped. So did her servitors, who likely had never seen her disconcerted. Her guards growled and hefted their weapons, angry without thinking at anyone who dared disturb her.

"Hold!" she said, and the guards froze in their places. Magda heard that sonorous voice address her: "Stranger woman with the copper-colored hair, I pledge you will take no harm here. I ask it of you, I do not command it: look at me."

Trembling, Magda obeyed. At the same time, she came back to herself enough to point her bracelet-camera at the goddess. It took only moments for stereophonic hell to break loose in the transceiver behind her ear as the people back at the *Jêng Ho* came to the same realization she had.

Norma Anderssen caught on first; she had used the tapes of Sabium as often as Magda. "That is the ruler from the *Leeuwenhoek*'s time," she said, her voice stumbling in disbelief.

Atanasio Pedroza was a split second behind her: "That is Sabium! How can she yet live?" He sounded as much indignant as astonished. After him came a swelling chorus of voices, until Babel rang in Magda's ear.

She reached up as if to scratch, pressed the transceiver to shut off reception, but let it keep sending to the *Jêng Ho.* Sudden silence fell inside her head. Out of the corner of her eye, she saw Kawar matching her gesture. Now the geologist had grasped the situation, or as much of it as anyone else. His mouth hung open in stunned surprise.

Magda was only peripherally aware of him. Through her own astonishment, she fought to focus her wits on the goddess. No, on Queen Sabium, she corrected herself, trying by the deliberate change of title to lessen the awe she felt. It did not help.

The goddess—the queen—waited. The byplay had lasted less than a minute. When Magda still did not speak, Sabium said, "The last person who called me by that name has been dust for more than a thousand years. There are days, there are weeks, when I do not remember I was born with it."

Any reply might have been wrong, disastrously wrong. Silence stretched. At last Sabium broke it. "In the very beginning of my days, I was ill, ill unto death."

Magda heard shocked intakes of breath from the locals. The goddess—it was impossible not to think of her as such—ignored them. She went on. "Two men from a far-off land—or so they said they were—cured me, where all hope had failed. Now *you* know my ancient, forgotten name. One of you"—she pointed toward Kawar—"is of the same sort as one of those. The other man then had skin like dark, polished wood. I had never imagined such a one, nor had I imagined any person with hair like metal."

Her finger turned toward Magda. "I ask you, then, if the two of you are of the people of those earlier strangers. Tell me, and know I will know if you lie."

She might, Magda thought, a little wildly. If she had somehow lived a millennium and a half, she must have learned to see through people as through glass. No wonder, then, her eyes had that piercing quality. The anthropologist found herself unable to dissemble. "Yes."

Sabium's head bent very slowly. She turned to her retinue and gestured peremptorily. "Leave me. Yes, all of you; I would have speech with these strangers alone." Some of the locals were startled enough to protest, even to their goddess. She overrode them. "Go, and close the chamber doors behind you."

The locals went. The majordomo and other palace attendants scowled over their shoulders at the Terrans. Jealous of having their influence diluted, Magda thought, although what influence could mere mayfly mortals exert on their goddess?

The hinges of the chamber's doors squealed as they swung shut; they had not been used much or kept oiled. Magda was sure as many eyes as possible were pressed to the crack between the portals.

Sabium did not seem to care. She descended from her throne

and slowly and with immense dignity prostrated herself before the two Terrans. "Along with what was my name, death is a thing I seldom think of, not for me, not for years upon years upon years. But I would have died, I think, had your countrymen not saved me. Is it not so?"

"It is so," Magda muttered. Usually, doing fieldwork on a pretechnological world, she was conscious of the greater sophistication the Federacy's long history gave her. Now, though, it felt obscenely wrong to have this being on her knees. "Please, your, uh, divinity, get up."

Irfan Kawar echoed her; she heard the embarrassment she felt in his voice as well.

"No," Sabium said, still with that same calm self-possession. "I am called a goddess, and I suppose I am, for I do not die. But your people must truly be gods, or gods of greater power than myself, for I received the gift of eternal life from you."

"Queen—goddess—Sabium—" Magda's tongue was falling all over itself, and no wonder, because she had no idea what to say. Admitting the existence of space-traveling aliens violated every noninterference canon the Federacy had. But she could not see how letting Sabium think she was a god improved matters much.

"God damn David Ware to hell—this whole fucking mess is his fault," she said bitterly.

Sabium shook her head in incomprehension; Magda had spoken Federacy Basic, getting no relief from swearing in the local language. But Sabium understood the anger, if not the words. She said, "I have tried every day to deserve the gift your folk gave me, by ruling justly and seeing that my people live as well as they may. If I have not pleased you, spare them and punish me."

Magda winced. Suddenly she began to see why, fifteen hundred years before, Ware had thought this woman worth saving. She knew that was all he had intended. But what a mess his well-intentioned interference had left in its wake! It had twisted Bilbeis IV's whole historical and religious development out of shape.

While such dark thoughts filled her head, Irfan Kawar knelt and raised Queen Sabium. "You need have no fear of us," he told her. "We have not come to judge you." Magda winced again, this time in shame. The geologist was doing a better job than she was.

From outside the chamber came an anxious call: "Goddess, is all well?"

"Yes, of course; leave us be!"

"Let them in," Magda urged. "We can talk more whenever you

want. They must fear for your safety, closeted alone with two such, uh, unusual strangers."

A ghost of amusement touched Sabium's lips. "Unusual indeed. Nevertheless, you speak rightly." She swept down the aisleway and flung open the doors. Some of her attendants almost fell over her as they rushed in. She said, "I will talk further with these"—it was her turn to hesitate—"people. Quarter them in the suite nearest me, Bagadat, so I may have speech with them whenever I wish."

"It shall be done," the majordomo said. He bowed to the Terrans. "If you will come with me."

Apparently, if his goddess accepted the foreigners, Bagadat would do the same . . . or, Magda thought, he might try to make them quietly disappear, to preserve his own position. No, probably not; not with an immortal looking over his shoulder. She shivered. That was true in the most literal sense of the word.

The suite Sabium had assigned to them was plainly one reserved for high dignitaries. The furnishings were rich, the sofa and bed upholstered with cushions soft enough to sink into. The portrait bust of Sabium that sat on a table was very fine. Done in what Magda thought of as the classical style, it showed the goddess serenely at peace with herself and her world. She wore her hair long and straight; Magda hoped she would be able one of these days to use the style to date the piece.

At the moment, she had more urgent things to worry about. She plopped down on the couch with a groan, wishing she could hide under it instead. "Disaster!" she said. She waved her arms in a wild, all-encompassing gesture.

Irfan Kawar slowly shook his head, still stunned himself. "No one could have expected—this."

"Of course. But nobody knew *what* was going to happen, which if you ask me is a good reason for not doing anything."

As Pedroza had before, Kawar muttered, "Maybe it's coincidence."

"Oh, horseshit, Irfan; you don't believe that yourself." Magda knew her harshness hurt the geologist and was sorry, because he was a good man—but only somewhat, because she could not refuse to look facts in the face. She went on. "It was the stinking immunological amplifier, nothing else but. It just happened to work a wee bit better on Sabium than on us—a wee bit! I'm sure Atanasio will want to chop her into bloody bits to find out why."

That, unfortunately, reminded her she and Kawar had been out of touch with the *Jêng Ho* for several hours. She turned on the receiver part of her implant and promptly regretted it. Everyone back at the ship must have been going mad with frustration, and everyone started shouting hysterical advice at her at once.

She listened—or tried to—for only a couple of minutes, then switched off so violently, she hurt herself. "Idiots!" she snarled. "Halfway around the world from us and telling us what to do."

What with the turmoil in her own head, she had not noticed Kawar also turning on his receiver. He stood the din a few seconds longer before shutting it off again. He did hear one thing she'd missed: "They won't be halfway around the world for long—the *Jêng Ho* has been on the way here since the moment you recognized who the goddess was."

Magda only grunted. She liked the independence six thousand kilometers of distance gave her, but the move made sense. The action was here, with Hotofras abruptly a backwater.

Someone scratched at the door, which had a bar on the Terrans' side. Glad for the interruption, Magda raised the bar. Servants fetched in supper, bowed nervously, and left. The fare was similar to what nobles had eaten when the *Leeuwenhoek* was there: bread, boiled vegetables and roots, a stew of salt fish, with preserved fruit and sweet wine.

The Terrans had reached the tooth-picking stage when the scratching sound came again. Expecting more servants to fetch away the dirty dishes, Magda opened the door. Sabium stood there instead, alone.

"C-come in." Magda stepped aside, as wary as the palace servitors had been with her. She made no move to close the door, being unsure that was proper.

Sabium shut it. When she began to prostrate herself, Kawar stopped her. With an apologetic glance toward Magda, he said, "You do not need to humble yourself before us. Rather, we are in awe of you, hardly less than your own subjects. And why not? I am but forty-two years old, and my companion is—"

"Thirty-one," Magda supplied.

"I do not believe you," Sabium said. Then, studying them with that searching clarity of hers, she changed her mind. "No; I do. Say rather I do not understand."

Again Magda saw the quality in this woman that had led David Ware to find her worth saving. And he was dishonored dust these many centuries, and here she stood yet.

For a moment the anthropologist was tempted to tell Sabium everything, but she did not: she could not make herself believe one interference justified another. Instead, she said, "Queen . . . goddess . . . have you ever sent out couriers with messages they could not speak of, save to their own superiors who were to receive them?"

"Of course."

"Think of us in such a light, then. Much of what we know, we may not speak."

"You say you are messengers of the gods, then, not gods yourselves?"

"We are messengers." Magda let it go at that, relieved she had not made a full confession. However brilliant and experienced Sabium was, it was in the context of her own culture. Asking her to assimilate the idea of the Federacy all at once was too much.

"That is marvel enough for me," Sabium said firmly. "My ships scoured the western coast, my artisans founded towns there in hopes of finding folk like unto those who had rescued me. And so they did, though long years after I proposed it."

"No wonder the city's name means 'search'!" Magda burst out. "All that time you were looking for Ware and Crouzet! They said they came from the west, didn't they?"

"If those were their names; I never knew them," Sabium said. "But yes, they said they were from the west. Here in this valley, we knew nothing of the west then. But though I never found a trace of my saviors, I never forgot them, either, or let my priests do so. If ever folk of strange aspect appeared, saying they were from a country of which we were ignorant, I wanted to meet with them, the more so if they had possessions unlike any of ours." She smiled. "And so you are here."

"So we are," Magda said, doing her best to hide her chagrin. Their "simple, foolproof" story could not have done a better job of advertising them to Sabium if they had concocted it for that very purpose.

She took a deep breath, forced herself to steadiness, and said, "We are glad to be here, for in you, Queen, we have found a greater marvel than any we know ourselves." She did not care whether Sabium was examining her for the truth in that—it was there.

"You are messengers, and you did not know of me?" Sabium paused. "I see it is so, though I do not see how. Well, if one tries to put it baldly, there is little to tell after the early years. You have said you know of my cure?"

At the Terrans' nods, Sabium continued. "Once I felt myself again, I went on as I always had, doing my best for Helmand. The years went by. People I had grown up with envied me at first, that

I kept my looks while their hair whitened and their faces wrinkled. I remember I thought nothing of it, past the flattery a queen always hears."

She stared back into the distant past she alone remembered. "Then one day I noticed—it seemed very sudden at the time—that my servants were the grandchildren of those I had first known and seemed no younger than I. They did not envy me any longer. They felt awe instead . . . as did I, when I began to realize my span of days, whatever it was, truly was longer than the usual run."

"Did you not fear overthrow in war, even if sickness would not come for you?" Kawar asked.

"Oh, indeed, and that overthrow almost happened more than once, when I was young. But Helmand survived. Eventually we came to win more easily, through alliances with our enemies' neighbors or by fighting before our foes were ready. By then I had begun to see how such things were managed, for already I was wiser than any king who opposed me."

Sabium poured a cup of wine and sipped reflectively. "I do not say I am more clever than any mortal; time and again the brilliance of some woman or man bringing a new thing before me will leave me dumbfounded. But what wit I have draws on lifetime after lifetime of experience, against the few paltry years that are all others can gain. And what is wisdom but wit tempered by experience?

"I did not die; after a while I did not lose. And after a while my people looked as much to me as to the gods I had always known. Bit by bit they forgot the old gods, and only I recall I became a goddess by their favor."

She drank again. Magda had been looking for a chance to interrupt. "You spoke of people bringing new things to you. We know you encouraged them to do so long ago—you have kept it up all this time?"

"Why, of course," Sabium said in faint surprise. "All manner of worthy things have come from such inventors, to make the lives of my people and me easier and more pleasant. Weapons of war, too, at need, which also helped our triumph. But I own I prefer the tools of peace, or of thought."

She gestured enthusiastically. "Why, do you know, a woman last year had observations to show the world and the moving stars go around the sun, and not all of them around us. Other astronomers are still measuring away, to see if she is right. What a marvelous thing if it were so!"

"Marvelous," Magda echoed. She tried to ignore the look of consternation Irfan Kawar sent her way, but it wasn't easy. With a civilization less than two thousand years old, Bilbeis IV was right at the edge of the scientific revolution.

No planet Magda knew of came close to matching that—Earth was as progressive as any, but in 1200 B.C. people on Earth were just getting around to finding out about iron. But then, no early culture on Earth or anywhere else she knew of had fostered invention for fifteen hundred years, either.

Sabium brightened. "Being messengers as you are, surely you would know the answer to our riddle. Is that why you have chosen to come now, to show us whether such a momentous change in the way we view the world is correct?"

"We're merely here to observe," Magda said.

The anthropologist had not had much hope Sabium would accept the lame evasion, but she did, and bowed her head as at a deserved rebuke. "Of course. What value to us if we are merely given knowledge without wrestling it from the fabric of the world for ourselves? You have great wisdom, to keep from interfering."

That made Magda want to laugh, or cry, or both at once. How would Sabium react if she ever learned that she herself was a product of interference? Would she say her greatness—which Magda could not deny—justified the meddling, or would she wish her world back to the slower but more proper course it would have taken had she died at her appointed time?

Magda did not know, and was afraid to ask.

Irfan Kawar had been thinking along a different line. He said to Sabium, "Perhaps you will have returned to us, then, the goods your priests confiscated at Hotofras? Some of them embody principles your people have not yet learned."

"Be it so," Sabium said at once. "When I leave you, I shall give the order to my servants."

"Keep the jewels, of course, as tribute to your own splendor," Magda said. She felt like kissing Kawar for his quick wits.

"I would not wish to impoverish you—" Sabium began.

"You do not," Magda said firmly.

Sabium acknowledged the gift with a dignity more than queenly. She departed a few minutes later, saying, "If it please you, I would speak with you again tomorrow. Though you may not speak of things I and mine do not yet know, surely there can be no harm in discussing the long-lost days. I never thought to meet anyone who knew of them but from my own tales, and to talk with such people is like seeing the reflection of a reflection of my own face. Sleep well now; use my servants as if they were your own." The door closed behind her.

"Whew!" Magda said when she and Kawar were alone again. That seemed to sum things up as well as anything. Her clothes were soaked with sweat, and not just from the heat.

The palace attendants who returned the Terrans' property looked at them with wide eyes and bowed as they might have toward their goddess. At Magda's dismissal, they fled. She hardly noticed. She was too busy strapping on her stunner. After so many months of being a politely held prisoner, she reveled in the feeling of freedom it gave her.

The transceiver behind her ear let out a hoot loud enough to hurt. She had almost forgotten about the override signal; only Captain Brusilov had the authority to use it. His harsh voice echoed in her head and in Kawar's: "We are down, safe and undetected, in the desert country north of Helmand—I mean, the Holy City. Escape at once, using your stunners if you have to: you did well to get them back. Get far enough out of the city so a flier can pick you up without any of the locals seeing it."

"Hey, wait!" Magda protested. "Don't we get any say in this?"

"You know I have the right to tell you no, Dr. Kodaly," Brusilov said with cold formality. "I will, however, appeal to your reason before doing so. Would you not agree the situation we have encountered"—as polite a way to say "crisis" as Magda had ever heard—"calls for discussion and analysis with all experts present?"

She bit her lip and glanced toward Kawar to see if he would back her in defiance. It looked unlikely. She sighed. "Very well."

The escape itself proved preposterously easy. The Terrans used their stunners through the chamber door to knock out any guards outside. There proved to be two, lying slumped against the wall. Magda set an empty wine jar between them to explain their unconsciousness.

The torchlit hallways were almost empty so late at night. A couple of servants bowed low to the Terrans. No one tried to stop them; it did not occur to anyone that the goddess's honored guests would want to leave without her permission. And once out of the palace, Kawar and Magda became just another couple of strangers, a bit stranger than most, wandering the streets of the Holy City.

The only mishap came when Kawar turned his ankle descending the hill of rubble on which the city sat. He stumbled on, his arm around Magda's shoulder. The night was hot and sticky. The contact should have been uncomfortable, but it was a relief to them both. Kawar did not let go even after they reached flat, smooth ground.

When the Holy City was well behind them, Magda keyed her transceiver. "You may as well come get us," she said. "This spot is as good as any."

"Half an hour," Brusilov said. He was not one to waste words.

Magda sat in the dust with a sigh of relief. Kawar sprawled, panting, beside her. In the darkness, she took a while to recognize the expression on his face. It was more than exhaustion; it was fear.

"What's the matter?" she asked.

"We'll have to cover this up," he blurted.

She gaped at him. "What? Are you crazy?"

"Not me. You were the one talking about the damned Purists a couple of days ago. What better club than Bilbeis IV for beating the Survey Service over the head?"

Magda drew in a thoughtful breath. There was a good deal of truth in that. Still, she answered slowly, "Strikes me we deserve to get beaten over the head for this one. We've managed to twist the history of a whole planet out of shape. How do you go about justifying that? People have to know we screwed up, and how badly we screwed up. Maybe getting it out in the open will keep it from happening again."

"But under Sabium, the planet is better off and farther along than it would have been without her. Why not leave well enough alone?" Kawar said, returning to the argument he had raised before.

"It won't wash," Magda said. "A bit of interference I could overlook; that's the kind of stuff the Purists howl about, and it doesn't mean a thing. But this is too big to sweep under the rug: a whole powerful religion—powerful, hell! Real!—that never should have been here, and a goddess who wouldn't be either, if it weren't for us. I just shiver in my shoes to think how lucky we were here."

"Make up your mind. If what Ware did was as terrible as you're making out, how can we be lucky now?"

"How? Easy—suppose he'd been a rotten judge of character along with being an altruistic idiot. That Bilbeis IV is what it is, is all thanks to Sabium. You saw her. She happens to be just what Ware thought she was—a wise, kindly woman. What if she hadn't been? What if she'd used her immortality to burn anybody with green hair or to wipe out all the people who spoke with a lisp? Think what we'd be facing now."

"Ware didn't know he was giving her immortality," Kawar protested.

"Yes, and that's the point—when you interfere, you don't know what's going to happen afterward. What do you want, us using planets full of people as smart as we are for laboratories? Count me out."

"Well, what do *you* want? The Service to go down the drain, and us with it? Is that better?" He reached almost pleadingly to touch Magda's face, but his hand faltered and stopped before it reached her.

Through her own hurt, she answered, "I don't know. But if I have to go down, I'd rather do it for the truth than nailed to a lie. And as for the Service, it can take care of itself. Bureaucracies are tough beasts."

"Yes, and one reason is that they find scapegoats when things go wrong. Three guesses who they'll pick here. I'm serious, Magda—we can't let word of what's happened here get out. Too much rides on it. I think a lot of the crew will agree with me, too."

Magda grunted. She knew where she could find one certain ally—Atanasio Pedroza. His Afrikaner rectitude wouldn't let him be a part of anything underhanded.

She would rather have had a leg taken off without anesthetic. She liked Irfan Kawar; once or twice she had imagined she was in love with him. The thought of lining up against him with someone she loathed made her guts clench. But she realized how hard Kawar was trying not to see the scope of the interference on Bilbeis IV. She could not deliberately blind herself the same way.

The flier came down beside them, quiet as a dream. Magda climbed wearily to her feet. When she offered Irfan Kawar a hand, he ignored her and struggled up by himself.

She shrugged and turned away, but her nails bit into her palms. It was going to be a long trip home.

IV

"Thank you so much, Chairman Koch," Assemblyman Valleix said. He was a Purist; his voice dripped sarcasm.

"It is my duty and my pleasure, sir," replied the plump middle-aged woman who was Chairman of the Survey Service. Paulina Koch's own voice was studiedly neutral. She wore her habitual gray—the better to blend into the background, her detractors said.

Valleix returned to the attack. "Isn't it a fact, Madam Chairman, that the natives of Rugi II learned of the moldboard plow through an indiscreet remark by one of your Survey Service operatives? That strikes me as a serious breach."

Paulina Koch did not smile. One of her subordinates had leaked that report to the aide of another, less prominent Purist months ago. Now it was going to come home to roost.

She let him blather along, listening with half an ear.

"Under the best of circumstances, the Survey Service strikes me as a luxury the Federacy can ill afford in these days of budgetary constraints. Such debacles as Rugi II only make matters worse. I ask you again, Madam Chairman, isn't it a fact that the natives of that planet learned about the moldboard plow from Service personnel?"

"No, I am afraid that is not a fact, Assemblyman." That he showboated by repeating his question only made springing the trap sweeter, though she did not let her face show it.

His eyebrows shot up. "I suppose you have evidence to support such a startling assertion." By his tone, he did not suppose so at all.

"Yes, Assemblyman, here it is." She produced a data card. "This will show that the moldboard plow was in fact invented on an island off the main continent of Rugi II and that it spread there through normal trade contacts at around the time of the last Survey Service examination of the planet. That accounts for its sudden appearance in areas where it had previously been unknown."

Valleix was a black man; had he been white, he would have blanched. He had tangled with Paulina Koch too often to suppose her data were anything but what she said they were. He was also painfully aware she had just made a fool of him throughout the Federacy. He cut his losses, nodding to the head of the subcommittee. "I request a day's recess to evaluate these documents."

"Granted. Madam Chairman, you will be available tomorrow?"

"Certainly, madam." Paulina Koch still did not smile or show any outward sign of triumph. She had been a bureaucrat too long for that. But having savaged one Assemblyman, she did not expect any problems from the others. The Survey Service's appropriation looked safe again.

Professor Fogelman breezed into the classroom fifteen minutes late, something he had done a lot in his undergraduate lecture course. Stavros Monemvasios was not surprised to find him acting the same way in his graduate seminar.

"Greetings, greetings, greetings." Fogelman peered around the room. The anthropology prof liked to show off. He started guessing students' home worlds by their looks and dress: "Iberia, Hyperion, Epirus, Saigon, Inshallah, Hyperion, Iowa—"

He came to Stavros and hesitated. "Alexander?"

Monemvasios grinned; Fogelman had made the same mistake in the undergrad course. "I'm from New Thessaly, sir." Unlike most men of his planet, he wore a beard.

"Damn!" The professor smacked his fist down on the lectern—he remembered, too. He got three of the last four people in the seminar right.

The one he missed was a girl from Earth—the University of Hyperion's anthro department drew students from all over the Federacy. "Earth! *Anyone* could come from Earth," Fogelman snorted, dismissing his error.

"Now for your first assignment," he said, and the students responded with predictable groans. "Even after you start doing your own fieldwork, comparative studies will require you to use Survey Service reports intelligently." He started tossing out data cards like a man dealing whist, one to each person in the classroom. "Fifteen-minute summaries of these next week. They're all fresh new reports—I just pulled them from the data net before I came. That's why I was late."

Stavros raised an eyebrow. Now he was surprised; Fogelman had never bothered with excuses before. He looked at the data card on his desk; it had no label. It could have been anything from a laundry list to the score for a symphony. He'd have to plug it into his computer to know for sure. No time for that now—he got sucked into argument and frantic note scrawling on just what the proper definition for "civilization" was.

The ringing bell took him by surprise. "See you all a week from now," Fogelman said. "I'm looking forward to the reports." A lot of profs would have been blowing smoke with that line, but he sounded as if he meant it. He grinned. "One of you has a real plum."

He was a good psychologist; Stavros was sure he wasn't the only student who hurried off to the dorm to see what world he'd drawn.

He brought the report up on the screen. The lead frame had a list of authors and a vid shot of the principal author. She was a redhead good-looking enough to make Stavros pause a moment before he started paying attention to the document itself. When he did, his jaw dropped. He whistled softly. "He wasn't kidding," breathed the young man from New Thessaly. "Bilbeis IV—"

Pleased with herself, Paulina Koch attacked the printouts in her IN basket with an energy alien to the dogged persistence that was her hallmark. She saw with relief that no red-flagged items were in there, and only a few with yellow warning tags. The Survey Service was orderly and efficient, as it should have been.

She disposed of the first two priority items in short order. One should never have had a flag; a deputy coordinator earned a black mark for not being able to make up his own mind.

The third paper with the yellow strip at the top made her frown. Why should she care in particular if the Survey Service ship *Jêng Ho* had come in to the Service base on Topanga from a routine survey of a world without space travel? Then she saw which world it was and punched for the full report.

The Survey Service had given itself a black eye on Bilbeis IV, no doubt about it. The Purists had been beating the Service over the head with David Ware's folly for fifteen hundred years. Fortunately, most interference canceled out in time, no matter how loud the Purists yapped. The odds were excellent that Bilbeis IV would be another case like that and could return to the obscurity it deserved.

The abstract came up on the screen. Paulina Koch read it. Disciplined as always, she started on the report itself. The phone buzzed several times while she was working through it. She was a trained speed-reader; the long document took her only about an hour and a half.

That was how long her career took to crumple, she thought when she was done. If Valleix howled for blood at the thought of giving a race a plow it had not had before, what would he say about giving a world a goddess? She knew the answer to that only too well: he would howl to shut down the Service. He'd have backing too, curse him, not just Purists but penny-pinchers of all stripes. She'd fought for years to keep that kind of unholy alliance from forming. Now it had a cause to coalesce around, one she knew would be strong enough to wreck the Service and her with it.

Even so, she thought she was in perfect command of herself until she tried to clear the report. She needed three stabs before she could hit the right button. At last the screen went blank and gray.

She also had to try several times before she got the extension she wanted.

"External Affairs," a deep voice said.

"Hovannis, will you come up here for a moment?" At least her voice gave away nothing, she told herself with lonely pride. Not that it mattered—not that anything would matter once the report came out. Still, rather than just yield to despair, she preferred to go on naturally as long as she could. "An interesting situation has arisen, one you'll want to see."

"On my way," Hovannis said briskly. The phone went dead. Hovannis was a capable man, Paulina Koch thought, well suited to running the Survey Service's External Affairs Bureau—Security, an organization less sensitive to public relations would have called it.

Stavros Monemvasios felt caffeine buzzing through his veins like current through wires. Excitement also energized him, perhaps more powerfully. Under both stimulants his exhaustion was rising, but he had no trouble shoving it down, though his clock told him the time was closer to sunrise than to midnight. He would be a zombie in class, but he did not care.

Fogelman couldn't have looked at the data cards before he dished them out. Stavros was certain of that. The report on Bilbeis IV was no plum; it was a bomb, waiting to go off and blow the Survey Service to smithereens.

Even as an undergrad, Stavros had learned about Bilbeis IV. It was the "don't" pounded into every would-be fieldworker, and carried two lessons with it. Breaking the rule of noninterference not only improperly influenced primitive worlds, it also guaranteed—and earned—professional death for anyone foolish enough to try it.

Improperly influenced . . . "Ho, ho, ho!" Stavros muttered. His lips skinned back from his teeth in a humorless grin. He would have backed that phrase in any understatement contest anywhere.

That anthropologist had cured Queen—what was her name? Sabium, that was it—Queen Sabium's cancer, all right. He'd cured her so well that there she still was, very much alive, fifteen hundred years later. No wonder a whole continent and part of another worshiped her as the undying goddess.

Stavros wished it weren't so late. He wanted to call Fogelman and scream in his ear. He reached for his phone. The anthropology prof had given his grad students his home code, and he wouldn't mind getting out of bed for news like this.

Then Stavros put the phone down. Rousting Fogelman would be fun, but coming into class in a week, all cool and innocent, and stunning everyone at once sounded even better. He plucked at his beard, trying to compose a couple of innocent-sounding opening sentences for his presentation. He chuckled. That wouldn't be easy.

He wondered just how many heads would roll at the Survey Service because of the Bilbeis IV report. He was no Purist, but he didn't relish the idea of having a whole planet's development yanked out of shape by external influences. And the only way the Service kept its budget so nice and fat was by insisting that kind of thing never happened, never *could* happen. Now that it had, a lot of people would need to cover their asses in a hurry.

He caught himself yawning enormously. Caffeine or no, work on the presentation would have to wait till tomorrow.

Roupen Hovannis did not read as fast as his boss, but he did not have to wade through the whole report, either. Paulina Koch brought the relevant, damning sections up on the screen one at a time.

"Enough," Hovannis said, waving for her to stop. He was a big, dark stocky man with a large hooked nose, heavy eyebrows, and a permanent five o'clock shadow even though he shaved twice a day. The thuggish exterior added to his effectiveness; people underestimated his intelligence.

"Reactions?" Paulina Koch asked after Hovannis had sat silent for some time.

"We are in major trouble if and when this report gets out." Paulina Koch frowned; she preferred bureaucratic circumlocutions to plain speech. But at the moment Hovannis did not care; for one of the few times in his career, he was shaken. He went on. "PK"—no one called the Chairman by her first name, not more than once—"when the Purists see it, they'll scream for our blood, and I think they'll get it. The document is plenty to drive everyone cool or lukewarm to us into the Purist camp, and to make our friends look for a good place to hide."

"Very much my own assessment, Roupen." Hovannis glanced at Paulina Koch with surprised admiration; she might have been talking about the pricing policy for oxygen tanks. "What response do you recommend we make, then?" she asked.

His grin was frightening. "I wish the damned ship had crashed before that crew of traitors ever got the chance to file their report."

"That, unfortunately, is not relevant at this point in time."

"I suppose not," Hovannis said regretfully.

"Still," the Chairman said, "I do not relish the prospect of standing up before the Assembly and telling them of the blunder we have found."

"David Ware got his a long time ago."

"Too long ago, I fear, for it to matter. We are the ones available now to be punished for his mistake."

Hovannis grunted. "The report ought to disappear from the files."

"I thought of that also. I concluded it would yield us no lasting benefit. Eventually the crew of the *Jêng Ho* will simply refile: probably when they notice no outcry has erupted from the report."

"But then we'll be ready for them." Once Hovannis had an idea, he ran with it. "If they start raising a stink, they'll do it through channels at first. Computer foulup explains anything once, especially since odds are those bastards don't even realize the mess they've landed us in. Hell, they may even be naive enough to believe the file got erased by accident twice. Any which way, we'll have bought ourselves some time."

"Maybe even enough to see us through this session of the Assembly," Paulina Koch mused. "Maybe. And an old scandal, even if unearthed, will not do us nearly so much damage next time as a fresh one now." She took her time to think it over and then slowly nodded. "Very well, Roupen. The critical issue, you understand, is to make certain the deletion is either invisible or, if by some mischance it should be noticed, cannot be traced to your intervention."

Hovannis nodded. "Depend on it. I'll handle the erasure myself." His smile did not touch his eyes. "After all, we don't need more people thinking about Bilbeis IV than are already."

"No."

"May I use your terminal?" The question was only formal.

"No," Paulina Koch said again. Hovannis stopped in surprise, his stubby-fingered hands poised over the keyboard. She went on. "Please note, Roupen, I have not told you what to do, and I can truthfully state that under oath. Nor do I care to see you do anything."

The External Affairs Director's eyes lit in anger, but it faded as he thought things through. He gave a grudging nod. "Sensible, from your seat."

"Indeed."

"All right." Hovannis wet his lips. Paulina Koch was one of the few people who made him nervous, and not because she outranked him. He had to work to bring out his next words: "Remember, though, PK, if the wave rolls over me, I won't be the last one to drown."

"Who said anything of waves? All we aim to do is keep the water calm and quiet. Thank you for coming up, Roupen. Now I hope you will excuse me; I have other business to attend to."

Paulina Koch watched him go. Her brows drew together very slightly. A capable man, yes, and one who could prove dangerous—no one had had the nerve to warn her that way in a long time. But their interests here ran in the same direction. And the dismissal she'd given him would keep him in his place a while.

She set the matter of Bilbeis IV aside and turned to the printouts still cluttering her desk. She could not ignore all of them because of a single problem elsewhere; that would have been bad management. She had kept the Survey Service running smoothly for nineteen years; she wanted to keep her seat at least that much longer.

Hovannis's abrupt return startled her. "Yes?" she said coldly. What was he doing back here?

"It's gone from our files."

"I assumed so. I did not need to hear that, nor want to. If you are seeking to implicate me in what you have done, you may have succeeded, but I assure you that you will not enjoy your success much."

"I'm not stupid enough to think I would, PK."

"Well, then? I assume this visit does have some reason?"

Hovannis started to sink into a chair, hesitated, waited for the Chairman's nod, then finished sitting. "You know that survey ships' reports, like most other government reports, go into open access."

"How could I not know that? It helps the Purists meddle." Paulina Koch had been maneuvering behind the scenes for years to get Survey Service records shifted to restricted access. The Purists were only part of her political consideration. Too many things happened on primitive planets that the public could not be expected to understand. Bilbeis IV was a perfect example. The Chairman nodded slowly, as if to herself. "You are, I presume, about to tell me seventeen people on thirteen different planets have already made copies of the report. If so, we are finished, and nothing to be done about it."

"If that were so, I'd still be downstairs, working on my vita so I could start looking for another job." That was candid enough to surprise a smile out of Paulina Koch. Hovannis noted it with some relief; it would soften the bad news. "One copy was accessed, less than half an hour before I dumped the file."

"Tell me the rest."

"Accessor is Isaac Fogelman, home planet Hyperion."

"Have you checked on him? I've heard the name, I think."

"Not yet. You needed to know ASAP."

"Mmp." The grunt told Hovannis he was forgiven. "Let's see what the data store tells us about him," Paulina Koch said. "No, don't leave, Roupen; seeing who uses Survey Service information will not incriminate me unduly." She punched buttons and grunted again. "University of Hyperion, anthropology department."

"Bad," the External Affairs Director said. People who chose teaching over fieldwork had no real notion of what conditions were like away from their keyboards and terminals. Most of them were Purists, and most of the ones who weren't were sympathizers.

Studying the readout, he saw Fogelman was like the rest. Several of his publications criticized Survey Service field technique, though he himself had stayed on Hyperion the last fifteen years. He was also a member of the Noninterference Foundation, a private watchdog group that monitored the Service. If he wasn't an out-and-out Purist, he came too close for comfort. "Bad," Hovannis repeated.

"Yes," the Chairman said. "When he makes his dramatic revelation, he will have the credentials to be taken seriously."

"If his copy of the text was to vanish also—"

"No," Paulina Koch said. Then she reconsidered. With the Service on the line, what did one meddling professor matter? "Well, perhaps—if he never has the chance to accuse us of anything. In this area, any publicity is bad publicity: the less anyone outside the Service thinks of Bilbeis IV, the better."

Hovannis agreed with her completely. "I've done some checking. The Service has contacts with a discreet individual on Hyperion, one who, by luck, operates out of New Westwood, the university town."

"Yes, that is fortunate," the Chairman agreed.

Hovannis waited for a more definite order, then realized he would not get one. "It will be attended to," he said. Bureaucratic language sometimes had its advantages; he could truthfully deny under oath that he had ever said he would do anything.

The discreet individual had already made electronic hash of all the data cards in Fogelman's study. Trashing the professor's entire data storage system was about the craziest commission he'd ever had, but he got paid for results, not questions. Very well paid in this case, certainly enough to keep him incurious.

The screen of Fogelman's terminal came on, filling the study with pale gray light. The discreet individual got to work again. Fogelman's security precautions were more than sufficient to keep amateurs from getting into his files, but the discreet individual was no amateur. Besides, he had been briefed about likely keywords and traps, which made the job go faster than it would have otherwise.

One thing the discreet individual had not been briefed about was Professor Fogelman's weak kidneys. As he usually did, Fogelman woke up in the middle of the night. The light downstairs bothered him. He sometimes left his computer up, but he thought he'd turned it off before he went to bed. Muttering to himself, he went down to check.

The discreet individual heard him coming, of course, and shot him through the head with a discreetly silenced weapon when he appeared in the study doorway. Fogelman lived alone; his neighbors would never notice the small noise he made falling. The discreet individual went back to what he had been doing.

When he was through, he efficiently ransacked the place—he

had not been paid not to—and left through the same window he'd used to enter.

Unlike the luckless Fogelman, he had no trouble sleeping when he got home.

Stavros was the first one to the seminar room, which showed how eager he was to get on with his presentation. Cooling his heels outside while the group inside finished, he wondered if eagerness was cause enough to drum him out of the grad students' union. It probably was, he decided.

The session in the room broke up, and the students came out excitedly discussing something or other that wasn't anthropology and made very little sense to Stavros. He pushed through them and found a seat.

One by one, the other members of the seminar drifted in. Some wanted to talk about their presentations. Others were too nervous about speaking in public to care to put out their conclusions more than once. Stavros kept quiet, too; he was saving his ammunition for Fogelman.

He was no poker player, though. "You look like the cat that ate the canary," the girl from Earth said. She was sitting across from him.

"The what?" he said foolishly, not following the idiom. What was her name? He'd only heard it at the meeting last week. "You're Andrea Dubois, aren't you?"

She smiled, pleased he remembered. She was a big pink blond girl and thus seemed strange to Stavros; most of New Thessaly's population was Hellenic, as slim and dark as he was. "How's this?" she said. "You look like someone sitting there waiting for the Academic Medal to go on your chest."

"I think I did a good piece of work." He still didn't want to talk about it, but she was pretty, obviously bright or she wouldn't be here, and so he didn't want the conversation to end either. "You speak beautiful Basic—you sound like the instruction tapes I learned from."

"Thanks." She smiled again. "I wish I could take more credit for it, but I just happen to come from Perth, and everyone in Australia talks this way. At home we call it English."

"I'm jealous."

"It's not as big an advantage as you think," Andrea said. "Because I use Basic all the time and never had to learn another language, I'll probably have more trouble than you in picking up alien languages."

"Well, maybe," Stavros said dubiously.

Without heat, they argued about it for a while until Andrea looked at her watch and said in some surprise, "Professor Fogelman is very late."

"He makes a habit of it." Stavros chuckled. But when Fogelman did not show up after another ten minutes, he began to wonder himself.

The door opened. But it was not Fogelman who came into the seminar room—it was one of the administrative aides from the anthropology department. The fellow looked shaken; his voice wobbled as he said, "May I have your attention, please?"

The class quieted. He went on, "I'm extremely sorry to have to tell you that Professor Fogelman died last night. His body has just been found at his home."

The seminar group exclaimed in shock and dismay. Stavros crossed himself. He had grown agnostic since coming to the university, but childhood habits still returned in times of stress. "What did he die of?" someone called.

The aide looked unhappier yet. "Professor Fogelman appears to have been murdered, apparently in the course of a robbery. Police investigations are continuing."

The second round of gasps and groans was louder and longer than the first. Stavros was too stunned even to join in. Fogelman had been too full of vigor—to say nothing of being too much a fixture on campus—to imagine him dead.

Andrea apparently accepted the idea more quickly, but then, Stavros didn't think she'd done her undergrad work on Hyperion, so she'd seen Fogelman only once or twice. "What does this do to our enrollment in the seminar?" she asked.

"Professor Richardson has agreed to take over the course," the aide said. Andrea looked relieved. Odds were the girl from Earth didn't know Richardson either, Stavros thought. Richardson specialized in physical anthropology, and thought the cultural half of the discipline a waste of time.

"Get ready for fifteen weeks of potsherds and middens," Stavros whispered to Andrea.

The aide left. The grad students trailed after him, still struggling to accept what they'd heard. "If I'd known he was going to get himself killed, I wouldn't have worked so hard," one said.

"Nice pragmatic fellow," Andrea said, rolling her eyes.

"We both know how he feels," Stavros said. "A lot of the time, I'd agree with him. Not now, though."

"No?" Andrea gave him a curious look. "You *are* carrying something big there, aren't you?"

Stavros hesitated. Sometimes professors ended up publishing work graduate students did. Sometimes other grad students pulled the same stunt. He sometimes thought anybody who wasn't a little paranoid had no business in grad school. But Andrea was right—he did have a blockbuster in his briefcase, and he felt he'd explode if he didn't show it to someone.

"Do you really want to see it?" he said. "Let's go over to the Bistro. What they do to *dolmades* is a crying shame, but they're cheap and close."

It was Andrea's turn to pause, but after a moment she laughed and said, "All right, you've got me curious. And what are dol-whatevers?"

"Grape leaves stuffed with lamb and rice. They're an ancient dish; the recipe goes back to Greece, the Earth region the settlers from New Thessaly came from. The cooks at the Bistro don't season them right, though."

"How long has New Thessaly been settled?" she asked.

He shrugged. "A couple of thousand years. Why?"

"Just that I'd be surprised if your people didn't use native spices in their cooking. Everybody does. For all you know, these *dolmades* may be more like the originals than the ones you're used to are."

That almost made him angry, as if she had somehow maligned his home planet. A few seconds of reflection showed she was right, but that did not help much. "Come on," he said gruffly.

Again, he didn't quite know how to take the appreciative noises she made over the Bistro's *dolmades.* After a couple of glasses of red wine, he worried less. He fiddled with his briefcase. "Are you ready yet?" he asked.

"Eager, eager, eager," she teased, but good-naturedly. "Yes, show me your great mystery, now that I'm not distracted by starvation."

He got out the hard copy of his paper, and ordered *baklava*—not even he could fault the way the Bistro made *baklava.* Andrea paid him the highest compliment of all: she left hers untouched while she read.

She looked up after a couple of pages. "You're sure you're not exaggerating this?"

"It's all straight from the report. If anything, summarizing it cuts the impact because so much of the documentation and supporting detail boils away."

She gave an absent nod; she was reading again. When she was

done, she knocked back the wine in her glass with a single gulp. "You weren't kidding," she said quietly. "What are you going to do now?"

He shook his head. "I just don't know. I was going to ask Fogelman, but now—what a mess this is."

He felt the inadequacy of the words, but Andrea understood what he meant. "If I were you, I'd be careful about showing this to a lot of people, at least ones you don't know you can trust."

"Don't be silly," Stavros started to say. He stopped. Knowing something important *could* be dangerous; New Thessaly's politics had proved that more than once. He touched her hand. "I'm not sorry you saw it."

"Good."

"Unfortunate the professor had to go downstairs at such an inopportune time," Paulina Koch remarked.

"Yes, very," Hovannis said. "Especially for him."

"No danger of any of that being traced to us?"

Hovannis snorted. "Not a chance. The deal went through an intermediary; our friend doesn't have any idea who he was working for. He didn't even know exactly what he was supposed to do—just to scramble the computer system was all the instructions he ever got. They may catch him; Hyperion has a fair constabulary. It won't do them any good."

"All right. That suffices, I suppose; you've already told me more than I ought to know."

"I apologize for the need," Hovannis said. The External Affairs Director left. Paulina Koch was very good at putting data in compartments. That was one reason she made such an effective Survey Service Chairman. She began raising the walls around the compartment that held the Bilbeis IV affair. Eventually, she was sure, those walls would be too high to see over, and she would forget whatever was behind them.

If Stavros hadn't taken off his headphones to change disks on the music player, he never would have heard the knock on the door. He rushed to open it, expecting Andrea. She had been over once to see the Survey Service report on Bilbeis IV and again the next day just to talk. Stavros hoped for something more.

"Hello!" he said enthusiastically—too enthusiastically, for standing in the hallway was not Andrea but a middle-aged oriental man whose face was vaguely familiar. Stavros's tongue stumbled over itself. "Er—yes?"

"I'm Van Shui Pong," the man said, "from Hyperion Newsnet." He dug out a holo ID, but Stavros did not need it. He had seen the other man now and then on the screen.

He stepped aside. "Come in, Mr. Pong. What could Hyperion Newsnet possibly want with me?" If anyone is less newsworthy than an anthropology grad student, he thought, whoever it is probably hasn't been born yet.

"It's Mr. Van," the newsman said with the air of someone who had said it a great many times. He had a round, good-natured face, but his eyes were disconcertingly keen when he turned them on Stavros. "You were one of Professor Isaac Fogelman's students, weren't you?"

The polite smile vanished from Stavros's face. "Yes. What of it?" Fogelman's murder hadn't even made the news.

"Very possibly, nothing," Van admitted. "There was something in the constabulary report strange enough to make me do a little checking on my own, though."

"What's that?" Stavros recovered his manners again. "Here, I'm sorry; sit down." He waved to the less disreputable of the two chairs in the dorm room.

"Thank you. As I say, it may well be nothing. Still, I find it strange that a burglar would take the time to dump an entire computer memory. Suppressing the internal surveillance program is normal, but this went far beyond that. There's no doubt it was done deliberately; all of Fogelman's data cards were blanked, too." The newsman rose in sudden concern. "Are you all right, Mr. Monemvasios?"

"Yes," Stavros said, but the word rang hollow in his own ears. He sat down himself, heavily. For the first time in his life, he knew what fear felt like.

Van saw his agitation. "You know something of this, or can guess?" he asked eagerly.

Stavros hesitated. Andrea's warning abruptly seemed much better advice than when she'd given it. Telling Van about the data card leaning against his computer could land him in genuine trouble that keeping quiet would avoid. But if Fogelman had been killed to make sure the report on Bilbeis IV never surfaced, then staying silent would only let the killers, whoever they were, get what they wanted. But, Stavros thought hopefully, most likely there was no connection between the burglary and the report but the long arm of coincidence. The Federacy was a big place; anything could happen, and probably would, somewhere.

Stavros got up. "You'd better see this and tell me what you think." Van followed him to the computer console. He put in the data card. The screen lit. No going back now, he thought. He did not feel the way he imagined investigators were supposed to feel. He just felt nervous.

Van Shui Pong went through the abstract of the report and got a couple of chapters into the body before he hit the pause button. When he looked over to Stavros, all the good humor had fallen from his features. "I take it you believe this document to be genuine," he said at last.

"Of course it's genuine," Stavros said indignantly. "I told you, Professor Fogelman gave it to me. His fingerprints must still be on the data card, if you doubt that."

"Not what I meant." Van held up a hand. "I am no anthropologist. Is this an authentic Survey Service document? The Service is an influential arm of the Federacy, and not forgiving to anyone with the gall to call it to account. I'd hate to have my career blighted for no good reason."

"Here—look at these, then." Stavros secured the data card with the Bilbeis IV report and took out a couple of others.

Van went through them as carefully as he had the first one, perhaps more so. "If it is a forgery, it's masterfully done," he conceded. "All right, I'm willing to spend the money to check one step further. To spend the newsnet's money, anyway—I'll have to go back to my office to use the accessor there. Do you want to come along?"

Nothing could have held Stavros back. He grabbed a cap. "Let's go." Accessors to link in with computer systems planets away were uncommon and exorbitantly expensive. Of course the university had one, and the local government, and Fogelman had doubtless used the anthro department budget, not his own, to get up-to-date data cards for his seminar. The newsnet setup might well be the only other one on Hyperion.

Stavros had never been to the newsnet office before. It reminded him of the way the university got the week before exams: both had the same air of intense concentration and near panic aimed at getting something important done on time.

"Better be good," somebody called as Van sat down in front of the accessor, "or they'll make you pay for it out of your own pocket."

"Funny, Flavius, funny." The newsman punched buttons, paused in thought, punched again. He gave Stavros an apologetic glance. "I haven't used this gadget in a while."

Despite the caveat, he did not take long to make the connection with the Survey Service archives. BILBEIS IV, MOST RECENT SURVEY REPORT, he typed.

SURVEY SERVICE REPORT—BILBEIS IV—FEDERACY STANDARD YEAR 1186 appeared at the top of the screen.

Stavros paid no attention to the text below. "That's not right! That's the old report—the one that tells how what's-his-name got this whole mess started."

Van typed, MORE RECENT REPORTS?

NO MORE RECENT REPORTS. The reply was immediate and uncompromising. Van looked at Stavros, who wanted to hide under his chair. He wondered where Fogelman had come by the data card, if not from the Survey Service. He could not imagine the professor manufacturing such a document or how he would go about it even if he wanted to. The video perfectly matched the first report's pictures and supported the text it accompanied.

"It's crazy," Stavros said. Van Shui Pong did not answer. Grasping at straws, the grad student suggested, "Ask when the next report from Bilbeis IV is due. The place must be up for resurvey—fifteen hundred years is the standard interval for pretechnological worlds."

Shrugging, Van typed in the question. NEXT REPORT EXPECTED WITH RETURN OF SURVEY SHIP *JÊNG HO*, was the response. Van shrugged again. "Your data card has that much right, at any rate."

"Well, when is the *Jêng Ho* coming back?" Stavros asked. Van entered that question, too. They both waited impatiently, hoping the reply would do something to clear up their confusion.

The screen stayed blank for some time. "Must be going through a different data base," Van said. The words were barely out of his mouth when the answer came: SURVEY SHIP *JÊNG HO* SCHEDULED TO RETURN FEDERACY STANDARD YEAR 2687:139.

"What's the current FSY date?" Stavros asked. The Federacy Standard Year, based on Earth's, had 365 days of 86,400 seconds each. It gave thousands of planets, each with its own natural period, a common way to reckon time. Like Hyperion, though, most of them used local time for everything but Federacy elections and other matters of off world importance. Stavros hadn't worried about FSY dating in months.

Van dealt with it more often; as a newsman, he used FSY datelines to see how recent stories set away from Hyperion were. But he did not have the FSY date at the tip of his tongue either. He fiddled with his watch, frowned, cleared it, tried again. "I knew I had to get this thing fixed," he muttered. "It says it's already FSY 2687:157."

"That's crazy," Stavros agreed. "Ask somebody else."

Van did, loudly. "It's 157," three people yelled back, one of them adding, "for another three hours, anyway."

"But that makes no sense," Stavros said. "If the *Jêng Ho* was due back from Bilbeis IV eighteen days ago, the crew must have filed its report already. Why isn't it on-line for accessing?"

"I'm beginning to think they did file," Van said, and he was not talking loudly at all now. "If the report you have is the real one, and it's missing from the Survey Service files, and your professor had all his data—to say nothing of himself—erased just after he pulled it out, what does that suggest to you?"

Stavros thought about it. "Trouble."

"To me, too." But Van sounded as though he enjoyed the prospect.

V

"You appear to have made a mistake, Roupen," Paulina Koch said.

"So I do," Hovannis replied stolidly.

"Is that all you have to say?" The Survey Service Chairman seldom let anger into her voice, but this was an exception. The first tape she'd just played from Hovannis was of some muckraker's story from the Hyperion Newsnet. It quoted at length from the Bilbeis IV report Hovannis had been so sure he'd squelched and then went on to scream cover-up. The second tape worried her more. She had just gotten that one. The story on it was much like the one from Hyperion, but it came from Fezzan, a dozen light-years away.

"What do you want me to do, jump off the top of the Survey Service tower?" Hovannis was finding that Paulina Koch no longer intimidated him as much as she once had. They were in the same starship now, even if it had sprung a leak. The thing to do was patch it, not argue. "I scrubbed the report, but I missed the notice of the *Jêng Ho*'s return date. The snoop spotted it and drew the right conclusions, that's all."

"I've been called into the Assembly for more questioning tomorrow," the Chairman said.

"And?" Hovannis waited for her to tell him she was throwing him out the air lock. If she tried, he had no intention of going alone.

"And I will deny everything, of course," she replied. "The initial report was bad enough. It would have cost us embarrassment, funding, and influence. Now we have suppressed evidence and involved ourselves in various other unsavory activities. If those are discovered, we stand to lose more than influence."

Hovannis gave her an admiring glance. "The whole thing is a forgery, then?" She had balls if she thought she could bring that off.

"From top to bottom. We have no record of any such report, so it could never have entered our files in the first place. Obviously, then, it must be a fabrication. How will the Assembly prove otherwise, from the computer records?"

"No way, of course." The External Affairs Director had already corrected his blunder; the *Jêng Ho* was now due to arrive any time, at least in the Survey Service data bank. He amended, "That's just from the computer records, though. If they start summoning the *Jêng Ho*'s crew, everything is out to lunch."

Paulina Koch smiled a wintry smile. "Not necessarily. They will take a while to think of that, and we already have."

"Yes, I see what you mean," Hovannis said. If and when he tackled that job, he planned to handle it so indirectly that no trace would ever lead back to him. He went on. "I just hope they don't decide to make another visit to Bilbeis IV and check things out firsthand."

He saw he had actually managed to amuse the Chairman. "I assure you, I shall not waste my time worrying about *that*," she said. "The controversy at the moment is over the report, after all, not the planet, and I intend to keep it focused there. Besides, can you imagine the cost?"

Hovannis nodded. Bureaucrats thought that way. Data cards and money were more real to them than barbarous worlds. He returned to more immediate concerns. "We ought to check out where Mr. Van Shui Pong is getting his information now that Fogelman's data base is gone."

"You really think it is?" Paulina Koch asked. "I'm beginning to wonder."

"I've used that person before, for one thing and another. He's reliable."

"If you're so sure, Fogelman must have passed it onto someone before your friend visited him. Not to this Van busybody, or we would have had him yapping at us sooner. To whom, then?" It was not really a question; the Chairman was thinking out loud. "To one of his students, perhaps, for a class project."

"Sensible," Hovannis said. "Fogelman pulled a lot of recent survey reports, not just the one on Bilbeis IV. We can check out why he wanted them without too much trouble. Then we start narrowing things down, and then, well, I suppose another visit from that discreet individual."

"Yes, overall that bears the potential for greatest benefit to the Service. With the focus of the infection removed, the hubbub should die down in fairly short order. Tend to it, Roupen; I have to prepare my testimony."

Tend to it, Roupen, Hovannis thought sourly as he left the Chairman's office. He would; his neck was on the block, too. But afterward, Paulina Koch would owe him a debt. He intended to collect.

Magda was in the shower when the phone chimed. She swore and stayed under the warm needle spray, hoping whoever was on the other end of the line would give up and go away.

Whoever it was had stubbornness to go with an exquisitely misplaced sense of timing. The chime kept ringing. Muttering under her breath, Magda turned off the shower, pulled her hair back from her face so it would not drip in her eyes, and shrugged on the robe she had hanging by the stall. Let this idiot figure out what he'd interrupted, she thought—maybe he'd be embarrassed enough to hang up in a hurry.

The minute she clicked on the screen and saw she was face to face with Atanasio Pedroza, she knew she had made a mistake. She had turned aside the biologist's advances all through the mission of the *Jêng Ho,* but he had not given up even after the ship had come back to the base on Topanga.

Now he did not look embarrassed; he looked as though he was picturing her wet naked body under the robe. She pulled it together so it covered more of her, but that proved wrong too, because it drew his attention to her breasts. The guardsmen who'd caught her in the bath on Bilbeis IV had been more polite.

"Hello, Atanasio," she said, sighing. "What is it?"

"Hmm? I'm sorry, Magda, I was too busy admiring." Even his voice had a leer in it, the anthropologist thought with distaste. He somehow never failed to set Magda's teeth on edge.

"*Will* you come to the point?" she snapped; patience had never been one of her long suits. She was also getting cold.

He looked hurt. "After we fought that report through together, I thought we might be able to get along better in other ways, too."

"Don't get your hopes up." To give Pedroza his due, he had fought hard for an honest report. He had rigid standards of right and wrong and the courage of his convictions. It was his personality outside those convictions that made Magda dislike him. "Just because we were able to work together once, Atanasio, doesn't mean I want to go to bed with you."

"I don't give up easily."

She grimaced. She knew that was true. Professionally, it was an asset; here, it was more a pain in the ass. He went on. "Soon I'll have a chance to try changing your mind under more pleasant circumstances than this semiconscious excuse for a planet offers."

Magda rather liked Topanga's relaxed pace, but that had nothing to do with the sharpness of her question. "What do you mean?"

"The whole crew has won a round trip to Carson Planet. Once a month here, they throw the names of all the incoming ships into the computer, and the *Jêng Ho* came out. Captain Brusilov delegated the arrangements to me."

That last sentence killed the pleasure the previous two had given Magda. She had been to Carson Planet before, and had enjoyed it. The place specialized not in industry or agriculture but in no-holds-barred fun: "Everything in Excess" was the local motto. Not surprisingly, it was one of the richer worlds in this part of the Federacy. However—

"I suppose you booked the two of us into the same cubicle on the flight out," she said. She had intended it as sarcasm, but Pedroza refused to meet her eyes. "You bastard, you didn't!"

"As a matter of fact, no," he said, flushing, but before she could be mollified he admitted, "You *are* in the one next to mine, and they do connect."

"You have your nerve. After the *Jêng Ho,* I'm not overjoyed being on the same planet with you, let alone the same starship—and being in the next cubicle is way, way too close. I'll stay here, thanks. Have yourself a good time."

"Everyone else I've gotten hold of is eager to go. We even got a credit advance to gamble with."

"I—don't—care," she said between clenched teeth. "Now, will you get off the damn phone and let me finish my shower?"

"I'll send the tickets and such over to you, in case you change your mind." He blanked the screen.

"Not bloody likely," she muttered. She took off her robe, flung it against the wall, and got back under the water. It did not wash away her foul mood, which was not helped by finding that Pedroza was as good as his word: a ticket for a tour ship, a reservation at one of the better Carson Planet hotels, and notification of her credit advance were sitting in the fax slot. She scowled at them, wishing

Pedroza were less stubborn, or at least that he would find someone else to pursue.

She dressed in a hurry and took a shuttle to the Survey Service field office. She could have done her business by phone, but she was too irked to stay in her apartment. Besides, she was also annoyed at the field office people, and snarling at them in person gave more satisfaction than fuming by phone.

"Any word on that report yet?" she snapped without preamble as she walked in. The report on Bilbeis IV had gone in to Survey Service Central days ago, but none of the explosions Magda expected was going off yet.

"Let me check," the clerk sighed. He fiddled with his terminal so slowly that Magda wanted to leap over the partition separating them and do it for him. He seemed oblivious to her impatience. After what could not possibly have been a year and a half, he looked up and said, "Central says the report never reached their files. Must be some computer trouble in the system somewhere."

"Oh, damnation," she said, loud enough to make people all over the office turn their heads her way. "Have you ever had trouble with the FTL link to that data base before?"

"No," the clerk said. "Of course, there's always a first time. I think you'll have to resubmit." He sounded almost pleased at the prospect. Fieldwork attracted adventurers; Survey Service offices drew routineers. The two groups often clashed.

Magda was not about to give the petty bureaucrat any more satisfaction than he'd already gotten. "All right," she said, so sweetly that he looked at her with sudden suspicion. "Of course, at the same time I expect you'll submit a notice of trouble in the system. Give me your supervisor's name, so I can notify him or her that it's coming."

The clerk grumbled at the prospect of work he couldn't do on automatic pilot, but Magda had him, and he knew it. He reluctantly coughed up his boss's name.

"Thank you very much," Magda purred. "I'll be back tomorrow with that data card." She kicked herself for not having brought it with her, but she really had thought the glitch was at her end, not in the computer network. Still, she was not altogether displeased as she rode back to her place. Not only did she know now where the trouble lay, she had also won the little duel with that officebound bungler.

Her roommate was home when she opened the door. She and Marie Roux had been friends during fieldwork training half a dozen years ago and then, as was the way of such things, had not seen each other since, though they had kept in touch with tapes. Finding each other on Topanga at the same time, they overrode the computer's temporary housing assignment to be together and talk about old times.

"Hi, Magda," Magda said.

"Hi, Marie," Marie said. They both laughed. They had been the only two redheads in their training group, and the instructors—and even some of the other recruits—had mixed up their names so often they started doing it themselves.

"I wish I *were* Magda," Marie said. "My ship couldn't win an overhaul, let alone the travel pool. Carson Planet—mmmm! I'm jealous." She waved at the goodies Atanasio Pedroza had sent.

"Do you want to go?" Magda asked. "Be my guest,"

"What? Don't be ridiculous, Magda. That trip is worth plenty, and besides, you'll have a good time."

"No I won't, because I wouldn't go if they paid me a bonus." Magda explained about Pedroza's unwelcome attentions, finishing, "So you see, Marie, that cabin will just be empty if you don't use it."

"You're serious, aren't you?" Marie said wonderingly. "I really would like to go, but—"

"But what? I told you already—go ahead, do it. You're not taking anything away from me, because I like Topanga without dear Atanasio about a hundred times better than Carson Planet—let alone the"—she checked the ticket—"*Clark County*—with him."

"But—" Marie began again, but Magda knew she was wavering when she shifted her approach. "Even if I did try to go, that prize is for the crew of the *Jêng Ho.* What do I do when somebody asks me what I'm doing there?"

"So long as it's not Atanasio, tell 'em the truth. They all know about him and me. For that matter, you can tell him, too. I have, often enough. He just doesn't listen."

"That's not what I meant. What do I do when they check my ID at the air lock?"

"Odds are they won't." Magda frowned, though, because they could, and she knew it. "Hmm, tell you what—take my spare credit card."

"I couldn't do that!"

"Why not? We've known each other a long time now; you're not going to steal me blind. You'll need it anyway, to tap into the line of credit that goes with the trip. All your other expenses are paid; you shouldn't need to dip into my account. If it makes you feel better, you can leave your spare behind as a hostage."

"I'd insist on that at the very least. Damn it, I'm so tempted now, but it still won't work. When your credit card goes into the computer, the screen will display your picture."

"Hi, Magda," Magda said again.

"I don't think we look alike," Marie said.

"Well, I don't either, but most people certainly seem to. After all these centuries of stirring genes around, redheads are so uncommon that hardly anybody looks past our hair. You're going to gamble *on* Carson Planet, for heaven's sake; are you afraid to gamble a little to get there?"

Marie threw her hands in the air. "All right. I give up. Thank you!" She hugged Magda. "I still think you're crazy, but when do I leave? Do I have time to pack?"

"Here, give me that ticket. I didn't even look." Magda quickly checked it. "You're all right. You're not due out till tomorrow morning."

"Plenty of time," Marie agreed. "One thing the Survey Service does teach you is how to live out of suitcases." She went over to the closet and with practiced efficiency started filling one. Her only hesitation came when she happened on something thin and filmy. She giggled and put it in.

Magda's back was turned. "What's funny?"

Marie displayed what she'd packed. "I was just thinking I might end up liking this Atanasio what's-his-name better than you do."

"Maybe," Magda said. She let it go at that; Marie was her friend. What she was thinking was, better you than me.

Stavros thumbed the remote unit; the holo screen came to life. "What's on?" Andrea asked. They were studying together. They both found Professor Richardson about as exciting as watching a shrub grow, and broken bits of pots did not much interest either of them, but Richardson expected her students to work.

"The news," Stavros answered.

That was plenty to make Andrea put down her notes. Hyperion Newsnet had been flailing away at the Survey Service for a couple of weeks now, with as yet no reply. The long silence from the immense government bureau made Stavros think of someone sticking a pin in a dinosaur. First the beast had to notice you were there at all, and then it would take a while longer to figure out what to do.

Of course, if it did decide to flick its tail, it was apt to squash you flat . . .

The lead story was local—an ore boat had capsized on some river over on the western continent, killing four sailors and losing a big cargo of rare-earth metals. "In offplanet news," the newswoman began, and Stavros tensed, but the item was about the crash of a starship full of gamblers trying to land at Carson Planet. "Three hundred seventeen people are known dead; the complete toll will not be known until the rubble has been cleared from what was until recently a spaceport terminal building."

"Four people here count for more than hundreds somewhere else," Stavros said scornfully.

"Isn't it the same on your world?" Andrea asked. "It is on Earth. Somebody here may know one of the ore haulers, or know someone who does. That makes that story more important in New Westwood than one that happens worlds away."

Stavros had not thought of it that way. Indeed, he had not thought much about it at all. He just knew he was impatient for some kind of response from the Survey Service, and frustrated because there was none. "I suppose you have a point. You know—"

He stopped. Van Shui Pong was on the screen. "In the continuing Survey Service scandal," Van declared, "Chairman Paulina Koch has at last issued a statement." Stavros's whoop drowned out Van's introduction of the Chairman.

"She looks so ordinary," Andrea said. Dowdy is a better word, Stavros thought. Paulina Koch reminded him of a gray dumpling. The suit she wore did not flatter her figure. The curtains behind her podium were bright blue, but she contrived to fade into the background nonetheless.

She was saying, "The Survey Service regrets the delay in response to these allegations, but did not believe they could possibly be taken seriously by anyone aware of the Service's long and successful record of integrity both within the Federacy and in its dealings with people at a pre-Federacy stage of culture. The Service must deny both the charges leveled in respect to activities conducted on the pre-Federacy world Bilbeis IV and those even wilder accusations relating to removal of data from storage. They are baseless, without foundation, and insusceptible to proof."

"What about the report on Bilbeis IV, then?" a newsman interrupted.

She gave him a chilly look. "The report that purports to be about Bilbeis IV, you mean. It is a forgery, and not a very clever forgery at that. Were I here to guess instead of telling you the facts as I know them, I might give you more than a fair idea of the perpetrators of the hoax."

Stavros grunted. He could predict where that line would lead the reporters. "Who?" three of them yelled together.

"Who else but the Purists?" the Chairman replied. "For almost as long as the Survey Service has existed, they have tried to curtail and even halt legitimate scientific inquiry. In the past, I did not question their motives, no matter how strongly I disagreed with their conclusions. When they stoop to tactics such as this, however, I can no longer sit idly by."

"Turn that off," Andrea said in disgust. "She's got them all eating out of her hand. Why won't they *see*!"

Stavros was reaching for the control when a newswoman called to Paulina Koch, "You haven't said anything about the Survey Service computer showing the *Jêng Ho* due back on 139 when it was already 157." The grad student decided to keep watching a while longer.

"Computer error is such a common excuse in a certain type of fiction that I am aware it is difficult to accept in fact," the Chairman said calmly, "but if it didn't occur, it would never have become such a cliché. An investigation into the nature of the error is now ongoing and will be published when complete. Any required modifications in hardware or software will of course be implemented."

At that, Stavros did turn off the holo, jabbing the switch with ferocity directed away from the image of Paulina Koch. She might as well have been coated with some fluorinated resin; nothing stuck to her. "No one even asked about Professor Fogelman," he said bitterly.

"What good would it do?" Andrea said. "I can figure out what she'd say already: that Fogelman's death was just a coincidence, and how can anyone possibly tell what was in his data store, as it has unfortunately suffered erasure—she'd never come right out and say anything as plain as 'been erased.' "

"You're right about that." At another time, he would have found her observation wryly amusing; now he was too angry to rise to the bait.

"I wish we could get hold of the *Jêng Ho*'s crew directly," she said, "instead of waiting for whatever the Survey Service decides to claim is their report."

Stavros sprang to his feet, rushed over to her, and gave her a hug. "Let's try! Van ought to know how to contact them without going through the Survey accessing system. They can't be in on this scheme of the Chairman's, or they never would have filed that report in the first place."

Andrea did not pull back right away. She looked Stavros in the eye—they were about of a height. "Good idea. Call Van."

"He doesn't like me to at night. He's usually busy working up his stories for the newscasts. I'll do it in the morning. No—you do it. You've earned the chance to be in on this."

"All right, I will." To Stavros's surprise, she added, "Thank you."

"Are you sure I'm doing you a favor? You were the one who told me this might get dangerous."

"It's already dangerous if we're right about Fogelman. But if we are, the Survey Service has already done a lot worse than cultural interference."

"Yes. We can't prove that, though."

Andrea clucked her tongue in annoyance. "We can't prove any of this, not when the chairman denies the report on Bilbeis IV is genuine. That's why we need to reach the people who wrote it; they can give her the lie. As a matter of fact, I'm surprised they haven't started squawking before this."

"So am I. It worries me."

"Me too, but I can't do anything about it now. What I can do—and you too—is get ready for the next quiz Richardson is going to drop on us. We ought to get those scrapers and tureens from Cappalli III up on the screen. Them, we can do something about right this minute."

Stavros laughed. "There's practicality for you." He fiddled with the controls. The screen lit, this time full of implements of bone and baked clay. "These are from the small continent in the northern hemisphere—what's its name?"

"Maximilian."

"That's right. I don't know what you're worrying about. You know the material a lot better than I do."

"I want to do a good job."

Even an anthropology grad student can examine only so many artifacts before the brain begins to numb. Andrea and Stavros reached that point at about the same time. She was the one who finally said, "Enough!" and turned off the text.

"What now?" Stavros asked.

"Let's check the entertainment menu. After all that, I need something mindless." She found a costume drama. Some of the costumes were hardly any costume at all. "Like that?" she asked ironically, noticing Stavros's sudden interest in the screen.

"More interesting than ladles and vials," he retorted. "Seriously, though, I was shocked silly the first time I saw bare breasts on the holo. They don't show that kind of thing on New Thessaly; the church is strong there."

"Were you?" Andrea raised an eyebrow. They watched the show sitting close together, as they had been while they were studying. When it was done, Stavros thought Andrea would leave. Instead, she leaned back in her chair and stretched lazily.

He slid an arm around her shoulder. She moved closer to him. "What else have you learned on Hyperion?" she asked.

"Shall we find out?"

Some time later, she leaned up on one elbow in his narrow bed. "You picked up all that in the last few years here?"

He sat up himself, offended. "Good God, no! After all, Andrea, I'm twenty-nine years old."

He watched the flush rise under her fair skin as she blinked in confusion. "But you said—"

"I said I didn't watch that kind of thing on New Thessaly. I didn't; my planet holds to keeping what it reckons private matters private. That doesn't mean we don't do them, though."

She laughed out loud. "You don't need to sound so defensive. I'm glad, that's all."

"Hmm. Prove it." Stavros tried to make his voice gruff, but he was laughing, too.

She poked him in the ribs. "How am I supposed to do that?"

"Think of something."

She did.

The discreet individual was not altogether pleased with the way things were going. It was not any failure to turn a profit that disturbed him. His fees, especially lately, were keeping him in a state of luxury that satisfied even his exacting standards.

Rather, his problem was figuring out a quiet way to earn this latest commission he had received. The woman who proposed it to him was the same person who had given him his last big job. She was so vague about this one that he was sure she was only an intermediary, and probably not the first in a chain.

Despite such precautions, he suspected he could make a good guess about where the chain's other end lay. He tried not to make the guess, even in his own mind. Some things, he felt instinctively, were better left uncontemplated.

The problem had two parts. Neither was easy, and the second, rare in his line of work, required him to draw his own conclusion and act on it. Bugging the comm lines into Hyperion Newsnet had been tough enough, but he was used to doing that. Now he had to decide just where Van Shui Pong was getting information he shouldn't have.

The discreet individual punched for the latest set of playbacks. A burst of static made him scowl. The next several conversations were garbled. The newsnet had most of the latest confidentiality protectors.

Not all of them, though. After a while, his electronics out-dueled the opposing defense systems and he was able to eavesdrop again.

He had done some discreet checking on Van's contacts and had found that two in particular had connections of interest to his carefully unthought-about employer. He had not been able to decide which of them knew more; they both knew too much.

He wondered whether it mattered. Dealing with one ought to teach the other to stop meddling. He was not wasteful: no point to getting rid of both of them unless he found himself without another choice.

In spite of his income, one luxury he could not afford was impatience. He wished he could; Van Shui Pong talked with a lot of people, most of them dull and most of them absolutely unconnected with this business.

At last Van got another call from one of the pair the discreet individual was interested in. After he finished listening to the taped conversation, he nodded thoughtfully. These people were doing their best to be difficult. In the abstract, he could almost wish their best to be good enough.

He was not, however, given to thinking in the abstract.

"He'll check," Andrea said with satisfaction as she switched off the phone. "He says it may take a while to work around the Survey Service network to get in touch with the *Jêng Ho*'s crew, but he thinks he can do it. He was boasting about his connections when he got a call on another line and had to give me a quick good-bye."

"All right," Stavros said. "I hope those connections come through."

"So do I. Reporters always boast about connections, whether they have them or not."

Stavros's long, dark face wore a frown well. Not for the first time, he had the feeling of being in over his head. Actually, he'd had that feeling from the moment he'd seen the report on Bilbeis IV. Running into it when thinking about a woman he cared for, though, was different from facing it when confronting a large, powerful, hostile organization.

He wondered how Andrea came to speak of reporters with casual familiarity. Van excepted, he had never dealt with one in his life. New Thessaly was not that kind of place. Gossip there was as incessant as anywhere else, but it was local and amateur, not industrialized.

Andrea was getting to know him well enough to guess some of the things behind his silence. She said, "Don't worry. We'll just do the best we can as long as we can, with us and with Bilbeis IV."

That was advice he might have heard on his home planet, and it was down-to-earth enough to shake him out of his apprehension. "Fair enough," he said. "I suppose that also applies to the quiz this afternoon."

"I wish you hadn't brought it up." She made a face at him. "I was just at the point of letting myself believe I could take it without doing any more studying. Now I suppose I'll have to get back to it."

"I know *I* need more work. You're good company." He turned on the computer. They sat down together. He looked at her sidelong. "Maybe you should pick out another spectacle instead."

"Ha! Not with that damn quiz waiting for me—no, don't pout, this is what you deserve for reminding me of it."

"All right." Stavros did get down to studying, disappointed but not really displeased. No matter what she knew about reporters, Andrea also knew what came first. That counted for more.

"Thank you for inviting me here today," Paulina Koch said. "It is always a privilege to provide information to this distinguished Assembly subcommittee."

"Thank you for agreeing to appear before us on such short notice, Chairman Koch," Assemblyman Valleix replied.

—Here you are, snooping again.—Damn straight, and maybe we'll nail you this time, too. The Chairman knew the real meaning of the opening amenities perfectly well. So did Valleix. The Purist was a blockhead but not, she thought, that big a blockhead.

He asked, "Have you any opening statement you care to read into the record?"

"Perhaps it would be better merely to respond to questions." Paulina Koch smoothed an imaginary wrinkle from the collar of her gray tunic.

"Very well. I will make the first question as general as I can, then, and ask how you respond to the allegations raised on Hyperion and other planets concerning Survey Service cultural interference on the pretechnological world Bilbeis IV."

"To that, sir, I have only the reply I already gave in public: that the report which—as you properly said—is *alleged* to deal with Bilbeis IV is not a product of Survey Service personnel and was produced to denigrate and cast doubt on the numerous successful activities of the Service."

Assemblyman Valleix nervously licked his lips. He remembered the last trap the Survey Service Chairman had set for him. If she blew him out of the water again here, not only would he look like a fool with elections coming up, but no one would dare tackle the Survey Service again for the next generation and a half.

His voice wobbled as he asked, "Have you conducted a thorough investigation through Service records to ascertain the truth of the statement you have just made?"

"Indeed we have, sir. Nothing in our data files gives any support whatever to the wild claims first raised on Hyperion and then copied by sensation seekers elsewhere. From that, one must conclude the supposed report to be fraudulent. The Survey Service is also conducting an investigation on Hyperion to attempt to discover the source of these scurrilous rumors."

"Yes, I can well believe that," Valleix said dryly. Paulina Koch sat quietly, waiting for his next question. If she heard his sarcasm—and he was certain she did—she never let on. "Perhaps computer specialists from outside the Service will have more luck accessing relevant documents than your own people."

"I hope they do," Paulina Koch said. "Our records are of course at their disposal." She was the perfect witness, polite, attentive; every fact Valleix wanted was at her fingertips.

He fought down the impulse to sigh. If anything ever had been in the Survey Service files, it was not there now, or the Chairman would never risk its being exposed. Still, he was slightly heartened. She had not flattened him by, say, producing a report on Bilbeis IV that showed everything normal there. Maybe she could not. "There remains the discrepancy between the arrival date of the *Jêng Ho* as first taken from Survey Service records by ah"—he paused to check his tickler screen—"by Hyperion Newsnet and that later offered as correct by your organization. Such alteration would seem to support the charge that information is being suppressed."

"Not, I would hope, sir, in the absence of any and all other data. Electronics are fallible, as has been made evident on several painful occasions in the history of the Federacy."

"That is true, Chairman Koch. Sometimes I think we rely too much on electronics. You would not take it amiss, then, if we were to summon some of the crew members of the *Jêng Ho* from, ah"—he glanced down at the note screen again—"Topanga, so they can testify as to what they witnessed on Bilbeis IV? Surely their ship will be in by this time."

"I would think so, sir. Of course I have no objection to such an action. Do whatever you can to uncover the truth here. That is also what we are trying to do, for the sake of our own good name. The wild claims this report makes are wholly inconsistent with the principles upon which we are conducting our operation."

"Thank you, Madam Chairman. I shall instruct the clerk of the subcommittee to issue and serve the appropriate subpoenas." This time Assemblyman Valleix did sigh. If the Chairman was so eager to let the crew people appear, odds were they'd back her up. Valleix turned to the head of the subcommittee. "I have no further questions of the witness at this time."

"Very well. Assemblywoman O'Kelly, you may proceed."

The clerk she had dealt with the day before looked up sourly from his tea as Magda came in. He grew even more unhappy when she walked around to his side of the desk. She took a data card out of her holdall and handed it to him. "I just want to make sure you don't have any trouble copying the document to the data base," she said innocently.

"I'm sure there will be no problem." He looked as if he wanted to erase her card but didn't quite dare. Instead, he put it in his terminal, punched two buttons, waited for a light to go from red to green, and handed it back to her. "It's in the system."

"Good. I hope that wasn't too difficult for you." Now the clerk looked as though he wished he had scrubbed the data card. She tossed him a note handwritten on a memo form. "This outlines the foulup and your part in it. Take it to your supervisor and be careful with it till she gets it—it's the only copy." Of course the memo would end up in the nearest trash can, but getting the report on Bilbeis IV to the attention of the Survey Service—and the public beyond the Service—counted for more than making a functionary's life miserable, however much fun the latter was.

After that, as had happened after the first time the *Jêng Ho*'s crew sent in the report, she had nothing to do but sit around and wait for the roof to blow off Survey Service Central. Even if a new assignment came through, she wouldn't be able to do anything about it until the rest of the crew got back from Carson Planet. But if she had to vegetate, Topanga was a nice place to do it. The climate was warmer and drier than she cared for. The locals had adapted. They never hurried; they made a point of taking things easy and viewed life with a relaxed detachment Magda envied without wanting to emulate.

She also did not care for the way they baked themselves under the sun. She preferred pale skin to bronze, and also preferred not to have to undergo skin cancer therapy every so often. The locals took that annoyance in stride, as they did everything else.

Thinking about the Topangans' indifference to malignancy brought Magda back inevitably to Queen Sabium. Had David Ware not meddled with her fate, she would have been a millennium and a half dead, and Bilbeis IV would be like any other pretechnological world.

Having met Sabium, though, Magda could understand his interference, if not condone it. Sabium was—something else. With time on her hands, Magda began a monograph detailing the effect of her reign. The work progressed only by fits and starts; Topanga's easygoing style proved infectious. Eventually Magda realized with a guilty start that a couple of weeks had gone by without her checking on what was happening with the report she had refiled. She went down to the field office to see what was up.

The clerk was friendlier than he had been the last time she had come in. Amazing what giving him something to throw away could do. He didn't even seem unwilling to check on the status of the report. "There shouldn't be anything wrong," he said reassuringly as he punched buttons. "Survey Service Central is a busy place, you know, and sometimes these things take a while to get a reaction."

"This one will get a reaction," Magda said.

The clerk's look said that Magda thought her little concerns were a lot more important in the grand scheme of things than they really were. She glared at him. Then the screen on his terminal lit. His brown face went smug as he glanced over to it—here he was, handing down the word from on high, Magda thought scornfully.

His smugness abruptly shattered. "What the—" he said, startled into a purely human reaction.

Magda walked around to see the screen for herself. He didn't scowl at her the way he had before when she took such liberties. REPORT FROM SURVEY SERVICE SHIP *JÊNG HO*: NOT IN FILES, she read.

"That's crazy," she muttered. She turned on the clerk. "You must have screwed up the transmission again, uh, Pandit." She had to read his name backward through the clear plastic plate on his desk; she'd never bothered noticing what it was before.

"I did not," he said angrily. "What are you doing, saying things like that? You hovered over me like some miserable vulture, and you didn't complain then."

"So I didn't," she admitted, taken aback by his hot response. "Well, what has gone wrong, then?"

"How should I know? Whatever it is, as far as Survey Service Central can tell, you and your whole crew are still in space. You'll have to retransmit one more time."

"Wonderful. The whole damn crew *is* in space, except for me. Captain Brusilov will nail my hide to the wall when he gets back, too. He'll have as much trouble believing back-to-back computer failures as I do."

"What else could it be?" said the clerk—Pandit, Magda reminded herself. She could not stay irritated at him; he sounded as puzzled as she was.

She said, "For all I know, the people at Central are scrubbing the damn thing on purpose every time it comes in." Pandit's expression said what he thought of that. Magda didn't believe it either. A little paranoia was all well and good, but letting it run wild was something else again. She sighed. "I suppose I'll have to bring it in again, won't I?"

"Unless you'd sooner save yourself the trip and just send me a copy through your computer."

"Not after all the trouble we've gone through already. I want to watch you again while you make the transmission to Survey Service Central."

"Whatever you say." It wasn't Pandit's problem.

"I'll see you tomorrow."

Magda went back to the apartment and made another halfhearted lunge at her monograph. Before long, she was looking for an excuse to quit. She turned on the news. She did not watch often; most of the time on Topanga it was comfortable chatter and not much else. Not this afternoon. A rubble-strewn crater filled the screen; disaster crews struggled frantically amid the debris.

The newswoman was saying, "—almost certainly dead, of course, are the 317 passengers of the ill-fated starship. The toll is expected to rise far higher as the ruins of the crowded terminal building yield their grim secrets. Here is a list of deaths confirmed by credit card recovery—"

"Vultures," Magda muttered. She reached out to switch off the screen.

"—in the crash of the *Clark County,*" the newswoman finished.

Magda's hand froze in the air. The rest of her also felt as if it had turned to ice.

Credit cards were nearly indestructible; men and women, sadly, not. Every so often, another name Magda knew would come up, setting her crying again. Irfan Kawar . . . Norma Anderssen . . . Captain Brusilov would never nail Magda's hide to the wall now. She even had tears for Atanasio Pedroza.

Then she saw her own name.

VI

Stavros opened the door and stepped back in surprise. "Hello! Come in."

"Thank you." Van Shui Pong had not phoned ahead. For that matter, he had not been back to the dormitory since the day he had first introduced himself. He nodded to Andrea, who was eating a candied orange. "Perhaps you and Stavros would like to go for a walk with me. The campus is a pleasant place; I don't get here often enough."

"A walk?" Stavros echoed foolishly. "It's close to midnight."

Van only waited. Andrea stood up and threw on her cloak. Muttering, Stavros got his cap and mantle out of the closet and closed the neck clasp. He and Andrea followed Van to the elevator.

The night was just this side of chilly. The air had a cool green smell, different from the way it smelled during the day. A few lights glowed in distant labs and offices. Still, the path the three walked was to the eye merely a pale snake coiling across dark lawns.

After a while, Van stopped. Stavros could hear the silence between the trills of Terran insects and Hyperion's own small night creatures. Van said, "I've finally managed to track down the crew of the *Jêng Ho.*"

"Have you? That's wonderful!" Stavros exclaimed. "Will they back their report?"

Andrea, though, found another question. "Why did you bring us out here to tell us that?" Even before Van answered, that dampened Stavros's first rush of excitement.

The reporter nodded somberly. "You begin to understand. Here I can hope, at least, that we are not overheard. I don't dare be so optimistic about your rooms anymore, Stavros."

The grad student took a moment to find a name for what he heard in Van's voice. "You're afraid."

"Yes, I am. You see, the *Jêng Ho*'s crew was aboard the *Clark County.*" When neither Stavros nor Andrea reacted, the newsman snorted in irritation. "Why do we go to so much trouble getting out the news when no one pays any attention to us? The *Clark County* is the ship that crashed on Carson Planet not so long ago. Something over three hundred people died, including all of the crewmembers of the *Jêng Ho.*"

"That proves the Survey Service is lying in its teeth," Stavros burst out. "If the *Jêng Ho* didn't get back till the day Paulina Koch claimed, how could the crew have gone on their junket and had that accident?"

"If it was an accident," Andrea said slowly.

Stavros felt the air rush out of him as if he had been kicked in the belly. "That makes too much sense for me to like," he said at last.

"And for me, too," Van said. "I was going to point it out to you people if you didn't come up with it for yourselves. Too many coincidences add up to scaring me a lot—if we keep pushing at this thing, I have a bad feeling we'll end up the same way your Professor Fogelman and twenty Survey Service crewfolk ended up. I'm sorry, but I've had enough. I wish you well if you want to go on, but you'll have to do it without me. My phone won't accept your calls any more; if I hadn't been afraid it was tapped, I'd have called you to tell you this. As is, we have a decent chance of talking in private here. Now I've talked, and now I'm going to leave."

"But, but—" Stavros sputtered to a halt and tried again. "But now we can prove the Service really is trying to suppress the report on Bilbeis IV. They lied about when the *Jêng Ho* came back, which meant the report I have is genuine. It can't mean anything else."

"No, it means one thing more, Stavros. It means the Service isn't just trying to suppress that report—they're doing it. Ask Fogelman, ask the *Jêng Ho*'s crew, ask three hundred other people on the *Clark County* if you doubt me . . . and if you can. I don't need to ask them: I get the message loud and clear."

Andrea said, "How can you back away from this, knowing what you know?" She did not sound angry; if she had, Van would never have answered her. She only sounded bewildered.

The newsman's reply came slowly and grudgingly. "I thought about all this. I've done nothing but think about it the last couple of days. I've lived with my ideals a good many years now. I've always believed in them, but I've found that if I have to choose between keeping my ideals and keeping alive, I'd sooner live. If I go on, I don't think I will, and if you go on, I don't think you will either."

"But—" Stavros had been saying that ever since they got out into the quiet dark. He felt stupid, but nothing better came to mind.

"No more buts." Van thumped him on the shoulder, reached to take Andrea's hand, but dropped his own when she drew back from him. He grimaced. "Good-bye, then." He strode quickly away.

Stavros stared after him, still trying hard not to believe any of what he'd heard. It sank in despite his best efforts. Van's fear was too real to ignore. So was the *Clark County.* "Three hundred some odd people dead," Stavros whispered. "They are playing for keeps."

"Three hundred some odd innocent people dead, on top of Bilbeis IV itself," Andrea said. "Can we let the Survey Service come away untouched after that?"

"Can we stop them?" Stavros did not feel anything like a hero. The longer he stood outside in the blackness, the better he understood Van Shui Pong.

"We have to," Andrea said indignantly.

"Yes, I suppose we do." Giving up would mean not calling the Survey Service to account for what it did on a good many thousand pre-Federacy worlds, to say nothing of leaving Paulina Koch in charge of that immense and powerful bureaucracy. But Stavros remembered Andrea's warning after she first saw the report on Bilbeis IV. Then he'd had to hesitate before he even took her seriously. Now she was proving only too good a prophet.

His shiver had nothing to do with the chill of the night.

"The problem appears to be contained within manageable limits," Paulina Koch remarked.

"Yes," Hovannis said. "The loss of the *Clark County* was a great tragedy."

"So it was." The Chairman did not ask her External Affairs Director any questions about that. Whatever he knew, he knew. She hoped it was nothing, but she did not want to find out.

Certainly, the Assembly probe had crashed with the *Clark County.* No one was in a position to contradict Survey Service testimony after that. A few people, Paulina Koch's informants said, made snide comments about the crash's convenience. No one made them to her face or on the record.

"Is there anything more?" she asked Hovannis.

"Nothing to speak of, PK. Hyperion Newsnet is finally calming down, as you may have noticed. I understand some small fuss or other is still going on there, but I expect that will fade out, too."

"All right." Paulina Koch dismissed Hovannis. She wondered how long she would be able to dismiss him and be sure he would obey. He knew too much, had done too much to help her cement her own position. One day, she thought, she might have to make certain he would stay silent. That carried its own risks. Roupen Hovannis was no one's innocent. Data could point an accusing finger even after a man was gone.

The Chairman's lips creased in a bitter smile. If she had not known of the power dead men carried, Bilbeis IV would have taught her all about it. That damned anthropologist had been dead more than fourteen hundred years, but the trouble his meddling had caused looked to be as immortal as the queen whose cancer he'd cured.

The smile disappeared. Paulina Koch drilled herself never to reveal too much. Behind the impassive mask she cultivated, though, her mind was still racing. More and more she thought she should have let the report on Bilbeis IV go public and simply taken whatever heat descended on her and on the Service because of it.

Too late for that. If it had not been too late from the moment the report vanished from the Service file, it had become so with the death of—what was his name?—Fogelman. She had managed to make herself believe that was necessary to protect the Survey Service for which she had worked so long and hard.

About the *Clark County* she did not want to think at all. Most of the people aboard the *Clark County* had never heard of Bilbeis IV. Well, they never would now, that was certain. And now she was not just protecting the Service but herself as well. Rehabilitation—she shuddered at a euphemism grimmer than any in the Survey Service lexicon—would be the least she could hope for if the truth came. No way but forward, then.

"But that's insane!" Magda yelled. She was tired of having people turn around to stare at her and even more tired of being in positions where she made them turn around to stare. More quietly, she went on, "Here I am in front of you, Mr. Peters."

"Yes, Ms., umm—" The credit manager's voice trailed away. He'd done that before, as if he wouldn't have to admit Magda was alive if he didn't speak her name. Peters reminded her of Paulina Koch, though he and the Survey Service Chairman looked nothing alike. Both of them had the same air of being not quite human, only projections of the organizations they represented.

"Mr. Peters, do I look dead?" she demanded.

"No," he admitted, not sounding pleased about it.

"Then why can't I make this stinking piece of plastic work? The red light goes on every time I try to use it. I've explained about how Marie was carrying my card when she went aboard the *Clark County.*"

"So you have. Unfortunately, you have not explained why no card authorized to Marie Roux has been unearthed on Carson Planet. If that card appears, it will facilitate the substantiation of your account and the restoration of your credit. Until then, I lack the authority to make that restoration, as the cancellation of your account was not originally implemented here. All I can do is pass on the discrepancy notice to our headquarters and allow them to make the determination."

"Where *are* your headquarters?" Magda asked dangerously.

"Why, on the capital world, of course."

"You officious idiot!" Magda shouted. Everyone in the office who hadn't been looking at her before was now. She was past caring. "Here I am, and you can't even tell I'm not dead? Make any check you want on me, for heaven's sake. If the ID doesn't match what's on my card, put me away and throw out the stinking key."

"I was going to suggest that in any case. It will bolster your account in the report I submit."

That was as far as he would go. Gradually Magda realized that he was not out to give her a hard time but that he would not stick his neck out one millimeter for her either. "How long will your miserable report take to go through?"

"I can't be sure. A couple of weeks perhaps, if the medical data are as you say. I'll hold off filing till I have them from you."

"A couple of weeks?" Magda echoed in dismay. "What am I supposed to do in the meantime, starve?"

She had meant it as a rhetorical question, but Peters took it literally. "If I might make a recommendation—"

"Please." By then Magda was ready to listen, seeing no way anything Peters said could make things worse.

"Well, then, I would suggest you use this Marie Roux's card, which is active, as your own while your credit identity is being reconfirmed. When that happens, or when her own death is established as fact, charges accrued can be transferred back to your account."

Magda knew he was trying to be helpful. She even knew he was giving her good advice. That didn't make it any easier to take. She had practically frog-marched Marie onto the *Clark County* in her place; if anyone but Pedroza had told her about the trip, she knew, she would have gone, and gone eagerly. But she hadn't, and Marie was dead instead of her. The thought of using her friend's card made her feel even worse than she did already—she hadn't felt like a ghoul before. And worse still, she knew she would do it. She left the credit office in a hurry.

The doctor who ran the medical checks on her that afternoon gave her a quizzical look. "You're paying me with *this* credit card so I can confirm you're the rightful user of *that* one?"

"Believe me," she told him, "it doesn't make any more sense to me than it does to you. Just rush those results over to Credit Superintendent Peters." She gave him the access code.

She went back to her apartment and for the most part stayed there. She lived as frugally as she could, not wanting to use any more of Marie's credit than necessary. She watched the screen more in ten days than she had in years—and discovered why she hadn't bothered. She did not watch the news.

Every morning she tried her own credit card. Every morning the system rejected it. She used the thesaurus program on her computer to generate page-long curses to call down on Peters's head.

The monograph got short shrift; Magda lacked the heart to work on it. She also kept delaying taking the report on Bilbeis IV back to the field office. Finally she made herself do it. She had no better monument to offer the crew of the *Jêng Ho.*

Riding the shuttle felt strange—she had grown too used to being cooped up. Pandit the clerk raised an eyebrow when she walked into the office. "You were so intent on transmitting this, and then you never came back. May I ask what happened?"

"I died," she said. "Ask your computer if you don't believe me."

His eyes widened as he made the connection. "The *Clark County*—"

"Exactly. I was supposed to be on it." Briefly, not naming names, she explained how she had stayed behind, and finished, "So if I had been on that ship, odds are this would have stayed shelved for good. Make sure Central gets it this time, will you, Pandit?"

"I don't know what went wrong the first two times." He sounded genuinely aggrieved; like Peters, he did not care for anything that upset his routine. Unlike the case of the credit representative, though, getting that routine back implied helping Magda, not frustrating her. He loaded the data card into his terminal and squirted its information across the light-years.

"Come in, Roupen. Do please sit down." Paulina Koch flicked an imaginary speck of lint from her gray blouse. Her slacks were a darker shade of gray, almost charcoal; that was as much extravagance as she allowed herself as far as clothes went. Anyone who thought of the Survey Service Chairman in a negligee—in itself an unlikely notion—would have imagined her in a gray one.

"What's up, PK?" Hovannis rumbled. Paulina Koch handed him a printout. His always dour features grew harsher still as he scanned it. "We've already scrubbed this twice," he observed. "If we do it again, whoever keeps filing the damned thing will really start wondering what's going on."

"It's already gone," the Chairman said, "though I leave to you the details of making the erasure invisible. We've involved ourselves too deeply in denying the authenticity of the report to have it linger in public files even for a moment."

"That's true," Hovannis agreed. They both knew what an understatement it was.

Paulina Koch hesitated before going on, as if searching for words. At last she said, "After the tragic loss of the *Clark County*, I had not expected to see this document surface again."

"Neither had I," Hovannis answered. They said no more than that; the subject was much too touchy to go into deeply.

"We have to be more thorough," the Chairman said.

"I'll look into it," Hovannis said.

Paulina Koch was checking another printout. She nodded to herself. "As I thought: the entire complement of the *Jêng Ho* is listed as having been aboard the *Clark County.*"

"I'll look into it," Hovannis repeated.

"Very well. Thank you for coming up." The Chairman's eyes had returned to her screen before Hovannis was out of her office.

VII

"Thank you." Andrea switched off the phone and savagely flung it against the back of one of Stavros's chairs. "Oh, that bastard!"

"Another one?" Stavros sighed. Both of them had grown very familiar with a stock set of responses over the last few days.

"She might as well have been a recording," Andrea said glumly. " 'I am sorry. You may even be right, but people are bored with Bilbeis IV, and what you have is not exciting enough to make them sit up and take notice again.' At least she didn't tell me it wasn't sexy enough to get on the news, the way some of them have."

"Trouble is, they're right. How do you make people care about eighteen days? You can't show them a picture of eighteen missing days the way you can of eighteen missing starships."

"But when they show the Survey Service is lying—"

"The way it looks, not everyone cares about that," Stavros said. "Do you know what one of the people I talked to told me? Something to the effect that of course government agencies lie, and the job of the news team was to catch them lying at something interesting. Without the *Jêng Ho*'s crew, we just can't do that."

Andrea set her hands on her hips. "You'd think the crash of the *Clark County* would wake them up."

"I know, I know." Stavros banged his fist against his thigh in frustration. "Trouble is, we shouted murder at the Survey Service over Professor Fogelman and weren't able to make it stick. Now it doesn't matter how loud we yell it, because no one's willing to pay attention anymore."

"Does that mean you want to give up?" Andrea asked.

"No, of course not." Stavros hoped he sounded indignant. He very much wanted the Service brought to account for all it had done. He was no longer confident that would happen, but he wanted it all the same. And even more, he wanted not to lose Andrea. If he quarreled with her over this, he was sure he would. So, suppressing his misgivings, he went on. "We'll keep trying."

"All right, then. Who's next on our list?"

He recalled it on the computer. "*The Unvarnished Truth.*"

"I've seen their output once or twice." Andrea looked unhappy. "Have we really sunk so low?" She retrieved the phone from where it leaned drunkenly against a wall and punched buttons. "Hello, this is Andrea Dubois. Could you please put me through to your managing editor? Yes, I'll wait . . . Hello? This is Andrea Dubois. I have important new information on the Bilbeis IV scandal—"

The discreet individual wanted to take those two idealistic idiots off to one side and pound some sense into them. Newsmen were notorious fools, but Van Shui Pong got the message once it was shouted loud enough. He might not have been able to put together two and two, but he could add one and three hundred-odd. Hyperion Newsnet was very quiet these days.

Sometimes the discreet individual thought about picking up some extra money blackmailing the Survey Service—after so long on the job, he could not escape realizing who was paying him. The Service would give him what he wanted, he thought; he had already shown he could keep his mouth shut.

But he kept on taking his fees and not pushing for more. The *Clark County* told him a story, too: he decided he did not want the Survey Service reminded of how much he knew. Sometimes being discreet and seeming slightly stupid looked a lot alike.

He wished the graduate students could understand that, and understand he was just the cutting edge of what they were up against. It wasn't going to happen, though. All their training went against it. They had to seem smart in class, so they thought they had to be smart all the time.

That, he knew, wasn't so smart itself.

One evening a week, Stavros had a class Andrea did not. Though his Basic was more than fluent and he also wrote it well, he kept working to improve. Being with Andrea so much showed him how much better he could do, and so he endured the composition course for the sake of the tricks it taught him. Andrea felt the class was helping his writing.

That night the instructor had been talking about adverbs and how to use them: in small doses, Stavros gathered. The instructor claimed the real skill lay in picking the right verb in the first place rather than in adjusting the meaning of one not so right with modifiers. Remembering some of his own papers, he decided the notion sounded reasonable. He wondered what Andrea would think of it.

"I'm back," he called as he opened the door to his rooms.

No one answered. His dark brows drew together. He and Andrea did not spend all their nights together, but she'd been there when he left, and he hadn't known she was going anywhere. He stepped toward the computer, wondering if she'd left a message.

He stumbled over a shoe and almost fell. That forced him to notice what a mess the place was. Stavros was not a neat housekeeper. Few men had occasion to learn such skills on New Thessaly. But nearly drowning in junk made him pay some attention to keeping things tidy, and his desire to keep Andrea happy had done more.

Leaving the place in such disarray was not like her, but Stavros did not think anything of it until he saw that his icons were missing. He had brought the hand-painted images of Christ, the Virgin, and John the Baptist with him from home. Though he was no longer devoutly Orthodox, the icons still served to remind him of New Thessaly: he felt good every time he glanced over at them. Now they were gone.

They were not the best work New Thessaly had to offer, but on Hyperion, where their like was rare, they were worth a fair amount. Stavros swore and dashed into the bedroom. He kept the rest of his valuables in a drawer under the bed.

Andrea's body sprawled across the mattress. For a moment, not understanding, Stavros thought she was asleep. Then he saw the blood under her head. He moaned, something he had heard of but never remembered doing.

The drawer under the bed was open. So was the little strongbox inside. Stavros noted all that peripherally, though later his recall of it would be perfect: disaster has a way of printing tiny details forever on the brain.

He stumbled forward to take Andrea's wrist, thinking there might be some hope she still lived. Her flesh was cool; it had begun to stiffen. He knew what death felt like. He staggered into the bathroom and was sick.

Mechanically, he rinsed his mouth. Tears streamed down his face. He did not realize he was crying until he went to pick up the phone and found he could not read the buttons.

The phone was next to the computer, where Andrea must have put it after her last useless call to the newsies. Stavros recalled the number for the police and had punched in the first three digits before he paused, scowling, and put the handset down again.

What had happened in his room bore every sign of being a random break-in and killing. But then, Professor Fogelman's death had looked the same way. Stavros turned on his computer. He could not access any of his files. They were not there to access—they were gone. If he hadn't made a habit of carrying the original data card with the report on Bilbeis IV around with him, it would have been lost too.

He had not thought he could be more afraid. Now he discovered he was wrong. A random burglar would not have lobotomized his computer. Someone from the Survey Service would. Van Shui Pong knew what to worry about.

Stavros started to call the police again and stopped for a second time. He suspected they might be more interested in him as a murderer than as the victim of a crime. He knew logically that he could prove his whereabouts when Andrea had been killed. Something old and watchful in him, though, warned that the police might not be thinking logically, not if the Service put enough quiet pressure on them. He thought the Service might do just that. After the *Clark County*, he could not afford to think otherwise.

He did not call the police. He packed a tote instead, the kind that looked as though it might be full of anything. He slung it over his shoulder and locked the door behind him. With luck, he had a couple of days to do whatever needed doing. Without it, he'd be scooped up before daybreak, and his running away would not look good.

He headed for the library to kill the rest of the night; he had to fight down hysterical laughter when the phrase occurred to him. The university library held several thousand volumes and was easily the largest of the three or four on Hyperion. It was the main storehouse for works that reached the planet in hard copy format and had not yet been entered into the data retrieval system.

Several archeological journals arrived in hard copy; the librarians were used to Stavros's dashing in at any hour of the day or night. He managed only one-word replies to their greetings but hoped he managed to seem merely busy, not distraught. He must have succeeded; they went about their business without looking at him twice.

The cool silent isolation, the musty smell of old paper, the rows of study carrels took him back to the ancient days when all scholarship took place in rooms of this sort. He dug a couple of periodicals off the shelf, went to the most distant carrel, and pretended to start reading.

He could not keep up the pretense long. He buried his face in his hands. His shoulders shook, but he wept very quietly. No one came over to see if anything was wrong. The handful of other people in the library at that hour were all intent on their own concerns.

After a while, exhaustion and reaction combined to waylay Stavros. He fell asleep, still slumped over the desk. That did make the librarians notice him, but only with amusement: they were used to it.

The eastern sky brightened toward dawn.

In theory, seats in the Assembly gallery were first come, first served. In practice, if the Chairman of the Survey Service wanted a seat, she got one. Today she wanted one. She could have had a better, closer view of the appropriations vote from the terminal in her office, but it would not have been the same. Paulina Koch had worked too hard for the victory not to want to enjoy it in person.

To her annoyance, the diehard Purists insisted on a formal roll-call vote. Any dozen Assembly members could do that, but it was an archaic rule hardly invoked once a session. They must have spotted her, she thought, and decided either to make her leave before the vote was done or else keep her in the chamber for hours. She did not intend to give them the satisfaction of leaving or even of seeming discomfited. She did note their names for future reference. Maybe they did not realize how well she would be able to repay such scores after the vote was done. If they didn't, they would soon.

And before long, even the Purists must have realized they'd made a mistake. The steady litany of ayes showed how strong the Survey Service was, better than an impersonal display of green lights on the tally board ever could. Even some of the men and women who had demanded the roll call began to waver at the end. When Assemblyman Valleix abstained, Paulina Koch needed all her self-control to keep from laughing.

After the last vote was cast and the appropriation overwhelmingly secured, the Chairman allowed herself to think of other things. These days Bilbeis IV was never far from her mind. She knew the silence she had imposed was only a temporary solution. Eventually calls for a new examination of the planet would come. She wondered if she could quell them. She did not think so; there had been enough quelling already. Yes, it had worked, but one reason it had was that it did not call too much attention to itself. More along the same lines would.

What then? The next best thing to no report on Bilbeis IV—maybe even better than no report on Bilbeis IV, now that she thought of it—would be a report that minimized the results of cultural interference there. That would give the Purists something to beat their breasts about without raising their paranoid suspicions the way a clean bill of health would. If she could not put together a tame Survey Service team that would see things her way, she did not deserve to be Chairman.

Thinking of lameness reminded her of Roupen Hovannis. The External Affairs Director was not nearly tame enough to suit her. Unfortunately, however, he was too useful to dispense with. So long as his interest and hers ran in the same direction, he was no problem. The tricky part would be keeping their interests aligned without giving him the idea that he could make her dance to his tune.

She had been a manager for a lot of years. The precise nature of the problem Hovannis posed was new to her, but it was not altogether different from others she had faced before. Again, if she couldn't handle it, what was she Chairman for?

Hovannis's henchmen were something else again. That discreet individual on Hyperion, for instance, was really too effective to suit her. No, that wasn't quite right. The trouble was, he had been used too often. Anyone with the talent he obviously owned would draw the proper conclusions from his assignments. She did not like that.

The chatter of librarians changing shifts was low-voiced, but enough to wake Stavros. He groaned and stretched. His joints creaked, protesting the contorted position in which he'd slept.

The police had not nailed him yet. That was the only bit of cheer he could extract from the situation. He stood up and stretched again but still felt old and arthritic.

"Long night?" one of the new librarians asked sympathetically as Stavros shambled toward the exit.

"You have no idea."

The librarian laughed. Stavros did not.

His stomach growled. He started to head for a food machine, then stopped. He would have to go hungry a while longer. The more he used his credit card, the plainer the trail he'd leave. He'd need to use it one more time, but no help for that. He'd have to hope nobody had found Andrea by then.

The university was surrounded by a couple of kilometers of greenery on all sides. Shuttles into New Westwood ran regularly, but no one paid walking students any mind.

Once he was among the buildings, he had to wait; for reasons no one remembered, banks did not open till halfway through the morning. Stavros needed one of the two human tellers for what he wanted to do. "I'd like to turn my account to cash, sir."

The teller's eyebrows rose. "The entire sum?"

"Yes. I'm afraid there's an emergency in the family—"

The teller let out an audible sniff. People had been talking about phasing out cash since long before the Federacy began. It hadn't happened yet, and wouldn't any time soon. Anonymous money was too convenient to do away with. Yet if someone insisted on paying cash, the suspicion usually was that he had a good reason to.

Stavros had rarely handled cash before. Holding the crisp paper with its holographic designs sent an atavistic thrill through him, as if he were carrying gold coins. A credit card was mundane by comparison.

"Let me have your thumbprint and signature on the receipt, sir," the teller said sourly.

The discreet individual said a loud, indiscreet word. He had not been sure he would be able to monitor Monemvasios's bank account; banks were even more jealous of their privacy than newsnets, and worked harder to keep it. But for the moment, at least, his trapdoor program was working. He saw the account drop suddenly to zero.

He hadn't thought cashing out would occur to Stavros Monemvasios. In the phone calls he'd tapped, Monemvasios had seemed on the tentative side, while his woman friend had been brisk and forthright. Mistaking hesitance for stupidity, though, was evidently an error.

And now Monemvasios was going to be a real nuisance to keep track of. The discreet individual scratched his head. What would the wretch be up to?

He hadn't gone screaming to the police. The discreet individual would have known about that. He wasn't sure whether to be pleased or disappointed. Like Stavros, he thought there was a fair chance they wouldn't look past their noses. That would have dealt with that very nicely.

With a pocketful of cash, Monemvasios had to be on the run. Where would he go? All he knew of Hyperion was the university and its surroundings. He'd probably try to get offplanet, most likely to his home planet. Hyperion had two space ports, one of them halfway around the world. A stakeout of the local facility might prove productive.

The discreet individual gathered a few tools of his trade and headed for the spaceport. He left others behind with regret. The spaceport was too public for them. He would have to be more subtle than usual. That did not bother him for long. Minimalism was part of his art, too.

Stavros spent part of his wad at a small appliance store down the street from the bank. The clerk who took his money gave him a curious look with his change. "You don't seem to have much use for that," she said.

"It's for a friend," he answered. He was lying. He went into the restroom. When he came out a few minutes later, he was clean-shaven for the first time in a dozen years. His face felt naked. To his own eyes, he seemed quite different and five years younger. He hoped others would see as much change and not see *him.*

The next thing was to eat. The first place he happened into served the sort of bland, vaguely greasy fare that would annoy no one and excite no one very much either. At the moment, Stavros did not care. He wolfed it down. He gulped coffee, too; his fitful sleep in the library had not been nearly enough.

He never had learned to like the coffee they brewed on Hyperion—he found it a thin, bitter brew. New Thessaly coffee was almost strong enough to drink with a fork and was full of sugar and heavy cream. Now he did not even grimace at the stuff in the foam cup. He was drinking it for caffeine, not flavor.

He had never bothered—or needed—to notice whether the ground shuttle had a cash slot. If it didn't . . . He set his jaw. The spaceport was a dozen kilometers away, maybe more. Walking would take hours he might not have.

Nothing ventured, nothing gained. He waited on a street corner until the spaceport shuttle came by. The scanner spotted his upraised thumb. The shuttle pulled to a stop. The doors hissed open. He sprang onto the step and looked anxiously at the control panel.

He sagged in relief. To the right of the credit card opening was another, smaller one marked CURRENCY. He fed in a bill. His change returned a moment later.

As the shuttle purred toward the spaceport, Stavros did some hard thinking. Getting offplanet was one thing; deciding where to go, something else again. His first impulse had been to run for home. Now he wondered how good an idea that was. If the police were already looking for him, that outbound line would be one of the first areas they'd cover.

What to do, then? Random flight held no appeal—it was too much like giving up. His fist clenched. He wanted to hit back if he could find a way. But how? If he went to the capital to beard Paulina Koch in her den, he knew the fate he could expect. Fogelman and the *Clark County* and now Andrea had taught him the same lesson they'd given Van Shui Pong. Unlike the newsman, though, he was too stubborn to be scared off.

If the capital was hopeless, Stavros had to find an alternative. By the time he snapped his fingers in sudden decision, he could see grounded starships in the distance. The *Jêng Ho* had sent its report from a world called Topanga. Maybe, just maybe, some of the crew had talked with the locals about it before they set out on the doomed *Clark County*.

Stavros had no idea where Topanga was. There were too many worlds in the Federacy to keep track of, unless one was Isaac Fogelman. And a fat lot of good his gift had done him in the end, Stavros thought.

The shuttle sighed to a stop outside a big terminal building. Stavros shouldered his tote and descended to the concrete. The terminal doors opened for him and the other passengers.

He went to an information outlet, and tapped in the name Topanga. It was, he found without surprise, not far from Carson Planet. It had no direct connection with Hyperion, but ships from both worlds touched on Enkidu. Stavros was in luck; a ship outbound for Enkidu lifted off tomorrow. He checked the fare column. Yes, he could afford it.

He walked over to the ticket line. The clerk processing orders frowned a little at the sight of so much cash. "May I see some identification, Mr., ah"—she looked down at her screen for the name Stavros had plucked out of the air—"Mr. Mesropinian?"

Stavros went through his wallet with fingers suddenly frozen. Getting caught using an alias would lead to more questions, questions he could not answer. He shifted his feet and made ready to bolt.

And then he came upon his old ID from New Thessaly. It bore

his picture and his name—but that, along with all the rest of the written information on the card, was in Greek. Affecting a nonchalance he did not feel, he put the card on the counter in front of the clerk.

Her frown deepened. "I'm sorry, sir, I can't read this."

"Is your ignorance my fault?" he said as cuttingly as he could.

He saw he'd angered her. "Let me have your luggage there, sir, for the contraband sniffer," she snapped. But the petty triumph faded from her face when he passed the tote to her without a word of protest. The sniffer's light went green, as Stavros had known it would. The only thing he was smuggling was information, the most deadly contraband of all but one without a smell.

The clerk looked as if she wanted to take things further, but the line was beginning to back up. "What's going on there?" someone called.

"*Is* anything wrong?" Stavros asked, softly this time.

"Well—" The clerk looked again at the all-clear light on the sniffer. "I suppose not." She punched keys with unnecessary violence and handed Stavros his ticket. But she could not resist a parting shot: "I do suggest, sir, that you obtain a more easily verifiable means of identifying yourself."

"I'll see to it," said Stavros, who had several, none of them, though, as valuable to him at this moment as that little incomprehensible piece of plastic.

The spaceport was studded with clocks, both FSY and local time. Twenty-nine hours to go, Stavros saw. He was not out of the woods yet. His main concern was staying inconspicuous; in a crowded spaceport, that shouldn't be too hard. All he needed to do was stake out a seat and look bored.

The discreet individual was wondering if he'd outsmarted himself. He had hooks into the spaceport information system, of course, but that was like saying he had a knitting needle lodged in a whale's fluke—he could not cope with the avalanche of data.

Restricting the incoming feed to travelers who paid cash helped some, but not enough. Too blasted many people came through the spaceport. Only a few of them, though, planned routes that would take them to New Thessaly or even the general direction of the planet. The discreet individual had his computer analyze the routing forms of cash customers going that way.

The conclusion became inescapable after awhile: none of those people was Stavros Monemvasios. Some were too old, others too female, and still others had papers an amateur could not fake on the spur of the moment.

All of which meant the discreet individual had miscalculated somewhere. He was still certain Monemvasios meant to get off Hyperion—what point to cashing out and then waiting around to be caught? And Monemvasios's home planet seemed the most logical place for him to go.

But logic and truth had at best a nodding acquaintance. The discreet individual always bore that in mind. He also had other things to do than worry about a student on the run. He decided to do some of them and come back to Monemvasios if inspiration struck.

As with peripheral vision, the mind is often sharper if it looks to one side of a problem. That evening, the discreet individual suddenly sat bolt upright. In guessing Monemvasios would head for New Thessaly, the discreet individual tacitly assumed his quarry would be trying to get away, nothing more.

What if that was wrong? What if Monemvasios was still in the mood to create problems? The discreet individual found that unlikely but believed in covering his bets. If it was so, where would Monemvasios go?

The discreet individual put the question another way—where offplanet could Monemvasios get backing for his claims? Not from the central bureaucracy of the Survey Service, that was for sure! Where had that miserable report come from? After a few minutes of searching through his files, he had the answer.

Then he had to reprogram his computer to examine cash customers en route to Topanga, or rather to Enkidu. When he found a certain S. Mesropinian, he smiled and picked up that attaché case. It was time to go back to the spaceport.

The preliminary screening gadgets at the terminal entrance never hiccuped as he walked through. The more sophisticated contraband sniffers that dealt with passengers' luggage would also have given his case a clean bill of health. Programmers, he thought smugly, did not know everything there was to know.

He queued up to use an information screen. The *Arminius,* the ship outbound for Enkidu, would be departing from sub-terminal seven—naturally, the one farthest from where he sat. He sighed and climbed onto the slidewalk that would take him there. All he'd need to do then would be to spot Monemvasios-Mesropinian and bump him a little. He'd have enough time for a getaway, but in a few minutes it would all be over.

Someone bumped *him* a little. "Beg your pardon," said a slim woman in business attire. She pushed past the discreet individual, adding her own walking speed to the steady roll of the slidewalk. He watched appreciatively; she had a nice backside.

Because she was so brisk, she soon put several people between herself and the discreet individual. Out of sight, out of mind, he thought as she disappeared. He went back to planning the credit-transfer scheme he could finally give full time to once Monemvasios was disposed of.

Waiting kept Stavros on edge. He migrated back and forth between the outgoing passengers' lounge and the cafeteria next to it. He was full to bursting by then, but each trip gave him an excuse for getting up and stretching his legs. That was easier than just sitting in one spot, headphones drowning out the world.

Or it would have been, except that every fifty-meter hike took him past the spaceport security guards. They ignored him, but each time he showed himself to them, he twisted with fear they wouldn't.

He was also, he noted ruefully, using the jakes a good deal.

The discreet individual glanced around the lounge. He saw no one who looked even a little like Monemvasios. Shrugging, he sat down to wait. The man he hunted could not be far away. He shivered. The air-conditioning was very high.

He stiffened. Was that skinny fellow walking out of the head the one? No, too short; no matter how desperate a man was, he could not shed ten centimeters.

There was Monemvasios, coming from the lunchroom! All he'd done was shave, but the discreet individual's first glance had slid right past him. Sometimes the least disguise was best.

The discreet individual got up, or started to. For some reason his legs did not want to work. He put his hands on the arms of his chair and pushed himself upright.

He shivered again. It's awfully cold in here, he thought. He took a step toward Monemvasios, staggered, caught himself. He took another step. This time he could not keep himself from sliding bonelessly to the floor.

His last conscious thought was that the woman who'd poisoned him really did have a fine behind. He never felt his head hit the ground.

✧ ✧ ✧

Someone screamed. Security guards rushed into the lounge. Stavros almost jumped out of his skin. His body took two involuntary half-running steps before he realized he was not the target of the guards' attention.

They gathered instead around a man who had crumpled on the thin carpeting. All Stavros could see of him was his shoes, for the guards screened his upper body from view. One guard was frantically massaging his chest, while another stooped to give mouth-to-mouth resuscitation.

The spaceport doctor came running in a couple of minutes later. She immediately pushed one of the security guards out of the way and got to work. Soon she rose again, her mouth twisted in a grimace of frustration.

Stavros reflexively crossed himself. At the doctor's direction, a couple of guards lifted the dead man and carried him away. The usual babble of the lounge was stilled. Background music, ignored a moment before, seemed loud and intrusive. Shivering as if he had taken a sudden chill, Stavros found a seat and waited for the *Arminius* to arrive.

The report was oblique, talking about a personnel transfer being satisfactorily expedited. Anyone who saw it on Paulina Koch's screen might have wondered why the Chairman had to deal with it herself but would have forgotten about it before he was out of her office.

The Chairman cleared the screen. Another loose end taken care of, and this time before any trouble resulted. Hovannis's discreet individual would never be anything but circumspect now. Better still, she had used her own contacts to arrange that, not going through the External Affairs Director. One day she might find it useful to have independent resources in that area.

She frowned, but only briefly. Bureaucratic language and patterns of thought made it easy for her to take an impersonal view of the operations she ordered carried out. She had trouble imagining people dead but could clearly see how her position and her agency had been protected by what she'd done.

And they had been protected. The appropriation was safe, the Purists discredited or ashamed of their own policies. The latest polls showed public approval of the Survey Service near an all-time high.

Now it was payback time. With her new power, she could make life very uncomfortable for the gadflies who'd been buzzing around the Service for years. Lately they'd thought they were vultures, come to pick her bones. It was time to remind them they were still small enough to swat.

What a delightful prospect, she thought.

Stavros had a bad moment boarding the *Arminius.* The steward who fed his ticket into the ship's computer nodded to him and said, "Glad to be aboard?"

"You'd better believe it!" he said fervently.

"Thought as much. You look like you're about three steps ahead of the executioner." The steward laughed at his own joke. Stavros managed a strained chuckle. The steward stepped aside and waved him into the ship.

Even after he was in his cabin, he did not feel altogether safe. The Hyperion police could still take him off the ship. If they came after him now, in fact, he could not even run. His stomach churned. He lay on the bunk and tried to relax. He couldn't. Pacing up and down in the narrow space between the bunk and the bulkhead helped more.

Because he was pacing, he never felt the *Arminius* lift off. He had to check his watch to realize he was in space. He had been running on nerves too long. As soon as he understood he was safe, at least for a while, he flopped to the bunk like a marionette whose puppeteer has dropped the strings.

"A chance," he said out loud. "A chance." Somewhere on Topanga, someone might have heard of the report on Bilbeis IV. And if someone had, he might yet call the Survey Service to account for Andrea—action had made him bottle up that hurt, but it came flooding back now full force—for Professor Fogelman, for the crew of the *Jêng Ho*, and for all the poor people who just happened to board the wrong starship at the wrong time.

The Service was huge and powerful, but it was not, must not be, beyond the reach of law. The Chairman had to be shown she and hers were not too big to swat.

What a delightful prospect, Stavros thought.

VIII

"Hello, Pandit," Magda said. "Let me guess—you've checked, and as far as Survey Service Central knows, you never sent in that report."

In the phone screen, the clerk's brown face grew even more troubled than it had been. "I am afraid that is correct. I tell you frankly, I have never seen another case like this. I don't know what to make of it. All the other documents I've processed have gone through flawlessly."

"It figures. Things have been going that way lately. As far as the credit system knows, I'm still dead, too. Something is screwed up in those computers, what's-his-name—Peters—says."

"I am sorry for your difficulties." Pandit actually sounded as though he meant it. Maybe he does, Magda thought; his orderly soul had to cringe for the chaos that had attached itself to her. He went on. "I suppose I can expect to see you again soon with our vanishing document?"

"No." Magda had decided to spread a little chaos herself. "I'm sick of this nonsense. I think I'm going to take the whole thing to the Noninterference Foundation and see what they make of it."

"You can't do that!" Pandit exclaimed in horror. Magda knew how he felt; giving information to the Noninterference Foundation was like going over to the enemy. The Foundation kept an eye on the way the Survey Service interacted with natives of pretechnological worlds. That would have been bad enough, but the private watchdog group got most of its support from the Purists, the people who thought the Service ought to keep off those worlds altogether.

Magda had about as much use for Purists as she did for cockroaches: to her they were two examples of pests the Federacy had never been able to eradicate. But that did not mean she thought the Survey Service ought to get away free when it made a mistake. Service personnel had interfered on Bilbeis IV, even if with the best of intentions, and the courses of billions of lives there had been changed as a result.

"Going through channels hasn't done me any good," she said. "I've told you before, Pandit—this report is important. One way or another, it has to get out."

"Yes, so you've said. All the same, do you feel like throwing away your career in a fit of pique over computer problems at Central? Think about the assignments you will draw when people know you collaborate with the Foundation."

Magda winced. What Pandit had suggested was illegal, of course. It was also very likely. For that matter, she wouldn't have wanted to ship with a known informer herself. "I've got good reason to go," she said, but her voice sounded defensive even to her.

"Yes, so you've said," Pandit repeated. "I'm sure you believe it, but remember, it is a step you cannot take back. May I suggest something?"

"Go ahead," Magda said grudgingly.

"Why not try once more to transmit your report through the proper channels? If you fail after four attempts, I do not suppose anyone could blame you for doing something irregular."

"As far as I'm concerned, they couldn't blame me after three." But despite her tough talk, Magda was secretly glad to have a chance to put off the trip to the Foundation. "Oh, all right. I'll see you before long. It had better go through this time, though; that's all I can say."

She broke the connection, picked up the data card, and rode the elevator down to the lobby of the apartment complex. The nearest shuttle stop was only a short walk from the building.

A few minutes later, a slim, swarthy man somewhere close to her own age joined her at the stop. His clothes were on the faded side and he wore a backpack. He looked tired. After a casual glance that told her that much, Magda ignored him, or tried to.

He did not make it easy, though. He kept looking stealthily in her direction and jerking his head away when she caught him at it. They were not the sort of glances a man gives a female stranger he finds attractive; Magda would have thought nothing much of those one way or the other. It was almost, she thought, as if the fellow was wondering whether he knew her. With all the strange goings-on of late, she did not like that, because she was sure she had never set eyes on him before.

The shuttle came sighing up just as the man looked to have worked up the nerve to speak to her. With a feeling of relief, she fed Marie Roux's credit card into the slot by the door; she wanted nothing to do with him. Her leeriness only increased when she heard the fare apparatus suck up a bill—he had paid his way aboard with cash. People who used untraceable money generally had a reason for it, and rarely a good one.

From habit, Magda sat near the front of the shuttle. She was soon kicking herself for it. Once, when she yawned and stretched, she caught the stranger staring at her from behind, though again he quickly looked away when he saw she had noticed him. After that she did not look back, but she imagined she felt his gaze on the back of her neck. It made for an unpleasant ride; she was glad to get off.

That did not last long. The stranger scrambled down as the shuttle was on the point of pulling away; its doors, which had started to close, hissed open for him. He had been holding his backpack in his lap and paused to resling it before leaving.

A trifle faster than she might have otherwise, Magda walked toward the Survey Service office, fortunately no more than a block and a half from the shuttle stop. She scowled—the stranger was still following her. If he tries anything cute, she told herself, I'll make him regret it. Like anyone who did Survey Service fieldwork, she had been well trained in unarmed combat.

All of which, she thought, would do her no good at all if he had a projectile weapon. But if he planned on shooting her, he'd already had plenty of chances.

That reasoning was reassuring, but only until he came into the office after her. Then he made her feel like an idiot, because he headed straight for the director's room in the back. She supposed that having two people come from the same shuttle stop to the Survey Service office wasn't twisting coincidence's arm outrageously.

Pandit spotted her and saved whatever document he was working on. "My screen is clear," he declared. "We are ready for another try—a successful one this time, I hope."

"So do I," Magda said, taking the data card from her hold-all, "but I'm not going to hold my breath. Central doesn't seem to want to know about Bilbeis IV."

She had forgotten the fellow who had been on the shuttle with her. He stopped in his tracks, turned, and walked back toward her. "You really are Magda Kodaly, aren't you?" he said.

"What if I am?" she said, her suspicion of him flaring again.

"I thought you were, but I didn't dare believe it. I thought you were dead."

"You aren't the only one," she muttered. He stared at her, not understanding. "Never mind. What do you want?"

"That's the report on Bilbeis IV you have there, the one from the *Jêng Ho*?"

"Yes. Who are you, anyway? How do you know about it? I've been trying for weeks to get it into Survey Service Central files, and I haven't had any luck yet. This is my fourth try."

Pandit had loaded the data card into his terminal and was about to hit the TRANSMIT button. "*Don't send it!*" the stranger exclaimed, so urgently that the clerk jerked his finger away in alarm. "Whatever you do, don't send it," the fellow repeated. He bent down, pushing Pandit aside, and took the card from the computer.

"Give me that back," Pandit said indignantly.

"No." The stranger stepped away from the terminal. He still had a tight grip on the data card. Magda tensed herself to grab it away from him. He noticed and handed it to her. "Here—it's yours. All I ask is that you don't transmit it until you've heard me out. You're in danger if it goes to Central—you may be in danger anyhow."

"Do you know," Magda said to nobody in particular, "I've had more melodrama in my life in the little while since we came back from Bilbeis IV than in all the time before that, and I don't like it one bit."

"I believe you," the stranger said with perfect seriousness. "So have I."

Magda studied him. He neither looked nor sounded like a madman . . . and things *had* been strange lately. "All right, talk," she said. "This had better be good."

"None of it is good," he said; again he seemed very tired. "I don't want to talk here, in front of Survey Service people." Pandit let out an indignant sniff. The fellow said, "Nothing personal. Believe me, you're better off not knowing any of this."

"All right, we'll find a public terminal and see what you're so excited about," Magda decided. She pointed warningly at Pandit. "Don't go away. I may be back very soon." Then she turned back to the stranger. "Who are you, anyway?"

He waited until they were back on the sidewalk outside before he answered. "My name is Stavros Monemvasios. I am—I *was*—

a grad student in anthropology at the University of Hyperion. My seminar group got assigned to summarize some newly arrived Survey Service reports."

Magda nodded; she'd had similar assignments herself before she escaped to fieldwork. She and Monemvasios walked into a bank. The terminals were next to the pay phones. "You haven't really told me anything yet, you know," Magda said as she stepped into a booth. It was on the crowded side for two.

"Yes, I do know. I want to show you instead." Stavros looked the terminal over and laughed ruefully. "You'll have to pay for it, though. This thing doesn't have a cash slot, and I cashed out my credit card to get off Hyperion without making myself conspicuous."

"Hmm." Magda gave him another hard look. Now he was practically admitting he'd done something shady on Hyperion. But she'd come this far . . . Clicking her tongue in exasperation, she shoved Marie Roux's credit card into the opening by the keyboard. The screen came on.

Stavros had been rummaging in his backpack. He pulled out a data card, fed it into the machine, and hit RECALL. The abstract of a document appeared.

"*Where did you get that?*" Magda was proud of herself. Instead of screaming the question, she let it out in a whispered hiss, but it was no less urgent for that.

"The report on Bilbeis IV, you mean? My prof gave it to me. I told you, it was my assignment. Go through it—make sure it's the same document the *Jêng Ho* submitted to Central."

Magda scrolled rapidly through the report, checking a page here, a page there. She was soon satisfied. "It's the same document." She was about to burst with questions and felt like reaching over to shake the answers out of Monemvasios. "How did your prof get it? And why isn't he screaming his head off about it?"

"He got it because Survey Service records are—or are supposed to be—public documents. And he isn't screaming about it because he's dead." The flat statement brought Magda up short. Stavros also paused before he went on and seemed to have to bring out his words by main force. "So is a woman who was in my class—she and I were trying to make people notice what this report means. We were also falling in love with each other, but that's another story. And so is everybody who was on the *Clark County*. That includes the whole crew of the *Jêng Ho,* or I thought it did until I met you. Do I need to draw any more pictures for you?"

"You're saying the crash wasn't an accident." Magda's voice sounded far away in her own ears.

"If it was, it was a mighty *convenient* accident for the Survey Service. Not even the Assembly can subpoena dead people or ask them awkward questions about a report the Service calls a fraud from top to bottom."

"A what?" Magda clenched her fists until her nails bit into her palms. "The hell it is! We worked our tails off on that thing."

"I believe you," Stavros said soberly. "I daresay I know it better than anyone else who wasn't there, and it's a devastating piece of work—which only makes it more dangerous to the Service if it's true, because it shows just how serious the results of the interference on Bilbeis IV were. So they're denying everything—and with the *Jêng Ho*'s crew gone, who's to contradict them?"

Magda shook her head, but it was reflex fighting reason. What Monemvasios said made a horrid kind of sense. It certainly explained why she had not been able to get the report on Bilbeis IV into the files at Survey Service Central. She said so, adding, "No wonder they kept deleting it, if they can't admit it's real."

"No wonder at all," Stavros agreed. "Fogelman—my prof—must have accessed it just minutes after it came in the first time, before the Chairman decided she had to erase it."

"The Chairman?" Magda said, startled. She had never had much use for Paulina Koch, but there was a big difference between thinking her hidebound and the things Monemvasios was implying.

"Haven't you seen any news?"

"No, not much," Magda admitted. "This isn't my planet, so I don't really care about what's happening locally, and the locals don't pay any more attention to what's going on offworld than they have to. Besides, the one time I did turn it on, the big story was the crash of the *Clark County*. After that, I just felt like finding a hole and pulling it in after me."

"I can understand that," Stavros said. He made a wry face. "For all I know, the story never even got here—the Federacy is a big place, with a lot going on. I liked to think we were making an enormous splash, but how could we tell for sure? We did get the Chairman to deny everything about Bilbeis IV in a news conference, though, and in front of an Assembly subcommittee. I suppose that counts for something."

"I should say so!" Paulina Koch shunned publicity. If she stood up in front of people to tell lies, Monemvasios really had hit a nerve, or rather, the report had. And the Chairman never would have done it if she hadn't known the report had disappeared—Stavros was right about that, too. Magda said contritely, "I'll have to recall the old news shows. Somebody here must have mentioned this mess at least once."

"Never mind that now," Stavros said. "Just tell me one thing: What was the FSY date when the *Jêng Ho* got back to Topanga and filed that report?"

"I'd have to check; I've gotten used to local time here. It's at the front of the document, though—we sent the report in as soon as we landed. Let me look." Magda moved the cursor to the beginning of the report. "That's what I thought I remembered. It was FSY 2687:139."

Stavros smacked fist into palm in triumph. "I thought so! We have them, then, on that, too! When I checked on Hyperion, it was 157, and the Survey Service computer said the *Jêng Ho*'s report wasn't in yet—they'd erased it the first time, you see. But they still listed the scheduled arrival date of your ship as 139; the scheduling information must have gone on a different data base from the report itself. That 139 disappeared not long afterward, when they realized it was there, but—"

Magda followed him perfectly. "We can beat them over the head with their missing eighteen days," she finished.

"Exactly!" For a moment, excitement lit Stavros's thin, worn features. He soon grew grim again. "Assuming we live to do it, of course. The way things have gone, that's not the best bet in the world."

"No," Magda agreed, shivering. "It's just accident that I wasn't on the *Clark County*." Even more quickly than she had with Pandit, she explained why she hadn't been.

Stavros nodded. "I have the feeling I got off Hyperion maybe one step ahead of the bastards who killed Fogelman and Andrea. I was the next logical target, even if the Hyperion police didn't try to hold me for Andrea's death. After everything else that's gone on, I was afraid the Survey Service had enough clout to make the constabulary think that way."

"I don't blame you," Magda said. "No wonder you've been using cash, come to that. Nobody can trace you that way."

"That's right. You're lucky yourself, even if it's a grisly kind of luck, having your roommate's credit card to use. You don't draw any attention to yourself with it. Even the coordinator at the local Service office thinks you're dead."

"Does she? She's an idiot, then. I've worked with her clerk since the *Clark County* crashed."

"She doesn't know about it. When I got to Topanga, I was just hoping to meet somebody who'd talked with the *Jêng Ho*'s crew, somebody who could help me show this report was genuine. The director gave me the address of what I gather is your apartment complex because several crewpeople had been staying there. 'Had been,' she said; she had no idea anybody was still there." Stavros stopped and looked alarmed. "Wait a minute. Have you tried sending the report on Bilbeis IV since the *Clark County* went down? I thought I stopped you."

"You did this time, but I'd already transmitted it once before that. I thought it was the last thing I could do for the *Jêng Ho.* What difference does it—" It was Magda's turn to break off abruptly. "You think they're going to come after me?"

"How can they afford not to? After everything they've done by now, they won't just lose their jobs if the truth comes out. They'll face rehab." Stavros and Magda both flinched at that.

"You're right, worse luck," Magda said. "Well, that tears it. Save your document there; I need to get a directory listing from the computer."

Stavros obeyed. "What are you going to do?"

"What I almost did earlier this morning: I'm going to take the whole miserable, stinking mess over to the Noninterference Foundation."

"Good!" Stavros exclaimed. "I wish Andrea and I had done that right from the start instead of going to the newsnets ourselves. We need somebody on our side big enough to stand up to the Survey Service."

"Big enough to step on us, too, maybe," Magda said. "I don't like the Foundation very much. They can talk about being disinterested till they're blue in the face, but everybody knows the Purists bankroll them."

"Purists." Stavros's voice showed his distaste. No one who wanted to do fieldwork on pretechnological planets thought well of the Purists. If the Purists had their way, they would get rid of the Survey Service altogether. A vocal minority of public opinion agreed with them.

"I know how you feel," Magda said. "I feel the same way, only more so, believe me. That's why I let Pandit talk me out of seeing the Foundation before. But the best shield I can think of against an assassin is publicity, and the Noninterference Foundation can give us that. They're good at it."

"And we don't have any better choices," Stavros said.

"That we don't." Magda stood up. "Let's go."

The local headquarters of the Noninterference Foundation was across town from the Survey Service office—not a good place for a watchdog, Magda thought sourly as she and Stavros took the long shuttle ride. She realized that was unfair; the real monitoring went on at Survey Service Central and outside the Federacy. She could not help being annoyed anyway.

To make things worse, the trip got interrupted when a horde of emergency vehicles, sirens screaming, tore across the shuttle's path. That did a splendid job of fouling up the traffic pattern.

Seeing Magda fidget, Stavros said, "The computer will fix things soon."

"Fat lot of good that does us now," she answered, but snapping at him did no more to relieve her concern than worrying about where the Foundation office was.

That office, when Magda and Stavros finally arrived, proved a good deal more luxurious than the one out of which the Survey Service operated. Looking around, Magda found herself with mixed feelings. A private organization needed to be affluent to take on a well-entrenched bureaucracy. On the other hand, these self-appointed advocates of poor, deprived people plainly had no experience of either poverty or deprivation themselves.

"What can I do for you people today?" asked a chunky bronze-skinned woman who, coming out of her office, saw the two newcomers standing irresolutely just inside the door. Neither of them replied at once. The woman repeated, "Can I help you? I'm Teresa Calderon; I'm a senior analyst here."

"This is about the recent report on Bilbeis IV," Stavros began. "I don't know if you've heard about it—"

"Oh, yes, aside from the Foundation's own bulletins, it's been in the news here," Teresa Calderon replied at once.

Magda wanted to kick herself. She asked carefully, "What is the position of the Noninterference Foundation on Bilbeis IV?"

"Frustration would probably be the best word for it; the Chairman has consistently denied the report's authenticity, and no one has been able to disprove what she says. After the *Clark County*, I don't expect anyone will. Speaking only for myself and not for the Foundation, it almost makes me believe some of the wilder claims that have been made in the affair."

"Believe them," Stavros said. Magda nodded.

Teresa Calderon's polite smile wavered. "Excuse me, but may I ask who you are?"

They told her.

The smile went out, to be replaced by incredulity. "One of you is dead, the other one wanted for murder," Calderon blurted.

"I'm getting tired of being told I'm dead," Magda said. At the same time, Stavros was exclaiming, "What did I tell you?"

When some measure of calm finally returned, Magda produced her own credit card, saying, "I can't spend money with this, but viewing it ought to convince you that I'm me." Teresa Calderon fed the card into a terminal. She looked from the picture on the screen to Magda, back again, and slowly nodded.

Stavros said, "I'm too many light-years from Hyperion to prove anything, but I was in a class when Andrea was killed. I don't know whether anyone went to the trouble of erasing that computer record, but people will remember if somebody bothers to ask them instead of jumping to conclusions."

By then, Teresa Calderon was almost beside herself with excitement. "This is the opening we've been after for years! We can finally show how the Survey Service has been deceitfully concealing its blunders and how its meddling has resulted in the exploitation of a whole planetful of innocent people for over a thousand years."

"That's not the word I'd use," Magda said sharply. She was reminded of why she mistrusted Noninterference Foundation people. The Federacy hadn't exploited Bilbeis IV; no one had been there at all between FSY 1186 and the visit of the *Jêng Ho.* That didn't mean the early interference had been right, but it had not been malicious.

The concealment afterward, of course, was something else again.

Stavros broke her train of thought—and probably forestalled a good, snarling argument—by yawning enormously. "I'm sorry," he said. "I haven't done a whole lot of sleeping since I got to Topanga—actually, Magda, what I have been doing is looking for you, but I didn't know it. I told you about that before. Anyway, I don't have a place to stay."

"Come back to my building, then," Magda said. "It's cheap—"

"It had better be!"

"—and I know there are vacant rooms. Ms. Calderon, you don't need us any more today, do you?" Magda looked at her watch. "It's later than I thought. You can get things rolling without us, I'm sure. For better or worse, we're allies for a while, it seems."

"So we are." Teresa Calderon sounded very little more pleased at the prospect than Magda was. That did not keep her from diving for a phone even before Magda and Stavros had left the office.

"Exploitation," Stavros muttered as they boarded the crosstown shuttle. He made it into a swear word.

"You caught that too, did you? Good. You might as well get used to it. We're going to be the Purists' little darlings for a while. That's not what I had in mind when I joined the Survey Service."

"I don't suppose you had murder in mind, either," Stavros said, and to that Magda had to shake her head. They rode in uneasy silence for some time after that and changed shuttles the same way.

"Wait a minute—we're not supposed to go down this street!" Magda exclaimed when the shuttle that usually went past her apartment complex took an unexpected turn.

Stavros pointed to the screen at the front of the passenger compartment. ROUTE CHANGED DUE TO TRAFFIC EMERGENCY AHEAD, it read. He and Magda looked at each other in alarm, both visualizing a Survey Service hijacking. The Service could probably foul up a shuttle route if it wanted to badly enough. No, scratch probably, Magda thought—the Service *could.*

She stabbed at the STOP AT NEXT CORNER button with her finger. Fearful sweat made it skid off the smooth plastic. She punched again, harder. Stavros was pressing the matching button on the arm of his seat. By the look in his eye, he didn't expect it to do any good either.

But the shuttle slid smoothly to a stop. The doors opened. Magda and Stavros scrambled down to the sidewalk with almost unseemly haste. They spun around, sure enemies would be lurking somewhere in the twilight. The shuttle disappeared down the street. Groundcars and lorries hissed by. No one paid the slightest attention to them.

Magda started to laugh and found she could not stop. Stavros finally had to hold her up. When the seizure was over at last, she stepped free of the arm he had around her shoulder. "Thanks," she said, wiping her eyes and rubbing at the pit of her stomach, which hurt. She told him, "If you ever had any doubts about whether I believed you, forget 'em. It's only taken me the afternoon to get as paranoid as you are."

"You're not paranoid when they're really after you," Stavros said grimly. "It's just as well you distracted me for a minute there; otherwise I expect I'd need a fresh pair of breeches." He did not sound as if he were joking.

"Let's get back to my complex," Magda said. She took a step and almost fell over; relief had left her giddy. She caught Stavros's arm, and he straightened her again. He was stronger than his skinny build would have made her think. "Thanks. We're just a couple of blocks away. Come on."

As they rounded the next to last corner, Magda stopped in her tracks. This was the route the shuttle should have taken, and she could see why it had been diverted. Police and people in emergency gear were everywhere. Something fell with a rending crash. An ambulance screamed past.

"Here, you can't come any farther," a harried-looking policewoman said, holding up a hand to stop Magda and Stavros.

"But I live down this way," Magda protested.

"What address?"

"It's the apartments at 141 Surf."

The policewoman's face changed. "I'm sorry," she said, but she made no move to let them by. Instead, she pointed down a side street. "Emergency shelter arrangements are that way."

"Emergency—" Magda left the word hanging.

"Honey, you can count yourself lucky you weren't home this afternoon. That building blew up; a lot of people are still trapped. They'll arrange temporary housing for you down that way"—the policewoman pointed again—"and see that you have a bed and a hot meal tonight."

Magda still tried to press ahead. "Isn't there any chance I could salvage some of my stuff from the ruins?"

"Honey, if you lived at 141, you don't have much to salvage. Now just go on, will you?" And stop making me trouble, Magda read between the lines. The policewoman went on, not unkindly, "Survivors will have a chance to search for their effects after we make sure things are stable. You'll be informed, I promise."

"Thanks." Numbly, Magda went in the direction the policewoman had pointed out.

"You see," Stavros said, following.

"Oh yes, I see." Magda's tone was still flat, stunned. Somehow that made her sound more menacing, not less. "I'm not the only one who will, either."

"I said that too, and look how well I've done," Stavros told her. "Now you know what you're up against—they're playing for keeps."

"So am I."

IX

"Thank you for coming here today," Paulina Koch said, looking out over the rostrum at the horde of video cameras. They peered back like so many long-nosed cyclopean beasts, and seemed more the masters than the servants of the people accompanying them. People and cameras alike were predators, she knew, and the blood they sought today was hers. The solid timber of the rostrum felt like a shield, holding them at bay.

"Chairman, do you have an opening statement?" called one of the reporters.

"No, I do not. I am here to respond to questions, and that is what I will do," Paulina Koch replied. She found no point to handing her foes free ammunition. Anything they wanted from her, they would have to earn. She pointed to one of the many upraised hands. "Yes, Mr. Karakoyunlu?"

The newsnet man was so surprised and excited at being called first that he forgot his carefully prepared question and blurted, "What about Bilbeis IV?"

Paulina Koch resisted—as many would not have—the temptation to reply, "Well, what about it?" Her answer was as painstaking as if the question had been a good one. "Bilbeis IV is a pretechnological world outside the Federacy. It was first visited by a Survey Service team in FSY 1186, at which time its civilization was early Bronze Age-equivalent."

"No!" Karakoyunlu was hopping up and down in frustration. "What about the *interference* on Bilbeis IV?" he shouted, hoping to make himself clear.

Again the Chairman chose to take him literally. "You are quite correct, of course. The anthropologist on that first expedition did interfere, contrary to all Survey Service policies and regulations, which even then were both clear and stringent. Upon his return to the Federacy, the individual in question could offer no acceptable defense for his actions and was quite deservedly cashiered." She chose another reporter. "Ms. Zedong?"

"What about the results of that anthropologist's interference on Bilbeis IV? Aren't they reflected in the recent report from the Survey Service ship *Jêng Ho,* and don't they show the interference caused a profound change in the planet's development, a change of exactly the sort the Survey Service is pledged to prevent?"

"Is that all one question?" Paulina Koch asked, raising some polite mirth. She grew serious at once, though, both because that was far more in her nature than frivolity and because she knew she could not seem to be evading the issue that had prompted the news conference. She said, "I presume, Ms. Zedong, you are referring to the report bearing the FSY date 2687:139."

"Of course, Chairman Koch. This is the report that first surfaced on Hyperion and is now vouched for by the Noninterference Foundation and by the one surviving crewmember of the *Jêng Ho*—"

"I'm sorry to disappoint you, but the Survey Service's position on that report has not changed since it—what was the word you used?—surfaced. Yes, that is apt. The person who brought it forward then is at the moment a fugitive from justice—a fugitive from a murder indictment, I might add. He hardly seems a trustworthy source."

"He denies it," three people said at once.

"Wouldn't you?" Paulina Koch retorted. She had strong doubts that this Monemvasios was guilty of anything—far more likely that was one of Roupen Hovannis's acquaintances—but she also knew she had told the precise truth: Monemvasios *had* run, and he *was* charged.

"Well, what about—" Zedong looked down to check her reminder screen. "—Magda Kodaly? She, after all, was present on Bilbeis IV and is the source of much of the critical data in the report."

"Certainly Magda Kodaly was a crewmember aboard the *Jêng Ho.* Whether the person using that name today has any right to it is another matter, however. Note that Magda Kodaly was reliably reported to have been killed in the tragic crash of the *Clark County,* and her credit card was recovered from the wreckage. Note also that the woman currently employing Kodaly's name has been using on Topanga the credit card of a certain Marie Roux. Nor did this alleged Kodaly respond to the recent subpoena sent to Topanga on behalf of the Assembly Subcommittee on Non-Federacy Contacts."

"Yes, but how much of an effort was made to serve that subpoena, Chairman Koch? After all, by then the *Clark County* had already gone down."

"So it had. As for what went into serving the subpoena, you would have to inquire at the Assembly. I am certainly not in a position to comment on the diligence of its employees." The small bit of sarcasm went down well; the newsnet people were avid for dirt on any segment of the Federacy government, not just the Survey Service. "You do understand, however, that I am not yet in a position to acknowledge that the person claiming to be Magda Kodaly is in fact she. If anything, her association with Monemvasios would tend to make me think otherwise . . . Mr. Salaam?"

"Isn't it a fact, Chairman Koch, that Kodaly's association with the Noninterference Foundation is what prejudices you against her?"

"Certainly not. The Noninterference Foundation is a public-spirited body with the highest ideals, many of which I share. The Survey Service has nothing to hide or to fear."

Salaam's eyes twinkled as he asked his follow-up question. "Chairman Koch, isn't it a fact that you wouldn't believe it if the Noninterference Foundation told you the sun was shining?"

"I would look outside, Mr. Salaam." Paulina Koch had not intended the reply to be funny and was taken aback by the laugh she got. She did not show it; she had schooled herself not to show anything. When the chuckles subsided, she nodded to another reporter. "Mr. Mir?"

"Hasn't Magda Kodaly taken steps to reestablish credit in her own name, and don't the physiological data she has submitted match those of the person who previously held credit under that name?"

"There you have the advantage of me, Mr. Mir. I would have to check on that." Again the Chairman spoke the truth, but not all of it. One of Hovannis's better computer people was still trying to change Magda Kodaly's credit system records. So far she had had no luck; the credit system's safeguards were the toughest in the Federacy. It was a losing battle, anyway. Sooner or later, Kodaly would be able to establish her bona fides.

Mir shrugged but was not through. "There is also the matter of the eighteen missing days, Chairman Koch."

Paulina Koch's expression of polite interest did not change. "To what eighteen days are you referring, Mr. Mir?"

"You and the Survey Service have insisted the report on Bilbeis IV is not genuine. It is, however, dated 2687:139. On 2687:157, on Hyperion, your computer reported to Hyperion Newsnet that the *Jêng Ho* had not yet come back from its mission to make a report. When asked when the ship would return, though, it gave a date of 2687:139. You stated at the time that this was computer error, yet Magda Kodaly insists that 139 is in fact the correct date of the *Jêng Ho*'s return. Your comments?"

Only that it appears you're able to add two and two, the Chairman thought. She tried to picture what the newsnet man's face would look like if she said that out loud. Too late if she intended to stay in the post she'd held so long—too late if she intended to stay free, for that matter. "I have seen nothing to make me change my mind, Mr. Mir, and you already know my reaction to the person claiming to be Magda Kodaly. It is remotely possible, however, I suppose, that an error has been made that is not accountable to computer malfunction. Accordingly, I have ordered Dr. Cornelia Toger, Survey Service Internal Affairs Director, to conduct a full investigation of any possible wrongdoing in this matter—which I stress I do not find likely—and to cooperate fully with any outside agencies conducting similar inquiries."

The newspeople sat up straighter—that was something they didn't know. They scribbled notes and muttered into recorders. Paulina Koch went on. "Dr. Toger will respond to your questions as to the nature of the inquiry now. I assure you that she is fully familiar with all aspects of the situation." She stepped away from the podium and beckoned Dr. Toger forward.

Dr. Toger did not know anything, did not suspect anything, and would not be allowed to find out anything. She fielded questions as best she could. She was earnest and sincere but very much out of her depth.

Paulina Koch listened to her luckless aide flounder. She realized she herself had had no questions about the immortal Queen Sabium. Down deep, she suspected, the reporters had trouble believing in the existence of a woman fifteen hundred years old, no matter what the report on Bilbeis IV said. She understood that. She had trouble believing it herself, and she knew only too well the report was real. Sabium would have been so much more . . . convenient as a legend.

When the conference was finally over, she went back to her office, where Hovannis waited. "What do you think, Roupen?"

He shrugged. "We're down, but we're not out. In a way, having the Noninterference Foundation weigh in against us does us a good turn. People know they hate us—it'll be easier to tar everything Kodaly says with their brush."

"Sensible plan." The Chairman nodded. "She's Survey Service herself, too, you know, even now. I wonder how much she cares for her new friends."

The talk-show host was suave without being oily, smooth without being facile. He had every hair perfectly in place. "Thank you for being with us, Ms. Kodaly," he said. "I'm sure you must be relieved to have formal use of your own name again."

"Yes, I certainly am, Mr. Vaughan." Magda's ears were full of the applause the audience had given her; she was still not used to being a celebrity. "Now that I've proved who I am, I can do a better job of proving just how accurate my colleagues' report on Bilbeis IV is."

"Of course." Vaughan nodded. "And of course you must agree with Dr. O'Brien that this kind of meddling on primitive planets can never be allowed to happen again."

Magda glanced toward the man sitting to the right of her on the couch. Peter O'Brien was the Foundation's head on Topanga, and fit the part: he was closing in on fifty and looked more like a well-fed executive than an activist. He was directing the media campaign against the Survey Service; he had pulled the strings to get Magda into the studio.

She did not resent O'Brien for appearing with her. The Noninterference Foundation was backing Stavros and her to make political capital for itself; she understood that. But she had no more intention of turning into a Foundation puppet than she'd had of turning a blind eye to what the Survey Service had done on Bilbeis IV.

She said, "I do agree with Dr. O'Brien on that, Mr. Vaughan, but—"

"Call me Owen, please," the emcee broke in. "Sorry to interrupt. But what, Magda? Tell us, please."

"But I don't necessarily feel the remedies he proposes are the right ones."

Beside her, O'Brien shifted in annoyance. Vaughan's eyes lit up. Magda had no idea what his politics were, but a good argument would liven up his show. "Why is that, Magda?"

"They're too drastic. The Survey Service monitors thousands of planets, almost every one of them with no trouble at all—in spite of what happened on Bilbeis IV—hell, partly *because* of what happened on Bilbeis IV back in FSY 1186. The Service takes the rule of interference very seriously. Disbanding it would be like cutting off your leg because you've an ingrown toenail."

"Dr. O'Brien, what do you think of—"

O'Brien did not need Vaughan to prompt him. "Magda's views reflect her training, naturally. I'd hoped the frantic concealment effort the Survey Service is making here would have opened her eyes to the cynicism inherent in all its policies."

"I don't see that." Magda was beginning to get angry; there was a difference between political capital and bullshit.

"Don't you?" O'Brien might look like a businessman and even act like one most of the time, but underneath that veneer he was still passionately convinced of the righteousness of his cause. "I'm referring to the cynical pretense that Survey Service fieldwork has no influence on planets where it occurs," he growled.

"It doesn't, and you know it perfectly well," Magda said. "You're acting as if you don't know a damned thing about the training we go through—"

"'We'?" O'Brien said icily. "I'm sure Paulina Koch would be pleased to hear you say that."

"Well, up yours, too. She's wrong, but that doesn't make you right, you sanctimonious know-nothing son of a bitch."

Owen Vaughan sat back, steepled his fingers, and kept his mouth shut. His sponsors had been complaining that nothing really juicy had happened on his show since the night the actress got drunk and threw a glass of brandy in the mullah's face. They'd have nothing to grumble about tonight.

"Doesn't it?" O'Brien shot back. "Why do we have any right to meddle in the affairs of people whose only crime is being culturally younger than we are? Let them develop their own way, I say, instead of corrupting them by our presence. I thought you would agree with me: you're the one who brought to the attention of the whole Federacy the sorry spectacle of millions of deluded people on Bilbeis IV following their false religion because of what the Survey Service did long ago."

"With Queen Sabium as she is, they have a lot better reason for believing what they believe than most worshipers I know." But even Magda backed away from that one in a hurry—she needed to swing people to her way of thinking, not alienate them. "Besides, you're making it sound as if all the primitive planets the Service visits are more Bilbeis IVs—"

"They are, just waiting to happen."

""They are not!" Magda slammed her fist down on the arm of her couch. "For one thing, Survey Service procedures are different from what they used to be: we've already talked about that. For another, there just aren't that many Sabiums around, or key situations where interference really affects a world's development."

"Where's your evidence for that?"

"Where's yours?" Magda retorted. "If interference were as widespread a problem as you claim, we'd see cases like Bilbeis IV every other year. And we don't. We don't. Most of the time, the Survey Service does a good job. But when it doesn't, it has to be called to account. That's why I'm here tonight. That's supposed to be the purpose of the Noninterference Foundation, too, as I recall, not wrecking the Service altogether."

"That is what we are for," O'Brien said, giving ground before her vehemence and also remembering she was valuable to him. "Where you and I differ is in judging how likely interference is. There's no doubt, though, that Bilbeis IV is a particularly flagrant case."

Magda nodded; she too was recalling that they had interests in common. "The worst of it, though, is the way Survey Service Central has done its best to sweep the report under the rug after the *Jêng Ho* submitted it. All my crewmates are dead, and so is the professor who first accessed it from public files . . . which it isn't in any more."

"There's such a thing as too much coincidence," O'Brien agreed. He did not say any more than that, not when he had no proof linking any deaths to Survey Service Central.

Owen Vaughan sighed imperceptibly. He had been hoping they would come to blows—*that* would have sent ratings through the roof on half the planets in the Federacy. But Vaughan was a practical man who took what he could get and knew how to cut things short when the heat went out of them. "Let's take a short break for these words from our sponsors," he said, "and we'll be right back."

Magda pounded on Stavros's door. They were staying in side-by-side furnished apartments in a building owned by a prominent contributor to the Noninterference Foundation. Both apartments still kept the air of sterility that such places have when uninhabited: neither Stavros nor Magda had enough in the way of belongings to dissipate it.

He took his time answering the door. Undoubtedly, Magda thought, he was checking the security camera first. She didn't blame him. She was cultivating the same habit herself.

"How did it go?" he asked. "You still have your makeup on."

"Yes, I know. I haven't even been in my own place yet—I'm too disgusted to sit by myself. You're in this same miserable boat with me; if anybody would understand, you're the one." She threw herself into a chair. Except for being blue instead of green, it was identical to the one in her apartment, right down to the scratchy upholstery.

"That bad, was it?"

"Worse. Let me put it like this: if this O'Brien person had Paulina Koch's job, we'd be in the exact same mess we are now. Well, maybe not, on second thought—Koch can keep her mouth shut and deny everything with a straight face. That's not O'Brien's style. He likes to hear himself talk, so he gives away more than she would. The other delightful thing is that he's a damned Purist and hardly bothers to hide it."

"I got that feeling, too, when I met him," Stavros said. "So much for the impartiality the Noninterference Foundation is supposed to show. Trouble is, we need him."

"I know, I know, I know. Otherwise I'd have loosened a few of his teeth for him. I still wish I had. He left a bad taste in my mouth."

Stavros got up. "Want to clean it out with a drink?"

"That's the first sensible idea I've heard since I got on camera." Magda held up a hand. "Wait a second, though—you don't like the sweet slop they drink here, do you?" Topangan taste in spirits ran heavily to liqueurs and creams, all of which Magda found cloying.

"Is vodka over ice all right?"

"Sure; that's fine."

Stavros went into the kitchen. Magda heard ice rattle in glasses. He brought the drinks back, handed Magda hers, and shook a few drops from a small bottle into his. It turned milky. "What's that?" Magda asked, intrigued.

"Anise extract," he answered. "It turns the stuff into poor man's ouzo. Everybody drinks ouzo on New Thessaly."

"I know what you mean. We're the same way with plum brandy on Kadar, where I come from." She held out her glass. "Let me try some." He gave her drink the same treatment he had given his.

Knocking back a good-sized swallow, she felt her eyes water. She tried not to cough, and almost succeeded.

"Are you all right?" Stavros asked anxiously.

"Takes getting used to," she said. She drank again, more cautiously. "Not bad, I suppose, but it must be a lethal hangover mix."

"Retsina—resinated wine—is worse."

Magda's stomach lurched at the very idea. The things some allegedly civilized people drank—

She glanced over to the screen above the apartment terminal. She had noticed it was on when she came in but had been too full of irritation to pay any attention to what Stavros was looking at. It was a sequence from the report on Bilbeis IV. She tried to recall whether it came from Irfan Kawar's ring camera or the one she had worn on the shattering day when they found the locals' undying goddess was in fact Queen Sabium of Helmand.

Stavros followed Magda's eye. "I don't know how many times I've been through that part of the report," he said. "I keep trying to get a feel for what it must be like to have lived so long and to have been the focus of a whole planet's devotion for—how long?—fifty or sixty generations."

"I know what you mean. I've been trying to do the same thing myself, ever since I met her. The other thing to keep in mind is that the tape can't convey more than a fraction of the presence she has. It really is as if she can see into your heart."

"I believe it," Stavros said. "There can't be much she hasn't seen, dealing with century after century of priests and courtiers and petitioners. There's nothing anywhere to compare her to: she's been the keystone of that planet's culture for almost as long as its had civilization."

"There's more to it, though." Magda was glad for the chance to talk about Sabium. The flap over Central's suppression of the report on Bilbeis IV had pushed the queen herself into the background, even in Magda's own mind, and Sabium was too remarkable for that. Stavros made a good audience, too; he had studied the report enough to be as familiar with Bilbeis IV as anyone outside the *Jêng Ho*'s crew could be. As familiar as anyone alive, Magda realized, was another good way to put it.

But he had not stood before Sabium's throne, had never felt the crashing awe that came with meeting the queen who had become divine. Magda struggled to put that into words. "It's not only the length of life Sabium's had. Even more of it, I think, is the person she was before we tinkered with her immune responses."

Stavros frowned. "I'm not sure I understand."

"I'm not sure I do, either. But even back in her mortal days, Sabium was a good queen. She cared about her people and about bettering the way they lived. The first Survey Service crew saw that—it's the main reason their anthropologist decided to cure her cancer. I suppose it's why he managed to talk the rest of them into it. And look at the mess he left behind."

"He didn't know—"

"No, he didn't." Magda cut off Stavros's beginning protest. "That's why you don't interfere—you don't know. I've sometimes shuddered, thinking how much worse things might have been if Sabium hadn't really been the able, kindly queen the first expedition thought she was."

"That hadn't occurred to me," Stavros said in a low voice. By his expression, he was going through the same set of appalling possibilities Magda had already imagined.

She said, "Here's something else to worry about: you're about the same age I am, aren't you—around thirty standard years?" She waited for him to nod and went on. "Did you ever have the feeling you're more distinctly *yourself* these days than you were, say, eight or ten years ago?"

Stavros nodded again. "Sure. The older I get, the more experience and knowledge I have to judge things by. My tastes are more settled, too: I like this kind of music and that kind of food. I expect I'll keep adding things as long as I live, but in the context of the structure I already have."

"That's exactly it—that's clearer than I ever thought it through, as a matter of fact," Magda said in surprised admiration. Because she was doing fieldwork while he was still a grad student, she automatically thought of herself as being more mature. His answer made her wonder. She continued more carefully, trying now to make each word count. "You and I have been growing into ourselves as adults for those eight or ten years. Sabium's been doing it more than a hundred times as long. As much as anything else, I think that's what makes her so intimidating—she's uniquely herself, uniquely an individual, in a way that no one who hasn't lived so long ever could be."

Stavros raised his glass in salute. It was nearly empty. "Well put," he said. "That's part of what I was looking for when I booted up the report tonight." He downed the rest of his drink and muttered something under his breath.

"I'm sorry, I didn't hear that," Magda said.

Stavros's swarthiness could not quite hide his flush. He hesitated, plainly of two minds about repeating himself, then blurted, "I wonder what she's like in bed."

Magda burst out laughing. "Well, there's one I hadn't thought of." She looked at the screen again. Sabium appeared no different from the way she had at the time of the first Survey Service visit to Bilbeis IV, fifteen centuries before: a handsome woman in the first years of middle age. Her gray-pink skin, blue hair, and the light down that grew on her cheeks were only exotic details. They might even make her more attractive to a man, not less, Magda thought. "She'd be interesting, I expect," she said.

"Even with the chance, I don't know if I would," Stavros said, "or could, for that matter. I can't imagine anything more inhibiting than thinking of how much experience I'd be measured against." He shivered in mock fright at the very idea.

"Don't worry about it," Magda advised. "It's not as if it's something that's likely to come up."

"I thought I just said that."

Magda snorted. She held out her glass. "Fix me another one, will you? I'll pass on the anise this time, though."

She was not surprised to end up sharing Stavros's bed that night. Alcohol had little to do with it; that the two of them were trapped in the same precarious situation counted for much more. She and Irfan Kawar had slept together when Sabium's priests conveyed them across the main continent of Bilbeis IV to meet the undying goddess. It had brought comfort to them both, and did again, until Magda thought of Kawar's dying on the *Clark County* with the rest of the *Jêng Ho*'s crew.

She did not want to remind herself of that, not again, not tonight. She turned to Stavros and touched his shoulder. "I don't think Sabium would complain." She was not exaggerating much; her knees felt pleasantly unstrung. He hardly seemed to notice the compliment, though. She wondered if she had pleased him. "What's wrong?" she asked.

He brought himself back to the here and now with a visible effort. Magda recalled she was not the only one with dark memories. "Sorry," Stavros said. "It's nothing to do with you, not really."

Any reassurance he'd meant to give collapsed with that two-word afterthought. He realized it at once and made an annoyed noise deep in his throat. Magda lay beside him, waiting till he was ready to go on. After a little while, he did. "I'm sorry, Magda. It's just that this reminds me too much of the way Andrea and I ended up making love with each other not so long ago."

"Oh." It was Magda's turn to be silent and thoughtful. She finally said, "You told me once—I think it was the first time we met, after we came out of the Survey Service office—that you were falling in love with her."

"Yes, I think so." Stavros's eyes went first distant, then furious. He sat up and slammed his fist into the mattress so hard that he and Magda both bounced. "And those bastards didn't just kill her, they landed the blame for it on me."

"You ought to talk with the Foundation people about that. There's bound to be a branch on Hyperion. Heaven knows I don't love them, but they have the money to dig out whatever they need to prove you were innocent—and once that's done, people are bound to start wondering just who did kill your Andrea, and why."

"You're right!" Stavros bounded out of bed. "Fogelman belonged to the Foundation. In fact, I think he was one of the higher-ups. And he was murdered, too, and all his data banks scrubbed. What burglar would bother? Andrea and I tried to bring that up on Hyperion, but no one took it seriously—until the *Clark County* crashed, and then all it did was scare people. Now, though—" His lips drawn back in a predatory grin, he started for the phone.

Magda coughed dryly. "Probably a good idea to put some clothes on first."

"Hmm? Oh!" Stavros clutched at himself.

"No need to hide from me, not now. Just pick up your pants." Watching while Stavros dressed, Magda saw she was forgotten for the moment. Now that he was reminded of his Andrea, she wondered whether he would have any more interest in her. If nothing else, life would be less lonely if he did.

She rolled onto the wet spot on the bed, swore, and then laughed. That was realism on the most basic level. Very few men, she thought, turned down the chance when it was there. That was realism, too. She got out of bed and went into the bathroom to clean up.

"It is always a privilege to meet with you, of course, Mr. Prime Minister," Paulina Koch said, smoothing an imaginary wrinkle on the sleeve of her gray smock, "but may I ask the reason for which you invited me to Government Mansion?"

Amadeo Croce matched her formality. "It is this Bilbeis IV matter, Madam Chairman." He tried to sound stern, and did not succeed well. Administrations came and went, but senior bureaucrats held the real, the lasting power in the Federacy. He and Paulina Koch both knew it.

"In what connection, sir?" the Chairman asked, deferential as protocol required. She would not flout his nominal authority, not now, not when the Survey Service needed every scrap of political help it could get.

Croce frowned a little. The expression did odd things to the lines on his face, which years of smiling at cameras had set in a mold of permanent affability. He said, "I feel the Service is, uh, unduly dilatory in dealing with the accusations of mishandling that have so persistently wrapped themselves around the situation relating to that planet."

"To which accusations are you referring?" Paulina Koch asked coolly. "The ones that allege Survey Service personnel guilty of everything from sabotage to murder to who knows what else? If you believe those, sir, I can only wonder why you called me here and not to the Office of Rehabilitation."

"No, no, of course not," Croce said, to Paulina Koch's well-hidden relief. One power the prime minister did have was control over the constabulary. It was a more brutal sort of power than the clashes of influence that formed the usual government shake-ups, but it was there. The Chairman had never had to fear it before. Now she did. She was the only one who knew it, but it still weakened her.

Her musings made her miss the prime minister's next sentence, which was also unlike her. "I beg your pardon, sir?" She had no great regard for Croce, but the apology was genuine; she did not like to slip.

"I was just saying that as far as I can see, no convincing evidence for anything past happenstance has surfaced concerning those charges. But the ones touching on Survey Service Central's handling of the report on Bilbeis IV itself do concern me."

"Given the nature of the people making those charges, sir, I must confess to wondering why. The Noninterference Foundation has been sniping at the Survey Service for several hundred years now—"

"I wasn't referring to the Foundation," Croce interrupted. "I meant the principals themselves, this Monemvasios person and the anthropologist off the *Jêng Ho* itself. If they are to be believed, Bilbeis IV has encountered interference in its development, interference caused by Survey Service personnel, and the report documenting that interference is genuine. And I have to tell you, the more they talk, the more credible they sound."

"It does appear that the person who claims to be Magda Kodaly may in fact be she," Paulina Koch admitted grudgingly. "As for the other one, though—"

The prime minister broke in again. "I know what you are going to say. I have information, however, that the authorities on Hyperion are dropping all charges against him: he definitely was in a classroom when his girlfriend's murder took place."

"Really?" Paulina Koch's eyebrows arched in surprise, but she had known that bit of news for a day and a half. Croce's interrupting her twice worried her more. Attuned as she was to the nuances of bureaucratic maneuvering, she read there the warning that he no longer felt as much need to conciliate her as he once had.

"Yes, it is true. And if this Monemvasios individual is to be believed, and if the woman Magda Kodaly was in fact aboard the *Jêng Ho,* I hope you will not be offended by my repeating that their view of the report on Bilbeis IV is also enhanced."

"Sir, I take no offense, but I respectfully have to disagree with you."

Croce raised an eyebrow. "You must tell me why."

"Even if Kodaly was in fact on Bilbeis IV, that says nothing about the accuracy of the document submitted as a report on the mission of the *Jêng Ho.* Kodaly was, if you recall, one of the two main actors in the wilder claims that the text of the document makes, and the interpretation of events going into those claims is almost exclusively hers. To put it as mildly as possible, her objectivity is suspect. If she were well-disposed to the Service, would she be associating with the Noninterference Foundation?"

"An interesting question," the prime minister said. Paulina Koch studied him with sudden sharp attention, thinking she scented irony, but his politician's face was proof against her scrutiny. He continued, "A pity we lack the remaining members of the *Jêng Ho*'s crew to give her the lie, is it not?"

"A great pity, and a great tragedy." Paulina Koch reminded herself that she still did not *know* exactly what had happened to the *Clark County.* She did not remind herself that she had not tried to find out. Ignorance felt more comfortable, to say nothing of safer.

"That being the case, however, I suppose you are going to accede to the Noninterference Foundation's request that they conduct a new investigation of the situation on Bilbeis IV, to ascertain precisely what that situation is."

Only the Chairman's wariness and experience let her evade the trap. She was sure her meeting with Croce was being recorded; a panicky shout of "No!" could be plenty to sink her, while a "Yes" was even more unthinkable. Her voice came out steady as she replied, "I have several reasons for believing that to be inadvisable." Down deep where it did not show, she was proud of her sangfroid.

"Let me hear them." If the prime minister felt disappointment, he was also a dab hand at not showing it.

Many sessions of testifying before the Assembly without notes had given Paulina Koch the knack of quickly organizing her thoughts. "First, of course, is the question of impartiality. The Noninterference Foundation's ties to the Purists are notorious, and have been only too evident throughout the present affair."

"That statement is self-serving, you realize."

"Yes." Paulina Koch was always ready to yield a small point to gain a large one. "That does not make it any less true."

Croce chuckled. "Well, maybe so. Go on."

"Thank you, sir. I also must remind you that for the Noninterference Foundation to undertake such a mission is in itself a contradiction in terms. Are the Foundation's people so steeped in moral purity that they can avoid causing the very kind of interference they claim to reject?"

"Were you to ask them, I am certain they would tell you so," the prime minister said. He had been in his profession far too long to have escaped cynicism.

"Yes, no doubt," Paulina Koch agreed as sardonically. "I was, however, asking you. I would also ask you to consider that while they spend so much of their time complaining about what we do, they lack the training for survey missions of the type we do routinely, let alone for one as delicate as this."

"I begin to see your drift."

Croce did not sound happy with it. Paulina Koch played her trump card. "Finally, think about whether you would be happy at the precedent set for a private organization's usurping here the function of a government bureau. Are you willing to have that happen whenever a publicity campaign whips people into a frenzy, deserved or not?"

The prime minister stiffened. That, thought the Chairman with the first real optimism she had felt during the meeting, had hit him where he lived. No official, elected or appointed, could warm to the notion of having authority taken out of his hands. "What do you suggest, then?" Croce asked.

"I suppose that in light of the hue and cry over Bilbeis IV, regular procedures must be set aside." The distaste in Paulina Koch's voice was twofold. Setting aside regular procedure was unpleasant to her in and of itself. And when doing so also involved having to retreat to a fallback position, that only made things worse. She did her best to maintain a bold front. "Any new survey team that visits the planet will have to be extraordinarily discreet. Survey Service personnel are the only logical choice for the mission."

She already had most of the crewmembers in mind—loyal, pliable souls one and all, people who would see only what did the Service the most good. Fallback positions were stronger when prepared in advance.

"I had thought you might say that." Amadeo Croce took a deep breath. "I must tell you that in the view of this administration, what you have suggested is not adequate. I shall so state on the floor of the Assembly. I would sooner have the Noninterference Foundation conduct the inquiry. The Survey Service is too deeply compromised to be the sole arbiter of its own affairs."

Behind her unrevealing features, Paulina Koch's mind raced. This was what Croce had summoned her here to tell her. Normally, the administration backed its bureau chiefs to the hilt; they were the ones who carried out the policies the politicians set. And Croce was no Purist, nor were the members of his cabinet. He had no strong ideological commitment to going after the Survey Service. He had simply scented weakness and decided to get clear of it.

"What plan do you have in mind, then, sir?" the Chairman asked, tasting gall.

"I shall propose a solution that would make Solomon proud," the prime minister answered. Seeing that the allusion meant nothing to Paulina Koch, he explained, "You are right in one way, Madam Chairman—we have to send a new mission to Bilbeis IV. I think you also make good sense when you advise against putting the expedition in the hands of the Noninterference Foundation. One of your people will retain overall command. But I will urge that the mission be made up half of Service personnel, half of individuals chosen by an independent agency, and for that role the Foundation seems the obvious choice."

The solution struck the Chairman as contrived; whoever this Solomon had been, he hadn't had much upstairs. On the other hand . . . she nodded slowly. A divided expedition could be counted on to produce an ambiguous report. At the moment, she—and the Survey Service—could hope for nothing better. A couple of other possibilities also occurred to her.

"Very well, sir," she said.

The prime minister had opened his mouth to argue her down. He shut it again in glad surprise.

"They're not going to get away with that!" Stavros exclaimed, staring at the formal hard-copy message he had just opened.

Magda read it over his shoulder. "You bet your life they're not." Her voice was full of the same furious disbelief that filled his.

Stavros took her cliché literally. "Yes, I have, and so have you. Is this the gratitude we get for it?" He read in a singsong voice: "'Thank you for your interest in participating in the renewed investigation of the planet Bilbeis IV. Unfortunately, these positions require more experienced individuals.'"

"There are no people more experienced with Bilbeis IV than the two of us," Magda said. "Me directly—hell, now I'm the only person in the Federacy who's ever been there—and you because you've been through our report until you probably know it better than I do. And so—" She took her anger out on the phone buttons.

A well-scrubbed young man's face appeared on the screen. "Noninterference Foundation."

"We're Kodaly and Monemvasios. Put us through to Dr. O'Brien right now. If he doesn't feel like talking to us—and he probably won't—tell him his other choice is listening to us on the newsnets later, and that he'll like that even less."

"Remind me not to let you get angry at me," Stavros whispered when the screen went momentarily black. "I think I'd sooner just stand in front of a shuttle and get everything over with at once."

Magda managed a grim chuckle. "I'll take that for a compliment. You know what we're going to hit him with?"

"A hammer, by choice," Stavros growled. His temper was not as quick as Magda's, but she had already found he was impossible to move from a position once he dug in his heels. He squeezed her hand, saying, "I think so. I'm with you all the way. I—"

He broke off abruptly, because Peter O'Brien's image replaced that of the Foundation underling. O'Brien eyed Magda with a singular lack of warmth. "What's this all about?" he demanded.

"I think you know," Magda said. She smiled a little when Stavros wordlessly held up the form letter; sure enough, he knew what she was up to.

"I am sorry." O'Brien did not sound sorry. "You must understand that we have to involve only the most qualified people on a project of the importance of this one. There is nothing personal involved."

"For one thing, I don't believe you. For another, where will you find anybody else who's met Queen Sabium, the undying goddess a whole planet worships? For a third, where would you be without Stavros and me? You owe us slots, and you will pay off, or I'm sure the newsnet people—and the whole Federacy—will be fascinated to hear how the high and mighty Noninterference Foundation shoved us to one side the minute we weren't useful to you anymore."

"Do you think you can blackmail me?" O'Brien snapped.

"Damn right I do," Magda said gleefully. "Fix it and fix it now, or we'll have other calls to make. Remember, the more you look like Purists, the less reason people will have to believe your side of the story. And kicking us off your crew will make you look an awful lot like a Purist to an awful lot of people. Me, I'm one of 'em."

"I'm another," Stavros added.

"Now," Magda said with a sweet smile, "shall we ring off and start getting hold of the newsnets?"

"I can't permit that," O'Brien said. "It would be—"

"Can't?" Stavros broke in. "Can't? How do you propose stopping us? The same way the Survey Service stopped Professor Fogelman and Andrea and the *Jêng Ho*'s crew? Do we ask for protection from you next?"

"No, of course not." O'Brien made a pushing-away gesture, as if to put distance between himself and Stavros's suggestion. For the first time, he seemed flustered. "We would never do, never think of such a thing. Of course you are free to do as you wish. It would hurt your cause as well as ours, though. Please think of that, please don't do anything you might come to regret—"

"You know what we want," Magda said implacably.

"Let me get back to you," O'Brien pleaded. "This is too big a decision for me to make on my own."

"We'll wait until tonight, no longer," Stavros told him.

"Tonight?" Now O'Brien looked horrified. "That's much too soon. Some of the people with whom I have to consult are offplanet, and—"

"Tonight." Stavros switched off the phone in the middle of O'Brien's protest. When it chimed again a moment later, he hit the REFUSE button. The noise cut off. He grinned a small-boy grin at Magda.

She hugged him. "You couldn't have backed me better! Nothing makes the Foundation angrier than being compared to the Service."

"I meant it." Stavros was still serious. "The minute any power group sees an edge, it grabs, and anybody in the way had better look out. And we aren't the kind of friends Purists feel comfortable with. That show you did with O'Brien must have made him sure of that."

"I don't want any Purists feeling comfortable with me," Magda snorted. "All they want to do is set every social science there is back a couple of thousand years. And speaking of setting back, you just cost the Foundation a nice tidy sum there."

"Yes, I know. If O'Brien does have to confer offworld—and he probably does—he'll need to use the FTL links, and those aren't cheap. But I figured that setting a deadline he'll have to scramble to meet would show him we weren't fooling."

"Smart." Magda was still discovering just how good an ally Stavros made. He was unprepossessing, especially at the moment—he was regrowing the beard he'd shaved off when he escaped from Hyperion. Unlike her, he was given to hesitating before taking something on. But once he committed, himself, he did not back away, and the rein he held on his temper let him keep getting in telling shots after she was reduced to outraged incoherence.

His single-mindedness could also be irritating. Once O'Brien was no longer an immediate concern, he went back to what he had been doing when the Foundation's letter arrived: poring over the report on Bilbeis IV. Magda draped herself against his back. "Shall we kill some time until they call us again?"

Without looking away from the screen, Stavros said, "Let's wait until we know whether we have anything to celebrate." She angrily strode away and had very little to say to him the rest of the afternoon. She would have got more satisfaction from her silence had he noticed it.

But they both dashed for the phone when O'Brien called back not long before sunset. "You win," he growled, and switched off himself.

"Probably making sure you didn't beat him to the—" Magda began.

Stavros found a very effective way to interrupt her. She never did finish the sentence. Sometimes, she thought a good deal later, single-mindedness was an advantage.

✧ ✧ ✧

Survey Service crews normally departed with no more fanfare than anyone else going off to do a job. The takeoff of the *Hanno* was different. It drew Assemblymen, Noninterference Foundation bigwigs, the Chairman of the Survey Service, and enough newsnet people to fill a luxury liner past takeoff weight.

Magda preferred the usual way. Everybody wanted to make a speech, and everybody's speech was running long. The only thing she was grateful for was that the crew got to sit down. A camera woman, on her feet for hours, had already passed out.

A black Assemblyman named Valleix was just finishing putting five minutes' worth of idea into a twenty-minute speech. Listening with one ear, Magda gathered that he was against the Survey Service and everything it stood for; he did not seem clear on what that was. The Foundation honchos up on the platform with him applauded lustily. Gritting her teeth at having to work with such people, Magda only wished he would shut up and go away.

Stavros might have been reading her mind. He leaned over and whispered, "I'd sooner be meeting interesting people instead of going through all this nonsense."

"Me, too." The crew of the *Hanno*, at least the half of the contingent that the Noninterference Foundation had chosen, was a high-powered group. Magda knew several members' work.

Paulina Koch was coming to the podium. Magda's feelings about the Chairman were still mixed; it was hard to think of her longtime boss, the head of the organization in which she had wanted to spend her whole career, as the enemy. At least Paulina Koch was not long-winded. She would say what she had to say and then quit. Magda turned and said as much to Stavros.

"A subtracter is also nice and straightforward," Stavros said. "All it does is kill you."

"What's a subtracter?"

"A big poisonous worm-type creature we have at home."

"We have something like that on Kadar, too. We call the thing an adder, after the Terran snake."

"I suppose one of our early settlers decided that didn't make much sense," Stavros said, "considering what it does. Greeks are very logical people." He grinned. "We also love to play with words."

The byplay had made Magda miss Paulina Koch's opening remarks. The Chairman was saying, "It is our hope that this mission will succeed in bringing back an unbiased account of conditions on Bilbeis IV, so that we can, if necessary, evolve new techniques for making contact with pretechnological cultures even more effective yet discreet than is the case at this point in time."

" 'If necessary'!" Stavros snarled. He was no friend of the Chairman's and never would be.

"In all candor, we initially doubted the necessity for a new visit to Bilbeis IV," Paulina Koch continued, "but we are now convinced that valuable data may be gleaned from it. It will also serve as a model of cooperation between our agency and organizations which hitherto have not always been in accord with us. From it we may learn to go forward in harmony."

"And I may learn to go into stardrive without a ship," Magda muttered. She had been in the Survey Service too long to believe the Service and the Noninterference Foundation were ever going to get along. She did not believe Paulina Koch thought so, either. The hypocrisy in the speech made her grimace; it reminded her all too much of the political games she had had to play herself lately.

Paulina Koch stepped down. Somebody else stepped up. More rhetoric spewed out for the cameras. Magda endured it, dose after dose. Finally it was done.

"At last, the point of the exercise," Stavros said as the crew of the *Hanno* followed their commander to the ship. As was customary, the commander paused at the top of the boarding ramp to greet the people with whom he would be traveling.

He was a dark, broad-shouldered man who looked more like an engine tech or a stevedore than any sort of leader. That was Magda's first impression of him, at any rate. She changed her mind when she saw his eyes, which were shrewd and opaque. He wore Survey Service coveralls.

"Captain Hovannis," she said, holding out her hand.

He did not take it. "Ms. Kodaly," he said. His voice was deep and rough. He did not shake Stavros's hand, either, and ignored the glare he got.

Stavros was still fuming as he got ready for lift-off. "Coldblooded bastard," he complained over the intercom.

"Screw him," Magda said. "He's Service, and he doesn't have any reason to like us. The angrier we let him make us, the happier he'll be. If I do get angry at him, I want it to be for my reasons, not his. Make sense?"

"Yes," Stavros said reluctantly.

"Relax, then. We're on our way."

"We are?"

Magda waved at her outside viewscreen. It showed the black of space.

Stavros laughed at himself. "I keep missing takeoffs."

"You're here, and that's what counts."

"No," he said. "What counts is when we get there."

Magda thought about it. "You're right."

X

"The disputed orchards, I find, do in law lie under the jurisdiction of the town of Khonsu. Yet because the representative of Shirik has shown that its townspeople have used these orchards for two generations without protest from Khonsu till now, they may still harvest up to one hundred *tals* of fruit per year there at no cost to themselves. Above that, they shall pay Khonsu at the market rate."

The spokesmen—actually, one was a woman—of the two towns bowed low before the glittering throne. "We thank the eternal goddess," they intoned. The words were ritual, but the goddess heard no great dissatisfaction in them. She had been able to give both sides something, which went a long way toward stifling resentment.

The claimants bowed again and walked out of the audience chamber side by side. No, there would be no further trouble there for a man's lifetime or two, the goddess thought. She turned to her majordomo. "They were the last for today?"

"Yes, goddess." Though the priest had served in the Holy City since before his beard sprouted, his voice was as full of awe as those of the petitioners from distant Khonsu and Shirik, who were seeing the goddess for the first and almost surely last time in their lives. He asked, "Will you return to your chambers now?"

"Not just yet, Bagadat. I will sit for a moment first." The goddess leaned back and smoothed a wrinkle in the fine white fabric of her robe. Suddenly the weight of the gold circlet on her brow seemed heavy and oppressive, though she could not remember the last time she had noticed it . . . perhaps not even since the days when she had been known as Sabium.

She needed all the discipline a millennium and a half had granted to keep from her face the complex concerns that thought evoked. The last meeting with the representatives of the higher gods, the ones who had given her eternal life, had been oddly inconclusive. The bronze-haired woman and bald-crowned man—strange, alien features only accented by their brownish-pink skins—had seldom been far from her mind in the two years since they mysteriously appeared and as mysteriously vanished.

What had puzzled her ever since was their youth and ignorance. Gods lived forever; even she, who had become divine only by the grace of more powerful deities, enjoyed that boon. Surely the same had to be true of divine messengers as well. Yet these claimed no more than a man's span of years and, by every subtle sign she had learned, were speaking the truth.

Moreover, she was convinced her own immortality had surprised and shocked them, though they knew of the events that had created it. She did not have many mysteries in her life; people had become transparent to her after so many years of observing them, guiding them. She worried away at the riddle of the messengers as at a piece of meat stuck between the teeth.

And as with a piece of meat, she was confident the mystery eventually would yield. The patience to wait for the fullness of time before acting was no small part of what had won Sabium dominion over most of her continent and a good portion of the smaller one to the east. Her rivals, being mere mortals, always moved too soon.

Behind her mask of calm, a wry smile stirred. Now she had no choice but to wait. She accepted that with the same resolution she had used long ago to face her own death. She rose from the throne. "I'm sorry, Bagadat; I've changed my mind. You may escort me after all."

The majordomo bowed very low. "Of course, goddess."

Paulina Koch ruled an empire older and vaster than Sabium's. Indeed, were it not for the Survey Service, Sabium's empire would never have come into being. Bureaucracies, too, have something of immortality about them and distill wisdom from the years. Had Paulina Koch been a person who framed mottoes and hung them on her wall, pride of place would have gone to the one that read, "When in doubt, do nothing."

The Chairman was not that sort of person. She loathed display in any form; all she wanted was to do her job, do it well, and be left alone. Most of the time she got her wish. Even after the mess about Bilbeis IV had blown up, she had guided the Service's appropriation through a hostile Assembly with her usual sharp skill.

But waiting would not always serve, and while the Survey Service might go on forever, Paulina Koch knew only too well her own tenure as Chairman—to say nothing of her freedom—would not last ten minutes past final confirmation of just how she had covered her tracks. It behooved her, then, to make sure those data stayed buried.

Cornelia Toger's report, which she had just reviewed, was no threat. The Internal Affairs Director hadn't been able to find anything wrong at Survey Service Central. Paulina Koch had not expected her to; the only reason Toger headed the internal investigation was her inability to see past her nose.

The Chairman almost laughed at her suggestion that the problem really lay on Topanga. Then she stopped, thoughtful. Pinning a piece of the blame there might not be a bad idea after all.

Getting Roupen Hovannis offplanet was a more certain insurance policy, though, she thought. For one thing, he would help keep a lid on this new investigation of Bilbeis IV. Self-interest was a perfect lever there: Hovannis knew his neck was on the line, too.

For another, now that he was gone, Paulina Koch had a better chance of teasing out of the computer whatever incriminating evidence he had on her. She knew it was in the system. Hovannis would have been a fool not to keep that kind of file, and Paulina Koch tolerated no fools in the Survey Service.

But data processing had been the key to her own rapid rise through the ranks. Hovannis was very good at hiding information. With no false modesty, she thought she was better at digging it out.

The trouble was, she had so much to go through. No one, and no army either, could hope to keep up with all the information the Federacy generated. And as External Affairs Director, Hovannis had access to almost all the veiling techniques the Survey Service had ever had to devise. If he wanted to conceal dirt in six-hundred-year-old committee meeting minutes against future need, he could change those documents without leaving any sign that their ancient obscurity had been disturbed.

Or so he thought. Still, there were ways. Like any safety-conscious administrator, Paulina Koch held a few tricks in reserve about which her subordinates knew nothing. Some, unfortunately, left traces behind—otherwise the Chairman would have been using them all along instead of having to wait until Hovannis was away from the scene.

Until she began her search project, she had had only an intellectual feel for the sheer size of the bureau she ran. Watching the computer spin its metaphorical wheels as it ground through enormous chaffheaps of data, though, gave her an emotional grasp as well, one she would just as soon not have had. Someone else might have given way to despair—what she was looking for might be *anyplace.*

Paulina Koch did not give way. In what free time she had from the day-to-day problems of running the Service, she refined a couple of search routines to make them harder to detect and, more important, faster.

Unlike Sabium, she knew she did not have all the time she needed.

Magda slammed her hand down on the table in disgust. "I don't know why I bother talking to you, Pierre," she snapped. "You're only using half the data we have, and the less important half, too."

Pierre Bochy gestured defensively. "You will forgive me, but I see no reason not to rely on language tapes, records of diet and dress, and the like. But I find a woman more than half as old as the Federacy much harder to take seriously."

"Survey Service hack," Stavros said, flipping his head back in a way that combined contempt and an effort to get a lock of hair away from his eyes.

Bochy rose, bowed with grace surprising in a man so portly, and stalked out of the small study compartment.

Magda sighed. "That's not going to help, Stavros." Ever since boarding the *Hanno,* she had worked to keep her temper under control. The *Hanno* was tense enough already. The Survey Service personnel looked on their counterparts from the Noninterference Foundation as a pack of meddling amateurs along only because of political pressure, while the Foundation contingent viewed the Survey Service team as, at best, hidebound button pushers and, at worst, wanton despoilers and murderers. No one seemed shy about saying so, either.

As Bilbeis IV neared, Magda found her good intentions fraying. Though she and Stavros were nominally part of the group from the Noninterference Foundation, they had few friends there. Most of the Foundation people were Purists, and mistrusted anyone who was not all for destroying the Survey Service. Magda's years with the Service only made her doubly suspicious to them.

Yet to the Survey Service staffers, she was a traitor for having gone over to the Foundation and, though no one would say so out loud, for airing dirty Service laundry in public. That bothered her less than she'd expected, and she took a long time to figure out why.

Stavros's rude crack summed it up as well as anything. The Survey Service people on the *Hanno* were . . . almost second-rate. If Magda had to guess, she would have said they were chosen much more for adherence to accepted views than for brilliance. Bochy was a case in point. He was competent enough, but his mind moved in preselected tracks.

Caught in her reverie, Magda did not notice the measuring stare Stavros sent toward her. Though they were allies in this, though she had given him no reason for it, he also worried about her coming from the Survey Service, worried that in the end her quarrel with the Service turned more on information suppressed than on lives suppressed.

He knew that was a paranoid thought; Magda had lost more people close to her than he had. But seeing the whole Service as an enemy, as he did, sometimes made him have trouble separating her from it. And thinking like a paranoid had kept him alive more than once lately.

Enough, he told himself firmly; he knew he was vaporing like a fool. Next he'd start hearing voices, and the ship's officers would fill him so full of happy pills he wouldn't care what day of the week it was, let alone anything else.

He touched Magda's arm, wanting to make amends the best way he knew how for thinking ill of her, even if she had no idea he'd done so. "Shall we go back to my cubicle?"

She glanced at the clock on the wall. "I'm supposed to be here another fifteen minutes, but why not?" she said sourly. "I don't know why they even bothered scheduling these briefing sessions in the first place."

"Well, thanks to their killing off everyone else who's ever been to Bilbeis IV, your opinions do have a certain value."

She laughed, but the mirth washed out before she was through. "You're getting as cynical as I am. Are you sure you want me to come along with you?"

"Yes." Stavros realized they were lovers more on account of the events that had thrown them together than for any more solid reason, but the pleasure and moments of forgetfulness they shared were no less desirable because of that.

"All right. Like I said, no one here pays any attention to me anyway. The Service people have their chunk that they can handle, and the Foundation people have theirs, and nobody wants to look any farther. Screw 'em all."

"No thank you," Stavros declared solemnly.

This time, Magda's laugh stayed happy. She took Stavros's hand and pulled him up from his seat. "Come on. Doesn't it make you feel like you're ditching a class?"

"I can't think of a better incentive," he said, smelling the clean fresh scent of Magda's hair. But though he bantered with her as they walked the *Hanno*'s corridors, some of the happiness had leached from him. Once or twice, back on Hyperion, he had cut class to sport with Andrea . . . who would still be alive had he not gotten that copy of the report on Bilbeis IV and recognized it for what it was.

His mood darkened further when he and Magda turned a corner and almost ran into Roupen Hovannis. The captain of the *Hanno* scowled his dark-browed scowl at them, then pointedly checked his watch. "Why aren't you at your assigned station?" he growled at Magda. It was only the second or third time he had spoken to her since the flight began. Stavros, as usual, he ignored altogether.

That suited Stavros fine. He distrusted Hovannis on general principles as being a creature of Paulina Koch's. But even without connection to the Chairman, the captain would have frightened him. There was no give anywhere to Hovannis. He even walked with his hard, stocky body leaning slightly forward, as if to bull obstructions out of his path.

No attitude could have been better calculated to get Magda's back up. She retorted, "Anyone who wants me that badly can call me in my cubicle. Sitting in that study chamber wastes its space and my time."

"I'll log your disobedience," Hovannis said stonily.

"Go ahead. While you're at it, log that a grand total of three people showed up in the last week and that none of them had any idea what questions to ask."

Shaking his head, Hovannis stamped away. Magda glared at his broad back, then surprised Stavros by chuckling under her breath. He said, "As far as I can see, that one's about as funny as a funeral."

"Nowhere near. I was just thinking, good luck to anybody who tries to call me in my cubicle, seeing as I'll be in yours."

Suddenly that prospect looked very good to Stavros again. "Let's go, then."

Afterward, Magda said with malicious glee, "We'll be landing in a couple of days. Then all the people who stayed away will wish they hadn't."

The phone chimed. "Usually that happens in the middle of things." Stavros got out of bed to pick it up. He answered the call, then, abruptly quite serious, turned to Magda. "It's for you: the Foundation's comparative theologian. She was surprised when she got me—thought she was punching for your cubicle."

"Then how in blazes did her call end up here? Our extensions aren't even close to being—" Magda paused as her brain caught up with her mouth. "Hovannis," she said slowly.

Her brows knit in a frown. She'd been thinking of the captain as someone with more muscle than brains. Now she saw that was judging him only by the impression his appearance gave. He had to have been the one who diddled with the call-forwarding system; undoubtedly he *had* been hoping she and Stavros would get interrupted. Yes, Hovannis was smarter than he seemed. That was worth remembering. He also had a mean streak.That was worth remembering, too.

As she did every so often, the goddess sifted through reports of prodigies that came to the Holy City. She did not believe, as she once had, that such things foretold the future; she had seen too much future unfold for that. But such fears and hopes still lurked in the hearts of her people. A soothing proclamation every so often, when something particularly strange happened, did no harm and some good.

Strange to mortals, at any rate, the goddess who had been Sabium amended mentally. After fifteen hundred years, the cries of alarm over misshapen animals and men and over such perfectly predictable matters as eclipses and transits all sounded very much alike. Sometimes she thought she would reward the reporter of a new kind of prodigy in the same way she did inventors. The drain on the treasury would be much smaller, that was certain.

Having thought that—not for the first time, nor for the hundredth—the goddess found herself only a short while later tugging in bemusement at the fine down on her cheeks. Several herders northwest of the Holy City had reported a great shape in the night sky, visible only because it blotted stars from view as it moved.

At first she thought a group of drovers had gone too deep into the ale pot. Then she noted that the reports had been turned in to priests in villages a fair distance apart. Those from villages farther east noted the prodigy in the western sky, while the westerly ones claimed it was in the east.

She tugged again, searching for a memory. Something of the same sort had come to her notice a couple of years before. She'd paid scant attention then, being still in a turmoil over the visit of the divine messengers. She stiffened. Could there be a connection? She was positive she'd seen nothing else like these messages, not in all her time on the throne.

She wondered if, around the time she had become immortal, similar news had come to the town that had been Helmand and was now the Holy City. She did not recall it offhand, but that meant little, given the span of years involved. She summoned Bagadat and told him to have a search made of the most ancient records. He hurried away, puzzled but as always obedient.

She was disappointed when no such report turned up, but not overwhelmingly so. Record-keeping had been catch as catch can in the early times; not only that, but in those days, with far fewer people about, drovers did not have to take their flocks so far into the northern desert. If something obscured the stars with no one there to see it, how would she ever find out?

She summoned Bagadat again. "Send word to the priests of Charsadda, Pauzatish, Izala—" She named several more northern hamlets; Bagadat's stylus scratched across wax as he scribbled notes. "Tell them visitors such as we last had two years gone by may soon come among us again, and bid them send on to me any strangers they reckon may be such."

"Yes, goddess." Bagadat's face was worried. He had never seen his divine mistress disturbed until the strangely colored foreigners appeared before her; he would have given much never to see her so again. All across the world, people loved and worshiped the goddess, but he was one of the lucky handful privileged to serve her person. He had never thought he might want more distance from her so he would not need to know she could be troubled.

Sabium—she thought of herself more that way since the divine messengers had reappeared than she had for centuries—sensed that and spoke quickly to reassure her chamberlain. "Have no fear, Bagadat. This meeting will find me better prepared than the last, I promise you."

Bagadat dipped his head in acquiescence. "Of course, goddess. I shall ready the dispatches at once." His back was straight as he left Sabium's presence; at bottom, like all those who worshiped her, he had confidence in her ability to meet any challenge. Over the generations, she had given them every reason for that confidence.

She felt less of it herself. Coming face to face with those who knew of her most ancient past had reminded her of how vulnerable she once was. Against her own folk, that was true no longer. The gods, she alone recalled, though, did what they would with mortals and could grant like powers to their messengers.

She was no longer a mortal, but she did not know where the balance of power lay. She would take what precautions she could.

Roupen Hovannis drained yet another cup of coffee. His eyelids still wanted to sag. He muttered something under his breath, dry-swallowed a wake-up pill, leaned back in his chair until the pill kicked in, then went back to studying.

He had thought the outward trip in the *Hanno* would be like a vacation: after the byzantine machinations of running the Service's External Affairs Bureau, keeping track of a couple of dozen scientists had to be a piece of cake.

That much, at least, was true. But it dawned on him only gradually that he might have to do more than keep track of them once they got to Bilbeis IV. With things as they were down there, he might have to get his feet muddy himself. And if he was going to do that, he had to conform as closely as he could to all the niggling Survey Service rules, or else blow the mission by bringing even the tame Service people down on his head. He had already learned more about the local unwashed barbarians and their language of clicks, coughs, and grunts than he ever wanted to know. All the same, he kept at it; as a security man, he had long ago learned that one could never tell beforehand which piece of data was the important one.

He had another reason, too. The more people saw him operating inside the rules, the less it would occur to them that he could step outside any time he chose.

The desert air seared the inside of Stavros's nostrils. He felt his eyeballs start to dry out. He blinked. In moments, the savage sun baked the moisture away again. Sweat sprang from every pore of his body. "Whew!" he said, wiping his forehead with the back of his hand. "I've been shipboard too long; I'm not used to real weather any more."

"You have to be born to this to get used to it," Magda answered. "Even then, the locals like to sleep for a couple of hours around noon." She dabbed at her face with a kerchief and looked down to examine the cloth. "This bloody makeup had better be as sweatproof as they promised; it's going to get a workout here. Not only that, my false cheek whiskers itch like hell. How can you stand that beard of yours?"

"It's not glued on, which helps, I suppose. I'm not used to the green tint in it, though." Nor was Stavros used to the grayish-pink skin dye, though he trusted it further than she did; if it had not come off in the shower, it would probably survive Bilbeis IV. He found her fuzzy cheeks more disconcerting—the last hairy face he had kissed had been his grandfather's.

The natives were humanoid enough that under most circumstances the crew of the *Hanno* could have gone without disguise, passing themselves off as travelers from a distant land. But nothing was normal about Bilbeis IV. With Sabium's priesthood alert to bring Terran-type humans to their goddess, more than usual discretion was called for. Even Hovannis wore makeup, though nothing could make his dour, craggy features much resemble anything Bilbeis IV produced.

For the moment, Stavros was content merely to forget the captain rather than worrying about him as he usually did. Doing fieldwork for the first time, getting sand in his boots from a world outside the Federacy, was exciting enough to make him unusually charitable. He said as much out loud.

"I know what you mean." Magda nodded. "I was so thrilled to be loose on my first planet that I almost killed myself out of sheer stupidity. I swaggered into a tavern and ordered the wrong kind of drink—like an idiot, I'd managed to forget the locals got high on methanol as well as ethanol. I'm just lucky the veteran I was with stumbled against me accidentally on purpose and knocked the mug out of my hand before I swallowed any."

That thrill never wore off, not completely, not if you were meant to be a Survey Service person. But experience tempered it for Magda. So did caution, here. No matter how big a technological advantage she had on Sabium, she did not feel safe matching wits with the goddess. Sabium's edge in wisdom, Magda was uncomfortably aware, was just as great.

She said, "I only hope we're far enough into the desert to let us practice being native without any real natives spotting us. If the locals see people walking into and out of a small mesa, then we might as well not have bothered turning on the *Hanno*'s camouflage screens."

Stavros glanced back at the ship. It looked like an outcropping of the yellow sandstone that underlay the dunes and emaciated plants thereabouts. "I think I trust the sensors that far."

"They're only as good as the people monitoring them." Magda rubbed a couple of new bites; whatever the sensors managed to pick up, they weren't worth a damn against flying pests. She scrubbed at her dyed skin with a wet finger. When she stayed gray-pink, she grunted in dubious satisfaction. "I am glad this stuff has a sunscreen in it; otherwise I'd be about ready to take out of the oven and eat."

Being darker under the makeup, Stavros was less concerned about sunburn. Still, the feeling of being stuck in a blast furnace had begun to outweigh his delight at working on a primitive planet. "I wouldn't mind some ice water."

"Or cold beer," Magda said. "Enjoy it while you can. Beer isn't the same at blood temperature." The memory of six months of such beer on the way to the Holy City made her shudder.

She gave a luxurious sigh at returning to cool, conditioned air, then sneezed several times in a row. She wiped her nose and scowled. She didn't like to be reminded of any little drawbacks of technology, not when she had just been counting on it as her big edge on Sabium.

As usual, an argument was going on in the lounge. Pierre Bochy, Magda thought, did not look good made up as a native of Bilbeis IV, not even in Survey Service coveralls. The dye turned his plump features the color of stewed pork. Which was also what the anthropologist was using for brains, Magda observed; he was blithering on again about how the local matriarchy was really no different from a good many others. "Take the Shadofa culture on Wasf II, for instance: quite similar in a large number of their beliefs and customs."

"How about historical development?" Magda broke in with a sweet, carnivorous smile. "The Shadofa hadn't made a new invention in two thousand years, never ruled more than part of one small island, and were losing ground there the last time the Service visited. Besides which, you'll forgive me for reminding you, their goddess isn't real."

"Not relevant," Bochy said blandly. "They believe in Acca without reservation; she has the same force in their lives that the eternal goddess does here." He would not speak Sabium's name.

His effrontery left Magda momentarily speechless, something not easy to accomplish. But Justin Olmstead, his opposite number from the Noninterference Foundation, returned to the attack he had been making when Magda came into the lounge. "I've urged you before, Pierre, don't refuse to face facts merely because you are a member of the organization responsible for the problem."

Olmstead's voice was deep, smooth, and mellow, his gray hair—now dyed gray-blue—perfectly in place. Even made up, he looked as though he would be more in place in front of a holo camera than in the field. From what Magda had seen of his professional work, in front of a camera was where he belonged. He was an excellent popularizer, though. More people knew his data cards and books than those of any three dozen serious researchers.

The Foundation had insisted on adding him to its contingent along with Magda and Stavros. Magda grinned to herself; she was getting to enjoy being considered unreliable. Still, she had to admit Olmstead was a shrewd choice. He would make a good talking head once the *Hanno* got back to the Federacy, always assuming he didn't get himself killed trying to be an anthropologist instead of just looking like one.

He did not overawe Bochy, however. "What are the facts?" The Survey Service man shrugged. "At the moment, they are in dispute; otherwise we would not be here. Have you so made up your mind that it is closed to anything new we may find?" Bochy was tenacious, Magda thought as she saw Olmstead frown; she would have reckoned him pigheaded had he come back at her that way.

Stavros broke in harshly, "How many people have died to keep these nonfacts of yours from ever coming to light? Isn't it a fact that your precious Service has been busy trying to bury the truth and the people who know it?"

Bochy shrugged again. "I know nothing of that. I was on a pre-Federacy world myself when the *Jêng Ho* was last here."

"Yes, I understand that," Stavros said, and surprised Magda by adding, "I apologize." After a moment he went on, "But doesn't it matter to you whether that's so?"

"Of course it matters to me. As I said, though, I had nothing to do with it." Bochy seemed to think he had made a complete answer. He turned away from Stavros; he was as eager to claw pieces out of the rich and famous Olmstead as the latter was to attack the minion of the corrupt Service. Stavros doubted that either saw the other as a human being. He wondered if Bochy saw anyone as a human being.

When, later, he said that to Magda, she shook her head. "I'm sure he's normal enough with his family and friends. But if he didn't see a Service screwup with his own eyes, it's not real for him. There was some phrase I ran across in an ancient lit class that puzzled me for years, until I joined the Service and saw the thing it pointed at. Bochy fits the type."

The ancient literature Stavros had read was mostly classical Greek. Doubting that Sophocles had been talking about Pierre Bochy, he raised a questioning eyebrow.

"'Good German,'" Magda told him.

The investigator was very young, very neat, and very self-assured. "Surely, Madam Chairman, you remember more about the day the report on Bilbeis IV reached Survey Service Central than is yet on the record," she said. "That was FSY 2687:139, if the precise date will help you."

"I doubt it," Paulina Koch said indifferently. The investigator had done her homework if she could pull the date out of the air like that, but the Chairman refused to let such a parlor trick rattle her. She went on, "If I'd thought the day somehow special, perhaps I would have taken more care to fix it in my mind. All I can say for certain is that I was busy. I usually am. For details, you will have to refer to the printout of the log I have submitted."

The investigator nodded and fought back a sigh. Sitting across the table in her trademark gray, Paulina Koch remained sweatless and elusive. She was taking exactly the right line, instead of falling into the trap that would have snared so many detail-oriented people: that of recalling far too much about a day supposedly ordinary.

No one, though, the investigator told herself firmly, was invulnerable. She tried to act as if she believed it. "About that printout, and others we have received from your staff," she resumed. "Analysis shows the paper on which they were printed is from a lot procured from a new supplier, one not yet sending shipments to Central on the dates the documents were produced."

"Let me check," the Chairman said. She tapped at the keyboard of the terminal beside her. "Ah, here we are."

The investigator came around the table to see. There on the screen was a requisition ordering a small trial shipment of the new paper. It showed the blasted stuff had been in use at Central on the days in question.

"Is there anything more?" the Chairman asked politely.

The investigator tried a different set of questions. Paulina Koch relaxed as much as she let herself relax these days. This line was not dangerous. The last one had been. Had she not happened to hold a couple of memos—an old one and a new one—side by side, she never would have noticed that they were printed on sheets of slightly different color and thought to insert that false requisition into the files. It would not stand up to close scrutiny, of course, but with luck it would not get any. Just having it in place should do the job.

That was a loose end tied up. She wondered how many were still around, lying there for her to trip over. Enough earnest young hatchetpeople like the one in front of her were out looking for them. She knew they were trying to penetrate her own private computer records, but so far—she thought—they'd had no luck at that. She had enough false trails there to bewilder the most resolute snoop.

She knew, though, that her precautions were not what kept her safe, not any more. The most important thing in her favor was a collective will to disbelieve that any bureaucracy could get out of hand to the extent of plotting murder. Concealment of faults, yes; any agency would do that without thinking twice. But such determined mayhem—

She could hardly blame the investigative team. Not so long ago, she would not have believed what she had done and ordered, either.

The woman pestering her gradually realized her latest line of questions was going nowhere. Paulina Koch almost felt tempted to laugh. Being asked about things of which she was actually innocent made for a pleasant novelty.

At last the investigator said, "Thank you for your time," and left. Paulina Koch went back to her office. Before she did anything there, she ran a scanner over herself to make sure the investigator hadn't managed to plant a bug on her. That was no baseless worry; it had happened more than once. She was clean this time, though.

Once satisfied of that, she rushed through the Service business that had piled up on her desk while she was away. She felt guilty at giving it such short shrift, but there was no help for it now. If she was going to go on guiding the Service, she had more important things to tend to.

The most important of those was penetrating Roupen Hovannis's files. She knew where they were now, or thought she did, but she was having no more luck accessing them than the outside investigators were with hers. Sure enough, he had his own undocumented entry codes.

Under other circumstances, Paulina Koch thought, she would have fired him for that.

The meeting broke up. Magda's head ached. She stayed in the conference chamber after most people had filed out. "I need a drink," she declared to anyone who would listen, which meant, in essence, to Stavros. She punched the refreshment panel and ordered anise-flavored vodka over ice.

He smiled when he saw the cloudy white liquid. "I'm corrupting you."

"Don't use that word, not when this whole mission smells like dead fish." Magda tossed down the drink at a gulp and threw the glass in a wastebasket. Being plastic, it denied her the satisfaction of shattering. She snarled and began ticking off points on her fingers. "Geology? The *Jêng Ho* did a first-rate job; everybody says so. Linguistics? Fine. Architecture? No problems. Biology? Good. There I won't argue; Atanasio Pedroza, may he rest in peace, was a bastard but a damned capable bastard. Then they get around to the anthro stuff, and all of a sudden dead fish is perfume by comparison."

"That's not quite true." Stavros knew Magda required careful handling when she was in one of these fits of temper. "They're ready enough to accept anything that doesn't touch too closely on Sabium."

"That doesn't leave bloody much, not on Bilbeis IV." She somehow contrived to look plump as she did a wicked imitation of Pierre Bochy, intoning, "'Further study and examination of this anomaly will be required before a final determination can be completed.' What really frosts me is Olmstead agreeing with him. Those two can't agree on which direction the sun comes up from, and now this." She felt—and sounded—betrayed.

Thinking that, Stavros got a handle on what had perplexed him as much as her. "If Olmstead agrees your data are valid, then what's he doing here? Confirming a Survey Service report? How much good would that do his career?"

Magda slowly nodded as she saw where Stavros was going. "Olmstead'd sooner be castrated with a microtome than admit the Service can do anything right. Whereas if *he* were to make the astounding discovery of an immortal goddess . . ." She let her voice trail away.

"With the tapes and books he churns out, he'd live fat for the rest of his life," Stavros finished for her.

"So he would. Yes, that fits very well." Magda nodded again. "And so off we'll all go, on pilgrimage to Canterbury."

"To where?"

"Never mind. More clutter from that class of mine; I must have it on the brain. I even thought about majoring in ancient lit once or twice, till I realized I'd have to teach for a living and that I liked fieldwork better." With the almost-ouzo warm in her, Magda tried to be optimistic. "One more band of pilgrims shouldn't be conspicuous, not with us in disguise and not with the number of people who go to the Holy City every year. It shouldn't be," she repeated, and tried to make herself believe it.

The goddess frowned, wondering whether the orders she'd passed to her priesthood had been too vague. She was not often guilty of overreacting, not after gaining perspective for so many years, but even she had scant experience to guide her when it came to dealing with the strange beings who had made her what she was.

Winnowing grain from chaff was the problem. Now more alert than ever to the presence of unusual strangers, some priests were sending her reports of anyone they spied who was even slightly out of the ordinary. Sabium had not realized so many of her subjects possessed large moles, lacked a digit or two, or had curiously stained teeth. A glance sufficed to consign most such sightings to the rubbish heap.

Some were harder to evaluate; even with instructions to send information as detailed as possible, all too many priests were maddeningly unclear. That problem seemed worse in the first messages now reaching her from the eastern continent, where her rule was newer and less firm. Before long, she decided to ignore news from the eastern land. Divine messengers, she reasoned, could come closer than that.

Had she not just reached that conclusion, she might have paid scant attention to another of the endless stream of reports. The people of whom it spoke, after all, had gray-pink skins and greenish or bluish hair like everyone else, not the exotic coloration of previous visitors. But they had arrived on foot at Mawsil, only a day's journey west of the Holy City, and no other pilgrims there remembered seeing them at any earlier stops in the Margush valley.

Sabium made a note to commend the priest who had written her; this woman, unlike so many others, had her wits about her. She had not just listened to travelers' gossip. Before sending word to the goddess, she had checked with the priesthood back in Rai, the town just west of Mawsil. On learning that no one there recalled this new band of pilgrims, she had observed them more closely.

They spoke with an odd accent—and the priest emphasized that she was familiar with most of the ways the dominant tongue of Sabium's realm could be flavored. More interesting still, they seemed to have more money than they knew what to do with. Yet they were walking, not riding on beastback or traveling in carriages or sedan chairs. They also seemed, the priest wrote, curiously unworn for people who must have come from far away.

The more Sabium studied the parchment, the more it intrigued her, especially when she remembered that the moving patch that obscured the stars had been seen fairly close to Mawsil. She wondered if the herders had seen the messengers' conveyance descending from the sky. That would have to be investigated.

A servant stood nearby. Servants were always at hand, except when the goddess chose privacy for herself. She turned to the woman and said, "Bring me Bagadat, please." The servant hurried away.

By the time the majordomo arrived, Sabium had the orders she would give clear in her own mind. She could see he was unhappy with them. But when he said, "Goddess, it shall be done," she knew he was telling the truth. Few mortals tried to lie to her; fewer still succeeded.

Mawsil, Stavros thought, was a tawdry town. Gateway to the Holy City, it was anything but holy itself. Its chief industry seemed to be separating pilgrims from cash. What really embarrassed him was how the people from the *Hanno* threw themselves into the spirit of the place. "Everyone's acting like a bunch of tourists," he complained to Magda, "running around buying everything in sight and gaping at all the fancy buildings. It's disgraceful."

This time she refused to take his side. "That's what you're supposed to do in Mawsil. If we weren't gathering great armloads of overpriced trinkets, the locals would be muttering behind their hands and wondering what was wrong with us. As is, we're effectively invisible."

"I suppose so," he said grudgingly. "It just doesn't seem very—"

"Scientific?" Magda suggested, grinning. "There's no law that says you can't have fun doing fieldwork, only one that says you can't make a spectacle of yourself. Someplace else, that might mean being quiet and contemplative. Here it means buying trash and oohing and ahhing over the sacred spot where Sabium—excuse me, the goddess—assumed the kingship of Mawsil. And since that last happened something like fourteen hundred years ago, it's worth a few oohs and ahhs."

"I suppose so." Now Stavros sounded more as if he meant it. "Tomorrow's the anniversary of that, by the way; there's a reenactment or some such ceremony planned."

"I suppose we ought to be there, then." Magda grinned again. "I wouldn't put it past the Mawsuli to hold an 'anniversary' once a month, to fleece each new crop of visitors. No, I take it back: Sabium would hear about that and put an end to it. But if they could get away with it, they would."

The entire contingent from the *Hanno* went to the plaza to watch the reenactment. It had something to interest anthropologists, historians, linguists, comparative theologians, and literary specialists. Also, they were supposed to be pilgrims, and that was the kind of thing pilgrims did.

Stavros whistled when he saw the rich display in the square and the large numbers of priests who joined the laity in celebrating the festival. "I owe the Mawsuli an apology, don't I? They must take this much of their faith seriously, anyhow."

"Maybe because it involves them," Magda suggested. "I have to admit I'm impressed. I didn't get to see this the last time I was here; the season was wrong. They have spent some money, haven't they?"

The plaza was gaudy with banners, streamers, placards, flags, fragrant branches. Behind them, Magda knew, the buildings were mud brick, as they had been when the *Leeuwenhoek* visited Bilbeis IV long ago. Nor were they much different to look at from those early structures. None of that surprised Magda. Hot-climate river-valley cultures built the same way almost everywhere; if something worked, people would find it.

But despite outward similarities, so much had changed. Iron, the alphabet, the very idea of progress. . . . Bilbeis IV had risen far and fast, thanks to Sabium.

Horns brayed, distracting Magda. A fat man came out onto the platform at one end of the square. He bawled something to the crowd through a megaphone. Thunderous, rapturous applause interrupted him. Magda and Stavros turned to each other. "What was that?" they said at the same time, each having caught perhaps one word in five.

"And now, ladies and gentlemen, our feature for the day," Magda guessed.

The robe, Magda saw, was much like the ones kings had actually worn when the *Leeuwenhoek* was here. Most cultures at this stage of development would have dressed the actor in contemporary clothes, having forgotten any other styles were ever worn. Sabium again, Magda thought. Not only was she pushing Bilbeis IV ahead, she also remained a link that gave it perspective on its past.

The horns blared out a fanfare, a theme that had once been the anthem of the kings of Helmand and now belonged to the goddess. "Nice touch," Stavros remarked, "though I suspect only Sabium gets the whole point anymore."

The fanfare rang out again. The actor playing the king of Mawsil fell to his knees. The crowd gasped and murmured excitedly as the native playing Queen Sabium made her appearance. She was wearing a robe as antique as the king's, but her simple, direct style contrasted curiously with his florid overacting. It might almost have been . . .

Observing the locals' reactions, Olmstead spoke in pontifical tones. "See the superstitious fervor with which they respond even to a representation of their living deity. The Survey Service has much to answer for, its machinations having propelled such primitives to a technological level far beyond their mental sophistication."

"Oh, shut up, you pompous fool," Magda snapped.

Olmstead glanced at her with what looked like scorn poorly masked by kindliness. "Even after exposing one of them, are you still blind to the fact that the Service makes such heinous blunders?"

"No, and I'm not blind to the fact that that's really Sabium up there either, the way you seem to be. Which gives the locals some excuse for being a little less restrained than usual, wouldn't you say?"

Olmstead, for once, said nothing at all, though his mouth silently opened and closed several times. The rest of the group from the *Hanno* made up for him; as they exclaimed and pointed, they were suddenly noisier than the natives around them.

Stavros had been paying more attention to the crowd than to what was going on up on the platform. Nowhere in any of the data on Bilbeis IV had he seen mention of a ceremony where so many priests mingled with the laity. He had been wondering why they were there until Magda's words made him stand on tiptoe and stare toward the platform again. He had never heard of the goddess's coming out of the Holy City, either. The priests had to be guards, to make sure nothing went wrong.

Someone took him by the right elbow: a priest, he saw as he turned in surprise. "What are you doing?" he asked. He had a moment of pleasure and pride: he got his grammar straight, and his voice did not squeak.

"You will come with us, please," the priest replied. To emphasize her words, another priest, this one a man, seized Stavros's other arm. He tried to shake free and could not.

As he struggled, he saw that all the Terrans had been netted with similar efficiency. No one else had been disturbed. No wonder Sabium's clergy were out in such force, he thought as the priests hustled him along. Finding out why too late seemed worse than never learning at all.

Magda, he saw, was going along quietly and without resistance. He remembered she had been taken by the clergy before. He managed to steer his way close to her and muttered his aphorism.

"Finding out too late, eh?" she echoed with a sardonic grin. "If you could come up with a better epigram for this whole bloody planet, I don't know what it'd be."

XI

Paulina Koch punched EXECUTE. She would not have minded implementing the command on the investigators who still peered at the Service like so many scavengers making sure the carcass they were going to eat was really dead. Hitting a computer button seemed a poor second best.

If this program runs, though, she thought, it may combine the literal and symbolic. She had thought that before, more than once, and been disappointed each time. Roupen Hovannis was even better than she had figured at covering his tracks.

The Chairman waited. Every time she had tried it before, her only reward had been a blank screen. Seconds stretched, but whether in the computer's circuits or only in her own mind she did not know. No matter how she armored herself against them, she was not immune to anticipation or hope.

Surely now, she told herself, things were taking longer to develop than they had before. . . . The screen lit. Paulina Koch nodded once in satisfaction. Hovannis had been clever, but not clever enough. Now that she had access to one of his files, the rest would yield more easily.

Then she began to examine what the External Affairs Director had stowed away for stormy times. Her pleasure gave way to cold anger. A copy of the *Jêng Ho*'s report on Bilbeis IV, complete with the original, suppressed FSY date—Hovannis hadn't wasted any time taking his own precautions, had he? Recordings of several conversations between the two of them. She listened to a few moments of each of them and frowned. Taken all together, they were even more damning than she remembered. Others were not in this file and had to be stored elsewhere.

She began the process of scrubbing the file—carefully, carefully, so that no trace it had ever existed was left behind. At last she knew she had done a proper job. And even while she was deleting that first dangerous chunk of information, her program, like a killer fish scenting blood in the water, had latched on to another. That one, she saw when she could look up from what she was doing, lurked in a completely different index. Clever, Roupen, she thought, but not clever enough.

She wondered how Hovannis was doing in the field. Now that his little data collection was being neutralized, an unfortunate accident might be much the tidiest thing that could happen to him. Had she been certain of breaking his codes, she would have arranged for one.

She still had hope. Hovannis was ruthless and able but, like herself, had risen though the Survey Service central bureaucracy. He had never been out on his own on a primitive planet. Any small mistake, Paulina Koch thought, could easily be his last.

"We apologize for the indignity to your persons," one of the priests told the people from the *Hanno.* She had said it at least a dozen times. She even sounded sincere.

"Give us back our clothes and gear, then," Pierre Bochy shouted. Other Terran voices echoed him. Once inside the temple, the priests had stripped the study team and confiscated everything they were carrying. A few people fought back and got lumps for their troubles. As Magda had already found out, the priesthood of the eternal goddess knew some decidedly unprimitive combat tricks.

A couple of male priests came in with armloads of robes. "Here, you may don these for the time being," the woman said as they began to pass them out. "They are finer than the ones you were wearing. As I have said already, your own garments and goods will be returned to you, along with a goodly reward to salve your tempers."

"Believe her; she's telling the truth." Magda had repeated that almost as often as the priestess had made her apology, and with almost as little effect. Whatever Sabium's priesthood was, Magda felt confident it was not vicious. As with so much on Bilbeis IV, that reflected the character of the goddess.

Stavros, at least, had followed Magda's lead and offered no resistance. He glanced down at himself as he belted the new robe, which was indeed of better quality than the one that had been taken from him. "I'm just glad we were thorough with the dye job."

She chuckled. "Yes, that would have been embarrassing, wouldn't it? I wonder what they'd have thought if they'd found us two different colors apiece, and that the hair hither didn't match the hair yon."

The priests had not gone so far as stripping off the Terrans' rings and bracelets, perhaps to help reassure their uninvited guests and perhaps, Magda thought, simply because it never occurred to them that such trinkets could be anything but what they appeared. The people of Bilbeis IV had gotten sophisticated quickly, but they were not to the point of looking for recorders and video cameras disguised as jewelry. Several men and women from the *Hanno* moved their arms and turned this way and that to capture their surroundings on tape.

A plump functionary stood in the doorway and clapped his hands for attention. Magda grew alert. This fellow had been at Sabium's court before; if he was here now, Sabium could not be far behind. A moment later, his words confirmed her thought: "Bow, all of you, bow before the eternal goddess!" Despite his best efforts, his voice was shaky.

"I'm glad he's nervous, too," Stavros muttered as he bent from the waist.

When he straightened, Sabium had taken her chamberlain's place. She was silently studying the group from the *Hanno.* Stavros had to work to keep from dropping his eyes when her gaze fell on him—and he was prepared for the moment, which Magda had not been when the *Jêng Ho* arrived. Tapes offered only the faintest suggestion of the calm majesty Sabium projected. She was, he thought, used to being worshiped, and used to deserving worship, too.

Once she released him by looking away, he found he was not the only Terran to have fallen under her influence. Nearly everyone seemed as awestruck as he was himself. The effect, he saw with ironic pleasure, was particularly strong among the Survey Service personnel, who had perhaps thought themselves immune. Pierre Bochy, for one, looked almost ready to go down on his knees.

"Serves the obfuscating bastard right," Magda answered when he whispered that to her.

She felt uneasy herself; Sabium's glance kept returning to her. "We have met before," Sabium said. It was not a question.

So much for disguise, Magda thought. "Yes, goddess."

"Is this your true seeming, or do you wear it merely to appear less noticeable among my people?"

"The latter, not that it seems to have worked any too well."

Magda's candor made Sabium smile, but the expression slowly faded as the goddess continued to look around the chamber. She turned back to Magda. "I fail to see your former companion, even in the guise you choose to wear now. Irfan was what he called himself, was it not?"

"Yes, goddess, that was his name." Magda felt sadness wash over her, sadness and rage at what had happened to Irfan Kawar. "I fear you will not see him again, goddess. He is dead."

The word hung in the air. Sabium recoiled, almost as if against physical attack. "Dead?" she whispered, sounding for once not the least bit queenly. "How can that be?"

Her priests glowered at Magda; seeing their goddess upset rocked their world. She suspected she understood better than they what the trouble was. Sabium must have assumed all her long, long life that people from the Federacy were at the very least messengers from the old gods she alone remembered. Learning they were mortal after all had to come as a shock. Next thing you knew, Magda thought, she might even wonder if they were fallible.

On the record, people from the Federacy looked quite a bit more fallible than Sabium had been for centuries. Fortunately, the goddess would still be a while realizing that.

Watching Sabium adjust to an idea that looked to change a millennium and a half of assumptions only made Magda admire her more. Had she been that old, she suspected she would have rejected out of hand anything that did not fit her view of how the world worked. The goddess showed no signs of that. Maybe, Magda thought, the continuing changes that sprang from her incentive-for-inventions scheme had helped keep her mind flexible. And maybe, too, she was simply an extraordinary individual, and not just for her length of years, either.

On second thought, that last was too obvious to need a "maybe" in front of it.

Sabium turned to her priests. "I will speak more with these strangers later. Feed and house them as you would yourselves, but do not let them leave." She looked at the group from the *Hanno* again and rubbed her chin. "Take their ornaments from them, and sequester those with their other belongings. Who but they can say where their power resides?" She left the chamber.

Magda swore under her breath as the priests confiscated her bracelets, which held a video link, and her earrings, which were just jewelry. The little transceiver implanted behind her ear still gave her an audio link with the *Hanno,* but a lot of data was going to go down the drain.

Stavros's trinkets, like everyone else's, were also a mixture of the technological and the innocuous. After he surrendered them, he said to Magda, "She doesn't miss much, does she?"

"Wouldn't do to count on it," Magda agreed soberly. She'd thought the jar of wine she and Irfan had planted between the guards they'd stunned when escaping from the Holy City would explain why those guards had fallen asleep at their post. Evidently not.

Pierre Bochy pushed his way through the crowd to Magda. His broad face was troubled. "I am beginning to think I may owe you an apology. If that is truly the Sabium from the days of the *Leeuwenhoek*—"

"If!" Magda's momentary pleasure vanished. She bristled. "What do you want, letters of fire across the sky?"

"Please." Bochy spread his hands placatingly. "Whoever she is, she is a most remarkable woman." With that, not even Magda could argue.

"It *is* Sabium, the one you mean." That was Nina Pertusi, the linguist from the Noninterference Foundation contingent. She sounded very sure of herself, and explained why a moment later: "I have—I mean, I had—a voiceprint comparator in my jewelry. There's a perfect match between this woman's voice and the old recordings of Sabium."

"Is there?" Bochy said.

Magda and Stavros could not resist a simultaneous triumphant, "You see?"

Servants soon fetched in food and drink. The meats and bread were strangely spiced but plainly well prepared and were served on silver. The beer was flat and the wine too sweet, but the locals liked them that way. Magda had tasted worse on some Federacy planets. She ate and drank her fill and used one of the chamber pots set against a wall without thinking twice about it.

Nina Pertusi approached her again. Magda was sure the linguist would have been scarlet without her makeup. "How can you do that so casually? I am almost ready to burst."

"Haven't you—" Magda began, and then reflected that maybe Nina hadn't. Linguists could get a lot done from tapes without going into the field. Magda patted her on the shoulder and said as kindly as she could, "Honey, when it's really a choice between bursting and going, you'll go, no matter who's around. The first time will be dreadful, the second one'll be mortifying, the third embarrassing, but after a while you won't think about it at all."

Nina made a small, wordless skeptical noise.

"It's true," Magda insisted. "Just remember, everyone else will be doing the same thing. That helps a lot. What they say about planets without soap is true—where everybody stinks, nobody stinks."

"I very much hope you are right," Nina said, "but I fear it will not come easily for me."

"Don't worry about it," Magda told her again. The whole Bilbeis IV affair, though, had taught the anthropologist not to say everything she thought. By the look of things, Nina Pertusi was liable to have plenty of time in Mawsil to learn to lose her inhibitions.

As a professional, Hovannis admired the efficiency with which the locals had scooped the party from the *Hanno* into captivity. He would have admired it even more if they had proceeded to send the survey team on to the next world with appropriately bloody rites. That would have made his job a lot simpler once the *Hanno* got back to civilization. From the reports he had reviewed, though, he gathered this Sabium creature didn't operate that way. Too bad.

Still, he felt like cheering when the goddess's minions confiscated everyone's data-gathering instruments. These scientists, he thought, wouldn't admit the sun had come up until they checked a recording of it. The less information they brought home, the better the Survey Service would end up looking.

But the more he monitored the tapes still coming in from the survey team's transceivers, the less happy he got. Nina Pertusi's confirmation that Sabium was Sabium did not bother him. She was, after all, from the Foundation. What really did matter there was sticking to the story that Survey Service Central had never found out about what was going on on Bilbeis IV until just before the *Hanno* took off.

That was why Hovannis scowled when he heard Pierre Bochy sucking up to that Kodaly bitch. If things hadn't gone wrong with her too many times, the Service—and Hovannis—wouldn't have been in this mess. Didn't Bochy and the rest remember which side of their bread had the butter? Probably not, he thought, even if Paulina Koch had picked them for that.

He slapped his desk drawer. The stunner in there looked—and scanned—as nonlethal as any of the others allowed on the *Hanno*. That only proved Hovannis knew more tricks than the people who made scanners. The stunner's range was hardly more than arm's length now, but it would do the job.

No matter what the Survey Service scientists thought, he was *not* going to let this mission get out of control.

The investigator gave Paulina Koch a more-in-sorrow-than-in-anger look that he must, she thought, have practiced in front of a mirror. He said, "I truly resent the necessity of having had to obtain a court order to gain access to these codes."

You've made me work for a living, which is strange and unpleasant, the Chairman translated mentally. Out loud, she answered in the same formal language he had used: this was on the record. "The Survey Service has maintained the principle of privileged information since its inception. Despite the ruling of the court, I still maintain it and strongly protest this seizure."

"But you will comply?"

"Reluctantly, I will." She handed him the data card with the listings he needed.

"Thank you, Madam Chairman. Though my unit should have had these ten days ago, I am certain they will still prove invaluable to our inquiry."

She politely inclined her head. The investigator left, clutching his prize. Paulina Koch had not been lying when she defended the idea of confidentiality, but she had known the Service's court fight was foredoomed. As the investigator said, all it had done was waste time. The Service lawyers had told her the same thing, but they went out and fought for her anyway. That was what lawyers were for.

No matter how many codes he had, though, he could not find data no longer in the system. Now Paulina Koch was certain she had scrubbed away all of Hovannis's poison. Ten days ago, she had not been.

She did not show any outward signs of relief. Even if such had been her style, things were still too tight for that.

If these truly are divine messengers, Sabium thought, they are doing an excellent job of concealing it. They ate, they drank—they drank quite a lot—they produced full chamber pots as foul as anyone else's. Among themselves they spoke a language no one knew, but from the sound of things they mostly used it to quarrel. The priests had already broken up three or four fights before they got well under way. Divinities, by Sabium's lights, ought to act better than that. She certainly tried to herself.

Were it not for the curious objects the priests had confiscated from the strangers, she would have judged them mere men, foreigners from some distant land masquerading as subjects of hers. But those enigmatic objects were like nothing known in her dominions. Whatever they were made of, it was neither wood nor metal nor pottery nor bone. Some could be felt to quiver, almost as if alive, when held in the hand.

None of which would have made them any more than strange, but when an incautious priest pushed a button she should not have, the two people beside her and two more in the next room were suddenly rendered unconscious. Every one of the strangers carried a device like the one that produced that remarkable effect. None of Sabium's scholars and savants had any idea how it worked or how to make anything like it.

The discovery had not surprised Sabium, not after the way the last two of these—personages—vanished out of her palace. And how, if not divine, had the woman changed her coloring so completely? Its implications, though, worried her. With powers such as the strangers possessed, where in the world did they come from? Why hadn't her own folk found them long before, or they her empire? Even more to the point, why had they not come as conquerors? They were no normal people, that was certain.

And if they weren't people and weren't gods either, what did that leave? The only way to find out, Sabium told herself, was to ask. She had seen she could read the strangers almost as if they were her own subjects; they could not hide their bodies' involuntary responses to her questions.

When the goddess came to a conclusion, she wasted no time acting on it. "Fetch me the woman who was here before, the one who then had hair the color of copper," she told Bagadat. "Bring her new companion as well, the lean young man."

The majordomo gave a doleful nod. He resented the strangers for disrupting the smooth routine of the palace and even more for vexing his deity. "Do you wish guards, goddess?"

"No, no," Sabium said impatiently. "There is no danger in these—personages; that is another thing about them that puzzles me. Go now, if you please. I assure you, I will be safe."

"As you say, goddess." Bagadat had trouble disbelieving her, but did not sound convinced, either.

"Why does she want me, too?" Stavros asked for about the fifth time as priests hurried him and Magda through torchlit passageways toward the goddess. They were perfectly polite and made no move to touch the Terrans, but Stavros thought they would simply drag him if he faltered or balked. When Sabium bade them do something, they were not used to getting no for an answer.

Magda, on the other hand, was by then out of patience with the question. "How should I know why?" she snapped. "For all I can tell, she's divined what you said back on Topanga and intends to invite you into bed with her."

For a moment, Stavros waited for the priests to react in horror to her words. Then he realized that, unlike him, she had spoken in Federacy Basic. Some of her slips of temper, he thought, were very calculated things. Annoyed, he shot back, "Then it's you who ought to be asking what you're along for."

"Maybe just to give helpful advice," she said sweetly.

He refused to be drawn. "With the experience Sabium has, I doubt she needs it."

"I didn't mean her," Magda murmured.

Feeling his cheeks grow hot, Stavros gave up. The banter was making him nervous anyway. Wondering what bedding a woman fifty times his age might be like was one thing back on Topanga: a topic of academic interest, so to speak. Even there, the prospect had been daunting. It was quite a bit more so when in the goddess's power.

Besides which, Sabium had shown about as much attraction for him as for one of the local draft animals, beasts that seemed to combine all the worst features of camels and zebras. In its own way, Stavros thought, that was reassuring.

Certainly the goddess's chamber was not set up for a seduction. Sabium waved the Terrans into chairs and seated herself in one facing them. A servant brought in wine and cakes, then silently departed.

"What would you do if I told you I had ordered you put to death?" the goddess asked without preamble.

Magda and Stavros exchanged appalled looks. Magda had been thinking for some time that Sabium was not showing the group from the *Hanno* the same deference Irfan Kawar and she had gotten, but there was a lot of difference between less deference and a death sentence.

"Are you telling us that, goddess?" she asked.

"Answer my question as I asked it." Sabium's face was an unrevealing mask; her words might have issued from one of the countless images of her that were reverenced over this whole continent.

"First I would ask why, then I would start trying to figure out how to evade your doom," Magda said.

Sabium's gaze swung to Stavros. "First I would ask if you are telling us that," he said after a moment's thought. That drive for precision was part of him, Magda thought, and a valuable part when he did not, as sometimes happened, let it run away from him. He got no reply from the goddess; seeing he would not, he sighed and resumed. "After that, I would do as Magda said, though in the opposite order."

Humanity returned to Sabium's features. "That is as good an answer as I could have hoped for," she said with a small, amused smile.

"Why are you trying to make us afraid, goddess?" Magda asked, sensing no trip to the headsman lay in the immediate future.

"To see what you are, of course." Secure for ages in her power, the goddess did not bother dissembling. "You and yours seek to hide your purposes from me, just as you hide your true appearance beneath colors that ape my people's."

Since that was exactly so, Magda kept her mouth shut.

"And you." Sabium returned to Stavros. "What do you really look like, without your false pigments?"

"Me? I am a dragon, goddess, about twice as tall as this temple," he said in a sober, reasonable voice. "I breathe fire."

She gaped at him, then burst out laughing. "Are you indeed? I must say, you hide it very well."

Seeing Sabium's mood softened, Magda dared ask, "What do you seek of us, then, goddess?"

"Still I do not know." Sabium frowned, as if she did not care to make that admission. "At times I feel in your folk the condescension a grown man might show watching children playing with toys. And yet at other times your comrades have in them more awe of me than my own people display. You would help me if you could explain how both these things can be true at once."

Magda knew she was treading on dangerous ground, even more so than in past conversations with the goddess. She picked her words with care. "For the first, I can only apologize; rude people are part of my nation, as they are of any other. For the second, well, your people know you, as they have for so long. Mine, on the other hand, have heard only travelers' tales. Those so often grow in the telling that the wonder is all the greater at finding them, this once, less than the truth."

"That is it precisely," Stavros agreed. He did not think he could have done such a smooth job of telling the literal truth without giving away the essential secrets behind it.

It did not do to count on too much in that regard, he discovered. Sabium's years let her fit together seemingly irrelevant bits of data as well as one of the mainframe computers back at the Federacy capital.

Her eyes measured Magda like a pair of locking calipers. "Yes, I know of travelers' tales. What I do not understand is where in the world they might have reached you. By the goods you carry, your people grasp the mechanic arts more deeply than my own, however hard we strive to learn. Yet we have found no land where that is so. Why have you not made yourselves known long before this?"

She no longer conceived of the Terrans as fellow gods, Magda noted; familiarity had bred contempt, at least that much. "We are a quiet, peace-loving people, goddess. We have little interest in other lands."

"Then why are you here?" Sabium's pounce was quick and deadly as a hunting cat's. "I think you have told me a lie. With the skills and devices you have"—the goddess was searching for the word "technology," which her language lacked—"you could not help gaining control over your neighbors without them, no matter how little you wanted to. I have listened to too many kings and princes proclaim how quiet and peace-loving they are, most of them just before they attacked me. No, those who have power will use it, and I do not see how you and yours could have gained your power anywhere in this world without brushing against my own folk more than you ever have."

Silence followed the goddess's words. Now neither Magda nor Stavros risked even a glance at the other; whatever they did or said could prove too disastrously wrong. For Sabium was right, of course: where technology existed, it would be used, and Bilbeis IV had no room for a technology—about which the goddess had only the slightest hints—to grow without impinging on her own state.

Magda wondered what that left. It left the existence of the Federacy, and precious little else she could see. She hoped Sabium's vision was not wide enough for her to make the same connection. It had not been when the *Jêng Ho* had been here.

No sooner had that thought passed through Magda's mind than

the goddess said, "How much simpler to believe all you oddly colored people spring from another world. Then we would have no report of you save when you wish it, and then you might own all sorts of strange arts without anyone around you learning of them." Her tone was musing, but Magda was not taken in by that. Sabium's centuries had left her better than a polygraph at gauging reactions to what she said.

This time, Stavros's thoughts ran along a slightly different track. As far as he could tell, the game was up when Sabium used the word "simpler." The goddess might not know Occam's razor by that name, but she had to use it.

Neither Terran, then, for whatever reasons, felt much past a sense of inevitability on hearing Sabium's sudden sharp intake of breath. "And I had thought myself but making an idle jest," she whispered. "You will tell me at once how you accomplish this marvel. Is it a magic spell, or is there after all some means of flying my folk are as yet too ignorant to have come across?"

"Do not belittle your own people, goddess," Stavros said. "They have learned very much very quickly." He conceded otherworldly status but hoped his praise of Sabium's subjects would keep her from noticing he had not responded to her main question.

He should have known better. For the first time, he heard menace and chilly warning in her voice. "I am not a child, to be evaded by such small, silly ploys. Answer, or learn of my displeasure." She sounded very much a goddess then, dreadful and remote. Stavros shivered. So did Magda, but she asked, "Are you sure that is truly your wish, Sabium?"

Again came that sudden indrawn breath, but on a rising note this time. Magda saw with relief that she had reached the person behind the divine façade. Only the Terrans—and Sabium herself—now recalled that name. Her subjects had forgotten it an age ago; to them, she was but the eternal goddess.

"I had thought it so," she replied slowly. "I take it you claim I am mistaken."

"Only that you may be." Magda fought for steadiness. "I would but remind you that what is given is often valued less than what is earned. Or have you not found it so?"

Sabium, who rarely hesitated, took a long time before saying, "You used the same argument when you were last here, or led me to find it myself. Perhaps it is so. I will think on it, then, before I demand your reply, and will also question others of your party." She nodded, as much to herself as to her guests. "Yes, that is what

I shall do. Return now to the quarters my priests have assigned you."

By this time, much to Nina Pertusi's delight, the Terrans were out of the central hall and in individual cubicles. Magda's and Stavros's had that convenient invention so many races stumble upon, the connecting door. He threw himself on the bed in her chamber, while she, too restless to sit still, paced back and forth. "Wonderful!" she cried, throwing her hands in the air. "Not only is she immortal, she's figured out the bloody Federacy, too. Next thing you know, she'll be running for the Assembly."

"I'd vote for her," Stavros said at once. "Wouldn't you?"

"In a minute," Magda agreed. "She'd do wonders for us. But picture the scene when the chaplain gives the invocation and she stands up and says, 'Thank you.'"

Stavros tried to, then gave up and laughed. After a while, he said, "It would never do. When was the last time you heard plain good sense in the Assembly?"

"The day they decided to go after Paulina Koch," Magda said, her voice suddenly savage.

But Stavros tossed his head in Greek disagreement. "They even botched that, or we wouldn't be here—they'd have accepted your last report and strung your dear Chairman up by the thumbs. Instead they sent out the *Hanno,* and this trip has done more to interfere with the development of Bilbeis IV than anything since the *Leeuwenhoek.* Before this, Sabium had no idea why she was the way she was or about anything off Bilbeis IV. Now she does, and—"

"—by the time some of the people we have with us are done jabbering at her, she'll know everything short of how to design a stardrive motor," Magda finished for him. She took off her sandals and hurled them against a wall. A guard knocked on the outer door and asked if everything was all right. Sighing, Magda reassured him. She turned back to Stavros. "I really feel like smashing this whole place up, but they'd probably break in the door and stop me. That wouldn't look good."

"No." Stavros rolled over onto his back. "Why don't you come here instead? With this leather strap arrangement underneath, the beds don't creak." He held out his arms.

"Well, why not?" Magda pulled her robe off over her head. "It's one way to work off my nerves." Hardly a romantic commitment, Stavros thought, but better than nothing. He had long since concluded he was not going to hear many words of romantic commitment from Magda. One day, back in the Federacy, with no one hot on his trail, he would worry about that. Not now.

Afterward, Magda leaned over and nipped him on the shoulder. He yelped. "What was that for?"

Her expression lay somewhere between mischief and malice. "I was just wondering if you still fantasized about having Sabium, now that you've met her."

He thought about it. After a moment, he tossed his head again. "Thank you, Magda, no. I only imagined I knew what intimidation was till I met her. I don't think I could manage it, even on divine command."

She snorted, a sound he had learned went with suppressed laughter. He poked her in the ribs. "'If it weren't for the honor of the thing, I'd rather walk,'" she quoted. He poked her again. He was getting tired of ancient literature.

"Good evening, sir. It was kind of you to invite me here again tonight. No, thank you, I don't care for anything to drink or smoke, but do by all means please yourself." Paulina Koch waited while the prime minister fixed himself a gin and tonic. Not even now, she knew, could she afford any relaxation from full alertness.

Amadeo Croce sipped, then set the drink down. "I appreciate your joining me on such short notice, Madam Chairman. Really, I should have invited you to Government Mansion more often."

"In my years at the Survey Service, I've been here many times, sir." When Croce only nodded and did not respond to the veiled barb, the Chairman felt her confidence grow. The prime minister was as much weathervane as executive; he shifted with the winds of power. By his manner, Paulina Koch had gained strength since their last meeting. But she was too old a hand to ask how the investigation of the Survey Service fared. Instead she made small talk and waited; let Croce lose face by having to bring it up first.

At last he did. "I am glad to see that no evidence has been unearthed to connect you with the unfortunate turn of affairs we have witnessed in regard to Bilbeis IV."

Not "that you are innocent," she noted, admiring the careful phrasing. The prime minister owned more subtlety than she'd thought. "I'm glad too, sir, and I know the reason no such evidence has been unearthed is that it never existed. Undoubtedly the entire contretemps will in the end be discovered to have originated from some clerk's inadvertent deletion of the report on Bilbeis IV before proper corrective actions could be implemented."

"So it would seem," the prime minister said. It did not sound like agreement. It sounded more like, "Well, we haven't been able to pin this one on you; too bad." Considering the way things could have gone, that would do nicely.

"A remarkable woman, Sabium, truly a remarkable woman," Justin Olmstead declared, his rich baritone rising slightly to show just how impressed he was. More than ever, Magda chalked him up as a pompous ass. Neither she nor any of the other Terrans sitting around the table, though, could readily disagree with him.

The priestly guards in the big audience chamber looked bored. The group from the *Hanno* preferred Federacy Basic to the local language. Magda was relieved Sabium still let the Terrans gather together. Even if she no longer thought them divine, she still had to keep some lingering respect. It was, Magda suspected as she half listened to Olmstead pointlessly rambling along, more than they deserved.

She abruptly sat bolt upright, and she was not alone—several Survey Service people who had been enduring Olmstead's drone also seemed to wake up at the same instant. Her bellowed, "You did *what*?" was, however, the loudest of the chorus.

"I told her something of the working of the Federacy's parliamentary system when she asked," the other anthropologist replied, taken aback at the uproar he had caused. "She asked how we chose our kings, and when I told her we had none, she was interested in what we used instead. She grasped the principle very quickly."

"I'll bet she did." Magda spoke in loud, clear tones for the record being continuously taped on the *Hanno*. "I charge Justin Olmstead, a Noninterference Foundation appointee, with interfering in the cultural development of Bilbeis IV." When she turned back to Olmstead, she was snarling again. "You blundering booby, why didn't you teach her nuclear physics, too, as long as you were about it?"

"I'll thank you to keep a civil tongue in your head," he said, scowling at her. "And what is this nonsensical talk of interference? I merely answered a few of her questions, in quite abstract terms."

"Yes—questions about things she'd never thought of before, and wouldn't have, without you. Service personnel get warned about that somewhere around the second day of training. And abstract ideas—say, like religions"—she smiled nastily as she rubbed his nose in what was especially obvious on Bilbeis IV—"can change societies just as much as technology."

"Oh, but Magda, he's with the Noninterference Foundation, as you said, so how could his motives be anything but good and pure?"

She stared at Pierre Bochy in surprised admiration. The stateliness with which he delivered the sarcasm only made it more effective. She had not thought he had it in him.

"Fortunately," Stavros put in, "Sabium has better sense than Justin here and won't necessarily rush out to try everything he blabs on about."

It always came back to that in the end, Magda thought. Because Sabium had good sense, things ran well on Bilbeis IV. As long as she was here, things would . . . and she looked likely to be here about forever. After so many centuries, Bilbeis IV was unimaginable without her.

The longer Roupen Hovannis listened to the scientific crew sing paeans to Sabium, the longer his face grew. Paulina Koch would not be grateful when the *Hanno* came back and filed a report that made the Survey Service look even worse than the *Jêng Ho*'s did. And when Paulina Koch felt ungrateful, bad things had a way of happening. Having caused a good many of them, Hovannis did not relish the prospect of being on the receiving end.

He wondered what the Chairman would do were she here now. Of one thing he was certain: sitting quietly in the *Hanno,* kilometers away from the action, was not her style. But once she got to Mawsil, what then?

However tempting the notion was, Hovannis decided he could not take out the whole scientific contingent. The affair had already seen too many such tragic but convenient accidents. One more would draw too much notice. Too bad, he thought. Even the supposedly pliable Survey Service group was out of control. Dealing with a reasonably authentic goddess was more than they were prepared to handle.

He wondered if he could arrange things through that chamberlain of Sabium's. That local—what was his name? Bagadat, that was it—plainly feared the Terrans for threatening whatever influence he had gained on his ruler. Reluctantly, Hovannis abandoned the idea. Sabium could read her people the way he read a printout. Knowing that, Bagadat would never even try to set up the job.

That moved Hovannis's thinking one step further down the line.

What would Bilbeis IV look like, he wondered, without Sabium? She had lived an enormously long time; not many people back in the Federacy, his gut feeling told him, would be upset or, more to the point, suspicious if she happened to pass away. Down deep, people who hadn't seen her in action could not believe she was what she was.

And if she died, how would the locals take it? Only one image occurred to him: they would act like ants after somebody kicked in their hill. In that chaos, all sorts of interesting and profitable opportunities might arise. At the very least, Bilbeis IV would stop looking so outrageously abnormal.

What had Pierre Bochy said? Hovannis had it on tape somewhere—something to the effect that lots of peoples worshiped immortal goddesses. Only Bilbeis IV really had one, though, and if she suddenly became as legendary as all the rest of them—

That would fix a lot of problems, Hovannis thought. Paulina Koch couldn't have come up with a neater solution. He took out his modified stunner and tucked it into a pocket of his coveralls.

He drew a few odd looks when he checked out a flier in Bilbeis IV disguise but Federacy clothing. The only people who would have asked serious questions, though, were already in detention in Mawsil. None of the technicians and engineers did more than scratch his head when Hovannis skimmed silently off into the night.

Stavros rolled the wooden die, thumped his thigh with his fist as he saw a four turn up, and took Magda's last man. She said something rude. "That's fifty-five you owe me now." He grinned.

She stared at him. "The hell you say. I was up fifty, not down—you only owe me forty-five now." Putting five a pop on one of the local board games made it more interesting. They'd been playing since Magda had begged a set from a priest not long after they had taken enforced residence at the temple. They'd also, evidently, kept their running totals running in opposite directions.

"Come on, Magda," Stavros protested. "Remember that hot streak I had a couple of nights ago?"

"Sure I do," she retorted. "Without it, you couldn't have afforded to get back to the Federacy. Weren't you bitching that I was going to end up owning your grandmother?"

"You'd be welcome to her; then you could put up with listening to how nothing that's happened to her in the last eighty-odd years has been her fault." Stavros set his jaw. "But you have to win her fair and square. I'm not going to let you cheat me out of her."

Magda started to laugh, then stopped. "Damn it, I'm not cheating." As absurd arguments have a way of doing, this one was turning serious. She took a deep breath. "You really think you're up on me?"

"Yes, I do. In fact, I'll put another fifty on it."

"You're on." Glaring at him, close to being really angry now, she kneaded the transceiver behind her right ear. "I'll show you," she muttered.

"What are you doing?"

"Calling the ship. You get in on this, too, so you can't say I'm diddling with the count. We'll listen to the tapes of our game sessions and figure out who owes whom what."

"That will take hours," he protested.

"Do you have any urgent appointments?" she asked, and he had to chuckle as he denied it. "All right, then." She waited and swore. "God, are they all asleep over there? Where is everybody?"

At that moment, she and Stavros heard a voice in their heads. "Richards here." Magda told the first officer what they wanted. "Can't do it," he said, "not right away, anyhow. Captain Hovannis is out of the ship."

"So?" Magda's voice was dangerously quiet.

"So no traffic from the ship to you people without his authorization. Standing orders. Sorry." He did not sound sorry. He sounded bored. Magda had not had much to do with him aboard the *Hanno,* but did not think he worried about standing orders, except with regard to how he was going to carry them out. Usually that was a good trait in a first officer. Now it was only frustrating.

"Get him on the comm circuit," Magda said.

"No, wait," Stavros broke in. "Where is he? What's he doing?"

"I don't know," Richards said. Plainly, he had never thought to wonder.

"We're just fooling around here," Magda said, "but what if somebody needed something really important? It's a silly order, Richards. Get me Hovannis and get him now; I'll tell him so myself."

"Very well." There was a pause before Richards came back on the circuit. For the first time, his voice held a trace of uncertainty. "He's not answering."

Magda rolled her eyes, a piece of dramatics unfortunately wasted because the first officer had no vision screen in front of him. "That's good. That's really good. In his absence you're in charge, right? Countermand that stupid piece of nonsense and give us what we need."

She was so intent on what was directly in front of her—and on proving herself right—that she did not worry about anything else. Stavros, more suspicious of Survey Service people generally and of Hovannis in particular, interrupted again. "You didn't answer me, Richards. Where is Hovannis? The flier must have a tracer on it, in case it crashes or something."

"It does," Richards admitted. He went off-circuit again. A couple of minutes later he said, "The machine is grounded a couple of kilometers outside Mawsil. Sorry I took so long; the tracer seems to be inactive, and I had to home on engine emissions. Otherwise, the flier is mechanically sound. Still no response from Captain Hovannis. Odd." From Richards, the word spoke volumes.

"What *is* he doing?" This time Stavros was talking to himself.

"Coming into Mawsil, sounds like," Magda said. "But why is he sneaking in instead of just coming ahead?" She suddenly cut Richards out of the conversation and gestured for Stavros to do the same. He cut off the first officer in midquestion, as puzzled as Richards was himself.

"What the—" Stavros began.

Magda's frantic gesture reduced him to silence again. She opened the outer door and nodded to the pair of guard-priests outside. "Would one of you please fetch me a slate and a lump of chalk?" The woman of the pair nodded back and ambled away; Sabium had made clear that her guests were to have any reasonable requests met. The little while the guard was gone seemed like forever to Magda.

She shut the door in the guards' bemused faces and scrawled a note to Stavros: *Hovannis here for no good reason. Why else sneak?*

"You're right! You have to be. He—"

Stavros shut up again; Magda was scribbling, *Richards can still listen—everything gets recorded. Is he safe?*

"I don't think it matters," Stavros said. "If Hovannis is coming here for reasons of his own, this will all be decided before Richards can raise him. And if what he's doing is against the rules, he won't call back to the *Hanno* to advertise it. Am I right?"

Magda hesitated, then conceded. "Seems reasonable."

"All right, then. The next thing we have to do is think, and think hard. Otherwise we'll go rushing off and maybe give him the opening he needs. My first guess would be that he's after us, or maybe after the whole group here, now that the rest of them know about Sabium, too. It would fit everything the murdering bastards who run the Service have done so far: Fogelman, and Andrea, and the *Clark County,* and your apartment complex, too."

Magda started to jump up, then stopped. "You're right and you're wrong at the same time. What does the Survey Service need most from Bilbeis IV?"

"A clean bill of health, and they're not likely to get one."

"Too bloody right they're not. But they won't get one from a dead crew of scientists, either. That would probably be one too many coincidences for anyone to swallow, don't you think? The Service can't afford more bad publicity; for once, they have an interest in keeping us healthy."

It was Stavros's turn to consider. "Well, maybe so," he said grudgingly. "All right, then, maybe Hovannis isn't coming here to slaughter us in our beds. He's not on his way to give us a great big kiss, either. He wouldn't have to skulk in to do that. What does that leave?"

"Nothing." Magda did not like the answer. Roupen Hovannis was not coming into Mawsil—or was inside by now, she thought uneasily—for any good purpose; Stavros was dead right there. But she was still sure Hovannis would not, could not, move on them. A decimated *Hanno* returning to Topanga would look even worse than a damning report. Magda balled her hands into fists. She felt as if her mind were running in a treadmill, a treadmill with no way off.

Then she saw there was one, after all. Stavros must have reached her conclusion at the very moment she did, for they both spoke the same word at the same time: "Sabium!"

They ran for the door together.

XII

Hovannis was sweating and swearing as he neared the city walls of Mawsi. He was also filthy; he had taken a couple of nasty falls walking in the darkness through fields and in a dirt roadway full of holes.

Though he did not realize it, he was lucky the town's gates were open. Most places locked themselves tight after nightfall. Had the eternal goddess not spent so much time in Mawsil, it would have done the same. But pilgrim traffic was beginning to shift away from the Holy City, and Mawsil had opened itself to accommodate the sudden—and profitable—influx.

All the same, the guard yawning in his sentry box cast a dubious eye on Hovannis as he trudged toward the town. "Why aren't you carrying a torch to light your way, fellow?" he called.

The true answer was that Hovannis had not thought of it; he had never had to worry about such things before. "It went out a ways back," he said lamely, adding, "When I fell in the last pothole."

The guard laughed. "A few potholes before that, by the look of you. What are you coming to Mawsil for?"

Despite Hovannis's bedraggled state, the question was strictly pro forma. The guard heard the same answer hundreds of times a day: "To see the goddess, of course." Had Hovannis taken a moment to consider, he would have realized that. But the topmost thing in his mind was that his mission had to stay secret. Not only that, he was offended that this native, this savage, dared question him. Thus his answer came out as a reflex snap: "None of your damned business!"

"No, eh?" The guard was suddenly alert. He hefted his spear.

"Come along with me, then. We'll make it my captain's business instead. You keep your distance there, too," he warned as Hovannis took a couple of steps toward him. "By the goddess, I'll stick you if you come any closer."

"I don't need to come any closer." Hovannis twisted the doctored stunner on his belt so it pointed at the local and squeezed the firing stud. He hoped he was close enough for the weapon to work. He was. The guard toppled bonelessly. Hovannis eased him to the ground so his mail shirt would not clatter, checked to make sure he was not breathing, and then, feeling a bit like a primitive warrior himself, sauntered into Mawsil.

He soon decided the best thing anyone could do with the place was bomb it and start over. It stank of sewage and smoke and unwashed people. Hovannis heard scuttlings in the darkness around him. Some were vermin; others, he was sure, were vermin that walked on two legs. He wished his stunner had more range.

The people he could see disturbed him almost as much as the ones he could not. Disease and injury did not leave their mark so openly on civilized worlds. He had never seen a woman with an empty eye socket before; now he spied two in the space of a couple of blocks. Till now, he had never thought himself fastidious. He was finding his standards for comparison had been deficient.

Relief flowed through him as he spotted the mud-brick building—ugly pile, he thought—where Sabium was staying. He gave the stunner an affectionate slap. The sooner this job was done, the sooner he was back aboard the *Hanno*, the happier he would be.

"Harm me? Why should he wish to harm me?" Sabium stared at the two—whatever they were—as if they had begun to speak in a foreign language she did not quite understand. She wished they did not wear the seeming of her own people; their true, alien colors would have helped remind her how strange their thoughts were.

"It has to do with the politics of our, uh, homeland," replied the woman called Magda. The goddess sensed she was telling the truth. A wave of sadness swept over Sabium. No matter what she had thought, no matter what she still wished, these were truly no gods after all. Yet their kind had made her immortal. She would have to think long and hard on what that meant.

No time now. The young man with Magda—"Stafros" was the best Sabium could do with his name—said, "This man means more than harm, goddess; I think he will kill you if he can."

Sabium's servants gasped at the blasphemy. The goddess saw that, like his companion, this "Stafros" was speaking the truth as he saw it. As he saw it—there was the rub. She could also tell he hated and feared this "Hofannis." Maybe even he did not know how much that influenced his perceptions, and if he did not, how could she?

A priest came into the chamber and bowed before her. "Goddess, I pray your forgiveness for disturbing you," the woman said, "but outside the temple is one who would have speech with you."

"Yes, I know," Sabium replied calmly.

The priest accepted that with barely a blink; the goddess was the goddess and had her ways. The priest resumed, "A street vagabond, or even a magnate, we should of course have turned away to ask for a regularly scheduled audience, but this man wears the garb described in your Rituals of Search: the trousers and tunic all in one, and all over pockets. He is colored as we are, but—" She eyed the two strangers with Sabium.

"Yes, that matters less than formerly," the goddess agreed. She took a deep breath. "I will see him. Prepare the audience chamber in all ways."

She had to raise her voice to finish. Magda and "Stafros" were trying to interrupt with shouted objections. Her servants stared in open-mouthed horror; no one ever interrupted the goddess. None of her subjects would even have thought to. The strangers might not be divine, but they were very strange. Sabium had thought that before, often enough.

Now it was a nuisance. "Silence," she proclaimed, and was gratified to find that the tone of command worked on the strangers, though more slowly than on her own people.

The priest had already gone to do her bidding. She turned to Bagadat, faithful, fearful Bagadat. "Have these two escorted into the chamber after me. Make sure the escorts are large and powerful. I will not tolerate interference from them."

For some reason, that touched off hysterical laughter in the woman called Magda. Neither she nor Stavros resisted the soldier-priests who took their arms. Bagadat paced along beside them, trying to look strong and stern and not succeeding very well.

Sabium set her hands on the arms of the throne in the audience chamber. They did not feel quite right; she realized they were not worn to conform to her flesh through centuries of use. Neither, sadly, was the seat, and a goddess, she knew instinctively, must not squirm. She sighed instead.

"Fetch in the stranger," she said.

✧ ✧ ✧

"Is she crazy? Does she want to die? Does she think we're kidding her?" Stavros said. He had lost track of how often he'd repeated that on the way to the audience chamber and now here inside it as they waited for Hovannis to arrive. His guards must have thought it some kind of prayer.

Magda had her own litany. "Goddam denim coveralls," she muttered over and over, which made little sense even to Stavros. But the Service's field costume had been standard so long that Sabium had seen it on the crew of the *Leeuwenhoek* . . . and she, above all others, had a special reason to remember it.

Set against that, comfort and practicality did not, for once, count for much. They should never have had the denims aboard the *Hanno.* Fine time to think of that now, she reflected bitterly, as the priests hustled her into the audience chamber.

Flanked by their keepers, she and Stavros were made to stand to the left of Sabium's throne. "Neither by word nor deed shall they meddle in the judgment of this man, for it is mine alone," the goddess warned their captors. She turned to the Terrans. "Know you shall answer to me if your accusations prove false."

A tide of despair washed over Magda. No matter how long Sabium had lived, she looked to be an innocent, after all. A planetful of people loved her, and she could not conceive of anyone who did not.

"Goddam denim coveralls," Magda said again. It did not help, but nothing else did, either.

Following the local priest, Roupen Hovannis felt as though he floated upon a rising tide of confidence. Ever since he had knocked over that guard, everything had gone well. He'd more than half expected to be kept cooling his heels till morning. As things were, though, he'd likely be back in his own bed by then.

He gave his stunner another slap, liking the idea.

The native, who smelled overdue for a fumigation, threw wide a door. "The goddess awaits you," the fellow declared.

Hovannis strode in. His eyes darted around the room, as they did when he entered any unfamiliar place. He spared not even an instant for the play of light and darkness on the filigreework walls; he wanted to see where the people were, the better to work out his upcoming getaway.

He spotted Stavros and Magda in the crowd to the left of the raised chair near the far wall. They did not make him hesitate.

Once Sabium unexpectedly expired, all the locals would rush to her. Then the traitor and her lover could meet misfortune, too. The stunner was silent. A couple of people falling down would attract no attention. If they didn't get up afterward, too bad—surely they had been trampled in the confusion.

Checking the place out took only moments. Then, at last, Hovannis looked toward Sabium. He was glad he had not glanced her way before, by accident; he surely would have revealed himself had he met her eyes unprepared. He found out what other Terrans had before: films just did not convey the awe she inspired. Perhaps part of it lay in the way she sat, as if she had all the time in the world. *Why not?* he thought—she did. Her gaze was the most arresting he had ever known, and he could never have told anyone why. But it was.

Still, he did not falter. He had kept secrets from Paulina Koch, and done it so well that she had never suspected. He had, in fact, kept secrets all his life; that was what an External Affairs Director, or even a security chief, got paid for. And did being an old primitive—or even an old, old primitive—make Sabium any less a primitive, or anything more than a primitive?

That he posed the question at all meant the answer was yes. He did not let it bother him. He had control over himself again. He did not think anyone else would notice he had lost it.

"What would you of me?" Sabium asked.

"Eternal goddess, I thank you for consenting to see me in such irregular fashion and at such an irregular time." He bowed and took a step forward. "I have traveled a great distance because of your glory." He bowed again, amused at actually telling the truth. He came another couple of steps closer to the throne. Soon, now . . .

Sabium was rarely puzzled, but these strangers had a gift for perplexing her. This one, by wearing clothes of his people's style rather than hers, set off further confusion in her, casting her memory back a millennium and a half to the pair whose cure for her illness had left her immortal.

Resolutely, she pushed that secondary confusion aside, for it only distracted her from the greater ambiguity surrounding this stranger: she could not read him. That was not because of his race; Magda and "Stafros" and the rest of them were no harder to gauge than her own people. But this one, this "Hofannis," drank in her examining glance and gave back nothing.

She sensed no violence in him. At first that reassured her and made her doubt the warnings the other two had given her. But the fellow did not seem particularly well-disposed to her, either. He was just—there. Her doubts returned.

"Why did you not come here at the same time as the rest of your countrymen?" she asked him.

"I had duties I could not set aside," he replied, slowly walking forward. "Still, knowing you are unique, I hurried through them so I could see you myself before we departed your land—with your gracious permission, of course."

Was he close enough now? Yes, probably, Hovannis thought. He took one more step, just to be sure. His hand drifted toward his stunner. No need to rush things now and spook Sabium. She would not know what a stunner was—not for long, anyway.

"What's he going to do, knock her out?" Magda whispered; she saw where Hovannis's hand was going. "He really has lost it—"

"It makes no sense," Stavros agreed, "unless that stunner isn't just a—" He stopped, appalled at where his mouth, without much intervention from conscious thought, had led him. He and Magda both opened their mouths to shout.

At last, as the stranger's hand approached the weapon that hung on his belt, Sabium read the tension in him and knew what it had to mean. She made a tiny gesture of her own.

The arrow that pierced the palm of Hovannis's right hand came as such a complete surprise that for a moment he only stared at it foolishly, as if wondering how it had come to lodge there. Then the pain reached him, and with it the realization he had been outguessed after all.

Another arrow struck him, this one in the right shoulder. The impact drove him back, away from Sabium. When he tried to use the arm, he found it was dead.

He snarled and tried to reach across his body with his left arm. But he was a long way from ambidextrous, and now the stunner's grip went away from his hand instead of fitting smoothly into it. That first hasty grab failed to pull the weapon free. He did not get another chance. The plump local who stood to one side of Sabium's throne jumped on him, hurling him to the floor. The native cursed and pummeled him.

The fellow was no warrior; with two good arms, Hovannis would have ruined him in seconds. Even wounded as he was, he took most of the local's punches on the top of his head and in other places that did him little damage. He drove a knee into his foe's soft middle, doubling him up with a grunt of pain. At last his hand closed on the stunner. He jerked it free and gave the local a full charge. The weight on top of him went limp.

Too late! Other natives were rushing up. Something—a foot or a club, Hovannis never knew which—exploded against the side of his head. The world spun into darkness.

When Magda and Stavros would have run forward to help bring down Hovannis, their guards restrained them, as if not trusting them not to take his side. "Let me go, you fools!" Magda shouted. She tried to break free. She failed, for Sabium's priests knew as many fighting tricks as she did.

Stavros, who did not, struggled less. Instead of writhing, then, he was watching as one of the priests bent by the fallen Hovannis to pick up his stunner. "Beware!" Stavros cried, urgently enough to pierce the din and chaos of the audience chamber and make the priest look his way. "Touch it wrongly and it may spit death."

"I think not," the priest said with a condescending smile. "We have made some study of these strange weapons you people carry. How you make them we have not learned, but we know they only cause sleep; they cannot slay."

"You stupid, trusting bastard," Magda yelled at him. She was still trying to get loose, but only by fits and starts. She was beginning to be convinced she couldn't.

Sabium spoke; at the sound of her voice, everyone else in the chamber fell silent. "See to poor Bagadat there beside that villain," she said. "If he but slumbers, you will be proved right. If he is dead, you shall add your thanks to mine, for then we shall both stand indebted to these strangers' warnings."

A few moments later, the priest said in a small voice, "He is dead, goddess." He put the stunner down very carefully, then bowed low to Stavros. "As the goddess says, I am in your debt."

That seemed to persuade the locals still holding Magda and Stavros that they could safely release them. "Goddess, where did the arrows come from?" Magda asked, her disposition improving quickly once she was free. "I thought you were doomed."

Sabium gestured at the filigree panels behind her throne. "Show yourselves," she commanded. Eyes appeared in several openings; arrows poked through others. "I am not unprotected," the goddess said. "I doubt if age or sickness may claim me, but I have never been so certain in the case of arms. The two of you having shown your concern, I took no chances."

Hovannis stirred and groaned, which served to recall the locals' attention to him. "He sought to kill the eternal goddess," one of them said, her eyes wide with horror at the thought. "For that he deserves death." A priest carrying a spear advanced on the downed Terran with deadly purpose.

"No," Sabium said. The priest halted, her spear poised above Hovannis. She obeyed her deity, but rebellion smoldered in her eyes. Then Sabium spoke again, and now her voice was that of the goddess passing sentence. "He wantonly slew my faithful majordomo Bagadat, who tried but to protect me. For *that* slaying, he deserves death."

The priest drove the spear home.

Magda almost cried out to protest the abrupt, unappealable sentence. Her mind was filled with thoughts of trials, of how Hovannis should be taken back to the Federacy to face justice there. But she could not speak of those things to Sabium, not without doing violence to the rule of noninterference. That rule had seen enough violence on Bilbeis IV. And so she hesitated for the bare instant between condemnation and execution, and then it was too late.

She did not feel very guilty. Hovannis's crime—and his attempted crime—were too blatant for that. Murder was foul enough in any case, but Sabium's death would have been a cataclysm to rock all of Bilbeis IV. And for what? For politics, she thought distastefully.

Stavros never had any impulse to cry out. As the spear went into Hovannis's vitals, he thought the External Affairs Director was getting exactly what he deserved. Then he watched, and listened to, and smelled, the man die. It took a long time and was worse than anything he had imagined. He had to look away. Hovannis's feet drummed and drummed in the ever-widening pool of blood that poured from his belly.

Finally he lay still. Only then did Sabium—who, unlike Stavros, watched to completion what she had ordained—turn her notice back to the two living Terrans in the audience chamber. She said, "I owe you a great debt for warning me this"—she nodded at the corpse—"was a miscreant. Had you not done so, I might have failed to take the precautions that saved me. Because you are who and what you are, I do not know with what gifts I might please you most. Therefore, I say to you, choose your own reward. If I may give it to you, I shall."

Magda and Stavros looked at each other. His mouth soundlessly shaped a word. She nodded; the same thought had been in her own mind. "Goddess," she said, "nothing would please us more than your having our belongings returned to us and our countrymen and letting us go home."

"It shall be done, of course," Sabium replied at once. "But is that all? Ask more of me than such a small thing."

"Goddess," Stavros said quietly, "freedom is never a small thing."

Sabium paused to consider that. "I think you may be right," she said at last.

Topanga's heat and sunshine reminded Magda of the vicious weather in the Margush valley but were less oppressive somehow: probably, she thought, because she could go into the cool indoors whenever she wanted. On Bilbeis IV, buildings were as hot inside as out and sometimes—especially at night—hotter.

Now she was out in the sun and reveling in it. She and Stavros stood outside the Survey Service field office while a swarm of holo cameras hummed and whirred around them. The data card she carried weighed no more than any other, but seemed heavier.

Someone called, "What do you think of what happened on Bilbeis IV?"

She'd answered that question a hundred times in the couple of days since the *Hanno* had come home. She had it down to half a dozen words now: "We were right the first time."

Stavros was willing to amplify that; media people were arriving on Topanga in a steady stream, and this poor woman might not have had a chance to ask anything before. "Even the scientists handpicked by the Survey Service acknowledge that serious interference, in technology and especially in religion and culture, did take place on Bilbeis IV," he said.

"Hard for them to get around it, when their own captain tried to get rid of the main evidence for that interference with a stunner he'd cooked up somehow into a deadly weapon," Magda agreed.

Peter O'Brien swung open the door to the office. "Here we are, back where it all began," the head of the local branch of the Noninterference Foundation said expansively. "Here the first true report on Bilbeis IV was delivered, and here we deliver the truth again. This time it will not be suppressed."

Magda wished he would shut up; for that matter, she wished he were not there at all. But the Foundation lost no chance to promote itself, and without it, she had to admit, the Service probably never would have felt enough pressure to send out the *Hanno.* In recognition of that, she decided not to step on O'Brien's foot as she and Stavros walked past him.

With as much good grace as she could muster, she endured more delay while the reporters jockeyed for position inside the small Survey Service office. She looked around. "Where's Pandit?" she demanded. "He's the clerk who took my report every time I sent it in to Central—only right he should do it again."

The coordinator in charge of the office looked embarrassed. The reporters looked delighted—here was something unrehearsed, while these formal events usually were stylized as *Noh* plays. The coordinator cleared her throat. "Ah," she got out, "intermediate clerk Pandit is in custody, charged with failing to properly transmit your report before. He was, it is alleged, a confederate of Roupen Hovannis."

"But that's absurd!" Magda said. "I saw him send it."

"Are you sure?" Stavros murmured. "Do you know what all the gadgetry back there does?"

She frowned. "It seemed simple enough."

The coordinator stepped forward and presented her better profile to the camera. "In any case, I will be pleased to handle the data transmission personally."

Reluctantly, Magda handed her the data card. She watched carefully as the coordinator fed the card into the machine and hit the TRANSMIT button. After a while, a light went from red to green. "The document has been acquired at Survey Service Central," the coordinator declared.

"She did the same damned thing Pandit did," Magda said mulishly.

"Have you an opening statement, Chairman Koch?" asked the reporter who was serving as moderator for the news conference.

"Yes, I do," Paulina Koch replied. A ripple of surprise ran through the Survey Service auditorium. Paulina Koch usually let reporters have at her as they would. Only a few veterans in the seats out there could remember the last time she'd broken that rule.

"Very well, then." The moderator stepped aside.

"I thank you, Mr. Mazyad." Paulina Koch took a deep breath and stepped up to the podium. This was it. If she got through this conference, she could ride out anything. If not . . . She built a wall around that thought. She would get through, because she had to.

She said, "To you, my friends"—if she was going to lie, might as well start early—"and through you to the people of the Federacy, I offer my apologies and pray your pardon. I, and through me you, have been betrayed. In all innocence, I told you that no deception was involved in the Survey Service's handling of the Bilbeis IV affair. It now appears I was in error.

"For reasons of their own, Roupen Hovannis and staff members of the External Affairs Division under his direction did attempt to destroy the report the survey ship *Jêng Ho* presented on Bilbeis IV. When their efforts began to come to light, they even engaged in acts of violence to hide their prior wrongdoing. Roupen Hovannis's death on Bilbeis IV itself came as a direct result of the last of those violent deeds.

"As Survey Service Chairman, I must of course take ultimate responsibility for the actions of all my subordinates. I stress, however, that I was unaware of Hovannis's machinations and was systematically lied to in my attempts to uncover the truth. The same applies to Dr. Cornelia Toger, whose investigative efforts were systematically hamstrung by Hovannis's henchmen."

Always a good idea to mix in a bit of truth, the Chairman thought. She went on. "Dr. Toger has offered me her resignation. I have not accepted it. She has done nothing wrong. Her next task, like mine, will be to restore effectiveness to the Survey Service and to restore public confidence in it. Now I will take questions."

"Have *you* offered to resign, Madam Chairman?" a woman called, springing up out of her seat in her eagerness to be recognized.

"No, Ms. Kluhan, I have not. I have confidence in my own innocence, and I feel I am still needed here. If Prime Minister Croce disagrees, I am sure he will make it known to me."

Actually, she was afraid Croce might have accepted a resignation. Requiring him to take the first step made things harder for him. No evidence focused on her. By now, she was sure she had done a good job of scrubbing the data banks.

"What are these mysterious 'reasons of their own,' Madam Chairman?" asked the next reporter at whom Paulina Koch pointed.

"Mr. Basualdo, I would not presume to act as speaker for the dead. Roupen Hovannis's motives, whatever they were, lie with him on Bilbeis IV. I would hope he acted out of a sense, however misguided, that he was serving the long-range best interests of the Survey Service. If so, he proved tragically in error. But let me say again, that is only my hope. We will never know."

That was all Paulina Koch had ever tried to do: serve the

long-range best interests of the Survey Service. If she survived this, she might even have succeeded. She wondered for a moment how Sabium would have done, were their positions reversed. Then, brushing aside such a nonessential thought, she fielded another question: "Yes, Mr. Goldberg?"

"What about the eighteen missing days?"

The little man looked smug, thinking he had caught her out. Now she had an answer, though, and one that did not incriminate her. "I must assume, Mr. Goldberg, that when Van Shui Pong"—she prided herself on having the reporter's name ready to bring forth—"accessed the correct arrival date of the *Jêng Ho,* it called attention to the blunder Hovannis's henchmen had committed in not altering it prior to that point in time. The error was then rectified, but not before the discrepancy had been noted."

Goldberg sat down, deflated. Paulina Koch pointed. "Yes, Ms. Wakuzawa?"

"Damn her, she has all the answers," Magda said, watching the Chairman demolish another questioner.

Stavros made a disgusted noise deep in his throat. "Yes, but do you believe any of them?" When Magda did not answer at once, he looked at her sharply.

"I'd like to," she admitted at last. "I've been with the Service my whole professional life. I'd like to think we're clean at the top."

"What are the odds, though? How could anyone think that the things they've done somehow magically stopped one rung below Paulina Koch on the ladder, and that she never looked down to find out why there was a stink under her feet?"

"I don't suppose I do," Magda sighed. "I'd like to, that's all. And there are plenty of people who will, just because they can't see past their noses."

"Everything worked out so bloody well for her—"

"That's what you get for hanging around with me," Magda interrupted. "You're starting to talk the same way I do."

But Stavros refused to be sidetracked. "She's piling all the blame on Hovannis, and he's not around anymore to give her the lie. It couldn't have worked out better for her if she planned it herself."

"What did you think of the Survey Service Chairman's performance last night?" asked the woman whose desk at Hyperion Newsnet was next to Van Shui Pong's.

"Didn't watch it," he answered shortly. Since leaving—"fleeing," he told himself in harsher moments, was really the proper word—the investigation of the Bilbeis IV affair, he had not paid much attention to it. He wanted to think that sprang from simple prudence. More likely, it was guilt.

Shaking his head in annoyance, he started working his way through the morning mail. A lot of the data cards he got ended up erased so he could reuse them; what some people thought newsworthy never stopped amazing him. Today's run of the stuff that didn't come through regular channels seemed especially bad. Fortunately, telling when something was tripe usually took only a few seconds.

He blanked the card that was in his terminal, took it out, inserted the next one in the stack. A man's face looked out of the screen at him. The fellow seemed vaguely familiar. Whoever he was, he needed a shave.

Then Van's boredom and faint contempt fell away, for the image declared, "I am Roupen Hovannis, External Affairs Director, Survey Service. If you are viewing this, I will be dead. If I were alive, it would be none of your damned snooping business, I promise you that."

Hovannis's laugh was full of scorn. Van Shui Pong felt anger rise in him but made no move to kill the data card. Hovannis had hooked him, sure enough. His eyes narrowed at what he saw, then went wide.

The reports, the screaming headlines and lead stories, kept coming in from all around the Federacy. Paulina Koch declined any comment for as long as she could, and for a bit longer than that. Each morning, more camera crews appeared outside Survey Service Central. Each morning, she strode past them as if they did not exist and went in to do her job.

Roupen Hovannis had buried his bombshells to avenge himself on her if she played him false. She had thought he would and had rooted from the computer several "dead-man" routines designed to spill information on word of his demise. Either she had missed some after all, or Hovannis had given copies to people to throw in the mails. It did not matter much either way.

She even saw the irony of her predicament. The bombshells were going off without proper cause: surely Hovannis had not expected he would die at Sabium's hands instead of hers. That did not matter much any more, either. What mattered was that everything was coming out, from the disposal of Isaac Fogelman to the destruction of the *Clark County* to the effort to change Magda Kodaly's credit records. And everything pointed straight back to her.

Still, she dared hope one day when she noticed a gap in the ranks of reporters in front of the Survey Service offices: were they getting tired of hounding her? Then she noticed the two men standing there, waiting for her to arrive. They wore the field-gray of the Rehabilitation Service. Not even reporters, the Chairman thought grimly, wanted to get close to rehab men.

She squared her shoulders. No point in hoping now. The only thing left was choosing how she went out. No point in whining either, not in public.

"May I make a statement?" she asked the taller man in gray.

She had the small satisfaction of seeing she had surprised him. She cherished it; she would get no more satisfaction for a very long time. After a moment, he politely dipped his head in assent. In public, rehab men were always polite. He did not even tell her to keep it short.

She turned to face the cameras for the last time. "Citizens of the Federacy," she began, and almost stopped in despair. How could she get across what she had tried to accomplish by doing as she had done? Only the thought that she would never get another chance helped her go on.

"Citizens of the Federacy," she said again, this time more firmly, "for two decades I have had the privilege of serving you as Chairman of the Survey Service. Throughout that time, I have striven to make the Service function as effectively as possible in all areas of its operation. On the whole, I believe I have been successful in that undertaking.

"In administering so large an organization, I have been required to make large numbers of decisions and judgments. In making them, I have tried to follow the principle of seeking only what was best for the Survey Service. Inevitably, I fear, not all decisions and judgments I was called upon to make have proved correct. That appears to have been the case in the matter of Bilbeis IV.

"I regret any injuries that may have occurred as a result of my decisions concerning that matter. I would remind you, however, that those decisions and judgments were made in what I believed at the time to be the best interests of the Survey Service, and to protect it from those who would seek to curtail its activities where no good cause exists.

"I am to be Chairman no longer, but the Survey Service will

remain, and will continue to perform its appointed tasks. I call on everyone, those who have supported me and those who did not, to put behind them the bitterness of the recent past and to support the organization I have been proud to lead for so long. That organization and its ideals must go forward, whatever becomes of me."

Her control held to the end. She had not been sure it would. She nodded to the rehab men. They moved in to take places on either side of her, two tall gray figures bracketing one short one, and led her away.

Stavros watched Paulina Koch disappear into the Rehabilitation Service groundcar. Then he ran the tape back to listen again to her parting statement. He shook his head wonderingly. "She's still talking her way around this whole thing. Some of her decisions weren't correct . . . injuries may have occurred. She ordered people dead. That's enough to create a little bitterness, wouldn't you say?"

"Yes," Magda said, but somehow the triumph she felt was muted. In stories, once the villains were gone, everyone proceeded to live happily ever after. Here and now, the trouble they had caused would go on being trouble. "The Purists are going to have just the kind of field day with the Service she started the stinking cover-up to prevent. The more she tried, the deeper she got."

"She should never have tried in the first place." Stavros thought for a moment. "Is 'hubris' a word in Basic, or just Greek?"

"Basic, too." On the screen, the rehab wagon purred away again. A commentator started making predictions about how the Survey Service would fare under the interim administration of Dr. Cornelia Toger. Magda switched him off. She could make her own predictions there. "The Service'll have a hell of a time. Toger's in way over her head. Maybe Sabium could straighten out this mess, but then, she'd have the time to do it."

"So she would." Stavros's eyes got a faraway look. "I wonder what Bilbeis IV will be like the next time the Survey Service checks it out."

"Now there's something to think about," Magda agreed, "but thinking won't take you far enough, I'm afraid. Sabium may still be around when the next survey team arrives, but you and I, my rather dear, won't be."

"Isn't that the truth!" Stavros chuckled. "'My rather dear,' eh? I rather like that." He gestured toward the screen. "Have you seen all you want of this?"

"Yes. We recorded it, so I can watch it again whenever I want."

"You have quite a taste for revenge, you know that? You'd make a good Greek; some of the feuds back in the mountains of New Thessaly got their start on Earth, or so the old men say."

"I like to be right, and when I am, I don't like anybody telling me I'm not. Speaking of which—" Magda went through the file of data cards and tapes she had brought off the *Hanno.* She ran one into a terminal, put on headphones, and started listening. Every so often, she made a tally mark.

"What are you doing?" Stavros asked. When she paid no attention, he pulled one earpiece away from her head and repeated the question.

She hit the PAUSE button. "What do you think? I'm going to find out who really owed fifty to whom. And if you owe me, by God, I'm going to collect!"

Sabium already had the desert scout's report nearly committed to memory, but she read it again all the same. A troop of scouts had gone north from Mawsil into the waste before the strangers departed the city. They shadowed them at the greatest possible distance, to learn what they could. Two did not return. The goddess had never learned to accept losses in her service easily. She made sure the scouts' families were provided for, but silver could not replace a man.

The rider whose words she was studying had not actually tried to stay close to the strangers at all. Instead, he'd almost killed his mount rushing far to the north, reasoning that the strangers, with their curious abilities, might be able to travel more quickly than they had shown. She made a note to reward him for his initiative.

He was soon proved right. They disappeared from their camp not long before dawn one night, with only briefly blotted stars to suggest something had swooped down from the air and carried them off. Most of the scouts came back then, baffled and afraid.

From a long way away, the one clever scout saw a flying sphere— "a ship, I would call it, not a creature," Sabium read, "for it had no wings—dash itself headlong into the side of a vertical bluff. But it did not tumble in ruins. Instead, it flew *into* the bluff, as if that were so much air."

Indeed, it might have been so; later, the scout saw people emerging from the rocks and then going back inside, with no sign of passageways or doors to explain how they did so. They did not spot him in turn; his mount was tethered behind an enormous boulder, while he himself moved only on all fours and wore the skin of a skulking desert predator across his back.

He waited the day away in the shade of a large bush. "Without it," he wrote matter-of-factly, "I would have died. But seeing that the strangers concealed the use of their powers under cover of darkness, I thought it best to wait for night to come."

His patience was rewarded, for about halfway through the first evening watch, the mesa he had been studying shimmered and vanished, to be replaced by a dark sphere many times vaster than the one the scout had seen before. Sabium tried to visualize the scene he described:

"By some art I cannot fathom, it rose silently into the air, as the smaller one had flown before. But it climbed straight up into the heavens rather than faring north or south, east or west. As it ascended, it appeared smaller and smaller, or so I judged by the stars it hid from sight. In the end I lost track of it; it must have grown too tiny to cover them any more. You in your wisdom, goddess, may know its destination. As for me, I am but a simple soldier and would not presume to guess."

A disingenuous soldier, Sabium thought as she set down his report. She could only guess where the sky ship was going herself; the strangers who crewed it had been closed-mouthed, most of them. All her guesses, though, were full of marvels.

She wondered how long she would have to wait before the strangers came to call upon her land again. As long as the time between their first two visits? That would try even a goddess's patience.

She looked up to the roof, and in her mind's eye through it, to the dome of the sky above. Once more she tried to see a huge sphere floating upward. She wondered how much her people would have to learn to build such a sphere for themselves.

She made herself a promise and spoke it aloud as if to seal it: "If they wait so long again, I shall go to visit them first."

She summoned her new majordomo and began to work to make the promise real.

Kaleidoscope

I've done a whole series of stories set in an alternate world where *Homo erectus* settled the Americas several hundred thousand years ago but the Indians never made it across the Siberian land-bridge (these stories are collected as *A Different Flesh,* Congdon & Weed, 1988). The presence of these subhumans—"sims"—and the Indians' absence would have made a profound difference in the way North and South America were settled by European colonists . . . and the way people looked at our place in nature. I've chosen this particular story because of the issues it raises—and because writing pastiche is so much *fun.*

AND SO TO BED

May 4, 1661. A fine bright morning. Small beer and radishes for to break my fast, then into London for this day. The shambles on Newgate Street stinking unto heaven, as is usual, but close to it my destination, the sim marketplace. Our servant Jane with too much for one body to do, and whilst I may not afford the hire of another man or maid, two sims shall go far to ease her burthen.

Success also sure to gladden Elizabeth's heart, my wife being ever one to follow the dame Fashion, and sims all the go of late, though monstrous ugly. Them formerly not much seen here, but since the success of our Virginia and Plymouth colonies are much more often fetched to these shores from the wildernesses the said colonies front upon. They are also commenced to be bred on English soil, but no hope there for me, as I do require workers full-grown, not cubs or babes in arms or whatsoever the proper term may be.

The sim-seller a vicious lout, near unhandsome as his wares. No, the truth for the diary: such were a slander on any man, as I saw on his conveying me to the creatures.

Have seen these sims before, surely, but briefly, and in their masters' livery, the which by concealing their nakedness conceals as well much of their brutishness. The males are most of them well made, though lean as rakes from the ocean passage and, I warrant, poor victualing after. But all are so hairy as more to resemble rugs than men, and the same true for the females, hiding such dubious charms as they may possess nigh as well as a smock of linen: nought here, God knows, for Elizabeth's jealousy to light on.

This so were the said females lovely of feature as so many Aphrodites. They are not, nor do the males recall to mind Adonis. In both sexes the brow projects with a shelf of bone, and above it, where men do enjoy a forehead proud in its erectitude, is but an apish slope. The nose broad and low, the mouth wide, the teeth nigh as big as a horse's (though shaped, it is not to be denied, like a man's), the jaw long, deep, and devoid of chin. They stink.

The sim-seller full of compliments on my coming hard on the arrival of the *Gloucester* from Plymouth, him having thereby replenished his stock in trade. Then the price should also be not so dear, says I, and by God it did do my heart good to see the ferret-faced rogue discomfited.

Rogue as he was, though, he dickered with the best, for I paid full a guinea more for the pair of sims than I had looked to, spending in all £11.6s.4d. The coin once passed over (and bitten, for to ensure its verity), the sim-seller signed to those of his chattels I had bought that they were to go with me.

His gestures marvelous quick and clever, and those the sims answered with too. Again, I have seen somewhat of the like before. Whilst coming to understand in time the speech of men, sims are without language of their own, having but a great variety of howls, grunts, and moans. Yet this gesture-speech, which I am told is come from the signs of the deaf, they do readily learn, and often their masters answer back so, to ensure commands being properly grasped.

Am wild to learn it my own self, and shall. Meseems it is in its way a style of tachygraphy or short-hand such as I use to set down these pages. Having devised varying tachygraphic hands for friends and acquaintances, 'twill be amusing taking to a *hand* that is exactly what its name declares.

As I was leaving with my new charges, the sim-seller did bid me lead them by the gibbets on Shooter's Hill, there to see the bodies and members of felons and of sims as have run off from their masters. It wondered me they should have the wit to take the meaning of such display, but he assured me they should. And so, reckoning it good advice if true and no harm if a lie, I chivvied them thither.

A filthy sight I found it, with the miscreants' flesh all shrunk to the bones. But *hoo!* quoth my sims, and looked close upon the corpses of their own kind, which by their hairiness and flat-skulled heads do seem even more bestial dead than when animated with life.

Home then, and Elizabeth as delighted in my success as am I. An excellent dinner of a calf's head boiled with dumplings, and an abundance of buttered ale with sugar and cinnamon, of which in celebration we invited Jane to partake, and she grew right giddy. Bread and leeks for the sims, and water, it being reported they grow undocile on stronger drink.

After much debate, though good-natured, it was decided to style the male Will and the female Peg. Showed them to their pallets down cellar, and they took to them readily enough, as finer than what they were accustomed to.

So to bed, right pleased with myself despite the expense.

May 7. An advantage of having sims present appears that I had not thought on. Both Will and Peg quite excellent ratters, finer than any puss-cat. No need, either, to fling the rats on the dungheap, for they devour them with as much gusto as I should a neat's tongue. They having subsisted on such small deer in the forests of America, I shall not try to break them of the habit, though training them not to bring in their prey when we are at table with guests. The Reverend Mr. Milles quite shocked, but recovering nicely on being plied with wine.

May 8. Peg and Will the both of them enthralled with fire. When the work of them is done of the day, or at evening ere they take their rest, they may be found before the hearth observing the sport of the flames. Now and again one will to the other say *hoo*!—this noise, I find, they utter on seeing that which does interest them, whatsoever it may be.

Now as I thought on it, I minded me reading or hearing, I recall not which, that in their wild unpeopled haunts the sims know the use of fire as they find it set from lightning or other such mischance, but not the art of its making. No wonder then they are Vulcanolaters, reckoning flame more precious than do we gold.

Considering such reflections, I resolved this morning on an

experiment, to see what they might do. Rising early for to void my bladder in the pot, I put out the hearthfire, which in any case was gone low through want of fuel. Retired then to put on my dressing gown and, once clad, returned to await developments.

First up from the cellar was Will, and his cry on seeing the flames extinguished heartrending as Romeo's over the body of fair Juliet when I did see that play acted this December past. In a trice comes Peg, whose moaning with Will did rouse my wife, and she much upset at being so rudely wakened.

When the calm in some small measure restored, I bade by signs, in the learning of which I proceed apace, for the sims to sit quietly before the hearth, and with flint and steel restored that which I had earlier destroyed. They both made such outcry as if they had heard sounded the Last Trump.

Then doused I that second fire too, again to much distress from Peg and Will. Elizabeth by this time out of the house in some dudgeon, no doubt to spend money we lack on stuffs of which we have no want.

Set up in the hearth thereupon several small fires of sticks, each with much tinder so as to make it an easy matter to kindle. A brisk striking of flint and steel dropping sparks onto one such produced a merry little blaze, to the accompaniment of much *hoo*ing out of the sims.

And so the nub of it. Shewing Will the steel and flint, I clashed them once more the one upon the other so he might see the sparks engendered thereby. Then pointed to one of the aforementioned piles of sticks I had made up, bidding him watch close, as indeed he did. Having made sure of't, I did set that second pile alight.

Again put the fires out, the wailing accompanying the act less than heretofore, for which I was not sorry. Pointed now to a third assemblage of wood and timber, but instead of myself lighting it, I did convey flint and steel to Will, and with signs essayed to bid him play Prometheus.

His hands much scarred and callused, and under their hair knobby-knuckled as an Irishman's. He held at first the implements as if not taking in their purpose, yet the sims making tools of stone, as is widely reported, he could not wholly fail to grasp their utility.

And indeed ere long he did try parroting me. When his first clumsy attempt yielded no result, I thought he would abandon such efforts as beyond his capacity and reserved for men of my sort. But persist he did, and at length was reward with scintillae like unto those I had made. His grin so wide and gleeful I thought it would stretch clear round his head.

Then without need of my further demonstration he set the instruments of fire production over the materials for the blaze. Him in such excitement as the sparks fell upon the waiting tinder that beneath his breeches rose his member, indeed to such degree as would have made me proud to be its possessor. And Peg was, I think, in such mood as to couple with him on the spot, had I not been present and had not his faculties been directed elsewhere than toward the lectual.

For at his success he cut such capers as had not been out of place upon the stage, were they but a trifle more rhythmical and less unconstrained. Yet of the making of fire, even if by such expedient as the friction of two sticks (which once I was forced by circumstance to attempt, and would try the patience of Job), as of every other salutary art, his race is as utterly ignorant as of the moons of Jupiter but lately found by some Italian with an optic glass.

No brute beast of the field could learn to begin a fire on the technique being shown it, which did Will nigh readily as a man. But despite most diligent instruction, no sim yet has mastered such subtler arts as reading and writing, nor ever will, meseems. Falling in capacity thus between man and animal, the sims do raise a host of conundrums vexing and perplexing. I should pay a pound, or at the least ten shillings, merely to know how such strange fusions came to be.

So to the Admiralty full of such musings, which did occupy my mind, I fear, to the detriment of my proper duties.

May 10. Supper this evening at the Turk's Head, with the other members of the Rota Club. The fare not of the finest, being boiled venison and some few pigeons, all meanly done up. The lamb's wool seemed nought but poor ale, the sugar, nutmeg and meat of roasted apples hardly to be tasted. Miles the landlord down with a quartan fever, but ill served by his staff if such be the result of his absence.

The subject of the Club's discussions for the evening much in accord with my own recent curiosity, to wit, the sims. Cyriack Skinner did maintain them creatures of the Devil, whereupon was he roundly rated by Dr. Croon as having in this contention returned to the pernicious heresy of the Manichees, the learned doctor reserving the power of creation of the Lord alone. Much flinging back and forth of Biblical texts, the which all struck me as being more the exercise of ingenuity of the debaters than bearing on the problem, for in plain fact the Scriptures nowhere mention sims.

When at length the talk did turn to matters more ascertainable, I spoke somewhat of my recent investigation, and right well-received my remarks were, or so I thought. Others with experience of sims with like tales, finding them quick enough on things practic but sadly lacking in any higher faculties. Much jollity at my account of the visible manifestation of Will's excitement, and whispers that this lady or that (the names, to my vexation, I failed to catch) owned her sims for naught but their prowess in matters of the mattress.

Just then came the maid by with coffee for the Club, not of the best, but better, I grant, than the earlier wretched lamb's wool. She a pretty yellow-haired lass called I believe Kate, a wench of perhaps sixteen years, a good-bodied woman not over thick or thin in any place, with a lovely bosom she did display most charmingly as she bent to fill the gentlemen's cups.

Having ever an eye for beauty, such that I reckon little else beside it, I own I did turn my head for to follow this Kate as she went about her duties. Noticing which, Sir William Henry called out, much to the merriment of the Club and to my chagrin, "See how Samuel peeps!" Him no mean droll, and loosed a pretty pun, if at my expense. Good enough, but then at the far end of the table someone, I saw not who, worse luck, thought to cap it by braying like the donkey he must be, "Not half the peeping, I warrant, as at his sims of nights!"

Such mockery clings to a man like pitch, regardless of the truth in't, which in this case is none. Oh, the thing could be done, but the sims so homely 'twould yield no titillation, of that I am practically certain.

May 12. The household being more infected this past week with nits than ever before, resolved to bathe Peg and Will, which also I hoped would curb somewhat their stench. And so it proved, albeit not without more alarums than I had looked for. The sims most loth to enter the tub, which must to them have seemed some instrument of torment. The resulting shrieks and outcry so deafening a neighbor did call out to be assured all was well.

Having done so, I saw no help for it but to go into the tub my own self, notwithstanding my having bathed but two weeks before. I felt, I think more hesitation stripping down before Peg than I should in front of Jane, whom I would simply dismiss from consideration but in how she performed her duties. But I did wonder what Peg made of my body, reckoning it against the hairy forms of her own kind. Hath she the wit to deem mankind superior, or is our smoothness to her as gross and repellent as the peltries of the sims to us? I cannot as yet make shift to enquire.

As may be, my example showing them they should not be harmed, they bathed themselves. A trouble arose I had not foreseen, for the sims being nearly as thickly haired over all their bodies as I upon my head, the rinsing of the soap from their hides less easy than for us, and requiring much water. Lucky I am the well is within fifty paces of my home. And so from admiral of the bath to the Admiralty, hoping henceforward to scratch myself less.

May 13. A pleasant afternoon this day, carried in a coach to see the lions and other beasts in the menagerie. I grant the lions pride of place through custom immemorial, but in truth am more taken with the abnormous creatures fetched back from the New World than those our forefathers have known since the time of Arthur. Nor am I alone in this conceit, for the cages of lion, bear, camel had but few spectators, whilst round those of the American beasts I did find myself compelled to use hands and elbows to make shift to pass through the crowds.

This last not altogether unpleasant, as I chanced to brush against a handsome lass, but when I did enquire if she would take tea with me she said me nay, which did irk me no little, for as I say she was fair to see.

More time for the animals, then, and wondrous strange ever they strike me. The spear-fanged cat is surely the most horridest murderer this shuddering world hath seen, yet there is for him prey worthy of his mettle, what with beavers near big as our bears, wild oxen whose horns are to those of our familiar kine as the spear-fanged cat's teeth to the lion's, and the great hairy elephants which do roam the forests.

Why such prodigies of nature manifest themselves on those distant shores does perplex me most exceedingly, as they are unlike any beasts even in the bestiaries, which as all men know are more flights of fancy than sober fact. Amongst them the sims appear no more than one piece of some great jigsaw, yet no pattern therein is to me apparent; would it were.

Also another new creature in the menagerie, which I had not seen before. At first I thought it a caged sim, but on inspection it did prove an ape, brought back by the Portuguese from Afric lands and styled there, the keeper made so good as to inform me, shimpanse. It flourishes not in England's clime, he did continue, being subject to sickness in the lungs from the cool and damp, but is so interesting as to be displayed whilst living, howsoever long that may prove.

The shimpanse a baser brute than even the sim. It goes on all fours, and its hinder feet more like unto monkeys' than men's, having thereon great toes that grip like thumbs. Also, where a sim's teeth, as I have observed from Will and Peg, are uncommon large, in shape they are like unto a man's, but the shimpanse hath tushes of some savagery, though of course paling alongside those of the spear-fanged cat.

Seeing the keeper a garrulous fellow, I enquired of him further anent this shimpanse. He owned he had himself thought it a sort of sim on its arrival, but sees now more distinguishing points than likenesses: gait and dentition, such as I have herein remarked upon, but also in its habits. From his experience, he has seen it to be ignorant of fire, repeatedly allowing to die a blaze though fuel close at hand. Nor has it the knack of shaping stones to its ends, though it will, he told me, cast them betimes against those who annoy it, once striking one such with force enough to render him some time senseless. Hearing the villain had essayed tormenting the creature with a stick, my sympathies lay all for the shimpanse, wherein its keeper concurred.

And so homewards, thinking on the shimpanse as I rode. Whereas in the lands wherewith men are most familiar it were easy distinguishing men from beasts, the strange places to which our vessels have but lately fetched themselves reveal a stairway ascending the chasm, and climbers on the stairs, some higher, some lower. A pretty image, but why it should be so there and not here does I confess escape me.

May 16. A savage row with Jane today, her having forgotten a change of clothes for my bed. Her defense that I had not so instructed her, the lying minx, for I did plainly make my wishes known the evening previous, which I recollect most distinctly. Yet she did deny it again and again, finally raising my temper to such a pitch that I cursed her right roundly, slapping her face and pulling her nose smartly.

Whereupon did the ungrateful trull lay down her service on the spot. She decamped in a fury of her own, crying that I treated the sims, those very sims which I had bought for to ease her labors, with more kindlier consideration than I had for her own self.

So now we are without a serving-maid, and her a dab hand in the kitchen, her swan pie especially being toothsome. Dined tonight at the Bell, and expect to tomorrow at the Swan on the Hoop, in Fish Street. For Elizabeth no artist over the hearth, nor am I myself. And as for the sims, I should sooner open my veins than indulge of their cuisine, the good Lord only knowing what manner of creatures they in their ignorance should add to a pot.

Now as my blood has somewhat cooled, I must admit a germ of truth in Jane's scolds. I do not beat Will and Peg as a man would servitors of more ordinary stripe. They, being but new come from the wilds, are not inured to't as are our servants, and might well turn on me their master. And being in part of brute kind, their strength does exceed mine, Will's most assuredly and that of Peg perhaps. And so, say I, better safe. No satisfaction to me for the sims on Shooter's Hill gallows, were I not there to see't.

May 20. Today to my lord Sandwich's for supper. This doubly pleasant, in enjoying his fine companionship and saving the cost of a meal, the house being still without maid. The food and drink in excellent style, as to suit my lord. The broiled lobsters very sweet, and the lamprey pie (which for its rarity I but seldom eat of) the best ever I had. Many other fine victuals as well (the tanzy in especial), and the wine all sugared.

Afterwards backgammon, at which I won £5 ere my luck turned. Ended 15s. in my lord's debt, which he did graciously excuse me afterwards, a generosity not looked for but which I did not refuse. Then to crambo, wherein by tagging *and rich* to *Sandwich* I was adjudged winner, the more so for playing on his earlier munificence.

Thereafter nigh a surfeit of good talk, as is custom at my lord's. He mentioning sims, I did relate my own dealings with Peg and Will, to which he listened with much interest. He thinks on buying some for his own household, and unaware I had done so.

Perhaps it was the wine let loose my tongue, for I broached somewhat my disjoint musings on the sims and their place in nature, on the strangeness of the American fauna and much else besides. Lord Sandwich did acquaintance me with a New World beast found in their southerly holdings by the Spaniards, of strange outlandish sort: big as an ox, or nearly, and all covered over with armor of bone like a man wearing chain. I should pay out a shilling or even more for to see't, were one conveyed to London.

Then coffee, and it not watered as so often at an inn, but full and strong. As I and Elizabeth making our departures, Lord Sandwich did bid me join him tomorrow night to hear speak a savant of the Royal Society. It bore, said he, on my prior ramblings, and would say no more, but looked uncommon sly. Even did it not, I should have leaped at the chance.

This written at one of the clock, for so the watchman just now cried out. Too wound up for bed, what with coffee and the morrow's prospect. Elizabeth aslumber, but the sims also awake, and at frolic meseems, from the noises up the stairway.

If they be of human kind, is their fornication *sans* clergy sinful? Another vexing question. By their existence, they do engender naught but disquietude. Nay, strike that. They may in sooth more sims engender, a pun good enough to sleep on, and so to bed.

May 21. All this evening worrying at my thoughts as a dog at a bone. My lord Sandwich knows not what commotion internal he did by his invitation, all kindly meant, set off in me. The speaker this night a spare man, dry as dust, of the very sort I learned so well to loathe when at Cambridge.

Dry as dust! Happy words, which did spring all unbidden from my pen. For of dust the fellow did discourse, if thereby is meant, as commonly, things long dead. He had some men bear in bones but lately found by Swanscombe at a grave-digging. And such bones they were, and teeth (or rather tusks), as to make it all I could do to hold me in my seat. For surely they once graced no less a beast than the hairy elephant whose prototype I saw in menagerie so short a while ago. The double-curving tusks admit of no error, for those of all elephants with which we are anciently familiar form but a single segment of arc.

When, his discourse concluded, he gave leave for questions, I made bold to ask to what he imputed the hairy elephant's being so long vanished from our shores yet thriving in the western lands. To this he confessed himself baffled, as am I, and admiring of his honesty as well.

Before the hairy elephant was known to live, such monstrous bones surely had been reckoned as from beasts perishing in the Flood whereof Scripture speaks. Yet how may that be so, them surviving across a sea wider than any Noah sailed?

Meseems the answer lieth within my grasp, but am balked from setting finger to't. The thwarting fair to drive me mad, worse even,

I think, than with a lass who will snatch out a hatpin for to defend her charms against my importuning.

May 22. Grand oaks from tiny acorns grow! This morning came a great commotion from the kitchen. I rushing in found Will at struggle with a cur dog which had entered, the door being open on account of fine weather, to steal half a flitch of salt bacon. It dodging most nimbly round the sim, snatched up the gammon and fled out again, him pursuing but in vain.

Myself passing vexed, having intended to sup thereon. But Will all downcast on returning, so had not the heart further to punish him. Told him instead, him understanding I fear but little, it were well men not sims dwelt in England, else would wolves prowl the London streets still.

Stood stock still some time thereafter, hearing the greater import behind my jesting speech. Is not the answer to the riddle of the hairy elephant and other exotic beasts existing in the New World but being hereabouts long vanished their having there but sims to hunt them? The sims in their wild haunts wield club and sharpened stone, no more. They are ignorant even of the bow, which from time out of mind has equipt the hunter's armory.

Just as not two centuries past we Englishmen slew on this island the last wolf, so may we not imagine our most remotest grandsires serving likewise the hairy elephant, the spear-fanged cat? They being more cunning than sims and better accoutred, this should not have surpassed their powers. Such beasts would survive in America, then, not through virtue inherent of their own, but by reason of lesser danger to them in the sims than would from mankind come.

Put this budding thought at luncheon today to my lord Sandwich. Him back at me with Marvell to his coy mistress (the most annoyingest sort!), viz., had we but world enough and time, who could reckon the changes as might come to pass? And going on, laughing, to say next will be found dead sims at Swanscombe.

Though meant but as a pleasantry, quoth I, why not? Against true men they could not long have stood, but needs must have given way as round Plymouth and Virginia. Even without battle they must soon have failed, as being less able than mankind to provide for their wants.

There we let it lay, but as I think more on't, the notion admits of broader application. Is't not the same for trout as for men, or for lilacs? Those best suited living reproduce their kind, whilst the trout with twisted tail or bloom without sweet scent die all unmourned leaving no descendants. And each succeeding generation being of the previous survivors constituted, will by such reasoning show some little difference from the one as went before.

Seeing no flaw in this logic, resolve tomorrow to do this from its tachygraphic state, bereft of course of maunderings and privacies, for prospectus to the Royal Society, and mightily wondering whatever they shall make of it.

May 23. Closeted all this day at the Admiralty. Yet did it depend on my diligence alone, I fear me the Fleet should drown. Still, a deal of business finished, as happens when one stays by it. Three quills worn quite out, and my hands all over ink. Also my fine camlet cloak with the gold buttons, which shall mightily vex my wife, poor wretch, unless it may be cleaned. I pray God to make it so, for I do mislike strife at home.

The burning work at last complete, homeward in the twilight. It being washing-day, dined on cold meat. I do confess, felt no small strange stir in my breast on seeing Will taking down the washing before the house. A vision it was, almost, of his kind roaming England long ago, till perishing from want of substance or vying therefor with men. And now they are through the agency of men returned here again, after some great interval of years. Would I knew how many.

The writing of my notions engrossing the whole of the day, had no occasion to air them to Lord Brouncker of the Society, as was my hope. Yet expound I must, or burst. Elizabeth, then, at dinner made audience for me, whether she would or no. My spate at last exhausted, asked for her thoughts on't.

She said only that Holy Writ sufficed on the matter for her, whereat I could but make a sour face. To bed in some anger, and in fear lest the Royal Society prove as close-minded, which God prevent. Did He not purpose man to reason on the world around him, He should have left him witless as the sim.

May 24. To Gresham College this morning, to call on Lord Brouncker. He examined with great care the papers I had done up, his face revealing nought. Felt myself at recitation once more before a professor, a condition whose lack these last years I have not missed. Feared also he might not be able to take in the writing, it being done in such haste some short-hand characters may have replaced the common ones.

Then to my delight he declared he reckoned it deserving of a hearing at the Society's weekly meeting next. Having said so much, he made to dismiss me, himself being much occupied with devising a means whereby to calculate the relation of a circle's circumference to its diameter. I wish him joy of't. I do resolve one day soon, however, to learn the multiplication table, which meseems should be of value at the Admiralty. Repaired there from the college, to do the work I had set by yesterday.

May 26. Watch these days Will and Peg with new eyes. I note for instance them using between themselves our deaf-man's signs, as well as to me and my wife. As well they might, them conveying far more subtler meanings than the bestial howlings and gruntings that are theirs in nature. Thus though they may not devise any such, they own the wit to see its utility.

I wonder would the shimpanse likewise?

A girl came today asking after the vacant maidservant's post, a pretty bit with red hair, white teeth, and fine strong haunches. Thought myself she would serve, but Elizabeth did send her away. Were her looks liker to Peg's, she had I think been hired on the spot. But a quarrel on it not worth the candle, the more so as I have seen fairer.

May 28. This writ near cockcrow, in hot haste, lest any detail of the evening escape my recollection. Myself being a late addition, spoke last, having settled the title "A Proposed Explication of the Survival of Certain Beasts in America and Their Disappearance Hereabouts" on the essay.

The prior speakers addressed one the organs internal of bees and other the appearance of Saturn in the optic glass, both topics which interest me but little. Then called to the podium by Lord Brouncker, all aquiver as a virgin bride. Much wished myself in the company of some old soakers over roast pigeons and dumplings and sack. But a brave front amends for much, and so plunged in straightaway.

Used the remains of the hairy elephant presented here a sennight past as example of a beast vanished from these shores yet across the sea much in evidence. Then on to the deficiencies of sims as hunters, when set beside even the most savagest of men.

Thus far well-received, and even when noting the struggle to live and leave progeny that does go on among each kind and between the several kinds. But the storm broke, as I feared it should and more, on my drawing out the implications therefrom: that of each generation only so many may flourish and breed; and that each succeeding generation, being descended of these survivors alone, differs from that which went before.

My worst and fearfullest nightmare then came true, for up rose shouts of blasphemy. Gave them back what I had told Elizabeth on the use of reason, adding in some heat I had expected such squallings of my wife who is a woman and ignorant, but better from men styling themselves natural philosophers. Did they aim to prove me wrong, let them so by the reason they do profess to cherish. This drew further catcalling but also approbation, which at length prevailed.

Got up then a pompous little manikin, who asked how I dared set myself against God's word insofar as how beasts came to be. On my denying this, he did commence reciting at me from Genesis. When he paused for to draw breath, I asked most mildly of him on which day the Lord did create the sims. Thereupon he stood discomfited, his foolish mouth hanging open, at which I was quite heartened.

Would the next inquisitor had been so easily downed! A Puritan he was, by his somber cloak and somberer bearing. His questions took the same tack as the previous, but not so stupidly. After first enquiring if I believed in God, whereat I truthfully told him aye, he asked did I think Scripture to be the word of God. Again said aye, by now getting and dreading the drift of his argument. And as I feared, he bade me next point him out some place where Scripture was mistaken, ere supplanting it with fancies of mine own.

I knew not how to make answer, and should have in the next moment fled. But up spake to my great surprise Lord Brouncker, reciting from Second Chronicles, the second verse of the fourth chapter, wherein is said of Solomon and his Temple, *Also he made the molten sea of ten cubits from brim to brim, round in compass, and the height thereof was five cubits, and a line of thirty cubits did compass it round about.*

This much perplexed the Puritan, and me as well, though I essayed not to show it. Lord Brouncker then proceeded to his explication, to wit that the true compass of a ten-cubit round vessel was not thirty cubits, but above one and thirty; I misremember the exact figure he gave. Those of the Royal Society learned in mathematics did agree he had reason, and urged the Puritan make the experiment for his self with cup, cord, and rule, which were enough for to demonstrate the truth.

I asked if he was answered. Like a gentleman he owned he was, and bowed, and sat, his face full of troubles. Felt with him no small sympathy, for once one error in Scripture is admitted, where shall it end?

The next query was of different sort, a man in periwig enquiring if I did reckon humankind to have arisen by the means I described. Had to reply I did. Our forefathers might be excused for thinking otherwise, them being so widely separate from all other creatures they knew.

But we moderns in our travels round the globe have found the shimpanse, which standeth nigh the flame of reasoned thought; and more important still the sim, in whom the flame does burn, but more feebly than in ourselves. These bridging the gap 'twixt man and beast meseems do show mankind to be in sooth a part of nature, whose engenderment in some past distant age is to be explained through natural law.

Someone rose to doubt the variation in each sort of living thing being sufficient eventually to permit the rise of new kinds. Pointed out to him the mastiffe, the terrier, and the bloodhound, all of the dog kind, but become distinct through man's choice of mates in each generation. Surely the same might occur in nature, said I. The fellow admitted it was conceivable, and sat.

Then up stood a certain Wilberforce, with whom I have some small acquaintance. He likes me not, nor I him. We know it on both sides, though for civility's sake feigning otherwise. Now he spoke with smirking air, as one sure of the mortal thrust. He did grant my willingness to have a sim as great-grandfather, said he, but was I so willing to claim one as great-grandmother? A deal of laughter rose, which was his purpose, and to make me out a fool.

Had I carried steel, I should have drawn on him. As was, rage sharpened my wit to serve for the smallsword I left at home. Told him it were no shame to have one's great-grandfather a sim, as that sim did use to best advantage the intellect he had. Better that, quoth I, than dissipating the mind on such digressive and misleading quibbles as he raised. If I be in error, then I am; let him shew it by logic and example, not as it were playing to the gallery.

Came clapping from all sides, to my delight and the round dejection of Wilberforce. On seeking further questions, found none. Took my own seat whilst the Fellows of the Society did congratulate me and cry up my essay louder, I thought, than either of the other two. Lord Brouncker acclaimed it as a unifying principle for the whole of the study of life, which made me as proud a man as any in the world, for all the world seemed to smile upon me.

And so to bed.

"Bluff" is based on the fascinating speculations Julian Jaynes put forward in *The Origins of Consciousness in the Breakdown of the Bicameral Mind.* They give rise to my favorite kind of aliens: those who think as well as people but not at all like them.

Not long after "Bluff" appeared in *Analog,* I got a letter from Professor Jaynes. I have to say that I opened the envelope with some trepidation. Much to my relief, I found inside a kind note telling me that he'd liked the story. So I must have done something right.

BLUFF

The pictures from the survey satellites came out of the fax machine one after the other, *chunk, chunk, chunk.* Ramon Castillo happened to be close by. He took them from the tray, more out of a sense of duty than in the expectation of finding anything interesting. The previous photo runs of the still-unnamed planet below had proven singularly dull.

There hadn't been a good shot of this river-valley system before, though. As he studied the print, his heavy eyebrows lifted like raven's wings. He felt a flush of excitement beneath his coppery skin, and damned himself for a fool. "Wishful thinking," he muttered aloud. Just the same, he slipped the print into the magnifying viewer.

His whoop brought people running from all over the *William Howells.* Helga Stein was first into the fax compartment: a stocky blonde in her late twenties, her normally serious expression now replaced by surprise. "*Mein Gott,* was that you, Ramon?" she exclaimed; Castillo was usually very quiet.

Most of the time he found her intensely annoying; he was a cultural anthropologist and she a psychologist, and their different approaches to problems that touched them both led to frequent arguments. Now, though, he stepped away from the viewer and invited her forward with a courtly sweep of his arm. "You'll see for yourself," he said grandly. He spoke Latin with a facility that left everyone else aboard the *Howells* jealous.

"What am I looking for?" she asked, fiddling with the focus, By then the other members of the survey team were crowding in: physical anthropologist Sybil Hussie and her husband George Davies, who was a biologist (they were married just before up-ship, and George had endured in good spirits all the stale jokes about practicing what he studied); Xing Mei-lin the linguist; and Manolis Zakythinos, whose specialty was geology.

Even Stan Jeffries stuck his head in to see what the fuss was about. "Found the mountain of solid platinum, did you?" the navigator chuckled, seeing Helga peering into the viewer.

She looked up, puzzlement on her face. "What is that in Latin?" she asked; the ship's English-speakers consistently forgot to use the international scholarly tongue. Grumbling, Jeffries repeated himself.

"Ah," she said, distracted enough to be polite instead of freezing him for his heavy-handed wit. "Interpreting such photos is not my area of expertise, you must understand; I leave that to Sybil or Manolis or Ramon who saw this first. But along the banks of this river there are I think cities set in the midst of a network of canals."

Yells like Castillo's ripped from the entire scientific crew. They all scrambled toward the viewer at the same time. "Ouch!" Sybil Hussie said as an elbow caught her in the ribs. "Have a care, there. This is no bloody rugby scrum—and try doing that into Latin, if anybody has a mind to."

At last, grudgingly, they formed a line. "You see?" Castillo said as they examined the print in turn. He was still voluble in his excitement. "Walled towns with major works of architecture at their centers; outlying hamlets; irrigation works that cover the whole floodplain. Judging by the rest of the planet, I would guess that this is its very first civilization, equivalent to Sumer or Egypt back on Earth."

They had known for several days that the world was inhabited, but nothing at a level higher than tiny farming villages had shown up on any earlier pictures—certainly no culture worth contacting. Now, though—

"A chance to really see how a hydraulic civilization functions, instead of guessing from a random selection of 5,000-year-old finds," Ramon said dreamily.

Mei-lin spoke with down-to-earth practicality: "A chance for a new dissertation." Her Latin was not as fluent as his, but had a precision Caesar might have admired.

"Publications," Helga and George Davies said in the same breath. Everyone laughed.

"Maybe enough art objects to make us all rich," Jeffries put in.

Manolis Zakythinos made a small, disgusted noise. All the same, the navigator's words hung in the air. It had happened before, to other incoming survey teams. There was always a premium on new forms of beauty.

Zakythinos slipped out. Thinking he was still annoyed, Ramon started to go after him, but the geologist quickly returned with a bottle of ouzo. "To the crows with the vile excuse for vodka the food unit turns out," he cried, his deep-set brown eyes flashing. "This calls for a true celebration."

"Call the captain," someone said as, amid cheers, they repaired to the galley. Most of them stopped at their cabins for something special; Sybil was carrying a squat green bottle of Tanqueray that she put between bourbon and scotch. Odd, Ramon thought, how her husband favored the American drink while Jeffries, who was from the States, preferred scotch.

Castillo's own contribution came from the hills outside his native Bogota. He set the joints, rolled with almost compulsive neatness, beside the liquor. Being moderate by nature, he still had most of the kilo he had brought, and had given away a good deal of what was gone.

Given a choice, he would sooner have drunk beer, but space restrictions aboard the *Howells* made taking it impossible. He sighed and fixed himself a gin and tonic.

He was, inevitably and with inevitable fruitlessness, arguing with Helga about what the aliens below would be like when the buzz of conversation around them quieted for a moment. Blinking, Ramon looked up. Captain Katerina Tolmasova stood in the galley doorway.

Always, Ramon thought, she had that way of drawing attention to herself. Part of it lay in her staying in uniform long after the rest of them had relaxed into jeans or coveralls. But she would have worn her authority like a cloak over any clothes, or none.

In any clothes or none, also, she would have drawn male glances. Not even George Davies was immune, in spite of being a contented newlywed. She was tall, slim, dark; not at all the typical Russian. But her nationality showed in her broad, high cheekbones and in her eyes—enormous blue pools in which a man would gladly drown himself.

It still amazed Ramon, and sometimes frightened him a little, that they shared a bed.

She came over to him, smiling. "I am to understand that we have you to thank for this, ah, occasion?" Her voice made a slow music of Latin. It was the only language they had in common; he wondered how many times in the past thousand years it had been used for lovemaking.

Now he shrugged. "It could have been anyone. Whoever saw the pictures first would have recognized what was on them."

"I am glad you did, even so. Making contact is ever so much more interesting than weeks in the endless sameness of hyperdrive, though the instructors at the Astrograd Starship Academy would frown to hear me say so." She paused to sip vodka over ice—not the rough ship's brew, but Stolichnaya from her private hoard, which went down like a warm whisper—then went on, "Also I am glad we have here beings without a high technology. I shall worry less, of nights." The weapons of the *Howells,* of course, were under her control, along with everything else having to do with the safety of the ship.

"I hope," he said, touching her hand, "that I can help keep you from worrying."

"It is a shame romantic speeches have so little to do with life," she said. She sounded a little sad. Seeing the hurt spring into his eyes, she added quickly, "Not that they are not welcome even so. My quarters would be lonely without you tonight, the more so as afterward we will be busy, first I guiding the ship down and then you with this new species. We shall not have much time together then; best enjoy while we may."

Pitkhanas, steward-king of the river-god Tabal for the town of Kussara, awoke with the words of the god ringing in his ears: "See to the dredging of the canals today, lest they be filled with silt!"

King though he was, he scrambled from his bed, throwing aside the light, silky coverlet; disobeying the divine voice was unimaginable. He hardly had a backward glance to spare for the superb form of his favorite wife Azzias.

She muttered a drowsy complaint at being disturbed. "I am sorry," he told her. "Tabal has ordered me to see to the dredging of the canals today, lest they be filled with silt."

"Ah," she said, and went back to sleep.

Slaves hurried forward to dress Pitkhanas, draping him in the gold-shot crimson robe of state, setting the conical crown on his head, and slipping his feet into sandals with silver buckles. As he was being clothed, he breakfasted on a small loaf, a leg of boiled fowl from the night before that would not stay fresh much longer, and a pot of fermented fruit juice.

Tabal spoke to him again as he was eating, echoing the previous command. He felt the beginnings of a headache, as always happened when he did not at once do what the god demanded. He hastily finished his food, wiped his mouth on the sleeve of his robe, and hurried out of the royal bedchamber. Servants scrambled to open doors before him.

The last portal swung wide; he strode out of the palace into the central square of Kussara. The morning breeze from the Til-Barsip river was refreshing, drying the sweat that prickled on him under the long robe.

Close by the palace entrance stood the tomb of his father Zidantas, whose skull topped the monument. Several commoners were laying offerings at the front of the tomb: fruits, bread, cheese. In the short skirts of thin stuff that were their sole garments, they were more comfortable than he. When they saw him, they went down on their knees, touching their heads to the ground.

"Praise to your father, my lord king," one of them quavered, his voice muffled. "He has told me where I misplaced a fine alabaster bowl."

"Good for you, then," Pitkhanas said. Dead no less than alive, his father always had a harsh way of speaking to him.

As now: "I thought you were going to see to the dredging of the canals today," Zidantas snapped.

"So I am," Pitkhanas said mildly, trying to avoid Zidantas's wrath.

"Then do it," his father growled. The old man had been dead for three years or so. At times his voice and manner were beginning to remind the king of Labarnas, his own grandfather and Zidantas's father. Labarnas rarely spoke from the tomb any more, save to old men and women who remembered him well. Zidantas's presence, though, was as real and pervasive in Kussara as that of Pitkhanas.

Surrounded by his attendants, the king hurried through the town's narrow, winding streets, stepping around or over piles of stinking garbage. The mud-brick housefronts were monotonous, but the two-story buildings provided welcome shade. Despite the breeze, the day was already hot.

Pitkhanas heard people chattering in the courtyards behind the tall blank walls of their homes. A woman's angry screech came from the roof where she and her husband had been sleeping: "Get up, you sot! Are you too sozzled to listen to the gods and work?"

The gods she spoke of were paltry, nattering things, fit for the lower classes: gods of the hearth, of the various crafts, of wayfaring. Pitkhanas had never heard them and did not know all their names; let the priests keep them straight. The great gods of the heavens and earth dealt with him directly, not through such intermediaries.

Kussara's eastern gate was sacred to Ninatta and Kulitta, the god and goddess of the two moons. Their statues stood in a niche above the arch, the stone images fairly bursting with youth. Below them, carts rumbled in and out, their ungreased axles squealing. Sentries paced the wall over the gate. The sun glinted off their bronze spearpoints.

The gate-captain, a scar-seamed veteran named Tushratta, bowed low before Pitkhanas. "How can this one serve you, my lord?"

"Tabal has reminded me that the canals need dredging," the king replied. "Tell some of your soldiers to gather peasants from the fields—three hundred overall will do—and set them to work at it."

"I hear you and obey as I hear and obey the gods," Tushratta said. He touched the alabaster eye-idol that he wore on his belt next to his dagger. They were common all through the Eighteen Cities, as channels to make the voices of the gods easier to understand.

Tushratta bawled the names of several warriors; some came down from the wall, others out of the barracks by the gate. "The canals need dredging," he told them. "Gather peasants from the field—three hundred overall will do—and set them to work at it."

The men dipped their heads, then fanned out into the green fields to do as they had been ordered. The peasants working at their plots knew instinctively what the soldiers were about, and tried to disappear. The warriors routed them out one by one. Soon they gathered the required number, most with hoes or digging-sticks already in their hands.

Pitkhanas gave them their commands, watched them troop off toward the canals in groups of ten or so. They splashed about, deepening the channels so the precious water could flow more freely. The king started to go back to the palace to tend to other business, then wondered whether he should stay awhile to encourage the canal-dredgers.

He paused, irresolute, glanced up at the images of the gods for guidance. Kulitta spoke to him: "Best you remain. Seeing the king as well as hearing his words reminds the worker of his purpose."

"Thank you, mistress, for showing me the proper course," Pitkhanas murmured. He went out to the canals to let the peasants see him at close range. His retinue followed, a slave holding a parasol above his head to shield him from the strong sun.

"His majesty is gracious," Tushratta remarked to one of the king's attendants, a plump little man named Radus-piyama, who was priest to the sky-god Tarhund.

The priest clucked reproachfully. "Did you not hear him answer the goddess? Of course he follows her will."

Kulitta's advice had been good; the work went more swiftly than it would have without Pitkhanas's presence. Now and then a man or two would pause to stretch or have a moment's horseplay, splashing muddy water at each other, but they soon returned to their tasks. "The canals need dredging," one reminded himself in stern tones very like the king's.

Because the goddess had told Pitkhanas to stay and oversee the peasants, he was close by when the sky ship descended. The first of it he knew was a low mutter in the air, like distant thunder—but the day was bright and cloudless. Then Radus-piyama cried out and pointed upward. Pitkhanas's gaze followed the priest's finger.

For a moment he did not see what Radus-piyama had spied, but then his eye caught the silver glint of light. It reminded him of the evening star seen at earliest twilight—but only for an instant, for it moved through the heavens like a stooping bird of prey, growing brighter and (he rubbed his eyes) larger. The noise in the sky became a deep roar that smote the ears. Pitkhanas clapped his hands over them. The sound still came through.

"Ninatta, Kulitta, Tarhund lord of the heavens, tell me the meaning of this portent," Pitkhanas exclaimed. The gods were silent, as if they did not know. The king waited, more afraid than he had ever been in his life.

If he knew fear, raw panic filled his subjects. The peasants toiling in the canals were screaming and shrieking. Some scrambled onto dry land and fled, while others took deep breaths and ducked under the water to hide from the monstrous heavenly apparition.

Even a few members of Pitkhanas's retinue broke and ran. The soldiers Tushratta had gathered were on the edge of running too, but the gate-captain's angry bellow stopped them: "Hold fast, you cowards! Where are your guts? Stand and protect your king." The command brought most of them back to their places, though a couple kept pelting back toward Kussara.

"Is it a bird, my lord?" Radus-piyama shouted through the thunder. The priest of Tarhund was still at Pitkhanas's side, still pointing to the thing in the sky. It had come close enough to show a pair of stubby wings, though those did not flap.

"Say rather a ship," Tushratta told him. Campaigning had, of necessity, made him a keen observer. "Look there: you can see a row of holes along either side, like the oarports of a big rivership."

"Where are the oars, then?" Radus-piyama asked. Tushratta shrugged, having no more idea than the tubby priest.

"Who would sail a ship through the sky?" Pitkhanas whispered. "The gods?" But they had not spoken to him, nor, as he could see from the fear of the men around him, to anyone else.

The ship, if that was what it was, crushed half a plot of grain beneath it when it touched ground about a hundred paces from the king and his retinue. A gust of warm air blew in their faces. The thunder gradually died. Several of Pitkhanas's attendants—and several of the soldiers—moaned and hid their eyes with their arms, certain their end had come. Had it not been beneath his royal dignity, the king would have done the same.

Tushratta, though, was staring with interest at the marks painted along the sides of the ship below the holes that looked like oarports. "I wonder if that is writing," he said.

"It doesn't look like writing," Radus-piyama protested. All the Eighteen Cities of the Til-Barsip valley used the same script; most of its symbols still bore a strong resemblance to the objects they represented, though rebus-puns and specific grammatical determinants became more subtle and complex generation by generation.

The gate-captain said stubbornly, "There are more ways to write than ours, sir. I've fought against the hill-barbarians, and seen their villages. They use some of our signs for their language, but they have signs of their own, too, ones we don't have in the valley."

"Foreigners," Radus-piyama snorted. "I despise foreigners."

"So do I, but I have had to deal with them," Tushratta said. Foreigners were dangerous. They worshiped gods different from those of the Eighteen Cities, gods who spoke to them in their own unintelligible tongues. And if they spoke with angry voices, war was sure to follow.

A door swung open in the side of the ship. Pitkhanas felt his hearts pounding in his chest; excitement began to replace fear.

Perhaps they were all inside the sky ship, having come to Kussara for some reason of their own. What an honor! Almost everyone heard the gods scores of times each day, but they were rarely seen.

A ramp slid down from the open doorway. The king saw a stir of motion behind it . . . and his hopes of meeting the gods face-to-face were dashed, for the people emerging from the sky ship were the most foreign foreigners he had ever seen.

He wondered if they *were* people. The tallest of them was half a head shorter than the Kussaran average. Instead of blue-gray or green-gray skins, theirs were of earthy shades, rather like dried mud bricks. One was darker than that, and another almost golden. Some had black hair like the folk of the Eighteen Cities and all the other peoples they knew, but the heads of others were topped with brownish-yellow or even orange-red locks. One had hair on his face!

Their gear was an unfamiliar as their persons. They wore trousers of some heavy blue fabric, something like those of the hillmen but tight, not baggy. Despite the heat, they were all in tunics, dyed with colors Pitkhanas had never seen on cloth. They held a variety of curious implements.

"Some of those will be warriors," Tushratta said as the royal party drew nearer.

"How can you tell that?" the king asked. To him the square black box one of them was lifting to his face—no, *her* face; by the breasts it was a woman, though what was a woman doing in the company of voyagers?—was as alien as the long, thin contraptions of wood and metal borne by the hairy-faced stranger and a couple of others.

"The way they carry them, my lord," the gate-captain answered, pointing to the trio with the long things. "And the way they watch us—they have something of the soldier to them."

Once it was pointed out to him, Pitkhanas could also see what Tushratta had noticed. He would never have spotted it for himself, though. "How can you observe so clearly, with the voices of the gods mute?" he said. That awful silence inside his head left him bewildered.

Tushratta shrugged. "I have seen soldiers among us and among the barbarians in the hills, my lord. My eyes tell me how these men are like them. Were the gods speaking, they would say the same, surely."

The golden-skinned stranger, the smallest of them all, descended from the ramp of the sky ship and slowly approached Pitkhanas and his followers. He held his hands out before him. The gesture was plainly peaceful, but not fully reassuring to the king; the foreigners, he saw, had only one thumb on each hand.

A moment later, the breath hissed from his nostrils in anger. "They insult me—it is a woman they send as herald!" This foreigner was so slimly made that only up close did the difference become apparent.

Hearing Pitkhanas's exclamation, one of the soldiers stepped forward to seize the offender. But before he could lay hands on her, she touched a button on her belt and shot into the air, hovering overhead at five times the height of a man.

The soldier, the attendants, the king gaped in astonishment. The sky ship was entirely outside their experience, too alien for them to gauge the power it represented. This, though— "Do not try to injure them again, or they will destroy us all!" Zidantas shouted to Pitkhanas.

"Of course, sire," the king gasped, putting his palms to his temples in relief that his dead father's voice had returned to him. "Do not try to injure them again, or they will destroy us all!" he called to his men, adding, "Abase yourselves, so they can see your repentance."

Heedless of their robes and skirts, his followers went to their knees in the soft mud of the field. Pitkhanas himself bowed from the waist, holding his eyes to the ground.

One of the strangers on the ramp of the sky ship called out something. His voice sounded like any other man's, but the words were meaningless to the king.

A soft touch on his shoulder made him look up. The foreign woman was standing before him, her feet touching the ground once more. She gestured that he should straighten himself. When he had, she bowed in return, as deeply as he had. She pointed to his men and motioned for them to rise too.

"Stand up," he told them.

As they were doing so, the woman went to her knees in the mud herself, careless of her rich, strange clothing. She got up quickly, echoing Pitkhanas's command with a questioning note in her voice.

He corrected her, using the singular verb-form this time instead of the plural. She understood at once, pointing to one man and repeating the singular and then at several and using the plural. He smiled, dipped his head, and spread his arms wide to show that she was right.

It began there.

✧ ✧ ✧

"May I speak with you, my lord?" Radus-piyama asked.

"Yes," Pitkhanas said, a little wearily. He could feel in his belly what was about to come from the priest. Radus-piyama had been saying the same thing for many days now.

Nor did he surprise the king; with more passion than one would have expected to find in his small, round frame, he burst out, "My lord, I ask you again to expel the dirt-colored foreigners from Kussara. Tarhund has spoken to me once more, urging me to set this task upon you, lest they corrupt Kussara and all the Eighteen Cities."

"The god has given me no such command," Pitkhanas replied, as he had all the previous times Radus-piyama had asked him to get rid of the strangers. "If I hear it from his lips, be sure I shall obey. But until then these people from the far land called Terra are welcome here. They bring many fine gifts and things to trade." His hand went to his belt. The knife that hung there was a present from the Terrajin; it was made from a gray metal that was stronger than the best bronze and held a better edge.

"Come with me to the temple, then," Radus-piyama said. "Perhaps in his own home you will know the god's will more clearly."

Pitkhanas hesitated. Tarhund spoke to him: "Go with my priest to my house in Kussara. If I have further commands for you, you should best hear them there."

"The god bids me go with you to his house in Kussara," the king told Radus-piyama. "If he has further commands for me, I should best hear them there."

Radus-piyama showed his teeth in a delighted grin. "Splendid, my lord! Surely Tarhund will show you the proper course. I had begun to fear that you no longer heard the gods at all, that you had become as deaf to them as the Terrajin are."

Pitkhanas made an angry noise in the back of his throat. "Not agreeing with you, priest, does not leave one accursed. Tushratta, for instance, prospers, yet he is most intimate with the Terrajin of anyone in Kussara."

Radus-piyama had begun to cringe in the face of the king's temper, but at mention of the officer he recovered and gave a contemptuous sneer. "Choose someone else as an example, my lord, not Tushratta. The gods have gradually been forgetting him for years. Why, he told me once that without his eye-idol he rarely hears them. Aye, he is a fit one to associate with the foreigners. He even has to cast the bones to learn what course he should take."

"Well, so do we all, now and then," the king reproved. "They show us the will of the gods."

"Oh, no doubt, my lord," Radus-piyama said. "But no one I know of has to use the bones as often as Tushratta. If the gods spoke to him more, he would have fewer occasions to call on such less certain ways of learning what they wanted of him."

"He is a good soldier," Pitkhanas said stiffly. Radus-piyama, seeing that he could not sway the king on this question, bowed his head in acquiescence. "To the temple, then," Pitkhanas said.

As usual near midday, the central square of Kussara was jammed with people. Potters and smiths traded their wares for grain or beer. Rug-makers displayed their colorful products in the hope of attracting customers wealthy enough to afford them. "Clear, fresh river-water!" a hawker called. "No need to drink it muddy from the canal!" He had two large clay jugs slung over his shoulder on a carrying-pole. Harlots swayed boldly through the crowd. Slaves followed them with their eyes or dozed in whatever shade they could find. More gathered at a small shrine, offering a handful of meal or fruit to its god in exchange for advice.

Pitkhanas also saw a couple of Terrajin in the square. The foreigners still drew stares from peasants new in town and attracted small groups of curious children wherever they went, but most of Kussara had grown used to them in the past year-quarter. Their odd clothes and coloring, the metal boxes they carried that clicked or hummed, were accepted peculiarities now, like the feather-decked turbans of the men from the city of Hurma or the habit the people of the town of Yuzat had of spitting after every sentence.

The Terraj called Kastiyo was haggling with a carpenter over the price of a stool as the king and Radus-piyama came by. "I know wood is valuable because you have to trade to get it," the Terraj was saying, "but surely this silver ring is a good payment." Kastiyo fumbled for words and spoke slowly, but he made himself understood; after tiny Jingmaylin, he probably had the best grasp of Kussara's language.

The carpenter weighed the ring in his hand. "Is it enough?"

"Who—ah, whom—do you ask?" the Terraj said.

"Why, my god, of course: Kadashman, patron of woodworkers. He says the bargain is fair." The carpenter lifted the stool, gave it to Kastiyo, and held out his hand for the ring.

The foreigner passed it to him, but persisted, "How is it you know what the god says?"

"I hear him, naturally, just as I hear you; but you will go away and he is always with me." The carpenter looked as confused as the Terraj. Then he brightened. "Perhaps you do not know Kadashman because you are not a woodworker and he has no cause to speak to you. But surely your own gods talk to you in much the same way."

"I have never heard a god," Kastiyo said soberly. "None of my people has. That is why we is—*are*—so interested in learning more about those of Kussara."

The carpenter's jaw dropped at Kastiyo's admission.

"You see?" Radus-piyama said to Pitkhanas. "Out of their own mouths comes proof of their accursedness."

"They have gods, or a god," the king answered. "I have asked them that."

Radus-piyama laughed. "How could there be only one god? And even if there were, would he not speak to his people?"

To that Pitkhanas had no reply. He and the priest walked in silence to the temple of Tarhund, the Great House, as it was called: after the shrine of Tabal, the tallest and most splendid building in Kussara. The temples towered over the palace of the steward-king, who was merely the gods' servant. The huge rectangular tower of mud-brick rose in ever smaller stages to Tarhund's chamber at the very top.

Together, Pitkhanas and Radus-piyama climbed the temple's 316 steps—one for each day of the year. Under-priests bowed to their chief and to the king, who could see the surprise on their faces at his unscheduled visit.

"Is the god properly robed?" Radus-piyama called when they were nearly at the top.

The door to Tarhund's chambers swung open. A priest whose skin was gray with age emerged, his walk a slow hobble helped by a stick. "That he is, sir," he replied, "and pronounces himself greatly pleased with his new vestments, too."

"Excellent, Millawanda," Radus-piyama said. "Then he will give our king good advice about the Terrajin."

Millawanda's eyesight was beginning to fail, and he had not noticed Pitkhanas standing beside Radus-piyama. The king waved for him not to bother when he started a shaky bow. "Thank you, my lord. Yes, Tarhund has mentioned the foreigners to me. He says—"

"I will hear for myself what he says, thank you," Pitkhanas said. He stepped toward the god's chambers. When Radus-piyama started to follow him, he waved him back; he was still annoyed that the priest had feared Tarhund was not speaking to him any more.

Tarhund stood in his niche, an awesome figure, taller than a man. Torchlight played off the gold leaf that covered his face, hands, and feet, and off the gold and silver threads running through the thick, rich cloth of his new ankle-length robe. In his left hand he held the solid-gold globe of the sun, in his right black stormclouds.

The king suddenly saw with horror that he had forgotten to bring any offering when the god summoned him. He groveled on his belly before Tarhund as the lowliest of his slaves would have before him. Stripping off his sandals with their silver buckles, he set them on the table in front of the god next to the gifts of food, beer, and incense from the priests. "Accept these from this worm, your servant," he implored.

Tarhund's enormous eyes of polished jet gripped and held him. The god's words echoed in Pitkhanas's ears: "You may speak."

"Thank you, my master." Still on the floor, the king poured out everything that had happened since the coming of the Terrajin. "Are they stronger than you, lord, and your brother and sister gods? When we first met them, their powers and strangeness silenced your voices, and we despaired. You returned as we grew to know them, but now you speak in one way to your priests and in another to me. What shall I do? Shall I destroy the Terrajin, or order them to leave? Or shall I let them go on as they would, seeing that they have done no harm yet? Say on; let me know your will."

The god took so long answering that Pitkhanas trembled and felt his limbs grow weak with fear. If the strangers *were* mightier than the gods— But at last Tarhund replied, though his voice seemed faint and far away, almost a divine mumble: "Let them go on as they would. Seeing that they have done no harm yet, they will keep on behaving well."

Pitkhanas knocked his forehead against mud-brick. "I hear and obey, my master." He dared another question: "My lord, how is it that the Terrajin hear no gods of their own?"

Tarhund spoke again, but only in a gabble from which the king could understand nothing. Tears filled his eyes. He asked, "Is it as Radus-piyama says, that they are accursed?"

"No." This time the god's answer came quick, clear, and sharp. "Accursed men would work evil. They do not. Tell Radus-piyama to judge them by their deeds."

"Aye, my master." Sensing that the divine audience was over, Pitkhanas rose and left Tarhund's chamber. Radus-piyama and Millawanda were waiting expectantly outside. The king said, "The god has declared to me that the Terrajin are not accursed. Accursed men would work evil. They do not, and they will keep on behaving well. Judge them by their deeds. This is Tarhund's command to me, and mine to you. Hear it always."

The priests blinked in surprise. But their obedience to the king was as ingrained as their service to Tarhund. "I hear you and obey as I hear and obey the god," Radus-piyama acknowledged, Millawanda following him a moment later.

Satisfied, Pitkhanas started down the long stairway of Tarhund's Great House. Had he conveyed his orders in writing, the priests might somehow have found a way to bend them to their own desires. Now, though, his wishes and Tarhund's would both be ringing in their ears. They would give him no more trouble over the Terrajin.

The tape of Ramon Castillo dickering with the Kussaran woodworker ended. The video screen went dark. Helga Stein lifted her headphones, rubbed her ears. "Another one," she sighed.

"What was that?" Castillo was still wearing his 'phones, which muffled her words. "Sorry." He took them off quickly.

"It's nothing," Helga said wearily. She turned to Mei-lin, who had been going over the tape with them. "Did I understand that correctly—the native calling on a deity named Kadashman at the decision-point?"

"Oh yes," the linguist answered at once. To Ramon she added, "You do very well with the language. He had no trouble following you at all."

"Thanks," he said; Mei-lin was not one to give praise lightly. But he had to object, "'Calling on' isn't quite what happened. He asked a question, got an answer, and acted on it. Look for yourselves."

When he reached to rewind the tape, Helga stopped him. "Don't bother; all of us have seen the like dozens of times already. The local's eyes get faraway for a few seconds, or however long it takes, then he comes out of it and does whatever he does. But what does it *mean*?"

"'Eyes get faraway,'" Ramon said. "That's not a bad way to put it, I suppose, but to me it just looks as though the natives are listening."

"To what?" Helga flared, her face going pink. "And if you say 'a god,' I'll brain you with this table."

"It's bolted to the floor," he pointed out.

"*Ach!*" She snarled a guttural oath that was emphatically not Latin, stormed out of the workroom.

"You should not tease her so, Ramon," Mei-lin said quietly. Trouble rested on her usually calm features.

"I didn't mean to," the cultural anthropologist replied, still taken aback at Helga's outburst. "I simply have a very literal mind. I was going to suggest that if she had to hit me, the stool I bought would serve better."

Mei-lin smiled a dutiful smile. "At least you and Sybil have your stools and other artifacts you can put your hands on to study. All Helga and I can do is examine patterns, and none of the patterns here makes any sense that I can find."

"You shouldn't expect an alien species to think as we do."

"Spare me the tautology," the linguist snapped; her small sarcasm shocked Castillo much more than Helga's losing her temper. "For that matter, I sometimes wonder if these Kussarans think at all."

Ramon was shocked again, for she plainly meant it. "What about this, then?" he said, holding up the stool. It was a fine piece of craftsmanship, the legs beautifully fitted to the seat, the dyed-leather seatcover secured by bronze tacks to the wood below. "What about their walls and temples and houses, their cloth, their fields and canals, their writing, their language?"

"What about their language?" she retorted. "As I said, you've learned it quite well. You tell me how to say 'to think' in Kussaran."

"Why, it's—" Castillo began, and then stopped, his mouth hanging open. "*No sé,*" he admitted, startled back into Spanish, a slip he rarely made.

"I don't know either, or how to say 'to wonder' or 'to doubt' or 'to believe' or any other word that relates to cognition. And any Kussaran who says, 'I feel it in my bones' suffers from arthritis. Your 'literal mind' would make you a wild-eyed dreamer among these people, Ramon. How can they live without reflecting on life? Is it any wonder that Helga and I feel we're eating soup with a fork?"

"No-o," he said slowly. Then he laughed. "Maybe their precious gods do their thinking for them." The laugh was not one of amusement. The problem of the gods vexed him as much as it did Helga. Where she fretted over failing to understand the locals' psychological makeup, he had the feeling he was seeing their cultural patterns only through fog—superficial shapes were clear, but whatever was behind them was hidden in the mist.

Mei-lin failed to find his suggestion even sardonically amusing. "There are no gods. If there were, our instruments would have detected them."

"Telepathy," Ramon probed, hoping to get a rise out of her.

She did not take the bait. All she said was, "Assuming it exists (which I don't), telepathy from whom? The bugs we've scattered around show that the king, the ministers, the priests talk to their gods as often as the peasants do—oftener, if anything. There are no secret rulers, Ramon."

"I know." His shoulders sagged a little. "In fact, the Kussarans who hold the fewest one-sided conversations are some of the soldiers and merchants—and everyone else looks down on them on account of it."

"Still, if they were all as interested in us as Tushratta, our job would be ten times easier."

"True enough." The gate-captain spent as much of his time at the *Howells* as his duties allowed. "I wouldn't be surprised if he's around so much because we have no gods at all and give him someone to feel superior to."

"You're getting as cynical as Stan Jeffries," she said, which canceled his pleasure at her earlier compliment. Feeling his face grow hot, he rose and took a hasty leave.

As he passed the galley, he thought there was some god working, and probably a malignant one, for Jeffries himself called, "Hey, Ramon, come sit in for a while. Reiko's engine-watch just started, and we're short-handed."

The inevitable poker game had begun when the *Howells* was still in parking orbit around Terra. Castillo rarely played. Not only were the regulars some of his least favorite people on the ship, they also won money from him with great regularity.

He was about to decline again when he saw Tushratta was one of the players. The Kussarans gambled among themselves with dice, and the soldier was evidently picking up a new game. He looked rather uncomfortable in a Terran chair: it was too small for him and did not quite suit his proportions.

"What does he use to buy chips?" Ramon asked, sitting down across from the native.

João Gomes, one of the engine-room technicians, said a little too quickly, "Oh, we give them to him. He just plays for fun."

Castillo raised an eyebrow. The technician flushed. Jeffries said, "Why fight it, João? He can always ask Tushratta himself. All right, Ramon, he buys it with native goods: pots and bracelets and such. When he wins, we pay off with our own trinkets: a pair of scissors, a pocketknife, a flashlight." He stared defiantly at the anthropologist. "Want to make something of it?"

That sort of dealing was technically against regulations, but Ramon said, "I suppose not, provided I get photos of all the Kussaran artifacts you've gotten from him."

"Naturally," Jeffries agreed. Faces fell all around the table. Castillo hid a smile. Of course the poker players had been planning to hide the small trinkets and sell them for their own profit when they got home. It happened on every expedition that found intelligent natives, one way or another. The anthropologist was also certain he would not see everything.

Tushratta pointed at the deck of cards. "Deal," he said in heavily accented but understandable Latin.

To keep things simple for the beginner, they stuck with five-card stud and one joker. "A good skill game, anyway," Jeffries said. "You can tell where you stand. You play something like seven stud, low in the hole wild, and you don't know whether to shit or go blind."

Ramon lost a little, won a little, lost a little more. He might have done better if he hadn't been paying as much attention to Tushratta as to the cards—or, he told himself with characteristic honesty, he might not. As was to be expected among more experienced players, the native lost, but not too badly. His worst flaw, Castillo thought, was a tendency not to test bluffs—a problem the anthropologist had himself.

When Tushratta ran low on chips, he dug in his pouch and produced a cylinder seal, a beautifully carved piece of alabaster about the size of his little finger designed to be rolled on a mud tablet to show that he had written it. The stake Gomes gave him for it seemed honest.

A couple of hands later, the Kussaran and Jeffries got into an expensive one. Ramon was dealing, but folded after his third card. Everyone else dropped out on the next one, with varied mutters of disgust.

"Last card," the anthropologist said. He tossed them out.

Someone gave a low whistle. Jeffries, grinning, had four diamonds up. A couple of chairs away, Tushratta was sitting behind two pairs: treys and nines.

"Your bet, Tushratta," Ramon said. The Kussaran did, heavily.

"Ah, now we separate the sheep from the goats," Jeffries said, and raised. But the navigator's grin slipped when Tushratta raised back. "Oh, you bastard," he said in English. He shoved in more chips. "Call."

Looking smug, Tushratta showed his hole card: a third nine.

"Ouch," Jeffries said. "No wonder you bumped it up, with a full house." Castillo was not sure how much of that Tushratta understood, but the Kussaran knew he had won. He raked in the pot with both hands, started stacking the chips in neat piles of five in front of him.

Jeffries managed a sour grin. "Not that you needed the boat," he said to Tushratta. He turned over his own fifth card. It was a club.

Laughter erupted around the table. "That'll teach you, Stan," Gomes said. "Serves you right."

Tushratta knocked several piles of chips onto the floor. He made no move to pick them up; he was staring at Jeffries's hole card as though he did not believe his eyes. "You had nothing," he said.

The navigator had learned enough Kussaran to follow him. "A pair of sixes, actually."

Tushratta waved that away, as of no importance. He spoke slowly, sounding, Ramon thought, uncertain where his words were leading him: "You saw my two pairs showing. You could not beat them, but you kept betting. Why did you do that?"

"It was a bluff that didn't work," Jeffries answered. The key word came out in Latin. He turned to Castillo for help. "Explain it to him, Ramon; you're smoother with the lingo than I am."

"I'll try," the anthropologist said; he did not know the word for "bluff" either. Circumlocution, then: "You saw Jeffries's four diamonds. He wanted to make you drop by acting as though he had a flush. He did not know you had three nines. If you only had the two pairs that were up, you would lose against a flush, and so you might not bet against it. That was what he wanted—that is what bluff is."

"But he did not have a flush," Tushratta protested, almost in a wail.

"But he seemed to, did he not? Tell me, if you had only had the two pair, what would you have done when he raised?"

Tushratta pressed the heels of his hands against his eyes. He was silent for almost a full minute. At last he said, very low, "I would have folded."

Then he did retrieve the chips he had spilled, carefully re-stacked them. "I have had enough poker for today. What will you give me for these? There are many more here than I had yesterday."

They settled on a hand-held mirror, three butane lighters, and a hatchet. Ramon suspected the latter would be used on skulls, not timber. For the moment, though, Tushratta was anything but warlike. Still in the brown study that had gripped him since he won the hand from Jeffries, he took up his loot and left, talking to himself.

Castillo did not think he was communing with his mysterious gods; it sounded more like an internal argument. "But he didn't . . . But he seemed to . . . But he didn't . . . Bluff . . ."

"What's all that about?" Jeffries asked.

When the anthropologist translated, Gomes chuckled. "There you go, Stan, corrupting the natives." The navigator threw a chip at him.

"I laughed with the rest of them," Castillo said as he recounted the poker game in his cabin that night, "but looking back, I'm not sure João wasn't absolutely right. Katerina, I'd swear the idea of deceit had never crossed Tushratta's mind."

Frowning, the captain sat up in bed, her hair spilling softly over her bare shoulders. Her specialty was far removed from Ramon's, but she brought an incisive, highly logical mind to bear on any problem she faced. "Perhaps he was merely taken aback by a facet of the game that he had not thought of before."

"It went deeper than that," the anthropologist insisted. "He had to have the whole notion of bluffing defined for him, and it hit him hard. And as for thinking, Mei-lin has me wondering if the Kussarans really do."

"Really do what? Think? Don't be absurd, Ramon; of course they do. How could they have built this civilization of theirs without thinking?"

Castillo smiled. "Exactly what I said this afternoon." He repeated Mei-lin's argument for Katerina, finished, "As far as I can see, she has a point. Concepts can't exist in a culture without words to express them."

"Just so," the captain agreed. "As Marx said, it is not the consciousness of men that determines their existence, but rather their social existence determines their consciousness."

You and your Marx, Castillo thought fondly. He did not say that aloud, any more than he would have challenged Manolis Zakythinos's Orthodox Christianity. What he did say was, "Here's Kussara in front of us as evidence to the contrary."

"Only because we do not understand it," Katerina said firmly, her secular faith unshakable.

Still, Ramon could not deny the truth in her words, and admitted as much. "Their gods, for instance. We may not be able to see or hear them, but they're real as mud-brick to the Kussarans."

"All primitive peoples talk to their gods," Katerina said.

"But not all of them have gods who answer back," the anthropologist replied, "and the locals certainly listen to theirs. In fact, they—"

His voice trailed away as his mind began working furiously. Suddenly he leaned over and kissed Katerina with a fervor that had nothing to do with lovemaking. He sprang out of bed, hurrying over to the computer terminal at his desk. Katerina exclaimed in surprise and a little indignation. He paid no attention, which was a measure of his excitement.

It took him a while to find the database he needed; it was not one he used often. When at last he did, he could hardly keep his fingers from trembling as he punched in his search commands. He felt like shouting when the readout began flowing across the screen.

Instead, he whispered, "I know, I know."

"You're crazy," Helga Stein said flatly when Ramon finished his presentation at a hastily called meeting the next morning. It was, he thought with a giddiness brought on by lack of sleep, a hell of a thing for a psychologist to say, but then Latin was a blunt language. And glances round the table showed that most of their colleagues agreed with her. Only Mei-lin seemed to be withholding judgment.

"Argue with the evidence, not with me," he said. "As far as I can see, it all points toward the conclusion I've outlined: the Kussarans are not conscious beings."

"Oh, piffle, Ramon," Sybil Hussie said. "My old cat Bill back in Manchester is a conscious being."

Castillo wished he was someplace else; he was too shy to enjoy putting forth a strange idea to a hostile audience. But he was also too stubborn to fold up in the face of mockery. "No, Sybil," he said, "your old Bill, that mangy creature—I've met him, you know—isn't conscious, he's simply aware."

"Well, what is the difference?" Manolis Zakythinos asked.

"Or, better, how do you define consciousness?" George Davies put in.

"With Helga over there waiting to pounce on me, I won't even try. Let her do it."

The psychologist blinked when Ramon tossed the ball to her, rather like a prosecution witness unexpectedly summoned by the defense. Her answer came slowly: "Consciousness is an action, not an essence. It manipulates meanings in a metaphorical space in a way analogous to manipulating real objects in real space. In 'meanings' I include the mental image a conscious being holds of itself. Consciousness operates on whatever the conscious being is thinking about, choosing relevant elements and building patterns from them as experience has taught it. I must agree with Ramon, Sybil: your cat is not a conscious being. It is aware, but it is not aware of itself being aware. If you want a short definition, that is what consciousness is."

Davies was already sputtering protests. "It's bloody incomplete, is what it is. What about thinking? What about learning?"

Reluctantly, Helga said, "One does not have to be conscious to think." That turned a storm of protest against her that dwarfed anything Ramon had faced. She waited for it to end. "I will show you, then. Give me the next number in this sequence: one, four, seven, ten—"

"Thirteen." The response came instantly, from three or four people at once.

"How did you know that?" she asked them. "Were you aware of yourselves reasoning that you had to add three to the last number and then carrying out the addition? Or did you simply recognize the pattern and see what the next element *had* to be? From the speed with which you answered, I'd guess the latter—and where is the conscious thought there?"

Abrupt silence fell round the conference table. It was, Ramon thought, an introspective sort of silence; the very stuff of consciousness.

George Davies broke it. "You picked too simple an example, Helga. Give us something more complicated."

"What about typing, then, or playing a synthesizer? In both of them, the only way to perform well is to suppress your consciousness. The moment you start thinking about what you are doing instead of doing it, you will go wrong."

That—thoughtful—silence descended once more. When Helga spoke again, she looked first toward Castillo, grudging respect in her eyes. "You've convinced me of the possibility, at least, Ramon, or rather made me convince myself."

"I like it," Mei-lin said with sudden decision. "It fits. The total lack of mental imagery in the Kussaran language has been obvious to me for weeks. If the Kussarans are not conscious, they have no need for it."

"How do they get along without consciousness?" Davies challenged. "How can they function?"

"You do yourself, all the time," Ramon said. Before the biologist could object, he went on, "Think of a time when you were walking somewhere deep in a conversation with someone. Haven't you ever looked up and said, 'Oh, we're here,' with no memory of having crossed a street or two or gone by a park? Your consciousness was busy elsewhere, and the rest of your intelligence coped for you. Take away the part that was talking with your friend and you have what the Kussarans are like all the time. They get along just fine on pattern recognition and habit."

"And what happens when those aren't enough?" Davies asked, stabbing out a triumphant finger. "What happens when a Kussaran turns his old familiar corner and the smithy's caught fire and the whole street is burning? What then?"

Castillo licked his lips. He wished the question had not come so soon, or so bluntly. No help for it now, though. He took a deep breath and answered, "Then his gods tell him what to do."

He had not known so few people could make so much noise. For a moment he actually wondered if the attack was going to be physical; George Davies and his wife bounced halfway out of their chairs as they showered him with abuse. So did Helga, who shouted, "I was right the first time, Ramon—you *are* crazy." Even Mei-lin was shaking her head.

"Shouldn't you hear me out before you lock me up?" Castillo said tightly, almost shaking with anger.

"Why listen to more drivel?" Sybil Hussie said with a toss of her head.

"No, he is right," Zakythinos said. "Let him back up his claim, if he can. If he can convince such a, ah, skeptical audience, he deserves to be taken seriously."

"Thank you, Manolis." Ramon had himself under tight control again; railing back at them would not help. "Let me start out by saying that what I'm proposing isn't new; the idea was first put forward by Jaynes over a hundred and fifty years ago, back in the 1970s, for ancient Terran civilizations."

Helga rolled her eyes. "*Ach,* that period. Gods from outer space, is it?"

"Nothing like that," Castillo said, adding with some relish, "Jaynes was a psychologist, as a matter of fact."

"And what sort of gods, if I may make so bold as to ask, would a psychologist have?" Sybil said in a tone calculated to put Helga's teeth on edge as well as Ramon's.

The cultural anthropologist, though, had his answer ready:

"Auditory and sometimes visual hallucinations, generated by the right side of the brain—the part that deals with patterns and broad perceptions rather than logic and speech. They would not be recognized as hallucinations, you understand; they would be perceived as divine voices. And, operating with the stored-up experience of a person's life, they would find the behavior pattern that fit any new or unexpected situation, and tell him what to do. No conscious thought would be involved at all."

"It is drivel—" Sybil began, but her husband was shaking his head.

"I wonder," he said slowly. "Kussaran life is organized neurologically on the same general pattern as Terran; dissection of native corpses and work with domestic animals clearly shows that. There are differences, of course—brain functions, for instance, seem to be arranged fore-and-aft, rather than axially as with us."

"That's your province, of course," Ramon said. If George was arguing on those terms, he had to be considering the idea.

"These 'divine voices,'" Helga said. "They would be related to the voices schizophrenics hear?"

"Very closely," Castillo agreed. "But they would be normal and universal, not something to be resisted and feared by the vestiges of the conscious mind-pattern. And the threshold for producing them could be much lower than it is in schizophrenics—anything unusual or unfamiliar would touch them off. So could the sight of an idol; that may be why Kussara is so littered with them."

Davies sat straighter in his chair, a mannerism he had when he was coming up with an objection he thought telling. "What possible evolutionary advantage could there be to a way of life based on hallucination?"

"Social control," Ramon answered. "Remember, these aren't conscious beings we're talking about. They cannot visualize a connected series of activities, as we do. The only way for one of them weeding a field, say, to keep at his job all day long without someone standing over him, would be to keep hearing the voice of a chief or king saying over and over, 'Pull them out!' "

"Hmm," was all the biologist said.

"And since the king is part of the system too," Helga mused, "he would hear the voices of whatever high gods his culture had. They would be the only ones with enough authority to direct him."

"Perhaps of his ancestors also," Ramon said. "Remember that shrine by Pitkhanas's palace—it's a monument to his father, the last king of the city. There are offerings there, as to the gods."

"So there are." The psychologist paused, her eyes going big and round. "*Lieber Gott!* For such beings, belief in an afterlife would come naturally, and with reason. If a woman still heard, for instance, her mother's voice after her mother had died, would her mother not still be alive for her, in a very real sense of the word?"

"I hadn't even thought of that," Ramon whispered.

George Davies remained unconvinced. "If this style of perception is so wonderful, why aren't we all still blissfully unconscious?"

Castillo gave credit where it was due. "A remark of Katerina's put me on this track. Work it through. As a society gets increasingly complex, more and more layers of gods get added, to take care of all social levels. Look at Kussara now, with a separate deity for the carpenters and one for every other trade. Eventually, the system breaks down under its own weight.

"Writing helps, too. Writing makes a more complicated society possible, but it also weakens the authority of hallucinations. It's easier to evade a command when it's on a tablet in front of you that can be thrown away than when the king's voice sounds in your ear.

"And finally, the structure is geared to stability. It would have to come apart during war and crisis. What good are the commands of your gods if you're dealing with someone from a different culture, with a different language and strange gods of his own? Their orders would be as likely to get you killed as to save you.

"And in noticing how oddly the foreigners acted, you might account for it through something different inside them. And once you conceived of strangers with interior selves, you might suppose you had one too; the beginning of consciousness itself, maybe."

"There is evidence for that," Mei-lin broke in excitedly. "Remember, Ramon, how you remarked that the Kussarans who talked least with their gods were warriors and traders? They are exactly the ones with the greatest contact with foreigners—they may *be* on the very edge of becoming conscious beings."

All the anthropologist could do was nod. He felt dazed; the others were running with his hypothesis now in ways he had not imagined. And that, he thought, was as it should be. The concept was too big for any one man to claim it all.

Still sounding sour, George said, "I suppose we can work up experiments to test all this, if it's there." That was fitting too. If the idea had merit, it would come through inquiry unscathed or, better, refined and improved. If not, it did not deserve to survive.

Ramon could hardly wait to find out.

✧ ✧ ✧

Holding his hands to his ears against the thunder, Pitkhanas watched the sky ship shrink as it rose into the heavens. It was the size of his fist at arm's length . . . the size of a night-flitterer . . . a point of silver light . . . gone.

The king saw how the great weight of the ship had pressed the ground where it had rested down half a forearm's depth. The grain that had been under it, of course, was long dead; the fields around the spot were rank and untended.

The fertility-goddess Yarris addressed Pitkhanas reproachfully. "That is good cropland. Set peasants to restoring its former lushness."

"It shall be done, mistress," he murmured, and relayed the command to his ministers.

His dead father spoke up. "Have warriors out to guard the peasants, to keep the men of Maruwas down the river from raiding as they did when you were a boy. See you to it."

Pitkhanas turned to Tushratta. "Zidantas warns me to have warriors out to guard the peasants, to keep the men of Maruwas down the river from raiding as they did when I was a boy. See you to it."

Tushratta bowed. "I hear you and obey as I hear and obey the gods." The king walked off, never doubting his order would be obeyed.

In fact, Tushratta did not hear the gods at all any more. Their voices had been slowly fading in his ears since his campaigns against the hillmen, but he knew to the day when they had vanished for good. "*Bluff*," he said under his breath. He used the Terraj word; there was nothing like it in Kussaran.

He missed the gods terribly. He had even beseeched them to return—and how strange a thing was that, for the gods should always be present! Without their counsel, he felt naked and empty in the world.

But he went on. Indeed, he prospered. Perhaps the gods still listened to him, even if they would not speak. In the half-year since they left him, he had risen from gate-captain to warmaster of Kussara—the previous holder of that office having suddenly died. With himself he had brought certain other officers—young men who looked to him for guidance—and the detachments that obeyed them.

He would, he decided, follow Pitkhanas's command after all—but in his own fashion. As leader of the soldiers in the fields he would pick, hmm, Kushukh, who was not loyal to him . . . but who did head the palace guards.

How to get Kushukh to leave his post? "*Bluff*," Tushratta muttered again. He still used the concept haltingly, like a man trying to speak a foreign language he did not know well. Standing as it were to one side of himself, seeing himself saying or doing one thing but intending another, took an effort that made sweat spring out on his forehead.

He would say . . . would say . . . His fist clenched as the answer came. He would tell Kushukh that Pitkhanas had said no one else could do the job as well. That should suffice.

And then, leading his own picked men, Tushratta would go to the palace and . . . He looked ahead again, to Pitkhanas's corpse being dragged away; to himself wearing the royal robes and enjoying the royal treasures; to lying with Azzias, surely the most magnificent creature the gods ever made. Standing outside himself for those images was easy. He had looked at them many, many times already.

After he had become king, Kushukh would prove no problem; locked in the old ways, he would hear and obey Tushratta just as he heard and obeyed the gods, just as he had heard and obeyed Pitkhanas. Tushratta was less certain of his own backers. He had not explained to them what a *bluff* was, as Kastiyo had for him. But he had repeatedly used the thing-that-seemed-this-but-was-that; he could not have risen half so quickly otherwise. They were quick lads. They might well see what it meant on their own.

If so—if he could never be sure that what one of them told him, what one of them did, was not a *bluff*—how was he to rule? They would not follow his orders merely because it was he who gave them. Must he live all his days in fear? That made him look ahead in a way he did not like, to see himself cowering on the throne he had won.

But why did he have to be the one cowering? If one of his backers tried to move against him and failed (and he would not be such easy meat as Pitkhanas, for he would always be watchful), why not treat that one so harshly that the rest were made afraid? No matter then whether or not they had his commands always ringing in their heads. They would obey anyhow, out of terror.

Would that be enough?

Tushratta could hardly wait to find out.

I've written eleven novels set in the world of the Empire of Videssos, and I'm working on one more. This is one of the few pieces of short fiction I've done that seemed to fit in that world. It's set a few hundred years before the events in *The Videssos Cycle,* and well to the east of anything that happened there. Like a good deal of what happens in Videssos, it has a real historical model—in this case from the pages of that most accomplished historian, Anna Comnena.

A DIFFICULT UNDERTAKING

Ulror Raska's son stood in the topmost chamber of the tall watchtower, staring out to sea. Like most Halogai, he was tall and fair. His shining hair hung in a neat braid that reached the small of his back, but there was nothing effeminate about him. His face, hard-featured to begin with, had been battered further by close to half a century of carousing and war. His shoulders were wide as a bear's. Until a few weeks ago, his belly had bulged over his belt. It did not bulge any more. No one inside the fortress of Sotevag was fat any more.

Staring out to sea kept Ulror from thinking about the Videssian army that sat outside the walls of the fortress. The sea ran east forever from Sotevag. Looking at it, Ulror could feel free for a while, even if these southern waters were warm and blue, not like the chill, whitecap-flecked Bay of Haloga he had watched so often from the battlements of his own keep.

Of course, in the north the harvest failed one year in three. Even when it did not, there was never enough, nor enough land, not with every family running to three, five, seven sons. And so the Halogai hired on as mercenaries in Videssos and the lesser kingdoms, and manned ships and raided when they saw the chance.

Ulror smacked a big fist into his open palm in frustrated rage.

By the gods, this chance had looked so good! With Videssos convulsed as two rival emperors battled, the island of Kalavria, far from the Empire's heartland, should have been easy to seize, to make a place where Halogai could settle freely, could live without fear of starving—it even reminded Ulror of his own district of Namdalen, if one could imagine Namdalen without snow. Chieftains whose clans had hated each other for generations joined in building and crewing the fleet.

The really agonizing thing was that, over much of the island, the men from the far north had managed to establish themselves. And here sat Ulror, under siege. He would not have admitted it to any of his warriors, but he expected Sotevag to fall. If it did, the Videssians would probably mop up the rest of the Halogai, one band at a time.

Damn Kypros Zigabenos anyway!

Kypros Zigabenos stood staring up at the walls of Sotevag, wondering how he was ever going to take the stronghold. His agile mind leapt from one stratagem to another, and unfailingly found flaws in each. From where he stood, the fortress looked impregnable. That was unfortunate, for he was all too likely to lose his head if it held.

An eyebrow quirked in wry amusement. Zigabenos had a long, narrow, mobile face, the kind that made him look younger than his forty-five years. Hardly any gray showed in his dark hair or in the aristocratic fringe of beard tracing the angle of his jaw.

He brushed a speck of lint from the sleeve of his brocaded robe. To wear the rich samite in the field was the mark of a fop, but he did not care. What was the point to civilization, if not the luxuries it made possible?

That they destroyed the opportunity to create such things was to him reason enough to oppose the Halogai. As individuals he valued highly many of the northerners, Ulror not least among them. Certainly Ulror was a better man than the fool and the butcher who each claimed to be rightful Avtokrator of the Videssians.

Both those men had called on him for aid. In a way, he thanked the good god Phos for the arrival of the Halogai. Their attack gave him the perfect excuse to refuse to remove men from Kalavria to take part in internecine strife. He would have done the same, though, if the invaders had not come.

But either the butcher or the fool would be able to rule Videssos, once the internal foe was vanquished. The Empire had survived for close to a thousand years; it had seen bad Emperors before. The eternal bureaucracy, of which Zigabenos was proud to be a part, held Videssos together when leadership faltered.

And that was something the Halogai, were their chieftains the best leaders in the world—and some came close—could never do. They knew nothing of the fine art of shearing a flock without flaying it. Like any barbarians, if they wanted something they took it, never caring whether the taking ruined in a moment years of patient labor.

For that Zigabenos would fight them, all the while recognizing and admiring their courage, their steadiness, aye, even their wit. When Ulror had sensibly decided to stand siege at Sotevag rather than risk his outnumbered, harried troops in a last desperate battle, Zigabenos had shouted to him up there on the battlements: "If you're so great a general, come out and fight!"

Ulror had laughed like one of his heathen gods. "If you're so great a general, Videssian, make me!"

The taunt still rankled. Zigabenos had surrounded the fortress, had even succeeded in cutting it off from the sea. The Halogai would not escape that way, or gain fresh supplies. But the storerooms and cisterns of Sotevag were full, thanks in no small measure to Zigabenos's own exertions the year before. Now he could not afford to wait and starve Ulror out. While he sat in front of Sotevag with forces he had scraped together from all over Kalavria, the northerners could do as they would through the rest of the island. Yet trying to storm the fortress would be hellishly expensive in men and materiel.

Damn Ulror Raska's son, anyway!

"They're stirring around down there," said Flosi Wolf's-Pelt, brushing back from his eyes the thick locks of gray hair that gave him his sobriquet.

"Aye." Ulror's eyes narrowed in suspicion. Till now, Zigabenos had been content to let hunger do his work for him. Like many Videssian generals, he played at war as if it were a game where the object was to win while losing as few pieces as possible. Ulror despised that style of fighting; he craved the hot, clean certainty of battle.

But there was no denying that what Zigabenos did, he did very well. He had chivvied Ulror's Halogai halfway across Kalavria, never offering combat unless the odds were all in his favor. He had even forced Ulror to dance to his tune and go to earth here like a hunted fox.

So why was he changing his way of doing things, when it had worked so well for him up to now?

Ulror pondered that as he watched the Videssians deploy. They moved smartly and in unison, as if they were puppets animated by Zigabenos's will alone. The Halogai lacked that kind of discipline. Even as the horns called them to their places on the battlements of Sotevag castle, they came out of the great hall in straggling groups of different sizes, getting in each other's way as they went to their assigned sections of the wall.

A single man rode past the palisade the Videssians had thrown up around Sotevag. He came within easy bowshot of the walls, his head bare so the defenders could recognize him. Ulror's lip twisted. Zigabenos might favor a spineless kind of warfare, but he was no coward.

"Your last chance, northerners," the Videssian general called, speaking the Haloga tongue badly but understandably. He did not bellow, as Ulror would have; still, his voice carried. "Surrender the fortress and yield up your commander, and you common soldiers will not be harmed. By Phos I swear it." Zigabenos drew a circle over his breast—the sun sign, symbol of the Videssian god of good. "May Skotos drag me down to hell's ice if I lie."

Ulror and Flosi looked at each other. Zigabenos had offered those same terms at the start of the siege, and been answered with jeers. No commander, though, could be sure how his troops would stand up under privation. . . .

An arrow buried itself in the ground a couple of strides in front of Zigabenos's horse. The beast snorted and sidestepped. The Videssian general, a fine rider, brought it back under control. Even then, he did not retreat. Instead he asked, "Is that your final reply?"

"Aye!" the Halogai yelled, shaking their fists and brandishing weapons in defiance.

"No!" Ulror's great shout overrode the cries of his men. "I have another."

Zigabenos looked his way, suddenly alert. The northern chieftain understood that look, and knew the Videssian thought he was about to turn his coat. Rage ripped through him. "The gods curse you, Zigabenos!" he roared. "The only way you'll get me out of Sotevag is stinking in my coffin!"

His men raised a cheer; the more bravado a Haloga showed

in the face of danger, the more his fellows esteemed him. Zigabenos sat impassive until quiet returned. He gave Ulror the Videssian salute, his clenched fist over his heart. "That can be arranged," he said. He wheeled his horse, showing the northerners his back.

Ulror bit his lip. In his own cold-blooded way, Zigabenos had style.

The palisade drew near. The space between Zigabenos's shoulder blades stopped itching. If that had been he in the fortress, no enemy commander who exposed himself would have lived to return to his troops. The Haloga notion of honor struck him as singularly naive.

Yet the trip up to the walls had been worth making. When the northerners once fell into corruption, they wallowed in it. They reminded the Videssian general of a man never exposed to some childhood illness, who would die if he caught it as an adult. His own troops, no more brave or honorable than they had to be, would never sink to the depths of a Haloga who abandoned his code of conduct.

No time for such reverie now, he told himself reproachfully. The trumpeters and fifemen were waiting for his signal. He nodded. As the martial music rang out, his command echoed it: "Forward the palisade!"

Half the Videssian soldiers picked up the stakes and brush surrounding the castle of Sotevag and moved ahead, toward the fortress walls. The rest of the men—the better archers in the army—followed close behind, their bows drawn.

The Halogai began shooting to harass the advance. The range was long and the stuff of the palisade gave some protection. Nevertheless, here and there a man dropped. The dead lay where they had fallen; the wounded were dragged to the rear, where the priests would tend them with healing magic.

Zigabenos gave a quiet order. The musicians sent it to the troops, who halted and began emplacing the palisade once more. "Give them a volley!" the general said. "From now on, they keep their heads down!"

The thrum of hundreds of bowstrings released together was the only pleasant note in the cacophony of war. Arrows hissed toward Sotevag. The Halogai dove for cover. Shouts of fury and screams showed that not all reached it.

One by one, the northerners reappeared, some standing tall and proud, others peering over the top of the battlements. Zigabenos gauged the moment. "Another!" he shouted.

The Halogai vanished again. "Marksmen only, from now on," the general commanded. "If you see a good target, shoot at it. Try not to waste arrows, though."

He had expected a furious answering fire from the besieged warriors, but it did not come. They were shooting back, but picking their marks as carefully as their foes. That made him want to grind his teeth. Ulror had learned too much, fighting against Videssians. Most of his countrymen would never have thought about saving arrows for a later need.

Zigabenos shook his head in reluctant admiration. He sighed, regretting the need to kill such a man. A race with the restless energy of the Halogai might go far, allied to Videssian canniness. Unfortunately, he knew the first place it would head for: Videssos the city, the great imperial capital. No lesser goal could sate such a folk. And so he would do his duty, and try to make sure it never came into being.

He waved. An aide appeared at his elbow. "Sir?"

"Muster the woodworkers. The time has come to build engines."

"I grow to hate the sounds of carpentry," Ulror said. The Videssian artisans were a quarter-mile away, out of reach of any weapons from inside Sotevag, but there were so many of them and they were chewing up so much timber that the noise of saw, hammer, axe, and adze was always present in the fortress.

"Not I," Flosi Wolf's-Pelt said.

"Eh? Why not?" Ulror looked at his companion in surprise.

"When the building noises stop, they'll be finished. Then they'll start using their toys."

"Oh. Aye." Ulror managed a laugh, as any northerner should in the face of danger, but even he could hear how grim it sounded. Frustrated, he shook his head until his braid switched like a horse's tail. "By the gods, I'd give two thumb's-widths off my prong for a way to strike at those accursed siege engines."

"A sally?" Flosi's eyes lit at the prospect; his hand went to the hilt of his sword.

"No," Ulror said reluctantly. "Look how openly the carpenters are working out there. See the cover off to the flanks? Zigabenos wants to tempt us into the open, so he can slaughter us at his leisure. I'll not give him his triumph so cheap."

Flosi grunted. "There's no honor in such tricks."

"True, but they work all the same." Ulror had lost too many men to ambushes to doubt that. Such tactics were of a piece with the rest of the way the Videssians made war, seeking victory at the least cost to themselves. To counter them, a man had to fight the same way, regardless of how much it went against his grain.

Flosi, though, still wanted to strike a blow at the enemy. "What of using sorcery on their engines?"

That had not occurred to Ulror. Battle magic almost always failed; in the heat of combat, men's emotions flamed strong enough to weaken the bite of spells. Only the most powerful wizards went to war, save as healers or diviners. And the one Haloga with Ulror who knew something of magic, Kolskegg Cheese-Curd, had a better reputation as tosspot than sorcerer.

When Ulror said as much to Flosi, his comrade snorted in disgust. "What do we lose by trying? If you don't aim to fight, why not throw yourself off the wall and have done?"

"I aim to fight," Ulror growled, pointing down into the outer ward, where men chopped logs and filled barrels with earth to build makeshift barriers if the walls should be breached.

"Defense," Flosi said scornfully.

Nettled, Ulror opened his mouth to snarl back, but stopped with his angry words still unspoken. How could he blame Flosi for wanting to hurt the Videssians? He wanted to himself. And who could say? Maybe Kolskegg could take the imperials by surprise. Ulror made for the stairwell, to track down the wizard. Behind him, Flosi nodded in satisfaction.

Kolskegg Cheese-Curd was a big, pockmarked man who, like Ulror, had been fat before the siege of Sotevag began. Now his skin was limp and saggy, like a deflated bladder. Something seemed to have gone out of his spirit, too, when the castle's ale casks ran dry. Living on well-water was torment for him.

His eyes widened in alarm as Ulror explained what he required. "You must be mad!" he burst out. "A hundredth part of such a magic would burn out my brain!"

"No great loss, that," Ulror growled. "How do you have the nerve to call yourself a wizard? What *are* you good for, anyway?"

"My skill at divination is not of the worst." Kolskegg eyed Ulror warily, as if wondering how much trouble that admission would get him into.

"The very thing!" the Haloga chieftain said, slapping him on the back. Kolskegg beamed, until Ulror went on, "Divine me a way to slip out of Zigabenos's clutches."

"But—my art is tyromancy," Kolskegg quavered, "reading the future in the patterns curds make as they separate out in new cheese. Where can I get milk?"

"One of the last two jennies foaled the other day. The colt went into the stewpot, of course, but we still need the mother for hauling wood and earth. She may not have dried up yet."

"Ass's milk?" Kolskegg's lip curled. Even poor sorcerers had standards.

"What better, for you?" Ulror said brutally. Losing patience, he grabbed Kolskegg by the arm and half-led, half-dragged him down to the ward, where the donkey was dragging a log up to the wall. The beast's ribs showed through its mangy coat; it was plainly on its last legs. It gave a sad bray as Kolskegg squeezed a few squirts of milk into a bowl.

"Butcher it," Ulror told his men; if they waited any longer, no meat would be left on those sad bones.

Seeming more confident once he had sniffed and tasted the milk, Kolskegg took Ulror back to his pack, which lay on top of his straw pallet. He rummaged in it until he found a small packet of whitish powder. "Rennet," he explained, "made from the stomach lining of young calves."

"Just get on with it," Ulror said, faintly revolted.

Kolskegg sat cross-legged in the dry rushes on the floor. He began a low, whining chant, repeating the same phrase over and over. Ulror had seen other wizards act thus, to heighten their concentration. His regard for Kolskegg went up a notch.

He noticed Kolskegg was not blinking. All the sorcerer's attention focused on the chipped earthenware bowl in front of him. Ulror tried to find meaning in the swirling pattern of emerging curds as the rennet coagulated the milk, but saw nothing there he could read.

Kolskegg stiffened. White showed round the irises of his staring blue eyes. "A coffin!" he said hoarsely. "A coffin and the stench of the grave. Only through a death is there escape." His eyes rolled up altogether and he slumped over in a faint.

Ulror's lips skinned back from his teeth in a humorless grin. Too well he remembered his roar of defiance to Zigabenos. The gods had a habit of listening to a man when he least wanted them to.

"I wish Skotos would drag that heathen down to the ice of hell now, instead of waiting for him to live out his span of days," Kypros Zigabenos said furiously, watching from the Videssian lines as Ulror dashed along the battlements of Sotevag, his blond braid flapping behind him. The barbarian ignored the hail of stones and darts with which the imperials were pounding the fortress. Buoyed by his spirit, the defenders stayed on the walls, shooting back with what they had and rushing to repair the damage from the bombardment.

Then, because he was an honest man—not always an advantage in Videssian service—Zigabenos felt he had to add, "But oh, he is a brave one."

"Sir?" said the servant who fetched him a cup of wine.

"Eh? Nothing." Zigabenos was irritated that anyone should have heard his mumblings. Still, he wished with all his heart for one of the Videssian missiles to dash out Ulror's brains.

Quite simply, the man was too good. Aye, he had let himself be penned here, but only as an alternative to worse. If ever he escaped, he might yet find a way to rally the Halogai and rape Kalavria away from the Empire. He was worth an army to the northerners, just as Zigabenos, without false modesty, assessed his own similar value to Videssos.

He snapped his fingers in happy inspiration. At his shout, a runner came trotting up. He sent the man over to the stone-throwers and ballistae. One by one, the siege engines stopped. Zigabenos took up a white-painted shield—a badge of truce or parley—and walked toward Sotevag's battered walls.

"Ulror!" he called. "Ulror, will you speak with me?"

After a minute or so, the northern chieftain shouted back, "Aye, if you'll talk so my men understand us."

"As you wish," Zigabenos said in the Haloga tongue. Another ploy wasted; he had deliberately used Videssian before to try to make Ulror's warriors doubt their leader. Very well, let them hear: "Come out of the fortress and I will still guarantee all your lives. And I pledge better for you, Ulror: a fine mansion, with a stipend to support a large band of retainers."

"And where will this fine mansion be? Here on the island?"

"You deserve better than this backwater, Ulror. What do you say to a residence at the capital, Videssos the city?"

Ulror was silent so long, Zigabenos's hopes began to rise. At last the northerner asked, "Will you give me a day's leave to think on it?"

"No," Zigabenos said at once. "You'll only use it to strengthen your defenses. Give me your answer."

Ulror boomed laughter. "Oh, how I wish you were a fool. I

think I will decline your gracious invitation. With civil war in the Empire, even if by some mischance I reached the capital alive, I'd last about as long as a lobster's green shell when you throw him in the boiling pot."

The Videssian general felt like snarling, but his face never showed it. "You have my personal guarantee of your safety," he said.

"Aye, and that's good as silver so long as I'm on the island, and worth nothing soon as I sail west, since both Emperors hate you for not sending 'em men."

Too good by half, Zigabenos thought. Without another word, he turned and walked away. But Ulror was still in the lobster pot. It remained only to bring him to the boil.

The cat crawled forward, its timber sides and roof covered with green hides to keep them from being burned. Fire arrows streaked from the Videssian archers toward bales of straw the Halogai had hung on the side of the wall to deaden the impact of the battering ram the cat protected. The northerners dumped pails of water and sewage, snuffing out the flames before they took hold.

Then the imperials manhandled their shed up to the base of the wall. The Halogai pelted it with boulders and spears, trying to create rifts in the hide covering through which boiling water and red-hot sand might find their way.

"There!" Ulror cried, pointing, and another stone thudded home. The din was indescribable. Through it all, though, Ulror heard the commands of the Videssian underofficer in the cat, each order delivered as calmly as if on parade.

He could not fathom that kind of courage. The hazards of the field—aye, he had their measure. This siege was harder, but here he had had no good choice. But how men could hold their wits about them advancing turtle-fashion into danger, knowing they would die if their shell was broken, was beyond him.

Like so many Halogai, he scorned the discipline Videssos imposed on her troops; no free man would let himself be used so. Now he saw what such training was worth. His own men, he knew, would have broken under the punishment the imperials were taking. Yet they stolidly labored on.

Rather than hearing the ram strike the wall, Ulror felt it through the soles of his feet. Chains rattled in the cat below as the Videssians drew their great iron-faced log back for another stroke. The wall shook again. Ulror could see the spirit oozing out of his warriors. They had gaily faced the chance of arrow or flying stone, but this methodical pounding stole the manhood from them. He wondered if he could make them fight in the breach. He had no great hope of it.

Just when he was telling himself he should have made what terms he could with Zigabenos, shrieks replaced the stream of orders coming from the cat. One of the smoking cauldrons the Halogai tipped down on it had found a breach of its own.

When the ram's rhythm missed a beat, the northerners above seemed to realize their doom was not inevitable after all. Ulror bellowed encouragement to them. They redoubled their efforts, working like men possessed.

Three soldiers grunted to lift a huge stone to a crenelation, then shoved it out and down onto the cat. The shed's sloping roof and thick sides had sent other boulders bouncing aside, but this one struck square on the midline. Along with the crash, Ulror heard a metallic snap as a chain holding the ram to the roof of the cat broke. Shouts of pain from the imperials it injured in its fall and curses from the rest were as sweet music in his ears.

Like a wounded animal, the shed began to limp away. Videssian shieldsmen stood at its open front, where the ram had swung. They protected their comrades from the missiles the Halogai rained on them. Whenever one was shot, another took his place. That was bravery Ulror could grasp. Even as he let fly at them, he hoped they would safely reach their own line. Zigabenos, he thought, would want them to fall to the arrows like so many quail. That was sensible, but he did not have the stomach for it.

The Halogai danced with joy as the cat withdrew, their heavy boots clumping on the stone walkways and stairs. "A victory," Flosi Wolf's-Pelt said.

"Aye, or so the lads think, anyway," Ulror answered quietly. "Well, that's worth something of itself, I suppose. It'll take their minds off the stale donkey tripes—the last of them left—and the handful of barley meal they'll be eating tonight."

"We hurt the cat," Flosi protested.

"So we did, and they hurt the wall. Which do you think the easier to repair?"

Flosi grimaced and turned away.

High overhead, a seagull screeched. Ulror envied the bird its freedom. Not too many gulls came near Sotevag any more. If they did, the Halogai shot them and ate them. Their flesh was tough and salty and tasted strongly of fish, but hungry men did not care. Ulror had stopped asking about the meat that went into the stewpots. He did know he had seen fewer rats lately.

Watching the gull wheel in the sky and glide away was suddenly more than Ulror could bear. He slammed his fist against the stone of the battlement, cursed at the pain. Ignoring Flosi's startled look, he rushed down the stairs and into the outer ward.

Kolskegg Cheese-Curd had been making what looked like a mousetrap out of sticks and leather thongs. He put the contraption aside as his chieftain bore down on him, asked warily, "Is there something I might do for you?"

"Aye, there is." Ulror hauled his reluctant wizard to his feet; his belly might be gone, but he still kept his bull strength. Paying no attention to the protests Kolskegg yammered, he dragged him through the gatehouse into the keep, and on into the chamber he had taken for himself.

The goosefeather mattress had belonged to the Videssian who once commanded here. So did the silk coverlet atop it, now sadly stained. Ulror flopped down on the bed with a sigh of relief, waved Kolskegg to a chair whose delicacy proclaimed it also to be imperial work.

Once Kolskegg had made himself comfortable, Ulror came to the point with his usual directness. "That was a true divination you gave me—that the only way I would leave Sotevag would be in my coffin?"

The wizard licked his lips, but had to answer, "Aye, it was."

To his surprise, his chieftain grunted in satisfaction. "Good. If Zigabenos's priests read the omens, they should learn the same, not so?"

"Aye." Kolskegg had been a warrior long enough to know not to volunteer more than he was asked.

"All right, then," Ulror said. "Give me a spell to turn me to the seeming of a corpse, stench and all, to let me get away. Then when I'm outside, you can take it off, or arrange in the first place for it to last only so long, or whatever you think best." He nodded, pleased at his own ingenuity.

The wizard's face, though, went chalky white. "Have mercy!" he cried. "I am nothing but a miserable diviner. Why do you set me tasks to strain the powers of the greatest adepts? I cannot do this; he who trifles with death in magic courts it."

"You are the only sorcerer I have," Ulror said implacably. "And you will do it."

"I cannot." As a weak man will, Kolskegg sounded querulous in his insistence.

"You will," Ulror told him. "If you do not, Sotevag will surely fall. And if the Videssians take me alive, I will tell them you worked your charms through their dark god Skotos. Once they believe that, you will wish you died fighting. No demon could serve you worse than their inquisitors."

Kolskegg shivered, for Ulror was right. As dualists, the imperials hated their deity's evil rival and dealt with legendary savagery with anyone who dared revere him. "You would not—" the wizard began, and stopped in despair. Ulror would.

The Haloga commander said nothing more. He waited, bending Kolskegg to his will with silence. Under his unwinking stare, the wizard's resolve melted like snow in springtime. "I will try," he said at last, very low. "Maybe at midnight, a spell I know might serve. It is, after all, only a seeming you seek."

He spoke more to reassure himself than for any other reason, Ulror judged. That was all right. "Midnight it is," Ulror said briskly. "I'll see you here then." He did not put any special warning in his voice. He had done his job properly, and did not need to.

The wizard returned at the hour he had set, stumbling in the darkness as he approached Ulror's door. Inside, the chieftain had a tallow dip lit. Not many lights burned in Sotevag at night; tallow and olive oil could be eaten, if a man was hungry enough.

Even in the red, flickering light, Kolskegg looked pale. "I wish I had a beaker of ale," he muttered under his breath. He fumbled in his pouch, finally digging out a chain that held a black stone with white veins. "An onyx," he said, hanging it round Ulror's neck. "The stone for stirring up terrible fantasms."

"Get on with it," Ulror said. He spoke more harshly than he had intended; Kolskegg's nervousness was catching.

The wizard cast a powder into the flame of the tallow dip, which flared a ghastly green. Kolskegg began a slow, rhymeless chant full of assonances. The stone he had set on Ulror's breast grew cold, so he could feel its chill through his tunic. He could also feel the little hairs at the nape of his neck prickling upright.

The chant droned on. Kolskegg began singing faster and faster, as if he wanted to get through the incantation as quickly as he could. In the end, his own fear of what he was doing undid him. His tongue slipped, so that when he meant to intone "thee," "me" came out instead.

Had he been wearing the onyx, the spell might have possessed him as he intended it to possess Ulror: as an unpleasant but impermanent illusion. But the Holga chieftain had the magical focus, not his wizard. Before Kolskegg could do more than gasp in horror at his blunder, the transformation struck him.

Ulror gagged on the stench that filled his chamber. He staggered outside and was sick against the wall of the keep. Several of his warriors rushed over, asking if he was all right.

One had the wit to offer a bucket of water. He rinsed his mouth, spat, rinsed again. The sour taste remained. His men began exclaiming over the graveyard reek that followed him into the inner ward.

"You will find a lich—not a fresh one—inside," he told them. "Treat poor Kolskegg with respect; he showed more courage dying at my order than ever he did in life."

As was his privilege, even after midnight, the blue-robed priest burst past Zigabenos's bodyguard and into the tent of the Videssian general. "Sorcery!" he cried, the firelight gleaming from his shaved pate. "Sorcery most foul!"

"Huh?" Zigabenos sat up with a start. He was glad he'd sent the kitchen wench back to her tavern instead of keeping her for the night. He enjoyed his vices, but had learned long since not to flaunt them.

His wits returned with their usual rapidity. "Say what you mean, Bonosos. Are the Halogai assailing us with magic?"

"Eh? No, your illustriousness. But they play at wizardry even so, a wizardry that stinks of Skotos." The priest spat on the ground in rejection of the wicked god, his faith's eternal enemy.

"The conjuration was not aimed against us? You are certain of that?"

"I am," Bonosos said reluctantly. "Yet it was strong, and of a malefic nature. It was not undertaken to curry favor with us."

"I hardly expected it would be," Zigabenos said; he had no intention of letting a priest out-irony him. "Still, so long as they do not send a blast our way, the Halogai are welcome to play at whatever they wish. Maybe it will go awry and eat them up, and save us the trouble."

"May the lord of the great and good mind hear and heed your prayer," Bonosos said, drawing Phos's sun sign on his breast.

Zigabenos did the same; his own piety, though he did not let it interfere with whatever he had to do, ran deep. After a moment he said, "Bonosos, I hope you had a reason for disturbing my rest, other than merely to tell me the Halogai have some fribbling spell afoot."

"Hardly fribbling." Bonosos's glare was wasted; to Zigabenos, he was only a silhouette in the doorway. But there was no mistaking the abhorrence in the priest's voice as he went on, "The conjuration smacked of necromancy."

"Necromancy!" Zigabenos exclaimed, startled. "You must be mistaken."

Bonosos bowed. "Good evening, sir. I tell the truth. If you do not care to hear it, that is none of my affair." He spun on his heel and stalked away.

Stiff-necked old bastard, the Videssian general thought as he settled back under his silk coverlet, and mad as a loon besides. The Halogai inside Sotevag had too many other things to worry about to bother with corpse-raising or anything like it.

Or did they? Zigabenos suddenly remembered Ulror's howl of defiance from the battlements. The northerner must have taken that for prophecy as well as brag. Zigabenos laughed out loud, admiring Ulror's ingenuity in trying to get around his own oath. Unfortunately for the Haloga, he thought, there was no way around it. The northerners fought bravely and, under Ulror's command, resourcefully. Against siege engines, however, bravery and resource only counted for so much. In a week, maybe less, maybe a day or two more, he would be inside Sotevag. And then Ulror's boast would be fulfilled in the most literal way imaginable.

Still chuckling, Zigabenos rolled over and went back to sleep.

After a sleepless night, Ulror stared out to sea, watching the rising sun turn the water to a flaming sheet of molten gold and silver. He regretted Kolskegg's death, and regretted even more that it had been in vain. Now, impaled on his own rash words, he found nothing else to do but face the prospect of dying.

He did not fear death. Few Halogai did; they lived too close to it, both at home and in battle on distant shores. But he bitterly regretted the waste. If only he could get free, rally the Halogai all across Kalavria . . . In pursuing him, Zigabenos really had concentrated his own forces too much—provided the northerners moved against him in unison. If not, he would go on dealing with them piecemeal, methodical as a cordwainer turning out boots.

Ulror ground his teeth. All he, all any of the Halogai, wanted was a steading big enough for a free man to live on and to pass down to his sons; a good northern woman to wife, with perhaps two or three of these island wenches to keep a bed warm of nights; a chance to enjoy the luxuries the imperials took for granted: wine grown on a man's own holding, a bathtub, wheat bread instead of loaves of rye or oats. If the Empire's god would grant him so much, he might even give worship to Phos along with his own somber deities.

Unless Zigabenos made a mistake, though, none of that would happen. And Zigabenos was not in the habit of making mistakes.

As had happened a few days before, a gull gave its raucous call high over Sotevag. This time the frustration was more than the Haloga chieftain could bear. Without conscious thought, in one smooth motion he reached over his shoulder for an arrow, set it to his bow, and let fly. His rage lent power to the shot. The bird's cry abruptly cut off. It fell with a thud to the dirt of the outer ward. Ulror stared malevolently at the dead gull—miserable, stinking thing, he thought.

"Good shooting," one of his warriors called, ambling over to pick up the bird and carry it off to be cooked.

"Hold!" Ulror shouted suddenly, rushing for a stairway. "That seagull's mine!" The warrior gaped at him, certain he had lost his mind.

An orderly came dashing into the tent, interrupting Zigabenos's breakfast. Paying no attention to the Videssian general's glare, he said breathlessly, "Sir, there's sign of truce over the main gatehouse of Sotevag!"

Zigabenos stood up so quickly that he upset the folding table in front of him. He ignored his valet's squawk of distress and hurried out after the orderly to see this wonder for himself.

It was true. Above the gate, a white shield hung on a spear. "They turned coward at the end," the orderly said, "when they saw what our engines were about to do to them."

"I wonder," Zigabenos said. It was not like Ulror to give in so tamely. What sort of scheme could the Haloga chieftain have come up with? No one had spied him on the walls for several days now. Was he planning a last desperate sally, hoping to slay Zigabenos and throw the Videssian army into confusion?

To forestall that, the general approached the fortress in the midst of a squadron of shieldsmen, enough to get him out of danger no matter what the Halogai tried. When he was within hailing distance, he called, "Well, Ulror? What have you to say to me?"

But it was not Ulror who came to stand by the northerners' truce shield. A raw-boned Haloga with gray hair took that place instead.

He stared down at Zigabenos in silence for a long moment, then asked, "Have you honor, imperial?"

Zigabenos shrugged. "If you need the question, would you trust the answer?"

A harsh chuckle. "Summat to that. All right, be it so. You'll do what you promised before, let the rest of us go if we yield you Sotevag and bring out Ulror?"

The Videssian general had all he could do not to cry out for joy. In exchange for Ulror, he was willing, nay eager, to let a few hundred barbarians of no special importance keep their lives. He was too old a hand, however, to let his excitement show. After a suitable pause, he demanded, "Show me Ulror now, so I may see you have him prisoner."

"I cannot," the Haloga said.

Zigabenos turned to leave. "I am not a child, for you to play tricks on."

"He is dead," the northerner replied, and Zigabenos stopped. The northerner went on, "He took a fever a week ago, but fought on with it, as any true man would. He died four nights past. Now that he is gone, we ask ourselves why we must sell our lives dear, and find no answer."

"You need not, of course," Zigabenos said at once. No wonder the Halogai had tried necromancy, he thought. But Ulror was tricksy, and who knew how far he would go to lend verisimilitude to a ploy? The Videssian general declared, "I will abide by my terms, save that I add one condition: as each man of yours leaves Sotevag, my wizards will examine him, to be sure he is not Ulror in sorcerous disguise."

The Haloga spokesman spat. "Do what you please. Victors always do. But I have told you you will not find him among them."

They haggled over details for the next hour. Zigabenos was lenient. Why not, with the one great northern chieftain gone and Sotevag about to return to imperial hands?

When noon came, the long-shut fortress gates swung open. As had been agreed, the Halogai came out two by two, in armor and carrying their weapons. They were all skinny, and many wounded. They could not help looking out toward the imperial lines; if Zigabenos wanted to betray them, he could. He did not want to. He expected to fight their countrymen again, and fear of a broken truce would only lead the Halogai to fight to the end from then on.

The Videssian general stood outside the gates with a pair of priests. The blue-robes had anointed their eyes with a paste made from the gall of a male cat and the fat of a pure white hen, an ointment that let them pierce illusion. They examined each emerging northerner, ready to cry out if they spied Ulror behind a veil of magic.

The gray-haired Haloga with whom Zigabenos had dickered came limping out. The general gave him a formal salute. He had developed some respect for this Flosi Wolf's-Pelt, for his spirit, his courage, and his blunt honesty. What sprang from those, though, was easy to anticipate. When the time came, he knew he would beat Flosi. With Ulror he had never been sure.

Flosi looked through him as if he did not exist.

The moment Zigabenos had been waiting for finally came. A dozen Halogai dragged a rough-built coffin behind them on a sledge. "Ulror is inside?" the general asked one of them.

"Aye," the man said.

"Check it," Zigabenos snapped to the priests who flanked him.

They peered at the coffin with their sorcerously enhanced vision. "That is truly Ulror Raska's son within," Bonosos declared.

So Ulror had been a prophet after all, Zigabenos thought, and look what it gained him. Something else occurred to the Videssian general. "Is the rascal dead?"

Bonosos frowned. "A spell to ascertain that will take some little time to prepare, and in any case I mislike touching on death with my sorcery—see how such an unholy effort profited the northerner here. I suggest you make your own examination to satisfy yourself. If he is four days dead, you will know it."

"Something in the air, you mean. Yes, I take your point." Zigabenos chuckled. He added, "Who would expect such plain sense from a priest?" Bonosos's frown turned to scowl. The Videssian general approached the coffin. "Pry up the top of the lid, you," he told one of the northerners.

Shrugging, the Haloga drew his sword and used it to lever up the coffin lid; nails squealed in protest. Through the narrow opening Zigabenos saw Ulror's face, pale and thin and still. The death smell welled out, almost thick enough to slice. "Shut it," Zigabenos said, coughing. He drew Phos's sun-circle on his breast, then saluted the coffin with the same formality he had offered Flosi.

Seeing how exhausted the pallbearers were, Zigabenos said kindly, "If you like, we will bury him for you here."

The Halogai drew themselves up; even in privation, they were proud men. One said, "I thank you, but we care for our own."

"As you wish." Zigabenos waved them on.

When the last northerner had left Sotevag castle, the general sent in a crack platoon to search it from top to bottom. No matter what the priests said, no matter what he had seen and smelled, maybe Ulror had found a way to stay behind and then drop over the walls and escape. Zigabenos did not see how, but he took no chances where Ulror was concerned.

Only when the platoon's lieutenant reported back to him that Sotevag was empty of life did he truly begin to believe he had won.

Hungry, worn, and battered as they were, the Halogai traveled slowly. Still, Kalavria was not a large island; by the end of the second day after they left Sotevag, they were at the end of the central uplands. They camped next to a swift, cool stream.

As the warriors shared the half-ripe fruits and nuts they had gathered on their march and hunters went into the undergrowth after rabbits, Flosi went up to Ulror's coffin. Wrinkling his nose at the stench emanating from it, he pried up the ends of a couple of boards with his dagger.

The coffin shook, as with some internal paroxysm. The boards Flosi had loosened flew up. Ulror scrambled out. The first thing he did was to dive into the water and scrub himself from head to foot with sand from the streambank. When he came splashing out, streaks of the mixture of chalk and grease with which he had smeared his face remained on it, but his natural ruddy color dominated once more.

One of his warriors threw a ragged cloak around him. "Food!" he boomed. "After two days with nothing but three stinking seagulls for company, even the rubbish we were eating back at Sotevag would taste good."

Flosi brought him some of their meager fare. He wolfed it down. One by one, the hunters returned. Fresh meat, even a couple of bites' worth, roasted over an open fire was the most delicious thing he had ever eaten.

His belly was still growling after all the food was gone, but he had grown used to that in Sotevag. He looked around again and again, admiring the stream, the trees, the little clearing in which the Halogai were camped. "Free," he breathed.

"Aye." Flosi still did not seem to believe it. "I thought we were ruined when your magicking with Kolskegg failed."

"And I." Ulror longed for wine, but after a moment he realized triumph was a sweeter, headier brew. He laughed. "We get so used to using sorcery for our ends, we forget what we can do without it. Once I thought of the scheme, my biggest worry was that Zigabenos would attack before the birds got ripe enough to use."

"A good thing you whitened your face, even so."

"Oh, indeed. Zigabenos is too canny for me to dare miss a trick against him," Ulror said. A swirl of the breeze brought the carrion reek his way. He grimaced. "I was afraid of one other thing, too. He might have noticed something wrong if he'd heard my 'corpse' puking its guts out."

"So he might." Flosi allowed himself a rare smile. He rose and started over to the opened coffin. "The birds have served their purpose. I'll toss them in the creek."

"Eh? Don't do that," Ulror exclaimed.

"Why not? What do you want them for? I wouldn't eat the smelly things if I'd stood siege for years, not a couple of months. Throw 'em away and have done."

"I have a better plan," Ulror said.

"What's that?"

"I'm going to send one back to Zigabenos behind a shield of truce." Ulror's eyes glowed with mischief. "I wish I could be there to see his face when he finds out how"—he grinned a huge grin; it felt monstrous good to be able to joke again—"how he's been gulled."

"Gulled, eh?" Kypros Zigabenos nodded at the noisome pile of feathers the smirking Haloga herald set before him. He would not give the barbarian the satisfaction of showing he felt anything at all at finding Ulror alive and free. Never in his life, though, had he come so close to dishonoring a truce shield. The northerner would never know by how little he had missed the lash, the thumbscrews, the red-hot bronze needles, and the rest of the ingenious torments the Videssians had devised over the centuries.

But only a vicious fool struck at the bearer of bad news. And so Zigabenos, his heart a cold stone in his breast, poured wine for the Haloga and laughed politely to hear how Ulror had duped him.

"Wait here a moment, if you will," he said to the warrior, and stepped out of his tent to speak to one of his guards. The man blinked in surprise, then saluted and hurried away, stringing his bow as he trotted.

Zigabenos returned to his unwelcome guest, refilled the fellow's cup, and went on with the urbane conversation he had briefly interrupted. Behind his smiling mask, he felt desperation building. He had staked too great a part of the imperial forces on Kalavria to finishing Ulror here. The Videssians scattered over the rest of the island were ragtag and bobtail. With his victorious army as a core, they would have sufficed. Now the Halogai would mop up, not he.

And then they would come for him. He wondered how fast his artisans could repair the damage his own engines had done to Sotevag, and what sort of supplies he could bring in. The Halogai were impetuous, impatient. They might not have the staying power to conduct a siege of their own.

But with Ulror leading them, they might.

The sentry with whom Zigabenos had spoken stuck his head into the tent. "I have one, your excellency."

"Very good. Bring it in." The general drew himself up straighter in his chair. Sometimes one won, sometimes one lost; no sane man expected nothing but triumph in his life. But win or lose, style mattered. He prayed the day might never come when he failed to meet misfortune with aplomb.

The bird the Videssian soldier brought in was smaller than the one Ulror had sent, with a deeply forked tail and a black cap. It was still warm. Zigabenos picked it up and ceremoniously offered it to the Haloga. "I hope you will be so kind as to present this to your master, with my compliments."

The northerner looked at him as if he had gone mad. "Just the bird, or shall I say something?"

"The latter." Zigabenos was an imperial, a man of anciently civilized race, and of high blood as well. This grinning blond lout here would never understand, but somehow he felt Ulror might appreciate the spirit in which he sent his message. "Tell him one good tern deserves another."

Sometimes ideas come in pieces. I got the first half of the idea for this one listening to a weather report while driving on the freeway: What if those constantly changing numbers were years instead of degrees? Once I got to a place where I could, I wrote down the notion. That gave me the background against which the story would be presented, but it took me two years to find a story to present. What you're about to read is the result.

THE WEATHER'S FINE

Tom Crowell goes into the little kitchen of his apartment, pulls a Bud out of the refrigerator. To save money, the place is conditioned to only the mid-seventies. He pulls off the ring tab and tosses it into the trash. Then he goes into the living room and turns on the TV news. The couch squeaks as he flops down onto it. Even in the mid-seventies, it isn't new.

As always, the weather is big news, especially in other parts of the country: "The old front sweeping down out of Canada continues to ravage our northern tier of states. It has caused widespread communications breakdowns. Authorities are doing their best to combat them, but problems remain far too widespread for portable generators to be adequate. This film footage, some of the little coming out of the area, is from Milwaukee."

The weatherman disappears from the screen, to be replaced by jerky, grainy black-and-white footage. The streets are tree-lined; horse carts and boxy cars compete for space. The men wear hats, and the women's skirts reach to the ground.

Not for the first time, Tom is glad he lives in southern California, where the weather rarely gets below the fifties. No wonder so many people move here, he thinks.

The weatherman comes back with the local forecast. The weather will be about standard for Los Angeles in April: mostly in the late sixties. Tom decides he won't bother with the conditioner in the car tomorrow. He looks good in long sideburns.

After the news, he stays in front of the TV. No matter where he sets the year conditioner, TV is pretty bad, he thinks. That doesn't stop him from watching it. Finally, he gives up and goes to bed.

He leaves the window down as he drives to work. The Doors, the Stones when they're really the Stones, the Airplane, Creedence—the music coming out of the car radio is better than it will be. The speaker, though, sounds tinny as hell. Trade-offs, Tom thinks.

He feels more businesslike when he gets into the buying office. The boss keeps the conditioner really cranked up. Eighties computer technology makes the expense worthwhile, he claims. Tom doesn't complain, but he does wonder, What price computers when the only links to the upper Midwest are telegraphs and operator-assisted telephones?

He sighs and buckles down to his terminal. It's not his problem. Besides, things could be worse. He remembers the horrible winter when Europe was stuck in the early forties for weeks. He hopes that won't happen again any time soon.

His pants start flapping at the ankles as he trots for his car at quitting time. He grins. He likes bell-bottoms. He remembers he has a cousin with a birthday coming up and decides to go to the mall before he heads home.

Everyone else in the world, it seems, has a cousin with a birthday coming up, too. Tom has to drive around for ten minutes before he can find a parking space. He hikes toward the nearest entrance. "Which isn't any too damn near," he says out loud. Living alone, he has picked up the habit of talking to himself.

Some people are getting up to the entrance, turning around and heading back toward their cars. Tom wonders why until he sees the sign taped to the glass door: SORRY, OUR YEAR CONDITIONER HAS FAILED. PLEASE COME IN ANYHOW. Maybe the people who are leaving really don't have cousins with birthdays coming up. Tom sighs. He does. He pulls the door open and goes in.

Sure enough, the conditioner is down. He doesn't feel the blast of air it ought to be putting out, doesn't hear its almost subliminal hum. The inside of the mall is stuck in the late sixties, same as outside.

Tom smells incense and scented candles. He hasn't been in a shopping center this downyear for a long while. He wonders what he can find for his cousin here-and-now. He smiles a little as he walks past a Jeans West, with its striped pants and Day-Glo turtlenecks. He doesn't go in. His cousin's taste runs more to cutoffs and T-shirts.

He climbs the stairs. The Pier 1 Imports is a better bet. No matter what the weather is like, they always have all kinds of strange things. The long-hair behind the counter nods at him. "Help you find something, man?"

"Just looking now, thanks."

"No problem. Holler if you need me."

The sitar music coming out of the stereo goes with the rugs from India that are hanging on the walls and the rickety rattan furniture in the center of the store. It's not as good an accompaniment for the shelves of German beer steins or for the silver-and-turquoise jewelry "imported from the Navajo nation." Wrong kind of Indians, Tom thinks.

He picks up a liter stein, hefts it thoughtfully, puts it down. It will do if he can't find anything better. He turns a corner, goes past some cheap flatware from Taiwan, turns another corner and finds himself in front of a display of Greek pottery: modern copies of ancient pieces.

He's seen this kind of thing before, but most of it is crude. This has the unmistakable feel of authenticity to it. The lines of the pots are spare and perfect, the painting elegantly simple. He picks up a pot, turns it over. His cousin doesn't have anything like it, but it goes with everything he does have.

Tom is just turning to thread his way through the maze toward the cash register when a girl comes round the corner. She sees him, rocks back on her heels, then cries. "Tom!" and throws herself into his arms.

"Donna!" he exclaims in surprise. She is a big armful, every bit as tall as his own 5'8", with not a thing missing—she's good to hug.

She tosses her head, a characteristic Donna gesture, to get her long, straight black hair out of her face. Then she kisses him on the mouth. When Tom finally comes up for air, he looks at the familiar gray eyes a couple of inches from his, asks, "Are you here for anything special?"

She grins. "Just to spend money." Very much her kind of answer, he thinks.

"Let me pay for this; then do you want to come home with me?"

Her grin gets wider. "I thought you'd never ask." They link arms and head for the front of the store. She whistles "Side by Side." Now he is grinning, too.

When he sets the pot on the counter so the clerk can ring it up, Donna exclaims over it. "I didn't even notice it before," she says. "I was too busy looking at you." That makes Tom feel ten feet tall as the long-hair gives him his change.

When they get to the glass door with the sign on it, he holds it open so she can go through. The only thing he can think when he sees what dark, patterned hose and a short skirt do for her legs is, Gilding the lily. Or lilies, he amends—she definitely has two of them. He admires them both.

He opened the passenger door to let her in, then goes around to his own side. He doesn't bother with the year conditioner. He likes the weather fine the way it is. He does keep having to remind himself to pay attention to his driving. Her skirt is even shorter when she's sitting down.

There is a parking space right in front of his building. He slides the car into it. "Sometimes you'd rather be lucky than good," he says.

Donna looks at him. "I think you're pretty good."

His right arm slips around her waist as they climb the stairs to his apartment. When he takes it away so he can get out his keys, she is pressed so tightly against him that he can hardly put his hand in his pocket. He enjoys trying, though. She doesn't seem unhappy, either. If anything, she moves closer to him.

She turns her head and nibbles his ear while he is undoing the deadbolt. After that, he has to try more than once before he can work the regular lock. Finally, the key goes in, turns. He opens the door.

The conditioned air inside blows on him and Donna. He can feel his memories shift forward. Because he stands outside instead of going straight in, it happens slowly. It's probably worse that way.

Now he looks at Donna with new eyes. She can't stand the seventies, even when she's in them. He always just goes on with his life, or tries to. And because of that, they always fight.

He remembers a glass shattering against a wall—not on his head, but only by luck and because she can't throw worth a damn. Her hand jumps up to her cheek. He knows she is remembering a slap. He feels his face go hot with mingled shame and rage. With a sound like a strangled sob, she turns away and starts, half stumbling, down the steps.

He takes a reflexive step after her. It moves him far enough from his apartment for the bad times to fade a bit in his mind. She stops, too. She looks at him from the stairs. She shakes her head. "That was a bad one," she says. "No wonder we don't hang out together all the times."

"No wonder," he says tonelessly. He feels beat up, hung over; too much has happened too fast. He is horny and angry and emotionally bruised, all at once. He walks down the stairs to Donna. She doesn't run or swing on him, which is something. Standing by her, he feels better. In the sixties, he usually feels better standing by her.

He takes a deep breath. "Let me go inside and turn the conditioner off."

"Are you sure you want to? I don't want you to mess up your place just for me."

"It won't be bad," he says, and hopes he isn't lying.

She squeezes his hand. "You're sweet. I'll try to make you glad you did."

The promise in that is enough to send him up the stairs two at a time. A couple of half-trotting steps to the walkway and he is in the apartment.

He was right. Doing it all at once is better than a little bit at a time, the way diving into a cold swimming pool gets you used to it faster than going in by easy stages. The memories come rushing back, of course. They always do. But in the fully conditioned mid-seventies of his apartment, they are older, mostly healed; they don't have the hurt they did before, when they were fresher.

He puts his hand on the chronostat, turns if off with a decisive twist of his wrist. Its hum dies. He's used to the background noise. He goes into the bedroom, opens the window to let outside air in faster. The mingling makes memories jump into focus again, but only for a moment: now they are going rather than coming.

When he walks back into the living room, the little calculator is gone from his coffee table. That's a good sign, he thinks. He glances at the chronostat needle. It's already down around seventy. He opens and closes the front door several times to bring in fresh air. The swirl is confusing, but only for a little while.

He looks at the needle again. Sixty-eight, he sees. That should be plenty good. Donna is still waiting on the stairs. "Come on in," he says.

"All right," she says. Now she takes the steps two at a time. She shows a lot of leg doing it.

"Wine?"

"Sure. Whatever you've got."

He opens the refrigerator. A half-gallon of Spañada is in there. He pours a couple of glasses, takes them into the living room.

"I like the poster," she says. It's a black-light KEEP ON TRUCKIN' poster, about the size of a baby billboard. When the conditioner is running, it isn't there. That doesn't matter to Tom if Donna likes it. He won't even miss the Chinese print that will replace it.

And then, as they have done a lot of times before, they head for the bedroom. Afterward, still naked, Tom wheels the TV in from out front. He plugs it in, spins the dial till he finds some news, then flops back onto the bed with Donna.

For a while, he doesn't pay much attention to the TV. Watching the flush fade from between Donna's breasts is much more interesting. He does hear that Minnesota is finally up into the thirties. "Not good, but better," he says, to show he has been following what's going on.

Donna nods; she really is watching. "Remember last winter, when it got below double zero and stayed there, and they had to try to get food to the markets with horses and buggies? People starved. In the United States, starved. I couldn't believe it."

"Terrible," Tom agrees. Then he has to start watching, too, because the weatherman is coming on.

As usual, the fellow is insanely cheerful. "The early seventies tomorrow through most of the metropolitan area," he says, whacking the map with his pointer, "rising into the mid- or late seventies in the valleys and the desert. Have a *fine* day, Los Angeles!" He whacks the map again.

Donna sucks in air between her teeth. "I'd better go," she says, catching Tom by surprise. She swings her feet onto the floor, turns her panties right side out, slides them up her legs.

"I'd hoped you'd spend the night," he says. He is trying to sound hurt but fears that the words have come out petulant instead.

Evidently not. Donna replies gently, "Tom, right now I love you very much. But if I sleep with you tonight—and I mean sleep—and we wake up in the early seventies, what's going to happen?"

His scowl says he knows the answer to that. Donna's nod is sad, but she stands up and starts pulling on her pantyhose. Tom aches at the thought of having her go, and not just because he wants her again. Right now, he really loves her, too.

He says, "Tell you what. Suppose I set the conditioner for sixty-eight. Will you stay then?"

He has startled her. "Do you really want to?" she says. She doesn't sound as if she believes it, but she does get back onto the bed.

He wonders if he believes it himself. The place won't be the same in the late sixties. He'll miss that little calculator. There should be a slide rule around somewhere now, he thinks, but a slide rule won't help him keep his checkbook straight. And that's just the tip of the iceberg. The frozen pizza will taste more like cardboard and less like pizza in the sixties. But—

"Let's try it," he says. Better cardboard with Donna, he thinks, than mozzarella without.

He shuts the bedroom window, goes out front to adjust the chronostat. It doesn't kick in right away, since the place is already around sixty-eight, but moving the needle makes him think again about what he's doing. A bookcase is gone, he sees. He'll miss some of those books.

"Hell with it," he says out loud and heads for the bathroom. While he is brushing his teeth, he starts rummaging frantically through the drawers by the sink. The toothbrush is still in his mouth; fluoridated foam dribbles down his chin, so that he looks like a mad dog. He stops as suddenly as he started. He does have a spare toothbrush, rather to his surprise. Donna giggles when, with a flourish, he hands it to her.

"When are you working these days?" she asks when she comes back to bed. "If it's close to when you had this place before—"

"No," he says quickly. He understands what she means. If he spends his office time reliving fights that are fresh to him, this will never fly, no matter how well they get on when they are home together. "How about you?" he asks.

She laughs. "I probably wouldn't have gone into the mall if I hadn't heard the year conditioner had broken down. I like the sixties. I work in a little record store called Barefoot Sounds. It suits me."

"I can see that," he says, nodding. Donna will never be a pragmatist. The more she stays out of the eighties, the better off she'll be. He yawns, lies down beside her. "Let's go to bed."

She smiles a broad's smile at him—there's no other word for it. "We've already done that."

He picks up a pillow, makes as if to hit her with it. "To sleep, I mean."

"Okay." She sprawls across him, warm and soft, to turn off the light. She has, he knows, a gift for falling asleep right away. Sure enough, only a couple of minutes later, her voice is blurry as she asks, "Drive me to work in the morning?"

"Sure." He hesitates. With a name like Barefoot Sounds, her record store sounds like a thoroughly sixties place. "If the weather changes, will I be able to find it?"

The mattress shifts to her nod. "It's year-conditioned. No matter what the weather's like outside, there are always sixties refugees popping in. We do a pretty good business, as a matter of fact."

"Okay," he says again. A couple of minutes later, he can tell that she has dropped off. He takes longer to go to sleep himself. He hasn't shared a bed with a woman for a while. He is very conscious of her weight pressing down the bed, of the small noises her breathing makes, of her smell. To trust someone enough to sleep with him, he thinks, takes more faith in some ways than just to go to bed with him. Suddenly, he wants her even more than he did before.

He lies still in the darkness. He has never yet met a woman who is eager just after she wakes up. Besides, he thinks, she'll be here tomorrow.

He hopes . . . Weather in the early seventies tomorrow. Nasty weather for him and Donna.

He falls asleep worrying about it. Sometime around two in the morning, the year conditioner kicks in. He wakes with a start. Donna never stirs. He reaches over, softly puts his hand on the curve of her hip. She mutters something, rolls onto her stomach. He jerks his hand away. She doesn't wake up. He takes a long time to go back to sleep.

The alarm clock's buzz might as well be a bomb going off by his ear. He needs a loud one. The adrenaline rush keeps him going till his first cup of coffee. The only thing that wakes Donna is his bouncing out of bed. He has forgotten what a dedicated sleeper she is.

But she has two plates of eggs scrambled, toast buttered, and the coffee perking by the time his tie is knotted. "Now I know why I asked you to stay," he says. "I just eat corn flakes when I'm here by myself."

"Poor baby," she croons. He makes a face at her.

While he is stacking the dishes in the sink, he asks, "So where is this Barefoot Sounds of yours?"

"Down in Gardena, on Crenshaw. I hope I'm not going to make you late."

He looks at his watch, calculates in his head. "I ought to make it. I won't bother washing up now, though. I'll get 'em tonight. Shall I pick you up? What time do you get off?"

"Four-thirty."

He grunts. "I probably can't get up that way till maybe half past five."

"I'll stay inside," she promises. "That way, I'll be sure to be glad to see you."

She does have sense, he knows, no matter how she sometimes hides it. "Sounds like a good idea to me," he says.

Just how good it is he discovers the minute they walk out the door. It's in the seventies, all right: the weatherman had it right on the button. By the time Tom and Donna get to the bottom of the stairs, they aren't holding hands any more.

He strides ahead of her, turns back to snap, "I don't have all day to get you where you're going, you know."

"Don't do me any favors." She puts her hands on her hips. "If you're in such a hurry, just tell me where the nearest bus stop is and take off. I'll manage fine."

"It's—" All that saves things is that he has no idea where the nearest bus stop is. Like a lot of people in L.A., he's helpless without a car. "Just come on," he says. In the seventies, she really does drive him crazy. The angry click of her heels on the walk tells him it's mutual.

He unlocks her door, goes around to unlock his, slides behind the wheel; he's not opening doors for her, not right now. He doesn't even look at her as she gets in. The engine roars to life when he turns the key, floors the gas pedal. He doesn't wait for it to warm up before he reaches for the year-conditioner switch. He has to change the setting; usually he keeps it in the eighties, to help him gear up for work.

The conditioner takes a while to make a difference; but little by little, the tense silence between Tom and Donna becomes friendlier. "My last car didn't have a year conditioner," he says.

She shakes her head. "I couldn't live like that."

He finds Barefoot Sounds without much trouble. It's at the back of a little shopping center where most of the stores are kept a lot newer. He shrugs. From what Donna says, the place pays the rent, and that's what counts. Besides, he likes sixties music.

"Maybe I'll stop in when I pick you up," he says.

"Sure, why not? I'll introduce you to Rick, the guy who runs the place." She leans over to kiss him, then gets out. He drives right off; he's left the motor running while he stops in the parking lot—he doesn't want the year conditioner to die.

But he doesn't like the look on Donna's face that he sees in the rearview mirror. The seventies are hard on them, and that's all there is to it. He hopes she does remember to wait for him in the store. If she stays outside, she'll be ready to spit in his eye by the time he gets there.

More likely, he thinks, she'll just up and leave.

If she does, she does; there's nothing he can do about it. He chews on that unsatisfying bit of philosophy all the way down the San Diego Freeway into Orange County.

When he gets out of the car, in the company lot, he hopes she *won't* be there in the afternoon. He hurries across the asphalt to the mirror-fronted office building, which is firmly in the eighties. A little more of this whipsawing and he won't be good for anything the rest of the day.

But he gains detachment even before he gets his computer booted up. As soon as he gets on line, he is too busy to worry about anything but his job. Now that the old front in the upper Midwest is finally breaking up, new orders come flooding in, and he has to integrate them into everything the system thinks it already knows.

He doesn't begin to get his head above water till lunchtime. Even then, he is too rushed to go out; he grabs a cheeseburger and a diet cola at the little in-house cafeteria. As he wolfs them down, Donna returns to the surface of his mind.

Being so far upyear gives him perspective on things. He knows that whenever the weather is in the early seventies, it'll be a dash from one year-conditioned place to another. Can he handle that? With eighties practicality, he realizes he'd better if he wants to keep her. He wonders what going from this long-distance indifference to a hot affair every night will do to him.

He also wonders what Donna is like in the eighties. He doubts he'll find out. She has made her choice, and this isn't it.

He has second thoughts again as he goes back out into the seventies at quitting time. But he has to go to his car anyhow, and as soon as it starts, he's all right again—he's left the year conditioner on. It's tough on his timing belt but good for his peace of mind.

Traffic is appalling. He's stoic about that. When the weather is in the eighties, things are even worse, with more cars on the road. When it drops into the fifties, the San Diego Freeway isn't there. Getting into town from Orange County on surface streets is a different kind of thrill.

He pulls into a parking space in front of Barefoot Sounds around 5:15. Not bad. Again he lets the year conditioner die with the engine without turning it off. He's trotting to the record store before the hum has altogether faded.

He's hardly out in the seventies long enough to remember to get hostile toward Donna. Then he's inside Barefoot Sounds and in the late sixties with a vengeance.

The place is wall-to-wall posters: a KEEP ON TRUCKIN' even gaudier than his, Peter Fonda on a motorcycle, Nixon so stoned his face is dribbling out between his fingers, Mickey and Minnie Mouse doing something obscene. Patchouli fills the air, thick enough to slice. And blasting out of the big speakers is "Love One Another," not the Youngbloods singing but a cover version: slower, more haunting, not one he hears much on the radio, no matter when he is. . . .

"My God!" Tom says. "That's H. P. Lovecraft!"

The fellow behind the cash register raises an eyebrow. He has frizzy brown hair and a Fu Manchu mustache. "I'm impressed," he says. "Half my regulars wouldn't know that one, and you're new here. Can I help you find something?"

"Only in a manner of speaking. I'm here to pick up Donna." Tom looks around. He doesn't see her. He starts worrying. There aren't many places to hide.

But the fellow—he must be the Rick she mentioned, Tom realizes—sticks his head behind a curtain, says, "Hon, your ride's here." *Hon?* Tom scowls until he notices that the guy is wearing a wedding ring. Then he relaxes—a little.

Donna comes out. The way her face lights up when she sees him makes him put his silly fears in the trash, where they belong. In the late sixties, he and Donna are good together. He whistles a couple of bars from the Doors song.

Rick cocks that eyebrow again. "You know your stuff. You should be coming in here all the time."

"Maybe I should. This is quite a place." Tom takes another look around. He rubs his chin, considering. "Who does your buying for you?"

"You're looking at him, my man," Rick says, laughing. He jabs himself in the chest with a thumb. "Why?"

"Nothing, really. Just a thought." Tom turns to Donna. "Are you ready to go?"

"And then some."

She's been waiting for him, Tom realizes. She can't be happy standing around while he chews the fat with her boss. "Sorry," he says. He nods at Rick. "Good to meet you."

"You, too." Rick pulls his wallet out of the hip pocket of his striped bell-bottoms. He extends a card, hands it to Tom. He may be a freak, but he's not running Barefoot Sounds to starve. "You ever get anywhere on that thought of yours, let me know, you hear?"

"I will." Tom sticks the card in his own wallet. Donna is at the door, tapping her foot. No matter how good he and she are, she is going to be one unhappy lady any second now. Maybe gallantry will help. With an extravagant bow, Tom holds the door open for her.

She steps through. "Took you long enough," she says. Her voice has an edge to it—she's outside, back in the early seventies. As he joins her, Tom feels his stomach start to churn.

This time, the tension breaks before it builds to a full-scale fight, thanks to Tom's car's being just a couple of steps away. They are inside and the year conditioner is going before they can do much more than start to glare at each other.

They both relax as it goes to work. Tom heads for his apartment. After a while, Donna asks, "What were you thinking about back there in the store?"

But Tom says, "Let it keep for now. It isn't ripe yet. Let's see how things go with us, then maybe I'll bring it up again."

"The curiosity will kill me." Donna doesn't push, though. In the seventies, she'd be all over him, which would only make him clam up harder. Luckily, she's thinking of something else when he pulls up in front of his building. The silence is guarded as they go up the stairs, but at least it is silence, and things are fine again once they're inside his place.

Come the weekend, Donna moves her stuff into his apartment. Without ever much talking about it, they fall into a routine that gets firmer day by day. Tom likes it. The only fly in the ointment, in fact, is his job. It's not the commute that bothers him. But he doesn't like not caring about Donna eight hours a day. He can deal with it, but he doesn't like it.

Finally, he digs out Rick's card and calls him. "You sure?" Rick says when he's done talking. "The pay would be peanuts next to what you're pulling down in your eighties job."

"Get serious," Tom says. "Every twenty-dollar bill I have in my wallet there turns into a five here."

Rick is silent awhile, thinking it over. At last, he says, "I'd say I've got myself a new buyer." He hesitates. "You love her a lot, don't you? You'd have to, to do something like this."

"In the sixties, I love her a lot, and she's a sixties person. If I want to stay with her, I'd better be one, too. Hell," Tom laughs, "I'm getting good on my slide rule again."

Donna's smile stretches across her entire face the first day they go into Barefoot Sounds together to work. This time, she holds the door open for him. "Come on in," she says. "The weather's fine."

"Yes," he says. "It is." She follows him in. The door closes after them.

This is the one story I've written that my wife has never read. Some of you know what dealing with a colicky baby is like. Rachel, our second daughter, was one. Colicky babies can make you paranoid—you start to think they're wailing just to drive you crazy. To a writer, a paranoid thought like that can be the springboard for a story. But Laura won't look at it. Can't say I blame her.

CRYBABY

This time, the steaks were rare enough when it started.

Pete Flowers had a potholder in his hand. He was opening the broiler door. Doug's wail went through him like the sudden malignant whine of a dentist's drill. Pete's hand jerked against the hot metal.

"Shit," he snarled, snatching it away. He put a week's worth of glare into the two long strides that got him to the kitchen sink. "You said he was really down this time."

"He *was*," Mary insisted. "He nursed like a champ. He burped. He was dry—you changed him yourself. And he didn't even wiggle when I put him in the crib. He didn't, Pete."

"Shit," Pete Flowers said again, softly this time. He hadn't heard everything his wife said, not over the splash of cold water on his burned hand. Doug was still crying, though. There wasn't any place in the condo where he couldn't hear that. God knows I know it, too, he thought, reaching for a dish towel. He gingerly dried his hand.

He looked so grim when he stamped past the dining room table that alarm sprang into Mary's tired blue eyes. "Where are you going?"

"To get him, where else?" He started down the hall toward the room that, up until six weeks ago, had been his cherished study.

Now the books were either in boxes or shoehorned into the master bedroom.

Not, he thought, that he had done much reading in Japanese history—or anything else that took longer to go through than *Bloom County*—lately. He'd had to go all the way up to the assistant dean for academic affairs at San Flavio State to get his sabbatical approved a year early. He'd fought the good fight gladly, eager to take a year off to help Mary with the baby. Now he wondered how good an idea it had been.

Doug's shrieks neared the pitch only dogs can hear. His father set his jaw so hard his teeth ground together. He turned on the light in the baby's room; even in Southern California, November twilight fades to darkness by six.

The baby's head was turned toward Pete. As usual, his frustrated anger met tough sledding when he looked at his son. Doug's hair—the first, incredibly fine growth of baby hair, now being rubbed away toward temporary baldness by his crib sheets—was even fairer than Mary's, but his eyes were already darkening from infant gray-blue toward Pete's own unspectacular brown.

He picked up Doug, slid a finger inside his Huggies. (Or was one of them just a Huggie—or even a Huggy? A fine point of language he'd never reached a firm conclusion about.)

Doug was dry, and still yelling. Pete didn't know whether to be pleased or not. He wouldn't have to change him, but at least he would have known what the kid's problem was if his finger had come out dripping with liquid poop.

He hoisted Doug up on his left shoulder, patted his back. "There, there," he crooned, "there, there." Maybe Doug would burp or fart or whatever he needed to do. He didn't sound gassy, though. Pete knew that cry. He wasn't drawing up his legs either. Pete sighed. Maybe Doug was yelling because he felt like yelling, too.

Mary, bless her heart, had the steaks on the table. She'd already cut hers into bite-sized pieces, so she could eat with one hand. She held out her arms. "I'll take him, Pete."

"Thanks." He got his hand behind Doug's head to cradle it, and hissed—it was the burned hand. He guided the baby into the crook of his wife's elbow. "Got him?"

"Yes. How's your hand?"

He looked at it. "Turning red. I'll live."

"Put some Cort-Aid on it."

"After dinner." He slathered A-1 Sauce on the steak, cut off a big bite. He made a dissatisfied noise, deep in his throat. "A little too done. He timed it just right."

"I'm sorry. I should have gotten up sooner."

"Never mind." Pete tried to sound as if he meant it. He hated overcooked beef. He ate his hamburgers rare too, which faintly revolted Mary. After five years of marriage, though, she had learned he fought change hard.

The steak tasted fine to her. She dropped a green bean on Doug. She was eating righthanded because she held him in her left arm, but even after forced intensive practice she wasn't good at it.

"He's calmed down, anyhow," she said, plucking the bean off Doug's THUMBSUCKERS ANONYMOUS T-shirt and sticking it in her mouth.

"Sure he has. Why not? His mission's accomplished—he's screwed up dinner."

Mary had a glass of Zinfandel halfway to her mouth. She put it down so hard a little splashed onto the tablecloth. "Oh, for God's sake, Pete," she said, her voice low and calm in the way that meant she'd be shouting if she weren't watching herself. "He's just a teeny tiny baby. He doesn't know what he's doing. All he knows is that something's bothering him."

"Usually he doesn't know what, though."

"Pete." This time she was a little louder: last warning.

"Yes, yes, yes." He gave in, settled down, and ate. But once lodged, the thought would not go away.

The first couple of weeks, of course, were chaos. Pete had thought he was ready. Looking back, he supposed he was, as ready as anyone could be who only knew about babies from hearsay. He started finding out how little that was even before Doug got home. Wrestling a car seat into place in the back of a two-door Toyota Tercel was an introduction of sorts.

But only of sorts. Doug had been born just past four in the morning, and seemed convinced night was day, and vice versa. That first dreadful night at home, he was awake—and yowling—almost all the time from one till five.

Even when he did catnap, it did Pete and Mary precious little good. They had the bassinet in their bedroom, and jumped every time Doug wriggled or breathed funny. Wriggling and breathing funny, Pete decided in a moment when he would have contemplated suicide had he been less tired, were about all newborns did. He soon revised that to include making frequent horrible messes.

Once was enough to teach him to keep a spare diaper over Doug's middle whenever he was changing him. "The fountains of Versailles," Mary called it; she was writing her dissertation on Voltaire. What Pete called it did not bear repeating, but then *he'd* had to wash his face.

The other thing Doug did was stay awake. Pawing through *The First Twelve Months of Life* one day, Pete protested, "The book says he's supposed to sleep seventeen to twenty hours a day." Before the baby was born, that had sounded reasonable. It even sounded as if it left parents a few hours a day to live their own lives.

"I don't think he's read the book," Mary said wanly. "Here, you take him for a while. My shoulder's getting sore from rocking him in my arms."

Pete took Doug. The baby squirmed and yarped and dozed off. Pete carried him into his room (the bassinet was in there now, though Doug still looked small and lost in a crib), set him down. Doug sighed. His mouth made little *suck-suck* sounds. Pete backed away and started down the hall.

He'd got about halfway to the front room when Doug let out an "Ooo-wah!" behind him. He stiffened in outrage. Then his shoulders sagged. He turned around and went back to pick up the baby.

"This all comes with the territory," he said when he reappeared, as much to himself as to Mary. Doug was already back to sleep in his arms. He tried to put him down again. This time he did not even get out of the room.

It was Mary's turn to console him. "It gets better."

"Sure it does," he said, and wondered if he would live that long.

But it did, some. Doug began to sleep, if not more, at least at more consistent times. He was awake for longer stretches during the day and less during the night, though he still wanted to be fed every couple of hours around the clock. Mary's fair complexion made the circles under her eyes seem darker than they really were, or so Pete told himself. As for him, the two staples of his life were Visine and caffeine.

Doug learned to smile. At first the expression was hard to tell from the one he wore when he had gas, but it soon became unmistakably an outlet for pleasure and the baby's first real communication other than screaming. Pete cherished it for that. The sight of his face or Mary's could touch it off.

Doug also developed another expression, a way of looking at things out of the corner of his eye. It made him look absurdly wise and knowing, as if he had a secret and was doing his best not to let on. Pete loved it. He would even smile when Doug assumed it while being cuddled after a crying bout. "All right, you self-satisfied little beast, that's more like it," he would say.

Doug seemed to reserve that smug look for him. Mary saw it much less often.

However much Pete came to love his son, though, he never got used to the hour after hour of banshee wails that marked Doug's bad days. Calling them colic gave them a name, but not one that really helped. In the moments he could grab, Pete read about colic with desperate intensity, trying to find some clue to making Doug feel better, or at least shut up.

The more Pete read, the less he found he knew. Colic wasn't the digestive upset people used to think it was. At least, the babies who were having fits didn't show any unusual intestinal activity. Also, breastfed babies got it as often as babies who used bottles. Colicky babies put on weight just as fast as any others.

They made a hell of a lot more noise, though.

Pete noticed early on that Doug owned an exquisite sense of timing. A couple of times Mary drove down to the Seven-Eleven to tide them over on diapers. Pete did the big Saturday shopping; he welcomed the chance to get out of the condo.

Both times, Doug had been out like a light when Mary left on the diaper run. Once he made Pete forget to put chili powder in a recipe, which wasn't the same without it. The other time, he caught his father with his hand on his zipper. Pete was about to burst by the time Mary got back. By then Doug was quiet, and looking smug.

Sometimes he wouldn't be quiet, no matter what. Those were the worst. Evolution designed a baby's cry to be noticed, to make its parents want to fix whatever was wrong. Evolution did not design parents to listen to a squawking baby at close range for hours, not and keep their marbles too.

They tried everything they could think of. Pete put a cotton ball in his left ear while he was toting Doug around. Sometimes, when the din was very bad, he put cotton balls in both ears. They didn't block Doug's racket, or come close. They did blunt the edge of it. Out of some perverse mommy equivalent of machismo, Mary refused to have anything to do with earplugs.

In any case, they were only for Pete's sake, as he put it one frazzled middle of the night. Except on the days when nothing helped, two things helped with Doug. One was bouncing him while sitting on the edge of the mattress. The other was cranking up the rock on the stereo. The rhythmic thump of the bass seemed to soothe him. He especially like Led Zeppelin, which dismayed Pete and horrified Mary.

Bouncing and Led Zep or not, though, Doug kept his gift for interrupting his parents, and Pete in particular. He wished he'd never thought, even as a sour joke, that the baby was doing it on purpose. It made him notice just exactly how often Doug's crying sabotaged things he needed to do or, worse, wanted to do.

The baby started yowling out of the blue one morning, for instance, just when Pete was shaving that impossible spot above the center of his upper lip. His hand jumped. He didn't quite slice off his lip, but he gave it the old college try.

"I haven't needed that much styptic pencil since I was fifteen years old and just learning how," he grumbled as he poured himself a bowl of Special K.

"There's still some blood under your chin," Mary told him. She was holding Doug, who by this time had calmed down considerably. He turned his head to try to follow his father across the kitchen as Pete walked over to wet a paper towel and watched him out of the corner of his eye while he dabbed at himself.

Pete threw the crumpled towel in the trash. He scowled back at his son. "Pleased with yourself?" He didn't sound as if he was kidding, or as if he was talking to a baby. He sounded more like someone talking to a fellow who had just done him a dirty trick.

Mary caught his tone. "For heaven's sake, Pete, he's just a baby. He doesn't know what he's doing."

"Yeah, you said that before. But enough things have happened with this crazy kid that I swear I'm beginning to wonder."

Mary felt Doug's diaper. "I can tell you what's happened with this crazy kid. I can also tell you that you're going to change him, because if I don't take a leak you'll have to change me too. Here." She thrust Doug at him.

He grinned a lopsided grin. "I'd have more fun putting the powder on you." She made a face back over her shoulder at him as she hurried down the hall.

Doug somehow missed interfering with dinner that evening, which gave Pete hope for the future. The baby nursed vigorously just after eight and was sound asleep (better yet, *soundless* asleep) by nine. Mary levered herself out of the rocking chair with her free hand, carried him over to his father on the couch. "Give him a kiss and I'll put him in his crib."

Pete leaned forward to kiss Doug's fine sparse fair hair. It had a sweet, clean smell that only had a little to do with being just washed. Pete knew he could do his own hair with Suave baby shampoo from now till doomsday and it would never smell like that. Doug was fresher-baked than he, and that was all there was to it.

Mary toted Doug away. He hadn't stirred for the kiss. "Down. That was almost too easy to stand," she said when she came back.

"Tell me about it. If it were this easy all the time, I'd like having the little critter around more." Pete saw her face cloud, said quickly. "I didn't mean it like that. But he is a strain."

"That he is." Mary stretched. Something in her back crackled. "Ooh. Nice. Now, what shall I do with this rare and priceless gift of privacy at a civilized hour?" Pete had an idea about that, but before he could say anything she went on, "I know—I'll take a shower. I think the flies were homing on me instead of the garbage when I took it out this afternoon."

Pete waited till the blow drier stopped whirring in the bathroom. Then he threw open the door, grabbed Mary around the waist, and lifted her off her feet. She let out an indignant squawk as he carried her away. "What are you doing, you maniac? You'll hurt yourself! Put me down, Pete, right now!"

He did, on the bed. Through the shirt he was pulling over his head, he told her, "What better way to spend an early evening when we're both awake and someone else isn't?" He fumbled with the brass button on his Levi's.

"I can't think of one." Mary sat up. "Here, let me help you."

"Much more help like that," Pete said a moment later, "and you'll have to wash these jeans." He kicked them off.

"Ah. I'll stop, then." Mary lay back again. Pete joined her on the bed. After a minute, she laughed. "My milk's letting down."

As always, Pete marveled at how sweet it was. Babies, he thought, had things a lot better than calves. They also got their milk in much more attractive containers.

His kisses drifted down her belly. He raised an eyebrow. "Shall I commit a felony for you?"

"What are you talking about?" Her golden hair slid across bare shoulders as she shook her head.

"Thanks to the wisdom of our duly elected Assembly, and to our know-nothing governor who wants to be president—*and* with a big hand for the Supreme Court—this" (he stopped talking; Mary murmured with pleasure) "is illegal again. Fortunately, it's not immoral or fattening."

After some little while, Mary pushed Pete down flat on the bed. Her eyes were enormous in the dim light. "You shouldn't be the only criminal in the family," she said softly. Her voice was low and heavy. He could feel the warmth of her breath on him.

Doug started to cry.

"Oh, no," Mary said. Pete heard something odd in her voice: not only annoyance over being interrupted, but also concern at how he would take it.

He surprised both of them by laughing, and by meaning it. "What the hell," he said, climbing back into his jeans. "I'll change him, or whatever he needs. He ought to go back to sleep pretty soon, and then, my lovely dear, I shall return."

"I'll be waiting," Mary promised.

"Of course you will. Dressed like that, where would you go?"

Her snort followed him into Doug's room. What the hell, what the hell, he repeated to himself: the kid's only a baby, after all. He wondered how often he'd said that in the last couple of months. Enough that if he'd had a dollar for every time, he could have afforded a nanny and not needed to worry about any of this, that was for sure.

Which was a damn sight more than he could say for his sex life. A dollar for each time there wouldn't have bought him dinner for one at any place fancier than the local Sizzler.

He stopped worrying about it as he stooped to pick up Doug. The baby really did sound upset, and the nightlight showed Pete that he had somehow managed to twist himself at right angles to the way Mary always set him down.

"All right, sport, what's going on here?" Doug yelled louder than ever as Pete lifted him. His father's hands under his chest squeezed the air from him until Pete shifted him into the crook of his left elbow. Pete stuck his right hand into Doug's diaper. The baby was dry. Pete frowned, just a little. There went the most obvious reason for Doug's distress.

"Maybe you spit up," Pete muttered. Doug's chin was damp, but then Doug's chin was often damp. This was only drool, not spit-up sour milk. Pete ran his hand over the crib sheet. It was dry too. Not only that, Doug threw out his arms and shrieked when his father bent down.

"I'm not going to drop you," Pete told him, though for an instant the prospect seemed tempting, if for no other reason than to get the little squawkbox away from his ear.

He felt Doug's forehead, to see if his son had a fever. Doug was cool. He stuck a finger in the baby's mouth, felt around to see if he was cutting a tooth. It was early, but still possible. It was possible, but not true.

"What's happening in there?" Mary asked from the master bedroom.

"Beats me." Pete remembered what he'd said at breakfast a couple of weeks before. "Maybe he's doing it on purpose."

He looked at Doug, who was still hollering—now probably in resentment at having something that wasn't a nipple shoved in his mouth. Then Doug met Pete's eye. He stopped crying for a moment, cocked his head to one side so he could peer up at his father out of the corner of his eye. It was his smug look, but something more was there, too. *Gotcha,* was what Pete thought.

"Why, you little sonofabitch!" he said.

He didn't realize he'd spoken out loud until Mary called, "What'd he do? Did he poop?"

Pete opened his mouth to answer, then left it hanging open. What was he going to tell her, that a nine-week-old baby had interrupted them because he was feeling mischievous? That he'd done it on purpose? She'd think he was crazy—he, Pete, not he, Doug.

If anyone else had told that to him, Pete thought, he wouldn't have believed it either. Doug started crying again. Now his face was just a baby face, eyes screwed shut, cheeks puffed out, mouth wide open. But Pete was sure of what he had seen. It was not an expression that belonged on the face of a baby too young to have teeth. The last time he'd seen it, when he was nineteen, his cousin Stan had just pulled a practical joke on him. He'd punched Stan.

"Pete?"

He had to say something. "I don't know what his problem is. He's just yelling and he won't shut up."

He heard Mary sigh. "I'm coming." She was just wearing jeans herself, which painfully reminded Pete of what wasn't happening. But she was only thinking about Doug now. "Here, let me have him."

Pete passed her the baby. He didn't stop crying when she took him. He didn't stop crying, in fact, until one in the morning. By then Pete and Mary had taken turns bouncing him till their legs were sore, and had danced him to rock 'n' roll until their next-door neighbor pounded on the living-room wall, something she'd never done before.

Pete was holding Doug when he finally gave up and fell asleep.

Pete was no longer interested in sex; he was no longer interested in anything but collapse. He carried Doug down the hall.

The baby's eyes opened. Pete cringed. Before Doug came along, his father had never imagined that anything that weighed twelve pounds and had trouble holding up its head could make him cringe. Now he knew better. He tried without much hope to brace himself for the next round of howls.

They didn't come. Instead, Doug gave him that knowing sidelong look again, sighed, and went back to sleep.

"Why, you little sonofabitch," Pete whispered. "You *did* do that on purpose." Another thing he had not known was how angry it was possible to get at a baby.

Doug slept for almost twenty minutes.

Thinking back, Pete decided the real war between his son and him began that night. He was a large, grown man. Logically, all the weapons should have been on his side. He told himself that, a lot, as he toted Doug around and wished and wished and wished the wailing, wiggling little creature in his arms would be quiet. Wishing did not do much good. Neither did logic. Doug was not equipped to understand logic. He was equipped to make noise, at a volume that would have put a stack of Marshall amps to shame.

Doug didn't seem out to drive *Mary* nuts. When it was just the two of them in the condo, he behaved like any other baby: sometimes he cried and sometimes he didn't. But she got the backwash of his feud with Pete. So did everyone else within half a mile, Pete thought.

Pete began to spend as much time as he could away from home. Trouble was, that wasn't really much. He wasn't the sort of person who got anything out of sitting in a bar for hours, soaking up beers. He was happier drinking at home: it was cheaper and the company (berserk bawling ghetto blaster excluded) better.

Tacking an extra ten minutes on a trip to the store or inventing an excuse to get away to the mall for half an hour just didn't do enough to help. Besides, Mary got stir-crazy too, all the more so when she was cooped up with Doug by herself. She started inventing excuses of her own.

Pete even called San Flavio State about ending his sabbatical early.

The department chairperson's laugh was not altogether kind. "Baby's not as much fun as you thought, Peter?" David Endicott turned serious. "It's not just that I'd look like a fool, having to go to the assistant dean irregularly to get her to undo something I'd gone to her to approve irregularly only six months ago. It really isn't; I hope you understand that. But we've already done the budget transfer, so we can't pay you till next September anyhow. This is the '80s, Peter. Soft money for that kind of thing just isn't there any more."

"I know. Thanks anyhow, David." Pete hung up. He took off his glasses, bent his head and rubbed his eyes with the heels of his hands. He'd known what Endicott would tell him before he picked up the phone. That he'd called regardless didn't seem a good sign.

Doug started up again, though he'd only been asleep a little while. Mary hadn't heard Pete on the phone, but she heard Doug. "Get him, will you?" she called from the kitchen. "My hands are greasy."

"All right." Pete walked slowly into his son's bedroom. He slammed his closed fist against the wall, as hard as he could. Pain shot up his arm.

"What was that?" Mary exclaimed.

That was your husband, not hitting his kid. Pete tried the taste of the words in his mouth, tried hearing them with Mary's ears. They would never do. They would frighten her. They frightened him.

"It's that bitch next door again," he answered after a pause he hoped she did not notice, "pounding for Doug to be quiet." He could not remember the last time he had lied to her about anything important.

"Well, she can go to hell, too," Mary said indignantly. The tigress defending her young, Pete thought. No, he could not have said what he almost told her. He would have to bear his secret, and his secret shame, alone.

He picked up Doug, who was now yowling indignantly at the slight delay. He put his face close to the baby's. Those small, wide, darkening eyes met his. "Will you please for God's sake just shut up?" he whispered. He did not know if he was taking the name of the Lord in vain or making one of the few honest prayers he had ever made in his life.

Doug actually did quiet down pretty fast; Pete's arms were automatically rocking him the way he liked—when he liked anything. His father was not reassured. Doug's face wore the smug expression he had come to know only too well.

"That wasn't too bad," Mary said when Pete toted the baby in a few minutes later. Doug was awake but not fussing. He tried to turn his head toward his mother's voice, and smiled in her direction. Mary smiled back; it was hard not to. Then she saw Pete's face. "Why so glum, hon?"

"Just tired, I guess." Pete knew he had shown weakness in the presence of the enemy. He also knew that was something else he could not tell his wife, not when the enemy was their son.

Mary could see what was going on, though, even if she did not understand it. When they went to bed that night, too worn for anything but whatever sleep Doug was going to let them have, she touched her husband's arm. "Pete, please don't take it so personally when Doug cries. I hate to watch you clamping your jaw when you carry him around. You act as though you think he deliberately sets out to provoke you."

"Sometimes I do wonder. His timing is awfully good." Pete kept his tone light on purpose. Mary could take his words as a routine complaint if she wanted . . . or she could ask just how serious he was. He was ready to cite chapter and verse to her, if she gave him half a chance.

"Pete." His heart sank. Her voice had that ring that sounds like patience but is really anything but. "He's just—"

"—a baby," Pete finished sourly.

"Well, he is." Mary was starting to sound angry. "Now let's go to sleep, shall we? We don't have time for this foolishness, not when Doug's liable to wake up any old time at all."

Pete was angry too, silently, frustratedly furious. It seemed to him that his wife had contradicted herself without so much as noticing. If Doug were "just a baby," they'd have some idea, at least, of when he'd be awake and when he'd be asleep. The only thing they were sure of now was that he'd pick the most inconvenient times possible.

That struck Pete as something nobody ought to find normal. Then something else struck him: fatigue, which laid him low as surely as if he had been sapped. For once, even Doug's howls failed to wake him. He never noticed Mary twice stumbling out of bed to nurse the baby. It was a splendid victory, and he did not know he'd won it.

The next few days made Pete wonder if he'd been wrong all along. Doug was amazingly civilized. He slept regular hours and was cheerful when he was awake. Pete paid him the ultimate compliment: "You wouldn't think it was the same baby."

Mary snorted but, he noticed, did not disagree.

The fragile hope Pete had nourished only made him hurt worse when it was dashed. His first stab at a Christmas list disintegrated in his mind when Doug let out a screech that should have burst from the iron throat of an insane calliope. Mary got to the baby before he did. He saw tears in her eyes. She'd had hopes, too.

"Hush, hush, hush," she murmured. She hugged Doug's little body against the softness of her breast, leaned his chin on her shoulder. She moved in the little dance steps that sometimes helped calm him. Nothing helped calm him today. Somehow Pete had thought it was going to be like that.

After a while, with an apprehensive look in her eye, Mary handed the baby to him and went into the kitchen to make dinner. Pete was fine with steaks and chops and hamburger, and had done most of the cooking since Doug was born. But Mary was a really good cook. She missed being in front of a stove; Doug's amiable spell had encouraged her to send her husband out for fancier food than he was up to making himself. Tonight she had something exotic and oriental planned for a pork roast.

That left Pete holding the baby. He carried Doug into the living room, turned on the stereo, and started going round and round the coffee table. The pile on the carpet was noticeably more beaten down there than anywhere else in the room.

"Hush, hush, hush, you little monster." Despite his words, his tone was a fair imitation of Mary's croon. He was determined not to let Doug get his goat—or not to let him know he had; listening to Doug at close range would have turned the back of Job's neck red. But Pete swayed and jiggled, as dedicated to calming his son as Doug was to driving him out of his tree.

He thought he was earning at least a draw. Doug's howls came further and further apart, and took on the rusty-hinge quality that showed the baby was getting tired. "Shh, shh," Pete sang. He turned his head. "How's dinner coming?"

"Getting there. How's he doing?"

"Not too bad." Pete glanced down at Doug. The baby's gaze met his with more directness and intelligence than ten-week-olds are supposed to show. Then Doug let out all the stops. Pete only *thought* he'd heard him cry before. He wished he'd been right.

He looked at Doug again. His son's face wasn't all screwed up, as baby's faces usually are when they pitch fits. Except for having his mouth open wide enough to let out all that horrible noise, Doug wasn't acting upset at all. He seemed . . . positively *smug.*

Rage filled Pete. "What sort of noise would you make if you really were hurting?" he growled. For a moment, the idea of dropping the kid just to find out looked awfully good. Almost without willing it, Pete felt his arm start to straighten to let go of Doug.

"Dinner," Mary called—shouted, rather, to be heard over the sound effects. "What was that you were saying to him?"

"Nothing." Saved by the bell, Pete thought. He wasn't sure whether he meant Doug or himself.

His legs felt very light as he carried Doug into the kitchen. He took a while to recognize the feeling, or rather to remember it. When he was a kid, they had felt that way whenever he was scared green and getting ready to run like hell. He was that scared again, but now he could not run.

He plopped Doug into his yellow plastic infant seat, setting him down with exaggerated care, as if to make up for his thoughts of moments before. He expected the baby to raise even more Cain at being put down, but Doug was mostly quiet while his parents ate. His few tentative yarps, though, sent worried jolts quivering through Pete. He wondered each time if this would be the one where the baby really let loose, and so he enjoyed the excellent pork roast less than he should have.

As he was filling the sink to soak the dishes, he wondered if Doug was beginning to learn subtlety to go with his brute-force hysterics. Babies learned things as they got older. Thinking about the sort of things Doug might like to learn filled Pete with dread.

In the two days that followed, Pete felt as if he were on a ship that had holed itself on submerged rocks: he sank slowly and on an even keel. The deck seemed stable and level under his feet, but he was going down all the same.

What made it even worse was that, as far as Mary could see, Doug was only a baby who cried too much. His outbursts didn't particularly interrupt her unless she was doing something with Pete, like eating lunch. He didn't yowl just to make her jump, or just to disrupt her train of thought.

And he didn't give that little aren't-I-clever-to-be-driving-you-bonkers stare out of the corner of his eye when she held him. By now, that expression infuriated Pete as much as Doug's crying. It was a constant reminder that his son was having sport at his expense. Sooner or later, Pete promised himself grimly, that would have to stop.

Had he been able to find boned chicken thighs on his last trip to Safeway, things might have turned out better. As it was, he'd brought home thighs with the bones still in. Mary had taken them out of the fridge to start defrosting early that afternoon, and was cutting the still partly frozen meat away from the bones. "This'll be good," she promised. "I'm just sorry you're stuck with Doug while I work on 'em."

"What?" Pete had heard maybe one word in three. Doug was squalling in his ear. Doug had been squalling in his ear for the past hour and a half, since he woke up from his latest nap. He wasn't hungry; he'd nursed for five minutes a while ago, and spit the nipple out. He wasn't wet, or poopy, or gassy, or warm, or cold, or anything. He was just ornery. Pete's tolerance for orneriness had worn very thin.

Mary turned away from the countertop to repeat herself. Doug yelled even louder, drowning her out again. He looked smugly up at his father. *What are you going to do about it?* his eyes seemed to say.

Pete heard the words in his head as plainly as if they were spoken aloud. "This," he answered, and threw the baby against the refrigerator.

The thud of the little body hitting the yellow-enameled metal door killed his fury like a bucket of icewater poured over a campfire. Horror replaced it. He took a step toward Doug, who for the moment was not crying at all.

"No!" Mary sprang at him. No linebacker could have done a better job of stopping him in his tracks. Linebackers, however, do not commonly carry knives. Rushing to defend Doug, Mary probably forgot she was still holding hers. It sliced a long furrow in Pete's sleeve, and in his arm.

The pain, and the sudden wet warmth of spilled blood, made him automatically grapple for the blade. He was bigger and stronger than Mary. He yanked it out of her hand. She fought back with more ferocity than he had dreamed was in her. They wrestled. She tripped him. They fell to the Solarion tile floor. He felt the knife go in.

There are not many places where a single knifethrust will kill at once. The soft flesh under the angle of the jaw is one of them.

"Mary?" Pete said. Even then, though, from the way she convulsed and suddenly stopped fighting him, he knew he would get no answer.

He pulled out the knife. His blood and Mary's were both on it, in a last terrible mingling. He sat on the floor of the kitchen, with Mary's body, and with Doug (Doug was crying again, and this time, by Christ, Pete knew why), and with the half-boned chicken thighs, and with the ruin of everything he had spent a lifetime building.

He looked at the knife again. It looked better to him now, better than whatever else lay ahead of him. He made sure he had a firm grip on it, drove it into his chest.

He took much longer dying than Mary, and hurt more than he had ever imagined he could, as his heart tried to beat around stainless steel. Consciousness finally faded. The last sound in his ears was Doug, crying.

Vicki Garreau fumbled with the car seat's catch as she took Doug out. Poor little fellow, she thought: he was too young to be coming home from the hospital for the second time, and to a new, unfamiliar home at that. Thinking about the baby made it easier not to think about what had happened to her sister and brother-in-law.

Doug squirmed and complained in Vicki's inexpert grasp. "Careful," her husband Jim said. He was hovering behind her, a big, thick-shouldered man with a coal-black handlebar mustache. "Don't hurt him."

"I'll try not to," she said. "He's just lucky to have only a cracked rib. Babies are tough little things, the doctor said."

"A good thing, too," Jim rumbled. The image of the dent in the refrigerator door would stay with him as long as he lived. He and Vicki had been trying to start a family of their own; after their nephew so suddenly and horribly became an orphan, they moved at once to start adoption proceedings.

"Shh. He's falling asleep again." Vicki carried him up the walk toward their house. As Jim hurried past her to open the door, she said softly, "If we hadn't lived a hundred and fifty miles away—" Try as she would, her mind, like his, kept coming back to Mary's kitchen.

Jim grunted and nodded. He opened the deadbolt, then the regular lock. He bent down to kiss his wife's hair as she brought the baby—their baby now, he thought—inside. She turned her head, managed a smile. He thought about how much she looked like her older sister, though her eyes were green, not blue.

She came out of the room that was now Doug's room a few minutes later. "I was just standing there watching him. He's sleeping like a little angel."

"Good. I put on a pot of coffee. After two and a half, three hours on the freeway, I need it."

"I won't turn down a cup myself."

The rich, dark smell filled the kitchen. Vicki got cups from the dish drainer. "I'll pour."

"Thanks."

She handed him his, and was pouring her own when Doug began to cry. She wasn't expecting it. The smooth brown stream wavered. "Ouch," she said. She popped a finger in her mouth. When she took it out, she was laughing. "We'll just have to get used to that, won't we?"

Most of this story is set in the town where I grew up, at a time when I was about four years old. To help my memory along, I was lucky enough to have my father's 1953 road atlas, which showed me how much of the Los Angeles freeway system that we take for granted today didn't exist a little more than a generation ago.

What sticks in my mind most about writing "Hindsight" is the night I finished it. I wrote the last few paragraphs at my in-laws' house about 12:30 A.M. just after Christmas 1983. Laura was deathly ill from stomach flu and couldn't do anything much about it because she'd found out she was pregnant a couple of weeks before. We were all supposed to leave at three in the morning to visit her relatives in San Francisco and give them the news. I went alone and was a zombie all the way up Interstate 5. Laura flew in a day or two later, mostly recovered. It was a sleepy, busy, happy time.

HINDSIGHT

Katherine tapped on the study door. "Mail's here."

"Be out soon," Pete Lundquist called, not looking up from his typewriter. He flicked the carriage return lever. The paper advanced a double space. A small part of his mind noticed that the ribbon needed changing; it was nearer gray than black. All his conscious attention, though, was focused on the novelette he was working on.

Another couple of paragraphs got him to the end of a section and, by luck, to the end of a page at the same time. A good enough place to stop for a while, he decided. He rolled the story out of the big Underwood office machine, peeled off the carbons one by one and put them in their stacks, and set the original on top of the typewriter to come back to later.

He stretched till his bones creaked. He was tall enough that his fingertips missed the ceiling only by a few inches: a thin stick of a man, with angular, not quite handsome features, very blue eyes, and a shock of blond hair that no amount of Wildroot or Vitalis could flatten for long. In a couple of weeks he would turn thirty, something he tried not to remember.

"How's it going?" Katherine asked when he finally emerged. That was not just interest in the story for its own sake. When a freelancer had trouble writing, steak turned to hamburger and hamburger to macaroni and cheese.

She relaxed, a little, as he said, "Not bad. I should be done in a couple of days, and get it out." He looked at her fondly. Physically they were total opposites; she was dark and inclined to plumpness, and he could rest his chin on the top of her head. But she had a good deal of the discipline that kept him steadily at the typewriter. With checks coming in on no schedule and for wildly varying amounts, she needed it.

"What's the good news today?" he asked.

"Not much." She displayed two envelopes and a magazine in a brown paper wrapper. "A gas bill, a check from *Interplanetary*—"

"The one should just about cover the other," he said sourly. *Interplanetary* paid late and not much and probably wasn't long for this world, but they had bought a short story he couldn't unload on any better market, so he had no real right to complain.

"—and the new *Astonishing*," Katherine finished.

"Aha!" he said. "Now I have the excuse I need for a break." She made a face at him; that just meant he would be busy later. She went into the kitchen to start dinner.

He lit a Chesterfield and sank into a shabby but comfortable overstuffed armchair with a sigh of contentment. It was a couple of minutes before four. He turned on the radio to catch the hourly news. The dial lit; he waited for the tubes to warm up and the sound to start.

He stripped off the *Astonishing*'s wrapper, turned to the table of contents. He didn't have anything in this month's issue, though he had been in the last one and would show up again in a couple of months. He saw with pleasure that there was a long novelette by Mark Gordian. He wondered what this one would be like. Gordian had mastered a number of different styles.

First things first, he thought. No one who read *Astonishing* put off the editorial. James McGregor could be—often tried to be—infuriating, but he was never dull.

As Pete read, he listened to the news with half an ear. Queen

Elizabeth's coronation dominated it. The Korean truce talks at Panmunjom dragged on and on. A new political party had been formed in the Philippines, and was promising great things. "And in sports," the announcer went on, "both the Seals and the Oaks fell further behind the Pacific Coast League–leading Hollywood Stars last night as—"

He was just turning to the Gordian story when the side door slammed. Not for the first time, he wondered how two small boys managed to sound like a platoon. "What's going on there?" he said, trying without much luck to sound stern.

"Daddy's out!" Wayne shouted joyfully. The six-year-old sounded as if Pete had just been released from jail. He came charging into the living room and flung himself at his father's lap. His brother Carl, who was seven, was right behind. Pete barely saved the *Astonishing* from getting squashed.

"And what have you two been up to?" he asked.

"Playing with Stevie next door," Carl answered. "His cousin Philip is visiting him from Denver. He's nine. He can throw a curveball."

"That's nice," Pete said. "Go wash your hands. With soap." He got nervous whenever his boys made a new friend—who knew whether the kid might be bringing infantile paralysis with him? The polio season was just starting, but it was already worse than last year's, and there had been almost 60,000 cases in 1952.

Pete did not get back to the *Astonishing* until he was done drying the dinner dishes and putting them away. He threw on a cardigan sweater; northern California late spring evenings were nothing like the ones he had grown up with in Wisconsin. But neither were the winters, thank God.

He flipped to the Gordian story. It was called "Reactions," which might mean anything. With Gordian, you never could tell—take the serial with the innocuous name "Watergate," for instance. Critics—serious critics—talked about the book version in the same breath with *1984.* To Pete, though, it was science fiction at its best, straightforward extrapolation of how difficult government skulduggery would inevitably become when copy machines and recorders were everyday items.

It also made Joe McCarthy hopping mad, something else Pete approved of.

It was hard to see how the same author could also write "Houston, We Have a Problem," a gripping tale of an early moon flight gone wrong, and *Tet Offensive,* a future war gone wronger. Barring the exotic hardware, that one looked disquietingly possible too, if you noticed the page-four stories about the fun the French were having trying to hold on to Indochina.

But Gordian—damn him!—didn't confine himself to the near future. "Neutron Star" had had all the astronomers who read science fiction buzzing a couple of years ago (and there were a lot of them). So did "Supernova," though Pete found the casual way computing machines were handled in that one even more exciting. It was a yarn he wished he'd written himself.

There were literally dozens more, not all in *Astonishing* by any means; *Galactic* and *Strangeness and Science Fantasy* had their share too. "All You Zombies" made every other time-travel story obsolete. "Sunjammer I" and "Sunjammer II" struck Pete as the prose equivalent of a jazz pianist improvising on a theme. And "Time Considered as a Helix of Semi-Precious Stones" was a literary firework that defied description.

Ever since Gordian started selling in 1949, he'd turned out even more words than Asimov, and not a bad story in the bunch. All things considered, he was the one writer who made Pete feel inadequate.

He settled in and began to read. By the end of the third page, he felt his hair trying to stand on end. He had not been so afraid since he'd driven a tank-destroyer through the crumbling wreckage of the Third Reich. But that had been a simple fear, fear that a kid with a grenade or an old man with a *Panzerfaust* or some diehard in a Royal Tiger tank would make sure he never saw the States again. This—

Discipline or no, he got very little writing done that night.

He spent the next week in a fever of anticipation waiting for McGregor's reply to his letter. He'd sent it airmail, and stuck another red six-cent stamp on the self-addressed return envelope he enclosed with it. At the moment, answers worried him more than pennies.

When the note finally came, he gritted his teeth against the anticlimax. "Dear Pete," the *Astonishing* editor had written, "I'm very sorry that Gordian picked off an idea you thought was yours, but things like that happen all the time (you should see my slush pile!). I'm sure you still have enough fresh notions to keep you going. Let me see one of those. Best, Jim."

Pete threw the letter on the kitchen table. "He doesn't believe me," he said bitterly.

"Would you, on someone's word alone?" Katherine said. "I'm still not sure I do, and I've seen your outline for myself."

"I suppose you're right," Peter admitted. "I guess I just think of Jim McGregor as slightly more than human. Well, by Christ, I can show him."

He turned on his heel and hurried into the study. He ran a fresh piece of paper into the typewriter. "Dear Jim," he wrote, "I realize I should have sent the enclosed with my first letter to you. I trust you will take my word that it was drafted some months ago. If you find it interesting, let me know. Yours, Pete Lundquist."

He looked at the letter for a moment, added a P.S.: "I don't know when I would have gotten around to writing from this skeleton. I have several ideas ahead of it, and one or two of them look like novels. But it would have happened eventually, I'm sure. You tell me what that story would have looked like."

This envelope was a lot fatter than the last one, but he sent it airmail too.

Three days later the telephone rang at 6:30 A.M. The unexpected noise made Pete cut himself shaving. Holding a piece of tissue to his chin, he got to the phone a split second ahead of his wife. Their eyes met in shared alarm; calls at odd hours generally spelled trouble.

"Mr. Peter Lundquist, please," the operator said.

"Speaking."

The woman's next words were a blessed relief: "I have a long-distance person-to-person call from a James McGregor in New York City."

"Yes, go ahead," Pete said, and mouthed to Katherine, "It's McGregor."

"Ho-ho! The game's afoot, Watson."

He waved her to silence. The editor's voice came on the line, raspy not just with distance but also from too many cigarettes: "That you, Pete?"

"I'm here." He had to stop himself from adding, "sir." So did most people who talked with McGregor.

"I'm only going to ask you once, and I expect a straight answer: Are you pulling my leg?"

Pete enjoyed a certain reputation as a practical joker, which at the moment he could have done without. "No," he said.

"All right, then. In a way, I was hoping you were. As is, how do you feel about meeting me in Los Angeles next week?"

"Why Los Angeles?" Pete was not at his best early in the morning, and the three-hour time difference from New York only made McGregor's advantage worse.

The *Astonishing* editor's sharp sniff showed he was holding on to his patience with both hands. "Because this Mark Gordian writes out of a post-office box in a town called Gardena. It took some work with a big atlas to find the place, but it's about fifteen miles south of L.A. I'd like to have a word with Gordian—don't you think you would too?"

Pete gulped. "Put like that, I suppose I would. Uh, Jim . . . what do you think is going on?"

"I don't know." McGregor sounded angry at the admission. "The first thing that occurs to me is telepathy, and I don't much fancy that for an explanation either."

"Why not? If anyone's been urging more basic research in extrasensory perception lately, it's you."

"Research, yes. But if Gordian picked this out of your brain, he stands to everyone else on Earth like the Empire State Building to a girl's dollhouse. I edit science fiction; I never planned on living it."

That Pete understood down to the ground. He had majored in engineering at college, and drew a very firm line between what was real and what wasn't. He shivered as the implications began to sink in. "If Gordian's a telepath, how do we know he's not reading our minds right now?"

"We don't," McGregor said. "And I have another question for you: If Gordian's a telepath, why is he reading *your* mind instead of Einstein's or Eisenhower's or Albert Schweitzer's? You'll be driving down to L.A., won't you?"

"I guess so," Pete said absently. He was still chewing on the more important query; in conversation as in his letters, McGregor had a gift for going right to the heart of an issue.

"Good. Pick me up at the airport, then. I'll be getting in at about a quarter past five on Friday evening—it's Trans World flight 107. If you've come up with any good answers, give 'em to me then."

"All right," Pete said. He was talking to a dead line.

Pete left with first light Thursday morning. By starting early, he got into Los Angeles before dark. The ride south along U.S. 101 was both hot and dull. Radio stations faded in and out as he drove. A little above Santa Barbara, the road came down to the Pacific. It was pretty enough to tempt Pete to stay on the Coast Highway the rest of the way, but he went back to 101 when it jogged inland again below Ventura and ran east toward the San Fernando Valley.

Sepulveda Boulevard led him south through the Sepulveda Pass and into the more built-up part of Los Angeles. None of the famous freeways was anywhere close; the nearest one, the Harbor, stopped just south of downtown, though his map showed its projected route all the way out to San Pedro.

He checked into a motel in a suburban district called Westchester, used the change from his ten-spot to buy a sandwich and Coke at the coffee shop down the street, then came back, took a shower, and went to sleep.

The six-lane tunnel that took Sepulveda under the airport's runways had only been open for a couple of months. Pete could see how much easier it made access to the facility. It had also allowed the runways to be lengthened.

The big silver DC-6 rolled to a stop about half an hour late. The enormous propellors spun themselves to silence. The people who filed off the plane looked weary, and no wonder; counting a forty-five-minute layover in St. Louis, they had been traveling for ten hours.

"Jim!" Pete called, striding forward to shake the editor's hand. As always, he was disappointed that James McGregor looked nothing like Kimball Kinnison. McGregor was in his early forties, of average height and build. His sandy crewcut was going gray above his ears, and his hair thinned at the temples. When younger, his face had been beaky; now craggy was a better word. Only his eyes seemed lensman-keen, and even then one had to look sharply, for he wore heavy, dark-framed glasses.

"Good to see you," McGregor said. They had met several times at conventions and other gatherings, and Pete had dropped into the *Astonishing* office once while in New York on other business. They argued for two hours. Pete lost, over and over, but the experience gave him notions for three new stories, all of which McGregor bought.

"Let's get my luggage," the editor said, "and some food, and a drink, and then back to wherever you're staying. I have some things to show you, now."

"Okay," Pete said, but disappointedly, "if you don't want to go down to Gardena first."

"What for? All we have to go on is a post-office box number, and the post office is closed."

Pete shook his head in chagrin at not having thought of that, but McGregor was already going on: "Unless, of course, he has a phone number in the local book. Worth a try, don't you think?" They were passing a bank of telephones on the way to the baggage claim area; McGregor found a chained phone book for the right part of town, pawed through its dog-eared pages. "Gordan . . . Gorden . . . Gordillo—so much for that. Well, we're no worse off."

"No," Pete said, still slightly stunned. The *Astonishing* editor could no more help throwing off ideas than a fissioning plutonium atom could help spitting neutrons, and the results were about as explosive.

Over dinner at the coffee shop near the motel, the talk had nothing to do with the mysterious Mark Gordian. Perhaps because he was tired, McGregor was full of sarcasm about the rioting in East Germany ("Which shows where the workers stand in the workers' paradise."), the unmanned Navajo guided bomber ("It'll be obsolete before it flies. Rockets are faster than jets."), and the way CBS and NBC has handled the televising of Queen Elizabeth's coronation ("Imagine sending P-51s to meet the British jet that brought the film to Canada. The RCAF has jets of their own, and got their film to the lab first and on the air first. Naturally—jets are faster than prop jobs.").

"It's still remarkable, having seen it the same day it happened," Pete insisted.

"Oh, no doubt. Me, though, I'll take one of Arthur Clarke's relay satellites, and see it the same minute it happens." The thing about McGregor, Pete thought, was that "good enough" would not do for him—he insisted on perfection. Sometimes he managed to wring it out of people, too.

Back at the motel, the editor unlocked the suitcase he had parked by the bed before going out to eat. He pulled out a fat manila folder. "What's in there?" Pete asked.

"A couple of manuscripts I've got from Gordian that I pulled out of the file. Look them over; I'd like to hear what you think of them." McGregor plainly had no intention of saying anything more for a bit; he sat in the motel room's shabby armchair puffing on an Old Gold while Pete sprawled full-length on the bed, reading.

"'The Hole Man,' eh?" Pete said. "That's a nice piece of work—gloomy, but nice."

McGregor only nodded and waited.

Pete felt flustered, as if facing a one-man oral exam committee without having studied. He nervously stacked the pages the editor had given him.

His fingers caught wrongness his eyes had missed. "Funny paper," he remarked; all four edges were rough, as if they had been torn off from perforations. "I've heard of typing paper sold in a roll, so you can run it into your typewriter continuously and rip off each sheet as you finish, but that would have smooth sides."

"So it would," McGregor said. "I don't understand this either, but I noticed it. Keep going."

After a few minutes, Pete said, "That's a high-quality ribbon he's using." He wasn't sure what made him notice that—probably a twinge of guilt at the decrepit state of his own.

"It's what they call a carbon film ribbon," McGregor explained. "They use them for legal documents and other things that might need to be photostatted. The things are hard to find and hideously expensive, because you can only go through them once. I've never had stories typed on them submitted before, I can tell you that."

"You've been researching this," Pete said accusingly.

"Guilty as charged. I can also tell you that one of New York's better detectives looked at some of these pages and couldn't match the typeface to anything in his collection. He was so surprised he didn't charge me."

"Curiouser and curiouser."

"Isn't it? The gumshoe did notice something I flat-out missed. You're not spotting it, but it's pretty obvious when it gets pointed out to you."

Pete stared without result at the pages in front of him. "All right, I give up. What is it?"

"Look at the right margin."

"My God! It's justified!" Pete felt like kicking himself for not noticing that right away. Every typescript he'd ever seen had a ragged right margin, but the pages of "The Hole Man" were so consistent and seemed so natural the way they were that their strangeness slipped by him.

"Very good," the *Astonishing* editor said. "Again, there's a gadget that will pull off the same stunt, but it's hard to come by—and why on Earth would you bother? The result's pretty, sure, but more trouble than it's worth."

"I'd say so." Pete sat up on the bed and took out a cigarette—he needed something to calm his nerves. He tapped the end of the Chesterfield on the nightstand to tamp down the tobacco; filtertips struck him as vaguely effeminate, and made the smoke taste like sawdust anyway. After a couple of deep drags, he said, "Whatever Gordian is, I don't think he's a telepath."

McGregor peered at him over the tops of his glasses. "Why's that?"

"It's not so much all this." He waved at the papers beside him. "This only helps confirm *what* I really decided on the drive down here—about 'Reactions,' I mean."

"How's that?"

"How would I put it? Something like this, maybe: there's more in the story you printed than I've thought of yet. The ideas, the world, even the names match, but the story has a depth of detail that I wouldn't begin to worry about until I actually started writing."

The editor steepled his fingertips. "And so? What conclusions do you draw?"

"Me? I'd rather not," Pete said, shaking his head. "I'd sooner believe in mind-reading."

For the first time, he saw McGregor angry at him. "If you reject the data, what do you work from then? A Ouija board, or the entrails of a sheep?"

"That's not fair," Pete protested. He felt himself flushing. "The whole thing is impossible."

"It is? Then why are we in Los Angeles?"

Pete had no good answer to that. McGregor got up and swatted him on the shoulder. "Nothing we can do about it at the moment, anyway. Maybe things will clear up when we meet Gordian. For now, though, I'd just as soon go to bed. I'm still running on East Coast time."

"Fair enough," Pete said, but he was a long time falling asleep.

"This is part of the fourth largest city in the country?" McGregor said incredulously as Pete passed the airport going south on Sepulveda.

"Well, actually, no," Pete answered. "According to that map on your lap, this is the sovereign city of El Segundo." There were streets and houses on the west side of Sepulveda; most of the east side was simply a field, brown under the summer sun and full of tumbleweeds.

"Mostly oilwells, from what I can see of it."

"It does look that way." Pete turned left onto El Segundo Boulevard. He drove for about a mile before coming on more houses. Then, just west of Hawthorne High School, the Chevy bumped over the streetcar tracks.

"Signs of life," McGregor said. "A few, anyway." About four miles later, Pete turned right on Vermont and headed south. The street was wide and looked as if it ought to be important, but it had a dirt center divider and there were good long stretches of field along it. It did, however, boast of a supermarket, a liquor store across the street, and a couple of large, garish buildings that identified themselves as "clubs." "Wonder what those are," McGregor said.

"Poker parlors," Pete said, pleased as always when he knew something the *Astonishing* editor didn't (it didn't happen very often). "Under California law, draw poker's a game of skill, and it's local option whether to allow it or not. This Gardena makes a bundle off the taxes the clubs pay."

Gardena Boulevard, where the post office was, was as much of a business district as the little town had. There was a Rexall drugstore on the corner at Vermont, a small department store and a jeweler's a little farther west, and then a pink stucco Bank of America, its gold Old English lettering gleaming in the morning sun.

But even Gardena Boulevard had its share of houses, mostly white clapboard buildings that dated from well before the war. The post office was next to one of those, just west of a narrow street called Budlong. Pete pulled in front of it; there was plenty of room to park. "Now what?" he said as he killed the engine.

McGregor was wrestling with the road map; as Pete might have expected, his competence extended to refolding one of the damned things. He tossed it into the glove compartment. "Now," he said, "we go in and wait for Mr. Gordian to open box one forty-eight."

"And get ourselves thrown out by the postmaster when we hang around for six or eight hours looking for somebody who doesn't show up."

"Nonsense. Writers haunt mailboxes; it's part of the disease. As for the postmaster, leave him to me."

"I suppose I have to." They were already walking up the low, broad steps into the building.

But it proved just as the editor had predicted. When the gaunt fellow behind the counter asked, "Help you gents?" McGregor said, "Yes. Could you tell me what time you usually put mail in your boxes? We're supposed to meet someone here then."

The man accepted that as casually as McGregor had said it. "Usually about eleven," he answered. "You've got some time to use up."

"Any place we could get a cup of coffee?" Pete asked, not wanting to be entirely left out.

"There's a delicatessen down the block there," the man said. He pointed west. "Reckon they can help you."

The coffee at Giuliano's was scalding hot and strong enough to growl, but good. While Pete and McGregor were drinking it, a Japanese man wearing a suit and hat came in; a lot of the people on the street in Gardena were Orientals. The man bought half a pound of cotto salami, paid the clerk and thanked him, and walked out.

"Acculturation." McGregor chuckled. His gaze sharpened, as if coming into focus. "Hmm—seems to me you could do something with that. Suppose you had an alien race, now, just coming into contact with technologically superior Terrans—"

The resulting conversation had the deli clerk listening, pop-eyed, from behind his counter and Pete frantically scribbling notes. He barely remembered to look at his watch. "It's half-past ten," he said. "We'd better get back, in case they're early today."

The *Astonishing* editor got up (to the clerk's obvious disappointment), but was not a man easily derailed from his train of thought. "All very well," he said as they walked back toward the post office, "but what about the attitude of the aliens' priests? No matter how much Terran gadgets eased life for their people, wouldn't they see them as black magic? And how would that affect their society?"

"You could take different approaches to that," Pete said. "The priests might even be right, for their special set of circumstances."

"So they might. My God, there's no one right answer! What I want to see is a good, solid, internally consistent story that carries its underlying assumptions—whatever those are—as far as they can go."

A couple of people were already waiting by the post office boxes, and several more came in after Pete and McGregor. "They can't *all* be writers," Pete whispered behind his hand.

The editor rolled his eyes. "You'd be amazed."

At five after eleven a mailman with a fat bag and a jingling ring full of keys pushed through the small crowd and began filling the boxes. McGregor nudged Pete in the ribs, but he had also seen the envelopes going into number 148.

Pete looked round, wondering which (if any) of the men near him was the mysterious Mark Gordian. Surely not the bald little man in overalls; he looked as if he didn't read anything, let alone write. The fellow who looked like a doctor was more likely, or the muscular man wearing a loud tie.

He got a lesson on how much such speculation was worth when the person who opened the box proved to be a freckled, redheaded woman with glasses. She might have been a couple of years younger than he was, and looked comfortably casual in a rust-colored blouse and green pedal pushers.

McGregor chuckled beside him. "I suppose there's no reason Gordian can't be married."

"I guess not," Pete agreed. He was taken aback all the same; he had used so much energy thinking about Mark Gordian the writer and Mark Gordian the enigma that Mark Gordian the person was outside his reckoning.

The woman paid no attention to him or McGregor. They followed her outside. She was opening the mail. One envelope plainly had a check in it; that went into her purse. After she opened another one, she said, "Oh, shit," crumpled up the sheet of paper inside, and threw it away. She did not seem angry, merely irritated; it was how a man would swear. Pete blinked.

Her car was parked a couple of spaces down from his Chevy. He frowned a little; she drove a cheap, ugly Volkswagen Bug. Having spent several months getting shot at by Germans, he did not care for the idea of buying automobiles from them.

She was unlocking the car door when he called, "Excuse me, are you Mrs. Gordian?"

For a second she did not react. Then she looked up in surprise. "I don't think I know you," she said, "but yes, I'm Miss Gordian." Pete felt stupid for not noticing she wore no ring, and only a little better because McGregor had missed it too.

The editor nodded to her in apology. He said, "You are related to Mark Gordian, aren't you?"

Her eyes narrowed. Pete thought she was going to drive away without answering, and got ready to dive into his car after her. Instead, though, she began to ask, "Who are—" She stopped. "You're James McGregor." It sounded like an accusation.

"Yes." He indicated Pete. "This is Peter Lundquist."

Her eyebrows shot up. "Why, so it is!" she exclaimed. It was as if she recognized him, and he was sure he had never seen her before. She hesitated again. "Why are you looking for Mark Gordian?"

Pete gave it to her in one word: "'Reactions.'"

He could see it hit home. "Oh," she said, and kicked at the sidewalk. "Oh, shit." This time it sounded like resignation. "You were already working on it?"

His heart thuttered inside his chest. He forced himself to steadiness. "Yes."

"*Are* you related to Mark Gordian?" McGregor persisted.

One corner of her mouth quirked upward. "In a manner of speaking. I *am* Mark Gordian."

Pete had never seen the *Astonishing* editor with a foolish expression on his face, but suspected he bore a similar one on his own. McGregor's rally was a visible thing. "Fair enough, I suppose," he said. "There's E. Maine Hull, after all, and C. L. Moore, and I understand Andre Norton is a woman too. Pleased to meet you, 'Mark.'"

She was still studying the two of them. "I'm not nearly sure I'm pleased to meet you. Who else knows you're here?" It was a sharp challenge; Pete thought her close to bolting again.

"My wife, of course," the editor said, and Pete echoed him. McGregor added, "There's a detective back in New York who's interested in the typewriter you use."

"I daresay he would be." She chuckled without much humor. "No one else? Not the FBI or the CIA?"

Pete spread his hands. "What would we have to show them? They'd laugh themselves sick at us Buck Rogers types. And besides," he added with characteristic independence, "what business is it of theirs, anyway?"

"Yes, you would be one to say that, wouldn't you?" Again he had the feeling she knew a good deal about him. She nodded slowly, as if coming to a decision. "All right, follow me home if you like. If anyone is, you're entitled to an explanation." She did not wait for an answer, but stooped to get into the Volkswagen. Its raucous air-cooled engine roared to life.

About ten minutes later she pulled into the driveway of a freshly built tract house; the front lawn still had the half-threadbare look that tender new grass gives. Pete parked his Chevrolet across the street. She was locking her car while he and McGregor walked over.

She waved at the house. "Isn't it splendid? I've only been in about four months. Eleven thousand five hundred dollars and a four-and-a-half percent loan."

"Everything is too expensive these days," Pete said sympathetically.

She turned red and made a peculiar strangled noise that perplexed him until he saw she was trying not to laugh. "Never mind," she said. "Care for some lunch? I'm no great cook, but sandwiches are easy, and there's beer in the refrigerator."

"Sold," McGregor said at once. Pete nodded too.

"Come on, then."

For a reason Pete had trouble naming, the inside of her house disappointed him. It was pleasant enough, with Early American furniture, Raphael prints on the walls, and a number of well-filled bookcases—nothing out of the ordinary. Then he realized that was the problem. He had expected something strange, and did not know what to make of this blatant normality.

She led him and McGregor into the kitchen, slapped ham, dill pickle, and mustard on rye bread, used a churchkey to open three cans of Burgermeister. For a few minutes they were all busy eating. "That was good," Pete said, wiping his mouth. "Thanks, uh—your name isn't really Mark, is it?"

She smiled. "It's Michelle, as a matter of fact."

Almost at the same time, the two men got out their cigarettes and looked round for an ashtray. They did not see one. Michelle Gordian's smile disappeared. "I'd rather you didn't smoke in the house," she said, a trifle sharply. McGregor shrugged and put his pack away. So, reluctantly, did Pete; his nicotine habit was much stronger than the editor's.

Michelle put the few dishes in the sink, then said, "Why don't we go back into the living room? It's more comfortable there."

She waved them to the couch, sat down herself in a rocking chair facing them. She came to the point with a directness Pete was not used to in a woman: "Just what is it you think I am?"

He had to try twice before he got the words out: "A time-traveler." Speculating about the impossible was much easier than proposing it—that implied belief.

"Why?" She effortlessly controlled the conversation; for once even McGregor did not seem eager to break in. As much as anything else, that helped make Pete take the preposterous idea seriously.

He plowed ahead, outlining the strangeness he and the *Astonishing* editor had found. As he spoke, he knew how absurd he had to sound. He waited for Michelle to burst into laughter. But instead she was leaning forward in the rocker, following him intently. He thought of her for the first time as an attractive woman; interest brought her features to life.

When he had stumbled to a halt, she was silent for most of a minute. As had been true outside the post office, though, once she made up her mind she went with it all the way. "You're right, of course," she said briskly.

McGregor had been gathering himself while Pete was talking.

"I'd like to see more proof than a peculiar typewriter and a story that corresponds too well to an outline," he said. "I've been burned before. And forgive me, but nothing here looks the least bit, ah, extratemporal. That goes for what I take to be your study, too, from what I saw of it from the kitchen."

"I'm not that careless," Michelle said, "even if I obviously wasn't careful enough. I have neighbors and friends who visit me; what would they make of a disc drive or a VCR?"

Nonsense words and letters, Pete thought. McGregor's snort said he agreed with that judgment. He shook his head with sarcastic mock sadness. "So, of course, you have nothing to show us."

Michelle Gordian's eyes sparked angrily. "I didn't say that," she snapped. She rummaged in her purse, took out a thin white plastic rectangle about the size of a driver's license, fiddled with it for a moment, and tossed it to her guests. "Go ahead—it's on. Just punch the numbers and functions and signs."

There was an inch-long strip of silvery stuff at the top of the card, with an angular dark gray zero at the right edge. Pete pressed the 7, and almost dropped the card when, silently and without any fuss, the matching number took the zero's place. McGregor leaned over and punched the radical sign. The 7 disappeared in turn, to be instantly replaced by 2.6457513.

"That," the editor said softly, "is the most astounding thing I have ever seen in my life."

Pete hardly heard him. He had used desktop electric calculators before, bulky machines half as big as a typewriter, was used to the whirr of their motors, the ratcheting thunk of turning gears and cams, the wait for everything to finish in a multidigit multiplication. But here for the asking, at the press not even of a button, was 2.6457513. He had met the future, and he was in love.

When Michelle held out her hand for the incredible little device, he did not want to give it back. All he could think of to say was, "If you're used to machines like this, how can you stand living in 1953?"

McGregor, as was his way, carried that thought a step further: "How many centuries in the future are you from?"

One of her carroty eyebrows rose. "I'm sorry to disappoint you, but only about thirty-five years." When the two men exclaimed in disbelief, she said, "Think of this, then: What would the best aeronautical engineer in the world have made of an F-86 jet fighter in 1918? The more technology grows, the more it can grow. You both know that."

"Yes, but I never had my nose rubbed in it like this before," McGregor muttered.

Pete did not look at it that way. The idea of the future had drawn him long before he began writing about it. Now he had held a piece of it in his hand, had touched the warm palm and fingers of it with his own.

He had to know more. "What else can you show us?" he breathed. "What were those things you named, a 'VCR' and and a, uh, 'disc driver'? You must have them here, or you wouldn't have mentioned them."

"Disc drive," she corrected absently. "Yes, I have them. Whether you should see them or not—well, having come this far, I suppose you deserve to know the rest. Come on out to the garage with me."

She led them through the kitchen and service porch. As they walked down the steps into the backyard, she locked the door behind them. "Why bother?" Pete said. "We aren't going to be gone all that long, are we?"

She looked surprised, then sheepish. "Force of habit. Something else I brought with me from the 1980s, I'm afraid."

McGregor cleared his throat. "Which brings up another point. Pete asked how you live here; I'm more interested in why. And why so secretly? With what you know, why not give the United States the help we need against the Reds?"

Something changed in her face. She was younger than Pete, years younger than the editor, but living through her life in the future (My God—she wouldn't even be born yet! Pete thought) had left her more streetwise, more cynical than both of them together. His misgivings stirred again.

She said bleakly, "Why do you think the government deserves that kind of edge?"

"Why don't you?" McGregor demanded after a short, stunned pause. The hostile edge was back in his voice, and Pete did not blame him.

Michelle was unabashed. "For one thing, *Watergate* wasn't exactly fiction. All I did was change some names. Do you want to know who President Cavanaugh really is?" She paused for dramatic effect, then told them.

McGregor winced. "I will be damned," Pete said.

She continued inexorably, "Does the name Klaus Barbie mean anything to either of you?"

"The Butcher of Lyon," Pete exclaimed. "I went through there not long after the Nazis left. What about him?"

"He's living in South America now, because he was a resource to our intelligence agencies and we helped spirit him away from the French. Just about thirty years from now, he'll finally get captured and we'll get around to apologizing to France."

Pete started to say, "I don't believe it," but the words stuck in his throat.

"Shall I go on?" Michelle asked McGregor. "Or will you believe I have some reason for doing things like I am?"

"You have an unpleasant way of making your points," he said, but took the argument no further.

She unlocked the garage door, swung it up, turned on the light, and closed it behind the three of them. The front third of the garage held the same sort of stuff Pete's did: a couple of trashcans, a lawnmower, some gardening and hand tools, a pile of boxes filled with miscellaneous junk. The rest was walled off. A door had been cut in the wall; a stout deadbolt gleamed above the knob.

"This is where I do my real work," she said as she unbolted and unlocked it.

She reached for a light switch just to the side of the door. Pete was not sure what to expect—probably something like the inside of a flying saucer. It wasn't like that. The general impressions reminded him of his own working area: office furniture, lots of books and records. There was an amenity he wished he had thought of for himself—a small refrigerator—in one corner.

The more he looked, though, the stranger things got. The television set was no model he had seen before, and he did not know what the small box, full of knobs and buttons, attached to it was. The radio, record player, and speakers were similarly recognizable but not familiar, and seemed somehow naked out by themselves without a cabinet.

And the gadget on the desk had a keyboard, but if its mother was a typewriter, she had been unfaithful with a TV set. Wires led to a couple of other unfamiliar machines—no, wait, there was paper in one of them. "No wonder your paper looks like that!" Pete said. "You've got little side-strips for the holes to mesh with the sprockets of the electric printer, and then you just peel them off. How clever!"

"That was the hardest thing to install," she remarked. "I don't want to say much about how I travel, but I can't bring anything back with me that I can't carry. These days I mostly stay here, anyway, unless I need something I can only get uptime. Happens I like it here."

Pete walked over to the desk. There was a magazine on it, next to the keyboard-*cum*-screen. He did not recognize the title, or the emblem prominently displayed on the cover: a stylized rabbit's head in a bow tie. "Gala 33rd Anniversary Issue!" the magazine proclaimed. The date (seeing that gave him chills) let him make a quick subtraction.

"It's almost ready to begin." The connection with his own times was cheering, in a way. Then he noticed something else. "This cost *five dollars*?" he said in horror.

"It's not as awful as it sounds," Michelle reassured him. "In terms of 1953 money, it's somewhere between a dollar and a dollar and a half."

He frowned. Not even the postwar inflation had been as bad as that. Some things in the future looked to be mixed blessings after all.

He picked up the magazine. "May I?"

"Go ahead," she said. There was something in her voice he could not quite read. She kept her face carefully blank as she went on, "In some ways it will probably interest you more than it does me."

The first few pages were mostly ads. The quality of the color reproduction surpassed anything 1953 could offer. Pete gaped at the lines of the cars. They were the most blatantly different element, though fashions had also changed, women's hairstyles were new, and mustaches and beards were common on men.

The magazine fell open naturally at the center. A very pretty girl smiled out at Pete. "Ah, I see what you meant; it's like *Esquire*," he said, and opened the foldout.

He closed it in a hurry, scarlet to the roots of his hair. "Where did you get this, this pornography?" he stammered.

He turned even redder when he saw how hard she was trying not to laugh at him. "By my standards, it isn't pornography; in fact, it's very mild, compared to some others," she said gently. "And I bought it at the same place I got my little calculator—the Rexall's at the corner of Vermont and Gardena Boulevard."

"You bought it yourself? You didn't have a man get it for you? I don't believe it. How could you show your face anywhere afterward?"

"Women do a lot of things in my time that they can't do here-and-now." She eyed him with disconcerting directness, smiled so that her lips parted very slightly. Did that mean what he thought it did? He was not sure he wanted to know. He had never seriously looked at another woman since he married Katherine, but there was no denying he felt drawn to Michelle Gordian now. He could not tell where his interest in her for her origin stopped and his interest in her as a person—and as a woman—began.

He was grateful when she changed the subject, and suspected her to be aware of it. She said, "Anyhow, the pictures weren't the reason I bought the magazine. It has a Clarke story in it that I want to use."

For a moment, all that did was to convince Pete that the publication wasn't obscene, at least in its own context: he could not imagine Arthur Clarke publishing in anything that was. Then the full meaning of her words hit him. "You're saying you've plagiarized all your work, then?" he asked coldly. "So that's why you came back here—to make an easy living off what other people have done." His liking for her flickered and blew out.

"It certainly looks that way," McGregor put in. Where exotic technology had lured Pete, with editor's instinct McGregor had been drawn to the bookshelves. Most of the volumes there were pocket books. Some of the writers' names were familiar, others not. The books were shelved alphabetically by author's last name; Pete's glance flicked to the L's. He was startled to see how much he had done—would have done?—will have done? He gave up on the right verb form.

In any case, McGregor was holding several books in his hand. He showed one to Pete. "You'll notice it's called *Neutron Star,*" he said. "It also has 'At the Core' and 'The Handicapped' in it. Here's another one: *The Hugo Winners, Volume V,* with 'Not So You'd Notice.' I can go on for a while, if you like."

He looked at Michelle Gordian as at some particularly unpleasant insect, an expression Pete understood completely. He had always reckoned thieves of other people's work beneath contempt; that the authors of the stories stolen here could have no chance to prove these words their own only made it worse.

Pete could not even bring himself to respect the way Michelle stood up to the scorn he and McGregor directed at her. "Don't you want to hear my reason for doing what I'm doing?" she asked.

"Does it matter?" Pete ground out. He felt ashamed of his thoughts of a few minutes before.

"It's obvious anyway," McGregor said. "It's one of the oldest clichés in science fiction—the time-traveler using special knowledge to get rich. I never thought I'd see anyone actually do it, that's all."

" 'Get rich?' " Michelle echoed. It was her turn to flush now, but from anger rather than embarrassment. "Not likely, at three cents a word and down. If money were what I wanted, there are easier ways than spending so much time in front of my word processor." Seeing their uncomprehending looks, she jabbed a thumb at the mutant typewriter.

Pete thought of his own troubles making ends meet, but her expostulation did nothing to move McGregor. "What then?" the editor snapped. "Look at the name you've built for yourself here and now. Who are you up in your own time?"

He plainly thought the question rhetorical, but she answered it. "An up-and-coming SF author, if you must know. You've been picking books off the shelves; why don't you get mine out?" There were four of them, three novels and a collection of stories, published, Pete noticed, under her own name. She said, "You can see I don't have to steal everything I do. That's come in handy, because some of what I've sold wouldn't be publishable in a science fiction magazine in the 1980s."

Pete pointed to the magazine with the rabbit on the cover. "After seeing *that*, I'd think you could get anything into print."

She smiled. "In that sense, you can, pretty much. But not everything I've written myself is science *fiction,* if you see what I mean."

"Oh." Pete and McGregor looked at each other. The writer asked in a low voice, "Which ones are real?"

"To hell with that." McGregor made an impatient gesture. He peered at Michelle over the top of his glasses. "You're saying you have some reason besides the strictly personal for doing what you're doing."

Relief showed on her face. "Yes, I do."

"It had better be a good one."

"I think it is."

The *Astonishing* editor waited, but she said nothing more. Finally he barked, "Well?"

"Think it through for yourself," she said. Nothing could have been better calculated to engage his interest. "You, too, Pete," she urged. "You must have read a fair number of the stories I've had published—I won't call them mine if that offends you. What do they have in common?"

Not much, was Pete's first thought. They were too diverse—and no wonder, if they actually came from many different pens.

But McGregor saw what she was driving at. He was more used to considering a number of stories together than Pete. He said slowly, "If I had to pick any one thing, it would be the way your characters attack problems. They all have a knack for applying knowledge logically."

"Thanks," she said. "That's one of the main ideas I've been trying to get across." She turned to Pete, asked with seeming irrelevance, "You have school-age kids, don't you?"

"A couple of boys," he nodded. "Why?"

"How are they learning to read?"

He made a sour face. "About how you'd guess—this current idiocy of pictures and 'looking at the shape of the whole word,' whatever that means. It doesn't matter. When Carl turned four, I bought an old phonics reader at a secondhand bookstore and taught him myself, the right way; I did the same for his brother a year later. They're both near the top of their classes now."

"I'm sure they are. But what about the children whose parents didn't bother? How well are they going to do when they come across an unfamiliar word? You're a good SF writer—extrapolate. What happens when those kids grow up? What happens when some of them become teachers and try to teach *their* sons and daughters to read?"

Pete thought about that, and did not like the answer he came up with. "You're telling us that's how it's going to be?"

"I'm afraid I am. You can watch out for something called 'new math,' too, which is just as delightful as reading through pictures."

"Thirty-odd years isn't that long a time," McGregor protested. "When the Roman Empire fell in the west, it took generations for the decline in literacy to become as widespread as you're implying. And we're starting at a much higher level than the Romans ever reached."

"True enough," Michelle said, "but then, the Romans were carrying on as best they could, trying to preserve what they had with the barbarians at the gates."

She stopped there, letting the two men follow her train of thought for themselves. "You mean we don't?" Pete said. His fist clenched; the notion that the United States, having surmounted the Depression and World War II, put western Europe back on its feet, and contained the Reds in Korea, could suffer a loss of will, was enough to infuriate him.

As was so often true, James McGregor asked the question that needed asking. "What went—er, goes—wrong?"

"My hindsight isn't long enough to be sure," Michelle said, "but I can put my finger on a couple of things. One is education, as I said. Another is the hangover from the war in Vietnam."

"In where?" the editor said, but Pete's memory jogged back to his thoughts when he was about to read "Reactions." He exclaimed, "Oh, my God! *Tet Offensive*!"

McGregor stared from one of them to the other. "You're not telling me that one's based on fact?" he demanded of Michelle. At her nod, he gave a rueful laugh. He said, "You know, when you sent it to me, I almost bounced it because it seemed too unlikely for the readers to believe. The only things that saved it were the gadgetry on the one hand and the fact that it was internally self-consistent on the other. No wonder, I guess." He was still shaking his head.

"No wonder at all," Michelle said. "The war is one of the reasons a magazine can cost five dollars. There wasn't—won't be—enough money to pay for guns and butter both, so the printing presses tried to make up the difference."

"That always happens," Pete said.

"Yes, but I think it was the least of the damage," Michelle replied. "What is it Heinlein says?—it doesn't matter if a hamburger costs ten dollars as long as there's plenty of hamburger. The harm done the country's institutions was worse."

"The riots and marches and such?" Pete asked; they had only been sketched in as background to the story, but they formed a constant counterpoint to the fighting that occupied center stage.

"Those are just the outward signs of what I mean," Michelle said. "To this day I'm not sure whether the war was right or wrong in itself, but it was certainly botched. People got very cynical about everything the government did (Watergate helped there too), and a lot of them automatically opposed it or thought it was stupid when it tried to do anything at all.

"And with contempt for the government went contempt for organization and standards of every sort. That aided and abetted the failure of education, I fear. And naturally, with the emphasis on the importance of the individual, anything that didn't produce immediate, obvious benefits had hard sledding. Even the space program had rough going—once weather satellites and communications satellites were in place, people took them for granted and didn't think about all the R&D it took to get them up in the first place. What can I tell you? The interest of the country just swung away from science and technology. There's no prettier way to put it than that."

"That can't be strictly true," Pete protested. "What about all these things?" He waved at the television, the contraption wired to it, the—what had she called it?—word processor.

She pointed at them one at a time in turn, saying, "Made in Taiwan, made in Japan (nobody in the United States manufactures videocassette recorders—we can't compete), made in Japan . . . the microcomputer is American-built, but the Japanese models are just as good and getting better—and cheaper."

Seeing their stricken expressions, she went on gently, "It's not all bad, up when I come from. Blacks—no, I'm sorry, Negroes is the polite word now—and women have many more opportunities than here-and-now, and a lot take advantage of them. Many people who would die or be crippled today can be saved."

"'Heart Transplant' will come true, then?" McGregor asked.

"Oh, yes, but it's just the most dramatic one of a whole range of new techniques. . . . What else? Well, we're still holding the line against the Russians. I expect we will, a while longer. That's not a bad thing; they're smoother then than they are now, but no nicer."

"All very interesting, I'm sure," the editor said, "but it still doesn't answer the question we've had all along: Why *are* you here?"

"I thought I was explaining that," she said. "I'm trying to change the future, of course." Her voice took on a fresh urgency, as if she were a lawyer trying to convince two magistrates of the justice of her case. "We missed coming so much further than we did by so little. The moon program petered out—"

That drew a grunt from McGregor and sent a wave of anguish through Pete. He did not want to believe it, but it fit horridly well with everything else Michelle had told them.

He pulled his attention back to what she was saying: "Compared to my time, education, interest, and (maybe most important) purpose are still strong here and now. I'm just trying to nudge things along a little bit, to get across the idea that the best way to solve a problem is to apply knowledge to it, as you said, Mr. McGregor. That's true both of my own stories and of the ones I've taken from other writers."

"And you've also slipped some of your special knowledge into them," the editor said.

"Of course. An amazing number of the people who read SF are engineers and scientists themselves; that's more true now than it will be in my time. If they pick up a notion or two from one of my near-future pieces, and act on them now instead—you see what I'm driving at, I think. I've done my best to describe hardware and techniques as precisely as I could."

"Using science fiction to save the world, eh?" McGregor said. "Much as I hate to say it, isn't that a trifle naive?"

"If ideas don't do the trick, what will?" Michelle retorted. The *Astonishing* editor grunted again.

A considerable silence fell before Pete nerved himself to ask, "Any luck?"

"I still have hope," was all she said. "Do you really want to find out more than that?"

"No, I suppose not," he said, and wondered if he meant it. He decided he did. Knowing what lay ahead was too much like losing his free will. He shuddered at the burden Michelle Gordian had taken on herself.

McGregor must have been thinking along the same lines, for he said to her, "What can I do to help?"

"The best thing would be to forget that this whole visit ever happened," she answered. "For God's sake, don't be any easier on my stories because of it. If they aren't worth reading, nobody'll care—or even find out—what's in them."

His grin was wolfish. "You needn't worry about that. If I start publishing stories that aren't worth reading, the magazine goes under and I either starve or have to start making an honest living for myself."

She made a face at him. "Fair enough." Stepping past Pete, she opened the door that led out to the mundane world of 1953.

"Excuse me." When they were walking back to the house, Pete took out his cigarettes, gratefully sucked in the harsh smoke. Seeing Michelle's expression of distaste, he quoted,

" 'Tobacco is a dirty weed.
It satisfies no normal need.
It makes you thin, it makes you lean,
It takes the hair right off your bean.
It's the worst darn stuff I've ever seen. I like it.' "

"The more fool you," she told him, but she waited until he had had enough and crushed the butt under his heel.

Once they were inside, McGregor said feelingly, "I hope no one will argue with me when I say that calls for another drink. A very dry Martini, if you have the makings."

"I'll wave the vermouth at it as I toss in the cherry," she promised. "Anything for you, Pete?"

"I wouldn't turn down another beer."

She handed it to him, made the editor's drink and a gin and tonic for herself. She watched McGregor take a cautious sip. "Is that all right?"

"I'll let you know when my eyes uncross," he wheezed, but the glass rapidly emptied.

After he was done, he seemed impatient to be gone. Pete thought he wanted to talk privately about the amazing day, but he said very little on the drive back to the motel. At last Pete said, "What is it, Jim? I've never seen you knock back a drink so fast, and I've never heard you so quiet."

"You didn't pay a lot of attention to the books back there, did you?"

"No, not really. Why?"

"I wish I hadn't." There was a long pause. "One of them was called *The James McGregor Memorial Anthology.*"

"*The*—oh, Jim!"

"Yeah. It's good to know I'll be well thought of, I suppose."

Pete could only admire the editor's composure. Even a kidnapper facing the gas chamber could hope his sentence would be commuted; this one, though indefinite, was certain. Pete hesitated, then asked, "Did you, uh, look at the copyright date?"

"The hell I did!" McGregor said, echoing Pete's feelings exactly: "That's a chunk of the future I have no desire to know more about, thank you very much."

"What will you do now?"

"What would you expect? Get a flight back to New York and go on with *Astonishing,* of course. There's certainly nothing I'd rather do." He fished his wallet out of his pocket, pawed through it. "Where's that Trans World reservation-and-ticket number? Oh, here it is—MIchigan 8141. I'll have to give them a call when we get back to our digs."

They were pulling into the motel parking lot when Pete said reflectively, "Things aren't going to be as simple—or as good—up ahead as I'd hoped, from what Michelle says."

The editor laughed at him. "Remember what de Camp put in the mouth of one of his characters? Something to the effect that a truthful traveler coming back from heaven would report its charm greatly overrated."

"Well, maybe so. Still, I'm not sorry she's trying to bend the future a bit. Imagine reaching the moon and then cutting back on space exploration. It's crazy!"

"You get no arguments from me. If I thought you were wrong,

I'd be calling the FBI now, not TWA." Pete turned off the ignition. They got out of the car. McGregor went on, "Let's get ourselves packed. Our wives will be missing us."

"So they will," Pete agreed, but he was disturbed to find himself thinking as much of Michelle Gordian as of Katherine.

The big propellers began to spin, slowly at first but then blurring toward invisibility. Even behind the steel and glass of the terminal, the roar of the radial engines sank into a man's bones. The airliner rolled west along the runway. It sprang into the air; the landing gear folded up into its belly.

Wishing McGregor well, Pete walked back through the terminal toward the parking lot off Century Boulevard. He passed the row of telephones in which the editor had searched in vain for "Mark" Gordian's number. He hesitated, took out a dime, and went over to an unused phone.

He dialed with a rising sense of trepidation. He heard three rings, four, five; he was about to hang up, more relieved than not, when his call got answered. "Hello?"

"Michelle?"

"Yes, this is Michelle Gordian. Who's calling, please?" She sounded out of breath; she had probably come running in from outside, he thought, to pick up the phone.

"This is Pete Lundquist, Michelle."

"How did you get my number?" she demanded, both anger and alarm in her voice.

"I saw it on your telephone yesterday," he said apologetically. "I have a good memory for such things."

"Oh." She seemed mollified, but only a little. "What is it you want, then?"

Not altogether sure of the answer to that himself, he decided to take her literally. "I've been thinking of the conversation we had yesterday, and—"

"—you decided you really want to know what's going to happen after all," she interrupted. Again he heard her full of the cynicism that appeared to come so easily to the future. She said, "You were smarter before, I promise you."

"I believe it," he said quickly. "It's just that—well, there I was in a room full of machines from your time, and every one of them turned off! I felt like Tantalus and the bunch of grapes. All I was going to ask was to see them work just once. Anything more than that I'll cheerfully stay ignorant of."

The line was silent so long that he said, "Hello?"

"I'm here," she answered. "Well, why not? The worst part of living back here is the loneliness. My neighbors are friendly, but we have so little in common with one another, and I don't dare show them what I have in the garage. Either they wouldn't understand or they'd expose me. You're enough different that—tell you what. I was just going out to the garage to work on a story of my own when you called, and that'll probably keep me busy through the afternoon. Why don't you come over around nine tonight? Come straight out to the garage; I'll probably still be in there anyhow."

"Nine o'clock," he repeated. "I'll be there." He hung up. Everything is okay, he told himself fiercely; I'm only going to have a look at marvels I won't have the chance to see again. But the interior dialog would not stop: In that case, why are your palms so sweaty? came the next question. His response was to ignore it.

As things worked out, he was late; never having gone directly to Michelle Gordian's house, he lost his way a couple of times, and streetlights were few and far between. When he finally did arrive, he thought she had changed her mind and was going to meet him in the house: behind drawn drapes, the lights were on. But no one came to the door when he rang the bell. He went back around the house to the garage.

Michelle was at the word processor when he entered her sanctum. She waved without turning around, saying, "With you in a couple of minutes. I'm working through a tough part, and it's taking longer than I thought it would. Sorry."

He didn't answer. He was not sure she could hear him: a record was spinning on the turntable, and she was listening to it through a pair of earphones. Instead, he walked over to the green-glowing screen in front of which she was sitting. As he came up, she muttered an obscenity under her breath, punched a couple of keys. Pete stared—on the screen, a paragraph had disappeared. A letter at a time, a new version began taking shape.

"I want this gadget!" he cried in honest envy, thinking of scissors and paste and snowdrifts of crumpled paper in his wastebasket.

She could hear—he saw her smile at him. "I think that'll do it," she said. She hit different buttons. A light on the small rectangular box next to the screen came on; the box started chuckling to itself. "Storing what I've written on the floppy disc," she explained, taking off the earphones. "I'll print it out tomorrow."

He must have looked like a small boy who had just lost his candy. "Oh, you really were interested in the machines, then?" she said.

He nodded, but felt his face grow hot at her ironic tone.

She waited until the disc drive had fallen silent, typed out a new command. Pete jumped as the printer started purring like a large mechanical cat. Paper rose at an astonishing rate. "How fast does it type?" he asked.

"About three hundred words a minute, I think," she said indifferently.

He peered into its works, exclaimed, "It's printing left-to-right and right-to-left!"

"Why not? It's quicker that way. It's not as if it knows what it's doing, or anything like that. It's just a tool, like an automobile."

"Yes, but I'm used to automobiles, and I'm not used to this." He changed the subject. "Was the record you had on from your time or mine?"

"Mine, or at least you would say so. Actually, it's pretty old. It's from, uh"—she looked at the back of the cardboard sleeve—"1978."

"That's new enough for me," he laughed. He took the record cover, turned it over. The design on the front was the same as that on the other side: a stylized street lined with geometric shapes running like a purple-pink bend sinister across a black background. "'Robin Trower. Caravan to Midnight,'" he read. "May I hear it?"

He was surprised when she hesitated. "I don't know if I ought to do this to you," she said. "It's only rock-and-roll, but I like it."

"Only what?"

"Never mind. Popular music."

"It's okay," he reassured her. "I like Bach and Vivaldi, sure, but I can listen to Perry Como too."

For some reason, that seemed to fluster her more. "It's not—like Perry Como."

"Is Robin Trower a girl singer, then, like Rosemary Clooney? That's all right."

"He's an Englishman who plays electric guitar," Michelle said flatly.

"Oh." If she thought she was going to put him off, she was wrong. The idea of futuristic technology married to music only intrigued him more. "Sounds fascinating."

His determination made her throw her hands in the air. "All right. Don't say you weren't warned." She set the earphones on his head. They were padded with red sponge rubber, lighter and more comfortable than the ones radiomen had used during the war. "You might as well listen to the first side first," she said, flipping the record in her hands. He saw it flex, and guessed it was unbreakable. He wished some of the hard shellac platters he'd once owned had been.

Then the needle—housed in a more elaborate cartridge than current phonographs employed—was dropping. Pete heard it hiss on the opening grooves of the record, listened to the syncopated thump of drums. He just had time to realize that the sound was marvelously clear before the snarling whine of the guitar made him jump straight up. Then everything was happening at once—guitar, drums, and a singer who attacked his song like a man going after a snake with an axe.

Michelle had the volume up very high. Pete felt as if he were listening to a jet engine warming up in stereophonic sound (something he knew only from a few big movie theaters). "It's not like Perry Como at all," he said. He could hardly hear himself talk. He saw Michelle's lips move, but made nothing of her reply.

He had almost snatched the earphones off at the first stunning jolt, but he soon realized that this Robin Trower knew exactly what he was doing and had his unruly instrument under control. The music was so strange he could not tell whether he liked it or not, but he recognized talent when he heard it.

The song—it was called "My Love (Burning Love)," he saw on the sleeve—came to an appropriately fiery end. In the brief moment of silence between tracks, Michelle said, "The next one's quieter."

"Jesus, I hope so." He lifted off the earphones. "Too strong for my blood, I think," he said, adding reflectively, "That's what I'd call real zorch."

He was obscurely pleased that he had managed to puzzle her. "Real what?"

"It's what the young hepcats say when they mean something like 'strange and marvelous,'" he explained. "There's a bop-talking San Francisco disk jockey named Red Blanchard who's their hero up where I live. Bunch of crazy kids, the kind who dye their hair green or wear purple lipstick or red eyebrow pencil—what's so funny?"

"Nothing, really," she got out after a while. "*Plus ça change, plus c'est la même chose,* that's all." She studied him. "What would you like now?"

He hesitated but played safe. "If this is your record player, what can your TV do?"

She shrugged, turned it on. The picture filled the screen much more quickly than on the sets with which he was familiar, and it was very sharp, but the difference seemed of degree rather than of kind. He was disappointed. He must have shown it, for she said,

"Remember, it can only give back the signal it's getting. However—" She went over to her desk, took out a plastic case a little larger than a fat paperback. "A videocassette," she said, loading it into the box attached to the television.

"Magnetic tape?" Pete asked, and at her startled nod he said smugly, "They were talking about it in *Time* last month."

"That'll teach me to show off. I ought to tell you this is old too. I've seen it a million times, but I never mind watching it again."

He did not answer. He was staring at the words flowing across the starry background: "A long time ago, in a galaxy far, far away . . ." The story background being laid out mattered much less to him than the fact that the lettering was glowing gold. There had been talk of color TV for years, but unexpectedly seeing one was something else again.

Michelle brought her desk chair over next to his. He felt about seventeen, at the movies with a date. The headlong action of the space opera he was watching only added to the feeling; it reminded him of a film made by splicing several months' worth of serials together.

Halfway through, he burst out, "My Lord, that's Alec Guinness!" The actor's snow-white beard brought home the inexorable passage of time even more starkly than the calculator card Michelle carried; Pete wondered what the years would do to *him*.

"What did you think?" she asked when the tape was done.

"The Hollywood word is 'colossal,' isn't it? The color, the trick photography—unbelievable. I almost hate to quibble about how thin the plot is."

"A man of taste." She sighed. "It's so much fun, though, I don't want to admit that you're right."

He glanced down at his watch. "It's almost one," he said in disbelief. "I ought to be getting back to the motel." He rose and stretched. "Thank you for a really marvelous time,"

The hackneyed formality of the phrase made the evening seem more like a date than ever. Without much conscious thought, Pete put his arms around Michelle to try for a good-night kiss.

He got more than he bargained for. Her body molded itself to his; he could feel the soft firmness of her breasts against his chest. And the kiss, instead of the prim peck he had expected, left delighted thunder in his brain when he finally came up for air.

Michelle pulled back, just a little. "The hardest thing for me living back here, I think, is having a relationship," she said.

"A wh—a what?" he stammered, still half-stunned by the yielding warmth of her under his hands—but not too stunned to respond, another part of him noted clinically.

"Most men here and now treat a woman as if she were a child," Michelle said, "and even with the ones who might not, how can I get close? I have too much to hide. But you already know my secret, and you've been looking forward for years. It's a damned attractive combination." She swayed toward him again.

The directness of her approach, though, did more to put him off than to arouse him; he was used to the game being played another way. "Easy there," he said, disengaging.

"It was pure intellectual curiosity, then, that brought you back here tonight?" she said with stinging sarcasm. "Tell me that was all, but wipe the lipstick off first."

He could still taste it on his lips. "I can't tell you that," he admitted, knowing miserably that he was going to regret whatever happened next, either way.

An army buddy had once told him, "The hardest thing in the world is turning it down when it's there for the taking." "How do you know?" he'd asked—"Ever done it?" "Me? Hell, no—and don't that prove my point?" His buddy would not have had a second thought here.

His buddy, though, had not spent his entire adulthood building a life with one woman. Though it took all Pete's will, he turned toward the door of Michelle's study.

Her voice pursued him. "You run, and you don't even know what you're missing."

The promise in that almost stopped him again. From everything he had seen, her era was much looser than his. There were things he had never dared ask of Katherine. . . . But then, why had Michelle Gordian chosen to live in 1953 if not for its virtues, such as they were?

"I know what I have," he said quietly, and walked into the night.

Gardner Dozois and Susan Casper asked me for a Jack the Ripper story for an anthology they were putting together. It was, I think, only the second time I'd ever been asked, so I said yes right away. Then I had to come up with a story idea. I wasn't sure I could; up to that time, I'd just taken ideas as they came rather than aiming toward a specific subject. But I began to think about Jack, about how and why he might have done the insanely vicious things he did. Once I found an answer to that, the story almost wrote itself.

GENTLEMEN OF THE SHADE

The gas flame flickered ever so slightly within its mantle of pearly glass as Hignett opened the door to fetch us in our port and cheeses. All five of us were in the lounge that Friday evening, an uncommon occasion in the annals of the Sanguine Club and one calling therefore for a measure of celebration.

As always, the cheeses went untouched, yet Hignett will insist on setting them out; as well reverse the phases of the moon as expect an English butler to change his habits. But some of us quite favor port, I among them. I have great relish for the fashion in which it makes the sweet blood sing through my veins.

Bowing, Hignett took his leave of us. I poured the tawny port with my own hand. For the toast to the Queen, all of us raised glasses to our lips, as is but fitting. Then, following our custom, we toasted the Club as well, after which those of us who care not for such drink may in honor decline further potations.

Yet whether or not we imbibe, the company of our own kind is precious to us, for we are so few even in London, the greatest city the world has known. Thus it was that we all paid close heed when young Martin said, "I saw in the streets last evening one I reckon will make a sixth for us."

"By Jove!" said Titus. He is the eldest of us, and swears that oath from force of habit. "How long has it been since you joined us, Martin, dear chap?"

"Myself?" Martin rubbed the mustache he has lately taken to wearing. "I don't recollect, exactly. It has been some goodish while, hasn't it?"

"Six!" I exclaimed, suddenly finding new significance in the number. "Then two of us can be away and still leave enough for the whist table!"

Amidst general laughter, Titus said, "Ah, Jerome, this unwholesome passion of yours for the pasteboards does truly make me believe you to have Hoyle's blood in you."

"Surely not, after so long," I replied, which occasioned fresh mirth. I sighed in mock heaviness. "Ah, well, I fear me even so we may go without a game as often as not. But tell us more of the new one, Martin, so as to permit me to indulge my idle fancy."

"You will understand I was upon my own occasions, and so not able to make proper enquiry of him," Martin said, "but there can be little doubt of the matter. Like calls to like, as we all know."

"He noted you, then?" Arnold asked, rising to refill his goblet.

"Oh, I should certainly think so. He stared at me for some moments before proceeding down Buck's Row."

"Buck's Row, is it?" said Titus with an indulgent chuckle. "Out chasing the Whitechapel tarts again like a proper young buck, were you?"

"No denying they're easy to come by there," Martin returned. In that he was, of course, not in error. Every one of us in the Club, I am certain, has resorted to the unfortunate "widows" of Whitechapel to slake his lusts when no finer opportunity presented itself.

"A pity you did not think to have him join you, so you could hunt together," remarked Arnold.

The shadow of a frown passed across Martin's countenance. "I had intended to do so, my friend, yet something, I know not what, stayed my hand. I felt somehow the invitation would be unwelcome to him."

"Indeed!" Titus rumbled indignantly. "If this individual spurns the friendship of an honored member"—"You honor me, sir," Martin broke in. "Not at all, sir," our Senior replied, before resuming—"an honored member, as I say, of what is, if I may speak with pardonable pride, perhaps the most exclusive club in London, why then, this individual appears to me to be no gentleman, and hence not an appropriate aspirant for membership under any circumstances."

Norton had not taken part in the discussion up to this time, contenting himself with sitting close to the fire and observing the play of the flames. As always when he did choose to speak, his words were to the point. "Nonsense, Titus," he said. "Martin put it well: like calls to like."

"You think we shall encounter him again, then, under circumstances more apt to let us judge his suitability?"

"I am certain of it," Norton replied, nor in the end did he prove mistaken. I often think him the wisest of us all.

The evening passed most pleasantly, as do all our weekly gatherings. Our practice is to meet until midnight, and then to adjourn to seek the less cerebral pleasures the night affords. By the end of August, the sun does not rise until near on five of the clock, granting us no small opportunity to do as we would under the comforting blanket of night.

For myself, I chose to wander the Whitechapel streets. Past midnight, many London districts lay quiet as the crypt. Not so Whitechapel, which like so much of the dissolute East End of the city knows night from day no more than good from evil. The narrow winding streets that change their names from block to block have always their share of traffic. I sought them for that, as I have many times before, but also, I will not deny, in the hope that I might encounter the personage whom Martin had previously met.

That I did not. I supposed him to have sated himself the night before, and so to be in no need of such peregrinations now—here again, as events transpired, I was not in error. Yet this produced in me only the mildest of disappointments for, as I have said, I had other reasons for frequenting Whitechapel.

The clocks were just striking two when I saw coming toward me down Flower and Dean Street a likely-seeming wench. Most of the few lamps that such a small, dingy lane merits were long since out, so she was nearly upon me before realizing I was there. She drew back in startlement, fearing, I suppose, me to be some footpad, but then decided from my topper, clawhammer, and brocaded waistcoat that such was not the case.

"Begging your pardon, guv'nor," she said, smiling now, "but you did give me 'arf a turn, springing from the shadows like that." She smelled of sweat and beer and sausage.

I bowed myself nearly double, saying, "It is I who must apologize to you, my dear, for frightening so lovely a creature." This is the way the game is played, as it has been from time immemorial.

"Don't you talk posh, now!" she exclaimed. She put her hands on her hips, looking saucily up at me. She was a fine strong trollop, with rounded haunches and a shelflike bosom that she thrust my way; plainly she profited better from her whoring than so many of the skinny lasses who peddle their wares in Whitechapel. Her voice turned crooning, coaxing. "Only sixpence, sir, for a night to remember always."

Her price was more than that of the usual Whitechapel tart, but had I been other than I, I daresay I should have found her worth the difference. As it was, I hesitated only long enough to find the proper coin and press it into her hand. She peered down through the gloom to ensure I had not cheated her, then pressed her warm, firm body against me. "What's your pleasure, love?" she murmured in my ear, her tongue teasing at it between words.

When I led her to a wall in deeper darkness, she gave forth a tiny sigh, having I suppose hoped to ply her trade at leisure in a bed. She hiked up her skirts willingly enough, though, and her mouth sought mine with practiced art. Her hands fumbled at my trouser buttons while my teeth nibbled her lower lip.

" 'Ave a care," she protested, twisting in my embrace. "I'd not like for you to make me bleed." Then she sighed again, a sound different from that which had gone before, and stood stock-still and silent as one made into a statue. Her skirts rustled to the ground once more. I bent my head to her white neck and began to feed.

Were it not for the amnesic and anaesthetic agent contained within our spittle, I do not doubt that humans should have hounded us vampires to extinction a long age ago. Even as is, they remain uneasily aware of our existence, though less so, I own to my relief, in this teeming faceless metropolis of London where no one knows his neighbor, or cares to, than in the hidden faraway mountains and valleys whence our kind sprang and where folk memory and fear run back forever.

When I had drunk my fill, I passed my tongue over the twin wounds I had inflicted, whereupon they healed with the same rapidity as does my own flesh. The whore stirred then. What her dreams were I cannot say, but they must have been sweet, for she declared roundly, "Ah, sir, you can do me any time, and for free if you're hard up." Greater praise can no courtesan give. She seemed not a whit perplexed at the absence of any spunk of mine dribbling down her fat thighs; doubtless she had coupled with another recently enough beforehand so as not to miss it.

She entreated me for another round, but I begged off, claiming adequate satisfaction, as was indeed the case. We went our separate ways, each well pleased with the other.

She had just turned down Osborn Street toward Christ Church and I was about to enter on Commercial Street when I spied one who had to be he whom Martin had previously encountered. His jaunty stride and erect carriage proclaimed him recently to have fed, and fed well, yet somehow I found myself also aware of Titus's stricture, delivered sight unseen, that here was no gentleman. I could find no concrete reason for this feeling, and was about to dismiss it as a vagary of my own when he also became aware of my presence.

His grin was mirthless; while his cold eyes still held me, he slowly ran his tongue over his lips, as if to say he was fain to drink from my veins. My shock and revulsion must have appeared on my features, for his smile grew wider yet. He bowed so perfectly as to make perfection itself a mockery, then disappeared.

I know not how else to put it. We have of course sometimes the ability briefly to cloud a mere man's mind, but I had never thought, never imagined the occasion could arise, to turn this power upon my own kind. Only the trick's surprise, I think, lent it success, but success, at least a moment's worth, it undeniably had. By the time I recovered full use of my faculties, the crass japester was gone.

I felt angry enough, nearly, to go in pursuit of him. Yet the sun would rise at five, and my flat lay in Knightsbridge, no small distance away. Reluctantly I turned my step toward the Aldgate Station. As well I did; the train was late, and morning twilight already painting the eastern horizon with bright colors when I neared home.

The streets by then were filling with the legions of wagons London requires for her daily revictualing. Newsboys stood on every corner hawking their papers. I spent a penny and tucked one away for later reading, time having grown too short for me to linger.

My landlady is of a blessedly incurious nature; so long as the rent is promptly paid and an appearance of quiet and order maintained, she does not wonder at one of her tenants not being seen abroad by day. All of us of the Sanguine Club have digs of this sort: another advantage of the metropolis over lesser towns, where folk of such mercenary nature are in shorter supply. Did they not exist, we should be reduced to squalid, hole-and-corner ways of sheltering ourselves from the sun, ways in ill-accord with the style we find pleasing once night has fallen.

The setting of the sun having restored my vitality, I glanced through the paper I had purchased before. The headlines screamed of a particularly grisly murder done in Whitechapel in the small hours of the previous day. Being who and what I am, such does not easily oppress me, but the details of the killing—for the paper proved to be of the lurid sort—did give me more than momentary pause.

I soon dismissed them from my mind, however, being engaged in going up and down in the city in search of profit. Men with whom I deal often enough for them to note my nocturnal habit ask no more questions on it than my landlady, seeing therein the chance to mulct me by virtue of my ignorance of the day's events. At times they even find their efforts crowned with success, but, if I may be excused for boasting, infrequently. I have matched myself against their kind too long now to be easily fooled. Most of the losses I suffer are self-inflicted.

I could be, I suppose, a Croesus or a Crassus, but to what end? The truly rich become conspicuous by virtue of their wealth, and such prominence is a luxury, perhaps the one luxury, I cannot afford. My road to safety lies in drawing no attention to myself.

At the next gathering of the club, that being Friday the seventh, only four of us were in attendance, Martin having either business similar to mine or the need to replenish himself at one of the multitudinous springs of life abounding in the city. By then the Whitechapel slaying was old news, and occasioned no conversation; none of us, full of the wisdom long years bring though we are, yet saw the danger from that direction.

We spoke instead of the new one. I added the tale of my brief encounter to what Martin had related at the previous meeting, and found I was not the only one to have seen the subject of our discussion. So also had Titus and Norton, both in the East End.

Neither appeared to have formed a favorable impression of the newcomer, though as was true with Martin and myself, neither had passed words with him. Said our Senior, "He may eventually make a sixth for us, but no denying he has a rougher manner than do those whose good company now serves to warm these rooms."

Norton being Norton was more plainspoken: "Like calls to like, as I said last week, and I wish it didn't."

Of those present, only Arnold had not yet set eyes on the stranger. He now enquired, "What in him engenders such aversion?"

To that none of the rest of us could easily reply, the more so as nothing substantial backed our hesitancy. At last Norton said, "He strikes me as the sort who, were he hungry, would feed on Hignett."

"On our own servant? I should sooner starve!"

"So should we all, Arnold, so should we all," Titus said soothingly, for the shock in our fellow's voice was quite apparent. Norton and I gave our vigorous agreement. Some things are not done.

We decided it more prudent for a time not to seek out the newcomer. If he showed any greater desire than heretofore for intercourse with us, he could without undue difficulty contrive to make his path cross one of ours. If not, loss of his society seemed a hardship under which we could bear up with equanimity.

Having settled that, as we thought, to our satisfaction, we adjourned at my urging to cards, over which we passed the balance of the meeting, Arnold and I losing three guineas each to Norton and Titus. There are mortals, and not a few of them too, with better card sense than Arnold's. Once we broke up, I hunted in Mayfair with good enough luck and went home.

Upon arising on the evening of the eighth, my first concern was a paper, as I had not purchased one before retiring and as the newsboys were crying them with a fervor warning that something of which I should not be ignorant had passed during the hours of my undead sleep. And so it proved: at some time near 5:30 that morning, about when I was going up to bed, the Whitechapel killer had slain again, as hideously as before, the very least of his atrocities being the cutting of his victim's throat so savagely as almost to sever her head from her body.

Every one of the entrepreneurs with whom I had dealings that evening mentioned of his own accord the murders. An awful fascination lay beneath their ejaculations of horror. I had no trouble understanding it. A madman who kills once is frightening, but one who kills twice is far more than doubly so, the second slaying portending who could say how many more to come.

This fear, not surprisingly, was all the worse among those whom the killer had marked for his own. Few tarts walked the streets the next several evenings, and such as did often went in pairs to afford themselves at least what pitiful protection numbers gave. I had a lean time of it, in which misfortune, as I learned at the next meeting of the Club, I was not alone. For the first time in some years we had not even a quorum, three of our five being absent, presumably in search of sustenance. The gathering, if by that name I may dignify an occasion on which only Arnold and I were present, was the worst I remember, and ended early, something hitherto unknown among us. Nor did my business affairs prosper in the nights that followed. I have seldom known a less pleasant period.

At length, despite our resolutions to the contrary, I felt compelled to visit the new one's haunts in the East End. I suspect I was not the first of us driven to this step. Twelve hundred drabs walk the brown-fogged streets of Whitechapel, and hunger works in them no less than in me. Fear of the knife that may come fades to insignificance when set against the rumbling of the belly that never leaves.

I did then eventually manage to gain nourishment, but only after a search long and inconvenient enough to leave me rather out of temper despite my success. Not to put too fine a point on it, I should have chosen another time to make the acquaintance of our new associate. The choice proved not to be mine to make: he hailed me as I was walking toward St. Mary's Station on Whitechapel Road.

Something in the timbre of his voice spoke to me, though I had not heard it before; even as I turned, I knew who he was. He hurried up to me and pumped my hand. We must have made a curious spectacle for those few people who witnessed our meeting. Like all members of the Sanguine Club, I dress to suit my station; moreover, formal attire with its stark blacks and whites fits my temperament, and I have been told I look well in it.

My new companion, by contrast, wore a checkered suit of cut and pattern so bold as to be more appropriate for the comedic stage than even for a swell in the streets of Whitechapel. Of his tie I will say nothing save that it made the suit stodgy by comparison. His boots were patent leather, with mother-of-pearl buttons. On his head perched a low-crowned billycock hat as evil as the rest of the rig.

I should not have been surprised to smell on his breath whiskey or more likely gin (the favored drink of Whitechapel), but must confess I could not. "Hullo, old chap," he said, his accent exactly what one would expect from the clothes. "You must be one o' the toffs I've seen now and again. The name's Jack, and pleased t'meetcher."

Still a bit nonplused at such heartiness where before he had kept his distance, I rather coolly returned my own name.

"Pleased t'meetcher," he said again, as if once were not enough.

Now that he stood close by, I had the chance to study him as well as his villainous apparel. He was taller than I, and of younger seeming (though among us, I know, this is of smaller signification than is the case with mankind), with greasy side-whiskers like, you will I pray forgive me, a pimp's.

Having repeated himself, he appeared to have shot his conversational bolt, for he stood waiting for some response from me. "Do you by any chance play whist?" I asked, lacking any better query.

He threw back his head and laughed loud and long. "Blimey, no! I've better games than that, yes I do." He set a finger by the side of his nose and winked with a familiarity he had no right to assume.

"What are those?" I asked, seeing he expected it of me. In truth I heartily wished the encounter over. We have long made it a point to extend the privileges of the Sanguine Club to all our kind in London, but despite ancient custom I would willingly have withheld them from this Jack, whose vulgarity disbarred him from our class.

This thought must have been plain on my face, as he laughed again, less good-naturedly than before. "Why, the ones wiv dear Pollie and Annie, of course."

The names so casually thrown out meant nothing to me for a moment. When at last I did make the connection, I took it to be no more than a joke of taste similar to the rest of his character. "Claiming yourself to be Leather Apron, sir, or whatever else the papers call that killer, is not a jest I find amusing."

"Jest, is it?" He drew himself up, offended. "I wasn't jokin' wiv yer. Ah, Annie, she screamed once, but too late." His eyes lit in, I saw, fond memory. That more than anything else convinced me he spoke the truth.

I wished then the sign of the cross were not forbidden me. Still, I fought to believe my fear mistaken. "You cannot mean that!" I cried. "The second killing, by all accounts, was done in broad daylight, and—" I forbore to state the obvious, that none of our kind may endure Old Sol.

"Oh, it were daylight, right enough, but the sun not up. I 'ad just time to do 'er proper, then nip into my 'idin' place on 'Anbury Street. The bobbies, they never found me," he added with scorn in his voice for the earnest bumbling humans who sought to track him down. However much I found the thought repugnant, I saw he was truly one of us in that, his sentiment differing perhaps in degree from our own, but not in kind.

I observed also once more the relish with which he spoke of the slaying, and of his hairsbreadth escape from destruction; the sun is a greater danger to us than ever Scotland Yard will be. Still, we of the Sanguine Club have survived and flourished as we have in London by making it a point never to draw undue attention to ourselves. Being helpless by day, we are hideously vulnerable should a determined foe ever set himself against us. I said as much to Jack, most vehemently, but saw at once I was making no impression upon him.

"Aren't you the toffee-nose, now?" he said. "I didn't ask for no by-your-leave, and don't need one of you neither. You bloody fool, they're only people, and I'll deal wiv 'em just as I please. Go on; tell me you've not done likewise."

To that I could make no immediate reply. I have fed innumerable times from victims who would have recoiled in loathing if in full possession of their senses. Nor am I myself guiltless of killing; few if any among us are. Yet with reflection, I think I may say I have never slain wantonly, for the mere sport of it. Such conduct must inevitably debase one who employs it, and in Jack I could not help noting the signs of that defilement. Having no regard for our prey, he would end with the same emptiness of feeling for his fellows (a process I thought already well advanced, by his rudeness toward me) and for himself. I have seen madness so many times among humanity, but never thought to detect it in one of my own.

All this is, however, as I say, the product of rumination considerably after the fact. At the time I found myself so very unnerved as to fasten on utter trivialities as if they were matters of great importance. I asked, then, not that he give over his cruel sport, but rather where he had come by the apron that gave him his sobriquet in the newspapers.

He answered without hesitation: "Across the lane from where I done the first one is Barber's 'Orse Slaughter 'Ouse—I filched it there, just after I 'ad me bit o' fun. Fancy the fools thinkin' it 'as some meanin' to it." His amusement confirmed what I had already marked, that he found humanity so far beneath him that it existed but for him to do with as he wished.

Again I expostulated with him, urging him to turn from his course of slaughter.

"Bloody 'ell I will," he said coarsely. "'Oo's to make me, any road? The bobbies? They couldn't catch the clap in an 'orehouse."

At last I began to grow angry myself, rather than merely appalled, as I had been up to this point. "If necessary, my associates and I shall prevent you. If you risked only yourself, I would say do as you please and be damned to you, but your antics threaten all of us, for if by some mischance you are captured you expose not only your own presence alone but reveal that of your kind as well. We have been comfortable in London for long years; we should not care to have to abandon it suddenly and seek to establish ourselves elsewhere on short notice."

I saw this warning, at least, hit home; Jack might despise mankind, but could scarcely ignore the threat his fellows might pose to him. "You've no right to order me about so," he said sullenly, his hands curling into fists.

"The right to self-preservation knows no bounds," I returned. "I am willing to let what is done stay done; we can hardly, after all, yield you up to the constabulary without showing them also what you are. But no more, Jack. You will have us to reckon with if you kill again."

For an instant I thought he would strike me, such was the ferocity suffusing his features. I resolved he should not relish the attempt if he made it. But he did not, contenting himself instead with turning his back and wordlessly taking himself off in the rudest fashion imaginable. I went on to the station and then to my home.

At the next meeting of the Club I discovered I had not been the only one to encounter Jack and hear his boasts. So also had Norton, who, I was pleased to learn, had issued a warning near identical to mine. If anything, he was blunter than I; Norton, as I have remarked, is not given to mincing words. Our actions met with general approbation, Martin being the only one to express serious doubt at what we had done.

As the youngest among us (he has been a member fewer than two hundred years), Martin is, I fear, rather more given than the rest of us to the passing intellectual vagaries of the mass of humanity, and has lately been much taken with what they call psychology. He said, "Perhaps this Jack acts as he does because he has been deprived of the company of his own kind, and would be more inclined toward sociability in the world as a whole if his day-to-day existence included commerce with his fellows."

This I found a dubious proposition; having met Jack, I thought him vicious to the core, and not likely to reform merely through the good agency of the Club. Norton confined himself to a single snort, but the fashion in which he rolled his eyes was eloquent.

Titus and Arnold, however, with less acquaintance of the newcomer, eagerly embraced Martin's suggestion: the prospect of adding another to our number after so long proved irresistible to them. After some little argument, I began to wonder myself if I had not been too harsh a judge of Jack, nor did Norton protest overmuch when it was decided to tender an invitation to the Club to him for the following Friday, that is to say September twenty-first.

I remarked on Norton's reticence as we broke up, and was rewarded with a glance redolent of cynicism. "They'll find out," he said, and vanished into the night.

It was with a curious mingling of anticipation and apprehension that I entered the premises of the Club for our next meeting, an exhilarating mixture whose like I had not known since the bad nights when all of mankind was superstitious enough to make our kind's every moment a risk. Titus was there before me, his features communicating the same excitement I felt. At that I knew surprise afresh, Titus having seen everything under the moon: he derives his name, after all, from that of the Roman Augustus in whose reign he was born.

"He'll come?" I asked.

"So Martin tells me," replied our Senior.

And indeed it was not long before good Hignett appeared at the lounge door to announce the arrival of our guest. Being the perfect butler, he breathes discretion no less than air, yet I could hear no hint of approval in his voice. What tone he would have taken had he known more of Jack I can only imagine. Even now his eye lingered doubtfully on the newcomer, whose garments were as gaudy as the ones in which I had first met him, and which contrasted most strikingly with the sober raiment we of the Sanguine Club commonly prefer.

After leaving the port and the inevitable cheeses, Hignett retired to grant us our privacy. We spent some moments taking the measure of the stranger in our midst, while he, I should think, likewise took ours. He addressed us first, commenting, "What a grim lot o' sobersides y'are."

"Your plumage is certainly brighter than ours, but beneath it we are much the same," said Martin, still proceeding along the lines he had proposed at our previous session.

"Oh, balls," Jack retorted; he still behaved as though on the Whitechapel streets rather than in one of the more refined salons London boasts. Norton and I exchanged a knowing glance. Titus's raised eyebrow was eloquent as a shout.

Martin, however, remained as yet undaunted, and persisted, "But we are. The differences between you and us, whatever they may be, are as nothing when set against the difference between the lot of us on the one hand and those among whom we dwell on the other."

"Why ape 'em so, then?" asked Jack, dismissing with a sneer our crystal and plate, the overstuffed chintz chairs in which we sat, our carpets and our paneling of carved and polished oak, our gaslight which yields an illumination more like that of the sun (or so say those who can compare the two) than any previously created, in short all the amenities that serve to make the Sanguine Club the pleasant haven it is. His scorn at last made an impression upon Martin, who knew not how to respond.

"Why should we not like our comforts, sir?" Titus, as I have found in the course of our long association, is rarely at a loss for words. He continued, "We have been in straitened circumstances more often than I can readily recall, and more than I for one should care to. Let me remind you, no one compels you to share in this against your will."

"An' a good thing, too—I'd sooner drink 'orseblood from Barber's, I would, than 'ave a digs like this. Blimey, next you'll be joinin' the bleedin' Church o' Hengland."

"Now you see here!" Arnold, half-rising from his seat in anger, spoke for all of us. Horseblood is an expedient upon which I have not had to rely since the Black Death five and a half centuries ago made men both too scarce and too wary to be easily approached. To this night I shudder at the memory of the taste, as do all those of us whom mischance has at one time or another reduced to such a condition. I almost found it more shocking than the notion of entering a church.

Yet Jack displayed no remorse, which indeed, as should by this point be apparent, played no part in his character. "Get on!" he said. "You might as well be people your own selves, way you carry on. They ain't but our cattle, and don't deserve better from us than they give their beasts."

"If what Jerome and Norton say is true, you give them rather worse than that," Titus said.

Jack's grin was broad and insolent. "Aye, well, we all have our sports. I like making 'em die monstrous well, better even than feeding off 'em." He drew from his belt a long sharp blade, and lowered his eyes so as to study the gleaming, polished steel. Did our reflections appear in mirrors, I should have said he was examining his features in the metal.

"But you must not act so," Titus expostulated. "Can you not grasp that your slayings endanger not you alone, but all of us? These cattle, as you call them, possess the ability to turn upon their predators and hunt us down. They must never suspect themselves to be prey."

"You talk like this bugger 'ere," said Jack, pointing in my direction. "I were wrong, guv'nor, an' own to it—it's not men the lot of yez are, it's so many old women. An' as for Jack, 'e does as 'e pleases, an' any as don't fancy it can go play wiv themselves for all 'e cares."

"Several of us have warned you of the consequences of persisting in your folly," said Titus in a voice like that of a magistrate passing sentence. "Let me say now that you may consider that warning to come from the Sanguine Club as a whole." He looked from one of us to the next, and found no dissent to his pronouncement, even Martin by this time having come to realize our now unwelcome guest was not amenable to reason.

"You try an' stop me and I'll give yer what Pollie an' Annie got," Jack shouted in a perfect transport of fury, brandishing the weapon with which he had so brutally let the life from the two poor jades. We were, however, many to his one, and not taken by surprise as had been his earlier victims. Norton seized the knife that sat among Hignett's despised cheeses. Of the rest of us, several, myself included, carried blades of our own, if not so vicious as the one Jack bore.

Balked thus even of exciting terror, Jack foully cursed us all and fled, being as I suspected too great a coward to attack without the odds all in his favor. He slammed the door behind him with violence to make my goblet of port spring from the endtable where it sat and hurtle to the floor. Only the quickness of my kind enabled me to save it from destruction and thus earn, though he would never know of it, Hignett's gratitude.

The crash of Jack's abrupt departure was still ringing in our ears when Martin most graciously turned to me and said, "You and Norton appear to have been correct; my apologies for doubting you."

"We shall have to watch him," Titus said. "I fear he will pay no heed to our advice."

"We shall also have to keep watch over Whitechapel as a whole, from this time forth," Arnold said. "He may escape our close surveillance, yet be deterred by observing our vigilance throughout the district."

"We must make the attempt, commencing this very night," Titus declared, again with no disagreement. "That is a mad dog loose on the streets of London, mad enough, I fear, to enable even the purblind humans of Scotland Yard eventually to run him to earth."

"Which will also endanger us," I put in.

"Precisely. If, however, we prevent his slaying again, the hue and cry over this pair of killings will eventually subside. As we are all gathered here now, let us agree on a rotation that will permit at least three of us to patrol Whitechapel each night, and" (here Titus paused to utter a heavy sigh) "all of us on our Fridays. Preservation here must take precedence over sociability."

There was some grumbling at that, but not much; one thing our years confer upon us is the ability to see what must be done. Hignett evinced signs of distress when we summoned him from downstairs long before the time usually appointed, and more upon being informed we should not be reconvening for some indefinite period. Not even the promise that his pay would continue heartened him to any great extent; he had grown used to our routine, and naturally resented any interruption thereof.

Having decided to patrol Whitechapel, we walked west along the south bank of the Thames past the Tower of London and the edifice that will upon its completion be known as Tower Bridge (and which would, were it complete, offer us more convenient access to the northeastern part of the city) to London Bridge and up Gracechurch Street to Fenchurch Street and Whitechapel. Once there, we separated, to cover as much ground as our limited numbers permitted.

Jack had by this time gained a considerable lead upon us; we could but hope he had worked no mischief while we were coming to the decision to pursue him. Yet the evening was still relatively young, and both of his previous atrocities had taken place in later hours, the second, indeed, so close to sunrise as to seem to me to display a heedlessness to danger suitable only to a lunatic among our kind.

I prowled the lanes near Spitalfields Market, not far from where I had first set eyes on Jack after supping off the young whore, as I have already related. I should not have been sorry to encounter her there once more, since, I having in a manner of speaking made her acquaintance, she would not have shied from my approach, as did several ladies of the evening, and I was, if not yet ravenous, certainly growing hungry.

It must have been nearing three when I spied Jack in Crispin Street, between Dorset and Brushfield. He was coming up behind a tart when I hailed him; they both turned at the sound of my voice. "Ah, cousin Jack, how are you these days?" I called cheerily, pretending not to have noticed her. In my most solicitous tones, I continued, "The pox troubles you less, I hope?"

"Piss off!" he snarled. The damage to his cause, however, was done, for the whore speedily took herself elsewhere. He shook his fist at me. "You'll pay for that, you bugger. I only wanted a bit of a taste from 'er."

"Starve," I said coldly, our enmity now open and undisguised. Would that keeping him from his prey might have forced that fate upon him, but we do not perish so easily. Still, the hunger for blood grows maddening if long unsatisfied, and I relished his suffering hardly less than he the twin effusions of gore he had visited upon Whitechapel.

He slunk away; I followed. He employed all the tricks of our kind to throw me off his track. Against a man they would surely have succeeded, but I was ready for them and am in any case no man, though here I found myself in the curious position of defending humanity against one of my own kind gone bad. He failed to escape me. Indeed, as we went down Old Montague Street, Arnold fell in with us, and he and I kept double vigil on Jack till the sky began to grow light.

The weakness of our plan then became apparent, for Arnold and I found ourselves compelled to withdraw to our own domiciles in distant parts of the city to protect ourselves against the imminent arrival of the sun, while Jack, who evidently quartered himself in or around Whitechapel, was at liberty to carry out whatever outrage he could for some little while before finding it necessary to seek shelter. A similar period of freedom would be his after every sunset, as we would have to travel from our homes to the East End and locate him afresh each night. Still, I reflected as I made my way out of the slums toward Knightsbridge, in the early hours of the evening people swarmed through the streets, making the privacy and leisure required for his crimes hard to come by. That gave me some small reason, at least, to hope.

Yet I must confess that when nightfall restored my vitality I departed from my flat with no little trepidation, fearing to learn of some new work of savagery during the morning twilight. The newsboys were, however, using other means to cry their papers, and I knew relief. The concern of getting through each night was new to me, and rather invigorating; it granted a bit of insight into the sort of existence mortals must lead.

That was not one of the nights assigned me to wander through

Whitechapel, nor on my next couple of tours of duty there did I set eyes on Jack. The newspapers made no mention of fresh East End horrors though, so the Sanguine Club was performing as well as Titus could have wished.

Our Senior, however, greeted me with grim and troubled countenance as we met on Fenchurch Street early in the evening of the twenty-seventh, preparatory to our nightly Whitechapel vigil. He drew from his waistcoat pocket an envelope which he handed to me, saying, "The scoundrel grows bolder. I stopped by the Club briefly last night to pay my respects to Hignett, and found this waiting there for us."

The note the envelope contained was to the point, viz.: "You dear chums aren't as clever as you think. You won't catch me if I don't want that. And remember, you haven't found my address but I know where this place is. Give me trouble—not that you really can—and the peelers will too. Yours, Jack the Ripper."

"The Ripper, is it?" My lip curled at the grotesque sobriquet, and also at the tone of the missive and the threat it conveyed. Titus perfectly understood my sentiments, having no doubt worked through during the course of the previous night the thought process now mine.

He said, "We shall have to consider harsher measures than we have contemplated up to this point. A menace to the Club is a menace to us all, individually and severally."

I nodded my affirmation. Yet to suppress Jack we had first to find him, which proved less easy than heretofore. Norton and I met in the morning twilight of the twenty-eighth at St. Mary's Station without either one of us having set eyes on him. "He may be staying indoors for fear of our response to his note," I said, having first informed Norton of the letter's contents.

My dour colleague gloomily shook his head. "He fears nothing, else he would not have sent it in the first place." Norton paused a while in silent thought—an attitude not uncommon for him—then continued, "My guess is, he is merely deciding what new atrocity to use to draw attention to himself." I did not care for this conclusion but, in view of Jack's already demonstrated proclivities, hardly found myself in position to contradict it.

The night of Saturday the twenty-ninth found me in the East End once more. Most of the previous evening, when under happier circumstances the Sanguine Club would have met, I spent beating down a most stubborn man over the price of a shipment of copra, and was sorely tempted to sink teeth into his neck afterward to repay him for the vexation and delay he caused me. I had not thought the transaction would take above an hour, but the wretch haggled over every farthing. Titus was most annoyed at my failure to join our prearranged patrol, and I counted myself fortunate that Jack again absented himself as well.

Early in the evening I thought I caught a glimpse of Jack by London Hospital as I was coming down Mount Street from Whitechapel Road, but though I hastened up and down Oxford Street, and Philpot and Turner which come off it, I could find no certain trace. Full of vague misgivings, I turned west onto Commercial Road.

Midnight passed, and I still had no idea of my quarry's whereabouts. I had by chance encountered both Martin and Arnold, who shared the night with me, and learned of their equal lack of success. "I believe he must still be in hiding, in the hope of waiting us out," Arnold said.

"If so," I replied, "he is in yet another way a fool. Does he think us mortals, to grow bored after days or weeks and let down our guard?"

The answer to that soon became all too clear. At one or so a great outcry arose on Berner Street, scarcely a hundred yards from Commercial Road where I had walked but a short while before. As soon as I heard the words "Leather Apron," I knew Jack had chosen to strike again in defiance not only of human London, but also of the Sanguine Club, and also that he had succeeded in evading us, making good on the boast in his recent note.

I started to rush toward the scene of this latest crime, but had not gone far before I checked myself. I reasoned that Jack could scarcely strike again in or close to such a crowd, if that was his desire, but would take advantage of the confusion this murder engendered, and of the natural attraction of the constabulary in the area to it. It was Norton's reasoning that made me fear Jack would not be content with a single slaying, but might well look at once for a fresh victim to demonstrate everyone's impotence in bringing him to heel.

My instinct proved accurate, yet I was unfortunately not in time to prevent Jack's next gruesome crime; that I came so close only served to frustrate me more thoroughly than abject failure would have done. I was trotting west along Fenchurch Street, about to turn down Jewry Street to go past the Fenchurch Street Station, as the hour approached twenty of two, when suddenly there came to my nose the thick rich scent of fresh-spilled blood.

Being who I am, that savory aroma draws me irresistibly, and I am by the nature of things more sensitive to it by far than is a man, or even, I should say, a hound. Normally it would have afforded me only pleasure, but now I felt alarm as well, realizing that the large quantity required to produce the odor in the intensity with which I perceived it could only have come from the sort of wounds Jack delighted in inflicting.

I followed my nose up Mitre Street to a courtyard off the roadway, where, as I had feared, lay the body of a woman. Despite the sweetness of the blood-tang rising intoxicatingly from her and from the great pool of gore on the paving, I confess with shame to drawing back in horror, for not only had she been eviscerated, but her throat was slashed, her features mutilated almost beyond identity, and part of one earlobe nearly severed from her head.

I had time to learn no more than that, or to feed past the briefest sampling, for I heard coming up Mitre Street the firm, uncompromising tread likely in that part of the city to belong only to a bobby, footpads and whores being more circumspect and men of good conscience in short supply. I withdrew from the court, thankful for my ability to move with silence and not to draw the eye if I did not wish it. Hardly a minute later, the blast of a police whistle pierced the night as humanity discovered this latest piece of Jack's handiwork.

As I once more walked Mitre Street, I discovered the odor of blood to be diminishing less rapidly than I should have expected. Looking down, I discovered a drop on the pavement. I stooped to taste of it; I could not doubt its likeness to that which I had just tried. A bit further along the street was another. I hastened down this track, hoping also to discover one of my fellows to lend me assistance in overpowering Jack. As if in answer to my wish, up came Martin from a sidestreet, drawn like me by the pull of blood. Together we hastened after Jack.

The drippings from his hand or knife soon ceased, yet the alluring aroma still lingering in the air granted us a trail we could have followed blindfolded. I wondered how Jack hoped to escape pursuers of our sort, but soon found he knew the East End better than did Martin or myself, and was able to turn that knowledge to his advantage.

On Goldstone Street, in front of the common stairs leading to Numbers 108 to 119, stood a public sink. It was full of water, water which my nose at once informed me to be tinctured with blood: here Jack had paused to rinse from this hands the traces of his recent deeds. Martin found also a bit of bloodstained black cloth similar to that of a garment the latest unfortunate victim had worn.

At the base of the sink, close by the piece of fabric, lay a lump of chalk. I picked it up and tossed it in the air idly once or twice, then, thinking back on Jewry Street where I had been when first I detected Jack's newest abomination, was seized by inspiration. The Jews of London form a grouping larger than we of the Sanguine Club, yet hardly less despised than we would become were Jack's insanity finally to expose our identity to the general populace. How better, thought I, to distract suspicion from us than by casting it upon others themselves in low repute? Above the sink, then, I chalked, "The Jewes are the men who will not be blamed for nothing," a message ambiguous enough, or so I hoped, to excite attention without offering any definite information. And when Martin would have removed the bloodstained cloth, I prevailed on him to replace it, to draw the eyes and thoughts of the constabulary to my scrawled note.

Martin and I then attempted to resume our pursuit, but unsuccessfully. In washing himself and, I believe, cleansing his blade on the rag from his victim's apron, he removed the lingering effluvium by which we had followed him, and forced us to rely once more on chance to bring us into proximity to him. Chance did not prove kind, even when we separated in order to cover more ground than would have been possible in tandem. Just as he had bragged, Jack had slain again (and slain twice!), eluding all attempts to stay his hand.

I was mightily cast down in spirit as I traveled homeward in the morning twilight. Nor did the clamor in the papers the next evening and during the nights that followed serve to assuage my anxiety. "Revolting and mysterious," "horrible," and "ghastly" were among the epithets they applied to the slayings; "Whitechapel horrors," shrieked *The Illustrated Police News.* It was, however, a subhead in that same paper which truly gave me cause for concern: it spoke of the latest "victim of the Whitechapel Fiend," a designation whose aptness I knew only too well, and one which I could only hope would not be literally construed.

Titus must also have seen that paper and drawn the same conclusion as had I. When I came to myself on the evening of the second I found in my postbox a note in his classic hand. "Henceforward we must all fare forth nightly," he wrote, "to prevent a repetition of these latest acts of depravity. We owe this duty not only to ourselves but to our flock, lest they suffer flaying rather than the judicious shearing we administer."

Put so, the plea was impossible to withstand. All of us prowled the sordid streets of Whitechapel the next few nights, and encountered one another frequently. Of Jack, however, we found no sign; once more he chose to hide himself in his lair. Yet none of us, now, was reassured on that account, and when he did briefly sally forth he worked as much mischief, almost, without spilling a drop of blood as he had with his knife.

We failed to apprehend him in his forays, but their results soon became apparent. The lunatic, it transpired, had not merely written to us of the Sanguine Club, but also, in his arrogance, to the papers and the police! They, with wisdom unusual in humans, had suppressed his earliest missive, sent around the same time as the one to us, perhaps being uncertain as to its authenticity, but he sent another note after the horrid morning of the thirtieth, boasting of what he termed his "Double Event." As the police had not yet announced the murders, not even men could doubt its genuineness.

Once more the press went mad, filled with lurid rehashes and speculations, some claiming the Ripper (for so he had styled himself also in his public letters) to be a man seeking to stamp out the vice of prostitution (presumably by extirpating those who plied the trade), others taking varying psychological tacks which intrigued our faddish Martin with their crackbrained ingenuity and left the rest of us sourly amused, still others alleging Jack a deranged *shochet.*

"Your work takes credit there, Jerome," Titus remarked to me as we chanced upon each other one evening not far from the place where Jack's last victim had died. "A madman of a ritual slaughterer fits the particulars of the case well."

"The Jews always make convenient scapegoats," I replied.

"How true," Titus murmured, and again I was reminded of the Caesar for whom he had been named.

Other, darker conjectures also saw print, though, ones I could not view without trepidation. For those Jack himself was responsible, due to a bit of sport he had had with the police after his second killing. After slaying Annie Chapman, he had torn two rings from her fingers and set them with some pennies and a pair of new-minted farthings at her feet. This he had wasted time to do, I thought with a frisson of dread, as the sun was on the point of rising and ending his amusements forever! It naturally brought to mind black, sorcerous rituals of unknown but doubtless vile purpose, and thoughts of sorcery and of matters in any way unmundane were the last things I desired to see inculcated in the folk of London.

I did my best to set aside my worries. For all Jack's dark skill, murder no longer came easy in Whitechapel. Aside from us of the Sanguine Club, the constabulary increased their patrols in the district, while a certain Mr. George Lusk established a Whitechapel Vigilance Committee whose membership also went back and forth through the area.

Neither constables nor committee members, I noted during my own wanderings, refrained from enjoying the occasional streetwalker, but the women themselves took more pleasure from those encounters than they should have from a meeting with Jack. The same also holds true for the whores we of the Club engaged. As I have previously noted, the wounds we inflicted healed quickly, the only aftereffect being perhaps a temporary lassitude if one of us fed overdeep because of unusual hunger.

Jack may have taken a hiatus from slaughter, but remained intent on baiting those who so futilely pursued him. October was not yet a week old when he showed his scorn for the Whitechapel Vigilance Committee by means of a macabre gift to its founder: he sent Mr. Lusk, in a neatly wrapped cardboard box, half the kidney of his latest victim, with a mocking note enclosed.

"He will be the ruin of us all," I said gloomily to Martin upon the papers' disclosure of this new ghoulery. "Would you had never set eyes on him."

"With that I cannot take issue," replied my colleague, "yet this lapse, however revolting humans may find it—and I confess," he added with a fastidious shudder, "to being repelled myself at the prospect of eating a piece from a woman's kidney—however revolting, I say, it does not add to any fears directed toward us, for none of our kind would do such a deed, not even Jack, I should say."

"One never knows, where he is concerned," I said, and Martin's only response was a glum nod.

As October wore on, more letters came to the papers and police, each one setting off a new flurry of alarm. Some of these may indeed have been written by Jack; others, I suspect, sprang from the pens of men hardly less mad than he, and fully as eager for notoriety. Men have so little time to make their mark that such activity is in them at least faintly comprehensible, but for

Jack, with years beyond limit before him, I offer no explanation past simple viciousness. In his instance, that was more than adequate.

Still, despite sensations such as I have described, the month progressed with fresh slayings. Once I dashed a couple of furlongs down Old Montague Street into Baker's Row, drawn as on the night of the Double Event by the scent of blood, but discovered only a stabbed man of middle years with his pockets turned out: a matter in which the police were certain to take an interest, but not one, I was confident, that concerned me.

My business affairs suffered somewhat during this period, but not to any irreparable extent; at bottom they were sound, and not liable to sudden disruption. I thought I would miss the weekly society of the Sanguine Club to a greater degree than proved to be the case. The truth is that we of the Club saw more of one another in our wanderings through Whitechapel than we had at our meetings.

October passed into November, the nights growing longer but less pleasant, being now more liable to chill and to wet fogs. These minor discomforts aside, winter long has been our kind's favorite season of the year, especially since coming to this northern latitude where around the December solstice we may be out and about seventeen hours of the twenty-four, and fifteen even in the mid-autumnal times to which my narrative now has come. Yet with Jack abroad, the increased period of darkness seemed this year no boon, as I was only capable of viewing it as a greater opportunity for him to sally forth on another murderous jaunt.

On the evening of the eighth, then, I reached Whitechapel before the clocks struck five. By the time they chimed for six, I had already encountered in the narrow, gridless streets Norton, Arnold, and Titus. We tipped our hats each to the other as we passed. I saw Martin for the first time that night shortly after six. We were complete, as ready as we might be should the chance present itself.

The night gave at the outset no reason for supposing it likely to prove different from any other. I wandered up toward Bishopsgate Station, having learned that the whore who was Jack's latest victim had been released from there not long before her last, fatal encounter. "Ta-ta, old cock, I'll see you again soon!" she had called drunkenly to the gaoler, a prediction that, unfortunately for her, was quickly proven inaccurate.

Wherever Jack prowled, if indeed he was on the loose at that hour, I found no trace of him. Seeing that so many prostitutes passed through the station, I made it a point to hang about: Jack might well seek in those environs an easy target. Whores indeed I saw in plenty thereabouts but, as I say, no sign of Jack. When the clocks struck twelve, ushering in a new day, I gave it up and went to hunt elsewhere.

Walking down Dorset Street near twelve-thirty, I heard a woman with an Irish lilt to her voice singing in a room on one of the courtyards there. I paused a moment to listen; such good spirits are rarely to be found in Whitechapel. Then I continued east, going by London Hospital and the Jews' Cemetery, my route in fact passing the opening of Buck's Row onto Brady Street, close to the site of Jack's first killing.

That area proved no more profitable than had been my prior wanderings of the night—no more profitable, indeed, than the whole of the past five weeks' exertions on the part of the Sanguine Club. True, I am more patient than a man, but even patience such as mine desires some reward, some hint that it is not employed in pursuit of an *ignis fatuus.* As I lacked any such hint, it was with downcast mien that I turned my steps westward once more.

My nostrils began to twitch before I had any conscious awareness of the fact. I was on Wentworth Street between Commercial and Goulston, when at last my head went suddenly up and back, as I have seen a wolf's do on taking a scent. Blood was in the air, and had been for some little while. Yet like a wolf which scents its prey at a distance, I had to cast about to find the precise source of the odor.

In this search I was unsurprised to encounter Norton, who was coming down Flower and Dean Street toward Commercial. His features bore the same abstracted set I knew appeared on my own. "Odd sort of trail," he said without preamble, as is his way.

"It is." I tested the air again. "The source lies north of us still, I am certain, but more precise than that I cannot be. It is not like the spoor I took from Jack's last pleasantry."

"A *man* could have followed that, from what you said of it," Norton snorted, and though he spoke in jest I do not think him far wrong. He continued, "Let us hunt together."

I agreed at once, and we proceeded side by side up Commercial (which in the dark and quiet of the small hours belied its name) to a corner where, after deliberation, we turned west onto White Street rather than east on Fashion. Well that we did, for hurrying in our direction from Bishopsgate came Titus. His strides, unlike our own, had nothing of doubt to them. Being our Senior, he is well-supplied with hunters' lore.

"Well met!" he cried on recognizing us. "This way! We have him, unless I miss my guess!" Practically at a run, he swept us north along Crispin Street to Dorset, the very ground I had patrolled not long before.

The scent trail was stronger now, but remained curiously diffuse. "How do you track with such confidence?" I asked.

"That is much blood, escaping but slowly to the outside air," Titus replied. "I think our quarry has taken his atrocious games indoors, in hopes of thwarting us. He has been—you will, I pray, pardon the play on words—too sanguine in his expectations."

His proposed explanation so precisely fit the spoor we were following that I felt within me the surge of hope I recently described as lacking. A much-battered signboard on the street read "Miller's Court" ; it was the one from which I had earlier heard song. A light burned in Number 13. From that door, too, welled the scent which had drawn us; now that we had come so close, its source could not be mistaken.

As our tacit leader, Titus grasped the doorknob, Norton and I standing behind him to prevent Jack from bursting past and fleeing. Jack evidently had anticipated no disturbances, for the door was not locked. On Titus's opening it, the blood smell came forth as strongly as ever I have known it, save only on the battlefield.

The scene I glimpsed over Titus's shoulder will remain with me through all my nights. Our approach had taken Jack unawares, he being so intent on his pleasure that the world beyond the squalid little room was of no import to him. A picture-nail in his hand, he stared at us in frozen shock from his place by the wall.

Both my eyes and nose, though, drew me away from him to the naked flesh on the bed. I use that appellative in preference to body, for with leisure at his disposal Jack gained the opportunity to exercise his twisted ingenuity to a far greater and more grisly extent than he had on the streets of Whitechapel. The chamber more closely resembled an abattoir than a lodging.

By her skin, such of it as was not covered with blood, the poor wretch whose abode this presumably had been was younger than the previous objects of his depravity. Whether she was fairer as well I cannot say, as he had repeatedly slashed her face and sliced off her nose and ears to set them on a bedside table. The only relief for her was that she could have known none of this, as her throat was cut; it gaped at me like a second, speechless mouth.

Nor had Jack contented himself with working those mutilations. Along with her nose and ears on that table lay her heart, her kidneys (another offering, perhaps, to George Lusk), and her breasts, his gory handprints upon them. He had gutted her as well.

Not even those horrors were the worst. When we interrupted him, Jack was engaged in hanging bits of the woman's flesh on the wall, as if they were engravings the effect of whose placement he was examining.

The tableau that held us all could not have endured above a few seconds. Jack first recovered the power of motion, and waved in invitation to the blood-drenched sheets. "Plenty there for the lot o' yez," said he, grinning.

So overpowering was the aroma hanging in the room that my tongue of itself ran across my lips, and my head swung toward that scarlet swamp. So, I saw, did Titus's. Norton, fortunately, was made of sterner stuff, and was not taken by surprise when Jack tried to spring past us. Their grapple recalled to our senses the Senior and myself, and I seized Jack's wrist as he tried to take hold of his already much-used knife, which, had it found one of our hearts, could have slain us as certainly as if we were mortal.

In point of fact, Jack did score Norton's arm with the blade before Titus rapped his hand against the floor and sent the weapon skittering away. Norton cursed at the pain of the cut, but only for a moment, as it healed almost at once. The struggle, being three against one, did not last long after that. Having subdued Jack and stuffed a silk handkerchief in his mouth to prevent his crying out, we dragged him from the dingy cubicle out into Mitre Court.

Just then, likely drawn by the fresh outpouring of the blood scent from the newly opened door of Number 13, into the court rushed Martin, and the stout fellow had with him a length of rope for use in the event that Jack should be captured, an eventuality for which he, perhaps inspirited by youthful optimism, was more prepared than were we his elders. We quickly trussed our quarry and hauled him away to obtain more certain privacy in which to decide his fate.

We were coming out of Mitre Court onto Dorset Street when I exclaimed, "The knife!"

"What of it? Let it be," Titus said. Norton grunted in agreement.

On most occasions, the one's experience and the other's sagacity would have been plenty to persuade me to accede to their wishes, but everything connected with Jack, it seemed, was out of the ordinary. I shook my head, saying, "That blade has fleshed itself in you,

Norton. Men in laboratories are all too clever these days; who knows what examination of the weapon might reveal to them?"

Martin supported me, and my other two colleagues saw the force of my concern: Why stop Jack if we gave ourselves away through the mute testimony of the knife? I dashed into Number 13 once more, found the blade, and tucked it into the waistband of my trousers. I found coherent thought in that blood-charged atmosphere next to impossible, but realized it would be wise to screen the horrid and pathetic corpse on the bed from view. Accordingly, I shut the door and dragged up a heavy bureau to secure it, only then realizing I was still inside myself.

Feeling very much a fool, I climbed to the top of the chest of drawers, broke out a pane of glass, and awkwardly scrambled down outside. I hurried to catch up to my comrades, who were conveying Jack along Commercial Street. As he was most unwilling, this would have attracted undue attention from passersby, save that we do not draw men's notice unless we wish it.

We turned off onto Thrawl Street and there, in the shelter of a recessed doorway, held a low-voiced discussion. "He must perish; there is no help for it," Martin declared. To this statement none of us dissented. Jack glared mute hatred at us all.

"How then?" said I. I drew forth Jack's own knife. "Shall I drive this into his breast now, and put an end to it?" The plan had a certain poetic aptness I found appealing.

Martin nodded approvingly, but Titus, to my surprise, demurred. He explained, "Had I not observed this latest outrage, Jerome, I should have no complaint. But having seen it, my judgment is that the punishment you propose errs in the excessive mercy it would grant."

"What then?" I cast about for some harsher fate, but arrived only at the obvious. "Shall we leave him, bound, for the sun to find?" I have never seen the effects of sunlight on the flesh of our kind, of course; had I been in position to observe it, I should not now be able to report our conversation. Yet instinctively we know what we risk. It is said to be spectacularly pyrotechnic.

Jack's writhings increased when he heard my proposal. He had dared the sun to kill for his own satisfaction, but showed no relish for facing it without choice. Our Senior coldly stared down at him. "You deserve worse."

"So he does," Norton said. "However much the sun may pain him, it will only be for a little while. He ought instead to have eternity to contemplate his failings."

"How do you propose to accomplish that?" asked Martin. "Shall we store him away in the basement of the Sanguine Club? Watch him as we will, one day he may effect his escape and endanger us all over again."

"I'd not intended that," replied Norton.

"What then?" Titus and I demanded together.

"I say we take him to the Tower Bridge now building, and brick him up in one of its towers. Then every evening he will awaken to feel the traffic pounding close by, yet be powerless to free himself from his little crypt. He will get rather hungry, bye and bye."

The image evoked by Norton's words made the small hairs prickle up at the nape of my neck. To remain forever in a tiny, black, airless chamber, to feel hunger grow and grow and grow, and not to be able even to perish . . . were he not already mad, such incarceration would speedily render Jack so.

"Ah, most fitting indeed," Titus said in admiration. Martin and I both nodded; Norton's ingenuity was a fitting match for that which Jack had displayed. Lifting the miscreant, we set off for the bridge, which lay only a couple of furlongs to the south of us. Our untiring strength served us well as we bore Jack thither. His constant struggles might have exhausted a party of men, or at the least persuaded them to knock him over the head.

Although we draw little notice from mortals when we do not wish it, the night watchman spied our approach and turned his lantern on us. "'Ere, wot's this?" he cried, seeing Jack's helpless figure in our arms.

We were, however, prepared for this eventuality. Martin sprang forward, to sink his teeth into the watchman's hand. At once the fellow, under the influence of our comrade's spittle, grew calm and quiet. Titus, Norton, and I pressed onto the unfinished span of the bridge and into its northern tower, Martin staying behind to murmur in the watchman's ear and guide his dreams so he should remember nothing out of the ordinary.

The other three of us fell to with a will. The bricklayers had left the tools of their trade when they went home for the night. "Do you suppose they will notice their labor is further advanced than when they left it?" I asked, slapping a brick into place.

Titus brought up a fresh hod of mortar. "I doubt they will complain of it, if they should," he said, with the slightest hint of chuckle in his voice, and I could not argue with him in that.

Norton paused a moment from his labor to stir Jack with his foot. "Nor will this one complain, not while the sun's in the sky.

And by the time it sets tomorrow, they'll have built well past him." He was right in that; already the tower stood higher than the nearby Tower of London from which the bridge derives its name. Norton continued, "After that, he can shout as he pleases, and think on what he's done to merit his new home."

Soon, what with our unstinting effort, Jack's receptacle was ready to receive him. We lifted him high, set him inside, and bricked him up. I thought I heard him whimpering behind his gag, but he made no sound loud enough to penetrate the masonry surrounding him. That was also massive enough to keep him from forcing his way out, bound as he was, while the cement joining the bricks remained unset. He would eventually succeed in scraping through the ropes that held him, but not before daybreak . . . and the next night would be too late.

"There," said Norton when we had finished, "is a job well done."

Nodding, we went back to reclaim Martin, who left off charming the night watchman. That worthy stirred as he came back to himself. He touched his grizzled forelock. "You chaps 'ave a good evenin' now," he said respectfully as we walked past him. We were none too soon, for the sky had already begun to pale toward morning.

"Well, my comrades, I shall see you this evening," Titus said as we prepared to go our separate ways. I am embarrassed to confess that I, along with the rest of us, stared at him in some puzzlement over the import of his words. Had we not just vanquished Jack? Seeing our confusion, he burst out laughing: "Have you forgotten, friends, it will be Club night?" As a matter of fact, we had, having given the day of the week but scant regard in our unceasing pursuit of Jack.

On boarding my train at St. Mary's Station, I found myself in the same car as Arnold, who as luck would have it had spent the entire night in the eastern portion of Whitechapel, which accounted for his nose failing to catch the spoor that led the rest of us to Jack; he had entered the train at Whitechapel Station, half a mile east of my own boarding point. He fortunately took in good part my heckling over his absence.

After so long away, our return to the comforts of the Sanguine Club proved doubly delightful, and stout Hignett's welcome flattering in the extreme. Almost I found myself tempted to try eating cheese for his sake, no matter that it should render me ill, our kind not being suited to digest it.

Despite the desire I and, no doubt, the rest of us felt to take the opportunity to begin to return to order our interrupted affairs, all of us were present that evening to symbolize the formal renewal of our weekly fellowship. We drank to the Queen and to the Club, and also all drank again to an unusual third toast proposed by Titus: "To the eternal restoration of our security!" Indeed, at that we raised a cheer and flung our goblets into the fireplace. A merrier gathering of the Club I cannot recall.

And yet now, in afterthought, I wonder how permanent our settlement of these past months' horrors shall prove. I was not yet in London when Peter of Colechurch erected Old London Bridge seven centuries ago, but recall well the massive reconstruction undertaken by Charles Lebelye, as that was but a hundred thirty years gone by; and there are still men alive who remember the building of New London Bridge in its place by John Rennie, Jr., from the plans of his father six decades ago.

Who can be certain Tower Bridge will not someday have a similar fate befall it, and release Jack once more into the world, madder and more savage even than before? As the French say, "*Tout passe, tout casse, tout lasse*"—everything passes, everything perishes, everything palls. We of the Sanguine Club, to whom the proverb does not apply, know its truth better than most. Still, even by our standards, Jack surely will not find freedom soon. If and when he should, that, I daresay, will be time for our concern.

Lest unwary readers reckon this story the product of a diseased mind, they should know it is the product of two. My longtime friend Kevin R. Sandes must bear his full share of responsibility for its contents; so must the Anheuser-Busch Corporation. I don't normally compose surrounded by potables. This once, it seemed to work.

THE BORING BEAST

An excerpt, O Prince, from an ancient chronicle:

A brisk westerly breeze drove the galley *Wasteful* into the port of Zamorazamaria. At the *Wasteful*'s helm stood Condom, the Trojan, one massive fist clamped round the wheel. The other clutched a skin of wine. Six feet and a span in height, he would have been taller yet had the fickle gods favored him with a forehead. Only a leather kilt hid his bronze skin and bulging thews from the sun. His hide was crisscrossed with scars, all too many of them self-inflicted.

A sudden roll spoiled his aim, spilling wine over his face and down his lantern jaw. Muttering an oath, he groped for a rag—and the ship's ram crunched into the side of a beamy merchantman tied up at a Zamorazamarian quay.

Condom took in the situation with one fuddled glance. "Back oars!" he bellowed. The ram pulled free, and the merchantman, a six-foot hole torn in her flank, promptly began to sink. Her crew scrambled like fleas on a drowning dog, cursing and screaming and diving over the side.

"What's going on here?" shrilled Captain Mince, emerging from his cabin. "How is a person to sleep with this crashing about? Why, I was thrown clear out of my hammock, and I ripped my new culottes." He fingered the pink silk regretfully. The cries of the foundering ship's sailors drew his gaze. "Condom, how clumsy of you!" he exclaimed, slapping the barbarian's muscly buttocks.

"Captain, I told you I'd break your arm if you did that again."

"You know I despise rough trade. Let's see if we can't give these dears some help, shall we?"

While Mince bickered with the dripping, furious merchants, his crew, Condom among them, roared into the dives and brothels of the decaying harbor district. The Trojan got hopelessly lost in the twisting back streets of Zamorazamaria. He put his faith in his innate barbarian instincts. Stepping up to the first man he saw, he wrapped an overmuscled arm round the fellow's neck and growled, "Tell me where the nearest grogshop is before I tear your head off!"

The man's mouth moved soundlessly. His hands scrabbled at Condom's flexors. The mighty warrior loosed his grip a trifle. Gasping, the man wheezed, "The Lusty Widow is two doors down. Its name is spelled out right in front."

Condom could not read six different languages. "Thanks, bud!" he said, giving his benefactor a slap on the back that sent him reeling into the curbside offal. Condom swaggered down the street until, with the keen-honed senses of the barbarian, his nose caught the sweet scent of beer.

Shaking his square-cut mane of black hair from his dull blue eyes, he strode into the tavern and threw himself into a chair. It collapsed. He picked himself up, only to face the irate proprietress bearing down on him with a bludgeon. She had time for one quick curse before Condom, whose sense of chivalry was rude indeed, decked her with a right. He snarled, "I want beer and I want quiet. After three bloody months cruising with Captain Mince, I *need* beer!"

She crawled away to fetch it. Condom settled back in a new, stronger chair for some serious drinking. Little did he suspect (which was true most of the time) that he was being watched from afar. Know, O Prince, that in long-ago Zamorazamaria lived the infamous necromancer, wizard, and unholy priest Sloth-Amok. He dwelt in his dark Tower of the Bat like a spider in its web, controlling the lives and destinies of the port city's inhabitants.

Sloth-Amok was a tall, dingy man, with scaly shoulders and aloof, toadlike features. From warty skull to webbed feet, his skin was a deep, venomous green. His bulbous eyes peered into a scrying-cauldron of cold split pea soup. "Heh-heh." He chuckled, flicking a fly from his eyebrow with his long pink tongue. He turned to his familiar, whose name was Gulp, saying, "'Tis a pity one so stupid as Condom, the Trojan, must die, but die he shall, for I have read in the guano of a thousand starlings that he is the only man alive who might thwart my schemes."

His familiar leered evilly and slobbered, "Can I help, master? Does master want poor ugly Gulp to help?"

"Indeed you may, good Gulp. And I know how." The wizard strode to a table across the chamber; it was there that he conducted his most fiendish experiments. The wooden surface was strewn with eye of newt, toe of frog, wing of bat, ring of bat, rope of bat, mobile of bat, and other exotica. The sorcerer produced a bowl filled with puffy-looking purple stuff. "This is it, Gulp!"

"'It,' master?"

"Yes, it! You bear in your gnarled paws the downfall of Condom, the Trojan."

"It seems no more than a common plum duff, your malignity."

"You are wrong, good Gulp, for there is nothing common about it. You gaze upon a masterpiece of inventive sorcery: the world's first exploding plum duff!"

Gulp blinked, swallowed nervously. "An exploding plum duff? Will it work, master?"

"Do you doubt me, worm in the pomegranate of life? Of course it will work. Never has it failed me."

"But, master, you said this was the first—"

"Never mind what I said, dolt of a familiar. We must now prepare your steed." Sloth-Amok's lithe, webbed fingers moved in the intricate passes of a spell he alone knew. Gulp cowered, terrified by the abyssal forces the great sorcerer so easily overcame. There was a puff of smoke, a reek of tuna, and a thirty-foot flying fish lay flopping on the stone floor of Sloth-Amok's chamber.

Gulp gulped. "Master, are you sure—"

"Quick, fool," Sloth-Amok cried, pressing the deadly pudding into his familiar's sweaty palm. "Look not a gift fish in the mouth. Ere it perish, mount and fly to the Lusty Widow!"

Condom was still swilling swinishly when Gulp, wearing a fearful expression and loud pantaloons, slunk into the tavern. Outside in the street his mount was gasping its last. Condom looked up muzzily. "Hey," he said. "You look familiar."

"I am."

"Have a beer."

Gulp set his murderous yummy under Condom's chair while the Trojan drank, then drained his own tankard and fled. A cry of dismay floated into the grogshop when he found his charger covered by a wriggling carpet of starving dockside cats. He scuttled down the street and back toward Sloth-Amok's lair.

He had not been gone long when Condom discovered the plum duff. "Blow my nose!" he exclaimed. "This must be a gift from the gods!" Not pausing to think twice (or even once), he downed the entire bowlful. He sat back with a contented sigh and raised his jack to his lips, but, before he could swallow, Sloth-Amok's hideous plan went into effect. The plum duff exploded.

Now, during his tour aboard the *Wasteful,* Condom had acquired a cast-iron stomach (in fact, he had won it at dice). Thus the Trojan, instead of spattering off the walls of the Lusty Widow, but felt his innards give a tremendous jerk.

Trembling, he leaped to his feet. He opened his mouth to gasp for air, but found himself belching instead. The deep bass roar echoed through the city. Birds fell from the sky, stunned by the concussion. And Condom, internal tremor satisfied, thumped his chest, sat down, and drank more beer.

Sloth-Amok had seen everything in his vat of soup. He shrieked with rage and danced about his chamber, ripping warts from his forehead and hurling them to the floor. The scrying-cauldron erupted, splattering split peas over his second-best robe. "What's this," he cackled, peering into the seething mass. "By the earwax of Hiram, god of small puddles, Condom shall not escape me!"

The Trojan was still feeling the aftereffects of his cataclysmic belch when a mysterious figure sat down beside him, its form and features hidden by a dark robe and hood. With the inborn suspicion of the barbarian, Condom growled, "Hey, you got another one of them plum duffs like the last fellow brung? It was good!"

A soft, serious voice answered him: "Of plum duffs I know nothing, good sir. I seek a mighty warrior, yclept Condom, the Trojan. Know you such a man?"

His low brow furrowed, as if in thought. "I heard the name somewheres. . . . Wait a minute! That's me!"

"Truly? Then you must come with me, and quickly, for my mistress is in desperate peril!"

"Where's that? I don't know my way past the docks too good."

The stranger swept back the hood of the robe. She proved to be a beautiful maiden, her fine features twisted in an exasperated pout. She rose, saying, "Come with me, great hero. My mistress, the princess Zamaria, has great need for aid only a champion like yourself can provide."

"Zamaria, huh?" Lustful thoughts ran through Condom's head like pigs through a wallow: if this was a serving-wench, the princess had to be even more luscious. "Sure thing, honey. Take me to her." He fumbled at his purse (a gift from Captain Mince), but the maiden impatiently drew a gold bracelet from her arm and tossed it on the table.

In his sanctum Sloth-Amok laughed to himself. He hurried to a book of lore, riffling its pages to the cantrip he had in mind. Once sure it was within his capacity, he slammed the book shut and began the spell.

Quickly mixing philosopher's stone (kidney, he thought, would be better than gall), tongue of toad, parsley, sage, rosemary, and a pinch of potent garfunkel root, he simmered them at medium heat for two minutes, tossed in a maraschino cherry, and cried out words of power. His magic done, he sank back on a bed of nails, exulting, "At last! Now the Trojan twit is done forever!"

A pit suddenly yawned beneath Condom. Princess Zamaria's maidservant sprang back with a shriek of horror, but the stalwart Trojan, unfazed at this terrifying apparition, stooped and picked it up. "Geez, this musta come from a sleepy peach," he said, chucking it into the gutter.

Baring his unbrushed teeth in an agony of frustrated fury, Sloth-Amok threw a year's supply of freeze-dried dragon blood, two sorcerous tomes, and a slightly used dwarf into his furnace. Little millipedes scurried from his leggings.

The serving-maid and Condom entered the royal palace through a secret doorway opening in the middle of a crumbling, ivy-covered wall. She led the Trojan through what seemed like miles of dank halls. His feet hurt; had he had any idea how to get out of the palace, he would have given the whole adventure up as a bad job. At last they came to a broad oaken door. The maid shut it in his face, ordering him to wait. Sulkily, he composed himself to obey.

She reappeared a few moments later. "You may come with me," she said.

The barbarian was more than willing to comply, for she had doffed her concealing mantle for a long blue gown that barely covered her breasts and clung provocatively to her rounded haunches. But when he tried to clasp her to his furry bosom, she evaded him with an ease bespeaking long practice and an oiled skin.

She led him to a jewel-encrusted door and bade him enter. "These are the private chambers of her majesty, Princess Zamaria.

A court function prevents her from being present. Still, within are all the implements you will require to succor Zamorazamaria in her hour of need." Condom's own implement was making his kilt rise; he tugged it back into place and entered the Princess Zamaria's boudoir.

Flickering lamps illuminated a chamber of unbelievable magnificence. The walls were covered with tapestries depicting men, women, and a variety of animals writhing in fantastic variations on the act of love. A huge round bed, piled high with pillows, silks, and furs, stood in the center of the room. The Trojan leaped onto it. "By Crumb, this is the life!" He leered at Zamaria's maid. "Now, my little oyster, what can I do to—uh, *for*—you?"

"O Condom, you must be the shield and protector of my mistress!" she cried. "Only you can save Zamorazamaria from utter ruin. The foul necromancer Sloth-Amok"—("Bigot!" sneered the wizard, who was watching all in his magical kettle)—"has the princess's fiancé, Elagabalus, in captivity, and is demanding her hand from her father, King Philiboustros. His limitless supplies of gold, created by the black arts, have corrupted everyone who might otherwise have braved a rescue. . . ." What fools these mortals be! Sloth-Amok thought. Making gold was easy; bullion cubes dropped into boiling water sufficed for all his needs. "Condom, you must save Elagabalus from Sloth-Amok's evil clutches. Any reward the kingdom can offer will be yours!"

"What do I hafta do?" he panted, lecherous visions still dancing in his head.

She did not seem to notice his burning gaze. "Were Elagabalus but free of the Tower of the Bat, he and Zamaria could wed and save the kingdom from the sorcerer's wicked domination. The omens have shown you to be the only man with a prayer of rescuing him, if you but will."

"I will! I will!"

"Truly, it is a task only a fool or a hero would undertake with so little hesitation," she said, giving him the benefit of the doubt. "The Tower of the Bat is easy to enter, but hard to leave.

"We have, indeed, only the dying babbles of men who have pressed beyond the outworks, but it is known that in the topmost pinnacle of the Tower of the Bat squats the invincible Boring Beast, which must be slain ere Elagabalus is saved. Will you aid Zamorazamaria in her hour of need, O Condom? It must be now, for if Elagabalus is not freed, King Philiboustros will give my mistress's hand to Sloth-Amok tomorrow."

The princess's hand did not much interest Condom, but if she was anything like her maidservant, he had a good healthy yen for her adjacent giblets. Still, there was that damned danger. He paused a while for thought; his reasoning advanced with the sluglike pace that marks the barbarian. "I'll do it!" he said at last.

The serving-maid's lips parted in the first smile he had won from her. She bent down and, wincing, kissed him passionately. "Gracious Condom!" she said, skipping back before he could pin her to the bed. "There is not a moment to lose if the kingdom is to be saved. Listen closely, for I have here a charm to aid you. . . ."

An hour later Condom was crouched before the frowning gate of Sloth-Amok's fortress. He was frowning himself, trying to remember what the charm was for.

After ascending the feared Thirteen Steps (these were made from the skulls and bones of virgins over the age of seventy-three, a story in itself), Condom at last confronted the Tower of the Bat. Having searched in vain for a knocker (he kept thinking of Zamaria's wench), he smote the door with his huge fist.

Only silence answered.

He drew his mighty axe and began to chop away at the ironbound wood. Suddenly, a small panel above the door flew open. One of Gulp's beady little eyes peered through. "What are you doing, you idiot? Can't you read the sign?"

Condom squinted up at Gulp. "I don't see no sign."

"Under your feet, cretin."

Condom looked down. "'Welcome'?" he guessed.

"No, lackwit. It says, 'Go away!' is what it says. So go away!" Gulp slammed the panel shut, leaving the barbarian with a perplexed scowl on his face. He muttered something impolite and resumed his assault on the door.

Gulp reappeared. "No one home!" he snapped, and vanished.

"Why didn't you say so in the first place?" Condom grumbled peevishly. He started down the dolorous stairway, but paused and turned back. "I don't care if you're there or not. Here I come!"

Chips flew as the axe smashed into the rock-hard timbers. "What do you think you're doing, you overthewed oaf?" Gulp cried. "Who in the seventeen distinct and different hells do you think you are?"

"I'm, uh, Condom, the Trojan, and if you don't get out of my way, I'll chop pieces off you, too." With a last brutal stroke, the barbarian reduced the entranceway to the Tower of the Bat to a pile of fagots. Gulp fled, screeching in dismay.

The Trojan climbed the Tower's gloomy stair to its end, only to find himself in a place any man in full possession of his faculties would have paid his soul as ransom to avoid: the chamber of the Boring Beast.

Know, O peerless Prince, that though the Beast is long vanished from this world, his progeny live on: the dealer who at great length extols the virtues of a worthless slave, the mage full of praise for his latest worthless nostrum, or your minister of finance. But the Boring Beast, O Prince, surpassed these in its capacity for ennui to the same degree as Your Radiance surpasses his humble servant, myself. For the dread Beast was wont to drone on and on over this and that, saying nothing whatever at such inordinate length as to freeze the ardor of the doughtiest warriors—and these brave men and bold, and not to be despised in battle, and men who always fought at the fore and never gave way . . . I crave pardon, O Prince, for even the thought of the Boring Beast conjures up its image. Suffice to say, any fool caught in its spell could no more escape than bird from mesmerizing snake. And into its dominion the Trojan now thrust himself.

At first he had no notion of aught amiss; the chamber he entered seemed deserted, save for a pile of gray furs in one corner. Condom paid the drab heap scant heed. Nor did he dwell on the row of still bodies before it, once-mighty men now no more than mummified skin stretched drum-tight over dry bones. The spell of the Beast had held them enthralled until they perished.

And now its colorless voice threatened the Trojan with the same desiccation. The Beast was talking, it seemed, of the state of its bowels, but so dull were its words that little meaning came to him, only a monotonous drone that made his mouth sag open in a huge yawn. In his chamber, Sloth-Amok peered, chuckling, into the scrying-kettle as he watched the Boring Beast ensorcel the barbarian.

Condom's eyelids began to droop; so, unbeknownst to him, did those of Sloth-Amok. The great sorcerer had never before witnessed the Beast toying with a victim, and found himself quite unable to resist the field of tedium it projected. With a soft snore, he fell face-first into the split peas.

As fate would have it, Condom put up a stronger resistance to Elagabalus's dreary guardian. He had forgotten the charm he had been given, small white tablets created specifically against this menace by the renegade mage Amphet-Amun. But his own resources were not so meager as might be thought. For one thing, he had often hunted wild bores through the forests of his native land. For another, he had the true barbarian distrust of speeches; as he himself had trouble stringing more than three words together, he naturally found listening to anyone else's long-winded talk unpleasant. Stifling a yawn, he moved toward the Boring Beast, languidly raising his axe. "Will you for Crumb's sake shut up?" he growled.

The Beast did not yet understand that its soporific techniques were failing. "Now I have always found that a brew of salt water and radishes makes a good cathartic," it informed him confidentially.

"Enough!" Condom roared. His gleaming blade bit deep into the Boring Beast's flabby gray flesh. Its cry of agony, this once, produced no ennui; not since the day it had bored its eggshell open had it been so rudely beset. Again and again Condom smote the insipid monster. At last his axe pierced its bladder of boredom. Pent-up anesthetic gases hissed free. The Beast fell with a final low, inane wail; within moments Condom swooned beside it.

When he woke, his head ached abominably, both from the aftereffects of the gases which had sustained the Beast and from the onset of a devastating hangover. He rose, groaning; even the dim light of the Beast's chamber seemed far too bright. And from the door behind the monster's corpse came insistent pounding and a voice whose words were muffled by the thick wood of the portal.

Condom wished the noise would go away, but whoever was making it kept right on. He also raised his voice, so the Trojan finally understood what he was saying: "Who has come to rescue Elagabalus?"

With a will, the barbarian took his axe to the door. He tried to ignore the racket he was making. As soon as he had hacked through the stout timbers, a pale hand snaked through the hole to turn the outer knob, which, the Trojan discovered, had not been locked. The door swung open and Elagabalus stepped out.

He was a tall, slim young man, dressed in fine silks now soiled from having been worn for days on end. Also of silk was the cloth over his eyes, for he was blind. "Good sir," he said, extending his hand in Condom's general direction, "I congratulate you, though I know you not. Any warrior stout enough to vanquish the Boring Beast must be a hero indeed. Know, sir hero, that you have saved Elagabalus, prince of Hypodermia and the intended husband of Zamorazamaria's fairest princess." He paused, waiting for his rescuer to introduce himself.

Condom's care for such social graces, however, was minimal.

"Come on!" he shouted, grabbing the blind prince's arm with such sudden force that Elagabalus all but fell. Elagabalus perforce followed the Trojan as he began stumbling down the stairs toward freedom.

In another part of the Tower of the Bat, Gulp sidled into Sloth-Amok's private quarters, to find the dreaded wizard snoring into his split peas. "Wake up, your maleficence!" he exclaimed.

"Wuzzat?" Sloth-Amok's head rose from the scrying-cauldron. He flicked his face nearly clean with a few quick strokes of his batrachian tongue. As full consciousness returned, he peered into the vat of soup, confidently expecting to find Condom as inert as he himself had been a moment before.

Instead he saw the barbarian and Elagabalus dashing down the Thirteen Steps. "To the palace!" Elagabalus cried, the taste of liberty lighting his aristocratic features.

Sloth-Amok cursed Condom so vilely that Gulp's toenails curled. Froggy eyes bulging, the wizard plowed through his library for a spell hideous enough to wreak proper vengeance on the Trojan.

The sentries at the palace gate stared at the mismatched pair blundering toward them. "Mithrandir!" their captain swore, not sure whose fantasy he was in. He hefted his spear threateningly.

Elagabalus's quick ear, though, recognized the officer's voice. "Do you not know me, Faex?" he said. "It is I, Elagabalus, saved for Zamaria from the foul clutches of Sloth-Amok."

Faex looked the blind prince over. "Well, damn me if you're not," he said. "This is great news." He turned to one of his troopers. "Clunes, move your buns; fetch the princess here at once. Tell her past all hope her fiancé is rescued!"

Sloth-Amok found the volume he was seeking, the great *Treasury* of s'tegoR. He riffled through its baleful pages, at last coming to the section he needed. Raising the book above his head, he cried out, "1014.7!" in a voice like thunder.

A horde of demons, fiends, devils, satans, devas [*Zoroastrian*], shedus [*Biblical*], gyres [*Scot.*], bad or evil spirits, unclean spirits, hellions [*colloq.*]; cacodemons, incubi, succubi; jinnis or jinnees, genies, genii, jinniyehs [*fem.*]; evil genii; afreets, barghests (even Sloth-Amok was unclear about what barghests were, O Prince, but he had summoned them, and they came), flibbertigibbets, trolls; ogres, ogresses; ghouls, lamiai, and Harpies vomited from the bowels of the Tower of the Bat. The Tower groaned, suffering from a bad case of mixed metaphor; the horde, yeeping, gibbering, roaring, and making whatever noise barghests make, stormed through the streets of Zamorazamaria after Condom. The townsfolk who saw them disappeared, for the most part permanently.

Horns blared inside the palace, trumpeting a royal fanfare. Peering into the entrance hall, Condom saw the princess's serving-maid hurrying toward him, amazed delight on her face. His heart, among other things, leaped. He opened his arms and lumbered forward. "Hey, sweets, look, I done it, see? I done it!"

She sidestepped with a dancer's adroitness, went gracefully to one knee before Elagabalus. "Welcome, your highness, in the name of my mistress, Princess Zamaria." She glanced behind her. "She comes to greet you even as I speak."

The guardsmen bowed low, eyes on the polished marble floor. Condom, untroubled by effete civilized notions like politeness, gaped at the mountain of flesh wallowing toward him. Zamaria waddled, she wobbled, she wheezed; her vast rolls of fat shook like the gelatin that dances round a cold ham. And like a five-pound sausage stuffed into a three-pound skin, her huge bulk was shoehorned into a cloth-of-gold gown that clung mercilessly to every curve.

"My darling!" she cried to her fiancé, her voice harsh as a raven's caw.

Condom spoke with the rude frankness that marks the barbarian. "By Crumb, buddy, it's a good thing you're blind," he told Elagabalus. "If you could see, you'd run miles, and I ain't kidding."

All heads snapped his way, then, as if drawn by some irresistible fascination, swung toward the Princess Zamaria. Her finger stabbed at the Trojan. "Kill him!" she screeched. "Kill him, kill him, *kill him!*"

"Shit!" said Condom, and Faex leaped at him with a vicious spearthrust. But the Trojan, with no thoughts to slow his reflexes, sprang to one side and brought down both hands, club-fashion, on the back of the captain's neck. Faex smashed to the ground, pike flying from nerveless fingers. And Condom, still acting on instinct, seized Zamaria's maidservant, slung her over his shoulder, and dashed down the street, a hundred guardsmen pouring after him.

If they had carried bows, he would have been pincushioned, but they had swords and pikes, and had to close with him to finish him off. Breath sobbing in his throat and the serving-wench in his ear, he reeled round a corner, the guards just a few strides behind. Then the Trojan, with a grunt of fright, whirled and dashed back the way he had come, straight toward the startled palace guards. But they had no chance to hack him down, for hard on his heels was the slavering spawn of Sloth-Amok's conjuration.

Both sides forgot Condom, their common quarry, as they smashed together. "Demons, fiends, devils, satans!" a soldier shrieked. He would have gone through the whole catalog, but a deva killed him. Another guardsman, quicker-witted, exorcised a whole squadron of jinnees with a bottle of vermouth. Three flibbertigibbets danced maniacally up one side of a trooper and down the other. They were not much use as far as fighting went, but spread chaos far and wide.

A cursing guardsman slashed at the monster in front of him. "What *is* that thing?" panted one of his squadmates, who had just unstrung a Harpy.

"A barghest," the soldier said—someone, at least, knew one when he saw one.

"Well, buy it a drink, then!" the other shouted. A lamia tore out his throat a moment later, and there was nobody to say he did not deserve it.

Caught in the center of the maelstrom, Condom kicked and pounded his way toward the edge. In the struggle for survival, none of the combatants paid him any special heed. He had almost won free when an ogre loomed before him. Zamaria's serving-maid swooned as it extended a misshapen, gore-dripping paw toward the Trojan. It roared, "Say, you look like a cousin of mine. You from Darfurdadarbeda?"

"Nah, my folks ain't from that far out in the Styx," Condom said.

"Oh. Sorry, bud. You still look like her, though." With a berserk bellow of rage, the ogre returned to the fray.

Condom sprang onto a stallion that was tied nearby to help the plot along, dug his heels into its side, and galloped for the city gates. A few angry shouts rose behind him, but guardsmen and creatures were still locked in fatal embrace (save, perhaps, for those troopers clutching succubi). The sounds of fighting faded in the distance.

The gate guards did not hinder the Trojan's flight. Burly barbarians with gorgeous, half-clad wenches draped over their saddlebows were two a copper in those days, if the tales that come down from them are to be believed.

The maidservant was awake and squirming when Condom reined the blowing stallion to a halt. The city was far away. The road ran through a glade of quiet, almost unearthly beauty. Tall, slim pines stood silhouetted against the flaming sky of sunset; thrush and warbler sang day's last sleepy songs. And to one side stretched a broad expanse of soft emerald grass.

With a slow smile, Condom dismounted from the great horse. The maid's waist was supple under his fingers as he helped her descend. He laid a hand on her arm, gently guiding her toward the inviting meadow. Her warm flesh was smooth as silk.

She kicked him in the crotch.

He was still writhing on the ground when she clambered aboard the stallion, wheeled it about, and trotted back toward Zamorazamaria. After a while he could sit up. He tried to laugh gustily and think thoughts full of primitive nobility, thoughts on meeting misfortune with stoic equanimity and on the instability of fortune, but his groin hurt and he was none too good at thinking anyhow. He crawled off into the woods and was sick instead.

Twice now, I've used ideas that originally appeared as bits of background in one story to give me another. My novel *Noninterference* (Del Rey, 1988) sprang from a bit of background business in a novelette that never sold. And something in another story of mine ("Herbig-Haro," my first sale to Stan Schmidt at *Analog*) seemed worth expanding into a story of its own. "The Road Not Taken" is the result: a first-contact story, but not of the usual sort.

THE ROAD NOT TAKEN

Captain Togram was using the chamberpot when the *Indomitable* broke out of hyperdrive. As happened all too often, nausea surged through the Roxolan officer. He raised the pot and was abruptly sick into it.

When the spasm was done, he set the thundermug down and wiped his streaming eyes with the soft, gray-brown fur of his forearm. "The gods curse it!" he burst out. "Why don't the shipmasters warn us when they do that?" Several of his troopers echoed him more pungently.

At that moment, a runner appeared in the doorway. "We're back in normal space," the youth squeaked, before dashing on to the next chamber. Jeers and oaths followed him: "No shit!" "Thanks for the news!" "Tell the steerers—they might not have got the word!"

Togram sighed and scratched his muzzle in annoyance at his own irritability. As an officer, he was supposed to set an example for his soldiers. He was junior enough to take such responsibilities seriously, but had had enough service to realize he should never expect too much from anyone more than a couple of notches above him. High ranks went to those with ancient blood or fresh money.

Sighing again, he stowed the chamberpot in its niche. The metal cover he slid over it did little to relieve the stench. After sixteen days in space, the *Indomitable* reeked of ordure, stale food, and staler bodies. It was no better in any other ship of the Roxolan fleet, or any other. Travel between the stars was simply like that. Stinks and darkness were part of the price the soldiers paid to make the kingdom grow.

Togram picked up a lantern and shook it to rouse the glowmites inside. They flashed silver in alarm. Some races, the captain knew, lit their ships with torches or candles, but glowmites used less air, even if they could only shine intermittently.

Ever the careful soldier, Togram checked his weapons while the light lasted. He always kept all four of his pistols loaded and ready to use; when landing operations began, one pair would go on his belt, the other in his boot tops. He was more worried about his sword. The perpetually moist air aboard ship was not good for the blade. Sure enough, he found a spot of rust to scour away.

As he polished the rapier, he wondered what the new system would be like. He prayed for it to have a habitable planet. The air in the *Indomitable* might be too foul to breathe by the time the ship could get back to the nearest Roxolan-held planet. That was one of the risks starfarers took. It was not a major one—small yellow suns usually shepherded a life-bearing world or two—but it was there.

He wished he hadn't let himself think about it; like an aching fang, the worry, once there, would not go away. He got up from his pile of bedding to see how the steerers were doing.

As usual with them, both Ransisc and his apprentice Olgren were complaining about the poor quality of the glass through which they trained their spyglasses. "You ought to stop whining," Togram said, squinting in from the doorway. "At least you have light to see by." After seeing so long by glowmite lantern, he had to wait for his eyes to adjust to the harsh raw sunlight flooding the observation chamber before he could go in.

Olgren's ears went back in annoyance. Ransisc was older and calmer. He set his hand on his apprentice's arm. "If you rise to all of Togram's jibes, you'll have time for nothing else—he's been a troublemaker since he came out of the egg. Isn't that right, Togram?"

"Whatever you say." Togram liked the white-muzzled senior steerer. Unlike most of his breed, Ransisc did not act as if he believed his important job made him something special in the gods' scheme of things.

Olgren stiffened suddenly; the tip of his stumpy tail twitched. "This one's a world!" he exclaimed.

"Let's see," Ransisc said. Olgren moved away from his spyglass. The two steerers had been examining bright stars one by one, looking for those that would show discs and prove themselves actually to be planets.

"It's a world," Ransisc said at length, "but not one for us—those yellow, banded planets always have poisonous air, and too much of it." Seeing Olgren's dejection, he added, "It's not a total loss—if we look along a line from that planet to its sun, we should find others fairly soon."

"Try that one," Togram said, pointing toward a ruddy star that looked brighter than most of the others he could see.

Olgren muttered something haughty about knowing his business better than any amateur, but Ransisc said sharply, "The captain has seen more worlds from space than you, sirrah. Suppose you do as he asks." Ears drooping dejectedly, Olgren obeyed.

Then his pique vanished. "A planet with green patches!" he shouted.

Ransisc had been aiming his spyglass at a different part of the sky, but that brought him hurrying over. He shoved his apprentice aside, fiddled with the spyglass's focus, peered long at the magnified image. Olgren was hopping from one foot to the other, his muddy brown fur puffed out with impatience to hear the verdict.

"Maybe," the senior steerer said, and Olgren's face lit, but it fell again as Ransisc continued, "I don't see anything that looks like open water. If we find nothing better, I say we try it, but let's search a while longer."

"You've just made a *luof* very happy," Togram said. Ransisc chuckled. The Roxolani brought the little creatures along to test new planets' air. If a *luof* could breathe it in the airlock of a flyer, it would also be safe for the animal's masters.

The steerers growled in irritation as several stars in a row stubbornly stayed mere points of light. Then Ransisc stiffened at his spyglass. "Here it is," he said softly. "*This* is what we want. Come here, Olgren."

"Oh my, yes," the apprentice said a moment later.

"Go report it to Warmaster Slevon, and ask him if his devices have picked up any hyperdrive vibrations except for the fleet's." As Olgren hurried away, Ransisc beckoned Togram over. "See for yourself."

The captain of foot bent over the eyepiece. Against the black of space, the world in the spyglass field looked achingly like Roxolan: deep ocean blue, covered with swirls of white cloud. A good-sized moon hung nearby. Both were in approximately half-phase, being nearer their star than was the *Indomitable.*

"Did you spy any land?" Togram asked.

"Look near the top of the image, below the ice cap," Ransisc said. "Those browns and greens aren't colors water usually takes. If we want any world in this system, you're looking at it now."

They took turns examining the distant planet and trying to sketch its features until Olgren came back. "Well?" Togram said, though he saw the apprentice's ears were high and cheerful.

"Not a hyperdrive emanation but ours in the whole system!" Olgren grinned. Ransisc and Togram both pounded him on the back, as if he were the cause of the good news and not just its bearer.

The captain's smile was even wider than Olgren's. This was going to be an easy one, which, as a professional soldier, he thoroughly approved of. If no one hereabouts could build a hyperdrive, either the system had no intelligent life at all or its inhabitants were still primitives, ignorant of gunpowder, fliers, and other aspects of warfare as it was practiced among the stars.

He rubbed his hands. He could hardly wait for landfall.

Buck Herzog was bored. After four months in space, with five and a half more staring him in the face, it was hardly surprising. Earth was a bright star behind the *Ares III*, with Luna a dimmer companion; Mars glowed ahead.

"It's your exercise period, Buck," Art Snyder called. Of the five-person crew, he was probably the most officious.

"All right, Pancho." Herzog sighed. He pushed himself over to the bicycle and began pumping away, at first languidly, then harder. The work helped keep calcium in his bones in spite of free-fall. Besides, it was something to do.

Melissa Ott was listening to the news from home. "Fernando Valenzuela died last night," she said.

"Who?" Snyder was not a baseball fan.

Herzog was, and a Californian to boot. "I saw him at an Old-Timers' game once, and I remember my dad and my grandfather always talking about him," he said. "How old was he, Mel?"

"Seventy-nine," she answered.

"He always was too heavy," Herzog said sadly.

"Jesus Christ!"

Herzog blinked. No one on the *Ares III* had sounded that excited since liftoff from the American space station. Melissa was staring at the radar screen. "Freddie!" she yelled.

Frederica Lindstrom, the ship's electronics expert, had just gotten out of the cramped shower space. She dove for the control board, still trailing a stream of water droplets. She did not bother with a towel; modesty aboard the *Ares III* had long since vanished.

Melissa's shout even made Claude Jonnard stick his head out of the little biology lab where he spent most of his time. "What's wrong?" he called from the hatchway.

"Radar's gone to hell," Melissa told him.

"What do you mean, gone to hell?" Jonnard demanded indignantly. He was one of those annoying people who think quantitatively all the time, and think everyone else does, too.

"There are about a hundred, maybe a hundred fifty, objects on the screen that have no right to be there," answered Frederica Lindstrom, who had a milder case of the same disease. "Range appears to be a couple of million kilometers."

"They weren't there a minute ago, either," Melissa said. "I hollered when they showed up."

As Frederica fiddled with the radar and the computer, Herzog stayed on the exercise bike, feeling singularly useless: What good is a geologist millions of kilometers away from rocks? He wouldn't even get his name in the history books—no one remembers the crew of the third expedition to anywhere.

Frederica finished her checks. "I can't find anything wrong," she said, sounding angry at herself and the equipment both.

"Time to get on the horn to Earth, Freddie," Art Snyder said. "If I'm going to land this beast, I can't have the radar telling me lies."

Melissa was already talking into the microphone. "Houston, this is *Ares III.* We have a problem—"

Even at light-speed, there were a good many minutes of waiting. They crawled past, one by one. Everyone jumped when the speaker crackled to life. "*Ares III,* this is Houston Control. Ladies and gentlemen, I don't quite know how to tell you this, but we see them too."

The communicator kept talking, but no one was listening to her anymore. Herzog felt his scalp tingle as his hair, in primitive reflex, tried to stand on end. Awe filled him. He had never thought he would live to see humanity contact another race. "Call them, Mel," he said urgently.

She hesitated. "I don't know, Buck. Maybe we should let Houston handle this."

"Screw Houston," he said, surprised at his own vehemence. "By the time the bureaucrats down there figure out what to do, we'll be coming down on Mars. We're the people on the spot. Are you going to throw away the most important moment in the history of the species?"

Melissa looked from one of her crewmates to the next. Whatever she saw in their faces must have satisfied her, for she shifted the aim of the antenna and began to speak: "This is the spacecraft *Ares III*, calling the unknown ships. Welcome from the people of Earth." She turned off the transmitter for a moment. "How many languages do we have?"

The call went out in Russian, Mandarin, Japanese, French, German, Spanish, even Latin. ("Who knows the last time they may have visited?" Frederica said when Snyder gave her an odd look.)

If the wait for a reply from Earth had been long, this one was infinitely worse. The delay stretched far, far past the fifteen-second speed-of-light round trip. "Even if they don't speak any of our languages, shouldn't they say *something*?" Melissa demanded of the air. It did not answer, nor did the aliens.

Then, one at a time, the strange ships began darting away sunward, toward Earth. "My God, the acceleration!" Snyder said. "Those are no rockets!" He looked suddenly sheepish. "I don't suppose starships would have rockets, would they?"

The *Ares III* lay alone again in its part of space, pursuing its Hohmann orbit inexorably toward Mars. Buck Herzog wanted to cry.

As was their practice, the ships of the Roxolan fleet gathered above the pole of the new planet's hemisphere with the most land. Because everyone would be coming to the same spot, the doctrine made visual rendezvous easy. Soon only four ships were unaccounted for. A scoutship hurried around to the other pole, found them, and brought them back.

"Always some water-lovers every trip." Togram chuckled to the steerers as he brought them the news. He took all the chances he could to go to their dome, not just for the sunlight but also because, unlike many soldiers, he was interested in planets for their own sake. With any head for figures, he might have tried to become a steerer himself.

He had a decent hand with quill and paper, so Ransisc and

Olgren were willing to let him spell them at the spyglass and add to the sketchmaps they were making of the world below.

"Funny sort of planet," he remarked. "I've never seen one with so many forest fires or volcanoes or whatever they are on the dark side."

"I still think they're cities," Olgren said, with a defiant glance at Ransisc.

"They're too big and too bright," the senior steerer said patiently; the argument, plainly, had been going on for some time.

"This is your first trip offplanet, isn't it, Olgren?" Togram asked.

"Well, what if it is?"

"Only that you don't have enough perspective. Egelloc on Roxolan has almost a million people, and from space it's next to invisible at night. It's nowhere near as bright as those lights, either. Remember, this is a primitive planet. I admit it looks like there's intelligent life down there, but how could a race that hasn't even stumbled across the hyperdrive build cities ten times as great as Egelloc?"

"I don't know," Olgren said sulkily. "But from what little I can see by moonlight, those lights look to be in good spots for cities—on coasts, or along rivers, or whatever."

Ransisc sighed. "What are we going to do with him, Togram? He's so sure he knows everything, he won't listen to reason. Were you like that when you were young?"

"Till my clanfathers beat it out of me, anyway. No need getting all excited, though. Soon enough the flyers will go down with their *luofi*, and then we'll know." He swallowed a snort of laughter, then sobered abruptly, hoping he hadn't been as gullible as Olgren when he was young.

"I have one of the alien vessels on radar," the SR-81 pilot reported. "It's down to 80,000 meters and still descending." He was at his own plane's operational ceiling, barely half as high as the ship entering atmosphere.

"For God's sake, hold your fire," ground control ordered. The command had been dinned into him before he took off, but the brass were not about to let him forget. He did not really blame them. One trigger-happy idiot could ruin humanity forever.

"I'm beginning to get a visual image," he said, glancing at the head-up display projected in front of him. A moment later he added, "It's one damn funny-looking ship, I can tell you that already. Where are the wings?"

"We're picking up the image now too," the ground-control officer said. "They must use the same principle for their in-atmosphere machines as they do for their spacecraft: some sort of antigravity that gives them both lift and drive capability."

The alien ship kept ignoring the SR-81, just as all the aliens had ignored every terrestrial signal beamed at them. The craft continued its slow descent, while the SR-81 pilot circled below, hoping he would not have to go down to the aerial tanker to refuel.

"One question answered," he called to the ground. "It's a warplane." No craft whose purpose was peaceful would have had those glaring eyes and that snarling, fang-filled mouth painted on its belly. Some USAF ground-attack aircraft carried similar markings.

At last the alien reached the level at which the SR-81 was loitering. The pilot called the ground again. "Permission to pass in front of the aircraft?" he asked. "Maybe everybody's asleep in there and I can wake 'em up."

After a long silence, ground control gave grudging assent. "No hostile gestures," the controller warned.

"What do you think I'm going to do, flip him the finger?" the pilot muttered, but his radio was off. Acceleration pushed him back in his seat as he guided the SR-81 into a long, slow turn that would carry it about half a kilometer in front of the vessel from the spacefleet.

His airplane's camera gave him a brief glimpse of the alien pilot, who was sitting behind a small, dirty windscreen.

The being from the stars saw him, too. Of that there was no doubt. The alien jinked like a startled fawn, performing maneuvers that would have smeared the SR-81 pilot against the walls of his pressure cabin—if his aircraft could have matched them in the first place.

"I'm giving pursuit!" he shouted. Ground control screamed at him, but he was the man on the spot. The surge from his afterburner made the pressure he had felt before a love pat by comparison.

Better streamlining made his plane faster than the craft from the starships, but that did not do him much good. Every time its pilot caught sight of him, the alien ship danced away with effortless ease. The SR-81 pilot felt like a man trying to kill a butterfly with a hatchet.

To add to his frustration, his fuel warning light came on. In any case, his aircraft was designed for the thin atmosphere at the edge of space, not the increasingly denser air through which the alien flew. He swore, but he had to pull away.

As his SR-81 gulped kerosene from the tanker, he could not help wondering what would have happened if he'd turned a missile loose. There were a couple of times he'd had a perfect shot. That was one thought he kept firmly to himself. What his superiors would do if they knew about it was too gruesome to contemplate.

The troopers crowded round Togram as he came back from the officers' conclave. "What's the word, Captain?" "Did the *luof* live?" "What's it like down there?"

"The *luof* lived, boys!" Togram said with a broad smile.

His company raised a cheer that echoed deafeningly in the barracks room. "We're going down!" they whooped. Ears stood high in excitement. Some soldiers waved plumed hats in the fetid air. Others, of a bent more like their captain's, went over to their pallets and began seeing to their weapons.

"How tough are they going to be, sir?" a gray-furred veteran named Ilingua asked as Togram went by. "I hear the flier pilot saw some funny things."

Togram's smile got wider. "By the heavens and hells, Ilingua, haven't you done this often enough before to know better than to pay heed to rumors you hear before planetfall?"

"I hope so, sir," Ilingua said, "but these are so strange I thought there might be something to them." When Togram did not answer, the trooper shook his head at his own foolishness and shook up a lantern so he could examine his dagger's edge.

As inconspicuously as he could, the captain let out a sigh. He did not know what to believe himself, and he had listened to the pilot's report. How could the locals have flying machines when they did not know contragravity? Togram had heard of a race that used hot-air balloons before it discovered the better way of doing things, but no balloon could have reached the altitude the locals' flier had achieved, and no balloon could have changed direction, as the pilot had violently insisted this craft had done.

Assume he was wrong, as he had to be. But how was one to take his account of towns as big as the ones whose possibility Ransisc had ridiculed, of a world so populous there was precious little open space? And lantern signals from other ships showed their scout pilots were reporting the same wild improbabilities.

Well, in the long run it would not matter if this race was numerous as *reffo* at a picnic. There would simply be that many more subjects here for Roxolan.

✧ ✧ ✧

"This is a terrible waste," Billy Cox said to anyone who would listen as he slung his duffel bag over his shoulder and tramped out to the waiting truck. "We should be meeting the starpeople with open arms, not with a show of force."

"You tell 'em, Professor." Sergeant Santos Amoros chuckled from behind him. "Me, I'd sooner stay on my butt in a nice, air-conditioned barracks than face L.A. summer smog and sun any old day. Damn shame you're just a Spec-1. If you was President, you could give the orders any way you wanted, instead o' takin' 'em."

Cox didn't think that was very fair either. He'd been just a few units short of his M.A. in poli-sci when the big buildup after the second Syrian crisis sucked him into the army.

He had to fold his lanky length like a jackknife to get under the olive-drab canopy of the truck and down into the passenger compartment. The seats were too hard and too close together. Jamming people into the vehicle counted for more than their comfort while they were there. Typical military thinking, Cox thought disparagingly.

The truck filled. The big diesel rumbled to life. A black soldier dug out a deck of cards and bet anyone that he could turn twenty-five cards into five pat poker hands. A couple of greenhorns took him up on it. Cox had found out the expensive way that it was a sucker bet. The black man was grinning as he offered the deck to one of his marks to shuffle.

Riffff! The ripple of the pasteboards was authoritative enough to make everybody in the truck turn his head. "Where'd you learn to handle cards like that, man?" demanded the black soldier, whose name was Jim but whom everyone called Junior.

"Dealing blackjack in Vegas." *Riffff!*

"Hey, Junior," Cox called, "all of a sudden I want ten bucks of your action."

"Up yours too, pal," Junior said, glumly watching the cards move as if they had lives of their own.

The truck rolled northward, part of a convoy of trucks, MICVs, and light tanks that stretched for miles. An entire regiment was heading into Los Angeles, to be billeted by companies in different parts of the sprawling city. Cox approved of that; it made it less likely that he would personally come face-to-face with any of the aliens.

"Sandy," he said to Amoros, who was squeezed in next to him, "even if I'm wrong and the aliens aren't friendly, what the hell good will hand weapons do? It'd be like taking on an elephant with a safety pin."

"Professor, like I told you already, they don't pay me to think, or you neither. Just as well, too. I'm gonna do what the lieutenant tells me, and you're gonna do what I tell you, and everything is gonna be fine, right?"

"Sure," Cox said, because Sandy, while he wasn't a bad guy, was a sergeant. All the same, the Neo-Armalite between Cox's boots seemed very futile, and his helmet and body armor as thin and gauzy as a stripper's negligee.

The sky outside the steerers' dome began to go from black to deep blue as the *Indomitable* entered atmosphere. "There," Olgren said, pointing. "That's where we'll land."

"Can't see much from this height," Togram remarked.

"Let him use your spyglass, Olgren," Ransisc said. "He'll be going back to his company soon."

Togram grunted; that was more than a comment—it was also a hint. Even so, he was happy to peer through the eyepiece. The ground seemed to leap toward him. There was a moment of disorientation as he adjusted to the inverted image, which put the ocean on the wrong side of the field of view. But he was not interested in sightseeing. He wanted to learn what his soldiers and the rest of the troops aboard the *Indomitable* would have to do to carve out a beachhead and hold it against the locals.

"There's a spot that looks promising," he said. "The greenery there in the midst of the buildings in the eastern—no, the western—part of the city. That should give us a clear landing zone, a good campground, and a base for landing reinforcements."

"Let's see what you're talking about," Ransisc said, elbowing him aside. "Hmm, yes, I see the stretch you mean. That might not be bad. Olgren, come look at this. Can you find it again in the Warmaster's spyglass? All right then, go point it out to him. Suggest it as our setdown point."

The apprentice hurried away. Ransisc bent over the eyepiece again. "Hmm," he repeated. "They build tall down there, don't they?"

"I thought so," Togram said. "And there's a lot of traffic on those roads. They've spent a fortune cobblestoning them all, too; I didn't see any dust kicked up."

"This should be a rich conquest," Ransisc said.

Something swift, metallic, and predator-lean flashed past the observation window. "By the gods, they do have fliers, don't they?" Togram said. In spite of the pilots' claims, deep down he hadn't believed it until he saw it for himself.

He noticed Ransisc's ears twitching impatiently, and realized he really had spent too much time in the observation room. He picked up his glowmite lantern and went back to his troopers.

A couple of them gave him a resentful look for being away so long, but he cheered them up by passing on as much as he could about their landing site. Common soldiers loved nothing better than inside information. They second-guessed their superiors without it, but the game was even more fun when they had some idea of what they were talking about.

A runner appeared in the doorway. "Captain Togram, your company will planet from airlock three."

"Three," Togram acknowledged, and the runner trotted off to pass orders to other ground troop leaders. The captain put his plumed hat on his head (the plume was scarlet, so his company could recognize him in combat), checked his pistols one last time, and ordered his troopers to follow him.

The reeking darkness was as oppressive in front of the inner airlock door as anywhere else aboard the *Indomitable,* but somehow easier to bear. Soon the doors would swing open and he would feel fresh breezes riffling his fur, taste sweet clean air, enjoy sunlight for more than a few precious units at a stretch. Soon he would measure himself against these new beings in combat.

He felt the slightest of jolts as the *Indomitable*'s fliers launched themselves from the mother ship. There would be no *luofi* aboard them this time, but rather musketeers to terrorize the natives with fire from above, and jars of gunpowder to be touched off and dropped. The Roxolani always strove to make as savage a first impression as they could. Terror doubled their effective numbers.

Another jolt came, different from the one before. They were down.

A shadow spread across the UCLA campus. Craning his neck, Junior said, "Will you look at the size of the mother!" He had been saying that for the last five minutes, as the starship slowly descended.

Each time, Billy Cox could only nod, his mouth dry, his hands clutching the plastic grip and cool metal barrel of his rifle. The Neo-Armalite seemed totally impotent against the huge bulk floating so arrogantly downward. The alien flying machines around it were as minnows beside a whale, while they in turn dwarfed the USAF planes circling at a greater distance. The roar of their jets assailed the ears of the nervous troops and civilians on the ground. The aliens' engines were eerily silent.

The starship landed in the open quad between New Royce, New Haines, New Kinsey, and New Powell Halls. It towered higher than any of the two-story red brick buildings, each a reconstruction of one overthrown in the earthquake of 2034. Cox heard saplings splinter under the weight of the alien craft. He wondered what it would have done to the big trees that had fallen five years ago along with the famous old halls.

"All right, they've landed. Let's move on up," Lieutenant Shotton ordered. He could not quite keep the wobble out of his voice, but he trotted south toward the starship. His platoon followed him past Dickson Art Center, past New Bunche Hall. Not so long ago, Billy Cox had walked this campus barefoot. Now his boots thudded on concrete.

The platoon deployed in front of Dodd Hall, looking west toward the spacecraft. A little breeze toyed with the leaves of the young, hopeful trees planted to replace the stalwarts lost to the quake.

"Take as much cover as you can," Lieutenant Shotton ordered quietly. The platoon scrambled into flowerbeds, snuggled down behind thin tree trunks. Out on Hilgard Avenue, diesels roared as armored fighting vehicles took positions with good lines of fire.

It was all such a waste, Cox thought bitterly. The thing to do was to make friends with the aliens, not to assume automatically they were dangerous.

Something, at least, was being done along those lines. A delegation came out of Murphy Hall and slowly walked behind a white flag from the administration building toward the starship. At the head of the delegation was the mayor of Los Angeles; the President and governor were busy elsewhere. Billy Cox would have given anything to be part of the delegation instead of sprawled here on his belly in the grass. If only the aliens had waited until he was fifty or so, had given him a chance to get established—

Sergeant Amoros nudged him with an elbow. "Look there, man. Something's happening—"

Amoros was right. Several hatchways which had been shut were swinging open, allowing Earth's air to mingle with the ship's.

The westerly breeze picked up. Cox's nose twitched. He could not name all the exotic odors wafting his way, but he recognized sewage and garbage when he smelled them. "God, what a stink!" he said.

✧ ✧ ✧

"By the gods, what a stink!" Togram exclaimed. When the outer airlock doors went down, he had expected real fresh air to replace the stale, overused gases inside the *Indomitable.* This stuff smelled like smoky peat fires, or lamps whose wicks hadn't quite been extinguished. And it stung! He felt the nictitating membranes flick across his eyes to protect them.

"Deploy!" he ordered, leading his company forward. This was the tricky part. If the locals had nerve enough, they could hit the Roxolani just as the latter were coming out of their ship, and cause all sorts of trouble. Most races without hyperdrive, though, were too overawed by the arrival of travelers from the stars to try anything like that. And if they didn't do it fast, it would be too late.

They weren't doing it here. Togram saw a few locals, but they were keeping a respectful distance. He wasn't sure how many there were. Their mottled skins—or was that clothing?—made them hard to notice and count. But they were plainly warriors, both by the way they acted and by the weapons they bore.

His own company went into its familiar two-line formation, the first crouching, the second standing and aiming their muskets over the heads of the troops in front.

"Ah, there we go," Togram said happily. The bunch approaching behind the white banner had to be the local nobles. The mottling, the captain saw, was clothing, for these beings wore entirely different garments, somber except for strange, narrow neckcloths. They were taller and skinnier than Roxolani, with muzzleless faces.

"Ilingua!" Togram called. The veteran trooper led the right flank squad of the company.

"Sir!"

"Your troops, quarter-right face. At the command, pick off the leaders there. That will demoralize the rest," Togram said, quoting standard doctrine.

"Slowmatches ready!" Togram said. The Roxolani lowered the smoldering cords to the touchholes of their muskets. "Take your aim!" The guns moved, very slightly. "Fire!"

"Teddy bears!" Sandy Amoros exclaimed. The same thought had leaped into Cox's mind. The beings emerging from the spaceship were round, brown, and furry, with long noses and big ears. Teddy bears, however, did not normally carry weapons. They also, Cox thought, did not commonly live in a place that smelled like sewage. Of course, it might have been perfume to them. But if it was, they and Earthpeople were going to have trouble getting along.

He watched the Teddy bears as they took their positions. Somehow their positioning did not suggest that they were forming an honor guard for the mayor and his party. Yet it did look familiar to Cox, although he could not quite figure out why.

Then he had it. If he had been anywhere but at UCLA, he would not have made the connection. But he remembered a course he had taken on the rise of the European nation-states in the sixteenth century, and on the importance of the professional, disciplined armies the kings had created. Those early armies had performed evolutions like this one.

It was a funny coincidence. He was about to mention it to his sergeant when the world blew up.

Flames spurted from the aliens' guns. Great gouts of smoke puffed into the sky. Something that sounded like an angry wasp buzzed past Cox's ear. He heard shouts and shrieks from either side. Most of the mayor's delegation was down, some motionless, others thrashing.

There was a crash from the starship, and another one an instant later as a roundshout smashed into the brickwork of Dodd Hall. A chip stung Cox in the back of the neck. The breeze brought him the smell of fireworks, one he had not smelled for years.

"Reload!" Togram yelled. "Another volley, then at 'em with the bayonet!" His troopers worked frantically, measuring powder charges and ramming round bullets home.

"So that's how they wanna play!" Amoros shouted. "Nail their hides to the wall!" The tip of his little finger had been shot away. He did not seem to know it.

Cox's Neo-Armalite was already barking, spitting a stream of hot brass cartridges, slamming against his shoulder. He rammed in clip after clip, playing the rifle like a hose. If one bullet didn't bite, the next would.

Others from the platoon were also firing. Cox heard bursts of automatic weapons fire from different parts of the campus, too, and the deeper blasts of rocket-propelled grenades and field artillery. Smoke not of the aliens' making began to envelop their ship and the soldiers around it.

One or two shots came back at the platoon, and then a few

more, but so few that Cox, in stunned disbelief, shouted to his sergeant, "This isn't fair!"

"Fuck 'em!" Amoros shouted back. "They wanna throw their weight around, they take their chances. Only good thing they did was knock over the mayor. Always did hate that old crackpot."

The harsh *tac-tac-tac* did not sound like any gunfire Togram had heard. The shots came too close together, making a horrible sheet of noise. And if the locals were shooting back at his troopers, where were the thick, choking clouds of gunpowder smoke over their position?

He did not know the answer to that. What he did know was that his company was going down like grain before a scythe. Here a soldier was hit by three bullets at once and fell awkwardly, as if his body could not tell in which direction to twist. There another had the top of his head gruesomely removed.

The volley the captain had screamed for was stillborn. Perhaps a squad's worth of soldiers moved toward the locals, the sun glinting bravely off their long, polished bayonets. None of them got more than a half-sixteen of paces before falling.

Ilingua looked at Togram, horror in his eyes, his ears flat against his head. The captain knew his were the same. "What are they doing to us?" Ilingua howled.

Togram could only shake his head helplessly. He dove behind a corpse, fired one of his pistols at the enemy. There was still a chance, he thought—how would these demonic aliens stand up under their first air attack?

A flier swooped toward the locals. Musketeers blasted away from firing ports, drew back to reload.

"Take that, you whoresons!" Togram shouted. He did not, however, raise his fist in the air. That, he had already learned, was dangerous.

"Incoming aircraft!" Sergeant Amoros roared. His squad, those not already prone, flung themselves on their faces. Cox heard shouts of pain through the combat din as men were wounded.

The Cottonmouth crew launched their shoulder-fired AA missile at the alien flying machine. The pilot must have had reflexes like a cat's. He sidestepped his machine in midair; no plane built on Earth could have matched that performance. The Cottonmouth shot harmlessly past.

The flier dropped what looked like a load of crockery. The

ground jumped as the bombs exploded. Cursing, deafened, Billy Cox stopped worrying whether the fight was fair.

But the flier pilot had not seen the F-29 fighter on his tail. The USAF plane released two missiles from point-blank range, less than a mile. The infrared-seeker found no target and blew itself up, but the missile that homed on radar streaked straight toward the flier. The explosion made Cox bury his face in the ground and clap his hands over his ears.

So this is war, he thought: I can't see, I can barely hear, and my side is winning. What must it be like for the losers?

Hope died in Togram's hearts when the first flier fell victim to the locals' aircraft. The rest of the *Indomitable*'s machines did not last much longer. They could evade, but had even less ability to hit back than the Roxolan ground forces. And they were hideously vulnerable when attacked in their pilots' blind spots, from below or behind.

One of the starship's cannon managed to fire again, and quickly drew a response from the traveling fortresses Togram got glimpses of as they took their positions in the streets outside this parklike area.

When the first shell struck, the luckless captain thought for an instant that it was another gun going off aboard the *Indomitable.* The sound of the explosion was nothing like the crash a solid shot made when it smacked into a target. A fragment of hot metal buried itself in the ground by Togram's hand. That made him think a cannon had blown up, but more explosions on the ship's superstructure and fountains of dirt flying up from misses showed it was just more from the locals' fiendish arsenal.

Something large and hard struck the captain in the back of the neck. The world spiraled down into blackness.

"Cease fire!" The order reached the field artillery first, then the infantry units at the very front line. Billy Cox pushed up his cuff to look at his watch, stared in disbelief. The whole firefight had lasted less than twenty minutes.

He looked around. Lieutenant Shotton was getting up from behind an ornamental palm. "Let's see what we have," he said. His rifle still at the ready, he began to walk slowly toward the starship. It was hardly more than a smoking ruin. For that matter, neither were the buildings around it. The damage to their predecessors had been worse in the big quake, but not much.

Alien corpses littered the lawn. The blood splashing the bright green grass was crimson as any man's. Cox bent to pick up a pistol. The weapon was beautifully made, with scenes of combat carved into the grayish wood of the stock. But he recognized it as a single-shot piece, a small-arm obsolete for at least two centuries. He shook his head in wonderment.

Sergeant Amoros lifted a conical object from where it had fallen beside a dead alien. "What the hell is this?" he demanded.

Again Cox had the feeling of being caught up in something he did not understand. "It's a powderhorn," he said.

"Like in the movies? Pioneers and all that good shit?"

"The very same."

"Damn," Amoros said feelingly. Cox nodded in agreement.

Along with the rest of the platoon, they moved closer to the wrecked ship. Most of the aliens had died still in the two neat rows from which they had opened fire on the soldiers.

Here, behind another corpse, lay the body of the scarlet-plumed officer who had given the order to begin that horrifyingly uneven encounter. Then, startling Cox, the alien moaned and stirred, just as might a human starting to come to. "Grab him; he's a live one!" Cox exclaimed.

Several men jumped on the reviving alien, who was too groggy to fight back. Soldiers began peering into the holes torn in the starship, and even going inside. There they were still wary; the ship was so incredibly much bigger than any human spacecraft that there were surely survivors despite the shellacking it had taken.

As always happens, the men did not get to enjoy such pleasures long. The fighting had been over for only minutes when the first team of experts came thuttering in by helicopter, saw common soldiers in their private preserve, and made horrified noises. The experts also promptly relieved the platoon of its prisoner.

Sergeant Amoros watched resentfully as they took the alien away. "You must've known it would happen, Sandy," Cox consoled him. "We do the dirty work and the brass takes over once things get cleaned up again."

"Yeah, but wouldn't it be wonderful if just once it was the other way round?" Amoros laughed without humor. "You don't need to tell me: fat friggin' chance."

When Togram woke up on his back, he knew something was wrong. Roxolani always slept prone. For a moment he wondered how he had got to where he was . . . too much water-of-life the night before? His pounding head made that a good possibility.

Then memory came flooding back. Those damnable locals with their sorcerous weapons! Had his people rallied and beaten back the enemy after all? He vowed to light votive lamps to Edieva, mistress of battles, for the rest of his life if that was true.

The room he was in began to register. Nothing was familiar, from the bed he lay on to the light in the ceiling that glowed bright as sunshine and neither smoked nor flickered. No, he did not think the Roxolani had won their fight.

Fear settled like ice in his vitals. He knew how his own race treated prisoners, had heard spacers' stories of even worse things among other folk. He shuddered to think of the refined tortures a race as ferocious as his captors could invent.

He got shakily to his feet. By the end of the bed he found his hat, some smoked meat obviously taken from the *Indomitable,* and a translucent jug made of something that was neither leather nor glass nor baked clay nor metal. Whatever it was, it was too soft and flexible to make a weapon.

The jar had water in it: *not* water from the *Indomitable.* That was already beginning to taste stale. This was cool and fresh and so pure as to have no taste whatever, water so fine he had only found its like in a couple of mountain springs.

The door opened on noiseless hinges. In came two of the locals. One was small and wore a white coat—a female, if those chest projections were breasts. The other was dressed in the same clothes the local warriors had worn, though those offered no camouflage here. That one carried what was plainly a rifle and, the gods curse him, looked extremely alert.

To Togram's surprise, the female took charge. The other local was merely a bodyguard. Some spoiled princess, curious about these outsiders, the captain thought. Well, he was happier about treating with her than meeting the local executioner.

She sat down, waved for him also to take a seat. He tried a chair, found it uncomfortable—too low in the back, not built for his wide rump and short legs. He sat on the floor instead.

She set a small box on the table by the chair. Togram pointed at it. "What's that?" he asked.

He thought she had not understood—no blame to her for that; she had none of his language. She was playing with the box, pushing a button here, a button there. Then his ears went back and his hackles rose, for the box said, "What's that?" in Roxolani.

After a moment he realized it was speaking in his own voice. He swore and made a sign against witchcraft.

She said something, fooled with the box again. This time it echoed her. She pointed at it. "'Recorder,'" she said. She paused expectantly.

What was she waiting for, the Roxolanic name for that thing? "I've never seen one of those in my life, and I hope I never do again," he said. She scratched her head. When she made the gadget again repeat what he had said, only the thought of the soldier with the gun kept him from flinging it against the wall.

Despite that contretemps, they did eventually make progress on the language. Togram had picked up snatches of a good many tongues in the course of his adventurous life; that was one reason he had made captain in spite of low birth and paltry connections. And the female—Togram heard her name as Hildachesta—had a gift for them, as well as the box that never forgot.

"Why did your people attack us?" she asked one day, when she had come far enough in Roxolanic to be able to frame the question.

He knew he was being interrogated, no matter how polite she sounded. He had played that game with prisoners himself. His ears twitched in a shrug. He had always believed in giving straight answers; that was one reason he was only a captain. He said, "To take what you grow and make and use it for ourselves. Why would anyone want to conquer anyone else?"

"Why indeed?" she murmured, and was silent a little while; his forthright reply seemed to have closed off a line of questioning. She tried again: "How are your people able to walk—I mean, travel—faster than light, when the rest of your arts are so simple?"

His fur bristled with indignation. "They are not! We make gunpowder, we cast iron and smelt steel, we have spyglasses to help our steerers guide us from star to star. We are no savages huddling in caves or shooting at each other with bows and arrows."

His speech, of course, was not that neat or simple. He had to backtrack, to use elaborate circumlocutions, to playact to make Hildachesta understand. She scratched her head in the gesture of puzzlement he had come to recognize. She said, "We have known all these things you mention for hundreds of years, but we did not think anyone could walk—damn, I keep saying that instead of 'travel'—faster than light. How did your people learn to do that?"

"We discovered it for ourselves," he said proudly. "We did not have to learn it from some other starfaring race, as many folk do."

"But *how* did you discover it?" she persisted.

"How do I know? I'm a soldier; what do I care for such things? Who knows who invented gunpowder or found out about using bellows in a smithy to get the fire hot enough to melt iron? These things happen, that's all."

She broke off the questions early that day.

"It's humiliating," Hilda Chester said. "If these fool aliens had waited a few more years before they came, we likely would have blown ourselves to kingdom come without ever knowing there was more real estate around. Christ, from what the Roxolani say, races that scarcely know how to work iron fly starships and never think twice about it."

"Except when the starships don't get home," Charlie Ebbets answered. His tie was in his pocket and his collar open against Pasadena's fierce summer heat, although the Caltech Atheneum was efficiently air-conditioned. Along with so many other engineers and scientists, he depended on linguists like Hilda Chester for a link to the aliens.

"I don't quite understand it myself," she said. "Apart from the hyperdrive and contragravity, the Roxolani are backward, almost primitive. And the other species out there must be the same, or someone would have overrun them long since."

Ebbets said, "Once you see it, the drive is amazingly simple. The research crews say anybody could have stumbled over the principle at almost any time in our history. The best guess is that most races did come across it, and once they did, why, all their creative energy would naturally go into refining and improving it."

"But we missed it," Hilda said slowly, "and so our technology developed in a different way."

"That's right. That's why the Roxolani don't know anything about controlled electricity, to say nothing of atomics. And the thing is, as well as we can tell so far, the hyperdrive and contragravity don't have the ancillary applications the electromagnetic spectrum does. All they do is move things from here to there in a hurry."

"That should be enough at the moment," Hilda said. Ebbets nodded. There were almost nine billion people jammed onto the Earth, half of them hungry. Now, suddenly, there were places for them to go and a means to get them there.

"I think," Ebbets said musingly, "we're going to be an awful surprise to the peoples out there."

It took Hilda a second to see what he was driving at. "If that's a joke, it's not funny. It's been a hundred years since the last war of conquest."

"Sure—they've gotten too expensive and too dangerous. But what kind of fight could the Roxolani or anyone else at their level of technology put up against us? The Aztecs and Incas were plenty brave. How much good did it do them against the Spaniards?"

"I hope we've gotten smarter in the last five hundred years," Hilda said. All the same, she left her sandwich half-eaten. She found she was not hungry any more.

"Ransisc!" Togram exclaimed as the senior steerer limped into his cubicle. Ransisc was thinner than he had been a few moons before, aboard the misnamed *Indomitable.* His fur had grown out white around several scars Togram did not remember.

His air of amused detachment had not changed, though. "Tougher than bullets, are you, or didn't the humans think you were worth killing?"

"The latter, I suspect. With their firepower, why should they worry about one soldier more or less?" Togram said bitterly. "I didn't know you were still alive, either."

"Through no fault of my own, I assure you," Ransisc said. "Olgren, next to me—" His voice broke off. It was not possible to be detached about everything.

"What are you doing here?" the captain asked. "Not that I'm not glad to see you, but you're the first Roxolan face I've set eyes on since—" It was his turn to hesitate.

"Since we landed." Togram nodded in relief at the steerer's circumlocution. Ransisc went on, "I've seen several others before you. I suspect we're being allowed to get together so the humans can listen to us talking with each other."

"How could they do that?" Togram asked, then answered his own question. "Oh, the recorders, of course." He perforce used the English word. "Well, we'll fix that."

He dropped into Oyag, the most widely spoken language on a planet the Roxolani had conquered fifty years before. "What's going to happen to us, Ransisc?"

"Back on Roxolan, they'll have realized something's gone wrong by now," the steerer answered in the same tongue.

That did nothing to cheer Togram. "There are so many ways to lose ships," he said gloomily. "And even if the High Warmaster does send another fleet after us, it won't have any more luck than we did. These gods-accursed humans have too many war-machines."

He paused and took a long, moody pull at a bottle of vodka. The flavored liquors the locals brewed made him sick, but vodka he liked. "How is it they have all these machines and we don't, or any race we know of? They must be wizards, selling their souls to the demons for knowledge."

Ransisc's nose twitched in disagreement. "I asked one of their savants the same question. He gave me back a poem by a human named Hail or Snow or something of that sort. It was about someone who stood at a fork in the road and ended up taking the less-used track. That's what the humans did. Most races find the hyperdrive and go traveling. The humans never did, and so their search for knowledge went in a different direction."

"Didn't it!" Togram shuddered at the recollection of that brief, terrible combat. "Guns that spit dozens of bullets without reloading, cannon mounted on armored platforms that move by themselves, rockets that follow their targets by themselves . . . And there are the things we didn't see, the ones the humans only talk about—the bombs that can blow up a whole city, each one by itself."

"I don't know if I believe that," Ransisc said.

"I do. They sound afraid when they speak of them."

"Well, maybe. But it's not just the weapons they have. It's the machines that let them see and talk to one another from far away; the machines that do their reckoning for them; their recorders and everything that has to do with them. From what they say of their medicine, I'm almost tempted to believe you and think they are wizards—they actually know what causes their diseases, and how to cure or even prevent them. And their farming: this planet is far more crowded than any I've seen or heard of, but it grows enough for all these humans."

Togram sadly waggled his ears. "It seems so unfair. All that they got, just by not stumbling onto the hyperdrive."

"They have it now," Ransisc reminded him. "Thanks to us."

The Roxolani looked at each other, appalled. They spoke together: "What have we done?"

The next two short fantasies both have their roots in medieval literature. "The Castle of the Sparrowhawk" is based on a tale told by that champion teller of tales, Sir John Mandeville, in his *Travels*—a volume I heartily recommend to anyone who enjoys marvels, whether real, imagined, or—best of all—real and imagined so commingled that the one is impossible to tell from the other.

THE CASTLE OF THE SPARROWHAWK

Sir John Mandeville heard the tale of the castle of the sparrowhawk, but only from afar, and imperfectly. If a man could keep that sparrowhawk, which dwelt in the topmost tower of the castle, awake for seven days and nights, he would win whatever earthly thing might be his heart's desire. So much Mandeville knew.

But he lied when he put that castle in Armenia. Armenia, surely, was a strange and exotic land to his readers in England or France or Italy, but the castle of the sparrowhawk lay beyond the fields we know. How could it be otherwise, when even Mandeville tells us a lady of Faerie kept that sparrowhawk?

Perhaps we may excuse him after all, though, for the tale as he learned it did involve an Armenian prince—Mandeville calls him a king, to make the story grander, but only the truth here. Natural enough, then, for him to set that castle there. Natural, but wrong.

You might think Prince Rupen of Etchmiadzin had no need to go searching for the castle of the sparrowhawk. He was young. He was strong, in principality and in person. He was brave, and even beginning to be wise. His face, a handsome face in the half-eagle, half-lion way so many Armenians have, was more apt to be seen in a smile than a scowl.

Yet despite his smiles, he was not happy, not lastingly so. He felt that nothing he owned was his by right. His principality he had from his father, and his face and form as well. Even his bravery and the beginnings of wisdom had been inculcated in him.

"What would I have been had I been born an ugly, palsied pig-farmer?" he cried one day in a fit of self-doubt.

"Someone other than yourself," his vizier answered sensibly.

But that did not satisfy him. He was, after all, only *beginning* to be wise.

In the east, the line between the fields we know and those beyond is not drawn so firmly as in our mundane corner of the world. Too, in the tortuous mountains of Armenia, who knows what fields lie three valleys over? And so, when Rupen, armed with no more than determination—and a crossbow, in case of dragons—set out to seek the castle of the sparrowhawk, he was not surprised that one day he found it.

But for a certain feline grace, the grooms and servants of the castle were hardly different from those he had left behind at Etchmiadzin. They tended his horse, fed him ground lamb and pine nuts, and gave him wine spiced with cinnamon. He drank deeply and flung himself on the featherbed to which they led him. To hold the sparrowhawk wakeful seven days and nights, he would have to go without sleep himself. He stored it away now, like a woodchuck fattening itself for winter.

No one disturbed his rest; he was allowed to emerge from his chamber when he would. After he had eaten again, the seneschal of the castle asked leave to have speech with him. The mark of Faerie lay more heavily on that man than on his underlings. In the fields we know, his mien and bearing would have suited a sovereign, not a bailiff. So would his robes, of sea-green samite shot through with silver threads and decked with pearls.

Said he to Rupen, "Is it your will to essay the ordeal of the sparrowhawk?"

"It is," the prince replied.

The seneschal bowed. "You have come, no doubt, seeking the reward success will bring. My duty is to inform you of the cost of failure; word thereof somehow does not travel so widely. If the bird sleeps, you forfeit more than your life. Your soul is lost as well. The prayers of your priests do not reach here to save it."

Rupen believed him absolutely. The churches of Armenia with their conical domes had never seemed more distant. For all that, he said, "I will go on."

The seneschal bowed again. "Be it so, then. Honor to your courage. I will take you to the lady Olissa. Come."

There were one hundred and forty-four steps on the spiral stair that led to the sparrowhawk's eyrie. Prince Rupen counted them one by one as he climbed behind the seneschal. His heart pounded and his breath came short by the time they reached the top. The seneschal was unchanged; he might have been a falcon himself, by the ease with which he took the stairs.

The door at the head of the stairway was of some golden wood Rupen did not know. Light streamed into the gloomy stairwell when the seneschal opened it, briefly dazzling Rupen. As his eyes took its measure, he saw a broad expanse of enameled blue sky, a single perch, and standing beside it one who had to be Olissa.

"Are you of a sudden afraid, then?" the seneschal asked when Rupen hung back. "You may yet withdraw, the only penalty being that never again shall you find your way hither."

"Afraid?" Rupen murmured, as from far away. "No, I am not afraid." But still he stayed in the antechamber; to take a step might have meant pulling his eyes away from Olissa for an instant, and he could not have borne it.

Her hair stormed in bright waves to her waist, the color of the new-risen sun. Her skin was like snow faintly tinged with ripe apples. The curves of her body bade fair to bring tears to his eyes. So, for another reason, did the sculpted lines of her chin, her cheeks, the tiny curve of her ear where it peeped from among fiery ringlets. He thought how the pagan Greeks would have slain themselves in despair of capturing her in stone.

Her eyes? Like the sea, they were never the same shade twice.

He stood until she extended a slim hand his way. Then indeed he moved forward, as iron will toward a lodestone. When she spoke, he learned what the sound was that silver bells sought. "Knowing the danger," she asked, "you still wish to undertake the ordeal?"

He could only nod.

"Honor to your courage." Olissa echoed the seneschal; it was the first thing that recalled him to Rupen's mind since he set eyes on her. Then the man of Faerie was again forgotten as she went on, "I will have provender fetched here; you must undertake the test alone with the sparrowhawk."

The thought that she would leave filled him with despair. But when she asked him, "Will you drink wine at meat?" he had to think of a reply, if only not to appear a fool before her.

"No, bring me water or milk, if you would," he said. He would not have chosen them in Armenia, but he feared no flux here. He felt bound to explain, "Come the seventh day, I shall be drowsy enough without the grape."

"A man of sense as well as bravery. It shall be as you wish, or even better."

Already Rupen heard servants on the stairs, though no sign he could detect had summoned them. Along with the flaky loaves and smoked meats, they set down ewers the fragrance of whose contents made his nose twitch.

"Fruit nectars," Olissa said. "Does it please you?"

He bowed his thanks. Against the liquid elegance of the seneschal, his courtesy seemed a miserable clumsy thing, but he gave it as a man will give a copper when he has no gold to spend.

She nodded to him, and he felt as if the Emperor of Byzantium and the Great Khan had prostrated themselves at his feet. Saying, "Perhaps we shall meet again in seven days, you and I," she stepped past him to join the seneschal in the antechamber at the head of the stairs.

The door of the golden wood was swinging shut when Rupen blurted out a final thought: "If no one is here to watch me, how will you know if I fail?"

He had hoped for a last word from Olissa, but it was the seneschal who answered him. "We shall know, never fear," he said, and the iron promise in his voice sent a snake of dread slithering through Rupen's bowels. Soundlessly, the door closed.

With the glory of Olissa gone, Rupen turned to the sparrowhawk for the first time. It stared back at him with fierce topaz eyes, and screeched shrilly. He had flown hawks, and knew what that cry meant. "Hungry, are you? I was not sure the birds of Faerie had to eat."

Among the supplies the castle servants had brought was a large, low, earthen pot with a lid of openweave wickerwork. Small scuttling sounds came from it. When Rupen lifted the lid, he found mice, brown, white, and gray, scrambling about inside. He reached in, caught one and killed it, and offered it to the sparrowhawk. The bird ate greedily. It called for more, though the tip of the mouse's tail still dangled from its beak.

Rupen shook his head. "A stuffed belly makes for restfulness.

We'll both stay a bit empty through this week." The sparrowhawk glared as if it understood. Perhaps, he thought, it did.

As dusk fell, it tucked its head under a wing. He clapped his hands. The sparrowhawk hissed at him. He lit a torch and set it in its sconce. It burned with the clean, sweet smell of sandalwood.

That night, drowsiness did not trouble Rupen, who was sustained by imaginings of Olissa. He felt fresh as just-fallen snow when dawn streaked the eastern sky with carmine and gold. The sparrowhawk, by then, was too furious with him to think of sleep.

Noon was not long past when he fed it another mouse. Soon after, the first yawn crept out of hiding and stretched itself in his throat. He strangled it, but felt others stirring to take its place. Presently they would thrive.

To hold them back, he began to sing. He sang every song he knew, and sang them all once again when he was through. The din sufficed to keep the sparrowhawk awake through most of the night. Eventually, though, it grew used to the sound of his voice, and began to close its eyes. Seeing that, he fell silent, which served as well as a thunderclap. The bird started up wildly; its bright stare had hatred in it.

That was how the second day passed.

Prince Rupen stumbled through the third and fourth days as if drunk. He laughed hoarsely at nothing, and kept dropping the chunks of bread he cut for supper. He was too tired to notice they had not gone stale, as they would have in the fields we know. The sparrowhawk began to sway on its perch. Some of the luster was gone from its bright plumage.

On the fifth day, it took Rupen a very long time to catch the bird its mouse. The mice were wide awake. When at last he had the furry little creature, he started to pop it into his own mouth. Only the sparrowhawk's shriek of protest recalled him to himself, for a little while.

He remembered nothing whatsoever of the sixth day.

Sometime in the middle of the last night, he decided he wanted to die. He lurched over to the edge of the eyrie's floor and looked longingly at the castle courtyard far below. The thought of forfeiting his soul for failing the ordeal did not check him, nor did the certainty that suicides suffered the same fate. But he lacked the energy to take the step that would have sent him tumbling down.

He did not remember why he kept snapping his fingers in the sparrowhawk's face. The bird, by then, lacked the spirit even to bite at him. Its eyes might have been dull yellow glass now, not topaz. Both of them had forgotten the mice.

The sun came up. Rupen stared at it until the pain penetrated the fog between his eyes and his brain. Tears streamed down his cheeks, and continued to flow long after the pain was past. He had no idea why he wept, or how to stop.

Nor did the sound of footsteps on the stairs convey to him a meaning. Yet when the door swung open, he somehow contrived a bow to the lady Olissa.

She curtseyed in return, as lovely as she had been a week before. "Rest now, bold prince," she murmured. "You have won."

The seneschal sprang out from behind her to ease Rupen to the slates of the floor, his first snores already begun. Olissa paid the man no attention, but crooned to the sparrowhawk, "And thou, little warrior, rest thyself as well." The bird gave what would have been a chirp had its voice been sweeter, and pushed its head into the white palm of her hand like a lovesick cat. Then it too slept.

The seneschal said, "To look at him lying there, this mortal now has in his possession his heart's desire."

"Ah, but he will not reckon it so when he wakes," Olissa replied.

The sun sliding fingers under his eyelids roused Rupen. He sprang up in horror, certain he was doomed. Ice formed round his heart to see the perch he had so long guarded empty.

Olissa's laugh, a sound like springtime, made him whirl. "Fear not," she said. "You have slept the day around. The ordeal is behind you, and you have only to claim your reward."

"You did come to me, then," Rupen said, amazed. "I thought surely it was a dream."

"No dream," she said. "What would you?"

He was not yet ready for that question. "The sparrowhawk—?" he asked.

His concern won a smile from her. "It is a bird of Faerie, and recovers itself more quickly than those you may have known. Already it is on the wing, hunting mice it does not have to scream for."

Rupen flushed to be reminded of his vagaries during the trial. That reminded him of his present sadly draggled state. "As part of my reward, may I ask for a great hot tub and the loan of fresh clothing?"

"It shall be as you desire; you are not the first to make that request. While you bathe, think on what else you would have.

I shall come to your bedchamber in an hour's time, to hear you."

The soaps and scents of Faerie, finer and more delicate than the ones we know, washed the last lingering exhaustion from his bones. His borrowed silks clung to him like a second skin. As he combed his hair and thick curly beard, he noticed the mirror on the wall above the tub was not befogged by steam. He wished he could take that secret back with him to Etchmiadzin.

He started when the soft knock came at the bedchamber door. At the first touch of the latch, the door opened as silently as all the others in the castle of the sparrowhawk. The lady Olissa stepped in. As if it were a well-trained dog, the door swung shut behind her.

She watched him a moment with her sea-colored eyes. "Ask for any earthly thing you may desire, for you have nobly acquitted yourself in the task set you."

Had it been the seneschal granting him that boon, Rupen would have answered differently. But he was a young man, and quite refreshed, so he said, "Of earthly things, Etchmiadzin fills all my wants. Therefore—" His resolve faltered, and he hesitated, but at last he did go on, all in a rush: "—I ask of you no more than that you share this bed with me here for a night and a day. I could desire nothing more."

Still her eyes reminded him of the sea, the sea at storm. Almost he quailed before her anger, and was steadied only by the thought that she would despise him for his fear.

She said, "Beware, mortal. I am no earthly thing, but of the Faerie realm. Choose you another benison, one suited to your station."

"Am I not a prince?" Rupen cried. He was only beginning to be wise. "In truth, I would ask for nothing else."

"For the last time, can I not dissuade you from this folly?"

"No," he said.

"Be it so, then," she said with a wintry sigh, "but with this gift you demand of me I shall give you another, such as you deserve for your presumption. Etchmiadzin will not so delight you on your return; you will come to know war and need and loss. And ten years hence I charge you to think upon this day and what you have earned here now."

Her words fell on deaf ears, for as she spoke she was loosing the stays of her gown and letting it fall to the floor. Rupen had imagined how she might be. Now he saw what a poor, paltry, niggling thing his imagination was. Then he touched her, and that was past all imagining.

Afterward, riding back to Etchmiadzin, he wished he had asked for a year. On the other hand, half an hour might have served as well, or as poorly. Anything less than forever was not enough.

He returned by the road he had taken into Faerie, but somehow he did not enter the fields we know where he had left them. Yet he was still in Armenia, only a few days' journey from his principality. He had half looked for a greater vengeance.

Then he found his border closed against him, and his onetime vizier holding the throne of his ancestors. "If a prince go haring into Faerie rather than look after his own land, he does not deserve to rule," the usurper had told the nobles, and most said aye and swore him allegiance.

But not all. Prince Rupen soon mustered a band of warriors and undertook to regain by force what had once been his by right. Fighting and siege and murder engulfed the land of Etchmiadzin that had been so fair. By his own hand Rupen slew a cousin who had been a dear friend. He watched comrades of old die in his service, or live on maimed.

And in the end it did not avail. Etchmiadzin remained lost. By the time he admitted that in his heart, Rupen had lived the soldier's life so long that he found any other savorless. From a nest high in the hills—to its sorrow, Armenia has many of them—he and his swooped down into the valleys to seize what they might.

Sometimes Rupen was nearly as rich as a bandit chief as he had been in the castle of Etchmiadzin. More often he went hungry. There were white scars on his arms, and along his ribs, and a great gash on his cheek and forehead that was only partly hidden by the leather patch covering the ruin of his left eye-socket.

He seldom thought of Faerie. Few even of the hard-bitten crew who rode with him had the nerve to bring up his journey to the castle of the sparrowhawk. After a while, most of those who had known of it were dead.

Then one day, as the lady Olissa had decreed, full memory came flooding back, and he knew in astonishment that a decade had passed. He thought of the tiny space of time he had spent in her arms, of his life as a prince before, and the long years of misfortune that came after. He thought of what he had become: ladder-ribbed, huddled close to a tiny fire in a drafty hut, drinking sour wine.

He thought of Olissa again. Not even the folk of Faerie see all the future, exactly as it will be. "I'd do it over again, just the same way," he said out loud.

One or two of his men looked up. The rest kept on with what they were doing.

A couple of things came together in "The Summer Garden." One is its model—it springs from a tale in Boccaccio's *Decameron*. The other was my falling in love, just about the time when I wrote the piece, with a woman who did not fall in love with me. These things happen. One of the advantages of being a writer is having the chance to work them out on paper.

A different version of this story appeared in the February 1982 *Fantasy Book* as "The Summer's Garden." The editor liked the idea but did not approve of its high, almost Dunsanian style and demanded a complete rewrite. He also introduced sundry other changes, most of them, I think, gratuitous. For better or worse, this is the way I think "The Summer Garden" ought to read.

THE SUMMER GARDEN

In the Empire of Kar V'Shem, in the town of Sennar, through which flow the laughing waters of the River Veprel, there lived the merchant Ansovald. A warm, good-hearted man, he had grown nearly rich from his trade in the furs and honey that the River Veprel brought down from the fabled North, and his home was in the finest quarter of the city, not too far from the marketplace but not too close to the church. With him dwelt his wife Dianora, the delight of his life. Her skin was fairer than the whitest linen, her eyes more green than the verdant jade which now and then appeared from out of the trackless East, her hair the blue-black of the midnight sky, and her nature . . . ah, with her nature we press close to the heart of the matter, for she was of that rare breed who can bear to give hurt to no living creature.

Being such as one, it is only natural that Dianora shared with her dear husband some years of wedded bliss. Nor should it surprise us to learn that her beauty and warmth attracted the notice of others in the town of Sennar beside the merchant Ansovald. Toward these she was, as was her way, unfailingly kind, but, as she truly loved her husband, unfailingly unavailable. One by one, some sooner, some later, they came to understand this and troubled her no more. All save Rand.

Now Rand was a belted knight, a veteran of wars and sanguinary single conflicts, yet withal a poet and dreamer as well. The experiences of his life had forged in him a singleness of purpose not easily matched in all the Empire of Kar V'Shem, let alone the sleepy town of Sennar. Thus when his sonnets fell on deaf ears and his gifts were discreetly returned, he did not grow downhearted—as had so many before him—but paid court to Dianora with greater vigor than before, reckoning the prize he sought all the more valuable for its difficulty of attainment.

The lady was unwilling simply to tell him to be gone; she did not wish to wound his feelings, recognizing his manly qualities even if they tempted her not. Instead, through a maidservant she sent him a message, as follows: "Know that to prove your deep love for me, you must produce in dead of winter a garden full of summer's fruits and flowers. Then I shall be yours to command, but until and unless this be done, you must cease importuning me." Confidently expecting that Rand would find the assigned task as difficult as she deemed it, she banished the knight from her thoughts, glad she had found a way to dismiss him without harshness and certain he would not pester her again.

But no sooner had her servant delivered the note and departed than Rand struck scarred fist against strong palm and spoke. "I shall do it," he vowed, though there was none to hear him. The arduousness of the task did not daunt him as the lady Dianora had hoped; in his wanderings he had seen more marvels than she had ever imagined, she who had never strayed more than a mile or two beyond the sheltering walls of the town of Sennar.

Undaunted Rand may have been, but also uncertain as to how to proceed, for he himself had no notion of how such a wonder as that required of him might be produced. How could one call into being the fragrance and beauty of a summer garden in a world all drear with cold and ice? All the savants and sages to whom he put the question owned themselves baffled. And so for a year and more he remained thwarted, until the mage Portolis took it in his mind to visit Sennar.

When he learned of the arrival of so famous a thaumaturge as Portolis, Rand wasted no time in making his acquaintance and setting forth the problem which had so long tormented him. After he had spoken, Portolis scanned his face. Rand would sooner have faced some men's swords than the wizard's eyes, for they were gray and hard as the granite ramparts of the mountains of Rincia, behind which the sun god sought his bed each day. But it ill-behooved a belted knight to show any trace of fear, and so Rand sat unflinching.

At length the wizard nodded slowly. "I can do this thing," he said, "yet the price of its success may be more than you would willingly pay."

Quoth Rand, "For the love of my lady Dianora no price could be too great."

The knight thought he saw a glint of irony kindle for a moment in the terrible eyes of Portolis, but it faded so quickly he could not be sure. "Are you certain of this?" the wizard asked. Rand had been gripped by his obsession for long and long, and could do nothing else but nod. "Be it so, then," Portolis said. "My fee—which must be paid in advance, as the components of this spell are quite costly—is seven thousand seven hundred seven and seventy kraybecks of gold."

Rand blanched, for after paying so great a sum he would be left in poverty. But his resolve was firm and his voice steady as he answered, "I shall deliver it to you on the morrow."

"Next week will suffice," the wizard said idly. "It is still some time before Midwinter Day, at which time, the gods willing, I shall do as you have requested."

As events transpired, the knight was glad Portolis had not required payment on the following day: to meet the magician's price he was compelled to mortgage both mansion and lands. He dismissed servant after servant, no longer able to afford their keep, until at last he was left with but one retainer, a stolid old fellow named Fant. Together they dwelt miserably in one small room of Rand's palatial home, for the knight lacked the wherewithal to heat the entire building. Rand bore his self-inflicted pauperhood proudly, for his heart, if not his body, was warmed by visions of Dianora in his arms; what, if anything, Fant did for like sustenance, it never occurred to Rand to inquire.

Unmoved by the slide of his client into penury, the wizard's preparations for his spell proceeded apace. More than once he left the town of Sennar for some days, arousing fear in the heart of Rand that he was being deluded by some traveling mountebank. But he always returned, and he expressed grave satisfaction whenever the knight queried his progress.

Midwinter Day, when at length it came, dawned clear and cold, the pale sun seeming wan and weak in a steel-blue sky. The entire surround of the town of Sennar was white and still. Even the laughing River Veprel, whose scurrying waters had long defied the icy hand of winter, lay prisoned under a palm-thick sheet of ice. An unsmiling 'prentice of the mage Portolis called upon Rand and Fant to repair to a certain spot by the banks of the river, where, he said, all was ready for the effort, saving only their presence.

Seen from without, the walls of Sennar lost for Rand the aspect of comfort and reassurance they had always before possessed. A warrior born, he had misread Dianora's relegation as challenge, and to his infatuate mind the fortifications formed the perfect metaphor for her heart. In this belief he was most sincere and, poor soul, most mistaken, for the woman's only thought had been to spare him pain.

Vermilion ribbon delineated the area in which the conjuration was to take place. Inside, pentacles had been scribed in snow. Marching around them in intricate geometric patterns, half a dozen chanting acolytes swung thuribles, charging the frosty air with pungent incenses.

Alone and still in the center of this stir stood Portolis. The north wind frisked playfully through gray tendrils of his beard, but there was nothing of play in his proud hawk face as he greeted Rand. "I ask you once more, sir knight," said he, "if you wish me to proceed?"

"Did I not, would I have beggared myself for you?" Rand demanded harshly. The mage looked him full in the face, then curtly bowed. So loud was Rand's heart pounding in his breast, he was surprised Portolis made no remark on it.

The wizard raised his arms. The acolytes froze, silent in their places, as if seized of a sudden by winter. Through the thunder in his veins Rand heard the wind's thin whisper die, as if the very universe held its breath. His voice ringing like a deep-toned bronzen bell, Portolis began the spell over which he had labored long, his pale fingers flying through its intricate passes like things independently alive.

Rand had never thought on what it might be like to be in the midst of an unfolding miracle. A glow like the distillation of a thousand sunrises suffused the air, conjoined with a scent like that of attar of roses but a thousand times more sweet, a thousand times more delicate, a scent to penetrate to the root of the heart and set it winging free. Portolis's voice was the perfect backdrop to the bedazzlement of Rand's senses, for though he knew not the tongue in which the wizard sang, he felt tears of joy course down his cheeks and fall hot and steaming in the snow.

Snow? As the mists of the enchantment faded, Rand looked down to find his boots no longer coated with rime but cushioned by a carpet of greenest grass. He cried out in wonder and delight: within Portolis's scarlet-lined square, summer reigned. Looking spent and drawn, the wizard leaned against a veritable apple tree full of ruddy fruit. A blue butterfly wheeled round his head; startled perhaps by a blink, perhaps by nothing at all, it darted away, out beyond the confines of his magic, and fell, an azure icicle, to the snow.

The knight all but thought himself still bemused, for hard by the apple tree was one laden with plump pears, next to that a fragrant-leafed orange tree, and beside it bearers of peaches, apricots, and purple figs, soft and deliciously ripe. The perfumes of fruit and trees mingled with those of the flowers clustering round them: roses red as maidens' lips (and Rand's heart throbbed, to think of Dianora), others yellow as the sun, tulips like bells of flame, lilies of every size, shape, and hue, and wild tropic blooms that the knight, traveled though he was, could never have hoped to name.

Filled with awe, Rand touched the smooth, gray-brown bark of the fig and stroked a parchmentlike leaf. He nipped off a tiny piece between thumb and forefinger and watched, entranced, as beads of white sap formed to seal off the injury he had worked. He questioned his senses no longer. Everything round him was too real, too detailed, to be a mere vision, even one produced by so gifted a warlock as Portolis.

Forethoughtfully having brought along a wicker basket, the knight now filled it with the choicest products of the wondrous summer garden. He handed it to his servant, bidding him repair to the town of Sennar, present it to the lady Dianora as token of the knight's true love, and lead her back to the paradise whose creation Rand had caused.

So intent was Rand on watching his servant near the gates of Sennar that he failed to hear Portolis come up beside him. "So," the wizard said, his voice a tattered ghost of itself, "you have your garden and soon shall have your woman, if that be your desire. Will you then be content?"

"Again and again you ask me this, as if to say it will not be so," Rand cried angrily. "Why do you hound me? I have spent all my substance to gain my lady's submission and love. Once achieved, how could they not fill me with delight?"

The wizard did not reply.

✧ ✧ ✧

As Fant came up to the gates, their guardsmen, in recognition of the marvel of which he was a part, grounded their spears, doffed conical helms, and bowed low in salute until he was past. "Well, well," he said to himself. "This consorting with magicians is not such a bad thing, no matter what I may have thought in the past. When has a poor servant ever before been greeted like a baron? No, like a prince or better!" And with a fine indolent wave to its warders, he entered the town of Sennar.

When he reached the home of Ansovald the merchant, Fant was greeted with some surprise by the maidservant who had delivered Dianora's message to his master. Recognizing him at once, she said, "You've not come this way in some time. What can I do for you now?" Before an answer could cross his lips, she went on, "Don't stand there and let all the warm out; it's rare cold today. Come in and toast your bones by the fire."

"I'm glad to do that," he replied, and spent the next several minutes savoring the delicious heat. Then, recalling his mission, he handed the maid his basket, saying, "My master bids me deliver this token to your lady and escort her back to the spot where he awaits her."

"Does he indeed?" she said with a toss of her head. "The cheek of the man!" Now, as it happened, she was altogether ignorant of the content of the message she had delivered to Rand so long ago, though she could scarcely have been unaware of his feelings toward her mistress. She commented, "It will take more than a hamper of fruit to change my lady's mind about your knight, I warrant."

Fant shrugged. "That's not for me to say, nor you either," he answered. "Could I ask for a mug of hot wine? I'm chilled clean to the marrow."

"You're as bad as your master." The maid sniffed, but she put some over the fire to heat. While Fant waited with ill-concealed eagerness, she took up the basket and carried it upstairs to the lady Dianora.

The lady had been weaving, and was not sorry to be interrupted. "What have you there for me?" she asked, seeing the basket but not yet understanding what it contained. Her maid repeated Fant's message, punctuated with condemnations of Rand's arrogance and his servant's insolence, and departed, leaving Dianora alone to struggle with her conscience.

She was flattered and complimented beyond all measure by

Rand's devotion to the cause of winning her, and she knew full well what his adherence to that cause had cost him, for his sudden and inexplicable slide into poverty had for weeks been one of the paramount topics of conversation in the town of Sennar. But despite his evident adoration, her heart was in her husband's keeping only, and she no more desired to lie with the knight in love than she had when she made her rash promise so long ago. Yet that promise had been freely given, extorted or coerced from her in no way, and how with honor could she now refuse to keep it? To do so would work far more grievous hurt on Rand than even the coldest and most summary rejection a year and a half ago. Bitterly she repented of her imprudent words, but that repentance no more effaced them than a sparrow's shadow made to disappear the Rincian granite whereon it fell.

When her servant returned to take her reply to Fant, she found she had none to give.

It was not much later that the merchant Ansovald, according to his custom, returned from the marketplace to lunch with his wife. Though she did what she could to conceal her distress, Ansovald soon noticed it and asked what troubled her. With a great show of indignation, she denied that anything was wrong. This deceived the merchant not at all but alarmed him no little, for if in their years of marriage he had come to rely upon anything, it was his wife's candor.

Therefore he persisted, and ere long had the entire story from her, though toward its end she was in tears. When he had heard everything, he was silent for a long time. His fingers curled his beard into ringlets, as was his unconscious custom while deep in thought. He had long known Dianora had admirers other than himself, and the notion did not much upset him; indeed, in his secret heart he was rather proud of it, as reflecting favorably upon his own manhood. Whether or not she occasionally succumbed to temptation mattered less to him than it might to other men, for he was fully assured of both her love and her discretion, and was sure she would do no injury to himself or to their union. Furthermore, he knew her pledge to Rand had been made not in expectation of its eventual fulfillment, but in the hope that it would, without wounding the knight, make him realize that his attentions were superfluous.

All of which considerations were now wide of the mark, as Rand had, by whatever means, met the conditions imposed upon him.

Ansovald felt nothing but admiration for his perseverance and ingenuity, however unfortunate he found their target. Moreover, as a reputable merchant, he was a man to whom agreements of any sort were sacred trusts, to be carried out by all parties to the best of their ability.

Accordingly, once he had relieved his wife's fears and kissed her tears away, he told her, "I see but one thing which can in honor be done. You must indeed go to Rand, explain to him the motive behind your promise, and pray him not to hold you to it."

The lady Dianora nodded; this was the same conclusion she herself had reached. However . . . "And if he insist?"

Ansovald sighed; he did not much care for the position toward which his logic inexorably led him. "If he must have that which he has sought so long and so hard, I see no easy way to say him nay this once. You need have no fear of me because of it; I will think none the worse of you, happen what may. A woman's faithfulness lies in her heart, not between her thighs." Barely believing her ears, Dianora marveled at her husband's forbearance. Ansovald's words were nothing less than heresy in that time and place, where most men would forthwith have sent away their wives at the faintest hint of scandal.

The merchant rose from the table, belting his long marten-fur coat round his ample middle. He stooped to kiss his wife once more, saying gruffly, "Go on with you, now. Soonest begun, soonest done." And then he was gone, hurrying back to his stall in the marketplace without the slightest trace of concern in face or step.

Far longer than he had expected or hoped did Rand wait in the summer garden for his beloved. He spoke no more to the mage Portolis, having less and less liking for him as hour succeeded hour and the wan sun began to wester. Had the sorcerer known even before the outset of his project its inherent futility, and carried on for his enrichment alone, or perhaps to make the knight a laughingstock? If so, thought Rand, he might well rue it, sorcerer or no: cold steel was proof against most magics.

Such were the shapes of his gloomy reflections, when suddenly his heart gave a great leap: that was surely Fant coming out through the gate of Sennar, and with him Dianora! The knight's features, so long dour, lit with delight, and when he shot a quick glance toward Portolis he spied a flush of interest livening the wizard's sallow and exhausted features. Ha! Rand thought: I have won, even against the old fool's prognostications.

Without giving Rand a word, a nod, any acknowledgment of

his presence, Dianora walked through the summer garden, now bending to test a flower's fragrance, now rising to touch a leaf, to test the ripeness of a dangling fruit. When her inspection was complete, she squared her shoulders beneath their mantling furs and stood at last before him.

"My love!" he cried, taking both her hands in his. It was all he could do to keep from clasping her to him then and there, so often had this moment been prefigured in his thoughts and dreams. "You are mine at last!"

Her emerald gaze was sorrow-filled, but she answered him firmly. "I am yours this day, if that be your will; such was my pledge to you. But you must know I am not your love, nor have I ever been. My heart lies only with my husband, the merchant Ansovald, as it has always. Do you not see, my lord Rand, that your love for me is as out of season as is this garden in the midst of a world of snow?"

Her words pierced Rand's exultation to the marrow, and he stood for a moment bereft of speech, like a man sore wounded and only just aware of it. "But you are here—" he began, and then faltered into silence once more.

"Yes, I am here," she said, and Rand knew the bitterness in her voice was directed as much against herself as at him. "Sir knight, why could you not understand I meant but to discourage you without doing you harm, not to spur you on? If you must have your way with me, be it so, but I yield myself solely from faith to my foolish promise, not from love of you."

And now, too late, the knight understood Portolis's warnings and the trap he had laid for himself. In his passion he had failed to distinguish between satisfying his body's lust and the love of the heart within it. He had indeed won Dianora's submission, but he had no hope—had never had a hope—of winning the love that would make that submission something more than a few moments of meaningless sensual pleasure. He freed her hands; his own, like dead things, fell to his sides. "Go," he said, his voice betraying little of the anguish he felt. "I release you from your pledge. I have yet to bed a woman unwilling, and would scarcely start with so fine a one as you, who would suffer me for your word's sake alone. Go," he repeated, but now his grief made of the word a ghastly whisper.

Her gratitude he endured with soldier's courage, but as Fant escorted her back to her home in Sennar, the knight swung round to face Portolis with fierce accusation. "You foresaw this!"

But the mage shook his head. "Not so," he said gravely. "That all might not turn out as you had wished, yes, I saw that, but needed scant magic to do so. It was pikestaff plain your love was not returned, else what need had you of me? Yet who could have foretold such generosity and greatness of soul as was displayed by the lady Dianora in freely offering that which she had no reason to give but to honor a word she had thought unfulfillable, or by yourself in willingly abandoning a goal you had unswervingly sought and beggared yourself to achieve? I own I am baffled as to how to comport myself in the face of such unselfishness. For your heart I have no salve save the healing hand of time, but out of gratitude for what you have taught me of magnanimity, you shall find when you return to your home the seven thousand seven hundred seven and seventy kraybecks of gold you devoted to this enterprise. I think, Sir Rand, you shall prosper to the end of your days."

The knight tried to decline this unexpected boon, but the mage Portolis was insistent, maintaining that any lesser action would leave him meanspirited in his own eyes. Not much later he departed the town of Sennar, never to return, but his magic stayed on. Forever after, the garden he had brought into being was sere and bare in summer, but bore abundantly when everywhere else frost held sway.

Nor was he a mean prophet, as Rand soon became one of the wealthiest men in the town of Sennar. His name became known all through the Empire of Kar V'Shem, for there was no work of philanthropy in which he failed to play a major role. In time he took a wife, and it is not to be doubted he loved her very much indeed. But until the end of his long and illustrious life, each year's Midwinter Day found him in Portolis's enchanted garden: the fruits thereof were out of season, but no denying they were sweet.

Alternate history stories are not really about the alternate worlds in which their authors set them. They're about our own world, as seen through the funhouse mirror of a changed past. They're thought experiments, testing the parameters of ideas in frameworks different from our own. "The Last Article" is an example of the type: a confrontation of extremes which, in our world, never met—and just as well, too.

THE LAST ARTICLE

Nonviolence is the first article of my faith. It is also the last article of my creed.

—Mohandas Gandhi

The one means that wins the easiest victory over reason: terror and force.

—Adolf Hitler, *Mein Kampf*

The tank rumbled down the Rajpath, past the ruins of the Memorial Arch, toward the India Gate. The gateway arch was still standing, although it had taken a couple of shell hits in the fighting before New Delhi fell. The Union Jack fluttered above it.

British troops lined both sides of the Rajpath, watching silently as the tank rolled past them. Their khaki uniforms were filthy and torn; many wore bandages. They had the weary, past-caring stares of beaten men, though the Army of India had fought until flesh and munitions gave out.

The India Gate drew near. A military band, smartened up for the occasion, began to play as the tank went past. The bagpipes sounded thin and lost in the hot, humid air.

A single man stood waiting in the shadow of the Gate. Field Marshal Walther Model leaned down into the cupola of the Panzer IV. "No one can match the British at ceremonies of this sort," he said to his aide.

Major Dieter Lasch laughed, a bit unkindly. "They've had enough practice, sir," he answered, raising his voice to be heard over the flatulent roar of the tank's engine.

"What is that tune?" the field marshal asked. "Does it have a meaning?"

"It's called 'The World Turned Upside Down,'" said Lasch, who had been involved with his British opposite number in planning the formal surrender. "Lord Cornwallis's army musicians played it when he yielded to the Americans at Yorktown."

"Ah, the Americans." Model was for a moment so lost in his own thoughts that his monocle threatened to slip from his right eye. He screwed it back in. The single lens was the only thing he shared with the clichéd image of a high German officer. He was no lean, hawk-faced Prussian. But his rounded features were unyielding, and his stocky body sustained the energy of his will better than the thin, dyspeptic frames of so many aristocrats. "The Americans," he repeated. "Well, that will be the next step, won't it? But enough. One thing at a time."

The panzer stopped. The driver switched off the engine. The sudden quiet was startling. Model leaped nimbly down. He had been leaping down from tanks for eight years now, since his days as a staff officer for the IV Corps in the Polish campaign.

The man in the shadows stepped forward, saluted. Flashbulbs lit his long, tired face as German photographers recorded the moment for history. The Englishman ignored cameras and cameramen alike. "Field Marshal Model," he said politely. He might have been about to discuss the weather.

Model admired his sangfroid. "Field Marshal Auchinleck," he replied, returning the salute and giving Auchinleck a last few seconds to remain his equal. Then he came back to the matter at hand. "Field Marshal, have you signed the instrument of surrender of the British Army of India to the forces of the Reich?"

"I have," Auchinleck replied. He reached into the left blouse pocket of his battledress, removed a folded sheet of paper. Before handing it to Model, though, he said, "I should like to request your permission to make a brief statement at this time."

"Of course, sir. You may say what you like, at whatever length you like." In victory, Model could afford to be magnanimous. He had even granted Marshal Zhukov leave to speak in the Soviet capitulation at Kuibishev, before the marshal was taken out and shot.

"I thank you." Auchinleck stiffly dipped his head. "I will say, then, that I find the terms I have been forced to accept to be cruelly hard on the brave men who have served under my command."

"That is your privilege, sir." But Model's round face was no longer kindly, and his voice had iron in it as he replied, "I must remind you, however, that my treating with you at all under the rules of war is an act of mercy for which Berlin may yet reprimand me. When Britain surrendered in 1941, all Imperial forces were also ordered to lay down their arms. I daresay you did not expect us to come so far, but I would be within my rights in reckoning you no more than so many bandits."

A slow flush darkened Auchinleck's cheeks. "We gave you a bloody good run, for bandits."

"So you did." Model remained polite. He did not say he would ten times rather fight straight-up battles than deal with the partisans who to this day harassed the Germans and their allies in occupied Russia. "Have you anything further to add?"

"No, sir, I do not." Auchinleck gave the German the signed surrender, handed him his sidearm. Model put the pistol in the empty holster he wore for the occasion. It did not fit well; the holster was made for a Walther P38, not this man-killing brute of a Webley and Scott. That mattered little, though—the ceremony was almost over.

Auchinleck and Model exchanged salutes for the last time. The British field marshal stepped away. A German lieutenant came up to lead him into captivity.

Major Lasch waved his left hand. The Union Jack came down from the flagpole on the India Gate. The swastika rose to replace it.

Lasch tapped discreetly on the door, stuck his head into the field marshal's office. "That Indian politician is here for his appointment with you, sir."

"Oh, yes. Very well, Dieter, send him in." Model had been dealing with Indian politicians even before the British surrender, and with hordes of them now that resistance was over. He had no more liking for the breed than for Russian politicians, or even German ones. No matter what pious principles they spouted, his experience was that they were all out for their own good first.

The small, frail brown man the aide showed in made him

wonder. The Indian's emaciated frame and the plain white cotton loincloth that was his only garment contrasted starkly with the Victorian splendor of the Viceregal Palace from which Model was administering the Reich's new conquest. "Sit down, *Herr* Gandhi," the field marshal urged.

"I thank you very much, sir." As he took his seat, Gandhi seemed a child in an adult's chair: it was much too wide for him, and its soft, overstuffed cushions hardly sagged under his meager weight. But his eyes, Model saw, were not a child's eyes. They peered with disconcerting keenness through his wire-framed spectacles as he said, "I have come to enquire when we may expect German troops to depart from our country."

Model leaned forward, frowning. For a moment he thought he had misunderstood Gandhi's Gujarati-flavored English. When he was sure he had not, he said, "Do you think perhaps we have come all this way as tourists?"

"Indeed I do not." Gandhi's voice was sharp with disapproval. "Tourists do not leave so many dead behind them."

Model's temper kindled. "No, tourists do not pay such a high price for the journey. Having come regardless of that cost, I assure you we shall stay."

"I am very sorry, sir; I cannot permit it."

"*You* cannot?" Again, Model had to concentrate to keep his monocle from falling out. He had heard arrogance from politicians before, but this scrawny old devil surpassed belief. "Do you forget I can call my aide and have you shot behind this building? You would not be the first, I assure you."

"Yes, I know that," Gandhi said sadly. "If you have that fate in mind for me, I am an old man. I will not run."

Combat had taught Model a hard indifference to the prospect of injury or death. He saw the older man possessed something of the same sort, however he had acquired it. A moment later, he realized his threat had not only failed to frighten Gandhi, but had actually amused him. Disconcerted, the field marshal said, "Have you any serious issues to address?"

"Only the one I named just now. We are a nation of more than three hundred million; it is no more just for Germany to rule us than for the British."

Model shrugged. "If we are able to, we will. We have the strength to hold what we have conquered, I assure you."

"Where there is no right, there can be no strength," Gandhi said. "We will not permit you to hold us in bondage."

"Do you think to threaten me?" Model growled. In fact, though, the Indian's audacity surprised him. Most of the locals had fallen over themselves, fawning on their new masters. Here, at least, was a man out of the ordinary.

Gandhi was still shaking his head, although Model saw he had still not frightened him—a man out of the ordinary indeed, thought the field marshal, who respected courage when he found it. "I make no threats, sir, but I will do what I believe to be right."

"Most noble," Model said, but to his annoyance the words came out sincere rather than with the sardonic edge he had intended. He had heard such canting phrases before, from Englishmen, from Russians, yes, and from Germans as well. Somehow, though, this Gandhi struck him as one who always meant exactly what he said. He rubbed his chin, considering how to handle such an intransigent.

A large green fly came buzzing into the office. Model's air of detachment vanished the moment he heard that malignant whine. He sprang from his seat, swatted at the fly. He missed. The insect flew around a while longer, then settled on the arm of Gandhi's chair. "Kill it," Model told him. "Last week one of those accursed things bit me on the neck, and I still have the lump to prove it."

Gandhi brought his hand down, but several inches from the fly. Frightened, it took off. Gandhi rose. He was surprisingly nimble for a man nearing eighty. He chivvied the fly out of the office, ignoring Model, who watched his performance in open-mouthed wonder.

"I hope it will not trouble you again," Gandhi said, returning as calmly as if he had done nothing out of the ordinary. "I am one of those who practice *ahimsa*: I will do no injury to any living thing."

Model remembered the fall of Moscow, and the smell of burning bodies filling the chilly autumn air. He remembered machine guns knocking down Cossack cavalry before they could close, and the screams of the wounded horses, more heartrending than any woman's. He knew of other things too, things he had not seen for himself and of which he had no desire to learn more.

"*Herr* Gandhi," he said, "how do you propose to bend to your will someone who opposes you, if you will not use force for the purpose?"

"I have never said I will not use force, sir." Gandhi's smile invited the field marshal to enjoy with him the distinction he was making. "I will not use violence. If my people refuse to cooperate in any way with yours, how can you compel them? What choice will you have but to grant us leave to do as we will?"

Without the intelligence estimates he had read, Model would have dismissed the Indian as a madman. No madman, though, could have caused the British so much trouble. But perhaps the decadent Raj simply had not made him afraid. Model tried again. "You understand that what you have said is treason against the Reich," he said harshly.

Gandhi bowed in his seat. "You may, of course, do what you will with me. My spirit will in any case survive among my people."

Model felt his face heat. Few men were immune to fear. Just his luck, he thought sourly, to have run into one of them. "I warn you, *Herr* Gandhi, to obey the authority of the officials of the Reich, or it will be the worse for you."

"I will do what I believe to be right, and nothing else. If you Germans exert yourselves toward the freeing of India, joyfully will I work with you. If not, then I regret we must be foes."

The field marshal gave him one last chance to see reason. "Were it you and I alone, there might be some doubt as to what would happen." Not much, he thought, not when Gandhi was twenty-odd years older and thin enough to break like a stick. He fought down the irrelevance, went on, "But where, *Herr* Gandhi, is your *Wehrmacht*?"

Of all things, he had least expected to amuse the Indian again. Yet Gandhi's eyes unmistakably twinkled behind the lenses of his spectacles. "Field Marshal, I have an army too."

Model's patience, never of the most enduring sort, wore thin all at once. "Get out!" he snapped.

Gandhi stood, bowed, and departed. Major Lasch stuck his head into the office. The field marshal's glare drove him out again in a hurry.

"Well?" Jawaharlal Nehru paced back and forth. Tall, slim, and saturnine, he towered over Gandhi without dominating him. "Dare we use the same policies against the Germans that we employed against the English?"

"If we wish our land free, dare we do otherwise?" Gandhi replied. "They will not grant our wish of their own volition. Model struck me as a man not much different from various British leaders whom we have succeeded in vexing in the past." He smiled at the memory of what passive resistance had done to officials charged with combating it.

"Very well, *Satyagraha* it is." But Nehru was not smiling. He had less humor than his older colleague.

Gandhi teased him gently. "Do you fear another spell in prison, then?" Both men had spent time behind bars during the war, until the British released them in a last, vain effort to rally the support of the Indian people to the Raj.

"You know better." Nehru refused to be drawn, and persisted, "The rumors that come out of Europe frighten me."

"Do you tell me you take them seriously?" Gandhi shook his head in surprise and a little reproof. "Each side in any war will always paint its opponents as blackly as it can."

"I hope you are right, and that that is all. Still, I confess I would feel more at ease with what we plan to do if you found me one Jew, officer or other rank, in the army now occupying us."

"You would be hard-pressed to find any among the forces they defeated. The British have little love for Jews either."

"Yes, but I daresay it could be done. With the Germans, they are banned by law. The English would never make such a rule. And while the laws are vile enough, I think of the tales that man Wiesenthal told, the one who came here, the gods know how, across Russia and Persia from Poland."

"Those I do not believe," Gandhi said firmly. "No nation could act in that way and hope to survive. Where could men be found to carry out such horrors?"

"*Azad Hind*," Nehru said, quoting the "Free India" motto of the locals who had fought on the German side.

But Gandhi shook his head. "They are only soldiers, doing as soldiers have always done. Wiesenthal's claims are for an entirely different order of bestiality, one which could not exist without destroying the fabric of the state that gave it birth."

"I hope very much you are right," Nehru said.

Walther Model slammed the door behind him hard enough to make his aide, whose desk faced away from the field marshal's office, jump in alarm. "Enough of this twaddle for one day," Model said. "I need schnapps, to get the taste of these Indians out of my mouth. Come along if you care to, Dieter."

"Thank you, sir." Major Lasch threw down his pen, eagerly got to his feet. "I sometimes think conquering India was easier than ruling it will be."

Model rolled his eyes. "I *know* it was. I would ten times rather be planning a new campaign than sitting here bogged down in pettifogging details. The sooner Berlin sends me people trained in colonial administration, the happier I will be."

The bar might have been taken from an English pub. It was dark, quiet, and paneled in walnut; a dartboard still hung on the wall. But a German sergeant in field-gray stood behind the bar and, despite the lazily turning ceiling fan, the temperature was close to thirty-five Celsius. The one might have been possible in occupied London, the other not.

Model knocked back his first shot at a gulp. He sipped his second more slowly, savoring it. Warmth spread through him, warmth that had nothing to do with the heat of the evening. He leaned back in his chair, steepled his fingers. "A long day," he said.

"Yes, sir," Lasch agreed. "After the effrontery of that Gandhi, any day would seem a long one. I've rarely seen you so angry." Considering Model's temper, that was no small statement.

"Ah, yes, Gandhi." Model's tone was reflective rather than irate; Lasch looked at him curiously. The field marshal said, "For my money, he's worth a dozen of the ordinary sort."

"Sir?" The aide no longer tried to hide his surprise.

"He is an honest man. He tells me what he thinks, and he will stick by that. I may kill him—I may have to kill him—but he and I will both know why, and I will not change his mind." Model took another sip of schnapps. He hesitated, as if unsure whether to go on. At last he did. "Do you know, Dieter, after he left I had a vision."

"Sir?" Now Lasch sounded alarmed.

The field marshal might have read his aide's thoughts. He chuckled wryly. "No, no, I am not about to swear off eating beefsteak and wear sandals instead of my boots, that I promise. But I saw myself as a Roman procurator, listening to the rantings of some early Christian priest."

Lasch raised an eyebrow. Such musings were unlike Model, who was usually direct to the point of bluntness and altogether materialistic—assets in the makeup of a general officer. The major cautiously sounded these unexpected depths: "How do you suppose the Roman felt, facing that kind of man?"

"Bloody confused, I suspect," Model said, which sounded more like him. "And because he and his comrades did not know how to handle such fanatics, you and I are Christians today, Dieter."

"So we are." The major rubbed his chin. "Is that a bad thing?"

Model laughed and finished his drink. "From your point of view or mine, no. But I doubt that old Roman would agree with us, any more than Gandhi agrees with me over what will happen next here. But then, I have two advantages over the dead procurator." He raised his finger; the sergeant hurried over to fill his glass.

At Lasch's nod, the young man also poured more schnapps for him. The major drank, then said, "I should hope so. We are more civilized, more sophisticated, than the Romans ever dreamed of being."

But Model was still in that fey mood. "Are we? My procurator was such a sophisticate that he tolerated anything, and never saw the danger in a foe who would not do the same. Our Christian God, though, is a jealous god, who puts up with no rivals. And one who is a National Socialist serves also the *Volk,* to whom he owes sole loyalty. I am immune to Gandhi's virus in a way the Roman was not to the Christian's."

"Yes, that makes sense," Lasch agreed after a moment. "I had not thought of it in that way, but I see it is so. And what is our other advantage over the Roman procurator?"

Suddenly the field marshal looked hard and cold, much the way he had looked leading the tanks of Third Panzer against the Kremlin compound. "The machine gun," he said.

The rising sun's rays made the sandstone of the Red Fort seem even more the color of blood. Gandhi frowned and turned his back on the fortress, not caring for that thought. Even at dawn, the air was warm and muggy.

"I wish you were not here," Nehru told him. The younger man lifted his trademark fore-and-aft cap, scratched his graying hair, and glanced at the crowd growing around them. "The Germans' orders forbid assemblies, and they will hold you responsible for this gathering."

"I am, am I not?" Gandhi replied. "Would you have me send my followers into a danger I do not care to face myself? How would I presume to lead them afterward?"

"A general does not fight in the front ranks," Nehru came back. "If you are lost to our cause, will we be able to go on?"

"If not, then surely the cause is not worthy, yes? Now let us be going."

Nehru threw his hands in the air. Gandhi nodded, satisfied, and worked his way toward the head of the crowd. Men and women stepped aside to let him through. Still shaking his head, Nehru followed.

The crowd slowly began to march east up Chandni Chauk, the

Street of Silversmiths. Some of the fancy shops had been wrecked in the fighting, more looted afterward. But others were opening up, their owners as happy to take German money as they had been to serve the British before.

One of the proprietors, a man who had managed to stay plump even through the past year of hardship, came rushing out of his shop when he saw the procession go by. He ran to the head of the march and spotted Nehru, whose height and elegant dress singled him out.

"Are you out of your mind?" the silversmith shouted. "The Germans have banned assemblies. If they see you, something dreadful will happen."

"Is it not dreadful that they take away the liberty which properly belongs to us?" Gandhi asked. The silversmith spun round. His eyes grew wide when he recognized the man who was speaking to him. Gandhi went on, "Not only is it dreadful, it is wrong. And so we do not recognize the Germans' right to ban anything we may choose to do. Join us, will you?"

"Great-souled one, I—I—" the silversmith spluttered. Then his glance slid past Gandhi. "The Germans!" he squeaked. He turned and ran.

Gandhi led the procession toward the approaching squad. The Germans stamped down Chandni Chauk as if they expected the people in front of them to melt from their path. Their gear, Gandhi thought, was not that much different from what British soldiers wore: ankle boots, shorts, and open-necked tunics. But their coal-scuttle helmets gave them a look of sullen, beetle-browed ferocity the British tin hat did not convey. Even for a man of Gandhi's equanimity it was daunting, as no doubt it was intended to be.

"Hello, my friends," he said. "Do any of you speak English?"

"I speak it, a little," one of them replied. His shoulder straps had the twin pips of a sergeant-major; he was the squad-leader, then. He hefted his rifle, not menacingly, Gandhi thought, but to emphasize what he was saying. "Go to your homes back. This coming together is *verboten.*"

"I am sorry, but I must refuse to obey your order," Gandhi said. "We are walking peacefully on our own street in our own city. We will harm no one, no matter what; this I promise you. But walk we will, as we wish." He repeated himself until he was sure the sergeant-major understood.

The German spoke to his comrades in his own language. One

of the soldiers raised his gun and with a nasty smile pointed it at Gandhi. He nodded politely. The German blinked to see him unafraid. The sergeant-major slapped the rifle down. One of his men had a field telephone on his back. The sergeant-major cranked it, waited for a reply, spoke urgently into it.

Nehru caught Gandhi's eye. His dark, tired gaze was full of worry. Somehow that nettled Gandhi more than the Germans' arrogance in ordering about his people. He began to walk forward again. The marchers followed him, flowing around the German squad like water flowing round a boulder.

The soldier who had pointed his rifle at Gandhi shouted in alarm. He brought up the weapon again. The sergeant-major barked at him. Reluctantly, he lowered it.

"A sensible man," Gandhi said to Nehru. "He sees we do no injury to him or his, and so does none to us."

"Sadly, though, not everyone is so sensible," the younger man replied, "as witness his lance-corporal there. And even a sensible man may not be well-inclined to us. You notice he is still on the telephone."

The phone on Field Marshal Model's desk jangled. He jumped and swore; he had left orders he was to be disturbed only for an emergency. He had to find time to work. He picked up the phone. "This had better be good," he growled without preamble.

He listened, swore again, slammed the receiver down. "Lasch!" he shouted.

It was his aide's turn to jump. "Sir?"

"Don't just sit there on your fat arse," the field marshal said unfairly. "Call out my car and driver, and quickly. Then belt on your sidearm and come along. The Indians are doing something stupid. Oh, yes, order out a platoon and have them come after us. Up on Chandni Chauk, the trouble is."

Lasch called for the car and the troops, then hurried after Model. "A riot?" he asked as he caught up.

"No, no." Model moved his stumpy frame along so fast that the taller Lasch had to trot beside him. "Some of Gandhi's tricks, damn him."

The field marshal's Mercedes was waiting when he and his aide hurried out of the viceregal palace. "Chandni Chauk," Model snapped as the driver held the door open for him. After that he sat in furious silence as the powerful car roared up Irwin Road, round a third of Connaught Circle, and north on Chelmsford Road past the bombed-out railway station until, for no reason Model could see, the street's name changed to Qutb Road.

A little later, the driver said, "Some kind of disturbance up ahead, sir."

"Disturbance?" Lasch echoed, leaning forward to peer through the windscreen. "It's a whole damned regiment's worth of Indians coming at us. Don't they know better than that? And what the devil," he added, his voice rising, "are so many of our men doing ambling along beside them? Don't they know they're supposed to break up this sort of thing?" In his indignation, he did not notice he was repeating himself.

"I suspect they don't," Model said dryly. "Gandhi, I gather, can have that effect on people who aren't ready for his peculiar brand of stubbornness. That, however, does not include me." He tapped the driver on the shoulder. "Pull up about two hundred meters in front of the first rank of them, Joachim."

"Yes, sir."

Even before the car had stopped moving, Model jumped out of it. Lasch, hand on his pistol, was close behind, protesting, "What if one of those fanatics has a gun?"

"Then Colonel-General Weidling assumes command, and a lot of Indians end up dead." Model strode toward Gandhi, ignoring the German troops who were drawing themselves to stiff, horrified attention at the sight of his field marshal's uniform. He would deal with them later. For the moment, Gandhi was more important.

He had stopped—which meant the rest of the marchers did too—and was waiting politely for Model to approach. The German commandant was not impressed. He thought Gandhi sincere and could not doubt his courage, but none of that mattered at all. He said harshly, "You were warned against this sort of behavior."

Gandhi looked him in the eye. They were very much of a height. "And I told you, I do not recognize your right to give such orders. This is our country, not yours, and if some of us choose to walk on our streets, we will do so."

From behind Gandhi, Nehru's glance flicked worriedly from one of the antagonists to the other. Model noticed him only peripherally; if he was already afraid, he could be handled whenever necessary. Gandhi was a tougher nut. The field marshal waved at the crowd behind the old man. "You are responsible for all these people. If harm comes to them, you will be to blame."

"Why should harm come to them? They are not soldiers. They

do not attack your men. I told that to one of your sergeants, and he understood it, and refrained from hindering us. Surely you, sir, an educated, cultured man, can see that what I say is self-evident truth."

Model turned his head to speak to his aide in German: "If we did not have Goebbels, this would be the one for his job." He shuddered to think of the propaganda victory Gandhi would win if he got away with flouting German ordinances. The whole countryside would be boiling with partisans in a week. And he had already managed to hoodwink some Germans into letting him do it!

Then Gandhi surprised him again. "*Ich danke Ihnen, Herr Generalfeldmarschall, aber das glaube ich kein Kompliment zu sein,*" he said in slow but clear German: "I thank you, Field Marshal, but I believe that to be no compliment."

Having to hold his monocle in place helped Model keep his face straight. "Take it however you like," he said. "Get these people off the street, or they and you will face the consequences. We will do what you force us to."

"I force you to nothing. As for these people who follow, each does so of his or her own free will. We are free, and will show it, not by violence, but through firmness in truth."

Now Model listened with only half an ear. He had kept Gandhi talking long enough for the platoon he had ordered out to arrive. Half a dozen SdKfz 251 armored personnel carriers came clanking up. The men piled out of them. "Give me a firing line, three ranks deep," Model shouted. As the troopers scrambled to obey, he waved the halftracks into position behind them, all but blocking Qutb Road. The halftracks' commanders swiveled the machine guns at the front of the vehicles' troop compartments so they bore on the Indians.

Gandhi watched these preparations as calmly as if they had nothing to do with him. Again Model had to admire his calm. His followers were less able to keep fear from their faces. Very few, though, used the pause to slip away. Gandhi's discipline was a long way from the military sort, but effective all the same.

"Tell them to disperse now, and we can still get away without bloodshed," the field marshal said.

"We will shed no one's blood, sir. But we will continue on our pleasant journey. Moving carefully, we will, I think, be able to get between your large lorries there." Gandhi turned to wave his people forward once more.

"You insolent—" Rage choked Model, which was as well, for it kept him from cursing Gandhi like a fishwife. To give him time to master his temper, he plucked his monocle from his eye and began polishing the lens with a silk handkerchief. He replaced the monocle, started to jam the handkerchief back into his trouser pocket, then suddenly had a better idea.

"Come, Lasch," he said, and started toward the waiting German troops. About halfway to them, he dropped the handkerchief on the ground. He spoke in loud, simple German so his men and Gandhi could both follow: "If any Indians come past this spot, I wash my hands of them."

He might have known Gandhi would have a comeback ready. "That is what Pilate said also, you will recall, sir."

"Pilate washed his hands to evade responsibility," the field marshal answered steadily; he was in control of himself again. "I accept it: I am responsible to my Führer and to the *Oberkommando-Wehrmacht* for maintaining the Reich's control over India, and will do what I see fit to carry out that obligation."

For the first time since they had come to know each other, Gandhi looked sad. "I too, sir, have my responsibilities." He bowed slightly to Model.

Lasch chose that moment to whisper in his commander's ear: "Sir, what of our men over there? Had you planned to leave them in the line of fire?"

The field marshal frowned. He had planned to do just that; the wretches deserved no better, for being taken in by Gandhi. But Lasch had a point. The platoon might balk at shooting countrymen, if it came to that. "You men," Model said sourly, jabbing his marshal's baton at them, "fall in behind the armored personnel carriers, at once."

The Germans' boots pounded on the macadam as they dashed to obey. They were still all right, then, with a clear order in front of them. Something, Model thought, but not much.

He had also worried that the Indians would take advantage of the moment of confusion to press forward, but they did not. Gandhi and Nehru and a couple of other men were arguing among themselves. Model nodded once. Some of them knew he was in earnest, then. And Gandhi's followers' discipline, as the field marshal had thought a few minutes ago, was not of the military sort. He could not simply issue an order and know his will would be done.

"I issue no orders," Gandhi said. "Let each man follow his conscience as he will—what else is freedom?"

"They will follow *you* if you go forward, great-souled one," Nehru replied, "and that German, I fear, means to carry out his threat. Will you throw your life away, and those of your countrymen?"

"I will not throw my life away," Gandhi said, but before the men around him could relax he went on, "I will gladly give it, if freedom requires that. I am but one man. If I fall, others will surely carry on; perhaps the memory of me will serve to make them more steadfast."

He stepped forward.

"Oh, damnation," Nehru said softly, and followed.

For all his vigor, Gandhi was far from young. Nehru did not need to nod to the marchers close by him; of their own accord, they hurried ahead of the man who had led them for so long, forming with their bodies a barrier between him and the German guns.

He tried to go faster. "Stop! Leave me my place! What are you doing?" he cried, though in his heart he understood only too well.

"This once, they will not listen to you," Nehru said.

"But they must!" Gandhi peered through eyes dimmed now by tears as well as age. "Where is that stupid handkerchief? We must be almost to it!"

"For the last time, I warn you to halt!" Model shouted. The Indians still came on. The sound of their feet, sandal-clad or bare, was like a growing murmur on the pavement, very different from the clatter of German boots. "Fools!" the field marshal muttered under his breath. He turned to his men. "Take your aim!"

The advance slowed when the rifles came up; of that Model was certain. For a moment he thought that ultimate threat would be enough to bring the marchers to their senses. But then they advanced again. The Polish cavalry had shown that same reckless bravery, charging with lances and sabers and carbines against the German tanks. Model wondered whether the inhabitants of the *Reichsgeneralgouvernement* of Poland thought the gallantry worthwhile.

A man stepped on the field marshal's handkerchief. "Fire!" Model said.

A second passed, two. Nothing happened. Model scowled at his men. Gandhi's deviltry had got into them; sneaky as a Jew, he was turning the appearance of weakness into a strange kind of strength. But then trained discipline paid its dividend. One finger tightened on a Mauser trigger. A single shot rang out. As if it were a signal that recalled the other men to their duty, they too began to fire. From the armored personnel carriers, the machine guns started their deadly chatter. Model heard screams above the gunfire.

The volley smashed into the front ranks of marchers at close range. Men fell. Others ran, or tried to, only to be held by the power of the stream still advancing behind them. Once begun, the Germans methodically poured fire into the column of Indians. The march dissolved into a panic-stricken mob.

Gandhi still tried to press forward. A fleeing wounded man smashed into him, splashing him with blood and knocking him to the ground. Nehru and another man immediately lay down on top of him.

"Let me up! Let me up!" he shouted.

"No," Nehru screamed in his ear. "With shooting like this, you are in the safest spot you can be. We need you, and need you alive. Now we have martyrs around whom to rally our cause."

"Now we have dead husbands and wives, fathers and mothers. Who will tend to their loved ones?"

Gandhi had no time for more protest. Nehru and the other man hauled him to his feet and dragged him away. Soon they were among their people, all running now from the German guns. A bullet struck the back of the unknown man who was helping Gandhi escape. Gandhi heard the slap of the impact, felt the man jerk. Then the strong grip on him loosened as the man fell.

He tried to tear free from Nehru. Before he could, another Indian laid hold of him. Even at that horrid moment, he felt the irony of his predicament. All his life he had championed individual liberty, and here his own followers were robbing him of his. In other circumstances, it might have been funny.

"In here!" Nehru shouted. Several people had already broken down the door to a shop and, Gandhi saw a moment later, the rear exit as well. Then he was hustled into the alley behind the shop, and through a maze of lanes which reminded him the old Delhi, unlike its British-designed sister city, was an Indian town through and through.

At last the nameless man with Gandhi and Nehru knocked on the back door of a tearoom. The woman who opened it gasped to recognize her unexpected guests, then pressed her hands together in front of her and stepped aside to let them in. "You will be safe here," the man said, "at least for a while. Now I must see to my own family."

"From the bottom of our hearts, we thank you," Nehru replied as the fellow hurried away. Gandhi said nothing. He was winded, battered, and filled with anguish at the failure of the march and at the suffering it had brought to so many marchers and to their kinsfolk.

The woman sat the two fugitive leaders at a small table in the kitchen, served them tea and cakes. "I will leave you now, best ones," she said quietly, "lest those out front wonder why I neglect them for so long."

Gandhi left the cake on his plate. He sipped the tea. Its warmth began to restore him physically, but the wound in his spirit would never heal. "The Armritsar massacre pales beside this," he said, setting down the empty cup. "There the British panicked and opened fire. This had nothing of panic about it. Model told me what he would do, and he did it." He shook his head, still hardly believing what he had just been through.

"So he did." Nehru had gobbled his cake like a starving wolf, and ate his companion's when he saw Gandhi did not want it. His once-immaculate white jacket and pants were torn, filthy, and blood-spattered; his cap sat awry on his head. But his eyes, usually so somber, were lit with a fierce glow. "And by his brutality, he has delivered himself into our hands. No one now can imagine the Germans have anything but their own interests at heart. We will gain followers all over the country. After this, not a wheel will turn in India."

"Yes, I will declare the *Satyagraha* campaign," Gandhi said. "Noncooperation will show how we reject foreign rule, and will cost the Germans dear because they will not be able to exploit us. The combination of nonviolence and determined spirit will surely shame them into granting us our liberty."

"There—you see." Encouraged by his mentor's rally, Nehru rose and came round the table to embrace the older man. "We will triumph yet."

"So we will," Gandhi said, and sighed heavily. He had pursued India's freedom for half his long life, and this change of masters was a setback he had not truly planned for, even after England and Russia fell. The British were finally beginning to listen to him when the Germans swept them aside. Now he had to begin anew. He sighed again. "It will cost our poor people dear, though."

"Cease firing," Model said. Few good targets were left on Qutb Road; almost all the Indians in the procession were down or had run from the guns.

Even after the bullets stopped, the street was far from silent. Most of the people the German platoon had shot were alive and shrieking: as if he needed more proof, the Russian campaign had taught the field marshal how hard human beings were to kill outright. Still, the din distressed him, and evidently Lasch as well. "We ought to put them out of their misery," the major said.

"So we should." Model had a happy inspiration. "And I know just how. Come with me."

The two men turned their backs on the carnage and walked around the row of armored personnel carriers. As they passed the lieutenant commanding the platoon, Model nodded to him and said, "Well done."

The lieutenant saluted. "Thank you, sir." The soldiers in earshot nodded at one another: nothing bucked up the odds of getting promoted like performing under the commander's eye.

The Germans behind the armored vehicles were not so proud of themselves. They were the ones who had let the march get this big and come this far in the first place. Model slapped his boot with his field marshal's baton. "You all deserve courts-martial," he said coldly, glaring at them. "You know the orders concerning native assemblies, yet there you were tagging along, more like sheepdogs than soldiers." He spat in disgust.

"But, sir—" began one of them—a sergeant-major, Model saw. He subsided in a hurry when Model's gaze swung his way.

"Speak," the field marshal urged. "Enlighten me—tell me what possessed you to act in the disgraceful way you did. Was it some evil spirit, perhaps? This country abounds with them, if you listen to the natives—as you all too obviously have been."

The sergeant-major flushed under Model's sarcasm, but finally burst out, "Sir, it didn't look to me as if they were up to any harm, that's all. The old man heading them up swore they were peaceful, and he looked too feeble to be anything but, if you take my meaning."

Model's smile had all the warmth of a Moscow December night. "And so in your wisdom you set aside the commands you had received. The results of that wisdom you hear now." The field marshal briefly let himself listen to the cries of the wounded, a sound the war had taught him to screen out. "Now then, come with me, yes, you, Sergeant-Major, and the rest of your shirkers too, or those of you who wish to avoid a court."

As he had known they would, they all trooped after him. "There is your handiwork," he said, pointing to the shambles in the street.

His voice hardened. "You are responsible for those people lying there—had you acted as you should, you would have broken up that march long before it ever got so far or so large. Now the least you can do is give those people their release." He set hands on hips, waited.

No one moved. "Sir?" the sergeant-major said faintly. He seemed to have become the group's spokesman.

Model made an impatient gesture. "Go on, finish them. A bullet in the back of the head will quiet them once and for all."

"In cold blood, sir?" The sergeant-major had not wanted to understand him before. Now he had no choice.

The field marshal was inexorable. "They—and you—disobeyed the Reich's commands. They made themselves liable to capital punishment the moment they gathered. You at least have the chance to atone, by carrying out this just sentence."

"I don't think I can," the sergeant-major muttered.

He was probably just talking to himself, but Model gave him no chance to change his mind. He turned to the lieutenant of the platoon that had broken the march. "Place this man under arrest." After the sergeant-major had been seized, Model turned his chill, monocled stare at the rest of the reluctant soldiers. "Any others?"

Two more men let themselves be arrested rather than draw their weapons. The field marshal nodded to the others. "Carry out your orders." He had an afterthought. "If you find Gandhi or Nehru out there, bring them to me alive."

The Germans moved out hesitantly. They were no *Einsatzkommandos,* and not used to this kind of work. Some looked away as they administered the first *coup de grâce;* one missed as a result, and had his bullet ricochet off the pavement and almost hit a comrade. But as the soldiers worked their way up Qutb Road they became quicker, more confident, and more competent. War was like that, Model thought. So soon one became used to what had been unimaginable.

After a while the flat cracks died away, but from lack of targets rather than reluctance. A few at a time, the soldiers returned to Model. "No sign of the two leaders?" he asked. They all shook their heads.

"Very well—dismissed. And obey your orders like good Germans henceforward."

"No further reprisals?" Lasch asked as the relieved troopers hurried away.

"No, let them go. They carried out their part of the bargain, and I will meet mine. I am a fair man, after all, Dieter."

"Very well, sir."

Gandhi listened with undisguised dismay as the shopkeeper babbled out his tale of horror. "This is madness!" he cried.

"I doubt Field Marshal Model, for his part, understands the principle of *ahimsa*," Nehru put in. Neither Gandhi nor he knew exactly where they were: a safe house somewhere not far from the center of Delhi was the best guess he could make. The men who brought the shopkeeper were masked. What one did not know, one could not tell the Germans if captured.

"Neither do you," the older man replied, which was true; Nehru had a more pragmatic nature than Gandhi. Gandhi went on, "Rather more to the point, neither do the British. And Model, to speak to, seemed no different from any high-ranking British military man. His specialty has made him harsh and rigid, but he is not stupid and does not appear unusually cruel."

"Just a simple soldier, doing his job." Nehru's irony was palpable.

"He must have gone insane," Gandhi said; it was the only explanation that made even the slightest sense of the massacre of the wounded. "Undoubtedly he will be censured when news of this atrocity reaches Berlin, as General Dyer was by the British after Armritsar."

"Such is to be hoped." But again Nehru did not sound hopeful.

"How could it be otherwise, after such an appalling action? What government, what leaders could fail to be filled with humiliation and remorse at it?"

Model strode into the mess. The officers stood and raised their glasses in salute. "Sit, sit," the field marshal growled, using gruffness to hide his pleasure.

An Indian servant brought him a fair imitation of roast beef and Yorkshire pudding: better than they were eating in London these days, he thought. The servant was silent and unsmiling, but Model would only have noticed more about him had he been otherwise. Servants were supposed to assume a cloak of invisibility.

When the meal was done, Model took out his cigar-case. The *Waffen-SS* officer on his left produced a lighter. Model leaned forward, puffed a cigar into life. "My thanks, *Brigadeführer*," the field marshal said. He had little use for SS titles of rank, but brigade-commander was at least recognizably close to brigadier.

"Sir, it is my great pleasure," Jürgen Stroop declared. "You could not have handled things better. A lesson for the Indians—less than they deserve, too" (he also took no notice of the servant) "and a good one for your men as well. We train ours harshly too."

Model nodded. He knew about SS training methods. No one denied the daring of the *Waffen-SS* divisions. No one (except the SS) denied that the *Wehrmacht* had better officers.

Stroop drank. "A lesson," he repeated in a pedantic tone that went oddly with the SS's reputation for aggressiveness. "Force is the only thing the racially inferior can understand. Why, when I was in Warsaw—"

That had been four or five years ago, Model suddenly recalled. Stroop had been a *Brigadeführer* then too, if memory served; no wonder he was still one now, even after all the hard fighting since. He was lucky not to be a buck private. Imagine letting a pack of desperate, starving Jews chew up the finest troops in the world.

And imagine, afterward, submitting a 75-page operations report bound in leather and grandiosely called *The Warsaw Ghetto Is No More.* And imagine, with all that, having the crust to boast about it afterward. No wonder the man sounded like a pompous ass. He *was* a pompous ass, and an inept butcher to boot. Model had done enough butchery before today's work—anyone who fought in Russia learned all about butchery—but he had never botched it.

He did not revel in it, either. He wished Stroop would shut up. He thought about telling the *Brigadeführer* he would sooner have been listening to Gandhi. The look on the fellow's face, he thought, would be worth it. But no. One could never be sure who was listening. Better safe.

The shortwave set crackled to life. It was in a secret cellar, a tiny dark hot room lit only by the glow of its dial and by the red end of the cigarette in its owner's mouth. The Germans had made not turning in a radio a capital crime. Of course, Gandhi thought, harboring him was also a capital crime. That weighed on his conscience. But the man knew the risk he was taking.

The fellow (Gandhi knew him only as Lai) fiddled with the controls. "Usually we listen to the Americans," he said. "There is some hope of truth from them. But tonight you want to hear Berlin."

"Yes," Gandhi said. "I must learn what action is to be taken against Model."

"If any," Nehru added. He was once again impeccably attired in white, which made him the most easily visible object in the cellar.

"We have argued this before," Gandhi said tiredly. "No government can uphold the author of a cold-blooded slaughter of wounded men and women. The world would cry out in abhorrence."

Lai said, "That government controls too much of the world already." He adjusted the tuning knob again. After a burst of static, the strains of a Strauss waltz filled the little room. Lai grunted in satisfaction. "We are a little early yet."

After a few minutes, the incongruously sweet music died away. "This is Radio Berlin's English-language channel," an announcer declared. "In a moment, the news program." Another German tune rang out: the Horst Wessel Song. Gandhi's nostrils flared with distaste.

A new voice came over the air. "Good day. This is William Joyce." The nasal Oxonian accent was that of the archetypical British aristocrat, now vanished from India as well as England. It was the accent that flavored Gandhi's own English, and Nehru's as well. In fact, Gandhi had heard, Joyce was a New York–born rabblerouser of Irish blood who also happened to be a passionately sincere Nazi. The combination struck the Indian as distressing.

"What did the English used to call him?" Nehru murmured. "Lord Haw-Haw?"

Gandhi waved his friend to silence. Joyce was reading the news, or what the Propaganda Ministry in Berlin wanted to present to English-speakers as the news.

Most of it was on the dull side: a trade agreement between Manchukuo, Japanese-dominated China, and Japanese-dominated Siberia; advances by German-supported French troops against American-supported French troops in a war by proxy in the African jungles. Slightly more interesting was the German warning about American interference in the East Asia Co-Prosperity Sphere.

One day soon, Gandhi thought sadly, the two mighty powers of the Old World would turn on the one great nation that stood between them. He feared the outcome. Thinking herself secure behind ocean barriers, the United States had stayed out of the European war. Now the war was bigger than Europe, and the oceans barriers no longer, but highways for her foes.

Lord Haw-Haw droned on and on. He gloated over the fate of

rebels hunted down in Scotland: they were publicly hanged. Nehru leaned forward. "Now," he guessed. Gandhi nodded.

But the commentator passed on to unlikely-sounding boasts about the prosperity of Europe under the New Order. Against his will, Gandhi felt anger rise in him. Were Indians too insignificant to the Reich even to be mentioned?

More music came from the radio: the first bars of the other German anthem, "Deutschland über Alles." William Joyce said solemnly, "And now, a special announcement from the Ministry for Administration of Acquired Territories. *Reichsminister* Reinhard Heydrich commends Field Marshal Walther Model's heroic suppression of insurrection in India, and warns that his leniency will not be repeated."

"Leniency!" Nehru and Gandhi burst out together, the latter making it into as much of a curse as he allowed himself.

As if explaining to them, the voice on the radio went on, "Henceforward, hostages will be taken at the slightest sound of disorder, and will be executed forthwith if it continues. Field Marshal Model has also placed a reward of 50,000 rupees on the capture of the criminal revolutionary Gandhi, and 25,000 on the capture of his henchman Nehru."

"Deutschland über Alles" rang out again, to signal the end of the announcement. Joyce went on to the next piece of news. "Turn that off," Nehru said after a moment. Lai obeyed, plunging the cellar into complete darkness. Nehru surprised Gandhi by laughing. "I have never before been the henchman of a criminal revolutionary."

The older man might as well not have heard him. "They commended him," he said. "Commended!" Disbelief put the full tally of his years in his voice, which usually sounded much stronger and younger.

"What will you do?" Lai asked quietly. A match flared, dazzling in the dark, as he lit another cigarette.

"They shall not govern India in this fashion," Gandhi snapped. "Not a soul will cooperate with them from now on. We outnumber them a thousand to one; what can they accomplish without us? We shall use that to full advantage."

"I hope the price is not more than the people can pay," Nehru said.

"The British shot us down too, and we were on our way toward prevailing," Gandhi said stoutly. As he would not have a few days before, though, he added, "So do I."

✧ ✧ ✧

Field Marshal Model scowled and yawned at the same time. The pot of tea that should have been on his desk was nowhere to be found. His stomach growled. A plate of rolls should have been beside the teapot.

"How am I supposed to get anything done without breakfast?" he asked rhetorically (no one was in the office to hear him complain). Rhetorical complaint was not enough to satisfy him. "Lasch!" he shouted.

"Sir?" The aide came rushing in.

Model jerked his chin at the empty space on his desk where the silver tray full of good things should have been. "What's become of what's-his-name? Naoroji, that's it. If he's home with a hangover, he could have had the courtesy to let us know."

"I will enquire with the liaison officer for native personnel, sir, and also have the kitchen staff send you up something to eat." Lasch picked up a telephone, spoke into it. The longer he talked, the less happy he looked. When he turned back to the field marshal, his expression was a good match for the stony one Model often wore. He said, "None of the locals has shown up for work today, sir."

"What? None?" Model's frown made his monocle dig into his cheek. He hesitated. "I will feel better if you tell me some new hideous malady has broken out among them."

Lasch spoke with the liaison officer again. He shook his head. "Nothing like that, sir, or at least," he corrected himself with the caution that made him a good aide, "nothing Captain Wechsler knows about."

Model's phone rang again. It startled him; he jumped. "*Bitte?*" he growled into the mouthpiece, embarrassed at starting even though only Lasch had seen. He listened. Then he growled again, in good earnest this time. He slammed the phone down. "That was our railway officer. Hardly any natives are coming in to the station."

The phone rang again. "*Bitte?*" This time it was a swearword. Model snarled, cutting off whatever the man on the other end was saying, and hung up. "The damned clerks are staying out too," he shouted at Lasch, as if it were the major's fault. "I know what's wrong with the blasted locals, by God—an overdose of Gandhi, that's what."

"We should have shot him down in that riot he led," Lasch said angrily.

"Not for lack of effort that we didn't," Model said. Now that he saw where his trouble was coming from, he began thinking like a General Staff–trained officer again. That discipline went deep in him. His voice was cool and musing as he corrected his aide: "It was no riot, Dieter. That man is a skilled agitator. Armed with no more than words, he gave the British fits. Remember that the Führer started out as an agitator too."

"Ah, but the Führer wasn't above breaking heads to back up what he said." Lasch smiled reminiscently, and raised a fist. He was a Munich man, and wore on his sleeve the hashmark that showed Party membership before 1933.

But the field marshal said, "You think Gandhi doesn't? His way is to break them from the inside out, to make his foes doubt themselves. Those soldiers who took courts rather than obey their commanding officer had their heads broken, wouldn't you say? Think of him as a Russian tank commander, say, rather than as a political agitator. He is fighting us every bit as much as much as the Russians did."

Lasch thought about it. Plainly, he did not like it. "A coward's way of fighting."

"The weak cannot use the weapons of the strong." Model shrugged. "He does what he can, and skillfully. But I can make his backers doubt themselves, too; see if I don't."

"Sir?"

"We'll start with the railway workers. They are the most essential to have back on the job, yes? Get a list of names. Cross off every twentieth one. Send a squad to each of those homes, haul the slackers out, and shoot them in the street. If the survivors don't report tomorrow, do it again. Keep at it every day until they go back to work or no workers are left."

"Yes, sir." Lasch hesitated. At last he asked, "Are you sure, sir?"

"Have you a better idea, Dieter? We have a dozen divisions here; Gandhi has the whole subcontinent. I have to convince them in a hurry that obeying me is a better idea than obeying him. Obeying is what counts. I don't care a *pfennig* as to whether they love me. *Oderint, dum metuant.*"

"Sir?" The major had no Latin.

"'Let them hate, so long as they fear.'"

"Ah," Lasch said. "Yes, I like that." He fingered his chin as he thought. "In aid of which, the Muslims hereabouts like the Hindus none too well. I daresay we could use them to help hunt Gandhi down."

"Now that *I* like," Model said. "Most of our Indian Legion lads are Muslims. They will know people, or know people who know people. And"—the field marshal chuckled cynically—"the reward will do no harm, either. Now get those orders out, and ring up Legion-Colonel Sadar. We'll get those feelers in motion—and if they pay off, you'll probably have earned yourself a new pip on your shoulderboards."

"Thank you very much, sir!"

"My pleasure. As I say, you'll have earned it. So long as things go as they should, I am a very easy man to get along with. Even Gandhi could, if he wanted to. He will end up having caused a lot of people to be killed because he does not."

"Yes, sir," Lasch agreed. "If only he would see that, since we have won India from the British, we will not turn around and tamely yield it to those who could not claim it for themselves."

"You're turning into a political philosopher now, Dieter?"

"Ha! Not likely." But the major looked pleased as he picked up the phone.

"My dear friend, my ally, my teacher, we are losing," Nehru said as the messenger scuttled away from this latest in a series of what were hopefully called safe houses. "Day by day, more people return to their jobs."

Gandhi shook his head, slowly, as if the motion caused him physical pain. "But they must not. Each one who cooperates with the Germans sets back the day of his own freedom."

"Each one who fails to ends up dead," Nehru said dryly. "Most men lack your courage, great-souled one. To them, that carries more weight than the other. Some are willing to resist, but would rather take up arms than the restraint of *Satyagraha*."

"If they take up arms, they will be defeated. The British could not beat the Germans with guns and tanks and planes; how shall we? Besides, if we shoot a German here and there, we give them the excuse they need to strike at us. When one of their lieutenants was waylaid last month, their bombers leveled a village in reprisal. Against those who fight through nonviolence, they have no such justification."

"They do not seem to need one, either," Nehru pointed out.

Before Gandhi could reply to that, a man burst into the hovel where they were hiding. "You must flee!" he cried. "The Germans have found this place! They are coming. Out with me, quick! I have a cart waiting."

Nehru snatched up the canvas bag in which he carried his few belongings. For a man used to being something of a dandy, the haggard life of a fugitive came hard. Gandhi had never wanted much. Now that he had nothing, that did not disturb him. He rose calmly, followed the man who had come to warn them.

"Hurry!" the fellow shouted as they scrambled into his oxcart while the hump-backed cattle watched indifferently with their liquid brown eyes. When Gandhi and Nehru were lying in the cart, the man piled blankets and straw mats over them. He scrambled up to take the reins, saying, "*Inshallah,* we shall be safely away from here before the platoon arrives." He flicked a switch over the backs of the cattle. They lowed indignantly. The cart rattled away.

Lying in the sweltering semi-darkness under the concealment the man had draped on him, Gandhi peered through chinks, trying to figure out where in Delhi he was going next. He had played the game more than once these last few weeks, though he knew doctrine said he should not. The less he knew, the less he could reveal. Unlike most men, though, he was confident he could not be made to talk against his will.

"We are using the technique the American Poe called the 'purloined letter,' I see," he remarked to Nehru. "We will be close by the German barracks. They will not think to look for us there."

The younger man frowned. "I did not know we had safe houses there," he said. Then he relaxed, as well as he could when folded into too small a space. "Of course, I do not pretend to know everything there is to know about such matters. It would be dangerous if I did."

"I was thinking much the same myself, though with me as subject of the sentence." Gandhi laughed quietly. "Try as we will, we always have ourselves at the center of things, don't we?"

He had to raise his voice to finish. An armored personnel carrier came rumbling and rattling toward them, getting louder as it approached. The silence when the driver suddenly killed the engine was a startling contrast to the previous racket. Then there was noise again, as soldiers shouted in German.

"What are they saying?" Nehru asked.

"Hush," Gandhi said absently, not from ill manners, but out of the concentration he needed to follow German at all. After a moment he resumed, "They are swearing at a black-bearded man, asking why he flagged them down."

"*Why* would anyone flag down German sol—" Nehru began, then stopped in abrupt dismay. The fellow who had burst into their hiding place wore a bushy black beard. "We had better get out of—" Again

Nehru broke off in midsentence, this time because the oxcart driver was throwing off the coverings that concealed his two passengers.

Nehru started to get to his feet so he could try to scramble out and run. Too late—a rifle barrel that looked wide as a tunnel was shoved in his face as a German came dashing up to the cart. The big curved magazine said the gun was one of the automatic assault rifles that had wreaked such havoc among the British infantry. A burst would turn a man into bloody hash. Nehru sank back in despair.

Gandhi, less spry than his friend, had only sat up in the bottom of the cart. "Good day, gentlemen," he said to the Germans peering down at him. His tone took no notice of their weapons.

"Down." The word was in such gutturally accented Hindi that Gandhi hardly understood it, but the accompanying gesture with a rifle was unmistakable.

Face a mask of misery, Nehru got out of the cart. A German helped Gandhi descend. "*Danke,*" he said. The soldier nodded gruffly. He pointed with the barrel of his rifle—toward the armored personnel carrier.

"My rupees!" the black-bearded man shouted.

Nehru turned on him, so quickly he almost got shot for it. "Your thirty pieces of silver, you mean," he cried.

"Ah, a British education," Gandhi murmured. No one was listening to him.

"My rupees," the man repeated. He did not understand Nehru; so often, Gandhi thought sadly, that was at the root of everything.

"You'll get them," promised the sergeant leading the German squad. Gandhi wondered if he was telling the truth. Probably so, he decided. The British had had centuries to build a network of Indian clients. Here but a matter of months, the Germans would need all they could find.

"In." The soldier with a few words of Hindi nodded to the back of the armored personnel carrier. Up close, the vehicle took on a war-battered individuality its kind had lacked when they were just big, intimidating shapes rumbling down the highway. It was bullet-scarred and patched in a couple of places, with sheets of steel crudely welded on.

Inside, the jagged lips of the bullet holes had been hammered down so they did not gouge a man's back. The carrier smelled of leather, sweat, tobacco, smokeless powder, and exhaust fumes. It was crowded, all the more so with the two Indians added to its usual contingent. The motor's roar when it started up challenged even Gandhi's equanimity.

Not, he thought with uncharacteristic bitterness, that that equanimity had done him much good.

"They are here, sir," Lasch told Model, then, at the field marshal's blank look, amplified: "Gandhi and Nehru."

Model's eyebrow came down toward his monocle. "I won't bother with Nehru. Now that we have him, take him out and give him a noodle"—army slang for a bullet in the back of the neck—"but don't waste my time over him. Gandhi, now, is interesting. Fetch him in."

"Yes, sir." The major sighed. Model smiled. Lasch did not find Gandhi interesting. Lasch would never carry a field marshal's baton, not if he lived to be ninety.

Model waved away the soldiers who escorted Gandhi into his office. Either of them could have broken the little Indian like a stick. "Have a care," Gandhi said. "If I am the desperate criminal bandit you have styled me, I may overpower you and escape."

"If you do, you will have earned it," Model retorted. "Sit, if you care to."

"Thank you." Gandhi sat. "They took Jawaharlal away. Why have you summoned me instead?"

"To talk for a while, before you join him." Model saw that Gandhi knew what he meant, and that the old man remained unafraid. Not that that would change anything, Model thought, although he respected his opponent's courage the more for his keeping it in the last extremity.

"I will talk, in the hope of persuading you to have mercy on my people. For myself I ask nothing."

Model shrugged. "I was as merciful as the circumstances of war allowed, until you began your campaign against us. Since then, I have done what I needed to restore order. When it returns, I may be milder again."

"You seem a decent man," Gandhi said, puzzlement in his voice. "How can you so callously massacre people who have done you no harm?"

"I never would have, had you not urged them to folly."

"Seeking freedom is not folly."

"It is when you cannot gain it—and you cannot. Already your people are losing their stomach for—what do you call it? Passive resistance? A silly notion. A passive resister simply ends up dead, with no chance to hit back at his foe."

That hit a nerve, Model thought. Gandhi's voice was less detached as he answered, "*Satyagraha* strikes the oppressor's soul, not his body. You must be without honor or conscience, to fail to feel your victim's anguish."

Nettled in turn, the field marshal snapped, "I have honor. I follow the oath of obedience I swore with the army to the Führer and through him to the Reich. I need consider nothing past that."

Now Gandhi's calm was gone. "But he is a madman! What has he done to the Jews of Europe?"

"Removed them," Model said matter-of-factly; *Einsatzgruppe* B had followed Army Group Central to Moscow and beyond. "They were capitalists or Bolsheviks, and either way enemies of the Reich. When an enemy falls into a man's hands, what else is there to do but destroy him, lest he revive to turn the tables one day?"

Gandhi had buried his face in his hands. Without looking at Model, he said, "Make him a friend."

"Even the British knew better than that, or they would not have held India as long as they did," the field marshal snorted. "They must have begun to forget, though, or your movement would have got what it deserves long ago. You first made the mistake of confusing us with them long ago, by the way." He touched a fat dossier on his desk.

"When was that?" Gandhi asked indifferently. The man was beaten now, Model thought with a touch of pride: he had succeeded where a generation of degenerate, decadent Englishmen had failed. Of course, the field marshal told himself, he had beaten the British too.

He opened the dossier, riffled through it. "Here we are," he said, nodding in satisfaction. "It was after *Kristallnacht*, eh, in 1938, when you urged the German Jews to play at the same game of passive resistance you were using here. Had they been fools enough to try it, we would have thanked you, you know: it would have let us bag the enemies of the Reich all the more easily."

"Yes, I made a mistake," Gandhi said. Now he was looking at the field marshal, looking at him with such fierceness that for a moment Model thought he would attack him despite advanced age and effete philosophy. But Gandhi only continued sorrowfully, "I made the mistake of thinking I faced a regime ruled by conscience, one that could at the very least be shamed into doing that which is right."

Model refused to be baited. "We do what is right for our *Volk*, for our Reich. We are meant to rule, and rule we do—as you see." The field marshal tapped the dossier again. "You could be sentenced to death for this earlier meddling in the affairs of the Fatherland, you know, even without these later acts of insane defiance you have caused."

"History will judge us," Gandhi warned as the field marshal rose to have him taken away.

Model smiled then. "Winners write history." He watched the two strapping German guards lead the old man off. "A very good morning's work," the field marshal told Lasch when Gandhi was gone. "What's on the menu for lunch?"

"Blood sausage and sauerkraut, I believe."

"Ah, good. Something to look forward to." Model sat down. He went back to work.

I was shooting the breeze with a friend of mine one day when he said, "Why don't you put me in one of your stories?" So I did—sort of. I don't write mainstream fiction very often. I don't sell it very often, either; this story makes once. Thanks, Bob.

THE GIRL WHO TOOK LESSONS

Karen Vaughan looked at her watch. "Oh my goodness, I'm late," she exclaimed, for all the world like the White Rabbit. Her fork clattered on her plate as she got up from the table. Two quick strides took her to her husband. She pecked him on the cheek. "I've got to run, Mike. Have fun with the dishes. See you a little past ten."

He was still eating. By the time he'd swallowed the bite of chicken breast he'd been chewing, Karen was almost out the door. "What is it tonight?" he called after her. "The cake-decorating class?"

She frowned at him for forgetting. "No, that's Tuesdays. Tonight it's law for non-lawyers."

"Oh, that's right. Sorry." The apology, he feared, went for naught; Karen's heels were already clicking on the stairs as she headed for the garage. Sighing, he finished dinner. He didn't feel especially guilty about not being able to keep track of all his wife's classes. He wondered how she managed herself.

He squirted Ivory Liquid on a sponge, attacked the dishes in the sink. When they were done, he settled into the rocking chair with the latest Tom Clancy thriller. His hobbies were books and tropical fish, both of which kept him close to the condo. After spending the first couple of years of their marriage wondering just what Karen's hobbies were, he'd decided her main one was taking lessons.

Nothing that had happened since made him want to change his mind.

Horseback riding, French cuisine, spreadsheets—what it was didn't matter, Mike thought in the couple of minutes before the novel completely engrossed him. If UCLA Extension or a local junior college or anybody else offered a course that piqued her interest, Karen would sign up for it. Once in a while, she'd sign him up too. He'd learned to waltz that way. He didn't suppose it had done him any lasting harm.

Tonight's chicken breasts, sautéed in a white-wine sauce with fresh basil, garlic, and onions, were a legacy of the French cooking class. That was one that had left behind some lasting good. So had the spreadsheet course, which helped Karen get a promotion at the accounting firm she worked for. But she hadn't even looked at the epée in the hall closet for at least three years.

Mike shrugged. If taking lessons was what she enjoyed, that was all right with him. They could afford it, and he'd come to look forward to his frequent early evening privacy. Then he started turning pages in his page-turner, and the barking thunder of assault rifles made him stop worrying about his wife's classes.

He jumped at the noise of her key in the deadbolt. By the time she got in, though, he was back to the real world. He got up and gave her a hug. "How'd it go?"

"All right, I guess. We're going to get a quiz next week, he said. God knows when I'll have time to study." She said that whenever she had any kind of test coming up. She always did fine.

While she was talking, she hung her suit jacket in the hall closet. Then she walked down the hall to the bathroom, shedding more clothes as she went. By the time she got to the shower door, she was naked.

As he always did, Mike followed appreciatively, picking up after her. He liked to look at her. She was a natural blonde, and not a pound—well, not five pounds—heavier than the day they got married. He wished he could say the same.

He took off his own clothes while she was getting clean, scratched at the thick black hair on his chest and stomach. He sighed. Yes, he was an increasingly well-fed bear these days.

"Your turn," Karen said, emerging pink and glowing.

She was wearing a teddy instead of pajamas when he came back into the bedroom. "Hi, there," he said, grinning. After a decade of living together, a lot of their communication went on without words. She turned off the light as he hurried toward the bed.

Afterward, drifting toward sleep, he had a thought that had occurred to him before: she made love like an accountant. He'd never said that to her, for fear of hurting her feelings, but he meant it as a compliment. She was as competent and orderly in bed as out, and if there were few surprises there were also few disappointments. "No, indeed," he muttered.

"What?" Karen asked. Only a long, slow breath answered her.

Their days went on in that regular fashion, except for the occasional Tuesday when Karen came home with bits of icing in her hair. But the magnificent chocolate cake she did up for Mike's birthday showed she had really got something out of that class.

Then, out of the blue, her firm decided to send her back to Chicago for three weeks. "We just got a big multinational for a client," she explained to Mike, "and fighting off a takeover bid has left their taxes screwed up like you wouldn't believe."

"And your people want *you* to go help straighten things out?" he said. "That's a feather in your cap."

"I'll just be part of a team, you know."

"All the same."

"I know," she said, "but three weeks! All my classes will go to hell. And," she added, as if suddenly remembering, "I'll miss you."

Typical, thought Mike, to get mentioned after the precious classes. But he wasn't too annoyed. He knew Karen was like that. "I'll miss you too," he said, and meant it; they hadn't been apart for more than a couple of days at a time since they'd been married.

Next Monday morning, he made one of love's ultimate sacrifices—he took a half-day off from his engineering job to drive her to LAX through rush-hour traffic. They kissed in the unloading zone till the fellow in the car in back of them leaned on his horn. Then Karen scooped her bags out of the trunk and dashed into the terminal.

While she was away, Mike did a lot of the clichéd things men do when apart from their wives. He worked late several times; going home seemed less attractive without anyone to go home to. He rediscovered all the reasons why he didn't like fast food or frozen entrees. He got horny and rented *Behind the Green Door*, only to find out few things were lonelier than watching a dirty movie by himself.

He talked with Karen every two or three days. Sometimes he'd call, sometimes she would. She called one of the nights he stayed late at the office and, when he called her the next day, accused him of having been out with a floozie. "'Bimbo' is the eighties word," he told her. They both laughed.

Just when he was eagerly looking forward to having her home, she let him know she'd have to stay another two weeks. "I'm sorry," she said, "but the situation here is so complicated that if we don't straighten it out now once and for all, we'll have to keep messing with it for the next five years."

"What am I supposed to do, pitch a fit?" He felt like it. "I'll see you in two weeks." From his tone of voice, she might have been talking about the twenty-first century—and the late twenty-first century, at that.

However much they tried not to, the days crawled by. Another clichéd thing for a man to do is hug his wife silly when she finally gets off her plane. Mike did it.

"Well," Karen said, once she had her breath back. "Hello."

He looked at his watch. "Come on," he said, herding her toward the baggage claim. "I made reservations at the Szechuan place we go to, assuming your flight would be an hour late. And since you were only forty minutes late—"

"—we have a chance to get stuck on the freeway instead," Karen finished for him. "Sounds good. Let's do it."

"No, I told you, we'll have dinner first," he said. She snorted.

The world—even traffic—was a lot easier to handle after spicy pork and a couple of cold Tsingtao beers. Mike said so, adding, "The good company doesn't hurt, either." Karen was looking out the window. She didn't seem to have heard him.

When they got back to the condo, she frowned for a few seconds. Then her face cleared. She pointed to Mike's fish tanks. "I've been gone too long. I hear all the pumps and filters and things bubbling away. I'll have to get used to screening them out again."

"You've been gone too long." Mike set down her suitcases. He hugged her again. "That says it all." His right hand cupped her left buttock. "Almost, all anyway."

She drew away from him. "Let me get cleaned up first. I've been in cars and a plane and airports all day long, and I feel really grubby."

"Sure." They walked to the bedroom together. He took off his clothes while she was getting out of hers. He flopped down on the bed. "After five weeks, I can probably just about stand waiting another fifteen minutes"

"Okay," she said. She went into the bathroom. He listened to the shower running, then to the blow dryer's electric whine. When she came back, one of her eyebrows quirked. "From the look of you, I'd say you could just barely wait."

She got down on the bed beside him. After a while, Mike noticed long abstinence wasn't the only thing cranking his excitement to a pitch he hadn't felt since their honeymoon and maybe not then. Every time, every place she touched him, her caress seemed a sugared flame. And he had all he could do not to explode the instant she took him in her mouth. Snakes wished for tongues like that, he thought dizzily.

When at last he entered her, it was like sliding into heated honey. Again he thought he would come at once. But her smooth yet irresistible motion urged him on and on and on to a peak of pleasure he had never imagined, and then to a place past that. Like a thunderclap, his climax left him stunned.

"My God," he gasped, stunned still, "you've been taking lessons!"

From only a few inches away, he watched her face change. For a moment, he did not know what the change meant. Of all the expressions she might put on, calculation was the last he expected right now. Then she answered him. "Yes," she said, "I have. . . ."

The law for non-lawyers course did not go to waste. A couple of months later, she did their divorce herself.

Earthgrip

To Jim Brunet . . .
there is some truth
in what he says.

THE G'BUR

I

The prince of T'Kai let the air out of his book lungs in a hiss of despair. "Of course we will fight," K'Sed told the four human traders who sat in front of his throne. "But I fear we are done for." His mandibles clattered sadly.

The humans looked at one another. No one was eager to speak first. K'Sed watched them all, one eyestalk aimed at each. Jennifer Logan wished she were anywhere but under part of the worried alien's gaze. Being back at her university library was a first choice, but even her cabin aboard the merchant ship *Flying Festoon* would have done in a pinch.

At last Bernard Greenberg said, "Your Highness"—the literal translation of the title was *One With All Ten Legs Off The Ground*—"we will do what we may for you, but that cannot be much. We are not soldiers, and there are only the four of us." The translator on his belt turned his Spanglish words into the clicking T'Kai speech.

K'Sed slumped on his throne, a brass pillar topped by a large round cushion on which his cephalothorax and abdomen rested. His walking-legs—the last three pairs—came within centimeters of brushing the carpet and giving the lie to his honorific. His two consorts and chief minister, who perched on lower toadstool seats behind and to either side of him, clacked angrily. He waved for silence.

Once he finally had it, he turned all his eyes on Greenberg. Even after most of a year on L'Rau, the master merchant found that disconcerting; he felt as if he were being measured by a stereopantograph. "Can you truly be as weak as you claim?" K'Sed asked plaintively. "After all, you have crossed the sea of stars to trade with us, while we cannot go to you. Are your other powers not in proportion?"

Greenberg ran a hand over his bald pate. Just as he sometimes had trouble telling the crablike G'Bur apart, they only recognized him because he wore a full beard but had no hair on his crown.

"Highness, you have exposed the Soft One's cowardice!" exclaimed K'Ret, one of K'Sed's consorts. Her carapace darkened toward the green of anger.

"Highness, do not mistake thought for fear." That was Marya Vassilis. She was the best linguist on the *Flying Festoon*'s crew and followed the T'Kai language well enough to start answering before the translator was done. "We do not want to see the M'Sak barbarians triumph any more than you do. Where is our profit if your cities are overthrown?" She tossed her head in a thoroughly Greek gesture of indignation.

"But by the same token, Highness, where is the Soft Ones' profit if they die fighting for T'Kai?" put in B'Rom, K'Sed's vizier. He was the most cynical arthropod Jennifer had ever known. "For them, fleeing is the more expedient choice."

"Manipulative, isn't he?" Pavel Koniev murmured. The other humans glanced at him sharply, but he had turned off his translator. "Get us to feel guilty enough to do or die for T'Kai."

One of K'Sed's eyestalks also peered Koniev's way; Jennifer wondered if the prince had picked up any Spanglish. But K'Sed made no comment, turning all his attention back to Greenberg. "You have not yet answered my question," he pointed out.

"That, Highness, is because the answer is neither yes nor no," Greenberg said carefully. K'Ret gave a derisive clatter. Greenberg ignored it and went on, "Of course, my people know more of the mechanic arts than yours. But as you have seen on all our visits, our only personal weapons are stunners that hardly outrange your bows and slings."

"That might serve," K'Sed said. "If a thousand of the savages suddenly fell, stunned, as they charged—"

Greenberg spread his hands in regret. "A hundred, perhaps, Highness, but not a thousand. The guns have only so much strength in them. When it is gone, they are useless, except as clubs."

Without flesh surrounding them, it was hard for K'Sed's eyes to show expression, but Jennifer thought he gave Greenberg a baleful stare. "And your ship?" the prince said. "What excuse will you give me there?"

"It is armed," Koniev admitted. K'Sed hissed again, this time with a now-we're-getting-somewhere kind of eagerness. Koniev, who was weapons officer when the *Flying Festoon* was offplanet, went on, "The weapons, unfortunately, function only out in space, where there is no air."

"No air? There is air everywhere," K'Sed said. T'Kai astronomy was about at the Ptolemaic level. The locals believed the humans when they said they came from another world; they and their goods were too unlike anything familiar. Not all the implications, though, had yet sunk in.

"I think we are all looking at this problem in the wrong way," Jennifer said.

Her crewmates all looked at her in surprise. Her silence through the uproarious meeting up to this point was very much in character. It wasn't just because she was only twenty-two and an apprentice. Had she been twice as old and a master merchant—not that she ever wanted to become a master merchant—she would have acted the same way.

"Tell us," Greenberg urged, in a tone that said he thought she was so quiet because she didn't operate in the same world as everyone else. "What have you seen that we've missed?" She flushed and did not answer. He growled, "Come on. His Highness doesn't care how pretty you are. Don't keep him waiting."

"I'm sorry, Master Merchant," she said, flushing even harder. It wasn't her fault she'd been born blond and beautiful. She rather wished she hadn't been; it kept people from taking her seriously. But Greenberg was right—to the T'Kai, she was as hideous and alien as the rest of the Soft Ones. The master merchant's glare forced more words from her. "We know, don't we, that there isn't much we can actually do against the M'Sak—" Her voice was small and breathy, barely enough to activate the translator.

"*We* don't know that," B'Rom said, not deigning to turn even one eyestalk Jennifer's way. "You Soft Ones keep saying it, but we do not know it."

The interruption flustered her. She took a while to get going again. At last she said, "Maybe the M'Sak also doubt we are as harmless as we really are—"

Sixteen eyestalks suddenly rose to their full length; sixteen eyes bored into Jennifer's two. She stopped, glancing toward Greenberg for support. He nodded encouragingly. "I think you have their attention," he said. He was fond of understatement.

"But what do I tell them now?" she asked.

"I haven't the slightest idea," he told her. "How do you think we'd look tricked out with a paint job and enough false legs and teeth to impersonate four *f'noi*?" The *f'noi*, which looked like an unlikely cross between a tiger and a lobster, was the worst predator this continent knew.

"You're baiting me!" Jennifer said. From some people, they would have been fighting words. She wished she could sound fierce instead of disappointed.

Marya Vassilis stepped into the breach. "We don't yet know your barbarous foes well," she reminded the prince and his retinue. "You will have to advise us on how we can best appear terrifying to them."

"Maybe even the sight of your ship will be enough," K'Sed said hopefully. "I do not think any Soft Ones have traded directly with the M'Sak."

"Why should they?" observed D'Kar, K'Sed's other consort, with what the translator rendered as a scornful sniff. She wore gold bands round all her walking-legs and had two rows of yellow garnets glued to her carapace. "The M'Sak are such low wretches, they surely have nothing worth trading for."

"Let them eat cake," Koniev quoted. No matter how well the computer translated, it could not provide social context. *A good thing, too,* Jennifer thought as the talk at last turned serious.

When they got back to the suite the humans had been modifying to their comfort for the past several months, Jennifer flopped down on her air mattress and put a reader on her nose. The mattress, a washbasin, and a chemical toilet were great improvements over the local equivalents. T'Kai sleeping gear, for instance, resembled nothing so much as a set of parallel bars.

Greenberg said something to her. Her attention was on the reader, so she didn't pay much attention. He coughed. She looked up. Her eyes took several seconds to focus on the real world.

"Thanks for the notion that got us going there," he repeated.

"Oh. Thank you very much. I wasn't sure what would come of it, but . . ." She hesitated. As often happened, the hesitation became a full stop.

"But anything was better than staying stuck where we were," Greenberg finished. "Yes." He was resigned to finishing sentences for her by now.

She went back to the reader, but still felt his eyes on her. She was used to looks from men, but on this cruise Greenberg and Koniev both seemed to have taken to Marya, though she was fifteen years older than Jennifer and lovely by the canon of no human world. To Jennifer, that was more a relief than anything else.

Greenberg said something to her. Again, she noticed that he said it, but not what it was. He repeated himself once more. "What are you reading?"

"Heinlein—one of the early Future History books." She'd loved Middle English science fiction ever since she was a child. It was all English; her father had taught her the ancient speech so young that she read it as fluently as she did Spanglish. She was also still young enough to think that everyone ought to love what she loved. "Would you like to borrow the fiche when I'm through with it?" she asked eagerly.

"More of your dead languages?" Greenberg asked her. She nodded. "No, thank you," he said. His voice was not ungentle, but her face fell. He went on, "I'm more interested in what's really here than in some ancient picture of a future that never happened."

"It's not so much the future he creates, but the way he does it," she said, trying to get across the fascination that rigorous world building had for her.

He shook his head. "I haven't the time or the inclination for it now. Illusions are all very well, but the M'Sak, worse luck, are real. I just hope illusory threats can chase them away. I have the bad feeling they won't. There's going to be some very real fighting before long, I'm afraid."

Jennifer nodded. As the meeting with the prince and his court was breaking up, a messenger had come in with bad news: C'Lar, one of the northern towns of the T'Kai confederacy, had fallen to the M'Sak. The T'Kai and their neighbors had been peaceful for several generations now. As K'Sed himself was uneasily aware, they were no match for the vigorous barbarians now emerging from the northern jungles.

But K'Sed intended to try, and nobody on the *Flying Festoon* had even brought up the idea of backing the other side. For one thing, T'Kai *objets d'art* brought the crew a tidy profit, trip after trip; that would vanish with a M'Sak conquest. For another, the M'Sak were not nice people, even for crabs. Their leader, V'Zek, seemed to have taken Chingis Khan lessons—he was both ruthless and extremely able.

Jennifer worried about that until the Heinlein story completely occupied her, but it was a distant sort of worry. If worse came to worst, the *Flying Festoon* could always lift off and leave.

K'Sed, of course, would not be so lucky.

V'Zek came down from his shelter and stepped away from it to watch the full moon rise. Many of his warriors felt anxious away from the trees they were used to, but he took the southlands' open spaces as a challenge, and he never met a challenge any way but claws-first.

Thus he did not pull in his eyestalks when he was away from the posts that held up his shelter and the web of ropes that imitated the closely twined branches of the jungle. And, indeed, there was a certain grandeur in seeing the great yellow shield unobscured by twigs and leaves.

He stretched his eyestalks as far as they would go, a grasping-claw's length from his cephalothorax. He drew a knife and brandished it at the moon. "Soon everything you shine on will be mine."

"The Soft Ones may perhaps have something to say about that, my master," a dry voice beside him observed. He hissed in surprise. He had not heard Z'Yon come up. The shaman could be eerily quiet when he chose.

"Soft Ones," V'Zek said, clicking his scorn. "They did not save C'Lar, nor will they save T'Kai when we reach it. I almost wonder if they exist at all. So much open space makes people imagine strange things."

"They exist," Z'Yon said. "They are one of the reasons I sought you out tonight. What do you plan to do about them?"

The chieftain clacked discontentedly. Since C'Lar fell, he had known the Soft Ones were real, but had tried to avoid thinking of them. Z'Yon was useful, because the shaman made him look at hard questions. "I will deal with them, if they care to deal with me," V'Zek said at last. "Some of their trinkets are amusing."

He thought of the mirror some grandee had owned in captured C'Lar. It was his now, of course. He admired the perfect reflection it gave. It was ever so much clearer than the polished bronze that was the best even T'Kai made. He had not known what a handsome fellow he was.

But Z'Yon would not leave off. "And if they do not?"

"Then I will kill them." V'Zek was very straightforward. That made him a deadly dangerous warleader—he saw an objective and went right after it. It also suited him to lead the M'Sak, whose characters were mostly similar to his own, if less intense. Z'Yon, though, did not think that way: another reason he was valuable to his chieftain.

The shaman let V'Zek's words hang in the air. V'Zek suspected his carapace was turning blue with embarrassment. Who knew what powers the Soft Ones had? "No rumor has ever spoken of them as killers," he said, the best defense of his belligerence he could come up with.

"No rumor has ever spoken of anyone attacking them, either," Z'Yon pointed out.

V'Zek knew that as well as the shaman. He changed the subject, a chiefly prerogative. "Why else did you want to see me?"

"To warn you, my master." When Z'Yon said that, V'Zek grew very alert. The shaman had smelled out plots before. But Z'Yon went on in a way his master had not looked for. "When the moon comes round to fullness again, unless I have misreckoned, the great *f'noi* that lives in the sky will seek to devour it." The M'Sak were not as intellectually sophisticated as the T'Kai, but their seekers-after-wisdom had watched the heavens through the trees for many years.

The chieftain cared nothing for such concerns. A superstitious chill ran through him; he felt his eyestalks contract of themselves. "It will fail?"

"It always has," Z'Yon reassured him. "Still, you might spend some time warning the warriors this will take place, so they are not taken by surprise and perhaps panic-stricken."

"Ah. That is sensible. Claim yourself any one piece of loot from my share of the booty of C'Lar." V'Zek was open-clawed with his gifts; who would stay loyal to a chieftain with a name for meanness?

Z'Yon lowered and raised his eyes, a thank-you gesture. "I wish I could have told you sooner, my master, but the campaign has disrupted my observations, and I did not become certain enough to speak until now."

"It is of no great moment." V'Zek settled back on his walking-legs. "Fifty-one days should be adequate time to prepare the fighters. By then, if all goes well, we will be attacking the city of T'Kai itself."

"Yes, and that is why you will need to harden the warriors' shells against fear. Think on it, my master: When the *f'noi* in the sky wounds the moon with its claws, what color does the moon turn as its blood spreads over it?"

V'Zek thought. He had seen such sky-fights a few times, watching as Z'Yon and the other shamans beat drums to frighten away the sky-*f'noi*. "The color of bronze, more or less . . ." The chieftain paused. "You are subtle."

"You see it too, then: When the heavenly *f'noi* attacks the moon, it will become the color of the T'Kai banners. That is an omen which, without careful preparation, common warriors might well see as disturbing."

"So they might." V'Zek opened and closed his upper grasping-claws while he thought, as if he wished to rend something. His left lower claw was never far from the shortspear strapped to his plastron. "Suppose the omen means that T'Kai will fall to us. Suppose that, till the evil night, you put that meaning about."

"Shall I consult the moltings, to seek the true significance of the phenomenon?"

"For your own amusement, if you like." That lower claw moved closer to the shortspear; Z'Yon felt his small, fanlike tail, of itself, fold under the rear of his abdomen. He did not need the reflex to know he was afraid; he felt the fear in his wits as well as his body. His chieftain went on, "Of course, you will present it to our warriors as I have given it to you now."

"Of course, my master." Z'Yon backed out of V'Zek's presence. When—actually, just before—he had gone a seemly distance, he turned and hurried away.

V'Zek let the slight breach of etiquette pass. He glowered up at the moon. Nothing would interfere with his plans for conquest: not the Soft Ones, whatever they really were, and not the moon, either. *Nothing.*

Having made that vow to himself, he returned at last to his shelter. The ropes and poles were a poor substitute for the fragrant, leafy branches he was used to. He let out a resigned hiss and wondered again how the southrons bore living away from the forests. Maybe, he thought, they were such skillful artificers exactly because they were trying to make up for what they lacked.

The why of it did not matter, though. They had been making their trinkets and trading them back and forth for so long that they forgot claws had any other uses. C'Lar had fallen even more easily than V'Zek had expected.

He composed himself for sleep. C'Lar was only the beginning.

Up on the battlements, Marya giggled. Jennifer took the reader off her nose for a moment so she could watch T'Kai's army march out of the city. The host looked martial enough to her, if uncertainly drilled. She asked, "What's funny?"

"It's just that I've never seen such a lot of tin openers on parade," Marya said.

Bernard Greenberg said, "They're on the big side for tin openers," but now he smiled, too. Marya had a point. Being armored themselves, the G'Bur had developed an assortment of weapons reminiscent of those of Earth's Middle Ages: halberds, bills, and partisans. All of them looked like big pieces of cutlery on long poles. On L'Rau, piercing and crushing took the place of slashing.

Pavel Koniev swung a wickedly spiked morning star, but his expression was sheepish. He said, "When the locals gave me this, I had visions of smashing the M'Sak army single-handed. But if they're all toting polearms, I won't be able to get close enough to them to do any good."

Jennifer went back to her reader; if not being described in Middle English, archaic weapons held little interest for her. Greenberg was saying, "It's a personal defense weapon, like the shortspears they carry. If you're close enough to have to use it, odds are we'll be in a lot of trouble." Out of the corner of her ear, she heard him click off his translator, in case one of the natives nearby was eavesdropping. He also lowered his voice. "We probably will be."

Marya and Koniev followed the master merchant's example. Jennifer would have, but she was engrossed in her Heinlein again. Marya said, "They seem willing enough to fight—which is more than I can say for their prince."

"I'm afraid he knows more than they do," Greenberg said. Down below, a couple of K'Sed's warriors were clicking and clacking at each other loud enough to draw even Jennifer's notice. They had gotten the heads of their weapons tangled and were holding up their whole section. Greenberg went on, "They're amateurs—smiths and taverners and carapace-painters and such. The M'Sak are professionals."

"We're amateurs, too," Koniev said.

"Don't remind me," Greenberg told him. "I'm just hoping we're amateurs at a higher level, so we can match up against G'Bur professionals."

"A higher level indeed," Marya said. "With the *Flying Festoon* and our drones and such, we'll be able to keep track of the barbarians and their route long before they know where we are."

Greenberg said, "That will be for you to handle, Jennifer."

"Huh?" Hearing her name brought Jennifer back to the here and now. She lowered the reader from her nose and got the local sun full in the face. Blinking, she said, "I'm so sorry. What was that?"

"The drones." Greenberg sounded as if he were holding on to his patience with both hands.

"Oh, yes, the drones. Of course," Jennifer said. Unfortunately, she hadn't the faintest idea of what he wanted her to do with them. She knew he could tell, too. Her cheeks grew hot. When she wasn't preoccupied by her Middle English science fiction, she wanted to do well.

"I'll handle the drones, Bernard," Koniev said, seeing her confusion. "I've had experience with them."

"I know you have. That's why I'm giving them to Jennifer," Greenberg said. "She has to get some herself."

Koniev nodded. So did Jennifer; Greenberg had a way of making sense. Then she saw a sparkle of irony in Marya's dark eyes. She flushed all over again. Another reason Greenberg might want her back aboard the *Flying Festoon* was to keep her out of trouble. It didn't occur to her to wonder whether that meant trouble with the M'Sak or trouble with him.

Just then, K'Sed came over to the four humans. The prince of T'Kai had gone martial to the extent of carrying a ceremonial shortspear that did not look sharp enough to menace anything much more armored than a balloon. "Let us see what we can do," he said. For a moment, only Jennifer's translator picked up his words. Then the other traders switched theirs back on. The machines' flat tones did not make him sound martial.

Greenberg said, "Your Highness, we admire your courage in going forth to confront your enemies. Many princes might stay within the walls and try to withstand a siege."

"If I thought I could, Soft One, I would. But V'Zek, may his clasper's prongs fall out, would swallow my cities one by one, saving T'Kai for the last. Maybe the town can hold against him, maybe not. But the confederacy would surely die. Sometimes a bad gamble is all there is."

"Yes," Greenberg said.

"I thank you for making it better than it might be. Now I join my troops." K'Sed gestured jerkily with the shortspear and headed for the way down. That was neither stairs nor ramp, merely a double row of posts driven into the wall. With ten limbs, the G'Bur needed nothing more complex. Humans could use the posts, too, though less confidently.

"More to him than I thought," Koniev said as he watched the prince descend.

"He's brave enough, and bright enough to see what needs doing," Greenberg agreed. "Whether he has the skill and the wherewithal to do it is something else again. Maybe we can help a little there."

"Maybe." Marya sounded about as convinced as K'Sed but, like the prince of T'Kai, was ready to get on with it. "Shall we go down? Otherwise they'll leave without us, which won't make them like us any better." She lowered herself off the edge of the wall, grunted when her feet found purchase, and then rapidly climbed down.

Jennifer stuck her reader in a pocket and followed Marya's lead. She didn't think about what she was doing until her boots kicked up gravel in the courtyard below. Then she started to put her reader back on.

Greenberg came down beside her. He wiped his hands on the sides of his coverall and shook his head. "I don't like that. Hell of a thing for a spacer, isn't it—a bad head for heights?"

"It would be a nuisance, wouldn't it?" Jennifer said. "I just don't notice them."

"Nothing seems to get to you, does it?" Greenberg said. She shrugged and started to walk with the rest of the humans toward the T'Kai army. The warriors milled about under their standards: bronze-colored pennons bearing the emblem of the confederacy T'Kai ruled—a golden grasping-claw, its two pincers open. Greenberg coughed. "You won't be marching with us," he reminded her." You're going back aboard the *Flying Festoon,* remember?"

"Oh, that's right," she said, embarrassed. She'd forgotten all about it. The ship sat a few hundred meters away, its smooth silver curves contrasting oddly with the vertical dark stone curtain of the walls of T'Kai. Willingly enough, Jennifer hurried toward it.

Bernard Greenberg watched Jennifer head back to the *Flying Festoon.* Her curves contrasted oddly with the jointed, armored G'Bur all around her. He sighed. Try as he might, he could not stay annoyed with her. He walked on over to where K'Sed was haranguing his army.

The prince was less optimistic than most human leaders would have been, were they facing his predicament. Even his peroration sounded downbeat. "Warriors of T'Kai, we are fighting for our freedom and our lives. Fighting is our best chance to keep them; if we do not fight, we will surely lose them. So when the time comes, let us fight with all our strength."

He got no cheers, but the soldiers began tramping north, the humans with them. Heavy wagons drawn by *t'dit*—large, squat, enormously strong quasi-crustaceans—rumbled in a long column between troops of warriors. Choking clouds of dust rose into the sky.

"I wish I had a set of nose-filters," Koniev said, coughing.

"Get used to it," Greenberg waved his hand at the ground over which they were walking—bare dirt, sparsely sprinkled with small bushes here and there. Most of them, now, were sadly bedraggled. "No grasses, or anything like them," the master merchant went on.

"So?" Koniev said indifferently.

Greenberg stared at him. "So?" he echoed. "Next trip in, we'll have a load of grain genetically engineered to take advantage of the gap in the ecosystem—grain is just grass with big seeds, after all. I've had people working on that for a long time, but always on a shoestring, so it's taken a while. T'Kai would pay plenty for a new food crop like that . . . if there's any T'Kai left to sell it to in a couple of years. The M'Sak won't give a damn about it—what forest nomads would?"

Marya knew about the grain project. "We're not just trying to save T'Kai out of altruism, Pavel," she said.

"Well, I was hoping not," he said. "Where's the profit in that?"

Greenberg clapped him on the back. He had the proper merchant's attitude. Now if only Jennifer could find a fraction of it in herself . . .

Quiet and smooth, the *Flying Festoon* rose into the air. The ground screen showed G'Bur with eyestalks that seemed more than fully extended, G'Bur pointing grasping-claws at the trade-ship, a few G'Bur running like hell even though starships had been visiting L'Rau every few years for a couple of generations now.

Jennifer noticed the excited locals only peripherally. The novel she was reading interested her much more than they did. Only when the *Flying Festoon* reached the five thousand meters she had preset did she reluctantly lower the reader and get around to the job she had been assigned.

Three drones dropped away from the ship and slowly flew off: northeast, due north, and northwest. One of them, Jennifer thought, ought to pick up the advancing M'Sak army. When it did, she would have more to handle. Until then, she could take it easy. She got out the reader and put it back on. The novel engrossed her again.

Prestarflight writers, she reflected, had one thing wrong about trading runs. Nobody in a novel ever complained about how boring they were. But then, she supposed, nobody set out to write a deliberately boring book.

Not for the first time, she wished she'd never gotten involved with real traders. But it had seemed such a good idea at the time. A whole little academic community specialized in comparing the imagined worlds of Middle English science fiction with the way things had actually happened. She'd always intended to join that community and, at the end of her sophomore year, she'd had a notion original enough to guarantee her tenure before she turned thirty—no mean trick, if she could pull it off.

She had reasoned that her competition—ivory-tower types, one and all—hardly knew more about how things really worked outside the university than the old SF writers had. If she spent a couple of years on real fieldwork and coupled that unique perspective with a high-powered degree, what doors would not open for her?

And so she'd taken a lot of xenanth courses her last two years. Some of them, to her surprise, were even interesting. When the crew of the *Flying Festoon* decided to carry an apprentice, there she was, ready and eager.

Here she was still, bored.

She read for a while, took a shower she did not really need, and programmed the autochef for a meal whose aftermath, she realized with remorse, she would have to exercise off. She did, until sweat stuck her singlet and shorts to her. Then she took another shower. This one, at least, she had earned.

After all that, she decided she might as well check the drones' reporting screens. Night had fallen while she was killing time. She did not expect to find anything exciting, the more so as the drones would be only halfway to the jungle home of the M'Sak.

For a moment, the regular array of lights twinkling in the blackness did not mean much to her. *A town,* she thought, and checked the map grid to find out which one it was. COORDINATES UNMATCHED, the screen flashed.

"Oh, dear," she said, and then, finding that inadequate, followed it with something ripe enough to have made Bernard Greenberg blink, were he there to hear it.

She sent the drone in for a closer look. Then she called Greenberg. He sounded as if he were underwater—not from a bad signal, but plainly because she had awakened him. "I hope this is important," he said through an enormous yawn.

Jennifer knew him well enough to translate that: *it had better be* sounded in her mind. "I think so," she said. "You do want to know where the M'Sak are camped, don't you?" The silence on the comm circuit lasted so long, she wondered if he had fallen asleep again. "Bernard?"

“I’m here.” Greenberg paused again, then sighed. “Yes, you’d better tell me.”

V’Zek peered into the night. The tympanic membrane behind his eyestalks was picking up a low-pitched buzz that would not go away. Scratching the membrane with a grasping-claw did not help. The chieftain summoned Z’Yon. His temper rose when the shaman clicked laughter. Laughing around V’Zek was dangerous, laughing at him insanely foolhardy.

“Well?” V’Zek growled. He reared back so the other M’Sak could see his shortspear.

Z’Yon opened the joint between his carapace and plastron to let the chieftain drive home the spear if he wanted. V’Zek thought the gesture of ritual submission insolently performed, but his anger gave way to surprise when the shaman said, “I hear it, too, my master. The whole army hears it.”

“But what is it?” V’Zek demanded. “No sky-glider makes that sort of noise.”

Z’Yon opened the edges of his shell again, this time, V’Zek judged, in all sincerity. “My master, I cannot say. I do not know.”

“Is it a thing of the T’Kai?” V’Zek was worried. He expressed it as anger; no chieftain could show anything that looked like fear. “Can they smite us with it? Have you heard of their possessing such?” He looked as if he wanted to tear the answer from Z’Yon, with iron pincers if his own were not strong enough.

“Never, my master.” Now the shaman truly was afraid, which made his overlord a trifle happier. Z’Yon spoke more firmly a moment later. “My master, truly I doubt it is a T’Kai thing. How could they conceal it?”

“And more to the point, why? Yes.” V’Zek thought, but came up with no alternatives that satisfied him. “What then?”

“The Soft Ones,” Z’Yon said quietly. “Traveling through the air, after all, is said to be their art, is it not?”

The suggestion made sense to V’Zek. He wished it had not. When the other choice was thinking them creatures of near—or maybe not just near—supernatural powers, he had preferred to doubt that such things as Soft Ones even existed. After C’Lar, he could not do that any more. So he had thought of them as skilled artificers—their mirrors and such certainly justified that. But then, the T’Kai confederacy was full of skilled artificers. The difference between those of his own race and the strangers seemed one of degree, not of kind.

The T'Kai, though, he knew perfectly well, could not make anything that buzzed through the air. If the Soft Ones could . . . It had never occurred to V'Zek that the line between skilled artificers and creatures of near-supernatural powers might be a fine one.

Someone cried out in the camp, a shout of fear and alarm that tore the chieftain from his uncharacteristically philosophical musings. "There it is! The sky-monster!" Other yells echoed the first. Warriors who should have been sleeping tumbled out of their tents to see what the trouble was. Panic ran through the camp.

"By the First Tree, I see it myself," Z'Yon murmured. V'Zek aimed his eyestalks where the shaman's grasping-claw pointed. At first, he saw nothing. Then he spied the little, silvery box his army's campfires were illuminating. The buzzing came from there, sure enough. No, no T'Kai had made the thing, whatever it was. Every line, every angle screamed its alienness. V'Zek wanted to run, to hide himself under the leaves and branches of the forests of M'Sak, to imagine himself undisputed lord of all creation.

He did not run. He filled his book lungs till they pressed painfully against his carapace. "Warriors!" he bellowed, so loud and fierce that eyestalks whipped toward him all through the camp. "Will you flee like hatchlings from something that does you no harm?"

"How much you take for granted," Z'Yon said, but only V'Zek heard him.

He knew the shaman was right. He ignored him anyhow—he had only this one chance to rally the army to him before it fell apart. He cried out again. "Let us try to make it run off, not the other way round!" He snatched up a fair-sized stone, flung it with all his might at the thing in the sky, and wondered if he would be struck dead the next moment.

So, evidently, did his followers. The stone flew wide, but the thing floating in the air took no notice of it and did not retaliate. "Knock it down!" V'Zek shouted, even louder than before. He threw another stone. Again the buzzing device—creature?—paid no attention, though this time the missile came close to it.

Crazy confidence, fueled mostly by relief, tingled through V'Zek. "You see? It cannot harm us. Use arrows, not stones, and it will be ours!" He had led the M'Sak many years now, almost always in victory. As they had so often before, they caught fire from him. Suddenly the sky was full of rocks and arrows, as if the fear the northerners had felt were transmuted all at once to rage.

"My master, you have magics of your own," Z'Yon said, watching the frenzied attack on the sky-thing. V'Zek knew the shaman had no higher praise to give.

Praise, however, won no battles. The M'Sak roared as one when a stone crashed against the side of the sky-thing. It staggered in the air. V'Zek ached to see it fall, but it did not. An arrow hit the thing and bounced off. Another, perhaps shot by a stronger warrior, pierced its shiny skin. It lurched again.

Despite that, its buzzing never changed. And after a little while, it began to drift higher, so that not even the mightiest male could hope to hit it.

"A victory," V'Zek shouted. "We've taught it respect."

His warriors cheered. The thing was still there; they could see it faintly and still catch its sound, though that was muted now. But they had made it retreat. Maybe it had not been slain or broken or whatever the right word was, but they must have hurt it or it would not have moved away at all. The panic was gone.

But if V'Zek had managed to hold his army together, he still felt fury at the buzz which remained, to his way of thinking, all too audible. The sky-thing showed no sign of departing for good. It hung over the camp like, like—on a world where nothing flew and only a few creatures could glide, he failed to find a simile. That only made him angrier.

"What's it doing up there?" he growled. At first it was a rhetorical question. Then the chieftain rounded on Z'Yon. "Shaman, you lay claim to all sorts of wisdom. What *is* it doing up there?"

Z'Yon was glad he had been working through that question in his own mind. "My master, I do not think it came here merely to terrify us. Had that been the aim, it would be more offensive than it is. But for its, ah, strangeness, in fact, it does not seem to seek to disturb us."

V'Zek made an irregular clicking noise. The sky-thing was disturbing enough as it was. Yet Z'Yon had seen a truth: it could have been worse. "Go on," the chieftain urged.

"From the way it hangs over us—and keeps on hanging there—my guess is that somehow it passes word of us to the Soft Ones and, I suppose, to the T'Kai as well. I say again, though, my master, this is only a guess."

"A good one," V'Zek said with a sinking feeling. Hanging there in the sky, that buzzing thing could watch everything he did. At a stroke, two of his main advantages over T'Kai disappeared. His army was more mobile than any the city-dwellers could patch together, and he knew with no false modesty that he surpassed any southron general. But how would that matter, if T'Kai learned of every move as he made it?

He clicked again, and hissed afterward. Maybe things could not have been worse after all.

B'Rom peered into the screen Greenberg was holding. "So that is the barbarians' army, is it?" the vizier said. "Does their leader camp always in the same place within the host?"

"I'd have to check our tapes to be sure, but I think so," Greenberg answered cautiously; B'Rom never asked anything without an ulterior motive. "Why?"

The chief minister's eyestalks extended in surprise. "So I can give proper briefing to the assassins I send out, of course. What good would it do me to have them kill some worthless double-pay trooper, thinking all the while they were slaying the fierce V'Zek?"

"None, I suppose," Greenberg muttered. He had to remind himself that the M'Sak had not invaded the T'Kai confederacy for a picnic. Drone shots of what was left of C'Lar said that louder than any words.

B'Rom said, "Do you think our agents would be able to poison the barbarians' food, or will we have to use weapons to kill him? We would find fewer willing to try that, as the chances for escape seem poor."

"So they do." The master merchant thought for a moment, then went on carefully, "Excellency, you know your people better than I ever could. I have to leave such matters of judgment in your hands." He knew the translator would spit out the appropriate idiom, probably something like *in the grasp of your claws.*

The minister went click-click-hiss, sounding rather, Greenberg thought unkindly, like an irritated pressure cooker. "Do not liken me to the savages infesting our land." He glared at Greenberg from four directions at once, then suddenly made the rusty-hinge noise that corresponded to a wry chuckle. "Although I suppose from your perspective such confusion is only natural. Very well, you may think of yourself as forgiven." He creaked again and scurried away.

No doubt he's plotting more mischief, Greenberg thought. That was one of the vizier's jobs. The old devil was also a lot better than most G'Bur—most humans, too, come to that—at seeing the other fellow's point of view, very likely because he believed in nothing himself and found shifting position easy on account of that.

The T'Kai army moved out. Greenberg, Marya, and Koniev

tramped along with the G'Bur. Even the locals' humblest tools would have fetched a good price on any human world. The water-pots they carried strapped to their left front walking-legs, for instance, were thrown with a breathtaking clarity of line the Amasis potter would have envied. And when they worked at their art, the results were worth traveling light-years for.

The T'Kai treated their land the same way. The orchards where they grew their tree-tubers and nuts were arranged like Japanese gardens, and with a good deal of the same spare elegance. The road north curved to give the best possible view of a granite boulder off to one side.

Greenberg sighed. The M'Sak cared little for esthetics. They were, however, only too good at one art: destruction. The master merchant wished he had a warship here instead of his merchant vessel. He wished for an in-atmosphere fighter. Neither one appeared.

"I didn't think they would," he said, and sighed again.

"Didn't think what would?" Marya asked. He explained. She said, "How do the M'Sak know the *Flying Festoon* isn't a warship?"

"Because it won't blast them into crabcakes, for one thing."

"Will it have to? They've never seen it before. They've never seen anything like it before. If a starship drops out of the sky with an enormous sonic boom and lands in front of them, what do you think they'll do?"

Greenberg considered. As far as he knew, no offworlders had ever visited the M'Sak. He laughed out loud and kissed Marya on the mouth. She kissed him back, at least until a couple of G'Bur pulled them apart. "Why are you fighting?" the locals demanded.

"We weren't," Greenberg said. "It's a—"

"Mating ritual," Marya supplied helpfully.

The G'Bur clacked among themselves. The translator, doing its duty, laughed in Greenberg's ear. He didn't care. He thought what the G'Bur did to make more G'Bur was pretty funny, too.

Jennifer put down the reader. Naturally, Greenberg's orders had come just when she was getting to the interesting part of the book. She wished this Anderson fellow, who seemed to have a feel for what the trader's life was like, were on the *Flying Festoon* instead of her. As he was about a thousand years dead, however, she seemed stuck with the job.

She had all three drones over the M'Sak army now, flying in triangular formation. They stayed several hundred meters off the ground. That first night had not been the only time the barbarians attacked them, and they thought of more ploys than Jennifer had. One M'Sak climbed a tall tree to pump arrows into a drone she'd thought safely out of range. Greenberg would not have thought well of her had it gone down.

She made a sour face. She did not think Greenberg thought well of her, anyway. Too bad. No one had held a gun to his head to make him take her on. Just as she had to make the best of boredom, he had to make the best of her.

The M'Sak were approaching a wide, relatively open space with low bushes growing here and there. When L'Rau got around to evolving grasses, that kind of area would be a meadow. It would, Jennifer thought with a faint sniff, certainly be more attractive as a broad expanse of green than as bare dirt and rocks punctuated by plants.

But even as it was, it would serve her purpose. She did not want the M'Sak distracted from her arrival by anything.

She told the computer what she wanted the *Flying Festoon* to do. She was smiling as she picked up the reader again. She doubted the M'Sak would have trouble paying attention to her.

These days, V'Zek and his army almost ignored the drones that hung over them. Their buzzing still reached the chieftain's tympanic membrane, but he no longer heard it unless he made a deliberate effort. If the things were spying on him for the Soft Ones, then they were. He could do nothing about it, now that the drones kept out of missile range.

The M'Sak marched in a hollow square, with booty and prisoners inside. The army was smaller than it had been when it entered T'Kai territory, not so much from casualties as because V'Zek had left garrisons in the towns he had taken. He intended to rule this land, not just raid it. When the T'Kai finally came out to fight, he would still have enough warriors to deal with them.

"For that matter, they may just yield tamely," the chieftain said to Z'Yon, who was ambling along beside him. The shaman was not a large male, nor physically impressive, but had no trouble keeping up with the hulking youths who made up the bulk of V'Zek's army.

Z'Yon did not answer for a moment; he was chewing a *f'leg*-fruit he had snipped from a bush as he walked past. When he was done with it, he said, "I have to doubt that. The confederation is stronger to the south. I think they will try to meet us somewhere there."

"I begin to wonder. The southrons are such cowards," V'Zek said derisively.

"Such what?"

"Cowards," V'Zek said, a little louder. The noise from the sky was louder, too. The chieftain turned his eyestalks that way, wondering if the drones were dropping lower again for some reason of their own. If they were, he would have his troopers drive them up again—they should not be allowed to think they could get gay with the bold M'Sak.

But the sky-things were where they had always been.

"Don't take the T'Kai too lightly," Z'Yon warned. He also had to raise his voice. V'Zek felt his eyestalks shrink back toward his shell. That was not a thin buzz coming from the sky now; it was a roar. It got louder and *louder* and LOUDER. V'Zek's walking-legs bent under it, as if he had some great weight tied to his carapace.

Z'Yon pointed with a grasping-claw. V'Zek made an eyestalk follow it. Something else was in the sky that did not belong there. At first he thought it just a bright silver point, as if a star were to appear in daylight. But it got bigger with terrifying speed—it became a shining fruit, a ball, and then, suddenly, the chieftain realized it was a metal building falling toward him. No wonder his legs were buckling!

He no longer heard the noise of its approach, but felt it as a vibration that seemed to be trying to tear his shell from his flesh. He looked up again, willing one eye to follow the sky-building as it descended. Would it crush him? No, not quite, he saw.

The roar continued to build, even after the thing was down on the ground in front of the M'Sak host. Then all at once it ended, and silence seemed to ache as much as clamor had a moment before.

"The Soft Ones!" Z'Yon was shrieking.

V'Zek wondered how long the shaman had been talking, or rather, screaming. "What about them?" he said. His own voice echoed brassily on his tympanic membrane.

"It's their ship," Z'Yon said.

"Well, who cares?" the chieftain growled. Now that the accursed noise had stopped, he was able to think again, and the first thing he thought about was his army.

When he looked back over his cephalothorax and tail, he let out a whistle of fury. His army, his precious, invincible army, was in full flight, dashing in all directions.

"Come back!" he bellowed. He chose the one line that had even a tiny chance of turning the warriors. "The prisoners are escaping with our loot!"

That made eyestalks whip around where nothing else would have. He saw he had not even been lying: captives from C'Lar and other towns were scuttling this way and that, with baskets on their carapaces and in their grasping-claws. He sprang after one and swung down his axe. It bit through the poor fellow's shell, which was softened by recent privation. Body fluids spurted. The prisoner fell. V'Zek slew one of his own soldiers, one who was running.

The chieftain reared back on his hindmost pair of legs, waved the dripping axe on high. "Rally!" he cried. "Rally!" A few officers took up the call. V'Zek fought and killed another would-be fugitive. The warriors began to regroup. They had feared their master for years, the unknown from out of the sky only for moments.

Then an even louder voice came from the sky-thing, roaring in the T'Kai dialect, "Go away! Leave this land! Go away!"

V'Zek understood it perfectly well. Most of his soldiers could follow it after a fashion; the M'Sak language and that of the southrons were cousins. The chieftain thought the sky-thing made a mistake by speaking. Had it remained silent and menacing, he could not have fought it, for it would have given him nothing to oppose. This way—

"It's a trick!" he shouted. "It's the accursed T'Kai, trying to run us off without fighting us!"

"Doing a good job, too!" one of his fleeing soldiers cried.

The fellow was too far away for him to catch and kill. V'Zek had to rely on persuasion instead, a much less familiar technique. Still, with the full power of his book lungs, he said, "It hasn't harmed us. Will you run from noise alone? Do you run from thunder and lightning?"

"Not bad," Z'Yon said beside him. Then he, too, raised his voice. "If this is the best the T'Kai can do, you warriors should be ashamed. Our master has the right of it: a good thunderstorm back home is more frightening than this big hunk of ironmongery ever could be. If it smites us, that is the time to worry. Till then, it's only so much wind."

As an aside to V'Zek, he added, "If it smites us, I suspect we'll be too dead to worry about anything." But only the chieftain heard him; Z'Yon knew what he was doing.

Long-ingrained discipline, the fear of losing plunder, and the sky-thing's failure to do anything more than make threatening noises slowly won the day for V'Zek. The M'Sak reclaimed most of their captives and most of their loot. They re-formed their ranks and, giving the building that had fallen from the sky a wide berth, resumed their march south.

V'Zek wanted more than that. He wanted revenge for the sky-building's nearly having put paid to his whole campaign. He sent a squad of halberdiers against it. Their weapons were good for cracking shells; he wanted to see what they would do against that gleaming metal skin.

He never found out. The sky-thing emitted such a piercing screech that he, no short distance away, drew in his eyestalks in a wince of pain. His warriors dropped their polearms and fled. Most returned to their troop, but two dashed straight for Z'Yon: the shaman was the army's chief healer.

Z'Yon examined them, gave them a salve, and sent them back to the comrades. When he turned back to V'Zek, his hesitancy showed the chieftain he was troubled. "The salve will soothe a bit. It will do no more. Their tympanic membranes are ruptured."

"Deafened, are they?" V'Zek glowered at the flying building. He only glowered, though. If the thing really could be dangerous when provoked, he would not provoke it. He had more important things to do than pausing for vengeance in the middle of his attack on T'Kai.

But once he had broken the confederacy, he told himself, the Soft Ones—or whoever was in charge of the sky-thing—would pay for trying to thwart him. Anticipating that was almost as sweet as wondering how many days he could keep Prince K'Sed alive before he finally let him die.

Browns and greens chased each other across K'Sed's carapace as he looked at the M'Sak army in the vision screen. His eyestalks pulled in a little. He noticed and lengthened them again, but Greenberg caught the involuntary admission of fear. "They are still advancing," the prince said. The translator's flat tones could not sound accusing, but the master merchant knew what he would have felt in K'Sed's shoes.

Not, he thought, that the prince wore any. He shoved the irrelevance aside. "So they are, Highness," he said. If K'Sed felt like restating the obvious, he could match him.

"You said your ship would frighten them away," K'Sed said.

"Were I not used to it, the sight and sound of a ship falling from the sky would be plenty to frighten me away."

"Yes, Highness," Greenberg agreed. "I thought that would be true of the M'Sak as well." Out loud, he did not draw the obvious conclusion: that the invaders, or at least their leader, were braver than K'Sed. He hoped the prince would not reach that conclusion for himself. K'Sed was demoralized enough already.

His next words showed that to be true, but at least he was thinking in terms of the nation he led, rather than personally. "I wish we could fortify a strongpoint and force the M'Sak to attack us on ground of our own choosing. But I fear they would only go around us and keep on ravaging the countryside." Refugees from the north had spread lurid tales of the destructiveness of the M'Sak, tales that did not shrink in the telling. Sadly, recon photos confirmed them.

"Your Highness, I fear you are right." Anything that kept K'Sed focused on dealing with his problems seemed a good policy to Greenberg.

"And after all," the prince said, mostly to himself, "the savages are still some days' journey from us."

"So they are." Greenberg chose his words with care, not wanting to let K'Sed delude himself that he need do nothing, but not wanting to alarm him further, either. "And remember Your Highness, that we still shadow their every move. When our forces close with theirs—" not, Greenberg made sure, *when they attack us* "—we will know their every move. They cannot take us by surprise."

"That is true." K'Sed brightened a little. "We will be able to ready ourselves to meet them. I shall remind my officers of this."

As soon as the prince was gone, Greenberg called Jennifer. He'd grown to expect to have to wait for her to answer the signal. When she finally responded, he said, "From now on, I want to hear everything the M'Sak do. *Everything*, do you hear? We can't afford to let them get any kind of edge at all."

"I understand," she said after another pause. "I'll do the best I can."

"Keep the reader *off* your nose for a while, can you?" he said.

Still another pause, this time a hurt one. "I said I'd do my best, Bernard."

"All right." Against his best intentions, Greenberg felt guilty. "It's important, Jennifer. Try to remember that. A whole civilization could be riding on what you spot."

"I'll remember," she said. He had to be content with that.

✧ ✧ ✧

"We draw closer, my master," Z'Yon said. As the M'Sak moved further from their home, the land grew strange. These cool uplands—with only those trees that yielded nuts and tubers, and those in the neat orchards—were daunting. Even the shaman felt under his shell how far away the horizon was.

V'Zek rarely showed worry. This time was no exception. He made his eyestalks long as he peered south. The smellpores around his eyes opened wider; he seemed to be trying to sniff out the T'Kai. At last he said, "It will be soon."

Two of his eyes stayed where they were. The other two broke from their southward stare to glance up at the three drones that still shadowed his army, and at the flying building as well. The latter was just a silver dot in the sky now, but V'Zek knew its true size. He wondered absently how far up it was, to look so small. However far that was, it was not far enough.

Without his willing it, his grasping-claws clattered angrily. "They watch us," he said. His voice reminded Z'Yon of the hunting call of a *f'noi.*

"They are not very brave, my master," the shaman said, trying to ease the chieftain's gloom.

But V'Zek burst out, "How brave need they be? Knowing how we come, they can meet us at a spot of their own choosing. And when at last we fight them, they will see every move we make, as we make it. They will be able to respond at once, and in the best possible way. How can we gain surprise in a fight like that?"

"Warrior for warrior, we are better than they," Z'Yon said. But he knew, as did V'Zek, that that only meant so much. Fighting defensively, the T'Kai might hold their casualties close to even with those of the invaders. A few engagements like that, and the M'Sak were ruined. Unlike their foes, the T'Kai could levy fresh troops from towns and countryside. The M'Sak had to win with what they had.

The shaman turned one cautious eye toward his chieftain. He was in luck: V'Zek paid him no attention. The chieftain's eyestalks were all at full length, his eyes staring intently at one another—a sure sign of furious concentration.

Then V'Zek let out a roar like a *f'noi* that had just killed. "Let them see whatever they want!" he cried, so loud that half the army looked his way. He took Z'Yon's upper grasping-claws in his and squeezed till the shaman clattered in pain and feared for his integument.

V'Zek finally let go. He capered about like a hatchling, then, as if whispering some secret bit of magical lore, bent to murmur into the shaman's tympanum, "They cannot see into my mind."

Pavel Koniev leaped aside. The halberd's head buried itself in the ground where he had stood. The G'Bur hissed with effort, using all four grasping-legs to tug the weapon free. It lifted.

Too slow, too slow—before the local could take another swing with the long, unwieldy polearm, Koniev sprang close. The G'Bur hissed again, dropped the halberd, and grabbed for his shortspear. By then Koniev had jumped onto his back. He swung the mace up over his head.

The circle of spectators struck spearshafts against carapaces in noisy tribute to his prowess. The claps and whoops that Greenberg and Marya added were drowned in the din. Koniev scrambled down from the G'Bur and gave him a friendly whack where a grasping-leg joined his shell. "You almost split me in two there, N'Kor, even though that halberd just has a wooden head."

"I meant to," N'Kor said. Luckily, the soldier did not seem angry at having lost. "I thought it would be easy—I flattened you often enough when we started our little games. But you're learning, and you Soft Ones dodge better than I dreamed anything could. Comes of having just the two legs, I suppose." With their wide, armored bodies and three walking-legs splayed off to either side, the G'Bur were less than agile.

Of course, Greenberg thought as Koniev repeated his moves slowly so the locals could watch, the G'Bur weren't very fragile, either. A practice halberd would bounce off a carapace with the equivalent of no more than a nasty bruise, but it really might have done in Pavel.

"A good practice," Koniev was saying to N'Kor. "With the M'Sak so close, we need all the work we can get."

N'Kor made a puzzled noise that sounded like brushes working a snare drum. "But you have your little belt weapons that bring sleep from far away. You will not need to fight at close quarters."

"Not if everything goes exactly as it should," Koniev agreed. "How often, in a battle, does everything go exactly as it should?"

This time, N'Kor's clattering was a G'Bur chuckle. "Next time will be the first. As I said, for a trader you are learning."

"Hmm," was all Koniev said to that. He wiped sweat from his face with a yellow-haired forearm as he walked over to the other two humans. "What are they doing?" he asked Greenberg; the master merchant always kept the vision screen with him.

"Making camp, same as we are," he answered after a brief look at it.

"How far away are they?" Marya asked.

She and Koniev waited a moment while Greenberg keyed new instructions into the vision screen. The M'Sak camp vanished, to be replaced by a map of the territory hereabouts. Two points glowed on the map, one gold, the other menacing scarlet. "Fifteen kilometers, more or less," Greenberg said, checking the scale along one side of the screen.

"Tomorrow," Marya said thoughtfully. Her dark eyes were hooded, far away. Greenberg suspected he bore a similarly abstracted expression. He had been in plenty of fights and skirmishes, but all of them out of the blue, leaving him no time for anything but reaction. Deliberately waiting for combat was, in a way, harder than taking part.

Because humans needed less room than G'Bur, the tents they set up were dwarfed by the locals' shelters. But their three stood out all the same, the orange nylon fiery bright when compared to the undyed, heavy fabric that was the standard tent-cloth on L'Rau.

Marya opened her tent flap. She hesitated before going through and looked from Greenberg to Koniev. Daylight was fading fast now, and campfires were not enough to let the master merchant be sure she flushed, not with her dark skin. Had it been Jennifer, there could have been no doubt.

"Come in with me," Marya said quietly.

Now the two men looked at each other. "Which one?" they asked together. They laughed, but without much mirth. Till now, they had never had any trouble sharing her affection . . . but there might not be another night after this one.

Marya knew that, too. "Both of you."

Greenberg and Koniev looked at each other again. They had never done that before. Koniev shrugged. Greenberg smiled.

"Come on, dammit," Marya said impatiently.

As the closing tent flap brushed him, Greenberg reflected that he had already decided it was no ordinary night.

In the *Flying Festoon,* Jennifer read fantasy and wished she were with the three traders. She had heard them all together when she called to ask if they'd come up with any new notions on how to use the starship in the upcoming battle. They hadn't; flying low and creating as much confusion as possible was the best thought they'd had. Jennifer got the idea their minds were elsewhere.

They could have invited me down, she thought. There would have been nothing to landing the *Flying Festoon* outside the T'Kai camp and then finding the brilliant tents the humans used. Except for Prince K'Sed's huge pavilion, they were the most conspicuous objects in camp.

But they had not asked her to come down, and she would not go anywhere she was not asked. She felt the hurt of that implied rejection, and the sadness. The three of them had a world in which she was not welcome. *Maybe it's just because I'm younger than any of them,* she told herself. She did not believe it. No matter what courses she had taken, she was not a trader. Greenberg must be sorry he had ever chosen her.

She gave herself back to her fantasy novel. It reminded her that she had a place of her own, too, in an intellectual world where she was up and coming, not all too junior and none too skilled. It also reminded her, unfortunately, that the nearest center of that world was some light-years away.

She began a fantasy of her own, one where she saved the *Flying Festoon* from hideous danger in space. The traders were ready to go into cold sleep and unfurl the light-sail for a sublight trip back to civilization that would surely last centuries. Somehow, armed with no more than a screwdriver and determination, she saved the hyperdrive.

She managed to laugh at herself. Even before spaceflight, that would have made god-awful science fiction. Here and now, it was simply ridiculous. If anything went wrong, the best she could do was scream for help; all other alternatives were worse.

She turned down the temperature in her cabin till it was just above chilly, then dug out blankets and wrapped them tight around her. She finally fell asleep, but it was not the sort of warm embrace she wanted to enjoy.

II

"They aren't four times our size, are they?" Prince K'Sed spoke with a certain amount of wonder as he studied the drawn-up ranks of the enemy.

"You knew that, Your Highness," Greenberg observed, hoping to hearten the T'Kai leader. "You've received M'Sak ambassadors often enough at your court."

"Ambassadors are different from soldiers," K'Sed answered. Now he could see the M'Sak were G'Bur much like the ones he commanded, but it did not seem to hearten him.

Eyeing the force ahead, Greenberg understood why the prince remained apprehensive. The ranks of the M'Sak were grimly still and motionless, while the T'Kai milled about and chattered as if they were still on march or, better image yet, gabbing about this and that while they tried to outdo one another in the marketplace. For the most part, they *were* merchants, not soldiers, by trade. The M'Sak, unfortunately, were soldiers.

The master merchant slowly realized that went deeper than the discipline the northern warriors showed. Everything about them was calculated to intimidate. Even their banners were the green of an angry G'Bur, not the unmartial bronze under which the T'Kai mustered. Greenberg wondered how many such clues he was missing but that were playing on the psyches of K'Sed and his army.

And yet, the T'Kai owned an edge no soldiers on L'Rau had ever enjoyed. "They cannot hide from us," he reminded K'Sed. "We will know all their concealed schemes and be able to counter them." Only once the words were out of his mouth did he stop to think the one might not be the same as the other.

✧ ✧ ✧

Something of an odd color moved with a peculiar sinuous motion through the ranks of the T'Kai. V'Zek wondered if the southrons had lured ghosts to fight for them. Trying to suppress superstitious dread, he put the question to Z'Yon.

"Anything is possible, my master, but I have detected no signs of this," the shaman said. "I think you are seeing instead a Soft One."

V'Zek gave a clattery shudder of disgust. The Soft One moved like—like— V'Zek took a long time to find a comparison. Finally he thought of water pouring from a jug. That did not make him feel much better. Live things had no business moving like water pouring from a jug.

He waved to his drummers. Their thunder signaled his warriors forward. He spent only moments worrying about being watched from the sky. Once it was pike against pike, things would happen too fast for that to matter. And he felt fairly sure the sky-things could not read his thoughts. If they could, reading his hatred would have burned them down long since.

"They're advancing," Jennifer reported.

Greenberg's voice was dry as he answered, "I'd noticed. Let's check the screen and see what they're up to." After a pause, he spoke again. "Two lines, no particular weighting anywhere along them I can see. Whatever cards he's holding, he doesn't want to show them yet."

"No," Jennifer agreed. She paused herself, then added, "Maybe we shouldn't have let him get used to the idea of having the drones up there."

"Maybe we shouldn't. Why didn't you say something about that sooner?"

Jennifer hated blushing, but couldn't help it. Luckily, the link with Greenberg was voice-only. "I just thought of it now."

"Oh," Greenberg said. "Well, I didn't think of it at all, so how am I supposed to criticize you? We're all amateur generals here. I just hope it doesn't end up costing us. Do you suppose we shouldn't have shown the northerners the *Flying Festoon*, either?"

"We'll find out soon enough, don't you think?"

"Yes, I expect we will. This is a tad more empirical than I'd really planned on being, though. Wish us all luck."

"I do," Jennifer said. "You three especially, because you're on the ground."

The master merchant did not answer. Jennifer sighed. She sent the *Flying Festoon* whizzing low over the battlefield. The roar of cloven air filled the cabin when she activated the outside mike pickup. Then she shut it off again and turned on the ship's siren. It reverberated through the hull, even without amplification, and set her teeth on edge.

She studied the pictures the drones gave her. After reading about so many imaginary battles in Middle English, she fancied herself a marshal. She soon discovered the job was, as with most jobs, easier to imagine than to do. She found no magic strategic key to V'Zek's maneuvers. If anything, she thought him over-optimistic, advancing as he was against a strong defensive front: the T'Kai right was protected by a river, the left anchored by high ground and a stand of trees.

She wondered if he knew something she didn't, and hoped finding out wouldn't be too expensive.

B'Rom sidled up to Greenberg crabwise—an adverb the master merchant applied to few G'Bur but the vizier. "Soon now," B'Rom declared. The translator should have given his clicks, hisses, and whistles a furtive quality, but that, sadly, was beyond its capabilities.

"Soon what?" Greenberg asked, a trifle absently. Most of his attention was on the forest of oversized cutlery bearing down on the T'Kai. The *Flying Festoon*'s histrionics left his ears stunned. He hoped the M'Sak were quaking in the boots they didn't wear.

Then his head whipped around, for B'Rom said, "Soon the assassination, of course. What better time than when the savages are in the midst of their attack?"

"None, I suppose," Greenberg mumbled. His hand eased on the stunner. Maybe he wouldn't have to use it after all.

The racket overhead was appalling and confusing, but V'Zek was proud of the way his warriors pressed on toward the waiting enemy. The Soft Ones had blundered in showing their powers too soon. That relieved V'Zek: ghosts or spirits never would have made such a foolish mistake. The Soft Ones were natural, then, no matter how weird they looked. V'Zek was confident he could handle anything natural.

A warrior whose carapace was painted with a messenger's red stripes rushed up to the chieftain. V'Zek's eyestalks drew together in slight perplexity—what could be so urgent, when the two armies had not even joined? Then the fellow's left front grasping-claw pulled a war hammer from its concealed sheath under his plastron. He swung viciously at the M'Sak chieftain.

Only V'Zek's half-formed suspicion let him escape unpunctured. He sprang to one side. The hammerhead slammed painfully against him between right front and rear grasping-legs, but the chisel point did not penetrate. By the time the would-be assassin struck again, V'Zek had out his own shortspear. He turned the blow and gave back a counterthrust his enemy beat aside.

Then half a ten M'Sak were battling the false messenger. Before their chieftain could shout for them to take him alive, he had fallen, innards spurting from a score of wounds. "Are you all right, my master?" one of the soldiers gasped.

V'Zek flexed both right-side grasping-legs. He could use them. "Well enough." He looked closely at the still shape of his assailant. The curve of the shell was not quite right for a M'Sak. "Does anyone know him?"

None of the warriors spoke.

"I suppose he is of T'Kai," the chieftain said. The soldiers shouted angrily. So did V'Zek, but his fury was cold. He had wanted the southrons for what they could yield him and his people. Now he also had a personal reason for beating them. He reminded himself not to let that make him break away from his carefully devised plan. "Continue the advance, as before," he ordered.

"Some sort of confusion for a moment there around the chieftain." Jennifer's voice sounded in Greenberg's ear. With the M'Sak so close, he had put away the vision screen. He let out his breath in a regretful sigh when she reported, "It seems to be over now."

"Damn." Marya and Koniev said it together. All three humans were on the right wing—the right claw, they would say on L'Rau—of the T'Kai army, not far from the river. Since V'Zek led the invaders from their right, he was most of a kilometer away, out of their view.

Closer and closer came the M'Sak. They were shouting fiercely, but the din from the *Flying Festoon* outdid anything they could produce. "Shoot!" cried an underofficer.

G'Bur held bows horizontally in front of themselves with their front pair of grasping-claws, using the rear pair to load arrows—sometimes one, sometimes a pair—and draw the weapons. The M'Sak archers shot back at the T'Kai, lofting arrows with chisel-headed points to descend on their foes' backs.

Every so often, a warrior on one side or the other would collapse like a marionette whose puppeteer had suddenly dropped the strings. More commonly, the shafts would skitter away without piercing their targets. Exoskeletons had advantages, Greenberg thought.

An arrow buried itself in the ground less than a meter from his left boot. He shuffled sideways and bumped into Marya, who was unconsciously moving away from an arrow that had landed to her right. Their smiles held little humor. She said, "Shall we give them something to think about?"

Greenberg and Koniev both nodded. The three humans leveled their stunners at the M'Sak. The gun twitched slightly in the master merchant's hand as it fed stun charges one after another into the firing chamber.

One after another, M'Sak began dropping; pikes and halberds fell from nerveless grasping-claws. The invaders' advance, though, took a long moment to falter. Greenberg realized the M'Sak, intent on the enemies awaiting them, hadn't noticed their comrades were going down without visible wounds.

Then they did notice, and drew up in confusion and fear: for all they knew, the felled warriors were dead, not stunned. Greenberg took careful aim and knocked down a M'Sak whose halberd had a fancy pennon tied on below the head—an officer, he hoped. "Good shot!" Koniev cried, and thumped him on the back.

"I only wish we had a couple of thousand charges instead of a hundred or so," Marya said, dropping another M'Sak. "That would end that, and in a hurry, too."

By no means normally an optimist, Greenberg answered, "We're doing pretty well as is." The M'Sak left was stalled; had they been humans, the master merchant would have thought of them as rocked back on their heels.

The officers who led the T'Kai right did not have that concept—or heels, for that matter—but they recognized disorder when they saw it. "Advance in line!" they ordered.

The T'Kai raised a rattling cheer and moved forward. They chopped and thrust at their foes, who gave ground. For a heady moment, Greenberg thought the M'Sak would break and run.

They did not. Faced by an assault of a sort with which they were familiar, the invaders rallied. Their polearms stabbed out at the T'Kai, probing for openings. The opposing lines came to close quarters. For a long time, motion either forward or backward could be measured in bare handfuls of meters.

The humans stopped shooting. They had to be careful with charges, and friend and foe were so closely intermingled now that a shot was as likely to fell a T'Kai as an M'Sak. If the enemy broke through, stunners could be of value again. Without armor, the humans were useless in the front line.

Koniev laughed nervously as he watched the struggle not far away. He said, "I never thought there would be so much waiting *inside* a battle."

"I notice you're still holding your stunner, not your mace," Marya said.

Koniev looked down as if he had not been sure himself. "So I am." The mace was on his belt. He touched it with his left hand. "If I have to use this thing, odds are we'll be losing. I'd sooner win."

Greenberg's own personal defense weapon was a war hammer. He had almost forgotten it; now he noticed it brush against his thigh, felt its weight on his hip. He nodded to himself. He would just as soon go on pretending it wasn't there.

"The savages are mad, mad!" Prince K'Sed clattered, watching the M'Sak swarm up the slope toward his waiting soldiers. "All the military manuals cry out against fighting uphill." Like a proper ruler, he could stand on any walking-leg. He had studied the arts of war even though they bored him, but had never expected the day to come when he put them to practical use.

B'Rom clicked in agreement. "No law prevents our taking advantage of such madness, however." He turned to the officer beside him. "Isn't that so, D'Ton?"

"Aye, it is." But the general sounded a little troubled. "I had looked for better tactics from V'Zek. After all, he—" D'Ton had at least the virtue of knowing when to shut up. Reminding his prince and vizier that the enemy had won every battle thus far did not seem wise.

"Let us punish him for his rashness," B'Rom declared. D'Ton looked to K'Sed, who raised a grasping-claw to show assent.

The general scraped his plastron against the ground in obedience. He had no real reason not to agree with the prince and vizier. Knowing when and by what route the M'Sak were coming had let the army choose this strong position. Not taking advantage of it would be insanely foolish. He filled his book lungs. "Advance in line!"

Lesser officers echoed the command. Cheering, the prince's force obeyed. They knew as well as their leaders the edge the high ground gave them. Iron clashed and belled off iron, crunched on carapaces, and sheared away limbs and eyestalks.

With their greater momentum, the T'Kai stopped their enemies' uphill advance dead in its tracks. The two lines remained motionless and struggling for a long moment. Here, though, the stalemate did not last. The T'Kai began to force the M'Sak line backward.

"Drive them! Drive them! Well done!" D'Ton shouted. V'Zek truly had made a mistake, he thought.

Prince K'Sed, gloomy since the day he learned of the M'Sak invasion, was practically capering with excitement. "Drive them back to M'Sak!" he cried.

"Driving them back to level ground would do nicely," B'Rom said, but as he spoke in normal tones, no one but K'Sed heard him. The T'Kai warriors picked up the prince's cry and threw it at the foe. "Back to M'Sak! Back to M'Sak!" It swelled into a savage chant. Even B'Rom found a grasping-claw opening and closing in time to it. Irritated at himself, he forced the claw closed.

"Hold steady! Don't break formation! Hold steady!" V'Zek heard the commands echoed by officers and underofficers as the M'Sak gave ground. He wished he could be in the thick of the fighting, but if he were, he could not direct the battle as a whole. That, he decided reluctantly, was more important, at least for the moment.

"Back to M'Sak! Back to M'Sak!" The shout reached him over the din of battle and the yells of his own warriors.

"Amateurs," he snorted.

"They aren't fond of us, are they?" Z'Yon observed from beside him.

"They'll be even less fond of us if they keep advancing a while longer." *And,* V'Zek thought but did not say, *if my own line holds together.* He would never have dared try this with the T'Kai semirabble. Even with good troops, a planned fighting retreat was dangerous. It could turn unplanned in an instant.

But if it didn't . . . if it didn't, he would get in some fighting after all.

Being a trader was different from what Jennifer had expected. So was watching a battle. It was also a good deal worse. Those were real intelligent beings trying to kill one another down there. Those were real body fluids that spurted from wounds, real limbs that lay quivering on the ground after being hacked away from their former owners, real eyestalks that halberds and bills sliced off, real G'Bur who would never walk or see again but who were in anguish now and might well live on, maimed, for years.

She tried to detach herself from what she was seeing, tried to imagine it as something not real, something only happening on the screen. Koniev or Marya, she thought, would have no trouble doing that; about Greenberg she was less sure. She knew she had no luck. What she watched was real, and she could not make herself pretend it was only a screen drama. Too many of these actors would never get up after the taping was done.

So she watched and tried not to be sick. The really frustrating thing was that, in spite of having a full view of the whole battlefield, she could not fathom what, if anything, V'Zek was up to. The T'Kai right wing was holding; the left, by now, had actually advanced several hundred meters.

This, she thought with something as close to contempt as her mild nature allowed, was the sort of fighting that had made V'Zek feared all through the T'Kai confederacy? It only showed that on a world with poor communications, any savage could build up a name for himself that he didn't come close to deserving.

F'Rev had no idea what the battle as a whole looked like. The commander-of-fifty had his own, smaller problems. His troop was in the T'Kai center. The line he was holding had stretched thin when the army's left claw drove back the barbarians: it had been forced to stretch to accommodate its lengthened front.

Now it could not stretch any further. He sent a messenger over to the troop on his immediate right, asking for more warriors.

The messenger returned, eyestalks lowered in apprehension. "Well?" F'Rev growled. "Where are the reinforcements?"

"He has none to send, sir," the messenger said nervously. "He is as thin on the ground as we are."

"A pestilence!" F'Rev burst out. "What am I supposed to do now?"

V'Zek's guards almost killed the red-striped messenger before he reached the chieftain—after one try on their master's life, they were not about to permit another. But when the fellow's bona fides were established, he proved to bring welcome news.

"There's a stretch in the center, three or four troops wide, my master, where they're only a warrior or two thick," he told V'Zek.

Z'Yon, who heard the gasped-out message, bent before V'Zek so that his plastron scraped the ground. "Just as you foretold, my master," the shaman said, more respectful than V'Zek ever remembered hearing him.

The chieftain knew he had earned that respect. He felt the way bards sometimes said they did when songs seemed to shape themselves as they were sung, as if even the sun rose and set according to his will. It was better than mating, purer than the feeling he got from chewing the leaves of the *p'sta* tree.

Neither moment nor feeling was to be wasted. "Now we fight back harder here," he told the subchiefs who led his army's right claw. "We've drawn them away from their strongpoint; now we'll make them pay for coming out."

"About time," one of his underlings said. "Going backward against these soft-shells was making my eyestalks itch."

"Scratch, then, but not too hard. I want you to hold their left in place, make it retreat a little if you like, but not too far."

"Why not?" the subchief demanded indignantly.

"Because that would only hurt them. I intend to kill." V'Zek was already running full tilt toward the center. Here indeed was his chance to fight.

"The M'Sak aren't giving up any more ground on the left," Jennifer reported into Greenberg's ear. "I suppose the T'Kai charge has run out of steam now that they're down onto flat ground." A moment later she added, "The barbarians are shifting a little toward the center, or at least V'Zek is moving that way."

"Anything serious there, do you think?" the master merchant asked.

After her usual hesitation, Jennifer said, "I doubt it. What can he do that he hasn't already failed with on the left? He—" She stopped again. When she resumed, all she said was, "My God."

This time, Greenberg did not blame her for halting. He could not yet see what had gone wrong, but he could hear that something had. He snapped, "What is it, Jennifer?"

"They found a soft spot in the line somehow—the M'Sak in the T'Kai line, I mean." Another wait, this time for Jennifer to collect herself. "Hundreds of them are pouring through. They're turning in on the T'Kai left wing and—rolling it up, is that the phrase?"

"That's the phrase," the master merchant said grimly.

Along with Koniev and Marya, he ran to try to stem the rout. Long before he reached the rupture point, he knew it was hopeless. No mere thumb could repair this dike. The few M'Sak the humans dropped did not influence the battle in the least.

From the *Flying Festoon,* Jennifer said, "I'm sorry I didn't notice anything going wrong."

"I don't think there was anything *to* notice, Jennifer," Koniev told her. "V'Zek didn't find that soft spot in our line—he made it. He lured the left out till the T'Kai got overextended, and then—and now—"

"And now," Jennifer echoed ruefully. "A few minutes ago, I was thinking V'Zek a fool of a general for letting himself get driven down the slope. He must have done it on purpose. That makes me the fool, for not seeing it."

"It makes all of us fools," Greenberg said.

"But he shouldn't have been able to do it," Jennifer protested. "Humans are a lot more sophisticated than any G'Bur, let alone barbarians like the M'Sak. We had the drones watching every move he made, too."

"He managed, though, in spite of everything," Greenberg said. "And that makes him a very nasty enemy indeed."

No one argued with him.

"We are undone!" K'Sed cried. It was not a shout of panic, but rather of disbelief. "They tricked us!" The M'Sak surged against his line and pushed it back. Maybe, he thought much too late, he should not have called for pursuit down off the slope the T'Kai had held. Then, perhaps, he would not have had these screaming, clacking savages in his rear, rolling up his warriors like a moltling folding a shed piece of grasping-claw.

"I did not know trickery was against the rules," B'Rom said. The vizier made as much a point of pride at being unimpressed with everything as V'Zek did with being unafraid. He went on, "After all, we tried to do the same to the M'Sak with what we learned from the Soft Ones."

"The Soft Ones!" K'Sed shouted. "They tricked us, too! They said we would win if we fought here. This whole botch is their fault."

"Oh, twaddle, Your Highness."

K'Sed stared at B'Rom. Under other circumstances, that would have been lese majesty enough to cost the vizier his shell, one painful bit at a time. But now—K'Sed mastered his anger, though he did not forget. "Twaddle, is it?"

"Certainly." Whatever his shortcomings in behavior, B'Rom was no coward. "They told us nothing of the sort that I recall. They said this was a good place to fight, and it is. You can see that with three eyes closed, as can I. But they are traders, not generals—that, unfortunately, is not a deficiency from which V'Zek suffers."

"Unfortunately." K'Sed could play the game of understatement, too. Staying detached was not easy any more, though, not when the line was unraveling like a poorly woven basket and the guards were almost as busy behind the prince as in front of him. He did try. "All these unfortunate things being true, what do you recommend now?"

One of B'Rom's eyestalks pointed behind him and to the left. "Running for the forest yonder seems appropriate at the moment, wouldn't you say? We'll save a remnant that way, rather than all staying in the trap."

"Our right—"

"Is on its own anyway."

K'Sed hissed in despair. B'Rom had a way of being not just right, but brutally right. With a more forceful prince, he would have been killed long since. K'Sed wished he were that sort of prince. The T'Kai confederacy could use such a leader, to oppose V'Zek if for no other reason. He was as he was, though; no help for it. "Very well. We will fall back on the forest." He hoped all the practice he'd put in with the shortspear would stay with him.

Chaos also gripped the T'Kai right claw, if in a less crushing embrace. Still under assault from the M'Sak before them, the T'Kai warriors could do nothing to rescue their cut-off comrades. In fact, the northerners pouring through the gap where the center had been tried to roll them up and treat them like the left.

"Here they come again!" Marya shouted. The humans expended more precious stun charges. M'Sak fell. Others advanced past them. Dying in battle, even strangely, held few terrors for them. They did not know the stun guns were not lethal, but they had seen enough to be sure the weapons were not all-powerful.

Pavel Koniev perturbed them more than the stun guns could when he sprang out and shrieked "Boo!" at the top of his lungs. The cry was as alien to their clicks, hisses, and pops as his fleshy body was to their hard integuments. Not even their stories held ghosts as strange as he.

But the M'Sak were soldiers, and they were winning. As with the *Flying Festoon,* the mere appearance of the unknown was not enough to daunt them. They rushed forward, weapons ready. The humans snapped shots at them. As with any hurried shooting, they missed more often than they wanted to. And they had time to press trigger buttons just once or twice before the M'Sak were on them.

Marya's scream made the shout Koniev had let out sound like

a whisper. The warrior in front of her was startled enough to make only a clumsy swipe with his partisan. She ducked under it, stunned him at close range, then dashed up to crush the brain-nodes under his suddenly flaccid eyestalks.

Koniev did not use his stunner. He killed his foe with exactly the same move he had practiced on the way north. Then, orange body liquids dripping from his mace, he stood on the fallen M'Sak's carapace and roared out a challenge to the local's comrades. The challenge went unanswered.

Greenberg did not find out till later how his friends fared. At the time, he was too busy staying alive to pay them much attention. He threw himself flat to avoid a halberd thrust, then leaped up and grabbed the polearm below the head to wrestle it away from the M'Sak who wielded it.

That was a mistake. G'Bur were no stronger than humans, but their four grasping-limbs let them exert a lot more leverage. Greenberg found himself flung around till he felt like a fly on the end of a fisherman's line. He lost his grip and fell in a heap. The M'Sak swung up the halberd for the kill.

Before he could bring it down, he had to parry a blow from a T'Kai. The soldiers from the southern confederacy were frantically counterattacking. Greenberg scrambled to his feet. "Thanks!" he shouted to the warrior who had saved him. He doubted the local had done so out of any great love for humans. But if the right wing of the T'Kai army was to escape as a fighting force, it could not let itself be flanked like the luckless left. Greenberg did not care about why the local had rescued him. Any excuse would do.

The M'Sak gave ground grudgingly, but they gave ground. More and more of them went off to finish routing the left—and to plunder corpses. That was easier, more profitable work than fighting troops still ready to fight back. The T'Kai right broke free of its assailants and retreated south and east along the bank of the stream that protected its flank. The three humans trudged along with it.

Jennifer turned on the *Flying Festoon*'s spotlight. A finger of light stabbed down from the sky. The ship descended, its siren wailing. She wished it were a rocket like the ones she read about—then it might incinerate thousands of M'Sak with its fiery blast. Sometimes mundane contragravity was too safe to be useful.

By then, the M'Sak took the starship for granted. They ignored it until it came down on top of several of them and smashed them into wet smears beneath it. The rest scattered. Jennifer ordered the air lock open. Her comrades laughed in delight as they scrambled inside. "It's a weapon after all!" Greenberg shouted.

"Why, so it is," Jennifer said. "Do you want to start squashing them by ones and twos?"

After a moment, Greenberg shook his head. "Not worth it, I don't think—might as well go smashing cockroaches with an anvil."

"All right," she said. She looked in the viewscreen. "They are running away."

"Good. That will let this half of the army get loose." Greenberg ran a grimy forearm across his face. He was swaying where he stood. "I don't believe I've ever been this tired in my life. I think we'll spend the next couple of nights in the ship."

"All right," Jennifer said again. She stifled a small sigh. With everyone else aboard, she wouldn't get much reading done.

Jennifer walked along the wall of the little town of D'Opt. Her reader was in her pocket; Bernard Greenberg walked beside her. They both looked out at the M'Sak who ringed the place. Jennifer wished the barbarians seemed further away. D'Opt was barely important enough to rate a wall; its four meters of baked brick sufficed to keep out brigands. Keeping out V'Zek and his troopers was likely to be something else again.

Walking-claws clattered on the bricks, close by her. She turned her head. So did Greenberg. He had the higher rank, so he spoke to K'Sed. "Your Highness."

The prince did not answer for some time. Like the humans, he was looking out at the encircling enemy. At last he said, "I wish we were back in T'Kai City."

"So do I, Your Highness," Greenberg said. Jennifer nodded. T'Kai City's walls were twice as high and three times as thick as those of D'Opt, and made of stone in the bargain.

"You Soft Ones could have done more to help us get there," K'Sed said—crabbily, Jennifer thought. She supposed the prince was not to be blamed for his bad temper. K'Sed had certainly had a hard time of it. Skulking through the woods and fleeing for one's life were not pastimes for which princes usually trained.

But Greenberg said, "Your Highness, were it not for us, you would have no army left at all, and the M'Sak would be running loose through the whole confederacy. As is, you are strong enough still to force them to concentrate against you here."

"But not strong enough to beat them," K'Sed retorted. "That

only delays matters, does it not? Had we fought them somewhere else, we might have won."

The unfairness of that almost took Jennifer's breath away. For once, she did not hesitate. Before Greenberg could reply to the prince, she blurted, "But you might have lost everything, too!" *You likely would have lost everything,* she said to herself.

"We'll never know now, will we?" K'Sed sounded as if he thought he had scored a point. "And after the fight, you did little to keep the barbarians off us."

"We did what we could, Your Highness," Greenberg said. "I am sorry the M'Sak did not oblige us by holding still to be smashed one at a time."

His sarcasm reached the prince where Jennifer's protest had failed. K'Sed bent his left walking-legs, letting that side of his plastron almost scrape the bricks—a G'Bur gesture of despondency. "I knew this campaign was ill-omened when we undertook it. Even the moon fights against us."

It was late afternoon. Greenberg and Jennifer looked eastward. She rarely gave L'Rau's moon a thought—why worry about a dead stone lump several hundred thousand kilometers away? It looked as uninteresting now as ever: a gibbous light in the sky, especially pale and washed out because the sun was still up.

"What about the moon, Your Highness?" she said.

"When it grows full, three days hence, it will be eclipsed," K'Sed told her, as if that explained everything.

"Well, what of it?" She was so surprised, she forgot to tack on K'Sed's honorific. "You must know what causes an eclipse?"

The prince was distraught enough to miss her faux pas. He answered, "Of course—the passage of our world's shadow over the face of the moon. Every enlightened citizen of the towns in the confederacy knows this." K'Sed turned one eyestalk toward the soldiers swarming through D'Opt's narrow streets. "Peasants, herders, and even artisans, though, still fear the malign powers they believe to stalk the night."

"That is not good," Greenberg said.

Jennifer thought he'd come up with one of the better understatements she'd heard. As low-technology worlds went, L'Rau, or at least the T'Kai confederacy, was relatively free from superstition. But the key word was *relatively.* And because humans dealt mostly with nobles and wealthy traders, she did not have a good feel for just how credulous the vast majority of the locals were.

She had also missed something else. K'Sed pointed it out for her, literally, gesturing toward the bronze-hued T'Kai banners that still fluttered defiance at the M'Sak. "Perhaps our color is ill-chosen," the prince said, "but when the swallowed moon appears in that shade, how will the ignorant doubt it implies their being devoured by M'Sak? Truly, I could almost wonder myself." K'Sed *was* a sophisticate, Jennifer reminded herself, but even sophisticates on primitive planets found long-buried fears rising when trouble came.

"Maybe we could teach your soldiers—" Jennifer stopped, feeling Greenberg's ironic eye turned her way. She realized she'd been foolish. Three days of lessons would not overturn a lifetime's belief. She asked, "Do your warriors know the eclipse is coming, your Highness?"

"Sadly, they do. We tried to keep it from them, but even the M'Sak, savages though they be, have got wind of it. From time to time they amuse themselves by shouting it up to our sentries, and shouting that they will destroy us on that night. I fear . . ." K'Sed hesitated, went on, "I fear they may be right."

"Are you sure it is prudent to warn our foes of what we intend?" Z'Yon asked, listening to the M'Sak warriors yelling threats at the southrons trapped in D'Opt.

"Why not?" V'Zek said grandly. "We spread fear through their ranks, and anticipation of disaster. Having them with their eye-stalks going every which way at once can only help us. And besides, they cannot be sure we are not lying. Almost I find myself tempted to delay the assault until the darkening of the moon is past."

"That might be wise, my master," Z'Yon said.

"What? Why?" When V'Zek stretched his walking-legs very straight, as he did now, he towered over Z'Yon. His voice, ominously deep and slow, rumbled like distant thunder—*not distant enough,* the shaman thought. He sank down to scrape his plastron in the dirt. "Why?" V'Zek repeated. "Speak, if you value your claws."

"The moltings suggest, my master, that we may fare better under those circumstances."

"So you consulted the moltings, did you?" The chieftain let the question hang in the air.

Z'Yon felt its weight over him, as if it were the big metal sky-thing that had crushed a fair number of M'Sak to jelly. "You said I might, my master," he reminded V'Zek, "for my own amusement."

"For yours, perhaps. I, shaman, am not amused at your maunderings. On the given night we shall attack and we shall win. If you put any other interpretation on what the moltings say, you will no longer be amused, either; that I promise you. Do you grasp my meaning?"

"With all four claws, my master," Z'Yon assured him, and fled.

Jennifer watched Greenberg cut another piece from the juicy, rare prime rib. "The condemned man ate a hearty meal," he said, and cocked an eyebrow at her. "Is that a quotation from your ancient science fiction?"

She paused to swallow and cut a fresh piece for herself. The *Flying Festoon*'s autochef did right by beef and nearly everything else, though Koniev swore its vodka was good only for putting in thermometers. She answered, "No. I think it's even older than that."

"Probably is," Marya agreed. "It sounds as if any society would find it handy."

"No doubt," Greenberg said. "The T'Kai would certainly think it was relevant tonight." He told the others what he and Jennifer had learned from K'Sed.

Koniev nodded slowly. "I've heard the barbarians shouting their threats. I didn't take much notice; the translator garbles them a lot of the time, anyway. But they're not bluffing, then?"

"Not even a little bit," Greenberg said. "That's why we'll stay close by the ship. We may have to pull out in a hurry, and fighting my way back to the *Flying Festoon* through a mob of panicked or bloodthirsty G'Bur is something I'd rather not even have nightmares about."

"Sensible," Koniev said. Marya nodded a moment later.

"Too bad the T'Kai won't be able to take ship with us," Jennifer said.

"Yes—a good market will close down if the confederacy goes under," Marya said. "V'Zek won't be eager to deal with us, I'm certain."

"That's not what I meant!" Jennifer said angrily. She noticed the others staring at her and realized that until now she'd never been interested enough in what they were doing to get angry. She went on, "We'll be running away while the highest culture on this planet goes under. That counts for more than markets, if you ask me."

"Of course it does," Greenberg said. "I told you as much before, when you were setting out the drones, remember? Why do you think we've put so much effort into trying to save T'Kai? No matter how much money's on the line, I wouldn't do foot-soldier duty for a people I didn't like and respect. Do the characters in your old books care that much for profit?"

She bit her lip. "No, of course not—they're supposed to be true to life, you know."

"All right, then." Greenberg sounded relieved, maybe because he wanted her to stay involved. "What we've been trying to do, then, is—"

"Wait," Jennifer told him.

He, Koniev, and Marya stared again—she hardly ever interrupted. She ignored them. She got up from the table and dashed—again something new—for her cabin. Behind her, Koniev said, "What's twisting her tail?" She ignored that, too.

She returned a couple of minutes later with her reader set to the right part of the story she'd found. She held it out to Greenberg. "Here. Look at this, please. I think it's important."

Greenberg set the reader on his nose. He took it off again a moment later. "Jennifer, I'm sorry, but I can't make heads or tails of Middle English, or whatever the right name for this is. What are you trying to show me?"

She made an exasperated noise and took back the reader. She peered into it, then returned it to him. "This story is called 'The Man Who Sold the Moon.' Do you see the circle, here and on this page?" She hit the FORWARD button. "And here—" She hit it again, "—and here?"

"The one with '6+' printed inside it? Yes, I see it. What's it supposed to be, some sort of magic symbol?"

She told him what it was supposed to be. He and Marya and Koniev all looked at one another. "This Heinlein person didn't think small, I have to give him that," Greenberg said slowly. "But I still don't quite follow how you think it applies to our problem here."

She knew she looked disappointed; she'd expected Greenberg to catch fire from her own inspiration. It was almost poetically apt, she thought: she'd planned to use trading to help her study Middle English science fiction, and now the Middle English science fiction might help her fellow traders. She did some more explaining.

Koniev said, "Where would we get enough soot, or for that matter rockets?"

"We don't need rockets," Jennifer said, "and soot wouldn't do us much good here, either. Instead . . ."

She outlined her plan and watched the three traders think it over. Koniev spoke first. "It might even work, which puts it light-years ahead of anything else we've got going for us."

"Pulling out the *Flying Festoon* will be tricky, though," Marya said.

Greenberg said, "Some of us will have to stay behind, to show the T'Kai we aren't abandoning them." He sounded unhappy at the idea, but firm. "All of us but Jennifer, I think. This is her hobbyhorse; let her ride it if she can."

"And let her—and us—hope she'll be able to rescue us if she can't," Marya said.

Jennifer gulped. If her scheme didn't work out as advertised, she'd be a long way away when D'Opt fell. Academia hadn't prepared her for having lives rest on what she did. "It will work," she said. Her nails bit into the palms of her hands. She knew she'd better be right.

V'Zek sent the T'Kai female scuttling out of his tent when the guard called that Z'Yon would have speech with him. "This is important, I take it?" the chieftain rumbled. It was not a question. It was more like a threat.

Z'Yon stooped low, but managed to keep the ironic edge in his voice. "It is, unless you would sooner not know that the great sky-thing has departed from D'Opt."

"Has it indeed?" V'Zek forgot about the female, though her shell was delicately fluted and the joints of her legs amazingly limber. "So the Soft Ones give up on their friends at last, do they?" He wished the weird creatures were long gone; without their meddling, he would have overwhelmed T'Kai without having to work nearly so hard.

Then Z'Yon brought his suddenly leaping spirits down once more. "My master, the Soft Ones themselves are still in D'Opt. They have been seen on the walls since the sky-thing left."

The chieftain cursed. "They are still plotting something, then. Well, let them plot. The moon still grows dark and red tomorrow night, and the Soft Ones cannot alter that. And our warriors will fight well, for they know the darkened moon portends the fall of T'Kai. They know that because, of course, you have been diligent in instructing them, have you not, Z'Yon?"

"Of course, my master." The shaman suppressed a shudder. V'Zek was most dangerous when he sounded mildest. As soon as Z'Yon could, he escaped from the chieftain's presence. He wondered how many eyestalks he would have been allowed to keep had he not followed V'Zek's orders in every particular. Surely no more than one, he thought, and shuddered again.

V'Zek watched the shaman go. He knew Z'Yon had doubts about the whole enterprise. He had doubts himself. The Soft Ones alarmed him. Their powers, even brought to bear without much martial skill, were great enough to be daunting. He would much rather have had them on his side than as foes. But he had beaten them and their chosen allies before, and after one more win they would have no allies left. For a moment, he even thought about trading with them afterward. He wondered what they would want for the weapons that shot sleep as if it were an arrow.

But even more, he wondered what they were up to.

The guard broke his chain of thought. "My master, shall I fetch back the female?"

"Eh? No, don't bother. I've lost the mood. After we win tomorrow, we'll all enjoy plenty of these southron shes."

"Aye, that we will!" The guard sounded properly eager. V'Zek wished he could match the fellow's enthusiasm.

Jennifer looked at L'Rau in the viewscreen. The world was small enough to cover with the palm of her hand. Away from the *Flying Festoon,* the ship's robots were busy getting everything into shape for tonight. She'd had to hit the computer's override to force it to make the gleaming metal spheroids do as she ordered.

At last, everything was the way she wanted it. She still had a good many hours of waiting before she could do anything else. She got into bed and went to sleep.

Her last fuzzy thought was that Heinlein would have approved.

L'Rau's sun set. Across the sky, the moon rose. The shadow of the world had already begun to crawl across it. The M'Sak raised a clamor when they saw the eclipse. Their tumult sounded like thousands of percussion instruments coming to demented life all at once.

The translator could handle some of their dialect. Most of their threats were the same stupid sort soldiers shouted on any planet: warnings of death and maiming. But some M'Sak showed imaginative flair, not least the barbarian who asked the defenders inside D'Opt for the names of their females, so he would know what to call them when he got to T'Kai City.

The hubbub outside the walls faded. An enormous G'Bur came out from among the soldiers. This, Greenberg thought, had to be the fearsome V'Zek. "Surrender!" he shouted up at the T'Kai. He used the southern speech so well, the translator never hiccuped. "I give you this one last chance. Look to the sky—even the heavens declare your downfall is at hand."

Prince K'Sed waved a grasping-claw to Greenberg. The master merchant stepped out where the M'Sak could see him; he hoped the sight of a human still had some power to unsettle them. "You are wrong, V'Zek," he said. The translator, and amplifiers all along the wall, sent his reply booming forth, louder than any G'Bur could bellow.

"Roar as loud as you like, Soft One," V'Zek said. "Your trifling tricks grow boring, and we are no hatchlings, to be taken in by them. As the sky-*f'noi* makes the moon bleed, so we will bleed you tonight, and all T'Kai thereafter." The M'Sak warriors shouted behind him.

"You are wrong, V'Zek," Greenberg repeated. "Watch the sky if you doubt me, for it too will show T'Kai's power."

"Lie as much as you like. It will not save you." V'Zek turned to his troopers. "Attack!"

M'Sak dashed into archery range and began to shoot, trying to sweep defenders from the walls. The T'Kai shot back. Greenberg hastily ducked behind a parapet. He was more vulnerable to arrows than any local.

"What if you are wrong, Soft One, and your ploy fails?" Only B'Rom would have asked that question.

"Then we die," Greenberg said, a reply enough to the point to silence even the cynical vizier. B'Rom walked away; had he been a human, he would have been shaking his head.

Arrows ripped through the T'Kai banners above the master merchant. He glanced up. The grasping-claw that stood for the confederacy had a hole in it. Not liking the symbolism of that, he looked away.

Shouts and alarmed clatterings came from the wall not far away. The translator gabbled in overload, then produced a word Greenberg could understand. "Ladders!"

Though poles set into a wall sufficed for the G'Bur, when such aids were absent the locals, because of the way they were built, needed wider and more cumbersome ladders than humans used. That did not stop the M'Sak from slapping them against the walls of D'Opt and swarming toward the top. In fact, it made the defenders' job harder than it would have been in medieval human siege warfare—being heavier than scaling ladders made for humans, these were harder to topple.

Without exposing more than his arm, Greenberg expended a stun cartridge when the top of a ladder poked over the wall. The barbarian nearly at the level of the battlements tumbled back onto his comrades below. They all crashed to the ground. Cheering, the T'Kai used a forked pole to push over the suddenly empty ladder.

"Good idea!" Koniev shouted. He imitated Greenberg. Another set of crashes, another overturned ladder.

"I'd like it better if I had more than—" Greenberg checked the charge gauge, "—half a dozen shots left."

"Eight here," Koniev said. Marya was somewhere off around the wall's circuit. Greenberg hoped she would not stop an arrow. For that matter, he hoped he would not stop one himself.

"Ladders!" The cry came from two directions at once. The master merchant looked at the moon. L'Rau's shadow covered more than half of it, but totality was still close to an hour away. "Ladders!" This shout was further away. *Click-pop-hiss-click:* By now, Greenberg had heard the T'Kai word often enough to recognize it in the original, even if he needed electronics to reproduce it.

"Lad—" This time, the cry cut off abruptly after *click-pop*—an arrow must have found its mark. The M'Sak were throwing everything they had into this attack. Greenberg worried. Jennifer hadn't counted on the possibility of D'Opt's falling in a hurry. Neither had he. If that was a mistake, it was likely to be his last one.

"Forward!" V'Zek roared. "Forward!" He wished he could have gone up the first ladder and straight into D'Opt. Waiting behind the scenes for his warriors to do the job was the hardest part of being chieftain. He corrected himself: no, the hardest part was knowing he needed to hold back, and not giving in to the urge to go wild and slaughter.

If he suppressed that urge all the time, he wondered, would he be civilized? He found the idea ridiculous. He would only be bored.

He cast two critical eyes on the fighting, turned a third to Z'Yon, who was clipping a wounded M'Sak's shell so no sharp edges would further injure the soft tissues inside. His fourth eye, as it had been most of the night, was on the moon. The fully lit portion grew ever smaller.

"You were right, shaman," he said, an enormous concession from him. But even a chieftain felt small and insignificant when the natural order of the world turned upside down.

Z'Yon did not answer until he had finished his task—had his

prediction been wrong, he would have dared no such liberty. What would have happened to him had he been wrong was unpleasant to contemplate anyhow. He hoped he sounded casual rather than relieved when he said, "So it seems."

"The warriors truly know the meaning of the prodigy," V'Zek went on. "They fight bravely. I think they will force an entrance into the town not long after the whole moon goes into the jaws of the *f'noi* in the sky. You did well in instructing them and insuring that they would be of stout spirit for the battle."

"I did as you commanded, my master." Z'Yon's eyestalks tingled in remembered fright. A ladder went over, directly in front of the shaman and his chieftain. Injured M'Sak flailed legs in pain. One lay unmoving. "They fight well inside D'Opt, too."

"Doubtless their leaders and the Soft Ones have filled them with nonsense so they will not despair at our might," V'Zek said scornfully. "And see over there!" He pointed with a grasping-claw. "We've gained a stretch of wall! Surely the end cannot be far away."

"Surely not, my master." Z'Yon wished he had not taken omens with the moltings; he would have had no qualms now about being as excited as V'Zek. He tried to stifle his doubts. He had been wrong before, often enough.

The last bit of white disappeared from the moon. V'Zek shouted in a voice huge enough to pierce the tumult. "Now we hold the moment between our claws! Strike hard and T'Kai falls. The sky gives us victory!"

"The sky gives us victory!" the warriors cried, and redoubled their efforts. The dim red light made seeing hard, but cries of alarm from the walls showed places where the M'Sak were gaining fresh clawholds. Z'Yon decided he had been wrong again after all.

The last bit of white disappeared from the moon. "Now's the time, Jennifer," Greenberg said quietly into his comm unit. "Get things rolling, or the T'Kai have had it."

The pause that followed was longer than speed-of-light could account for. The master merchant started to call down curses on Jennifer's head. He wished he could take her damned reader and wrap it around her neck. He was starting to get more creative than that when she said, "Initiated."

He checked his watch. The delay had been less than fifteen seconds. All she'd done, obviously, was start the program before she answered him. He felt ashamed of himself. The fighting had screwed up his time sense.

He hoped he hadn't waited too long. T'Kai warriors fought desperately to keep the M'Sak from enlarging the two or three lodgments they had on top of the wall and to keep them from dropping down into D'Opt. If the southerners broke now, nothing could save them. But if he'd told Jennifer to start before the eclipse was total, odds were her scheme would have been wasted.

Too late for ifs now, anyhow. He wondered how long things would take at the *Flying Festoon*'s end. When he judged the moment ripe, he started the tape that was loaded into his translator. The amplifiers around the wall made all the battle din, all V'Zek's shouts, seem as whispers beside his voice. "The very heavens proclaim the glory of T'Kai! Look to the sky, you who doubt, and you will see the truth writ large on the face of the moon itself!"

The message repeated, over and over. In the spaces between, the master merchant heard what he most hoped for: quiet. T'Kai and M'Sak alike were peering upward with all their eyes.

"Hurry up, Jennifer, dammit," Greenberg muttered. He made sure the translator could not pick up what he said.

"... Look to the sky, you who doubt, and you will see the truth writ large on the face of the moon itself!" That roar might have been enough to frighten the M'Sak troops, had they not heard it before. More Soft One trickery, V'Zek thought, and handled as ineptly as the rest of their stunts.

Nevertheless, he looked. He could not help it, not with that insistent great voice echoing and re-echoing on his tympanic membrane. The moon remained dim and bronze—alarming, but alarming in a familiar way.

V'Zek laughed, loud and long. The last bluff had failed. No one but the *f'noi* in the sky could harm the moon, and from the *f'noi* it always won free in the end.

"Lies!" V'Zek shouted. "Lies!"

And as he watched, as he shouted, the moon changed.

A light-sail is nothing more than a gauze-thin sheet of aluminized plastic, thousands of kilometers across. When fully extended, it holds photons' energy as a seaboat's sail traps the wind. As it needs no internal power source, it makes a good emergency propulsion system for a starship.

Normally, one thinks only of the light-sail catching photons. No one cares what happens to them afterward. Jennifer did not think normally. A corner of her mouth twisted—on that, no doubt, she and Greenberg would agree. She'd realized the light-sail could also act as a mirror, and, with the ship's robots trimming it, a mirror of very special shape.

She'd been ready for more than a day. She was, in fact, reading when Greenberg called her, but she wasted no time getting things under way. The adjustment was small, tilting the mirror a couple of degrees so the light it reflected shone on L'Rau's moon instead of streaming past into empty space.

As soon as she was sure the robots were performing properly, she went back to rereading "The Man Who Sold the Moon."

The wait seemed to stretch endlessly. The M'Sak were not going to pause much longer, Greenberg thought, not with their chieftain screaming "Lies!" every few seconds. Then golden light touched the edge of the moon, which should have stayed bronze and faint upwards of another hour.

The light stayed at the edge only a moment. Faster by far than L'Rau's patient shadow, the radiant grasping-claw hurried to its appointed place in the center of the moon's disk, so that it became a celestial image of the emblem of T'Kai.

The warriors of the confederacy suddenly pressed against their foes with new spirit. The humans had promised a miracle, but few, Greenberg knew, believed or understood. Asking a planetbound race to grasp everything starfarers could do was asking a lot. But since the prodigy worked for them, they were glad enough to accept it.

As for the M'Sak— "Flee!" Greenberg shouted into the translator. "Flee, lest the wrath of heaven strike you down!" The barbarians needed little urging.

"Hold fast!" V'Zek shrieked. A warrior ran by him. The warrior also shrieked, but wordlessly. All his eyes were on the moon, the horrible, lying moon. V'Zek tried to grab him. He broke away from the chieftain's grip and ran on. V'Zek swung a hatchet at him, but missed.

The chieftain's mandibles ground together in helpless fury. Moments before, he had led an army fine enough to satisfy even him. Now it was only a mob, full of fear. "Hold fast!" he cried again. "If we hold, we will win tomorrow."

"They will not hold," Z'Yon said softly. Even the shaman, curse him, had three eyes on the sky. "And tomorrow, there will be ambuscades behind every tree, every rock. We daunted T'Kai before. Now we will be lucky to win back to our own forests again."

V'Zek's eyestalks lowered morosely. The shaman was likely right. The M'Sak had gone into every fight *knowing* these effete southrons could never stand against them. And they never had. But now—now the T'Kai, curse them, *knew* the very heavens fought for them. Worse, so did his own warriors.

He turned on Z'Yon. "Why did you fail to warn me of this?"

"My master?" Z'Yon squawked, taken aback. Too taken aback, in fact, for he blurted out the truth. "My master, I did tell you the moltings indicated the need for caution—"

"A pestilence on the moltings!" Before V'Zek was aware of willing his grasping-claw to strike, the hatchet he carried leaped out and crashed through Z'Yon's shell, just to the left of the shaman's center pair of eyestalks. Z'Yon was dead almost before his plastron hit the ground.

V'Zek braced and pulled the hatchet free. Killing Z'Yon, he discovered, solved nothing, for the shaman's words remained true. There was no arguing him out of them any more, either. And a little while later V'Zek, like his beaten, frightened warriors, fled north from D'Opt.

Until the sky-*f'noi* began to relinquish its grip on the moon, the hateful emblem of T'Kai glared down at them. Forever after, it was branded in their spirits. As Z'Yon had foretold—another bitter truth—few found home again.

L'Rau's sun grew visibly smaller, visibly fainter in the holovid tank as the *Flying Festoon* accelerated toward hyperdrive kick-in. Jennifer waited eagerly for it to disappear. Civilization lay on the other side of the starjump. "Back to the university," she said dreamily.

Bernard Greenberg heard her. He chuckled. "I won't miss L'Rau myself, I tell you that. Anytime you have to bring off a miracle to get out in one piece, you're working too hard."

He spoke to her differently now; he had ever since she'd brought the *Flying Festoon* back to the planet. He'd kissed her then, too, where before he'd hardly seemed to notice her as anything save a balky tool. *But I'm not balky any more,* she realized: she'd proved herself a part of the crew worth having. A kiss of acceptance was worth a hundred of the sort men tried to press on her just because of the way she looked.

"Speaking of miracles, that eclipse was visible over a whole hemisphere," Koniev said. "I wonder what G'Bur who've never heard of T'Kai made of it." He took a sip of ship's vodka. For once he was not complaining about it—a measure of his relief.

"Giving the next generation's scribes and scholars something new to worry about isn't necessarily a bad thing," Marya said. She moved slowly and carefully, but X-rays said she had only an enormous bruise on her shoulder from a slingstone, not a broken collarbone. Left-handed, she raised her glass in salute. "Speaking of which, here's to the scholar who got us out." She drank.

"And with a profit," Koniev said. He drank.

"And with a civilization saved and a market for our next trip," Greenberg said. He drank.

Jennifer felt herself turning pink. She drank, too. After that, even her ears heated. "Speech!" Marya called, which made Jennifer swallow wrong and cough.

"A pleasure to pound your back," Greenberg said gallantly. "Are you all right now?" At her nod, he grinned. "Good, because I want to hear this speech, too."

"I—don't really have one to make," she said with her usual hesitancy. "I'm just glad it all worked out." A moment later, she added, "And very glad to be going home."

"Aren't we all?" Greenberg said. Koniev and Marya lifted their glasses again, in silent agreement. The master merchant also drank. Then he asked, "What are you going to do, once you're back?"

"Why, go back to school, of course, and work on my thesis some more," Jennifer said, surprised he needed to ask. "What else would I do?"

"Have you ever thought about making another run with us?"

"Why ever would you want me to?" Jennifer said. She was not altogether blind to what went on around her, and a long way from stupid; more than once, she suspected, Greenberg must been been tempted to leave her on L'Rau.

But now he said, "Because nothing succeeds like success. This little coup of yours will win you journeyman status, you know, and a share of the profits instead of straight salary. And with your, uh, academic background—" Jennifer guessed he'd been about to say "odd academic background," but he hadn't—quite. "—you'd be useful to have along. Who knows? You might come up with another stunt to match this one."

"You really mean it, don't you?" She had trouble believing her ears.

"Yes, I do," Greenberg said firmly.

"We'd like to have you along," Marya agreed. Koniev nodded.

"Thank you," Jennifer said. "Thank you more than I can say." She went over and kissed Greenberg. She found she didn't mind at all when his arm slipped around her waist. But she still shook her head. "Once, for me, is enough. I feel very certain of that. The university suits me fine."

"All right," Greenberg said. "I'll see you get rated journeyman anyhow. You've earned it, whether you choose to use it or not."

"Thanks," she said again. "That's very kind. I won't turn you down. Not, mind you, that I ever *will* use it."

"Of course not," Greenberg said.

She looked at him sharply. As a master merchant, he was used to—and good at—manipulating people to get his way. *Not this time, you won't,* she thought.

THE ATHETERS

III

The tall fur crest above Gazar's eyes rippled slightly. With Atheters, Jennifer thought, that was supposed to mean they were going to get down to serious business. She hoped so. Gazar had shown her nothing but junk—well, not junk, but certainly nothing worth taking offworld—for the past two hours.

As the Atheter merchant rummaged through his wicker basket, Jennifer wondered, for far from the first time, what she was doing sitting cross-legged on a fat tree branch dickering with an alien who looked like a blue plush chimpanzee with a prehensile tail. She'd firmly intended to teach Middle English literature after a single trading run gave her a taste of the life Middle English science fiction writers tried to imagine.

That had been two trips ago, now. She still hadn't quite worked out why she'd signed up for her second trip. Had she really been *that* depressed about not getting the first teaching job she'd applied for?

She stopped the useless worrying as Gazar's big golden eyes—his least-chimplike feature—went wide. He'd found what he was looking for, then. With a fine dramatic sense, he held whatever it was concealed between his six-fingered hands. He started squawking. The translator Jennifer wore on her belt turned his words into Spanglish. "Here, my fellow trader, is something not many will be able to show you."

"Let me see—" Jennifer's soft, breathy voice didn't activate the translator. She tried again, louder. "Let me see it, please." The machine let out a series of raucous squawks and shrieks.

"Here." Crest erect with pride, Gazar opened his hands. "This is carved *omphoth* ivory, which of course means it is very, very old."

"Why 'of course'?" Had Gazar not made an issue of it, Jennifer would have taken him at his word. The ivory of the figurine was yellowed, the carving in a style unlike anything she had seen on Athet: it was vigorous, exuberant, unsophisticated but highly skilled. Back in civilization, collectors would pay a lot for it.

"Surely any nestling knows—" Gazar began. Then he let out a high-pitched screech that reminded Jennifer of forks on frying pans. To him, it was laughing. He was, in fact, laughing at himself. "But why should you, from the treeless wastes between the stars? 'Of course' because as soon as my earliest ancestors bravely crossed the Empty Lands into this forest, they began to hunt the *omphoth* that roamed here. No *omphoth* has been seen alive in more than a thousand winters."

"Oh." Jennifer was glad the alien would not notice her distaste. Humans, she was sure, had exterminated a lot more species than the Atheters, but they had also learned not to sound proud of it. Maybe, she thought, Gazar had an excuse. "Were these *omphoth* fierce animals, then, that killed and ate your people?"

"They were worse!" Gazar's tail writhed like a fat, pink worm, a sure sign of agitation. "They ate the trees! Fruit, leaves, branches, everything!"

That hit him where he lived, all right, Jennifer thought, in the most literal sense of the word. Atheters were arboreal by evolution and by choice. They only came down from their precious trees for stones and for copper and tin ores. Their domestic animals were as tree-bound as they were. No wonder they called the savannahs that alternated with their rain forests "the Empty Lands."

"No wonder you hunted them, then," Jennifer said soothingly. "What would you want in exchange for this figurine?"

"Ah, so here at last is something that interests you, then? I was beginning to think nothing did." Atheters understood sarcasm just fine. Gazar's tail twitched again, a different motion from the one it had made before; he was deciding how greedy he could be. "You must understand, of course, that because there are no more *omphoth,* the object is irreplaceable, and so doubly precious."

"I suppose so," Jennifer said. The flat tones of the translator made sure she sounded indifferent. She'd hoped Gazar wouldn't think of that.

"Oh, indeed!" Always raucous, his screeches were nearly apoplectic now. "In fact, I would not think of parting with it for less than half a dozen scalpels, two dozen *swissarmyknives*"—the Terran name came out in one squawked burst—"and, let me see, two, no, three bottles of the sweet tailtangler you humans brew."

He meant Amaretto, Jennifer knew. The Atheters were crazy about it. She also knew he had decided to be very greedy indeed. She gasped. The translator turned the noise into a scream of rage worthy of—what was that ancient mythical ape's name?—King Kong, that was it. That was how Atheters gasped. They were a noisy species. Jennifer said, "Why not ask for our ship, while you are at it?"

Gazar's grin exposed formidable teeth. "Would you sell it to me?"

"No. Nor will I give you everything that in your extravagance you demanded. Are you trying to empty all our stores so that we cannot deal with anyone else here?" The haggling went on for some time. It started to grow dark outside Gazar's hut of woven branches. Eventually they agreed on a price. Jennifer rummaged in her backpack. "Here are your two scalpels and fourteen knives. I will come back tomorrow with the bottle of tangletail," she said.

"I trust you so far," Gazar agreed.

"Now I must go back to my ship, while there is still some light." Jennifer stood up. She was not very tall by human standards, but she had to stoop to keep from bumping the ceiling of the hut.

Gazar scurried around to open the door for her, a courtesy she'd read of but one long obsolete on civilized worlds, where doors were smart enough to open themselves. "Until tomorrow," the Atheter merchant said.

"Yes." Jennifer started down the chain ladder the crew of the *Pacific Overtures* used to reach the lower branches of the big trees on which the locals lived. The Atheters carved what they reckoned hand-, foot-, and tailholds into the forest giants' trunks, but for humans, who unfortunately lacked both opposable big toes and any sort of tails, prehensile or otherwise, ladders were infinitely preferable.

Gazar peered anxiously after her. "Be careful down there," he called. "The *omphoth* may be gone, but there are all manners of dangerous beasts."

"I have my weapon that throws sleep," she reminded him. He smiled a big-toothed, reassured smile, then started screaming at the top of his lungs for customers. His shrieks were just a tiny part of the din; living as they did in an environment where they could rarely see far, Atheters advertised with noise.

Jennifer was relieved to descend to the relative quiet of the forest floor. She took out her stunner; she knew Gazar hadn't warned her just for politeness' sake. The ground featured not just the usual assortment of large mammaloid carnivores, but also poisonous lizardy things that struck from ambush out of piles of leaves. The thick boots she wore to protect herself against them were one more reason not to use the locals' routes up and down trees.

Being under those trees, Jennifer discovered, had other risks she hadn't thought of. Something whistled past her face, so close she could feel the breeze it raised, and smacked to earth just in front of her feet. She sprang back in alarm. Without her willing it, her finger went to the stunner's firing button.

But, she saw, it was only one of the big, knobby, hard-skinned fruits that fell from the Atheters' trees. As she looked around, she saw two or three more similar fruits and a couple of scraggly saplings that were not doing at all well as they tried to grow in the gloom cast by their elder relatives.

"A stupid seed," she muttered. Then she shivered. Stupid the seed certainly was, but had it fallen in a spot half a meter different, it would have smashed her skull. As she walked on, she cocked her head to look up every so often. Not just seeds fell from the Atheters' tree, but also rubbish the locals threw out.

After a few hundred meters, she emerged from the forest into a large clearing, almost big enough to be an independent patch of plain. In the middle of it, sunset gleamed off the metallic bulk of *Pacific Overtures.* Jennifer blinked; after forest twilight, the crimson sun-reflections from the ship were dazzling.

She hurried toward it. Less than a hundred meters away, she stumbled over something and nearly fell. As she caught herself, she saw she'd tripped on a stump completely overgrown by grass and low bushes. It had been a big tree once; now it was just a menace to navigation.

She sighed with animal pleasure the moment she got inside *Pacific Overtures.* After the humid heat of the jungle, conditioned air was a blessing. She shook back her long, blond hair, frowned at how heavy and limp with sweat it was. As she had before, she thought about cutting it short. But it helped the Atheters tell her apart from the other humans on *Pacific Overtures,* so she supposed it was worth the bother.

She was into the common room before she realized how much like a trader she was starting to think. Annoyed, she kicked at the carpet.

The scuffing noise made Sam Watson look up from the spice cones he was grading. His eyes lingered. That annoyed Jennifer all over again; hot, grubby, and none too clean, she felt anything but attractive. Men, though, usually seemed to think otherwise.

The once-over ended soon enough not to be offensive. "How'd you do?" Watson asked. "Get anything interesting?"

"As a matter of fact, I did." She took the ivory figurine from her beltpouch and set it on the table in front of him. "Have you ever seen anything like this before?"

He reached for it, then paused. "May I?" At her nod, he picked it up. He was a medium-sized, medium-brown man in his mid-thirties, five or six years older than Jennifer. She suspected he wore his bristly handlebar mustache for the same reason she kept her hair long: to give aliens something by which to recognize him. She couldn't think of any other reason for him to want a black caterpillar in the middle of his face.

The caterpillar twitched as he pursed his lips. "Can't say as I have," he said slowly. "That's an old, old style of carving."

"I thought so, too, though I hadn't seen it before," she nodded. "Gazar—the merchant I got it from—says the animal whose ivory it comes from is a thousand years extinct."

"I wouldn't be surprised, though I've never met a merchant, human or otherwise, who wouldn't stretch things for the sake of profit. Still, it's a pretty piece." He handed it back to her. "If it really is as old and rare as all that, it might even be museum quality."

"Do you think so?" Jennifer felt her pulse race, as if Watson had said a magic word. In a way, he had. Private collectors had only private wealth with which to buy. Museums could draw on the resources of whole planets. If they started bidding against one another, they could make a trader rich for life.

"*Might* be, I said." Watson jabbed a rueful thumb at his spice cones. "One thing certain—none of these is. Some will help make prime Athet brandy, some good brandy, and the rest rotgut. They'll all turn a profit, but no big deal."

"I suppose not." Jennifer daydreamed about what she could do with a really big profit. Heading the list, as always, was setting up—and then occupying—an endowed chair. She smiled, imagining the Jennifer Logan Endowed Chair for the Study of Middle English Science Fiction—maybe even of Middle English Literature, for her interests had broadened since she left the university. "But I'd need to find the *omphoths*' graveyard for that," she murmured.

Watson scratched his head. "The which? For what?"

"Never mind, Sam." Jennifer felt herself flushing. After so many years of ancient literature, she often found herself speaking a foreign language even when she used perfectly good Spanglish.

"All right." Watson shrugged. He was a pragmatic type who did not waste his time worrying about what was of no immediate use to him. That made him narrow, but within his limits acute. "Now that we know your ivory exists, we'll have to see if we can get more. Don't forget to tell Master Rodriguez about it."

"I won't. When do you suppose she'll be back?"

Watson shrugged again. "She's got some sort of complicated deal brewing with the treelords, so she may be gone days yet. Who can say?" He gave a wry chuckle. "Whatever she's up to, it's a lot bigger than the trinket exchange level we humble journeymen operate at."

"I suppose so." Jennifer still had mixed feelings about her rank. If she hadn't made journeyman at the end of her first run, she wouldn't have had anything to fall back on when her try at a real job went up in smoke. Maybe she would have tried again instead of signing up for another trip.

Watson, she knew, would have told her it was much too late to worry about such things now. He would have been right, too. That didn't stop her.

Now he glanced longingly back toward his spice cones. "I'd better finish these, so I can see exactly what I've got. Congratulations on the ivory. I'm most sincerely jealous."

She smiled. "Thanks." She headed on to her own cubicle and shut the door behind her. The figurine went into her strongbox. She walked down the hall to take a fast shower. Then she did what she did during most of her free time: she got out her reader and went from modern times back to the days before English changed to Spanglish. She might not be teaching the ancient literature, but she still loved it.

This new tale wasn't science fiction but, she discovered as she read, it did show respect for rational thought. She laughed a little, quietly, at a pleasant coincidence between past and present. Even across a gap of a thousand years, such things turned up now and again. They only made her enjoy her reading more.

Master Merchant Celia Rodriguez called a crew's meeting two afternoons later. Jennifer made sure she was in the common room at the appointed time; Master Rodriguez's tongue could degauss computer chips when she got annoyed. The other five merchants who made up the rest of *Pacific Overtures*' crew were equally punctual, no doubt for the same reason.

Jennifer loathed meetings, feeling they wasted time in which she could be doing something useful instead. Sitting through a great many of them had only made that feeling stronger. She got ready to look interested while she thought about her ancient scientific detective.

Celia Rodriguez's first words, though, made her sit up and take notice. "The civilization in this whole tract of forest is in deep trouble." Master Rodriguez's take-it-or-leave-it delivery was a good match for her looks: she was about fifty, heavyset, with blunt features and iron-gray hair she wore short. She badly intimidated Jennifer. Most loud, self-assured people intimidated Jennifer.

"What do you mean?" demanded Tranh Nguyen. He was also a master merchant, though junior to Rodriguez. "Judging from the records of earlier trade missions here, technology is improving, the standard of living is up, and population per tree keeps increasing." A couple of others, Sam Watson among them, nodded agreement.

"You're right," Rodriguez answered at once. "None of that matters at all, though, because the forest itself is dying back. Dim lights!" she told the ship's computer, and the common room went dark. "First image," she commanded. The computer projected a map onto the wall next to her. "The green shows the extent of this tract of forest at the time of the first landing on Athet, 250 years ago. Second image." The borders of the green patch changed shape. "This is about a hundred years ago. Note the losses here, here, and here. Note also that the open space in which we are sitting appears during that interval."

Jennifer thought of the stump she'd tripped over. That had seemed just one of the small things that made up a day. Now it looked more like a symptom of a much bigger problem.

So it proved. "Third image," Rodriguez said. The map changed again. "This is where we are today. See how much bigger this clearing has grown, and the appearance of these two further west. See also where grassland has replaced forest here, and in this sector. The next map is an extrapolation of where these trends will lead if they keep on for another two hundred years. Fourth image."

The new map that appeared beside the master merchant brought gasps of surprise and dismay from her colleagues. The broad expanse of forest that had dominated this part of the continent was gone, only a few small outcrops surviving like islands in a sea of grass.

"This, of course, spells catastrophe for the Atheter civilization here," Master Rodriguez said. "The locals are so tied to their arboreal life-style that they have a great deal of trouble adapting to life on the ground. Their most likely response to the failure of the trees would be to try migrating to the next big forest tract, a couple of hundred kilometers away. That tract is already settled; I doubt its inhabitants would welcome newcomers with open arms."

"Have you shown the treelords these maps?" Tranh Nguyen asked.

Rodriguez shook her head. "I prepared them last night, after our meeting. The treelords realize they have a problem, but not its extent. As you said before, they can support more people per tree than they once could, which has helped mask there being fewer trees in which to support them. But now they have begun to notice."

"What do they want us to do, then?" Nguyen went on, having the seniority to ask the questions the whole crew was thinking.

"We've spent 250 years building up our image here as the wise, powerful traders from the stars. Now they want us to live up to it." Master Rodriguez's smile was ironic. "They want us to make the forest grow bigger again. Not much, eh?"

This time, several people spoke at once. "How do they propose to pay for it?" It was the first question that flashed through Jennifer's mind, though she did not speak aloud. Her own smile was rueful. Yes, she thought like a merchant now, sure enough.

"I don't know," Rodriguez said. "I don't know if we can, for that matter, but even trying will be expensive. And Athet has never been what you'd call a high-profit world. For something of this scale . . ." She let the words hang.

"I don't like the idea of standing by and watching a civilization fall," Suren Krikorian said. He was a journeyman hardly senior to Jennifer, but came from a wealthy family—he did not need to worry about the consequences of speaking his mind.

"Neither do I," Celia Rodriguez replied. "I don't like the idea of bankrupting myself either, though. Even a preliminary study on the local problem will keep us here a lot longer than we'd planned, and that will be expensive. If we don't have something to show for it when we get back to *our* civilization, we'll all be badly hurt."

Krikorian scowled but did not answer. The master merchant was right, and everyone knew it. Jennifer suddenly got up and hurried away from the table. She remembered to say "Excuse me" just as she left the common room, but so softly she was afraid nobody heard her.

"I trust this will be interesting," Rodriguez said when she got back. By her tone, she did not trust any such thing.

Jennifer felt herself flush. "I—I hope so, Master Merchant," she said, wishing she could push arrogance into her voice whenever she needed it. She held up the *omphoth*-ivory figurine. "I—I was just thinking that if the Atheters have more pieces of this quality, they would help pay us for our time here."

Celia Rodriguez's voice changed. "May I see it, please?" Jennifer brought it to her. She examined it closely, then asked, "May I show it to the rest of our group?" Jennifer nodded. "Opinions?" the master merchant asked as she handed Tranh Nguyen the piece.

The merchants passed it from one to another. Finally, Sam Watson returned it to Jennifer. "Enough like this, and staying here may well be worth our while," Nguyen said. No one argued with him.

"I only hope there *are* enough pieces," Jennifer said. "The trader from whom I got this one told me that the animals from which the ivory came have been extinct for a thousand years."

"Have they?" Now calculation was in Rodriguez's voice, and something else as well—the purr of a predator that had just spotted dinner. "Then with a little luck, we may be able to clean out the whole supply. We'll sell a few pieces when we get back to civilization, leave the rest with our brokers while half a dozen other ships scurry out here to try to get in on the good thing. And when they come back empty—why, then we'll sell more, at four times the price."

Everyone in the common room grinned at Jennifer. She smiled back, a little uncertainly—attracting attention, even favorable attention, made her nervous. It did, however, beat the stuffing out of the other kind, she thought.

Gazar's crest rose. His tail thrashed. "Your people will be buying many *omphoth*-ivory pieces, you say?"

Jennifer nodded. "As many as they can. If you want more, if you want more to sell to us, now would be a good time to get them, before you have to compete with the lure of offworld goods."

"And if I do get them, you will trade those offworld goods to me?" The Atheter's golden eyes were big and yellow as twin full moons.

"Certainly," Jennifer said. "Provided, that is, that you remember the favor I have done you and keep your demands within the bounds of reason."

Gazar winced. "Now I understand why your teeth are so small, merchant from the stars—your sharp tongue long ago sliced off their points." He displayed his own formidable set of ivory.

"From you, I will take that as a compliment," Jennifer chuckled.

"I meant it as one," Gazar said. "You must understand me, even with advance notice I doubt I will be able to get a great many pieces. *Omphoth* ivory has become rare enough over the years that most of it, now, is in the treasury of one treelord or another. Still, some may be persuaded to fall from the branch."

"I hope so." Jennifer paused. "Speaking of falling from the branch, I almost had my head smashed in by a falling fruit the other day."

"I'm glad you escaped. Still, that shows the folly of going down to the ground, does it not?"

"Not what I meant." Jennifer reminded herself not to be annoyed. Just as she was a product of her environment, so Gazar was of his. "I would have thought that you treefolk would take care to harvest those fruits for yourselves, and not let the ground creatures have the benefit of them."

The Atheter made a horrible face. "Not even the crawlers in the leaves would want them. Our trees are wonderful. They are our lives, they are our livelihoods, they are our homes. But we do not eat their fruits. They taste dreadful."

"Oh. All right." Jennifer thought for a moment. "But you have many different kinds of large trees in this forest. Surely some must be of use to you."

"A few," Gazar said grudgingly, as if making an enormous concession. "Most, though, are truly foul—better for weapons, as you saw, than for food."

"You know best, I'm sure." Jennifer stood up, as well as she could inside Gazar's shop. "I'll come back again in a few days. I hope you'll have found some *omphoth* ivory by then."

"So do I," Gazar said. "My mate is pregnant with a new set of twins, and I expect we will need a larger house after they are born. The more offworld goods I get from you, the sooner I can buy it. Maybe I will buy a slave or two as well."

Jennifer was glad Atheters had trouble reading human expressions; she was afraid her revulsion showed on her face. *You are not here to reform these people,* she told herself. Until they industrialized, they probably would have slaves, and there was nothing she could do about it. No, not quite nothing—trading with them was bound to spur their own technology, which might hasten the day when slavery grew uneconomic here.

As she walked back to *Pacific Overtures* this time, she kept a wary eye on the treetops. When a big fruit crashed down into the bushes, maybe fifty meters off to her left, she almost jumped out of her skin. No missiles came any closer than that, though, for which she was duly grateful.

Back at the ship, she gave herself the luxury of a few seconds of gloating. A small private hoard of *omphoth* ivory couldn't help but improve her credit rating when she got back to civilization. A large private hoard would be nicer yet, but she knew she lacked the resources to get her hands on one.

Maybe next trip out, she'd score that really big coup . . . She stopped in dismay. That was thinking too much like a trader to suit her. If she got a decent stake out of this run, she'd be able to afford to look for an academic job.

"And if I land one," she said aloud, "I'll never again go to a world that doesn't have an automated information retrieval system."

Pleased at that promise to herself, she dug out her reader and returned to twentieth—or was it nineteenth?—century London. The more stories she read about this detective, the more she wanted to read. That surprised her; the fellow who wrote them had also turned out a lot of bad science fiction. But the detective and his amanuensis lived and breathed. These tales were what the writer should have been doing all along, instead of wasting his time on things he wasn't good at.

She put down the reader and fought back angry tears. What was she doing aboard *Pacific Overtures* except wasting her time on things she wasn't good at?

Tranh Nguyen made as if to bang his head against the corridor wall. "I don't know why the forest is shrinking," he growled. "As far as I can tell, the soil in the grasslands is the same as the soil where the trees still grow. It has the same mineral content, the same little wormy things crawling through it, the same everything."

"Not the same everything." Celia Rodriguez shook her head. "It doesn't have trees on it any more. We still have to find out why."

"Excuse me," Jennifer said—softly, as usual—as she tried to get past them.

Neither master merchant paid any attention to her. Tranh Nguyen said, "I know we have to, but I'm not sure we can. I do what the computer tells me to do, I compare the results of one sample to those from another, but if nothing obvious shows up,

I'm stuck. I can't make the intuitive leap—I'm a trader, after all, not an agronomist who might see more than is in the computer program."

"Excuse me," Jennifer said again.

"An agronomist!" Rodriguez clapped a hand to her forehead. "As if we could afford to haul an agronomist all the way out here! As if we could find an agronomist crazy enough to want to come! We have to be able to do this kind of work for ourselves, because if we don't, no one will."

"I know that as well as you do," Tranh Nguyen said. "Why carry the big computer library, except to make sure we can do a little of everything? A *little* of everything, though, Celia, not everything. We may really need a specialist here. Right now, I'm stymied."

"Excuse me," Jennifer said one more time.

Celia Rodriguez finally noticed she was there. She stepped out of the way. "Why didn't you say something?" she demanded.

Jennifer shrugged and walked by. She was often effectively invisible aboard *Pacific Overtures.* She much preferred that to the way things had been on her last trading run, when two male journeymen, neither of whom she wanted in the least, had relentlessly hounded her through the whole mission.

Sometimes she wished she were chunky and hard-featured like Celia Rodriguez instead of slim and curved and possessed of an innocent look she could not get rid of no matter how hard she tried. She would have enjoyed being valued for herself instead of just for her blue eyes. She'd never found a tactful way to say that to the master merchant, though, and so sensibly kept her mouth shut.

She let herself into her cubicle and closed the door after her. That cut off most of the noise from the corridor, where Rodriguez and Tranh Nguyen were still arguing. She carefully took off her backpack and set it on the floor. Then, grinning, she leaped onto her mattress and bounced up and down like a little kid.

When she was done bouncing, she got up again and opened the backpack. Inside, wrapped in a square of thick, native, printed cloth that was a minor work of art in itself, lay two fine *omphoth*-ivory figurines. One was a carving of an Atheter; but for its age, Jennifer would have guessed it a portrait of Gazar. It certainly captured the local merchant's top-of-his-lungs style—she could practically see the fur rising on the figurine's back.

That piece was excellent, but it paled beside the other. "This," Gazar had said, swelling up with self-importance, "is a veritable *omphoth,* carved from its own ivory to show later generations the sort of monsters we had to battle in those ancient days."

To a tree-dweller, Jennifer had to admit, it must have looked like a nightmare come to life. She thought of an elephant's head mounted on a brachiosaur's body, though the ears were small and trumpetlike, the tusks curved down, and the trunk—miraculously unbroken on the figurine—seemed to be an elongated lower lip rather than a nose run rampant. Such details aside, the carved *omphoth* certainly looked ready to lay waste to whole forests.

Imagining a full-sized one, Jennifer had trouble seeing how the Atheters ever could have killed it. When she had said as much to Gazar, he'd burst into epic verse in a dialect so antique that her translator kept hiccuping over it. Apparently a band of heroes had gone out into the Empty Lands, brought back an immense boulder, somehow manhandled it up into the treetops, and then dropped it on an *omphoth*'s head.

"Thus was the first of the monsters slain," Gazar had declaimed, "giving proof—could be done again." Jennifer remembered staring at her translator; the machine wasn't programmed to produce rhymes like that.

Now, though, she was more interested in the statuette than in the poetry its model had inspired. No matter how many treelords ransacked their collections for Celia Rodriguez, she did not think the master merchant would come up with a finer piece.

How much would the *omphoth* be worth? Enough to set up an endowed chair of Middle English literature? Jennifer knew she was dreaming. The whole hoard *Pacific Overtures* was bringing back might be worth something close to that, but her few private pieces wouldn't come close.

She sighed, rewrapped the figurines, and put them in her strongbox. One of these days, she told herself—most likely, just about the time when she would start forgetting her Middle English.

No, that was unfair. She loved the old language—although perhaps it wasn't older, she thought, surprised, than Gazar's hunting epic—and kept fresh her command of it. Fiche and a reader even a journeyman could easily afford.

She settled in with her scientific detective. This tale, part of what was called his memoirs, had to do with horse racing. Jennifer had seen a great many alien beasts on her trading runs, but never a horse. She had to struggle to work out from context what several of the words in the story meant; she was always rediscovering how large a vocabulary Middle English had. Even so, as she usually did, she got the gist of the piece and smiled at finding an exchange that had passed straight into Spanglish.

"'Is there any point to which you would wish to draw my attention?'

"'To the curious incident of the dog in the nighttime.'

"'The dog did nothing in the nighttime.'

"'That was the curious incident,' remarked Sherlock Holmes."

She finished "The Silver Blaze," loaded the fiche *Oxford English Dictionary* into the reader so she could look up a few words that had completely baffled her. But her mind kept going back to the dog that had not done anything. She frowned, trying to figure out why.

Then her eyes got wide. She reached under the bunk for her strongbox. She got out the two figurines she had just bought from Gazar. She looked from one of them to the other, then slowly nodded. This had to be how Holmes felt when all the pieces fell together. She quoted him again. "When you have eliminated the impossible, whatever remains, *however improbable,* must be the truth."

"Excuse me, Master Merchant." Jennifer had to say it three times before Celia Rodriguez noticed her. She didn't mind; she was used to that.

Finally Rodriguez looked up from her computer screen. "You want something, Jennifer?" She sounded surprised. Jennifer didn't mind that, either. She usually kept a low profile.

"Yes, I think so, Master Merchant. That is, I think I may know why this forest is shrinking."

Rodriguez slammed a meaty hand down on the panel in front of her. "Well, if you do, that's more than anyone else does. And I haven't seen you doing anything in the way of trying to find out, either. So how do you know? Divine inspiration?"

"No. I—I—" Jennifer had to work to keep her voice audible in the face of such daunting sarcasm. "I—I got the idea from a Middle English book I was reading."

The master merchant groaned. "Jennifer, I don't begrudge anyone a hobby. Tranh Nguyen keeps trying to beat the computer at chess. He'll keep trying till he's 105, if he lives that long. Me, I like to knit. That's even useful, every now and then. I've traded things I've made for more than they're worth. You have your ancient books. They're harmless, I suppose. But what can they possibly have to do with why this forest tract on Athet is getting smaller?"

"It's—a way of thinking. But never mind that now. You're right, Master Merchant, I haven't done much work on the problem till now. I'm sorry. But can you tell me if you have maps that show the boundaries of the forest from a long time ago? Long before we first landed here, I mean: back when the Atheters were first settling this territory."

"I think so, yes." Rodriguez fiddled with the computer. A map appeared on the screen, replacing the chart she had been studying. "As best we can tell now, this is the size of the forest about fifteen hundred local years ago. It started declining then, slowly at first, but more and more rapidly in the past millennium. The process was well under way when humans came here, for reasons we still can't fathom—no great climatic changes, no shifts in the nature of the soil, nothing."

The master merchant checked herself, glanced sourly at Jennifer. "Oh, I'm so sorry. Now you know why, out of your antique books. Enlighten me, please."

Jennifer took a deep breath. If she was wrong now, the fitness report Rodriguez turned in on her would make it next to impossible for her to fly again. After not getting a fair shot at one career, the prospect of washing out of another frightened her more than she was willing to admit, even to herself.

"I think it was—" She spoke so softly that Rodriguez had to lean forward to hear what she was saying. She involuntarily yelped, "—the *omphoth.*"

"The *omphoth*?" The master merchant looked disgusted. "You come in here, waste my time with this foolishness when I have serious work to do? The *omphoth,*" she said, as if to an idiot child, "have been extinct for a thousand years. You were the one who found that out. How can something that isn't here any more have anything to do with conditions now?"

"By not being here," Jennifer said. Rodriguez snorted and turned back toward the computer screen. "No, wait!" Jennifer said desperately. "The forests really started shrinking a thousand years ago—you said so yourself. And the Atheters here finished wiping out the *omphoth* a thousand years ago. Don't you think there's a connection?"

"Coincidence," Rodriguez snorted. But she did look at Jennifer again. Now she might have been talking to a clever child. "Be reasonable. The Atheters got rid of the *omphoth* because they kept eating up the forest. So why is it shrinking now that they're gone?"

"Yes, they ate the trees," Jennifer agreed. "They even ate the horrible fruits that the Atheters can't stand, that none of the animals that are still around want anything to do with. What happens to the fruits that fall to the ground now?"

"They sprout, of course."

"Yes." Jennifer nodded eagerly. She was so full of her idea, she was almost fluent. "They sprout. They sprout under the trees that dropped them in the rain-forest gloom. Not many grow up, and the ones that do only grow up in the same place trees had always been."

"So what do the *omphoth* have to do with any of that? If they eat those fruits, they digest them, don't they? That gets rid of them a lot more thoroughly than trying to grow in the shade."

"They digest the fruit, yes, but what about the seeds inside?" Jennifer asked. "Lots of plants on lots of worlds disperse their seeds by passing them through animals' guts. I looked that up when I first wondered if there was any connection between the *omphoth* disappearing and the forest shrinking back."

"Do they? Did you?" Now, at last, Celia Rodriguez began to seem interested.

"Yes. It makes sense here, too, in ecological terms. It really does, Master Rodriguez. The *omphoth* ate fruit nothing else here likes at all. Doesn't that probably mean they and the trees evolved together? The trees provided them a special food and in return they disseminated the seeds inside. And so when they disappeared, the seeds didn't get disseminated any more, and that's what I think has made this tract of forest get smaller."

"Hmm." The master merchant pulled out her lower lip, then let it snap back with a soft plop. "You've done your homework on this, haven't you?"

"Of course I have, Master Rodriguez." Jennifer knew she sounded surprised. If she was good at anything, it was research.

"Hmm," Celia Rodriguez said again. "Well, what do we do even if you're right? The *omphoth* are extinct. We don't have a time machine to bring them back."

"Ooh." It was like a blow in the belly—Jennifer hadn't thought that far ahead.

But once the master merchant had an idea, she was not one to let go of it. She said, as much to herself as to Jennifer, "They're extinct here, anyhow. But this isn't the only tract of rain forest on Athet, not by a long shot. It's just the one offworlders do the most business with. Maybe others have relatives of the *omphoth* still running around loose."

"It shouldn't be hard to find out," Jennifer said.

Celia Rodriguez barked a couple of syllables' worth of laughter. "No, not hardly," she agreed. "Even with our translators barely working, the way they act when they're still picking up new languages, the locals won't be in much doubt about whether they have *omphoth* around."

Jennifer thought of something else. "I hope the main hold is big enough to carry one. More than one, I mean, if we intend to establish them here."

"First things first." The master merchant laughed again. "Hope the stunners are strong enough to put them under. Otherwise I suppose we'll have to herd them across the however many hundreds or thousands of kilometers it is from where they are to here. And for that—" Rodriguez's tone was still bantering, but Jennifer had no doubt she meant what she said "—for that, I would definitely charge extra."

Something went crashing through the undergrowth far below the branch on which Gazar's establishment was perched. Then the something—Jennifer and Gazar both knew what it was; nothing else made that much racket—let out a bellow that sounded like a cross between a kettledrum and a synthesizer with a bad short in its works.

Gazar made a ghastly face. "Now I know why our heroic ancestors slew all the ancient *omphoth*—in the hope of getting a good night's sleep. The cursed beasts are never quiet, are they?"

"They don't seem to be," Jennifer admitted. The cries of the newly released animals could be heard even inside *Pacific Overtures.*

Out along the branch, Atheters shouted and screeched. Jennifer's translator screeched, too, protesting the overload. It did manage to pick up one call. "Come on out, Gazar, and look at the *omphoth*! Here it comes!"

"Why should I want to see the creature that torments my rest?" Gazar grumbled, but he went. Jennifer followed more slowly, the hobnails in the bottom of her boots helping to give her purchase on the branch.

Young Atheters squealed and clung to their mothers' fur as the *omphoth* lumbered by underneath. It took no notice of the excited locals in the tree; its attention was centered solely on food. It pulled up a bush, spat it out—it was still learning what was good in this new forest and what was not.

"It doesn't look the way an *omphoth* is supposed to," Gazar complained; having found that figurine for Jennifer, he fancied himself an expert. "It doesn't even have tusks."

He had a point, she supposed. The new beasts were not identical to their exterminated cousins. Not only were they tuskless, but their lower-lip trunks were bifurcated for the last meter or so of their length. They hardly had any tails, either, and their claws were smaller than those of the *omphoth* this forest had once known.

But in the one essential way, they were like the *omphoth* of old: they were ravenously fond of the big, knobby fruits the various trees here produced. The *omphoth* under Gazar's tree bent its head down so its forked trunk could grab fruit that had fallen to the ground. Wet chewing noises followed.

Then the *omphoth* reached up almost as high as the branch on which Jennifer was perched. If the baby Atheters had squealed before, they shrieked now. Jennifer could not blame them. The sight of that open pink maw only a few meters away made her want to shriek, too. The *omphoth* had dreadful breath.

It was not interested in snacking off the locals, though. All it wanted to do was pluck more fruit from any branch it could reach. Finally it stripped those branches bare and stamped away to look for more fodder.

Gazar turned around to display his hindquarters at it, a gesture of contempt he had never been rude enough to use on a human. He caught Jennifer's eye. "Some treetowns are even less happy with these beasts than ours," he said. "I only hope they are not so shortsighted as to try to get rid of them."

"Why would they do that?" Jennifer exclaimed in horror. "The *omphoth* are saving the forest for you."

"Saving the whole, aye, but damaging the parts. We have laws against building on branches lower than a certain height." Gazar blinked. "I suppose one reason we have those laws is the *omphoth* of long ago. I never thought about it till now. But not every treelord enforces those laws—without *omphoth,* they matter little. Now there are *omphoth* again, and they've already wrecked some houses that were low enough for them to reach."

"Oh. I'm sorry to hear that," Jennifer said. "Your people had better know, though, that we won't be around to get more *omphoth* for them if they go and kill these. You need to build up the herd, not destroy it."

"The treelords know that," Gazar said, still sounding a long way from happy at the prospect. "Armed males travel through the trees to guard the beasts from harm."

"I should hope so," Jennifer said. After all the trouble the crew of *Pacific Overtures* had gone through in stunning and transporting the great beasts, the idea of having them hunted down was appalling.

She took her leave from Gazar and climbed down the chain ladder to the ground. The *omphoth* was nowhere to be seen, although she could still hear it somewhere off deeper in the forest. She was glad it was not between her and *Pacific Overtures.*

Immense footprints and crushed bushes showed the beast's path. So did a huge pile of steaming, stinking, green dung. In the dung Jennifer saw several teardrop-shaped seeds.

She smiled. These particular seeds got no great advantage from their trip through the *omphoth's* gut. But *omphoth* also wandered out to the edges of the savannah country surrounding the forest. Seeds deposited there would be more likely to thrive. With luck, the forest would grow again.

Her smile grew broader. All too often preindustrial races wanted nothing more from traders than help in war against their neighbors. This time, though, the crew *of Pacific Overtures* had really accomplished something worth doing. They'd turned a profit on the deal, too. Jennifer had learned to think well of the combination. She hurried toward the ship.

An *omphoth* came out of the forest. Sam Watson stepped up the gain on *Pacific Overtures*' viewscreen. He and Jennifer watched the beast's pupils shrink in the sudden bright sun. It didn't seem to like the feeling much. With a bellow, it drew back into the shelter of the trees.

Watson yawned and stretched. "I'll almost miss the big noisy things," he said.

"Yes, so will I, but not their racket," Jennifer said.

"No, not that. Maybe the next ship in can see if coffee does for Atheters what it does for us. I suspect a good many of them will need it, though they're not what you'd call a quiet race themselves."

"Hardly." Thinking of Gazar, Jennifer knew that was, if anything, an understatement. After a moment, she went on, "Maybe we should have done some tests with the coffee in the galley. If it worked, they'd have paid plenty for it."

"Too late to worry about it now, what with us upshipping tomorrow. I wonder how much the ivory will end up bringing. The way Master Rodriguez has things lined up, we may take a while selling everything, but we'll get a lot when we finally do. It's especially nice," Watson added, "that the new kind of *omphoth* we've introduced here doesn't have tusks; the Atheters won't have the incentive of hunting them to carve more trinkets for traders."

"That's true," Jennifer said. "I wouldn't feel right if we'd brought them here just to have them killed off."

"No." Sam gave Jennifer an admiring look. She hardly noticed it; she was used to admiring looks from men, and used to discounting them, too. But this one proved different from most. "That was a lovely piece of analysis you did, Jennifer, working out the connection between the extinction of the old *omphoth* and the trouble the forest was having."

She felt her cheeks heat with pleasure. "Oh. Thank you very much."

"I ought to thank you, for bumping up our profits, and I suppose for the Atheters, too. How did you ever work out that the *omphoth* passed the seeds through their intestinal tracts and then out again?"

"That? It was—" Jennifer paused, knowing he wouldn't understand—he was just a merchant, after all, not a scholar of Middle English. She found she didn't care. "It was alimentary, my dear Watson."

THE FOITANI

IV

Ali Bakhtiar glanced toward the clock. A dark, arched eyebrow rose. "Isn't your first class at 0930, Jennifer? You're going to be late."

"I'm almost ready." Jennifer made sure one last time that she had all her notes. She took a couple of deep breaths, as if she were going to start lecturing then and there. "I hope the hall's well miked. My voice just isn't big enough to carry well by itself."

Bakhtiar smiled encouragingly. "You'll do fine." When he looked at the clock again, the smile faded. "But you'd better get moving."

"Here I go." Jennifer ran a hand through her long, blond hair. "Do I look all right?"

"That is a foolish question. You know you look wonderful." He stepped forward to kiss her; his hand slid down her back to cup her left buttock. He pulled her closer. The kiss went on and on.

Finally she twisted away. "You were the one who said I'd be late," she reminded him. She knew her looks drew men to her; she found that a nuisance as often as she enjoyed it. Living with Ali Bakhtiar the past year had at least given her an anchor. Seeing her on his arm kept a fair number of other men—not all, but a fair number—from pestering her. Even so, there were times when she wished she was still trading with aliens, to whom she was as peculiar as they were to her. It made life simpler.

But as she strode out of the apartment she and Bakhtiar shared, that sometimes-wish vanished. This would be her third semester of teaching Middle English science fiction at Saugus Central University. She still had trouble believing that, after close to ten years traveling the wilder reaches of the local arm of the galaxy, she actually had the academic job she'd wanted all along.

Sometimes you'd rather be lucky than good, she thought as she hurried toward and then across the university campus. She'd been about to set out on yet another trading run when word of the opening at Saugus Central came over the data net. The post would have been long filled by the time she got back, which meant she would have left on one more mission still, just to put more credit in her account. By the time the next job opening appeared, she might have been nearing master-trader status. Master trader was all very well—after some years of trading, she knew it was a title that had to be earned—but she much preferred putting *assistant professor* in front of her name.

Saugus was a good planet for hurrying. The weather here in the foothills was cool and crisp, the gravity was only about .85 standard, and the air held a little more oxygen than human beings had evolved to breathe. The clock in the classroom said 0929 when she stepped through the door. She grinned to herself. Being late on the first day didn't make a prof look good.

She got to the podium just as the clock clicked to 0930. "Good morning. I'm Dr. Logan," she said—she didn't believe in wasting time. "This is Middle English 217: Twentieth-century Science Fiction." Someone got up and left in a hurry. *In the wrong room,* Jennifer thought. Other students tittered.

"Can you all hear me?" Jennifer asked. Everyone nodded, even the students in the back of the hall. The miking was all right, then. Her voice was so light and breathy that it needed all the help it could get.

"All right. This course is part language, part literature. As you'll have noticed when you were registering, beginning and intermediate Middle English are prerequisites. Don't forget, the documents we'll be reading are a thousand years old. If you think you'll be able to get through them with just your everyday Spanglish, or even with an ordinary translation program, you can think again."

Someone else, a girl this time, walked out the door shaking her head. Jennifer felt the eyes of the rest of the class upon her. Most students muttered their notes into recorders with hush-mikes. A few stroked typers or scribbled on paper in the ancient fashion; in every class, she'd found people who remembered better when they wrote things down.

A couple of male students hadn't started taking notes at all. She could tell what was in their minds as well as if she were telepathic. It annoyed her. No only were they boys by her reckoning, but she'd been places and faced challenges they could hardly imagine. She knew they didn't care what she'd done. To them, she was only an attractively shaped piece of meat. That annoyed her even more.

She sighed to herself and went on, "That's not to say you won't find words—a lot of words—that look familiar. A lot of Spanglish vocabulary can be traced back to roots in Middle English. That's especially true of Middle English science fiction. Many, in fact most, of our modern terms relating to spaceflight come from those first coined by science-fiction writers. Remarkably, most of those coinages were made before the technology for actual spaceflight existed. I want you to think for a moment of the implications of that, and to think about the leap of imagination those writers were taking."

Some of them made the mental effort, she saw. She knew they were doomed to failure. Imagining what humanity had been like before spaceflight was as hard for them as willing oneself into the mind of an ancient Sumerian would have been for an ordinary citizen of the twentieth century.

She held up a sheet of paper. "I want to talk about the books we'll be reading this semester," she said. The back door to the lecture hall opened. She frowned. This was one of the times she wished she had a deep, booming voice. She hated latecomers interrupting her when she'd already started lecturing. She began, "I hope you'll be on time for our next—" but stopped with the complaint only half-spoken. The new students were not human.

The whole room grew quiet when the three of them walked in. They were dark blue and on the shaggy side. The door was more than two meters high, but they had to stoop to get under the lintel. The door was more than a meter wide, but they had to turn sideways to go through it. Their faces had short muzzles and impressive teeth.

"What species are they?" a student in the front row asked the fellow next to her. He shrugged and shook his head. Likely neither of them had ever been off Saugus before, Jennifer thought.

She knew the aliens' race. Of all the places she would never have expected to meet Foitani, though, a Middle English class on a human-settled planet of no particular importance to anyone ten light-years away came close to topping the list. Maybe, she thought, they were looking for the engineering department instead. She called, "How may I help you, Foitani?"

The three big blue creatures cocked their heads to one side, listening to the translators each wore. One of them answered, speaking softly in his own rumbling language. His translator turned the words to Spanglish. "Apologies for tardiness, honored instructor.

We concede the fault is ours; we will yield any forfeit your customs require."

"We will," the other two echoed.

"No—forfeits—are necessary," Jennifer said faintly. "May I direct you to the class you are seeking?"

The Foitan who had spoken first bared his teeth—or possibly hers; the differences between Foitani sexes did not show on the outside. Jennifer knew the gesture was the Foitani equivalent of a frown, but it made the alien look as if he intended to take a bite out of someone. She wished for the trader's stunner she seldom wore any more. The Foitan said, "Have we interpreted your symbology inaccurately? This hall is not for the teaching of Middle English two-one-seven?"

"You're enrolled in my class?" Jennifer heard herself squeaking, but couldn't help it. It wouldn't matter anyhow; translators were fine for meaning, but they filtered out tone of voice.

"So we ought to be," the Foitan answered, his own translator sounding grave as usual. "Our funds were accepted, our names inscribed in your computer banks. I am Thegun Thegun Nug; here beside me stand Aissur Aissur Rus and Dargnil Dargnil Lin."

Jennifer shoved notes aside. "Enrollment," she muttered. The list appeared on the screen set into the top of the podium. Sure enough, the three Foitani were on it. Human names came in such bewildering variety that she hadn't especially noticed theirs. "Very well," she said, "sit down—if you have the reading knowledge of Middle English this course requires."

The Foitani sat. They weren't so much bigger than the average human as to make human furniture impossible for them—just enough bigger to be intimidating, Jennifer thought. Aissur Aissur Rus said, "We will meet the language requirements of the course, honored instructor. We are Foitani, after all. We are practiced in dealing with languages far more ancient and different from modern speech than your Middle English."

She knew that was true. "Very well," she said again, and began talking about the books she would be assigning. Never had she had such perfect attention from students on the first day of class. After the ostentatious if somber politeness of the Foitani, it was as if all her human students feared they would be torn limb from limb if they got out of line.

Because she didn't have to pause even once, she got through all the material she'd planned to present in spite of the delay the Foitani had caused. Only after the three big aliens left the hall did the rest of the people there start chattering among themselves. Even then, their voices were low, subdued.

Jennifer went back to her office to see how the campus computers were doing on a couple of her pet research projects. The new printouts had some important data, but didn't interest her as much as they should have: With three Foitani—Foitani!—enrolled in her course, she had trouble getting excited about revised charts of de Camp's use of the colon rather than the comma to introduce quotations, or on a fresh stemma tracing the spread of the word "thutter" from Anderson to writers of the next generation like Stirling and Iverson.

After lunch, she taught one course in modern Spanglish literature and another in composition, neither of which excited her very much but both of which helped pay her half of the rent for the apartment she shared with Ali Bakhtiar. She told herself she would have gone through them without much thought no matter what; with three Foitani in her morning class to think about, she knew she wasn't giving the afternoon sessions her full attention.

When she got back to the apartment, Bakhtiar was already there. His last class—he taught imaging, both tape and film—got out half an hour before hers. All she wanted to do was exclaim about the Foitani. He listened, bemused, for several minutes; she was not usually the sort to gush. At last, he held up a hand. "Wait one second, please. Why are you so excited about having these three aliens in your class?"

"That's what I was telling you," Jennifer said. "They're Foitani."

"So I'd gathered," he answered with a wry quirk of that eyebrow. Sometimes she thought he practiced in a mirror, but she'd never caught him at it. "But who are the Foitani?"

She stared at him. "You really don't know?"

"Why should I?" he asked reasonably. "How many species of aliens do we know? Several hundred without hyperdrive, several dozen with it. That's on top of Allah only knows how many human-settled worlds. So why should I remember anything in particular about this one bunch?"

Jennifer knew he was right—humanity had spread too widely, learned too many things, for any one person to keep track of more than a tiny fraction of all there was to know. But somehow Bakhtiar's complete ignorance of the Foitani badly irked her. She wanted to exclaim over them and have him exclaim right back. How could he do that if he had no idea why she was exclaiming in the first place?

He saw something was wrong; after all, he had lived with her for a year. Spreading his hands to placate her, he said, "Tell me about them, then, if they're that important."

"Well, for one thing, we've only known they aren't extinct for about the past fifty years," Jennifer said. "They used to rule a big empire in toward the galactic center, a good many thousand years ago. Then they started fighting among themselves; I don't think anybody knows why. They kept right on doing it, too, till they'd wrecked just about all the worlds they lived on."

"Wait a minute." A light came on in Bakhtiar's eyes. "Didn't they run a holovid special on that three or four years ago? Secret of the lost race, or something like that? I remember watching it, but I'd forgotten the name of the race."

"I suppose they may have," Jennifer said. Three or four years ago, she'd been dickering with the Atheters over the price of *omphoth* ivory. "But yes, those were the Foitani. *Are* the Foitani," she corrected herself.

"Why have they enrolled in your Middle English class? What do they think they're going to get out of it?"

"I haven't the slightest idea," Jennifer said. "Of course, I don't know what about a third of my human students are going to get out of the class either, except for four units of credit."

Several years of trading missions among the stars had let her forget the time-serving students, the ones who took a course because they needed to fill a breadth requirement or because it happened to fit their schedules. The ones she'd remembered were the ones like herself, who enrolled in classes to learn something and worked hard at everything, for pride's sake if for no other reason. Saugus Central University had plenty of those. Unfortunately, it had plenty of the other sort, too, as she'd found to her dismay.

Ali Bakhtiar said, "Well, it's nice you had something out of the ordinary to liven up your day. Let's go have dinner, shall we?"

"Foitani in a Middle English class is more than something out of the ordinary," Jennifer said. But Bakhtiar was already walking into the kitchen and didn't hear her—the apartment wasn't miked. Glaring at his back, Jennifer followed him.

She wanted to talk more about the aliens after dinner, but he turned on a battleball game and was lost to the world for the next couple of hours. Battleball required the biggest, strongest bruisers humanity produced. The Foitani, Jennifer suspected, could have torn most of them in half without working up a sweat—assuming Foitani sweated in the first place.

She didn't care about battleball one way or the other. She sometimes watched because Ali liked it so much; it gave them something to do together out of bed. Tonight she didn't feel like making the effort. She went into the bedroom to work on the computer for a while.

When she found herself yawning, she shut down the machine. She needed a few seconds to return from the distant past's exciting imagined future to her own thoroughly mundane present. Somehow hardly anyone in Middle English science fiction ever got bored or had to go to the bathroom at an inconvenient time or worried about her credit balance.

As *she* went off to the bathroom, Jennifer reflected that her own credit balance was in pretty good shape. Thanks to the *omphoth* ivory, she had a good deal more to her name than if she'd landed the first academic job she'd tried for. And she had no business being bored, not with three Foitani to wonder about.

She hoped the Foitani would get around to explaining just what they were doing in a Middle English course. She didn't know enough about their customs to risk asking straight out, but she'd die of curiosity if they kept quiet all semester.

She spat toothpaste foam into the sink. In the front room, Ali Bakhtiar yelled, "Reload and spin, fool, before he gets you!" The battleball game was in the last five minutes, then. Jennifer made a sour face. If Ali thought battleball more interesting than the Foitani, that was his problem.

Even when she got into bed, the big blue aliens would not leave her mind. Thegun Thegun Nug, Aissur Aissur Rus, and—what was the third one's name? Dargnil Dargnil Lin, that was it. She wondered if they were males or females. She thought of them as males, but that was only because they were large and had deep voices: anthropocentric thinking, the worst mistake a trader could make.

But she wasn't a trader any more. She was doing what she'd trained to do—what she'd always wanted to do, she told herself firmly.

Ali Bakhtiar came to bed a few minutes later. Her back was to him. She breathed deeply and steadily. He stroked her hair and slid his hand down to the curve of her hip. Most of the time, she enjoyed making love with him. Tonight, though, she was still annoyed at him for not caring more about the Foitani. She kept on pretending to be asleep. If Bakhtiar tightened that hand so she'd have to notice it, he'd get all the fight he wanted and then some.

He didn't. He took it away, muttered something grumpy under

his breath that she didn't quite catch—*just as well, too,* she thought—and rolled onto his stomach. Moments later, he was snoring. As if to punish herself for feigning sleep, Jennifer lay awake for the next hour and a half.

The Foitani pulled their weight in the Middle English class. However they did it, they stayed up with the reading. They were certainly more familiar with human customs than Jennifer was with theirs; they asked good, sensible questions and seldom needed anything explained more than once.

Little by little, they started becoming individuals to Jennifer. Thegun Thegun Nug seemed to be senior to the other two; they deferred to him and let him speak first. Aissur Aissur Rus thought for himself. His interpretations of what he'd read were most apt to be off-base, but also most apt to be interesting and original. Dargnil Dargnil Lin, by contrast, was conservative: steady, sound, not likely to go far from the beaten path but perfectly reliable on it. The studies all three of them turned in were among the better ones she got from the class. No doubt they'd linked their translator programs with the printer, but humans whose first language wasn't Spanglish did that, too.

Jennifer spent the first couple of weeks in the course on stories that dealt with alien contact. Experience had taught her that students enjoyed the theme, enjoyed seeing how wildly wrong most ancient speculation was. That some writers came within shouting distance of what the future really looked like also piqued their interest.

"Remember, science fiction wasn't supposed to be prophesy," she said. "Trying to foretell—to guess—the future is a much older set of thought processes. Science fiction was different. Science fiction was a literature of extrapolation, of taking something—some social trend, some new technology, even some ideology—that existed in the writer's time and pushing it farther and harder than it had yet gone, to see what the world would look like then.

"Of course, a lot of it became trivial even within a few years after it was written. Social trends, especially, changed so fast that they rarely lasted long enough to be carried to the extremes writers imagined. As humans have always been, in the twentieth century they were sometimes radical, sometimes reactionary, sometimes sexually permissive, sometimes repressive. They'd go through two or three of these cycles in a person's lifetime, as we do today.

"Some writers, though, chose harder questions to ask: how

humanity would fit into a community of intelligent beings, some quite different from us; how we should treat each other under changed circumstances; what the relationship between government and individual should be. That's why writers like Anderson, Brin, and Heinlein can still make us think today, even though the worlds they imagined didn't come true."

Somebody stuck up a hand. "Why are the videos from that time at an intellectual level so much lower than the books?"

"That's a good question," Jennifer said approvingly. "The answer has to do with the economics of book and video distribution back then. Books made money with much smaller audiences than videos did, so they could target small segments—in the case of science fiction, generally the better-educated section—of the population, and present sophisticated ideas to them. Videos needed mass appeal. They borrowed the exotic settings and adventure of written science fiction, but seldom attempted to deal with serious issues."

"Another question, please, honored professor?"

"Yes, go ahead, Aissur Aissur Rus." Jennifer was always curious to hear what the Foitani would ask. Aissur Aissur Rus had a special knack for coming up with interesting questions.

He did not disappoint her now. "Honored professor, I taste the intellectual quality of the authors you mention, which is indeed praiseworthy. Yet others—Sturgeon, Le Guin—seem to write more pleasingly. Which carries the greater weight?" His bearlike ears twitched. Jennifer thought that meant he was pleased with himself.

"Before I answer, Aissur Aissur Rus, may I ask a question in return?" Jennifer said. He waved a hand back and forth in front of his face. She knew that meant yes. She went on, "How have you learned Middle English well enough to have a feel for its style?" Not many human undergrads, even with computer aids, developed that kind of sensitivity to a language not their own.

Aissur Aissur Rus said, "To prepare us for this class, honored professor, our people used a Middle English/Spanglish program, a Spanglish/Raptic program—Rapti, you should know, is a world that once lay at the edge of Foitani space—and finally one from Raptic into our own tongue. Eventually our machines acquired sufficient vocabulary and context cues to abandon the two intermediate programs; they began to read directly from Middle English into our speech. From that point, it was not hard for us to learn Middle English directly."

"I see," Jennifer said slowly. And indeed she did see how, but not why. What good was ancient science fiction to the Foitani?

She almost asked straight out. Before she did, though, she felt she had to deal with Aissur Aissur Rus's question. "In their own time, the writers you named—and some others like them—were often very highly esteemed indeed, exactly because they were such fine stylists. And to say they did not address serious issues is not true, either. But they are less often read now because their concerns are not as relevant to us today as those of other authors. Do you see?"

"Yes, I taste the distinction you are cooking, but I am not sure it is valid," Aissur Aissur Rus said. "Again I ask, which carries the greater weight, abstract artistic excellence or utility?"

"That is a question humans have asked for as long as they have examined their own art," Jennifer said with a smile. "No one has ever come up with a definitive answer."

"Questions have answers," Dargnil Dargnil Lin said reprovingly.

"That may be so, but often only on a case-by-case basis—and with something as subjective as artistic elegance, one man's answer is another man's error," Jennifer said.

"Before the Suicide Wars, the Great Ones would have known." Even through the translator's flat tones, Dargnil Dargnil Lin sounded sure of that.

"If the Great Ones were as great as that, why did they fight the Suicide Wars?" Aissur Aissur Rus asked. Jennifer did not think the remark had been meant for the class to hear, but the translator sent it forth all the same.

Thegun Thegun Nug said, "Enough. We interrupt the discourse of the honored professor." All three Foitani visibly composed themselves to listen. Jennifer found she had no choice but to go on with her lecture. *One day,* she told herself, *I* will *ask my questions of them.* It would not be that day, though.

"It's so frustrating," she said to Ali Bakhtiar when she got home from her last class. "They're good in class. They're *very* good. But *what are they doing there*?"

"I haven't the faintest idea," Bakhtiar answered, as he had every time she raised the issue. Now his patience showed signs of wearing thin. "I wouldn't lose sleep over it, either. If they want to spend good money to hear you talk about your musty old books, that's their problem, not yours."

"Musty old books? Problem?" Jennifer didn't know where to start being indignant at all that.

"You look silly standing there with your mouth hanging open," Bakhtiar said.

If she'd had her stunner on her belt, she would have given him a dose big enough to keep him out the rest of the night—and maybe for the week after that. Her mouth *was* open, she realized. She shut it. She wasn't indignant any more; she was furious. Usually anger made her come to pieces. Now she knew what she had to do. When she spoke again, her voice was even tinier than usual. "I'll start looking for my own apartment."

Ali Bakhtiar stared at her. "Don't do that!" he said in alarm. She watched his face, the way his eyes moved up and down her. The alarm wasn't for her, at least not the part of her that dwelt behind her eyes. It was concern that he wouldn't be able to sleep with her any more. As if to prove it, he reached out to take her in his arms.

She took one step back, then another. He followed. "You leave me be," she said. She hated her voice for quavering. Her eyes filled with angry tears. She hated them even more.

"You're just upset," Bakhtiar said smoothly. "If it'll make you feel better, I'll apologize. Come here, Jennifer; it's all right." He put his hands on her shoulders.

A moment later he reeled away, right hand clutching left wrist. Jennifer hoped she hadn't broken it. She'd never needed unarmed combat on any of the worlds she'd visited, but all traders learned it, to protect themselves from aliens and humans both. Now she was using it for the first time, not a five-minute walk from the peaceful campus where she'd wanted to spend her days in quiet research. She'd already learned life didn't always work out the way one thought it would.

She walked past Ali Bakhtiar to the phone. He flinched back from her as if she'd suddenly sprouted fangs and talons; his eyes said he'd never seen her before. Maybe he hadn't, not really—maybe all he'd paid attention to was the small, shapely body, the blond hair that fell to the small of her back, the blue eyes and clear features. She started getting angry all over again.

She keyed the number of a friend, a colleague in the dead languages department a few years older than she. "Ella? It's Jennifer. Is there any chance I could sleep on your couch for a few days? I've had a fight with my boyfriend and I'll be moving out of here as soon as I can."

"I don't see any reason why not," Ella Metchnikova answered, her almost baritone contralto booming in Jennifer's ear. "Come on over."

"Thank you, Ella dear. I will." Jennifer hung up, threw some books, disks, and papers into an attaché case, then tossed the case, a change of clothes, and her toothbrush into a blue plastic shopping bag. She paused at the door to look back at Ali Bakhtiar. "I'll be out of here just as quick as I can get a place. If you mess with my things, even a little bit, I won't hit you in the wrist next time. I promise you that."

Then she had an afterthought. She went past Bakhtiar again, this time into the bedroom. It spoiled her grand exit, but she did not care for melodrama in her own life anyhow. She found her stunner and dropped it into the bag, too. One more trip by her lover—her former lover, she amended to herself—and she was gone.

Ella Metchnikova lived only a few blocks away. Her apartment building—and her apartment—were nearly clones of the one in which Jennifer had lived; the same construction company must have put up both of them.

Ella was large and blustery. She hugged Jennifer when she came in, kissing her on each cheek. "You have my sympathy, if you want it," she said. "More likely you think you're well rid of him, and if you think that, you're probably right. Let me give you something more practical instead." She took a glass from the refrigerator and handed it to Jennifer.

Jennifer sipped cautiously. Ella had handed her glasses before. Sometimes they were tasty, sometimes anything but—one of Ella's hobbies were reconstructing drinks nobody had drunk for hundreds of years. There were often good reasons why nobody had drunk them for hundreds of years.

This one wasn't bad—smooth, a little sweet, not alcoholic enough to scorch her throat or make her eyes water. As she was supposed to, she asked, "What's it called?"

"A Harvey Wallbanger," Ella said. "Orange juice, ethanol, and a liqueur called Galliano that I just found a bottle of last week. I thought it was long since extinct, but somebody still makes it. Can't imagine why. It's death by itself—think of high-proof sugar syrup with yellow food coloring. But it is good for something, you see."

"Yes, so it is." Jennifer took a larger sip, then another one. Warmth spread from her stomach. "Thanks for taking me in on short notice."

"On no notice, you mean." Ella laughed. A moment later, the laugh got louder. "I didn't know anybody on this planet could blush."

Jennifer's cheeks only grew hotter. "I can't help it if I'm fair."

"I know you can't. I can't help laughing about it, either. Have you had dinner?"

Jennifer let Ella mother her. It took her mind off the sudden crash of her relationship with Bakhtiar and off the hideous nuisance of moving—although her trader training would come in handy there, for she was used to packing quickly and thoroughly. Her trader training kept coming in handy all sorts of ways, something she'd certainly not expected when she signed up as an apprentice. All she'd wanted was something out of the ordinary on her resumé.

After dinner, she accessed the realty data net to see what sort of apartment she could find. The results of the search annoyed her: with the semester well begun, the units nearest the campus were full up. "Nothing closer than three kilometers," she complained.

"Maybe I ought to take that one," Ella said, looking over her shoulder. "You could have this place. I need the exercise more than you do." She sighed. "No, it wouldn't do. Knowing me, I'd take the shuttle in instead of walking. Oh, well."

Still grumbling, Jennifer electronically arranged to move into the nearest apartment she'd found, though she put in a withdrawal option in case something closer to the university opened up before she took possession of the new place. She'd enjoyed walking to work. She could afford the penalty she'd have to pay if she used the option.

"When does it come vacant, three days from now?" Ella asked.

"That's right. I hope I won't be too much a bother till then," Jennifer said. She'd already started thinking about what she could give Ella to repay her kindness.

"Tonight's not a problem, and neither is tomorrow. But the day, or rather the night after that—well, I'd invited Xavier over, and . . . you know what I mean," Ella said.

"Oh, yes," Jennifer said quickly. Ella and Xavier had been lovers for a long time. Jennifer didn't know how long, but it was longer than she'd been on Saugus. "I'll find someplace else to be, even if I have to sleep in the office that one night. It has a couch, of sorts; that wouldn't be too bad, really. And I'll be going into the new place the next day, so I won't cramp you any more after that."

"You're sweet, Jennifer. Sometimes I think you're too sweet for your own good. That's why you surprised me when you said you were breaking up with Ali. What touched that off, if you don't mind my asking?"

Jennifer started to explain about the Foitani. Before she'd gone three sentences, she ran into the same wall of incomprehension with

Ella that had driven her out of the arms of Ali Bakhtiar. Even though humans had spread over several thousand light-years, most of them, if they traveled at all, went from one human-settled planet to another and had only sketchy dealings—if any—with the many other species who shared the galaxy with them. Ella knew a lot more about ancient distilling techniques than she did about the Foitani.

When Jennifer was done, her friend shrugged and said, "It doesn't seem like much of a reason to me, but you know best how *you* feel. And it sounds like something else would have happened if this hadn't."

"I suppose so," Jennifer said. "I guess I knew I was more or less marking time with Ali." She ruefully shook her head. "I hadn't expected to get my nose rubbed in it this way, though."

"You never do," Ella said. "I remember this fellow I was seeing about ten years ago . . ." The tale that followed went on for some time and was more lurid than the fiction Jennifer was used to reading.

When she tried to sleep in Ella's front room, Jennifer tossed and turned. She was still upset. Moreover, the couch was harder and narrower than her big bed. The room wasn't as dark as her bedroom, and the noises of ground traffic outside were louder. Someone in an apartment across the courtyard had a clock that chimed the hours. She listened to it announce midnight, then, a year or so later, one o'clock. Finally she slept.

Ella's alarm screamed like a banshee—worse than an Atheter, Jennifer thought fuzzily as her panic at the hideous noise faded and she realized what it was. Ella was either a serious sleeper or selectively deaf, because the clock squalled on and on until at last she yelled for it to shut up.

Jennifer winced at her red-tracked eyes after she got out of the shower. She felt as if she had a hangover, without even the remembered pleasure of getting drunk the night before. Moving as if underwater, she dressed in her one clean outfit—making a mental note to wash the shirt and skirt she'd worn yesterday—dove into a cup of coffee, gulped down a fruit bar, and headed for the university.

The caffeine and the thought of the material she was going to present made her more lively by the time her Middle English class rolled around. She was beginning a new unit today, which also pleased her; she felt as if she was turning over a whole new leaf in her life. That absurd jingle left her chuckling to herself as she strode into the lecture hall.

The chuckles disappeared before she reached the podium. She fixed the class with as steely a gaze as she could muster—not very steely, she knew down deep, but she did her best. In what she hoped was a stern voice, she demanded, "Who hasn't kept up with the reading for today?"

A few luckless souls, lazy and honest at the same time, raised their hands. "You'll have to do better than that," she told them. "You knew when you enrolled—you certainly knew when you saw the syllabus—your work load would be heavy here. You have to stay with the lectures if you expect to get full benefit from the course."

Thegun Thegun Nug and the other two Foitani had kept their big, thick-fingered hands down. Jennifer was sure it wasn't because they didn't want to admit they'd fallen behind. She almost used them as an example, to say to the rest of the class, *See, if they can keep up, you ought to be able to.* Only the thought that they might not want to be singled out held her back.

She said, "We're not going to look at imaginary aliens for a while. Instead, we'll consider science fiction's examination of a problem that was pressing for several generations: the risk that mankind would annihilate itself over local disputes on Earth before it acquired the technology to get off the planet."

All three Foitani sat straighter in their slight, too-small chairs. She thought of the history of their race and shivered a little: a species didn't have to be planet-bound to do a pretty fair job of annihilating itself.

"For those of you who did read the lesson," she went on, "we'll discuss *A Canticle for Leibowitz* first. Ever since it was written, many people have named it the best science fiction novel of all time. The section I want to examine now is the middle one, the one called 'Fiat Lux.'"

"What is the meaning of this heading?" Aissur Aissur Rus asked. "Our translator program broke down on it, making obscure references to ancient wheeled conveyances and soaps. This does not seem appropriate to the content of the book."

"It sure doesn't." Jennifer wondered how any program could come up with anything so farfetched. "Maybe the problem is that the heading isn't in Middle English but rather Latin, a still older human speech. 'Fiat Lux' means 'let there be light.'"

"Ah." That wasn't Aissur Aissur Rus; it was a human student. Several others also made notes. Jennifer silently sighed. *Lazy,* she thought. They should have had no trouble accessing the meaning of the phrase. Not only was Latin still used liturgically, it was an important ancestral tongue to Spanglish.

"'Fiat Lux' is particularly interesting for its blend of historical analogy and extrapolation," she said. "The role of the church in the piece is based on what the church actually did after the collapse of the Roman civilization earlier in Earth's history; the Romans, by the way, were the people who used Latin.

"But the civilization which Miller envisioned collapsing after nuclear war was his own, which had already become highly dependent on technology. As civilization restored itself, as it began to discover once more how the world worked, it also began to discover that it was in fact rediscovering, was only finding out what its ancestors had already known. Miller effectively paints into his book the intellectual turmoil this realization would create—"

Jennifer stopped there. She hadn't intended to, but one glance at the Foitani would have distracted anybody. They weren't making a racket, they weren't even jumping up and down, but they had come to full alert for the first time in her presence. When a large creature—three large creatures—with spiky ears and good teeth comes to full alert in a human's presence, the human comes alert, too. Three million years of biological programming was screaming *Wolves!* in her ears.

She needed only a moment to collect herself. Thanks to her time as a trader, she knew how to break free from the prejudice of shape. A small part of her mind noted that she was thanking her time as a trader rather often these days. That annoyed her, all the more so as she'd wished she was on a nice, quiet university campus while it was going on.

She said, "Is there a question?" Her voice was still light, but steady enough.

She'd expected the Foitani to be bursting with questions. They surprised her. They started when she spoke to them, then looked at each other, as if she'd caught them picking their noses—if doing that was bad Foitani manners.

Finally Thegun Thegun Nug said, "No, no questions at this time, honored professor. We were merely interested in the analogies between the world this author draws and the experiences of our own people."

"Very well, I'll go on," Jennifer said. The translator's tone was as bland as ever, but she knew she'd heard a lie just the same—or at least, not all of the truth. Something more than interest in analogies had stirred up the Foitani there. But if they didn't care to talk about it with a human, what could she do?

Distractedly, she got through the rest of the day's presentation. The discussion was less lively than she'd hoped, not least because the Foitani had stopped taking part. They paid close attention to everything she and the humans students said, though: their ears kept twitching. Maybe that was a reaction they couldn't control.

When Jennifer got back to Ella's apartment, she wanted to talk about the aliens' extraordinary reaction to *A Canticle for Leibowitz.* Ella didn't want to listen. Ella was planning tomorrow's extravaganza with Xavier and wanted to talk about that. Jennifer, who was sick of men in general and Ali Bakhtiar in particular, made a poor audience.

After she and her friend discovered they weren't going to communicate that evening no matter how hard they tried, Jennifer began playing with the computer and de Camp's colons again. She wondered if some of the works where commas appeared instead were the work of overzealous copy editors. Offhand, she couldn't think of a single twentieth-century author who had a good word to say for copy editors.

The next day in class, she talked more about *A Canticle for Leibowitz,* comparing it to other works that looked at the aftermath of atomic war: *Davy, The Postman, Star Man's Son.* "This subgenre of science fiction was played out by the end of the twentieth century," she said. "By then it had become plain that such a conflict would not leave the survivors, if there were survivors, in any condition to recover as quickly as earlier writers had imagined."

Again, the Foitani stirred. Again, Jennifer thought they would say what was in their minds. Again, they did not. She almost asked them straight out. Unfortunately, that seemed to lie in the unpleasant middle ground between foolhardy and suicidal. The Foitani had been willing, even eager to talk before. Why not now, with a topic that really hit them where they lived? Jennifer had no answers. Grumbling to herself, she finished her presentation and stalked out of the lecture hall.

She went through her other two classes on automatic pilot. Still on automatic pilot, she started back toward her own apartment. After a couple of hundred meters, she muttered, "Idiot!" under her breath and turned toward Ella's building. After another fifty meters, she said, "Idiot!" again, much louder this time. A student close enough to hear gave her a curious look. Her cheeks flamed. That seemed only to interest the student more—he was a young man.

Jennifer spun away and tramped with grimly determined stride back to her office.

It wasn't the ideal place to spend a night. The "couch of sorts" was considerably more disreputable—and shorter—than the one in Ella's apartment. But the rest room was only a couple of doors down the hall. For one night, it would do. *Tomorrow,* Jennifer thought, *I'll be in my own new apartment.* That made the idea of one uncomfortable evening—even the thought of a dinner at the university cafeteria—bearable.

The dinner turned out to be bearable, too. Jennifer's best guess was that the university food service would soon fire whoever was responsible for cooking something edible. She took her Coke—what else, she said to herself, would a professor of Middle English drink?—out into the evening twilight and walked across campus slurping on it.

Once back in her office, she dutifully set to work. No one yet had come up with a computer program for grading essays. She scribbled marginal comments in red ink. At least Spanglish orthography corresponded to sound; she didn't have to deal with the erratic spelling that had plagued Ancient and Middle English.

Twilight faded to darkness around her. At just after 2100, a security guard phoned. "Sorry, Professor Logan," he said when he saw her face. "Just checking—the IR telltale showed somebody was in there. As long as it's you, there's no problem."

"I'm so glad," she said, but he had already switched off.

She tried to recover her train of thought. This student actually showed some grasp of how Piper had put together his future history, and she wanted to make sure she cleared up the gaps in the girl's understanding.

Just when she had reimmersed herself in the essay, the phone chimed again. This time, it was Ali Bakhtiar. "What do you want?" Jennifer said coldly.

Bakhtiar flushed. "I want to apologize again," he said. "I've just met your Foitani, and they're at least as impressive as you said they were. At least." He looked more than a little shaken. He didn't look shaken very often.

"Wait a minute. You *met* them? How did you meet them?"

"They came over here looking for you. They said they wanted to talk with you about the class. They didn't seem much interested in taking no for an answer, if you know what I mean. Finally I convinced them you'd moved out. I sent them on to your friend with the deep voice—Ellen Metchnikova, is that right?"

"Ella," Jennifer corrected absently. "Oh, God. She's not going to be very happy to see them. She has company tonight."

"I gathered that," Bakhtiar said. "I called her place to warn you they were coming, and she didn't much want to talk. She kept the vision blank, too. She snapped out where you were and switched off. So now you know."

"Oh, God," Jennifer said again. Ella would be a long time forgiving her for this, if she ever did. "Thanks, Ali, I guess. Better to know they're on the way."

"Listen, is there any way you could forget about moving out and come back here?" Bakhtiar said. "I really am sorry about what I said before, and I—"

"No, Ali," Jennifer said firmly. She'd already done all the thinking she needed to do about that one. "I'm sorry, too, but I don't think we were going anywhere anyhow. Just as well to break it off now. I hope we can still be friends, but that's it."

Bakhtiar scowled. "I hate when women say that. Anyway, though, I thought you ought to know about these creatures of yours. Good luck with them."

"They're not my creatures," Jennifer said, but Bakhtiar, like the security guard, didn't wait on the line to give her the last word. Shaking her head, she stared down at the essay on Piper. "Where was I?"

Just when she thought she remembered, the phone chimed again. She muttered something under her breath and jabbed a thumb at the ACCEPT button. The vision screen did not light. *Ella,* she thought, and Ella it was. "Jennifer, three blue behemoths are on their way to visit you."

"Thanks, Ella. Ali just phoned to warn me he'd sent them to your place. I'm sorry about that," Jennifer added.

"You ought to be," Ella snapped. "I don't like being interrupted when I'm right on the edge, and I especially don't like being interrupted twice."

"Oh, dear." Jennifer swallowed a giggle.

"If you weren't my friend . . . Well, these Foi-whatevers look big enough to have you for breakfast instead of talking, if that's what they want. Maybe you should keep your door locked after all."

"Don't be silly, Ella. Go back to Xavier, and I hope nobody interrupts you any more."

"Better not," Ella said darkly. "Good-bye." As it was the first one she'd got in three calls, Jennifer cherished that good-bye. She went back to work on the essay, hoping to finish grading it before the Foitani arrived.

A few minutes later, the elevator down the hall beeped. *The Foitani,* Jennifer thought. She put aside the paper; maybe it was never going to get finished. As it went back onto the pile, her brows came together. To get into the building this late, you were supposed to have an authorization card for the elevator to read. Then she shrugged. Maybe the Foitani had ridden up with someone who had a card. They knew her name, after all; a little explaining would be all they'd need.

Someone knocked on the door—knocked so high up on the door that it could only have been a battleball centerliner or a Foitan. She hadn't heard footsteps in the hall, but then the Foitani didn't wear shoes. They were very smooth and quiet for beings so large, as if they were closer to their hunting ancestors than humans were.

Jennifer opened the door and looked up and up. Thegun Thegun Nug towered over her; behind him stood the other two Foitani. Close up, they really were intimidating. Without intending to, she took half a step back before she said, "Hello. What can I do for you this evening?"

"You can come with us," Thegun Thegun Nug said.

The flat tone of his translator made Jennifer unsure just how he meant that. "I'd sooner talk here," she answered.

"It was not a conditional request," Thegun Thegun Nug said. Only then did she notice he held something in his left hand; anthropocentrism made her automatically look toward the right first.

The something sparked. That was all Jennifer remembered for a long time.

When she woke up, she was on a starship. The realization filtered in little by little, with her returning consciousness. Perhaps it took longer than it should have, for she had a headache like a thousand years of hangovers boiled down into a liter. Her trading stunner would quietly put a person out for an hour or two and leave her feeling fine when she woke up. Whatever the Foitani used didn't work that way. Oh my, no. The first time she tried to sit up, her head felt as if it would fall off. She rather wished it would, so she could forget it for a while.

After a bit, she began to notice things other than her pounding skull. The gravity was a good deal higher than Saugus's comfortable .85. It wasn't a planet's g-field, either. She didn't know how she knew the difference—no star traveler had ever succeeded in putting it into words—but she knew. The air was more than conditioned; it had the perfect flatness a good recycling plant gives.

Everything pointed to its being a Foitani ship, too. The chamber that held her was bigger and had a higher ceiling than humans were likely to build. Even the plain, foam pad on which she lay was outsized. The light from the ceiling panel had an oranger cast than humans would have used.

She looked around; she had to close her eyes several times at the pain that turning her head cost her. But for the bare mattress, the only things in the chamber with her were three plastic trash bags. She crawled over to them, moving slowly and carefully because of both the higher gravity and her headache. The trash bags held everything she'd had at her office, from her toothbrush to her computer to the complete contents of her desk, right down to paper clips and small change.

With a gasp of delight, she found her stunner. The delight quickly disappeared. Given that she was on a Foitani ship which she had no idea how to fly, how much good was the stunner likely to do her? She would have traded it in an instant for a year's supply of tampons. Since no one appeared with the trade offer, she clipped the stunner onto her belt.

Then she looked around for a place to relieve herself. Somehow, no one in her Middle English novels ever worried much about that. Neither had she, until she went on her first trading run. Squatting in the bushes brought her down to basic reality in a hurry.

She picked the corner farthest away from the foam-rubber mat. If the Foitani didn't come in and give her somewhere better to go before she had to empty her bladder, they could clean up after her themselves.

She was uncomfortable but not yet urgent when a door appeared in the far wall of her chamber: one second it wasn't there, the next second it was. Thegun Thegun Nug stepped inside. Of itself, her hand reached for her stunner. "That will do you no good," the Foitan said.

Suddenly she wasn't so sure. Maybe she couldn't fly this ship herself, but if she knocked Thegun Thegun Nug out and threatened to start carving him into strips a centimeter wide, his henchbeings might be persuaded to turn around and take her back to Saugus. Since that was the best notion she had, she pressed the trigger button.

Thegun Thegun Nug bared his teeth, but uncooperatively refused to fall over in a large, blue heap. "I said that would do you no good," he told her. "Your weapon makes me itch, but it does not make me sleep. Foitani stunners use a different ray."

Jennifer's gonging head gave anguished testimony to the truth of that. Back to her next priority, then. "Take me to whatever you people use for a toilet."

Thegun Thegun Nug took her. He even walked out of the room and left her alone. "My folk do not require privacy for this function, but we have learned humans prefer it." The door in the wall did not disappear, though.

"Thank you so much," Jennifer said, acid in her voice. "Why couldn't you have left me with my privacy back on Saugus, instead of kidnapping me?"

Her sarcasm rolled off Thegun Thegun Nug's blue skin. Through the opening in the wall, he answered, "You are welcome. And you would not have come with us of your own free will from the world you call Saugus; you were content there. But we have need of you, have need of your knowledge. Thus we took you."

"Thanks a lot," Jennifer muttered. The sanitary arrangements were simple enough: a couple of round holes in the floor, each close to half a meter wide. She squatted over one of them. When she was done, she called Thegun Thegun Nug, "Do you have anything I can use to wipe myself clean? Something soft and absorbent, I hope."

"I will see," the Foitan answered after a moment. "My species' orifices do not have this difficulty." Now the doorway vanished. The Foitan stayed away for a quarter of an hour. When he returned, he brought a length of gauzy cloth. "This is from our first-aid kit. Use it sparingly. It is all we can afford to give you."

"How long will the flight be?" she asked. Thegun Thegun Nug did not answer. She tried another string of questions. "What do you mean, you have need of my knowledge? How do you know what I know? And what kind of good is the knowledge of a professor of Middle English to you, anyhow?"

Thegun Thegun Nug chose to respond to one of those questions. "You were recommended to us by another human."

That only created more confusion for Jennifer. "I was? By whom?"

"By one with whom we have worked. He came across a situation beyond his expertise, and suggested you were the one to employ. From all we have seen of you, the probability that he is correct seems, if not high, then at least significant. He will also give you such aid as he may: he is still within Odern space."

"Odern?" The translator had left the word unchanged.

"Odern is my planet," Thegun Thegun Nug said. "It is one of the 127 worlds within our former sphere that still support Foitani life, one of the nineteen where starflight has been rediscovered. Before the Suicide Wars," he added, "we had settled on several thousand worlds; the precise number is still a matter of dispute among our scholars."

Jennifer shivered. She tried to imagine how humanity would war with ninety-five percent of its planets swept clean of life. She also wondered what the Foitani had found important enough to fight about on such an enormous scale. Humans had battled over religion with similar ferocity, but the rise of technology had weakened religion's hold on mankind. Maybe the Foitani had kept their fanaticism after they reached the stars.

Thegun Thegun Nug said, "Analysis of our rations has shown that you may safely eat them. You need have no concern on that score."

"How nice." Jennifer set hands on hips, took a deep breath. "You haven't given me a single reason why I should have the least bit of interest in doing anything for you. And I tell you this: kidnapping me like this has given me an awfully big reason not to."

"You have been on our payroll since the day we enrolled in your class, honored professor," Thegun Thegun Nug said. "We will pay standard journeyman merchant's wages, either in your currency or trade goods—your choice."

"I wasn't talking about money," Jennifer said. "And you have gall, too, putting me on your payroll for something I have less than no interest in doing."

For the first time outside the lecture hall, she succeeded in impressing the Foitan. "Money is not a sufficient inducement?" he said slowly. "I had been given to understand—and nothing I observed on Saugus diminished my understanding—that humans are a mercenary species, willing even, at times, to take arms against their own race or kin-group for the sake of profit."

"Some humans are. This human isn't. Damn you!" Jennifer heard her voice breaking, but could not do anything about it. "I was doing what I wanted to do, at last, after years of not being able to. What right do you have to take me away from that?"

"The right of species self-interest," Thegun Thegun Nug said, "which to us is paramount. I might also point out that, at need, physical coercion is available to force you to our will."

Jennifer's stomach turned to a small, chilly lump of ice. She felt her knees wobble. She was sure, though, that the more weakness she revealed to this inexorable alien, the worse off she would be. She looked up into the Foitan's round, black eyes. "How well do you think I'd do for you if you tortured me into submitting?"

"Less well than if you cooperate voluntarily, I admit. Torture, certainly, would be a last resort. I am, however, perfectly prepared to take away from you all your possessions and leave you alone in your chamber until ennui induces you to evince a more constructive attitude. My race has been waiting for twenty-eight thousand years. A fraction of another matters little to us."

She had no doubt Thegun Thegun Nug meant exactly what he said. Being bored into cooperation was attractive only in comparison to being tortured. The worst of it was, the trader part of her wanted to go along with the Foitan. *No, the traitor part,* she thought. But how many merchants had won the chance to trade with the Foitani? If she looked at it the right way—*the wrong way,* the professorial part of her insisted—that was what she'd be doing, trading her knowledge for their goods, if she *did* know what the aliens thought she knew. If she couldn't skin them on that deal, she didn't deserve to be a journeyman.

"All right," she said. "If you think I'm worth risking an interstellar war to get, I'll do what I can for you—provided you let me go after I'm done."

"Certainly," Thegun Thegun Nug said at once. "As for risking war with humans, I will only say it is highly unsafe for ships flown by other species to enter Foitani space unescorted. It is not altogether safe for our own ships to fly. Many weapons from the Suicide Wars are in free orbit throughout our former domain, and hard vacuum is an excellent preservative."

"Wonderful," Jennifer muttered. Now all she had to do was worry about hitting a mine that had been floating free since the days when Cro-Magnon man chased woolly mammoths between glaciers back on Earth.

"It is not wonderful, but it is a fact," Thegun Thegun Nug said; none of the three Foitani had much of a sense of humor. "Our detectors should suffice to get us back to Odern, however."

"They'd better," Jennifer said. "If we blow up, I'll never forgive you."

Thegun Thegun Nug started to answer, then stopped and seemed to think better of it. At last he said, "Come. I will return you to your chamber."

"What happens the next time I need to relieve myself?"

"One of us will escort you here. Were our situations reversed, would you trust me unescorted on a human ship?"

Jennifer wanted to say she wouldn't trust the Foitan no matter what. That did not seem politic at the moment, regardless of how true it was. Without a word, she followed Thegun Thegun Nug out of the toilet chamber and back to her own. She thought hard about annoying her captors with toilet calls at every hour of the day and night. With some species, she might have tried it. Her best guess, though, was that the Foitani would simply stop coming after a while, leaving her to foul her chamber. She decided not to risk it.

Aissur Aissur Rus brought her a plastic pouch of food a couple of hours later. She looked at it without enthusiasm. It resembled nothing so much as dry dog food. "This will nourish you, and should cause no allergic responses," the Foitan said.

Of the three aliens, Jennifer thought Aissur Aissur Rus the most open. Hoping he would answer where Thegun Thegun Nug had not, she asked, "Why did you people grab me? What do you think I can do for you, anyhow?"

"As a matter of fact, taking you was my idea," he said.

She stared at him. After liking him the best, hearing that jolted her. "What is it you want from me?" she repeated.

"One of your human sages once said, 'I am a midget, standing on the shoulders of giants.' When we Foitani of the present days look at the deeds of the Great Ones before the Suicide Wars, we are midgets trying to see up to the shoulders of giants. Perhaps you can help us do that. If not, perhaps you can help us see around the giants' bodies to a new way."

Jennifer frowned. Thegun Thegun Nug had evaded her questions. Aissur Aissur Rus seemed to answer openly enough, but the answer did not mean anything to her. "Go away and let me eat," she told him.

"I did not know you required privacy for that," he said.

"I don't require it, but I'd be grateful. I have a whole lot of things I need to sort out in my mind right now. Please."

Aissur Aissur Rus studied her. The Foitan's eyes had no sclera, no iris, no pupil. They were completely black and completely unreadable. At last, without a word, he made the doorway appear in her wall, walked through it, and made it disappear after him.

She ate. The coarse, crunchy lumps in the plastic pouch tasted like what she thought dog food ought to taste like; they came from something that had been meat quite a while ago. She made herself go on eating till she was full.

When she was done, she looked up at the ceiling and said, "I would like something to drink, please." The Foitani had to have electronic eyes and ears in the chamber.

Sure enough, Aissur Aissur Rus brought her a jug a few minutes later. "This is pure water," he said. "You may drink it safely."

"Thank you," Jennifer said. "May I also have water for washing?"

"Perhaps when you go to the toilets, so it will run down into a disposal hole," Aissur Aissur Rus said. "How often do you usually wash? The human custom is once a day, is it not? I suppose that might be arranged."

"You might have thought beforehand about what I'd need," Jennifer said.

"We are not used to considering the needs of other species. It is not the Foitani way, and does not come easy to us."

"Really? I never would have noticed."

Irony bounced off Aissur Aissur Rus as if he were iron-plated. When he saw Jennifer had no more to say, he turned and left as abruptly as he had before. She drank the jug dry. The water was cold, and had the faint, unpleasant untaste of distilling. It did help to ease her headache.

The jug was made of soft plastic. She flung it against the wall nonetheless. It denied her the good satisfying crash she craved, falling to the ground with a dull thump. She walked over to it and kicked it as hard as she could. That helped, but not enough. She found a pen, drew a couple of black circles on the side of the jug to stand for Foitani eyes. She kicked it again. "Better," she said.

V

Jennifer's computer insisted the flight to Odern lasted twenty-three days and some hours after the aliens snatched her away from Saugus. She thought it felt more like twenty-three years. By the time the ship landed, she wished all the Foitani had succeeded in blasting themselves to hell and gone—and then another twenty kilometers farther, for luck.

For one thing, her period arrived while she was in space, with no possibility of privacy whatever. She didn't much feel like explaining to the aliens how her plumbing worked, but she didn't have much choice, either, not if she wanted to keep her clothes clean. This time, they gave her all the absorbent cloth she wanted without arguing; menstruation, evidently, was one aspect of humanity about which they hadn't informed themselves.

"You wanted me, you got me—just the way I am," she told Thegun Thegun Nug.

"As you say." The Foitan hesitated. "You are certain you are not wounded?"

"I'm certain."

"As you say," Thegun Thegun Nug repeated. Though his translator sounded flat as ever, he did not seem convinced. *Squeamish, are you?* Jennifer wondered. She wished she could break out in green, smelly spots, just to revolt him.

For another, she got thoroughly sick of kibbles and water as a standard diet. "You knew you were going to kidnap me," she snarled at Dargnil Dargnil Lin. "Why didn't you buy—or even steal—something edible for me?"

"These rations are both edible and nutritious," Dargnil Dargnil Lin answered primly. "They are adapted for human needs from our standard spacecraft fare."

"You mean you eat this stuff all the time when you're in space?" Jennifer asked. When Dargnil Dargnil Lin waved a hand in front of his face in the Foitani equivalent of a nod, she said, "That's the best argument against spaceflight I ever heard." Dargnil Dargnil Lin left quite suddenly. *Maybe,* Jennifer thought, *I've managed to annoy him for a change.* She hoped so.

The one good thing about the flight was that it met none of the infernal devices left over from the Suicide Wars. Having to go that far to find something good brought the rest of the journey into perfect perspective for Jennifer.

She did not even know the ship had touched down until all three Foitani appeared outside the disappearing doorway. "Come with us," Thegun Thegun Nug said.

"How can I say no?" Jennifer murmured. Not only did he have his two immense comrades to help enforce his wishes, he was also carrying that vicious Foitani stunner. Getting shot with it was better than dying, but only a little.

The Foitani led her in the direction away from the lavatory. That was her first hint something unusual had happened. Any hope she had of seeing more of the ship quickly went by the wayside; one stretch of blank corridor looked just like another. But the chamber they went into had big space suits in a rack to one side; in a human ship, that would have made it the air lock.

Thegun Thegun Nug touched a panel on the far wall. Another doorway opened. Sunlight poured in. So did fresh air. After more than three weeks of the recycled product, it smelled amazingly sweet. The doorway framed buildings and green hills. *The green hills of Odern,* Jennifer thought. She shook her head. Rhysling would not have approved.

Thegun Thegun Nug turned and went backward out the door. Since he didn't fall, Jennifer figured he was going down a ladder. Aissur Aissur Rus followed him. "Now you," Dargnil Dargnil Lin said. "I will come last." Since he also had a stunner, Jennifer did not argue.

The way down proved not to be a ladder, but rather rungs set into the side of the spacecraft. The rungs were made for people the size of Foitani, which is to say, they were much too far apart for Jennifer. She was enough meters off the concrete below to get nervous at the thought of missing one, which did nothing to improve her grip.

"Hurry, can't you?" Dargnil Dargnil Lin called from the air lock.

"No, I can't," she said through clenched teeth. By the time she reached the ground, sweat was pouring from her armpits, too. This was a lot harder than going down the wall on L'Rau. She wanted to stand where she was and catch her breath, but from the way Dargnil Dargnil Lin was descending behind her, he didn't care whether he landed on her or not. She skipped aside in a hurry.

Once on the ground, Dargnil Dargnil Lin reached up and slapped the side of the ship. The rungs vanished, leaving the side smooth once more. It had to be memory metal, Jennifer thought. On human worlds, the stuff was a toy. The Foitani would appear to have exploited the technology more intensively.

As soon as the rungs disappeared, her captors seemed to forget all about her. They faced the low, rounded, green hills behind the spaceport, bowed themselves almost double. Still bowed, they began a slow, mumbling chant. Their translators picked up some of it for Jennifer. "Great Ones, look kindly on us. We return to Odern our homeworld, faithful always to our mission to regain the glory you once knew. Though earthgrip holds you now, we shall redeem you. May your glory return speedily, Great Ones, speedily. So may it be."

"You worship the Foitani who lived before the Suicide Wars?" Jennifer asked when Thegun Thegun Nug and his companions decided to notice her again.

"Not worship so much as respect," Aissur Aissur Rus said, "and truly the deeds of the Great Ones deserve—no, demand—respect. The more we learn of them, the more we seek to emulate them, to restore our sphere to the grandeur it once knew."

To bring about the conditions that caused the Suicide Wars, whatever those were, Jennifer glossed mentally, with a slight internal chill. Aloud, she said, "Then you don't really believe the Foitani you call the Great Ones live inside those hills?'"

"Not now," Aissur Aissur Rus said. Before Jennifer could do more than start to frown, the Foitan went on, "But once they did. Those are not natural hills. Once a city stood there. We've mined it for millennia."

Jennifer glanced over to the hills once more, this time with fresh eyes. They still looked big enough and permanent enough to have been in place for millions of years. And this was after—how long had Thegun Thegun Nug said?—twenty-eight thousand years, that was it, of neglect and erosion. She tried to imagine the towers that must have existed before earth and plants and time had their way with them, tried and failed.

"Odern was but a minor world in our former sphere," Aissur

Aissur Rus added. "Others have remains far grander and far better preserved. But most of those worlds are dead, of course."

"Of course," Jennifer echoed softly. That internal chill grew and spread as she thought about what living as the scattered survivors of the galaxy's biggest slaughterhouse had to be like for the Foitani. No wonder they didn't have much of a sense of humor.

"Now come with us," Thegun Thegun Nug said. "We have reported our success to our kin-group chiefs. They and we will presently acquaint you with the other human in our employ."

The other human—Jennifer had forgotten about him. Of itself, her hand went to the stunner she still wore on her belt. It was no more than an annoyance to the Foitani, but the first time she saw this other human, she intended to flatten him—and to kick him while he was down, too.

The spaceport tarmac was full of big, blocky-looking Foitani ships. A couple of kilometers away, almost hidden by one of them, she saw a vessel that had to be human-built. It was the sort of medium-sized, medium-slow ship a trader who worked solo might fly. "He'll be *so* low, all right, when I'm through with him," she said under her breath.

Like the ships, the spaceport buildings were on what was to her a heroic scale. Foitani who carried things that looked a lot more lethal than stunners stood outside doorways. They touched their left knees to the ground as Thegun Thegun Nug and his comrades went by. Even from that position of respect, their fathomless black eyes bored into Jennifer. She wondered if she really did prefer these dispassionate stares of suspicion to the longing glances human males so often sent her way. Maybe not, she decided.

Inside the administrative center or whatever it was, Foitani tramped purposefully down corridors wide and tall enough to echo. Some were armed like the guards outside; others spoke into computers. They all went about their business with the serious intensity that seemed a hallmark of the species.

Thegun Thegun Nug stood outside a place marked by writing in the angular Foitani script. He spoke to the air. Jennifer did not know what he said; somewhere between the ship and here, he and his fellows had turned off their translators. The air answered, as unintelligibly. Thegun Thegun Nug spoke again. One of those unnerving now-you-see-it, now-you-don't doors opened in front of him.

Jennifer had never been inside a spaceport operations center, but every third holovid drama seemed set in one, so she had some idea what they were like. This was definitely the Foitani version of such a nerve center. Big blue aliens talked into microphones, listened to oddly shaped headsets that accommodated their erectile ears, and watched holographic displays. For a few seconds, no one paid any attention to Thegun Thegun Nug and his comrades.

Then a Foitan spotted Jennifer. He waved her captors toward what looked like another blank wall. By now she had learned blank walls didn't necessarily stay blank among the Foitani. Sure enough, this one didn't. A door appeared, this time opening onto what had to be the local equivalent of a boss's office. For one thing, it boasted carpeting, the first Jennifer had seen on Odern. For another, the desk behind which a Foitan stood seemed about as long and wide as the flight deck of an ancient aircraft carrier.

"You will pay your respects to Pawasar Pawasar Ras." Thegun Thegun Nug turned his translator back on as soon as the office door disappeared behind his party. He pointed to the Foitan behind the desk.

Jennifer nodded. "Hello, Pawasar Pawasar Ras." *If I had a stepladder, I'd spit in your eye.*

"I greet you, human," Pawasar Pawasar Ras said; Jennifer suspected that meant he was too important an executive to be bothered with remembering her name. "I trust your journey here was of adequate comfort."

You're pretty trusting, then, aren't you? was what she wanted to say. Since the Foitani who had kidnapped her already knew exactly how she felt about that, she kept her mouth shut.

Dargnil Dargnil Lin nudged her. A nudge from a Foitan was almost enough to knock her off her feet. "Answer the honored kingroup leader when he questions you," Dargnil Dargnil Lin said.

"I survived the journey," she said. Let this honcho make what he wanted of that.

Pawasar Pawasar Ras said, "You are doubtless of the opinion that you have seen a sufficiency of our kind." Jennifer's eyes opened wide: this was the first Foitan she'd met who had any of what humans reckoned common sense. Maybe it was rare enough in his species to make possessing it an automatic ticket to an important job like his. He went on, "Accordingly, I will let the human who has been working in cooperation with us explain the predicament he and we have encountered."

He touched something on his desk. A door appeared in a different wall of the office. Jennifer waited grimly. Whoever had set her up for this would have a lot more explaining to do than

Pawasar Pawasar Ras thought. He might even find himself in a brand new predicament of his own.

A man dressed in trader coveralls came through the doorway. Jennifer stared. She'd expected to know the fellow who had betrayed her. She'd never expected he'd be someone she liked. "Bernard!" The academic part of her dredged up a stupid Middle English joke. "What's a nice guy like you doing in a place like this?"

Bernard Greenberg looked sheepish, although the top of his head was devoid of wool. "Hello, Jennifer," he said. "I'm sorry. I didn't think they'd just up and grab you."

"Well, they bloody well did," she said, then added bitterly, "Were you so angry at me for going off to the university instead of staying a trader that you decided to get even? This isn't even; this is overkill."

"No, no, no." He plucked at his salt-and-pepper beard in distress. "It's not like that, Jennifer; really it's not. I thought they'd consult you. When they told me they were going to bring you here, I tried as hard as I could to talk them out of it. But their ship had already left for Saugus by then, and even if it hadn't, it's not easy to talk a Foitan out of anything. You may have noticed that."

"Now that you mention it, yes," she said with a sidelong glance at Thegun Thegun Nug. She studied Bernard Greenberg and decided she'd made a mistake. "I should be the one who says she's sorry, Bernard. It's not your fault—not all your fault, anyway. I just hit out at the first thing I could reach without climbing onto a box." She looked at Thegun Thegun Nug again. His translator was working, but if he caught what she'd meant as well as what she'd said, he gave no sign of it.

Pawasar Pawasar Ras said, "Enough, if you please; this is not an appropriate time or place for social intercourse. Human Bernard, be so good as to define the problem for your colleague here." *He knows* Bernard's *name,* Jennifer thought with what she knew to be a completely irrational stab of jealousy.

"If I could define the problem, honored kin-group leader Pawasar Pawasar Ras, I wouldn't need a colleague," Greenberg answered. Pawasar Pawasar Ras bared his teeth. Jennifer knew that was only a Foitani frown, but it carried more impact than anything a human could do. Greenberg turned back to Jennifer. "You know the Foitani are past-worshipers and scavengers both."

She nodded. "Given what they did to themselves so long ago, it's hardly surprising."

"No, it isn't. The local population on Odern has mined the

planet pretty thoroughly, when you consider how much of what used to be here has to have rusted away or whatever over the past umpty-thousand years."

Not enough, Jennifer thought. By the way Greenberg's mouth narrowed and lengthened ever so slightly—it wasn't a smile; it wasn't even close to a smile—Jennifer knew he'd picked up what she was thinking. No nonhuman would have noticed a change in his expression. She said, "I'm still not clear what this has to do with me."

"Scavenging turned into a whole different game for the local Foitani when they reinvented the hyperdrive," Greenberg said. "They had some idea which stars held planets their species had settled once upon a time. When they went out to look at those planets, they found that a lot of them were dead. Some had no Foitani left, some had no life at all—sterile. Fission bombs, diseases, asteroid strikes, poison gas—I don't know what all. The old imperial Foitani—"

"The Great Ones," Pawasar Pawasar Ras corrected.

"The Great Ones, I mean—well, they seem to have had a more advanced technology than we do now. They were great at killing, that's certain. And on a lot of those dead worlds, the toys they left behind survived in much better shape than on a place like Odern, where everything got reused over and over again as the world was sliding into barbarism. Now, on one of the planets that used to be part of the empire, they've come across something they can't handle."

"They said that themselves," Jennifer said. "They didn't explain it, though—they haven't explained much of anything. So what exactly are you talking about?"

"They've found an artifact they cannot try to use and stay sane. If they're within ten or twelve kilometers of it, they can't help trying to use it, either, whatever the hell it is. I've seen dozens of the poor bastards who tried. They aren't pretty. The ones on the fringes of the effect around the thing can fight the compulsion, but if they get too close, they're doomed. Finally they lost enough people to make them fortify the whole area. But they were still curious, so they hired a non-Foitan—me—to see what he could find out."

"And you went crazy, too," Jennifer said, "or you never would have given them my name."

Pawasar Pawasar Ras's eyes swung sharply toward Greenberg when Thegun Thegun Nug's translator turned that into the local language. "Does the other human speak accurately, human Bernard? Has the Great Unknown"—even with the translator, Jennifer could hear the capital letters—"affected your psychological integrity?"

"I do not think so, honored kin-group leader Pawasar Pawasar Ras," Greenberg answered. Jennifer had finally managed to get his goat; he gave her a dirty look as he went on, "You may have noticed that humans use irony more than Foitani do."

"This practice of saying one thing while meaning another is rank, manifest foolishness," Pawasar Pawasar Ras said.

"As may be," Greenberg answered mildly; he sounded used to soothing Pawasar Pawasar Ras every so often. He turned back to Jennifer: "I couldn't find anything about this artifact that would make anybody go insane, human or Foitan. If it's not a physical effect, what's left? Best bet, I figured, was something cultural. I've been a trader a long time; I know something about that sort of thing. But you know more. Not only do you have your trader background, you've got a working knowledge of all the hypothetical cases your old-time writers invented. And the more I dealt with this thing, the more hypothetical everything about it looked, if you know what I mean. So I mentioned your name to the Foitani."

The worst part was, it made sense. Jennifer tried to stay angry, but failed. She let out a long sigh. "And they took the ball and shot it toward the far goal," she said. "That does seem to be the way they do things."

"It certainly does." Greenberg cocked his head at her. "Shot the ball toward the far goal? I didn't know you followed battleball."

"An acquired taste. It's wearing off, believe me. Now that I'm here, there isn't any good way back without going along, is there?" She turned to Pawasar Pawasar Ras. "All right, where next?"

"To the world Gilver," he answered with almost robotic literality. "This is the world upon which the Great Unknown is situated."

"Any chance for research first?" she asked: she *was* an academic before anything else. "You've been studying your ancestors ever since the, ah, Suicide Wars. Did they leave behind any records that might help you understand this thing?"

"That is an intelligent question." Pawasar Pawasar Ras's ears twitched, so he was genuinely pleased. "We have not found any data related to the world Gilver that pertain to it. Dargnil Dargnil Lin here can assist you in examining our data bases, if you think that would be valuable. He is expert in the ancient archives."

"I would like to see them, yes," Jennifer said. She wondered if Dargnil Dargnil Lin was an exception, or if steady, solid, serious types among the Foitani gravitated toward jobs like archivist as they did with humans.

"See to it, Dargnil Dargnil Lin," Pawasar Pawasar Ras said.

"It shall be done, honored kin-group leader," Dargnil Dargnil Lin replied.

Striking while the iron was hot and the big boss in a cooperative frame of mind, Jennifer said, "I saw Bernard Greenberg's ship here at this spaceport, honored kin-group leader." If she was going to butter up Pawasar Pawasar Ras, might as well get him good and greasy. "May I stay aboard it? A human ship truly would be a more proper base for me." *And thanks to you, I'll never, ever keep a dog.*

"If the human Bernard does not object, you may do this," Pawasar Pawasar Ras said.

"I don't object," Greenberg said at once.

"Then you may make those arrangements, human," Pawasar Pawasar Ras said to Jennifer—he still didn't have her name. Though Foitani eyes were next to impossible to read, she felt his gaze intensify as he went on, "Do not think this will permit you two humans to plan a joint escape. Aside from the dangers inherent for non-Foitani flying through space once in the Great Ones' sphere, we have our own tracker and explosive device secured in the—the—what is the name of your ship, human Bernard?"

"The *Harold Meeker*, honored kin-group leader," Greenberg said.

"Yes, the *Harold Meeker*. Very well, then, human, ah—"

"Jennifer." *Took him long enough to ask,* Jennifer thought.

"Yes, Jennifer. You may proceed, then, human Jennifer, with your researches for a period not to exceed, ah, twenty Odern days, Dargnil Dargnil Lin to assist you as necessary. Then you and human Bernard shall travel to Gilver to continue in the attempt to analyze the Great Unknown. Thegun Thegun Nug, Aissur Aissur Rus, Dargnil Dargnil Lin, and I shall accompany you there."

Jennifer had expected the other three Foitani to go offworld with her if she left Odern. They were plainly her keepers. But Pawasar Pawasar Ras surprised her by including himself. From what she knew of big-wheel executives, they didn't often inflict themselves on actual research sites. "Why you?" she asked him.

"The Great Unknown is my project," Pawasar Pawasar Ras said, as if that explained everything. To him, it seemed to. To Jennifer, it showed the Foitani definitely were not human—not that she hadn't noticed that already.

Jennifer finished a salami sandwich. The meat was greasy, the bread bland. The mustard was tangier than she cared for. She washed down the sandwich with a glass of *vin* extremely *ordinaire.*

After Foitani rations, it all tasted wonderful. "Thank you, Bernard," she said. "I just may live. I may even decide I want to."

"Sorry there isn't more and better," Greenberg answered. "I've been in Foitani space long enough that I'm starting to run low myself."

"And I'll make you run out all the faster. I'm sorry."

"Don't be. You always did apologize too much; do you know that? If I hadn't opened my big mouth, you'd still be happily back on Saugus. Sharing real food with you is the least I can do to pay you back. We won't starve on what the Foitani eat—"

"However much we wish we would," Jennifer finished for him.

He studied her, one eyebrow raised. After Ali Bakhtiar's virtuoso displays of superciliosity, this was amateur night. The master trader said, "You've changed a bit since we flew together a few years ago. Then you wouldn't have interrupted or made sour jokes."

She shrugged. "I've finished growing up. I find I can manage all right for myself. Now to business, if you don't mind, because I don't want to spend one more second here than I have to. First off, is your ship bugged?"

"I assume so. Pity we don't know some arcane foreign languages we could use to talk privately," Greenberg said. Jennifer gave a rueful nod. Nobody bothered to learn to speak foreign languages these days, not with oral translator programs so widely available. She supposed she could make a stab at speaking Middle English, but the Foitani were more likely to understand her than Greenberg was.

"What is this Great Unknown thing, anyway?" she asked.

"If I knew, I would tell you," he answered. "If I knew, we could go home, come to that. But I don't know. I just hope we'll be able to find out. I keep worrying about what the Foitani may do if we can't—and we may not be able to. Nobody who isn't a Foitan has any real notion of what their ancestors were capable of, back before the Suicide Wars. I told you, though, it's pretty clear they were technologically ahead of where we are now."

"That won't help us understand them." Jennifer slowly shook her head. "They may have been ahead of us technically, but socially! Think of spending however many thousands of years they took to build up their empire, and then to blow it to bits, and themselves with it." She shook her head again, this time in horror. The Foitani seemed to have lived out every human's darkest nightmares.

Greenberg said, "To this day, they don't know why they started to fight. But once they got going, they did a good, thorough job, which is typical of the species. Pawasar Pawasar Ras says they undoubtedly intended to kill themselves off altogether; in a crazy sort of way, he thinks less of them for failing."

"The worst part of it is, now that I've been around Foitani a while, I can almost see the logic in that." Jennifer started to say something more, but found herself yawning instead.

"You may have more privacy aboard one of their ships, or in the spaceport," Greenberg said. "You'd certainly have more room. This isn't a big ship at all."

"If you want me to leave, I will. Otherwise I'd sooner stay here," Jennifer said. "I don't need a whole lot of privacy from you, do I? After all, we've flown together before."

"I'll set you up with a foam pad in the storeroom." Greenberg spread his hands. "I'm sorry, but that's the best I can do if you want any room to yourself."

"Drag the pad in here tonight, would you? After getting lifted the way I did, just being close to somebody human will feel good. I don't think you're going to molest me."

Greenberg grinned lopsidedly. "Tempting as the notion is—no." He rummaged in a compartment, pulled out the promised foam pad. Except for being smaller, it was identical to the one on which she had awakened inside the Foitani ship. Greenberg rummaged some more, let out a grunt of triumph. "I thought I had a spare pillow in here. And here's a blanket, too."

Jennifer took them. "Thanks. But do you know what the biggest pleasure being aboard your ship will be for me?" Without waiting for Greenberg to reply, she went on, "Having a toilet that fits my behind."

He laughed at that. "Yes, I've seen what the Foitani use. They'd be especially bad for you, wouldn't they?" He waved toward the refresher cubicle. "Help yourself."

"I don't mind if I do." She hesitated, then asked, "You wouldn't by any chance have tampons or anything like that?"

"I don't know if there are any in the sanitary supplies or not. I never needed to find out until now."

"Well, if you don't, I suppose I can improvise something or other. I did it once; I can do it again."

When she got out, Greenberg went in. She stripped down to her underpants, gave her grimy outfit an unhappy look, and then brightened—the *Harold Meeker* would be able to get clothes *clean*, not just stir the dirt around as she had been doing. She slid under the blanket.

Greenberg surprised her by stooping next to the foam pad and reaching out to touch her shoulder. She stiffened. Was he going to make advances now? She'd made love with him a few times on their first trip together, on the way home from L'Rau. But this was *not* the right time, not for her. She tried to figure out how to tell him that without hurting him or making him angry.

But all he wanted was to apologize again. "Jennifer, I'm so sorry. You should be back on your campus, doing what you wanted to do."

"It can't be helped," she said. Her dreams of elaborate revenge had collapsed when she found out how the Foitani learned of her, and from whom. While they lasted, though, they'd helped sustain her. With nothing in their place, she felt very tired. "Just let me sleep."

"Fair enough." Greenberg rose; Jennifer's eyes closed even as he did so. She heard cloth whisper when he pulled off his coveralls, then the muffled sound his body made pressing against the sofa bed. He must have touched the light switch, for the darkness behind her eyelids got blacker. "Good night," he said.

She thought she answered him, but she was never sure afterward.

Dargnil Dargnil Lin stood in front of a workstation. It had all the elements of the ones with which Jennifer was familiar—holoscreen, mike, keyboard, and printer—yet was in aggregate nothing like them. The Foitani had their own engineering traditions, which owed nothing to those of mankind.

"I suppose you will want to begin with our records pertaining to the Great Unknown," Dargnil Dargnil Lin said.

"I'd rather have more background first, if I could," Jennifer answered. "Can you show me something basic and general about your race as it was before the Suicide Wars?"

"Your time for research is limited." The translator was expressionless as always, but Jennifer thought she heard a sniff in the Foitan's voice. She looked up at him without saying anything. He bared his teeth at her. She kept waiting. At last he said, "Let it be as you wish, then." He spoke to the workstation. The screen lit. Dargnil Dargnil Lin said, "This is a history such as our adolescents use."

"Good." The video had more text to it than a comparable human one would have used, and Jennifer could not read the Foitani written language. But there were still plenty of pictures, and Dargnil Dargnil Lin's translator turned the soundtrack into Spanglish for her. She watched and listened and spoke low-voiced notes into her computer.

On a historical star atlas, she watched the empire of the Great Ones spread. The sound track attributed their unbroken run of success to their inherent superiority over all the races they encountered. She wondered whether the species was biologically programmed to think that way, the Foitani of Odern were imitating their ancestors, or if they were projecting their own attitudes back onto the Great Ones.

A few minutes of watching made her toss out that last possibility. The Foitani of long ago had definitely been in the habit of killing off races that proved obstreperous. They did not bother to hide or even to go out of the way to justify genocide; they simply went about it, with second thoughts as few and far between as if they were swatting flies.

"Can you stop the tape for a moment?" Jennifer said. Dargnil Dargnil Lin could. Jennifer asked him, "Would your people act that way again if you were strong enough?"

"Probably," he said. "We have not reached the heights the Great Ones achieved, however, and races such as your own appear more potent than any they faced. Thus we have had to begin to learn to treat with other species rather than simply rolling over them. It is not easy for us."

Jennifer bit back the sardonic retort that automatically came to mind. The Foitani could not help being what they were. Expecting aliens to act like humans was the easiest way for a trader to get into trouble. Moreover, mankind could not boast a spotless record among the stars, though humans had perpetrated their worst acts of savagery on themselves.

The same seemed true of the Foitani. The screen Jennifer was watching suddenly turned a dazzling white. She staggered back, hands to her eyes, as if caught by the blast of a real explosion. When she looked again, a phrase in the Foitani written language filled the screen. "The Suicide Wars," Dargnil Dargnil Lin read for her.

"I'd suspected that, yes," Jennifer murmured. Far more rapidly than it had grown, the Foitani empire crumbled. Most of the stars that had filled the holovid map went dark. A handful, scattered at random across two or three thousand light-years, kept glowing red. An even smaller handful burned with a yellow light.

"Those yellow dots are the worlds of our species that have relearned starflight," Dargnil Dargnil Lin said. "On the red, Foitani also survive, but in a state of savagery."

"But *why* did it happen?" Jennifer asked. "What made you fight like that?" The tape hadn't offered a clue; its narration merely recorded the event without analyzing what had brought it on.

"I cannot answer for certain, nor could anyone else on Odern," Dargnil Dargnil Lin said. "There are speculations, but who can truly hope to see into the minds of the Great Ones? Only when we can match their deeds will we be worthy to comprehend their thoughts."

Jennifer's mouth twisted in discontent. The Foitani were too busy venerating their past to try seriously to understand it. "May I speak without causing offense through ignorance of your customs?" she asked, one of the standard questions every trader learned.

"Speak," Dargnil Dargnil Lin said.

"If the Great Ones were as magnificent in every way as you make them out to be, why did they ever go and fight the Suicide Wars in the first place?"

"For reasons of their own, reasons which surely reflected their greatness," Dargnil Dargnil Lin answered. Jennifer filled her lungs to shout at him; that was less than no answer, for it shunted aside thought rather than inspiring it. But the Foitan was not through. "Some among us have speculated that the Great Unknown contains the full and proper response to your question, and that our failure to grasp merely reflects our degeneracy in comparison to our ancestors."

"That's—" Jennifer stopped. How did she know it was nonsense? She was no Foitan—*thank God,* she added to herself. She tried again. "That's interesting. What evidence do your scholars apply in support of it?" The idea of the Foitani of Odern as decadent descendants of the true race had a nasty appeal to her, not least because it made their behavior in snatching her the product of debased minds.

Dargnil Dargnil Lin said, "I will show you a tape and let you draw your own conclusions."

"Show me several tapes, ones with differing points of view. How can I decide what is true on the basis of a single report?"

"You are a scholar," Dargnil Dargnil Lin said, as if reminding himself. "Very well, let it be as you wish." For the next several hours, Jennifer viewed records of the Foitani discovery of the Great Unknown, and of speculations about it. When she was through for the day, she mentally apologized to the big, blue aliens. She'd thought them too staid to produce much in the way of crackpottery. Now she knew better. Given the proper stimulus, they could be as bizarre as any human ever born.

The Great Unknown was proper enough. She studied orbital views of it, then pictures taken at long range from the ground, and finally close-ups. "Those were obtained by remote-controlled cameras," Dargnil Dargnil Lin said of the last batch. "We have a great store of data, as you see. They do not lead us toward understanding, however."

The old Foitani seemed to have gone in for monumental architecture in a big way. Massive colonnades led toward an enormous column that leaped most of a kilometer into Gilver's sky. No weeds, no undergrowth marred the Great Unknown or its precinct, even after twenty-eight thousand years. Nor had Gilver's tectonic forces damaged either tower or colonnades. They might have been raised yesterday rather than in the late Pleistocene.

"Why didn't this thing get bombed along with the rest of the planet?" Jennifer asked.

"Something else we do not know," Dargnil Dargnil Lin said. "For your knowledge base, though, you should also observe some of the first of our people to come close enough to the artifact to feel its effect." He spoke into the microphone again.

After a few seconds of viewing, Jennifer had to turn away. Greenberg had been right; the Foitani who got too close to the Great Unknown weren't pretty. They hadn't just been damaged—they'd been destroyed. They drooled and shook and sucked on their toes and relieved themselves wherever they happened to be. Their muzzled faces gave not the slightest indication of surviving intelligence, nor could Dargnil Dargnil Lin's translator make sense of the shrieks and growls that sprang from their throats.

"This happened to *all* your people who got too close?" Jennifer said, gulping.

"All. The precise radius at which the Great Unknown began to grip them varied with the individual, but within it no one was safe."

"Hmm." Jennifer thought for a while. "And we know this didn't happen with Bernard. Does it happen to Foitani from worlds other than Odern who come to Gilver?"

"We do not know," Dargnil Dargnil Lin said. "We do not want to find out. To an alien such as yourself, all who still inhabit the Great Ones' sphere may rightly be known as Foitani. Well and good. But those who spring from other worlds are untrustworthy at best and outright abomination at the worst. Only we of Odern are the true descendants of the original race."

"Oh, my aching head," Jennifer said softly.

"Your head still distresses you? Perhaps it is an aftereffect of the ray Thegun Thegun Nug used to stun you. I hope you have an analgesic available."

"Never mind," Jennifer said, not surprised the translator had been too literal. All the surviving Foitani had been separated from one another for more than twenty thousand years. No wonder they'd have trouble getting along. After so much time, they wouldn't even all be of the same species any more. She asked, "When you deal with these other Foitani, what language do you use?"

"That of the Great Ones, so far as we understand it. It is the only speech we have in common, after all. Some worlds, among which Odern takes the lead, also use this tongue in everyday life in place of our former degenerate jargons. Others barbarously insist on maintaining the primitive languages they employed before coming into contact with more civilized Foitani."

"All right; thanks. I think I've seen enough for today, if that's all right with you." What with the spectacle of completely deranged Foitani and the realization that the Foitani of Odern were just one small part of a much bigger puzzle, Jennifer was sure she'd seen enough.

Bernard Greenberg clapped a rueful hand to his forehead when she told him what she'd learned. He said, "I should have thought of that. It's too easy to forget how long they spent isolated on their own planets."

"With luck, it won't matter," Jennifer answered. "After all, the Foitani from Odern are the only ones who know about Gilver, so they'll be the only ones we have to worry about."

"I suppose so," Greenberg said. "But if they learned of the place from records they dug up, there's always the chance some other bunch will, too."

Jennifer had tried not to think about that. "Bite your tongue."

The more she researched the Great Unknown, the more she concluded that was a good name for it. Fusion bombs had all but sterilized Gilver. They'd fallen all around the mysterious artifact, but not a single one had landed inside what she'd taken to calling the radius of insanity. The planet's ecosystem was still struggling to repair itself; parts of that continent had become almost lush with greenery. Within the radius of insanity, nothing grew. Mere life, apparently, was not allowed to disturb the Great Unknown.

"I can imagine achieving that effect for a limited time, with periodic maintenance," Dargnil Dargnil Lin said when Jennifer asked him about it. "But to continue since the Suicide Wars . . . no, human Jennifer, it is but another of the wonders the Great Ones left behind for us to marvel at."

Jennifer was sick of marveling at the Great Ones. She wanted answers, and the Foitani records on Odern held precious few of them. "I never would have believed it," she said when her last allotted research day was done, "but I'll be glad to go to Gilver, just to try and figure out what's really going on."

"More power to you, if you can do that on Gilver," Greenberg answered. "If you think Odern is boring, you haven't seen anything yet."

"I haven't seen anything of Odern, except the spaceport and the library. Neither one of them is likely to drive Earth or Redford's Star off the tourist itineraries."

He smiled at her. "You've changed; do you know that? You're not nearly the same person you were when you flew with me aboard the *Flying Festoon.*"

Jennifer mentally prodded herself. "It hasn't been that many years, Bernard. I don't feel different in any particular way."

"You are, though. Back then, when anybody said anything to you, you were as like as not to pull back into your shell and not even answer. You don't back away any more; you're a lot surer of yourself than you used to be."

"Am I?" Jennifer thought about it. "Well, maybe I am. I'm older now, after all. I was just a student when I took my first trading run." She laughed, mostly at herself. "All I wanted to do was get something out of the ordinary on my vita. I did that, all right. I've been to places most Middle English professors would run screaming from. Come to think of it, I wouldn't blame them. If I thought it would do any good, I'd run screaming out of here."

"It wouldn't do any good. But Odern is lively, next to Gilver. Here at least you have a whole planet full of people doing all the normal things people do. There are only two kinds of people—well, Foitani, but you know what I mean—on Gilver. They have soldiers, to guard something nobody else is supposed to know about, and they have scholars, to try to understand something they don't dare approach. Aissur Aissur Rus is from Gilver—he was the head of the research team there."

"I like him better than a lot of the others," Jennifer said.

"Yes, he's sharp," Greenberg agreed. "He thinks for himself, and that's unusual among the Foitani. They usually just go around trying to figure out what the Great Ones would have done. I suppose that's one of the reasons he got the job. Nobody here had any idea what the Great Ones were doing with the Great Unknown, so they had to get someone who could put his own slant on things. But that's not the point I was trying to make. Aissur Aissur Rus was so glad to get away from Gilver that he volunteered to be part of the team that brought you back here."

"That's great," Jennifer said. "But he's going back there with us, isn't he?"

"So he is, but I don't think it's because he really wants to. The Foitani run more toward a strong sense of duty than we do."

"After what they put themselves through with the Suicide Wars, it sounds like a survival characteristic for them. To pull themselves back up after something like that, they'd have to have been able to stick together."

"I suppose so." Greenberg yawned. "We'd better get some sleep. If your research is done, we'll probably be leaving for Gilver early tomorrow, or maybe even late tonight. The Foitani don't believe in wasting time. They could be in here any minute now, to install the course tape and the electronic countermeasures they hope will get us there without being blasted by something left over from the Suicide Wars."

"Of course, they have their own bomb aboard already," Jennifer said.

"There is that, yes. But we don't have to worry about it as long as we're good little boys and girls." Greenberg's voice was dry.

"That's great," Jennifer said again. She walked into the refresher cubicle. When she came out, Greenberg went in. She undressed, lay down on the foam pad—it never had gotten moved to the storeroom—and pulled the blanket up over her. She closed her eyes, but discovered that, though she was tired, she wasn't ready to sleep. The faint ammoniacal smell of the foam pad reminded her of the one she'd had on the Foitani ship, which in turn made her feel all over again how very much alone she was. But for Greenberg, she was the only human for too many hundred light-years. The *Harold Meeker*'s temperature was perfectly comfortable. She shivered under the blanket even so.

Greenberg came out of the refresher. He yawned again, stepping toward his sofa bed. If he had any worries like Jennifer's, he didn't show them. She suspected they were there; back aboard the *Flying Festoon,* he'd been good at keeping things to himself so his worries wouldn't worry others. It was one of the several traits for which she admired him.

She nodded to herself. "Bernard," she called softly, "do you really feel like sleeping right away?"

He stopped in midstride. His voice was controlled and careful when he answered, "Does that mean what I think it means?"

She nodded again, this time for him. "I think it means what you think it means."

"Jennifer, any man who didn't want to go to bed with you the minute he set eyes on you would need his vision correction adjusted. You know that," Greenberg said. Jennifer did know it. The knowledge had not always brought happiness; men found it too easy to separate her body from her, to want the one without caring about the other. But Greenberg was going on: "We have enough other things to worry about right now, so I want to know if you're sure. If it's going to complicate our lives a lot, it's more trouble than it's worth."

"If you have the sense to say something like that—and I was sure you did—then we should be able to manage, don't you think?"

"I hope so," he answered. He pulled off his shorts. The cabin of the *Harold Meeker* was small; two quick steps brought him to the foam pad. He got down beside her. She wadded up the blanket, threw it against the wall. He smiled. "I forgot just how lovely you are. I'd sort of kept from looking at you a lot—I didn't want to make a nuisance of myself, or more of a nuisance than I've already been for getting you dragged to Odern in the first place."

"That's foolish," Jennifer said. "It's not as if we haven't seen each other before. Trading ships are like that. And we're friends already, and more than friends, even if it was a while ago now."

"Quite a while ago now—getting close to ten years, isn't it? I didn't want to impose, and you were still upset about being here. But—" He didn't go on, at least not with words.

Jennifer savored what he was doing. She remembered from the *Flying Festoon* that he was seldom in a hurry—a rare virtue in men, she'd since found. Since he was about twenty years older than she was, she wondered if it was just that he was more thoroughly mature. More likely, it was that he was simply himself. Whatever it was, she enjoyed it.

Some considerable while later, she arched her hips so he could slide down her underpants. "Be careful with them," she said. "I only have the two pairs, and yours aren't made for the way I'm put together."

"I like the way you're put together."

"I noticed." Her hand closed on him.

"And I'll be careful," he promised. "How's that—and that—and that?"

Her underpants had only gotten as far as her knees, but she didn't care. "Mmm. That's—nice. Oh, yes. Right there, right there—"

The communicator buzzed harshly. "Oh, no," Jennifer said. Greenberg was a good deal more eloquent than that. The communicator ignored both of them. It kept on buzzing.

"Open your ship at once, humans. This is Pawasar Pawasar Ras speaking. I shall brook no delay." The electronic translator's tone was flat, but the words could hardly have been more peremptory. Pawasar Pawasar Ras went on, "We need to install important gear aboard the *Harold Meeker* immediately. Refusal to open the ship will be taken as evidence of conspiracy against the Foitani species."

"What do you suppose they do to conspirators against the Foitani species?" Jennifer asked.

Greenberg stroked her one last time. "I'm tempted to find out." But the moment was broken, and they both knew it. He got up from the foam pad and called out, "We will open the ship in a moment, Pawasar Pawasar Ras. You roused us from our rest, that's all."

"What rest?" Jennifer said. Then she giggled. "I was certainly roused, though."

"Shut up," Greenberg said over his shoulder as he dressed. She put her clothes back on, too. He ordered the air lock open. The alien, faintly spicy smells of Odern's air filled the cabin.

Two Foitani technicians came in. They filled the cabin, too, to overflowing. They installed their gadgetry, then ran some checks to make sure their artificial-intelligence system meshed with the *Harold Meeker*'s computers. One of them wore a translator. He said, "If you try to disable this system, you will also disable your own electronics. If by some accident you do not do that, you will remain altogether vulnerable to weaponry from the days of the Suicide Wars. I tell you this for information's sake. You may die if you like, but you should be aware of how and why this will come to pass."

"Thank you for being generous enough to warn us," Greenberg said.

"You are welcome." Like most Foitani, the technician was irony-proof. "You will lift off as soon as is practicable, which is to say, at once."

Greenberg drew himself to attention and spoke to the air: "Commence lift-off sequence."

"Automatic checklist commencing," the ship's computer answered.

"Wait for us to leave this cramped vessel, you fool," the Foitani technician exclaimed. "We are not ordered to fly to Gilver." For once, Jennifer saw an agitated Foitan.

"Sorry. Computer, cancel lift-off sequence," Greenberg ordered. He turned back to the technician. "You did tell me to lift off at once, did you not?"

"Yes, but—" The Foitan gave up. Along with his companion, he hastily departed from the *Harold Meeker.*

Greenberg grinned at Jennifer. "The best way to confuse them is to take them perfectly literally when they don't want you to. Only trouble is, they're so literal-minded themselves that you don't get as many chances as you'd like." The grin changed shape, just a little. "Which is true of other things as well. Where were we when we got so rudely interrupted?"

Jennifer stepped close to him, took his hand, and guided it. "I think," she whispered, "you were right about here."

The trip from Odern to Gilver was about as long as the one from Saugus to Odern had been. Other than that, the two journeys held no similarity. This time, Jennifer had pleasant human company aboard a human ship. All the facilities were designed for her species; she'd been glad to discover that the *Harold Meeker*'s sanitary supplies did include tampons.

She studied the material Dargnil Dargnil Lin had taken from Odern's library. The Foitani of Odern did very much seem to be spiritual descendants of their long-destroyed imperial ancestors: they were stern, humorless, efficient, and basically unwilling to recognize other species as anything but creatures to be exploited. *I can testify to that,* she thought.

Nothing in the data gave her any great insight into the Great Unknown. If the Foitani thought she'd step off the *Harold Meeker* with the answer to their problem all wrapped up with a bow around it, they were going to be disappointed. She took malicious glee at the idea of disappointing them, glee tempered only by the realization that disappointed Foitani were also liable to be dangerous Foitani.

The idea of stepping off the *Harold Meeker* without the answer made something else occur to her. "What became of the *Flying Festoon,* Bernard?" she asked. "Why aren't you still flying it?"

"I sold it after that first trip you took with me," he said, shrugging.

"Marya and Pavel both reached master status after that run, and they wanted commands of their own. I could have kept it and hired on some less experienced crewfolk, I suppose, but I didn't feel like it. So I sold it and got this smaller ship. I'm a jack-of-all-trades and I like my own company pretty well, so I thought I'd make a few runs by myself. I was turning a profit till this mess with the Foitani blew up. If we can figure out the Great Unknown, I'll make one yet. So will you."

Jennifer sighed. She'd been a trader long enough that turning a profit was important to her, too. She wondered if it was important enough to mean she had to satisfy the Foitani after all. Maybe it was. If they kept their bargain and let her take her pay in trade goods, she was more confident than ever that she could squeeze them till their black, ball-bearing eyes popped.

But she was not just a trader; and she didn't want to be a full-time trader. She spent a lot of time with her reader in front of her face, going through Middle English science fiction both to keep her grasp of the language sharp and to see if any of the science-fiction writers, with their elastic minds, had imagined a race analogous to the Foitani. That was a better hope than wading through the xenanthropology manuals: a glance there had told her what she already knew, that none of the other races with which humanity was acquainted resembled the blue-skinned aliens at all. Besides, Middle English was more fun to read than the manuals.

"Any luck?" Greenberg asked hopefully when she came up for air one day about halfway through the trip to Gilver.

She had to shake her head. "Nothing so far."

"Keep looking. I know how I used to sneer at you for reading that stuff, but the ideas you got from it really came in handy on L'Rau."

"I used ancient literature to help me on Athet, too: Sherlock Holmes it was that time, not properly science fiction at all. As somebody—Niven, I think it was—said back in the twentieth century, abstract knowledge never goes to waste."

Greenberg knew something about the twentieth century, but not enough. "Niven? I thought he was an actor, not one of your writers." The misunderstanding took several minutes to clear up. Finally Jennifer projected pictures of both men. "No, they're definitely not the same fellow," Greenberg admitted.

"There, you see?" she said. "They—" She stopped with a squawk, grabbing for the back of the sofa bed—the *Harold Meeker* was lurching under her feet as if caught on the ground during an earthquake. She felt the hair on her arms and at the back of her neck prickle up in alarm. Ships in hyperdrive had no business lurching. What was there to run into?

The viewscreen had been dark all through the journey; in hyperdrive, what was there to see? It was dark still, but dark in a different way, dark with the velvety blackness of space. A couple of stars gleamed, like tiny jewels set on the velvet.

Greenberg and Jennifer stared at each other. "Status report!" he snapped.

"Ship has returned to normal space," the computer answered. "Reason unknown."

They looked at each other again, this time fearfully. If they couldn't get back into hyperdrive, the way home was laser driver, light-sail, and frozen sleep. Inside human space, that was feasible; every human planet listened for rescue beacons and maintained rescue ships. Starting out from somewhere in the middle of the Foitani sphere, though, they could travel for ten thousand years before they ever got back to the edge of human space.

"Condition of hyperdrive engine?" Greenberg said urgently.

After a moment, the computer reported, "All systems appear to be performing satisfactorily. The hyperdrive, however, is not functional."

Greenberg made hair-tearing gestures. Jennifer stifled a nervous laugh—she wondered if he'd really pulled his hair before he went bald. Just then, what looked like a supernova blossomed in the viewscreen. Jennifer threw up her hands to protect her eyes. "Radiation!" the computer screeched. "Protective screens—" There was a pause of several seconds. "—holding."

The flat voice of a translator came from the comm speaker. "Foitani ship *Horzefalus Kwef* to human ship *Harold Meeker.* You may proceed in normal operation."

"First tell us what the hell just happened," Greenberg said. His own voice was shaky; Jennifer blamed him not at all.

"We have successfully destroyed a hyperdrive trap that dates from the days of the Great Ones. As soon as a ship is forcibly returned to normal space, a normal-space missile left behind in the area homes on it. That missile is now detonated. You may proceed."

For the third time in a couple of minutes, Jennifer and Greenberg stared at each other. She was not surprised that he found words first: "There's no way you can pull a ship straight out of hyperdrive like that!"

"On the contrary," the Foitan aboard *Horzefalus Kwef* answered, "there is a way. You have just seen it demonstrated. Our science has not succeeded in reconstructing what that way is. I gather from what I infer to be your surprise that human science has not either. But the Great Ones knew. I tell you once more, you may proceed. Failure to do so will be construed as lack of good faith."

"We're going, we're going," Greenberg said. He gave the computer the necessary orders. The *Harold Meeker* had no trouble returning to hyperdrive. Greenberg gaped at the blank black viewscreen and shook his head. He spoke to the computer again. "Save multiple copies of all data pertaining to this incident."

"It shall be done," the computer said.

Jennifer said, "Just knowing that a hyperdrive trap is possible is going to drive human engineers crazy for years. Nobody's ever even imagined such a thing. And you'll have the only tapes of one in action." The *Harold Meeker* was his ship; they were his tapes. Trading Guild regs spelled that out in words of one syllable; she was just a passenger here.

"*We'll* have," he corrected. "I wouldn't try to go all regulation on you. You wouldn't be in this mess if it weren't for me. And besides . . . those tapes have enough money in them for a lot more than two people."

"You don't have to do that," she said. "I didn't go into trading for the money. And all the same, I'm a long way from broke."

"You're also a long way from home, and that's my fault. Computer, log that any profits from tapes of the hyperdrive trap will be divided equally between journeyman trader Jennifer Logan and me."

"Logged," the computer said.

Jennifer saw that any further protest would be worse than useless. "Thank you, Bernard."

He brushed that aside. "Let's just see if we can get back to human space to turn the tapes into money. Right now, I have to say that's rather less than obvious."

Some people would not have been generous at all. That wouldn't have bothered Jennifer; the tapes belonged to Greenberg because he was shipmaster. Some people would have been generous and then expected something—probably a lot—in return. Very few people were like Bernard Greenberg, to be generous and then act as if nothing had happened. She thought that was wonderful, and knew he wouldn't want her to say so.

The rest of the trip to Gilver was uneventful. The only misfortune that took place was running out of human-style food and having to go over to Foitani rations. Jennifer crunched away at her kibbles with a singular lack of enthusiasm. "No, a plural lack of enthusiasm," she said a few meals later, "because there are lots of ways I don't like them."

Greenberg answered with a snort. Wordplay wasn't one of his virtues, or vices. People had been arguing about that since the days of Middle English, and longer. Puns were part of why Jennifer enjoyed Middle English science fiction in the original; Robinson, among others, was untranslatable into Spanglish because of them.

The hours followed each other, as hours have a way of doing. At last the computer announced that the *Harold Meeker* had reached Gilver's star system. The viewscreen went from blank blackness to velvety blackness; Gilver's sun blazed in the center of it. Gilver itself, a bright blue-green spark, shone in one corner. The computer swung the ship and boosted toward the planet on normal-space drive.

Alarms went off. "Missiles incoming!" the computer shouted. "Firing laser driver. Many hostile targets, converging on ship from many directions. Maneuvering to position laser driver. Firing . . . Maneuvering . . ."

"Human ship *Harold Meeker* to *Horzefalus Kwef,*" Greenberg called urgently. "What the bloody hell is going on? I thought you people said Gilver was a dead world except for the Great stinking Unknown. Where are all these ancient missiles from the time of the Great Ones coming from?"

While he and Jennifer waited for an answer, the ship's weaponry blasted three missiles. But more bored in. Then those, too, began winking off the screen, some just vanishing, others exploding in spheres of radioactive fire. Jennifer found herself wondering about the *Harold Meeker*'s shielding and wishing she were wearing something more protective than thin synthetic underwear and cotton coveralls cut down to fit her. A lead suit of mail might have been nice.

At last the *Horzefalus Kwef* deigned to reply. "Human ship, these missiles are not of Great One manufacture. We are under attack by elements of a fleet from the Foitani planet Rof Golan. These Foitani are vicious and treacherous by nature. They must somehow have stolen information that led them to Gilver. We shall endeavor to protect your feeble ship as well as—" The transmission cut off.

"Did they get hit?" Jennifer asked. She half hoped the answer would be yes. The *Horzefalus Kwef* might be protecting them from the Rof Golani ships, but if it was gone they could try to head back to human space. The Foitani electronics aboard gave them some chance of making it in one piece.

But after checking the telltales, Greenberg said, "No, they're still there. The other ships are jamming their radio traffic. There they go, down toward the surface of the planet. I think we'd better follow them."

Regretfully, Jennifer decided he was right. The screen and radar plot showed explosions and missiles all around the ship. The *Harold Meeker* was not built for war. The Rof Golani spacecraft plainly were; they had more acceleration and maneuverability than a peaceful ship would ever need. By the way it performed, *Horzefalus Kwef* seemed a match for them. Staying close to it seemed the best bet for survival.

Unintelligible words came from the speaker: a Foitani voice, but not one always calm and self-contained like those of the Foitani from Odern. This one screeched and cried and yelled. "What do you suppose he's saying?" Jennifer asked.

"Nothing we want to hear, and you can bet on that," Greenberg answered. He studied the radar plot. "There goes one of the bastards! And that wasn't a missile from *Horzefalus Kwef,* either. Our paranoid friends' ground installations have paid off after all."

"They certainly don't think much of other Foitani, do they?" Jennifer agreed. "And they do think this Great Unknown thing is worth protecting. They didn't want to get caught flat-footed if another Foitani world somehow found out about Gilver."

"Somebody has, all right," Greenberg said.

The viewscreen blazed white. Alarms yammered, then slowly quieted. "We cannot sustain another hit so close without serious damage," the computer warned. A moment later, it added, "Entering atmosphere."

Atmospheric fliers swarmed up from the base on Gilver. With the fight so close to the planet, they were of some use against spacecraft. Jennifer found herself cheering when one of the attacking ships blew up in a burst of supernova brilliance. She stopped all at once, surprised and a little angry at herself. "I never thought I'd be yelling for the miserable folk who kidnapped me," she said.

"When they're helping to save your one and only personal neck, that does give you a different perspective," Greenberg answered.

"So it does," she said, glad he understood and also impressed that he could preserve his wry slant on things when they might turn to radioactive incandescence in the next instant.

Horzefalus Kwef managed to get a signal through. "Human ship *Harold Meeker,* land between the two westernmost missile emplacements at our base. Dive below us now; we will provide additional cover for you."

Deceleration compensators whined softly to themselves as the computer guided the *Harold Meeker* toward the designated landing site. The base was on the night side of Gilver. Not too far away, a large circle of ground was illuminated bright as day; at its center, the white tower that was the heart of the Great Unknown stabbed outward toward the stars.

Jennifer caught her breath at the beauty of the scene. She knew then that the esthetic sense of Odern's Foitani was different from her own, and also, she was suddenly sure, from that of their ancient ancestors. None of the pictures in their data base had been taken at night.

"Landing," the computer announced. "Recommend you do not leave the ship at the present time. The risk of radiation exposure outside appears significant."

"Did you program it for understatement?" Jennifer asked. Greenberg chuckled softly and shook his head.

Having nothing else to do, they spent their first hour on Gilver making love. Just as they were hurrying toward the end, a missile made a ground hit close enough to shake the ship. Jennifer laughed softly.

"What is it?" Greenberg gasped above her.

"Stupid twentieth-century joke," she answered, clutching him to her. "Did the earth move for you, too?" Then, for a while that could never be long enough, all speech left her.

Afterward, as he was dressing, Greenberg said, "Now I know you were really meant to be a scholar and not a trader."

"Why, Bernard?"

"Because who but a born scholar would come up with thousand-year-old jokes at a time like that? And thousand-year-old stupid jokes—you were right."

"I told you as much aboard the *Flying Festoon.* You didn't believe me then; I guess that's why you upgraded me from apprentice to journeyman."

"Partly I didn't believe you, I suppose. But there was more to it than that. You showed me you were a good trader. You got done what needed doing. You didn't seem to do it the way anybody else would, but it works for you, and that's the only thing that counts in the long run."

"I was using ancient literature as my data base instead of traders' manuals. No wonder things I tried looked strange to you."

"That's not all of what I meant, either," he said. "Most traders—just about all traders—push hard at everything they do. Pushing is part of being a trader. You're not like that. You're more reserved, shy almost. You were shy then—less so now, I think. But you still got a lot of business done."

"It's how I am," Jennifer said.

"I like how you are." His eyes softened as he smiled at her.

The communicator had developed a way of spoiling tender moments, almost as if it were a baby that resented anyone else's getting attention. It did not break the pattern now. "*Horzefalus Kwef* to human ship *Harold Meeker.* We have beaten the Rof Golani pirates away. You may emerge and join our scientific team."

"Then again, we may not," Jennifer said, irked at getting interrupted yet again.

The communicator was silent only a moment. Then the Foitan on the other end said, "Our weapons are trained on you. You will emerge and join our scientific team."

This time, the look Greenberg shot Jennifer was reproachful. She felt suitably reproached; she'd known since her first contact with the species that the Foitani were humorless. Greenberg said, "Thank you, *Horzefalus Kwef.* Let us put on our suits, if you don't mind—the computer says it's 'hot' out there. Then we will emerge and join your scientific team." Sighing, he walked over to the air lock. Sighing even louder, Jennifer followed.

VI

The planet Gilver had obviously had little to recommend it even before the Foitani from Rof Golan attacked. Back in what on Earth was still the Pleistocene, the Foitani had done a much more thorough job on it during their Suicide Wars. They'd eliminated their own species from the planet, and come too bloody close to destroying the whole ecosystem. Life still clung to Gilver. It no longer thrived there.

Jennifer found depressing a landscape that showed more slagged desert than forest and grassland. When she looked east rather than west, though, she looked toward a landscape with no life at all: the precinct surrounding the Great Unknown was sterile as an operating theater. The column at the heart of the Great Unknown speared the sky, though the research facility of the Foitani from Odern was more than fifteen kilometers away. That seemed to be far enough to keep the big, blue aliens safe from the hideous insanity that plagued them closer to the gleaming white tower. Their instruments wandered the precinct of the Great Unknown and probed what they could; the Foitani themselves were barred.

"The instruments don't pick up any too much, either," Jennifer complained.

Aissur Aissur Rus said, "If instruments provided the data we need, we would not have been required to requisition your services."

She gave the Foitan reluctant credit for not being mealy-mouthed, but said, "If I'm going to do you any good at all"—*and if I'm ever going to get out of here,* she added mentally—"I'll have to examine your Great Unknown for myself."

"By all means," Aissur Aissur Rus said. "The human Bernard is already proficient with our ground vehicles. Before you enter the precinct of the Great Unknown, you would be wise to acquire a similar proficiency. Bear in mind that, should difficulty arise, you will have to effect your own rescue, as we shall be unable to come to your aid."

She had to admit that made sense. The ground vehicle proved simple to operate. It was a battery-powered sledge, tracked for good ground-crossing capability, and steered with a tiller. The size of the tiller was her only problem; she had to stand up to shift it from side to side.

She and Greenberg rode separate sledges into the area surrounding the tall, white pillar. The Foitani had not argued about that; they believed in redundancy, too. The vehicles purred forward side by side.

The radiation level had gone down in a hurry; the Foitani from Rof Golan had thrown neutron bombs, no doubt to make their own planned landing easier. Jennifer wasn't sorry it hadn't worked. One set of Foitani at a time was plenty.

After they'd gone four or five kilometers, she said, "We have more privacy here than we did on the *Harold Meeker.* Whatever we do, the Foitani aren't going to come after us to stop us."

"True enough," Greenberg said, "but what do you want to bet these chassis have explosives in them along with the motors?"

She thought it over. "You own a nasty, suspicious mind, and I've no doubt whatever that you're right."

They rode on. The sledges had one forward speed, slow, and one reverse speed, slower. Eventually they reached the beginning of one of the colonnaded paths that led inward to the Great Unknown's central column. The path, of gleaming gray stone, was as fresh as if it had been set in place the day before. Not even a speck of dust marred its surface. However the Great Ones had managed that, Jennifer wished her kitchen floor were equipped with a like effect.

The columns that supported the roof overhead gradually grew taller and thicker as they approached the central tower. The effect went from impressive to ponderous to overwhelming. Jennifer did not think that was merely because she was smaller than a Foitan. How any living creature could have felt anything but antlike on that journey was beyond her.

She said, "I don't like this. Why would the old-time Foitani want to make themselves into midgets? I've seen pictures of our own old monumental architecture—the pyramids of Egypt, the freeways of

Los Angeles—but none of it, not even the pyramids, sets out to deliberately minimize observers the way this thing does."

"The stuff you're talking about was done in low-tech days," Greenberg said. "I suppose the effects were worked out empirically, too—on the order of, it's big, so it must be impressive. The thing to remember about the old-time Foitani is, they knew exactly what they were doing. They had all our modern building techniques and then some, and they were able to figure out just how they wanted this thing to look, too. And if it works on us, just think what it does to their descendants."

Jennifer thought about the tapes she'd seen, then quickly shook her head. She preferred not to recall the drooling, mindless Foitani who had come to the Great Unknown. She tried to imagine instead what the colonnade might have been used for, back in the days of the great Foitani empire. She pictured hundreds of thousands of big, blue aliens triumphantly marching toward the column, and hundreds of thousands more standing on either side of the path and cheering.

That wasn't so bad. Then, though, her imagination went another step, as the imagination has a habit of doing. She pictured the hundreds of thousands of triumphal Foitani herding along even more hundreds of thousands of dejected, conquered aliens of other races. She pictured those other aliens going into the base of that clean, gleaming, kilometer-high column and never coming out again.

She shook her head once more. From everything she knew about the Great Ones, that latter image had a horrifying feel of probability to it. She asked Greenberg, "Is there any way to get inside the column?"

"The Foitani have done magnetic resonance imaging studies that show it's not solid—there are chambers in there," he answered. "None of their machines found an entrance, though, and I didn't either, the last time I was here."

"Might be worthwhile blasting a hole in the side," Jennifer said.

"Might get us killed for desecration, too," he pointed out. "They've been studying this thing for a long time. If they wanted to try blasting their way in, they would have done it by now. Since they haven't, I've operated on the assumption that they don't want to."

"A shaped charge wouldn't do that much damage," Jennifer said, but then she let it go. She feared Greenberg was right. The Great Unknown was the principal monument the imperial Foitani had left behind, at least so far as their descendants on Odern knew. If they'd wanted to break into it by brute force, they probably would have done so for themselves.

Now the column was very close. Greenberg drove right up to it, halted his sledge. Jennifer stopped beside him. She craned her neck and looked up and up and up and up. The experience made for vertigo. Her eyes insisted the horizontal had shifted ninety degrees, that she was about to fall up the side of the tower and out into space.

She needed a distinct effort of will to wrench her gaze away and look back to Bernard Greenberg. He smiled a little. "I did just the same thing the first time I came here, only more so," he said. "The next time I looked at my watch, ten minutes had gotten away from me."

Jennifer found that she wanted to look up the side of the tower again. She ignored the impulse until it sparked a thought. "Do you suppose this is what sets the Foitani off? Maybe it just hits them a lot harder than it does us."

"I don't think it's anything so simple," he answered regretfully. "For one thing, it doesn't begin to explain why they're *drawn* here from ten kilometers away."

"No, it doesn't," she admitted with equal regret. She climbed down from her sledge. "I'm going to look around for a while."

Her shoes scuffed on the polished gray pavement. But for the faint whistle of wind between columns of the colonnade, that was the only sound for kilometers around. If Gilver boasted any flying creatures, they stayed away from the precinct of the Great Unknown. Jennifer found herself missing birdcalls, or even the unmusical yarps of the winged beasts native to Saugus.

She also found herself deliberately keeping her back to the white tower so she would not have to look up it. As deliberately, she turned round to face it. She refused to let the Foitani intimidate her.

She walked over to the tower and kicked it hard enough to hurt. Greenberg gave her a quizzical look, which she ignored. She'd booted the water-bottle the Foitani had given her all the way across her chamber. She wished the tower would fly through the air the way the water-bottle had. It stubbornly stayed in place.

"As if anything that has to do with the Foitani ever paid the least bit of attention to what I wish," she said, more to herself than to anyone else. With her pique at least blunted, she climbed back onto her sledge, turned it about, and headed back down the colonnade road toward the Foitani base outside the radius of insanity.

"What are you doing?" Greenberg called after her. "You just got here."

"I've seen all I need to see, for now," Jennifer answered, "Enough to make me certain I'm not going to turn the Great Unknown into the Great Known by walking around and peering as if I were Sherlock Holmes."

"That's the second time you've mentioned him to me. Who was he?"

"Never mind. An ancient fictional detective." Not everyone, she reminded herself, read Middle English—or even Middle English authors translated into Spanglish—for fun. She went on, "Anyway, the point is that I need more data than my eyes will give me. If the Foitani here at their base don't have those data, nobody does."

"What if nobody really does?" Greenberg asked. He was coming after her, though. The Great Unknown didn't drive humans crazy, but that didn't mean anyone enjoyed being around it, either, especially by himself.

"If they don't have the data we need, then maybe we ought to think about manufacturing some shaped charges and getting inside the column to see what's hiding there. If the Foitani want to call that blasphemy or desecration, too bad for them. They can't blame us for not coming up with answers if they won't let us ask the right questions."

"Who says they can't?" Greenberg said. Past that, though, he did not try to change her mind. She wondered if he agreed with her or if he was just waiting for her to find out for herself.

About one thing he'd been right: if the Foitani base on Gilver wasn't the dullest place in the galaxy, that place hadn't been built yet. The base was mostly underground, which had served it well when the attack from Rof Golan came. It only served to concentrate the boredom, though, because the Foitani didn't seem to care much about getting out and wandering around. There Jennifer had trouble blaming them. Gilver had not been a garden spot before the fleet from Rof Golan hit it. It was worse now.

Jennifer decided to beard Aissur Aissur Rus first. Of the Foitani with whom she'd dealt, his mind was most open. When she proposed blasting a hole in the tower, he studied her for a long time without saying anything. At last, he rumbled, "I have been urging this course on my colleagues for some time. Some say they fear the tower has defense facilities incorporated into its construction and so are afraid to damage it. Others tell me frankly they believe the demolition would be a desecration. I prefer the latter group. Its members are more honest."

"If you won't test, how do you propose to learn?" Jennifer asked.

"Exactly the point I have been trying to make," Aissur Aissur Rus said. "Now that I have your support for it, perhaps I can persuade some of my stodgier fellows to see that it is only plain sense."

"Or maybe they'll oppose you even more because you have a non-Foitan on your side," Jennifer said, thinking aloud.

"Yes, that is certainly a possibility. On the other hand, the Foitani of Rof Golan have also evinced a strong interest in the Great Unknown. I would sooner be associated with a non-Foitan than with those savage beings who style themselves Foitani. So, I think, would others."

That righteous anger, delivered in the translator's toneless voice, made Aissur Aissur Rus seem more nearly human to Jennifer. Preferring the out-and-out infidel to the heretic, to one's own gone bad, had roots that went back to Earth and were ancient there.

"Let us take this up with Pawasar Pawasar Ras," Aissur Aissur Rus said, apparently fired with enthusiasm. "He always declined my requests when he stayed on Odern. Now that he has at last seen the Great Unknown for himself—and seen that the Rof Golani covet it—perhaps he can be made to feel as certain we can unravel its mysteries as if he were to find himself just within the radius of doom."

Radius of insanity was Jennifer's term for it, but she had no trouble following Aissur Aissur Rus. She looked up at him. He was staring away from her, staring at an empty spot a meter or so in front of the end of his muzzle. His gaze held enough intensity to make her shiver. She used once more the standard question she'd learned as a trader. "May I speak without causing offense through ignorance of your customs?"

Aissur Aissur Rus needed a moment to return to himself. Then he said, "Speak."

"Just—a feeling I had. Were you ever on the fringes of the radius of doom?"

His big, rather ursine head swung quickly toward her. "It is so. How could you have deduced it?"

"You used the comparison you made as if you understood exactly what it entailed."

Getting a Foitan from Odern to show alarm was not easy. Jennifer had seen that. Now she saw one who was alarmed and did not try to hide it. Aissur Aissur Rus's plushy blue fur rose till he looked even bigger than he was. He bared his teeth in a way different from, and more frightening than, the usual Foitani frown-equivalent. His eyes opened so wide that Jennifer saw they really did have a pale rim.

He paced up and down the chamber, working hard to bring himself back under control. At last he turned back toward Jennifer and said, "May I never have such an experience again. I knew the danger, but proved to be unfortunate. Most of us may safely work at a distance within my personal radius of doom. I went to discuss some instrument readings with a technician and found myself—"

He stopped. His fur stood on end again. He waited until it had subsided before he went on, "I found myself filled with insight such as I'd never had before. I knew—I could feel that I *knew*—exactly how to comprehend the Great Unknown. I started to go toward it, to implement my knowledge. I went by the most direct route. I threw a desk and table out of the way, tried to batter down a wall at a place where no door existed in it, kicked and clawed the technician when he had the ill luck to stand in my way. It took four of his fellows at the installation to cart me back to a safe distance, and I fought them at every step until my mind was free of the Great Unknown's thrall."

The account of his episode of insanity was all the more chilling because it came out in the translator's flat tones. Jennifer shivered. She bore Aissur Aissur Rus no great goodwill, particularly as he'd evidently been the one who instigated her kidnapping. But she would not have wished on anyone what the Great Unknown did to Foitani.

She asked, "When you were safe again, did you recall the insight you'd had within your radius of doom?"

"No, and that may be the worst of it. I still feel that if I returned there, I would *know* again; I gather others of my kind have had a similar reaction. But none ever succeeded in communicating this knowledge, and I doubt I would prove the lone exception." He whispered something in his own language. The translator made it come out as emotionlessly as everything else, but Jennifer supplied the exclamation point: "Oh, to be wrong!"

They went to see Pawasar Pawasar Ras, who fixed Aissur Aissur Rus with a black ball-bearing stare. "You have been advocating this course for some time."

"Yes, honored kin-group leader, I have," Aissur Aissur Rus said.

Pawasar Pawasar Ras turned to Jennifer. "Why do you take his part?"

"Because if you really do want answers about the Great Unknown and nothing you've tried has worked, then you'd better try something else. If you're not serious about this project, then you can go on doing the same old things for the next twenty-eight thousand years." She threw in the number with malice aforethought. Beside her, Aissur Aissur Rus's ears twitched, but he kept quiet. She finished, "Honored kin-group leader, you were serious enough about what your people are doing here on Gilver to come here yourself. The Foitani from Rof Golan seem serious about this place, too. So why won't you do what plainly needs doing?"

Pawasar Pawasar Ras bared his teeth at her. She stood firm, as she had with Dargnil Dargnil Lin in the library. Finally Pawasar Pawasar Ras said, "Had the Great Ones encountered your species, human Jennifer, they would have made a point of exterminating it. I must say I feel a certain sympathy toward such an attitude myself."

"I'll take that for a compliment," Jennifer answered coolly. Aissur Aissur Rus's ears twitched again. Now it was Jennifer's turn to try to stare down Pawasar Pawasar Ras. "Are you going to do what needs doing, or is this whole project just a sham?"

"Honored kin-group leader, what the human means is that—" Aissur Aissur Rus began.

"Don't soften what I said," Jennifer interrupted. "I meant it. If your people were willing to invade human space to snatch me to investigate this thing, why aren't you willing to do a proper job?"

"As we have noted, you do not think kindly of our species," Pawasar Pawasar Ras said. "Tell me this, then: Why do you care whether our project succeeds or fails? Indeed, I would expect you to hope we fail, so that you might gain a measure of revenge thereby."

Jennifer looked at the big, blue alien with the same reluctant respect she'd had to give him after they first met at the Odern spaceport. "You know which questions to ask, I must say. When your people first kidnapped me, I did hope you'd fail," she answered honestly. "I've changed my mind, though, for two reasons. First, digging out the answers you need looks like the only way I'm going to get back to Saugus. And second, I just flat-out hate the idea of any job being done poorly when it could be done right."

"At last, human Jennifer, you have found a characteristic the two of us share," Pawasar Pawasar Ras said. "Very well, then, it shall be as you suggest. We shall undertake to open the tower that is the centerpiece of the Great Unknown. Should matters not go as you hope, however, remember that a share of the responsibility remains yours even if, as kin-group leader, I make the ultimate command decision here."

"You sound as if you expect the tower'll start spitting out warriors from the age of the Great Ones, or something like that," Jennifer said. "For heaven's sake, it's been sitting here ever since the Suicide Wars."

"As you did, I will give two reasons for my concern, human Jennifer," Pawasar Pawasar Ras said. "First, the Great Ones built to last, as witness the hyperdrive trap that nearly took us all on our journey here. And second, the Great Unknown remains active at least in some measure, as witness its state of preservation and the radius of doom that surrounds it. Opening the tower will be in the way of an experiment, and in a proper experiment one learns what one had not known before. I will not deny my fear at some of the things the Great Unknown may teach us."

Jennifer thought about that. A line from a Middle English fantasy writer—was it Lovecraft? Howard?—floated through her mind: *do not call up that which you cannot put down.* Maybe it was good advice.

She shook her head. If she didn't take the chance, she didn't think she'd ever see Saugus again. She was willing to take a lot of chances to get back to human space. No matter how big the tower in the middle of the Great Unknown was, she didn't think it could hold enough old-time Foitani to overrun the entire human section of the galaxy. After what Pawasar Pawasar Ras had said, she wasn't as sure of that, but she didn't think so.

"Let's go on with it," she said.

"We will need to consult with some of our soldiers," Pawasar Pawasar Ras said. "They will best be able to gauge the type and strength of explosive likely to penetrate the tower while doing the minimum amount of damage."

"Possibly Enfram Enfram Marf. He is a specialist in ordnance," Aissur Aissur Rus suggested.

"Whomever you say." Jennifer paused, wondering whether she should trot out her all-purpose question again. She decided to: "May I speak without causing offense through ignorance of your customs?"

Pawasar Pawasar Ras and Aissur Aissur Rus's translators answered together. "Speak."

"I've met a good many Foitani by now. As far as I can tell, all of you have been males. If I'm mistaken, I beg your pardon, but if I'm not, why haven't I met any of your females?"

"As this question steps along, the claws of its feet press against delicate flesh," Pawasar Pawasar Ras said.

"Shall I attempt an answer, honored kin-group leader?" Aissur Aissur Rus asked.

"Please do," his boss answered.

Aissur Aissur Rus turned to Jennifer. She was ready to hear anything—perhaps even that storks brought baby Foitani from the lettuce patch like so much airfreight. Aissur Aissur Rus said, "I know that in your species, human Jennifer, as in most, gender is fixed for the life of the individual. This is not so among us. During approximately our first thirty years of life, we are female; for the balance, we are male. Thus you will not see females in places of importance among us, as they, by their nature, cannot acquire sufficient experience to justify such placement."

"Oh," Jennifer said. That made a certain amount of sense. She decided to tweak the Foitani. "You are aware that I'm female."

"Indeed," Pawasar Pawasar Ras said, apparently relieved that someone else had done the talking about actual details. "You are, however, also of another species. The denigration implied by that far outweighs any relating to your gender."

"Oh," Jennifer said again, in a different tone of voice. The Foitani didn't need to look down their muzzles at her gender to keep her in her place.

Even Aissur Aissur Rus seemed relieved not to have to talk about gender any more. He quickly changed the subject. "Let us proceed to Enfram Enfram Marf, human Jennifer. He is our explosives expert here, as I said."

"All right." Jennifer smiled a little at finding the Foitani, for all their differences from mankind, so Victorian about the way their bodies worked. Had she not studied Middle English, she wouldn't have had a word to describe their attitude; the term had not come forward into Spanglish. Something occurred to her. "Did the Great Ones operate the same way you do, Aissur Aissur Rus?"

"Certainly." Aissur Aissur Rus drew himself up even taller than he was already, a paradigm of offended dignity. "They were Foitani and we are Foitani. How could disparity exist between us?"

"I didn't mean to make you angry," Jennifer said, on the whole sincerely—she liked Aissur Aissur Rus best of the Foitani she'd met. "I was just asking."

"Very well, I shall assume the slight was unintentional. Now let us proceed to Enfram Enfram Marf."

The Foitani explosives expert was taller but thinner than Aissur Aissur Rus. He had a scarred muzzle that made him easy to recognize. All the Foitani seemed predatory to Jennifer; Enfram Enfram Marf seemed predatory even for a Foitan. He all but salivated when Aissur Aissur Rus explained why they were there. "I do not believe it," he said several times. "How did you persuade Pawasar Pawasar Ras to let us use the power we have? I thought he would just let us sit here forever, doing nothing."

"The opinions and suggestions of the human Jennifer aided materially in getting him to modify his previous opinion," Aissur Aissur Rus said. That made Jennifer like him even better. Plenty of humans wouldn't have shared credit with a friend from their own species, let alone with an alien they'd hijacked.

Enfram Enfram Marf turned to stare at her. "This ugly little pink and white and yellow thing?" Jennifer heard through Aissur Aissur Rus's translator. "Pawasar Pawasar Ras listened to this sub-Foitani blob where he would not hear you? Our sphere's a strange place, and no mistake."

The contempt behind the colorless words made Jennifer realize she really had been dealing with what passed for interspecies diplomats among the Foitani. If Enfram Enfram Marf thought like the average Foitan in the street, no wonder the Great Ones hadn't worried about genocide.

She smiled sweetly at the ordnance officer—she knew the smile was wasted on him, but used it for her own satisfaction—and said, "I'm female, too. How do you like that?"

Had Enfram Enfram Marf been human, he would have turned purple. He drew back a leg, as if to kick Jennifer across the room. "Wait," Aissur Aissur Rus said before the leg could shoot forward. "The human is still of use to us."

"Why?" Enfram Enfram Marf retorted. "Now that we have Pawasar Pawasar Ras's permission to open up the Great Unknown, we don't need this thing to gather data for us. We can go back to using machines; they'll be able to bring artifacts out past the radius of doom so we can properly study them."

"If all goes well, yes," Aissur Aissur Rus said. "But all may not go well. Machines are less flexible than intelligent beings, even now. Moreover, we acquired the human Jennifer not so much to gather data as to interpret it. She is expert in a peculiar form of extrapolation by storytelling that humans developed long ago, which may give her unusual insight into the reasons the Great Ones created the Great Unknown as they did."

"How could this creature understand the Great Ones when we, their descendants, do not?" Enfram Enfram Marf demanded. But his leg returned to the floor. He bared his teeth, then went on, "Oh, very well, Aissur Aissur Rus, let it be as you say. I shall begin calculating the proper weight, shape, and composition of the charge, based on what we know of the thickness and material of the tower's outer wall."

"Excellent, Enfram Enfram Marf. That is what we require of you."

"Nice to know that I'm useful," Jennifer remarked as Aissur Aissur Rus led her down the corridor. "Otherwise you would have let him kick me into the middle of next week."

Aissur Aissur Rus paused and looked down at Jennifer. After a moment, he said, "I will assume my translator should not have rendered that idiom so literally."

"Well, no," Jennifer admitted.

"Good. We did not believe humans capable of time travel. We are not able to travel in time ourselves, either, though there are some poorly understood indications that the Great Ones had that ability."

It was Jennifer's turn to stare. She had thought about pulling Aissur Aissur Rus's leg over what was indeed merely an idiom the translator program had missed—there wasn't a program around that didn't have a few of those annoying blank spots in it. Now she wondered if he wasn't telling her a tall tale to get even. The only trouble was, she didn't think Foitani minds—even that of Aissur Aissur Rus, who was the loosest, most freewheeling thinker she'd met among the aliens—worked that way.

She called him on it. "Time travel is as impossible—"

"As a hyperdrive trap?" he interrupted. She opened her mouth, then closed it again as she realized she had no good comeback to make. She thought of herself as quicker-witted than the Foitani, but this time Aissur Aissur Rus unquestionably got the last word.

The tracked sledge delivered the explosive charge against the side of the polished white stone, then rolled off. The charge clung to the stone. The sledge stopped a couple of hundred meters away. Jennifer and Greenberg crouched behind it, on the side facing away from the stone. Greenberg spoke into his communicator. "We're under cover, Enfram Enfram Marf."

The Foitani ordnance office did not waste time replying. An instant later, a sharp, flat *craaack* rang out. It was much less dramatic than Jennifer had expected. She lifted her head. The stone panel had a neat, almost perfectly round hole in it, about a meter and a half across.

"He knows his stuff," she said, less than delighted about giving Enfram Enfram Marf any credit whatever.

"Explosives people tend to, at least the ones who live long enough to get a handle on what they're doing," Greenberg said. He spoke into the communicator again. "This was a good test, Enfram Enfram Marf. If your figures for the column are accurate, we won't have any trouble getting inside when we try this on the Great Unknown."

Again Enfram Enfram Marf did not reply. Jennifer said, "He doesn't think anyone who's not a Foitan is worth talking to."

"That's his problem. His bosses think I'm worth talking to, and they thought you were worth kidnapping so they could talk to you. I'm not going to lose a minute of sleep worrying about what the high-and-mighty Enfram Enfram Marf thinks of me."

Jennifer was sure he meant it. She admired his detachment and wished she could share it. She asked, "How do you keep from taking what aliens say personally?"

"The same way I do with humans: I try to gauge whether the person who's talking has any idea of what he's talking about. A lot of humans are damn fools, and so are a lot of aliens, Enfram Enfram Marf included. Just because he knows his explosives, he thinks he knows everything. I don't know much, but I know he's wrong."

Jennifer grinned and clapped her hands. Greenberg gave her a curious look. She wondered how she was supposed to explain to him that his line of reasoning went back thirty-five hundred years to the *Apology* of Socrates.

Before she had a chance to try, the sledge speaker spoke up again. "Humans Bernard and Jennifer, this is Thegun Thegun Nug speaking. We shall have a charge ready for placement tomorrow. You will then proceed to begin exploration of the tower of the Great Unknown, relaying to us such data as you uncover."

To Jennifer's way of thinking, Thegun Thegun Nug had an unpleasant habit of assuming that everything would be exactly as he wished just because he said so. Greenberg did not let that bother him. He said, "Yes, we'll start exploring for you, Thegun Thegun Nug. We'll all learn something."

"That is the desired outcome," Thegun Thegun Nug agreed.

"What I want to learn is how to get out of here," Jennifer said.

For all she knew, the mike was still open. Thegun Thegun Nug didn't answer her. She hadn't expected him to. He'd known all along how she felt.

The two sledges purred away from the Foitani research base toward the Great Unknown. Enfram Enfram Marf's new shaped-charge device sat behind Bernard Greenberg. Jennifer was glad it didn't rest on her sledge. She didn't quite trust Enfram Enfram Marf not to touch a button and say it was an accident. A meter-and-a-half hole out of her middle wouldn't leave much. . . .

They'd only gone a couple of kilometers, barely even to the edge of the radius of doom, when a loud, warbling whistle began behind them. "What the devil is that?"

"It's a Foitani alarm," Greenberg answered.

"It sure alarms me."

Greenberg spoke into the communicator on the sledge. "Human Bernard to Foitani base: Why have you switched on your alarms?" He repeated himself several times.

For a long time—more than a minute—no answer came. Jennifer began to wonder if the Foitani had forgotten about them. Then the cool tones of the translator came over the speaker. "Humans Bernard and Jennifer, this is Pawasar Pawasar Ras. I suggest you take cover as expeditiously as possible. Gilver is once more under attack from the savages of Rof Golan. Vectors of incoming ships indicate that they may attempt to land ground forces on Gilver, most probably with a view to assaulting or capturing the Great Unknown."

"We'd better head back," Jennifer said. Fliers sprang into the sky from the Foitani base. Cloven air shouted far behind them. Missiles leaped off launchers.

Then, from nowhere, a flier shrieked overhead at treetop height. A string of what might have been finned eggs fell from its belly. Had it sought the two sledges, it would have blasted them to bits. But its target was a hardpoint a few hundred meters to the west, between the humans and the base. Explosions smote Jennifer's ears. With an instinct she didn't know she owned, she threw herself off her sledge and onto the roadway, flat on her belly.

More explosions came, some distant, some close enough to lift her off the ground and slam her back down. During one brief lull, she looked over and saw Greenberg beside her. She had no idea how or when he'd got there. Then more bombs fell. Shrapnel whispered overhead.

Greenberg put his mouth next to her ear. "We can't go back," he screamed through the din.

"We can't stay here, either," she screamed back. As if to underscore her words, a fragment of bomb casing went *spaang!* off the side of a sledge.

"Then we head for the Great Unknown," Greenberg said, still at the top of his lungs.

Jennifer thought it over, as well as she could think in the midst of chaos and terror. "Sounds good," she said. "Let's do it, if the bombing ever moves away from us. It's the one place on the planet where the Foitani can't come after us."

"The ones from Odern can't, anyhow," Greenberg said. "We just have to hope that holds for the ones from Rof Golan, too."

"I wish you hadn't said that," Jennifer told him. She glanced up at her sledge. "I also wish we had more kibbles and water along." They'd planned on staying at the Great Unknown for a couple of days if they succeeded in getting into the tower, so they weren't without supplies. She looked up at the plastic bag of kibbles again and fought back a laugh. She'd never imagined a day would come when she wanted more of them than she had. She'd never imagined most of the things that had happened to her since the day the Foitani walked into her class at Saugus Central University.

More bombs struck, so close that she felt the impact with her whole body much more than she heard it. She and Greenberg clutched each other, life clinging to life in the middle of mechanized death. He shouted something at her. She knew that, but she was too stunned and deafened to tell what it was. She looked at him and shook her head.

"I love you," he said again. She still could not hear him, but his lips were easy to read.

"Why are you telling me now?" she said, slowly and with exaggerated movements of her own lips so he could follow. "We're liable to get blown to bits any minute."

He nodded vehemently. "That's just why. I didn't want to die without letting you know."

"Oh." She supposed it was terribly romantic, but she needed to be able to think about it. Thought was impossible here; she was battered and deafened and more frightened than she'd ever been in her life. Holding on to him still seemed like a good idea, so she kept on doing it.

The explosions grew more distant. Jennifer detached herself from Greenberg, far enough to peer past the front of the sledge. Dirt rose in graceful fountains all around the research base. The base fought back; close-in guns chattered maniacally, blasting bombs and incoming missiles before they struck home.

"If we're ever going to move, this is probably the time to do it," she told Greenberg. "Nobody seems to be paying attention to us."

"Let's go, then," he said. "The farther inside the radius of insanity we are, the better I'll like it." They scrambled onto their sledges and sent them dashing ahead at their best—and only—forward speed. No healthy Foitan would have had the least trouble running them down.

Greenberg looked over his shoulder. "Good thing we didn't head back to the base," he said. Jennifer looked back, too. A troop-carrier had landed right about where they would have been if they'd tried to reverse their course. Foitani—presumably Foitani from Rof Golan—leaped out of it and scrambled for cover. They started firing with automatic weapons heavier than anything a human could have carried.

"I wouldn't have wanted to meet them up close, no," Jennifer admitted. *Meet* wasn't quite the right word, she thought. The Foitani didn't look like the sort who would have waited for formal introductions before they started shooting.

The sledges crawled along. The invaders seemed too busy trying to blast the research base off the face of Gilver to bother doing anything about them. Jennifer wondered if that was too good to last. A moment later, she wished she hadn't, because it was. Something *cracked* past her ear. Then another something smacked off the rear facing of the sledge, hard enough to make it shudder under her. It kept running, though.

She turned around again. A couple of big aliens were bounding after her and Greenberg. As she'd feared, they ran faster than the sledges. Nothing grew in the area of the Great Unknown. There was no place to hide, save possibly behind the massive columns of the colonnade. The only weapon she had was her stunner, which might make a Foitan scratch but assuredly would not stop him. In any case, the soldiers' hand weapons far outranged the feeble thing.

Greenberg had seen the Foitani, too. If he felt the same choking despair that cast its pall over her, he did not show it. In fact, he stood up on his sledge—it was slow enough and smooth enough to make that safe—and jumped up and down thumbing his nose at them. That only made them run harder—and all at once, Jennifer realized he wanted exactly that. "You're a genius, Bernard!" she shouted. She stood up on her sledge, too.

The Foitani from Rof Golan kept coming. All too soon, they were only a couple of hundred meters behind the sledges. The closer they drew, the more easily Jennifer could see they were not the same as Foitani from Odern. They were taller and leaner and nearer gray than blue. Their ears were larger. So were their muzzles—and their teeth. They had red marbles for eyes, not black ones. That made them seem all the fiercer as they bore down on the humans.

Their clawed feet slapped on the smooth stone of the processionway. Jennifer heard their harsh breathing closer, ever closer. She reached into her beltpouch for her stunner, though she knew a steak knife would have done more good. She put away the stunner. If these Foitani had decided to take them prisoner instead of slaying them out of hand, she would not try to change their minds.

The Foitani caught up with the sledges. They even smelled different from the Foitani of Odern—sharper, like ripe cheese, Jennifer thought as she waited to be seized. The Rof Golani Foitani ran past her and Greenberg, on either side of their sledges. They paid no attention whatever to the humans. Their red eyes were only on the tower ahead. Like two big machines, they pounded toward it.

Jennifer watched their backs recede ahead. "I think we may take it as proved that the Great Unknown affects more than one type of Foitani descendant," she said. She was proud of herself. The sentence came out as cleanly as if she were dictating an academic paper into the Middle English Scholars Association data net.

Greenberg gave her an odd look. "Yes, I think we may," he answered, half a beat late. "I think it's a good thing, too."

"So do I." Jennifer steered her sledge up next to his. She reached across and took his hand. Her own palm was cold and trembling. The vibration of the two sledges didn't let her tell if he also had the shakes, but he felt no warmer. After a moment, she added, "That was good thinking, luring them on into the zone of insanity. Now all they care about is the Great Unknown. Right now, they can keep it, as far as I'm concerned. I don't think I was made to be a soldier."

"Neither was I," Greenberg said. "I kept thinking about getting behind you and setting off Enfram Enfram Marf's shaped charge at the Foitani. By the time I decided it wasn't a good idea, they'd already gone by us."

"You still did better than I did," she said. "I forgot all about the stupid thing."

"That's not so good, Jennifer," he said seriously. "You should never forget about anything."

The sledges ground on toward the central tower. Jennifer kept looking back at the research base of the Foitani from Odern. The one good thing about the fighting that continued all around it was that the Foitani from Rof Golan weren't using nuclear weapons, as they had when they attacked from space. Maybe now, she thought, they were more interested in conquest than in annihilation. She hoped they would go on thinking that way; she had no confidence in the Great Unknown's ability to keep fallout from the local atmosphere.

Several other Foitani from Rof Golan strode the procession-way behind the first two. None passed the sledges, which by then were more than halfway from the outer edge of the radius of doom to the central tower. None shot at the sledges, either, for which Jennifer was duly grateful. A couple of kilometers from the tower, the sledges, slow but mechanically steady, repassed the first two Foitani soldiers. Their gray-blue fur was damp with sweat; their tongues lolled from their mouths. They did not glance at the machines or the humans aboard them, but kept trudging toward the tower at the best speed they could muster.

The tower grew closer and closer. The two sledges stopped a couple of meters away. Greenberg climbed down from his sledge, lifted the shaped charge Enfram Enfram Marf had given him, and carried it to the side of the immense white structure. He pressed it against the stone. Jennifer wondered if it would stick, as it had against the practice slab of stone. The material of the Great Unknown seemed much more than simple white marble. But stick the charge did.

Greenberg went back to the sledge and called the research base. "We have the entry charge in place. Please advise if we should proceed, under the circumstances." Only static came from the speaker. Either no one at the base was listening, or the Rof Golani were jamming the channel. Greenberg looked at Jennifer. "What do you think we ought to do?"

"I think we ought to blow it," she said without hesitation. "We're never going to have a better chance than this. I just hope it's not all for nothing anyway—if the Foitani from Rof Golan win, what's going to happen to the *Harold Meeker*?"

"That's such a good question, I've done my best not to think about it." Greenberg made a sour face. He ran wire from the charge back to the detonator. "We have a couple of hundred meters to retreat. Let's use them." The sledges went into reverse until the wire began to grow taut.

Greenberg dismounted again and got behind his sledge. Jennifer took cover, too. She said, "I'm just glad this thing doesn't have to be set off by radio from the base, the way the practice charge did."

He let out a wry chuckle. "That would rather ruin our day's work, wouldn't it?"

"You might say so, yes," she answered, trying to match him dry for dry. She heard the slap-slap-slap of Foitani feet on the processionway. The first two soldiers from Rof Golan were getting close again. "If you're going to do it, you'd better do it now."

Greenberg glanced back toward the Foitani. He nodded. "Right you are." He brought his thumb down on the blue firing button. He grunted—squeezing the contact closed took considerable effort. Not only were Foitani stronger than people to begin with, the firing button was rigged so it could not go off by accident.

After the bombardment she'd been through, Jennifer found the detonation of the shaped charge an anticlimax. Unlike munitions makers, blasting experts do not make their devices as strong as possible, only just strong enough to do a particular job. Even in quiet circumstances, the blast would hardly have made her jump.

She looked up over the top of the sledge. Just as in the practice run, Enfram Enfram Marf's charge had blown a neat, round hole in the white stone of the tower. Blackness lay beyond it.

Greenberg looked up, too, then grabbed the communicator. "Calling the research base. I don't know whether you can see it—for that matter, I don't know if you can hear me—but we have succeeded in making a breach in the base of the column at the center of the Great Unknown."

"This is Pawasar Pawasar Ras, human Bernard," the comm answered. Jennifer jumped—she hadn't expected a reply. Pawasar Pawasar Ras went on, "I regret that our project has been disrupted by the perfidious attack from the wretched pseudo-Foitani of Rof Golan. Nevertheless, we do continue to keep you and the Great Unknown under observation. We discern no evidence of damage to the column."

Jennifer looked up over the sledge again. So did Greenberg. "I see a hole," he said. "Do you see a hole?" She nodded. "Good," he told her, then spoke into the communicator once more.

"Honored kin-group leader, both of us think there's a hole in the side of that building. We're going to test it experimentally. How much do you want to bet that we get inside?"

"As a matter of fact, we may not be the first ones to do the testing," Jennifer added. The two Foitani from Rof Golan, still paying no attention to the humans or their sledges, tramped past them toward the tower.

"If you are somehow correct and there is an opening I cannot perceive, you must not permit the Rof Golani to exploit it. Use whatever means necessary to prevent their gaining entry," Pawasar Pawasar Ras said. The translator didn't let him sound agitated, no matter how upset he really was.

"How are we supposed to stop them?" Jennifer asked.

"Use whatever means necessary," Pawasar Pawasar Ras repeated.

Jennifer looked at the Foitani. Each of them was more than a meter and a half taller than she was. Each of them carried a weapon that could kill her at five times the range she could even make him itch. She looked at Greenberg. He'd been looking at the Foitani, too. Now his gaze swung back to her. She said, "Bullshit."

He nodded. "You'd better believe it." He spoke into the communicator. "Honored kin-group leader, we didn't sign up with you to commit suicide. You ought to know, though, that the Foitani from Rof Golan seem to be suffering from the same thing your people do when they get too close to the Great Unknown. They don't seem to be in any shape to relay whatever they learn to anybody."

A long silence followed. At last Pawasar Pawasar Ras said, "There may be some truth to this comment. Nevertheless—"

"No," Greenberg broke in, adding, "It's too late anyhow, honored kin-group leader. The first two Rof Golani have reached the tower."

The big, blue-gray Foitani dropped their weapons to press themselves against the smooth white stone of the wall. They were only five or six meters from the hole in its side, but gave no sign of noticing it. For several minutes, they seemed content just to stand there. Then, not getting more than a meter or so away from the edge of the wall, they began walking parallel to it, one of them behind the other.

They walked right past the hole. Their feet scuffed through the pieces of stone the shaped charge had blasted loose. They took no notice of them, either; as far as they were concerned, the area was as perfectly smooth as any other part of the processionway.

Greenberg turned to Jennifer. "I will be damned. They *can't* see that it's there."

Spanglish failed her. She fell back into Middle English. "Curiouser and curiouser." Then she said, "It makes me wonder whether the hole really is there after all."

"I can tell you two things about that," he answered. "Thing number one is that we know the Great Unknown makes Foitani crazy and we don't think it does that to us. Thing number two is, we can go and find out, so let's go and find out."

He stood up and walked toward the hole. Jennifer followed him. She saw the chunks of white stone that lay in front of it. Pretty soon, she kicked one of them. She felt it as her boot collided with it and heard it rattle away. All the same, she had the feeling she was approaching one of those holes quickly painted on the side of a mountain in an ancient animated fantasy video, the sort that would let whoever painted them go through and then turn solid again so a pursuer smashed himself against hard, hard rock. She stretched a hand out in front of her so she wouldn't hurt herself if the opening ahead proved not to be an opening.

She kicked another fragment of stone out of the way. This one clicked off the side of the tower. The noise seemed no different to her from the one the first stone had made, but the Foitani from Rof Golan hadn't noticed that one. They noticed this time. They spun around. Their red eyes blazed. They'd let their weapons fall when they came up to the column, but they still had fangs and claws and bulk. Roaring like beasts of prey, they charged at the two humans.

"Uh-oh," Greenberg said, which summed things up well enough. Running away from the Foitani didn't seem as if it would help. Greenberg and Jennifer ran for the hole instead. He shoved her in ahead of him. The rough stone at the edge of the hole ripped the knees out of her coveralls as she scrambled through. Greenberg dove after her scant seconds later, just ahead of the Foitani.

By then she had a fist-sized rock in her hand, ready to fling in the face of one of the aliens. At such a close range, she thought, she might even hurt him. Greenberg scrabbled around in the darkness for a rock for himself.

The Foitani came up to the hole and stared at it. They said something in their own language. Even without the moderating effect of the translator, Foitani from Odern sounded calm whether they were or not. As Jennifer had heard over the *Harold Meeker*'s radio, Foitani from Rof Golan yelled even when there was nothing worth yelling about. These two screamed back and forth at each other. Jennifer didn't need a translator to guess they were saying something like, "Where did the funny-looking critters go?"

Then she drew back her arm again to throw that rock, for a Foitan reached toward the hole. Those big, clawed hands came straight for her. If she waited any longer, she thought, the Foitan would pluck her straight out of her hiding place.

But his hands stopped, right where the surface of the wall had been before Enfram Enfram Marf's charge bit through it. Jennifer watched his palms flatten out against what to him was plainly still a solid surface. He turned to his comrade, gesturing as if to say, *Come on; you try it.*

The other Foitan tried it. His hands stopped where the wall should have been, too. He squawked something to his friend. Friend squawked back. They walked off, both of them shaking their heads.

Greenberg indulged in the luxury of a long, heartfelt, "Whew!" Then he said, "You don't know how glad I am that they'd put down their guns. I didn't care to find out whether bullets believed in hallucinations."

"Urk." Jennifer hadn't thought of that. After a moment, she added, "Who says I don't know how glad you are?"

Greenberg spoke into the communicator. "Research base, we are inside the central tower to the Great Unknown. I say again, we are inside." He repeated himself several times, but got no answer. He stuck the comm in his pocket. "Maybe the Foitani from Rof Golan are jamming again."

"Or maybe Pawasar Pawasar Ras and his friends can't hear you because you're calling from inside the tower and don't exist any more as far as they're concerned," Jennifer said.

He gave her a dirty look. "I was right after all when I first got to know you—reading all that ancient science fiction has twisted your mind."

"People used to say that about it then, too." Jennifer took out a hand torch and clicked it on. "As long as we're here, shall we see what *here* is like?"

Greenberg also got out a light." We don't want to shine these out through the hole," he told her. "If the effect that keeps the Foitani from seeing it is like a one-way mirror, bright light from this side could ruin it."

"All right," Jennifer said, "but if the effect is like a one-way mirror, how come the Foitani couldn't feel their way in, either?"

"I don't know. I'm just glad they couldn't. Aren't you?"

"Now that you mention it, yes." Jennifer turned around and played the torch on the far wall of the chamber. However disagreeable he was, Enfram Enfram Marf had been an artist with his shaped charge: that wall, only four or five meters from the blast, was hardly even scorched. The chamber itself was bare, but for the fragments of stone from the outer wall.

"We're lucky," Greenberg said. "Looks like we didn't damage anything much in here."

"We didn't, did we?" Jennifer looked around again. "This room is so bare, it's almost as if they emptied it out on purpose, knowing this was where we'd break in." The words hung in the air after she spoke them. She deliberately shook her head, "It couldn't be. The Suicide Wars happened twenty-eight thousand years ago."

"But what's been keeping the Great Unknown alive all that time?" Greenberg said, a note of doubt in his voice. "The Great Ones had a higher technology than ours."

"It couldn't be," Jennifer repeated.

What happened next made her think of the closing line of a classic Clarke story: "One by one, without any fuss, the stars were going out." This surprise was not on such a cosmic scale, but it more than sufficed for the occasion. One by one, without any fuss, the ceiling lights in the chamber came on.

"Oh, my," Jennifer whispered, and then, a moment later, "Oh, no." Nothing she'd seen about the empire of the Great Ones made her admire them or want them back. Much of what she'd seen had scared her spitless. And now an artifact—a big artifact—from the time of that empire was indubitably not just alive but awake. "Maybe if we leave, it'll go back to sleep," she said. "I think I'd rather face the Rof Golani than—this."

"You've got a point," said Greenberg, who had to have been thinking along with her. But when they turned around to scramble out through the hole the shaped charge had blasted, they discovered it was no longer there. The inner wall looked as if it had stayed undisturbed for twenty-eight thousand Foitani years.

Jennifer walked over to the wall, patted it much as the soldiers of Rof Golan had from the outside. It felt as solid as it looked. "Is it real?" she asked.

"What's 'real'?" Greenberg countered. People had been wondering that since long before the days of Pontius Pilate, Jennifer thought, and generally, like Pilate, washed their hands of the question. Before she could say that out loud, Greenberg went on, "It's real enough to keep us in here, which is what counts at the moment."

"I can't argue with you there," Jennifer said. None of the walls now, so far as she could tell, held any openings. But with the Foitani, that wasn't necessarily the way things were. If the Great Ones were as adept at memory-metal technology as their distant descendants from Odern, the chamber could have had a dozen doorways, or two dozen, or three.

Bernard Greenberg evidently reached the same conclusion at the same time. He went over to the wall opposite the reconstituted one that led to the outside, began rapping on it here and there, as the Foitani did when they used their unnerving entranceways. For all the rapping, though, nothing happened.

"Try higher up," Jennifer suggested. "They're bigger than we are, so the sensitive area should be farther off the ground than if we'd built this thing."

"If humans had built this thing, it would have come with holovid instructions," Greenberg said. All the same, he raised his hand most of a meter. That produced results. In fact, it produced them twice: two doors opened up, less than a meter apart. They led into different rooms, one into a chamber much like the one in which Jennifer and he stood, the other into a long hallway.

"The lady or the tiger," Jennifer murmured. One trouble with that was that Greenberg didn't know what she was talking about. Another was that the choice was more likely to be between two tigers. She turned to Greenberg. "Which way do you think we should go?"

He plucked at his graying beard. "That room looks like more of the same. The hall is something different. Let's try it and see what happens."

"Makes as much sense as anything," Jennifer said, "which isn't much. All right, let's do it."

They stepped into the hall together. Jennifer's hand was on her useless stunner. Years of reading Middle English SF left her ready for anything, from Niven-style matter transporters to an extravaganza of lights out of the classic video *2001.* Human technology was as advanced as any in this part of the galaxy . . . except, evidently, that of the Great Ones. Not knowing what to expect left Jennifer more than a little uneasy. She reached out to Greenberg and was not surprised to find him also reaching out to her.

They didn't find themselves all at once in another part of the building. They weren't surrounded and overwhelmed by flashing lights. The hallway was just a hallway. But when Jennifer looked back over her shoulder, the door that had let them in was gone.

Every so often, Greenberg reached up to rap on the hallway wall. For more than fifty meters, nothing happened when he did; he must not have been picking the right spots. Then, with the unnerving suddenness of Foitani doors, a blank space appeared where only wall had been.

Greenberg and Jennifer both jumped. When she looked into the room that instant door revealed, Jennifer felt like jumping again. The chamber held an astonishingly realistic statue or holovid slide of a Foitan.

"He's not quite the same as the ones from Odern or from Rof Golan," Greenberg said.

"No," Jennifer agreed. The image of the Great One was a little taller than either of the descendant races she'd met. Its fur was green-blue, not the gray-blue of the Rof Golani or the plain, pure blue of the Foitani from Odern. The shape of the torso was also a little different. The legs were rather longer. The Great One might not have been of the same species as the modern Foitani; it definitely was of the same genus.

"Everything we're doing in here seems stage-managed somehow," Greenberg said. "We've known all along that this is a center for the Great Ones. What else are we supposed to learn from seeing one almost in the flesh?"

"I don't know," Jennifer answered. "Maybe that—" She stopped with a gurgle as the statue or holovid slide of the imperial Foitan turned its head and looked straight at her.

VII

Without conscious thought, Jennifer pointed her stunner at the—no, it wasn't a statue—at the imperial Foitan and thumbed the firing button. Only later did she pause to wonder why she'd done anything so aggressively futile. If the Great One was a holovid projection or a robot simulacrum, the beam would do nothing whatever to it. Even if he was somehow alive, the most she could do was make him itch. All she knew was that she wanted a weapon, and the stunner was the best she had.

The Great One scratched vehemently, all over. "It's real," Greenberg said. He sounded as if he was accusing Jennifer.

"I'm glad you thought it couldn't be, too," she said. She put the stunner away. Enraging something with carnivore teeth and four times her weight didn't seem like a good idea.

The Foitan walked toward her. He didn't act outraged, just curious. He said something in his own language. The words didn't sound too different from the ones the Foitani from Odern used. The only trouble was that without a translator she couldn't understand any of them. She spread her hands, shook her head, and bared her teeth in a Foitani-style frown. "I wish I could wiggle my ears," she whispered to Greenberg.

A look of intense concentration came over him. His ears did wiggle, close to a centimeter to and fro. Jennifer stared at him. His smile was sheepish and proud at the same time. He said, "I haven't done that since I was a kid. I wasn't sure I still could."

Jennifer wasn't sure whether the ear wiggling did any good. The Great One stopped just in front of her and bent his knees so his eyes were on a level with hers. Those eyes were not quite the jet-black of the eyes of a Foitan from Odern; they were a deep, deep green-blue, an intensification of the shade of the Great One's skin and pelt. The color would have been stunning in human eyes. Here, it was simply alien.

"We come in peace," Jennifer said, knowing the alien would not understand. She also realized it was barely true; they'd blasted their way into the tower, and a good-sized battle was going on just outside the Great Unknown's radius of insanity. For that matter, more than a few armed Foitani from Rof Golan were inside the radius of doom, even if at the moment they were in no state to use their weapons.

Greenberg held his hands in front of him, palms out. Many races used that gesture to show they had peaceful intentions. Jennifer tried to remember if she'd seen it among the Foitani from Odern. She didn't think so. As far as she could tell, though, Foitani in general didn't have peaceful intentions all that often.

The Great One kept studying Greenberg and her. A visual examination didn't seem to satisfy the alien. The Great One sniffed at them, too, with as little regard for their modesty as a dog would have given them. Jennifer wished she hadn't spent the last several hours sweating and terrified after the Foitani from Rof Golan attacked the research base of their cousins from Odern.

Finally, to her relief, the Great One straightened up. He spoke a few words into the air. Holovid pictures of alien races appeared in front of him, one after another, as if in a video collage. Jennifer recognized a couple of species, but most were strange to her. Then the Foitan spoke again. The cavalcade of images stopped—with a pair of humans hanging in midair before the Great One.

"That's impossible," Jennifer whispered to Greenberg.

"Maybe not," he whispered back. "I've heard it claimed in traders' bars that the Foitani made it all the way to Earth. I never thought it was anything but a bar story, though."

The humans in the holovid display—a man and a woman—were a lot grimier than Jennifer had worried about being. They wore furs. The man carried a wooden spear with a stone point attached with sinews. The woman clutched a stone knife, or it might have been a scraper. They both looked scared to death.

The Great One examined them carefully as he had Jennifer and Greenberg. He even sniffed them in the same way, as if to confirm by another sense that they were of the same type. That puzzled Jennifer. Could a holovid come with a scent attachment? She supposed so, for a race with a sense of smell more sensitive than humanity's. On the other hand—

"Bernard," she whispered, "do you think those poor cave people could somehow still be alive in here?"

He started to shake his head, then stopped. "I don't know," he said slowly. "The Foitan sure seems to be. After that, all bets are off."

Jennifer wondered if the tower was some kind of Foitani museum—or zoo. At first, no doubt because she'd seen the two humans, the idea was horrifying. Then she remembered the notion she'd had the first time she came up to the tower, of countless aliens going in and never coming out. Imagining a museum or zoo was a lot more comfortable than thinking about—what was the Middle English expression? A Final Solution, that was it.

The Foitan spoke to the air again. The humans it had called up disappeared once more, whether back into data storage or storage of a more literal sort. The Great One gave Jennifer and Greenberg another once-over. He bared his teeth at them in a Foitani frown. "Wondering what we're doing here," Greenberg guessed.

"I'll bet you're right," Jennifer said. "Earth is a long, long way from Gilver. What are the odds of cave people ending up here on their own and on the loose?" Something else occurred to her. "I wonder if the Foitan knows he's been here twenty-eight thousand years."

Greenberg hissed. "That's a real good question. I wish I had a real good answer."

"I wish I did, too."

The Foitan came out of his study. He walked over to the far wall of the chamber and rapped on it. This time it wasn't a door that opened, only a drawer-sized space. The Great One reached in, pulled something out, pointed it at Jennifer and Greenberg. By the way he handled it, the object was obviously a weapon.

"Oh, shit," Greenberg said softly. "Whether it's twenty-eight thousand years or day before yesterday, the breed doesn't seem to have changed much some ways, does it? Oh, shit," he repeated.

Jennifer would have looked for better last words than that. But the Great One seemed to have second thoughts. Instead of firing, he gestured with the weapon. "I'm tired of being ordered around by Foitani," Jennifer said. With very little choice, however, she went down the hall in the direction the Great One indicated.

After about twenty meters, the Foitan stopped her and Greenberg. Another rap on the wall produced another doorway. The Great One ordered the humans into the new chamber. It reminded Jennifer of nothing so much as the library setup back on Odern: it was full of strange-looking holovid gear and computer equipment. Greenberg found another name for it. "Command post," he said.

His proved the better guess. The Great One said something. A bank of screens came to life: the view immediately around the tower at ground level. More than one screen showed gray-blue Foitani from Rof Golan pressed up against the side of the building. Some still carried the arms they had brought to Gilver to use against the Foitani from Odern. All of them, armed or not, had the lost-soul look of Foitani under the influence of the Great Unknown.

The Great One had seemed almost godlike in competence and confidence. Now for the first time Jennifer saw him discomfited. He stared at his Rof Golani umpty-greatgrandscions as if he could not believe, did not want to believe, his eyes. She wondered what the Great One thought of those distorted versions of himself, versions made all the more grotesque by their obvious insanity.

At a shouted command, the Great One shifted to a view that had to have come from the top of the tower. Far off in the distance, Jennifer saw the spaceport by the research base of the Foitani from Odern. She also saw atmospheric fliers, tiny specks in the screen, diving to attack the base.

One exploded in midair. The burst of light drew the Great One's notice. The magnification of the pickup increased. Now small-arms flashes were plainly visible. Jennifer tried to figure out what was going on. The Foitani from Odern—*her* Foitani—seemed to have established a defensive perimeter against their distant cousins from Rof Golan. As she watched, a missile streaked out from the base to blow up a Rof Golani armored vehicle.

The Great One watched, too—in horror, if Jennifer was any judge. When the Foitan spoke again, alarms started yammering. Alarm ran through Jennifer, as well. Not so long ago, she'd scoffingly suggested to Pawasar Pawasar Ras that the tower might be full of armed Great Ones waiting to get loose. Now she didn't feel like scoffing any more.

Her own personal Great One didn't wait for any of his hypothetical relatives to arrive. Another wave of his weapon sent Jennifer and Greenberg back down the hall the way they had come. He marched them past the chamber in which they'd found him, all the way to the end of the corridor. An offhand, almost contemptuous rap on the wall produced the doorway Greenberg had found after so much effort. The Great One's weapon ordered the humans back into the room by way of which they'd entered the tower.

The Great One looked at the outer wall. Jennifer wondered if he saw it smooth and unblemished or if he could tell the hole from the shaped charge was there. Pieces of stone from the explosion still littered the floor. If the Great One saw that wall as being smooth and unblemished, he'd have the devil's own time figuring out how the broken rock got there.

Several other Great Ones came rushing into the room. They were as like the first one as so many peas in a pod—almost even down to color, Jennifer thought irrelevantly. They were all armed, too, with weapons identical to the one the first old-time Foitan carried. One of them pointed his weapon at the outer wall. Jennifer didn't see him pull a trigger or press a button, but suddenly the hole—or a hole—was visible to her again.

"Did he make a new opening, or is that the same one Enfram Enfram Marf's charge blasted?" she asked Greenberg.

"I think it's ours," he answered, his eyes wide. "What does that make the Foitan's gun, though? An illusion-piercer? An illusion-creator?"

"Whatever it is, I don't want to be on the wrong end of it. If it makes me think I'm dead, I have the bad feeling I'd really end up that way."

"Me, too." Greenberg reached out to take her hand. She squeezed back. The contact was reassuring. She knew—she thought she knew—it was real.

A Great One stuck his head through the hole. It was barely wide enough for his shoulders to go through, but he managed to squeeze out. Jennifer wished Pawasar Pawasar Ras hadn't listened to her or to Aissur Aissur Rus. Here were the warriors of a long-forgotten day, free on Gilver once more.

One of the Great Ones pointed his weapon at Jennifer and Greenberg. He urged them toward the hole they'd made. They went. Greenberg scrambled out first. Jennifer came after him a moment later.

The Great One goosed her with his weapon to make her go faster. She squawked and almost fell as she popped out of the hole. Greenberg helped steady her, then moved her away from the opening before the next Foitan came through and stepped on her.

Imperial Foitani kept emerging. Jennifer wondered if the alarm had rung all through the tower, and how many Great Ones had been in suspended animation or whatever they used. She thought again of Pawasar Pawasar Ras's worries and how she'd pooh-poohed them. If she ever got the chance, she'd apologize to the kin-group leader.

No Foitani from Rof Golan had been within a couple of hundred meters of where the Great Ones were coming out. The gray-blue soldiers, caught in the spell of the Great Unknown, gaped as their green-blue forebears came out of what might have looked to them like solid rock.

Jennifer waited for the Rof Golani to fell to their knees and worship the returned Great Ones, or to perform some equivalent ritual. The Rof Golani pointed at the newcomers, shouting among themselves. One of them yelled something toward the revived imperial Foitani. A Great One answered. Without hesitation, the Foitani from Rof Golan began running toward the Foitani who had come out of the tower.

And, without hesitation, the Great Ones methodically began shooting them down. Most of the Foitani from Rof Golan were too befuddled to use their own weapons, but their bared teeth, outstretched claws, and bellows of fury said what they thought of the Great Ones. But that wholehearted hatred availed them not at all, for the imperial Foitani calmly continued their massacre.

One Rof Golani somehow kept enough presence of mind to remember he carried a weapon more lethal than those with which he'd been born. Bullets ricocheted from the wall just above the Great Ones' heads. Jennifer and Greenberg threw themselves flat. A moment later, an imperial Foitan killed the only gray-blue soldier who'd seriously tried to fight back.

Slowly, Jennifer got to her feet. The precinct that contained the Great Unknown seemed to sway around her. Her view of the Foitani was rocking, too. Far from reverencing the Great Ones, the Foitani from Rof Golan had tried to kill them on sight. The Great Ones hadn't wasted any time returning the favor, either, and by all indications so far, they were a lot deadlier than the Rof Golani.

An old-time Foitan walked over to the nearest Rof Golani corpse and stared down at it. Jennifer wished she were better at reading Foitani facial expressions. Then the Foitan removed all doubt about what he was thinking. As Enfram Enfram Marf had with Jennifer, he drew back his leg for a kick. Unlike Enfram Enfram Marf, he didn't stop himself. He kicked the dead Rof Golani as hard as he could. The body had to weigh something close to two hundred kilos. The kick rolled it over, twice.

Several other Great Ones abused the bodies of the Foitani from Rof Golan. One picked up the weapon the Rof Golani had managed to fire. He examined it for more than a minute, then threw it aside with unmistakable scorn. His own hand weapon emitted a beam of some sort; but for being dead, the Rof Golani looked fine.

Off in the western distance, the explosions round the research base of the Foitani from Odern kept rumbling. Fliers clashed above it: Rof Golani attacking, Foitani from Odern defending. A Great One pointed his weapon at one of those fliers. It was more than a dozen kilometers away, but it twisted in midair and crashed to the ground with a flash of purple light.

The rest of the old-time Foitani began swatting fliers out of the air as easily as if they'd been flies. Jennifer watched in appalled perplexity as the machines tumbled. "What's going on?" she demanded of Bernard Greenberg, who had no more answers than she did. "The Foitani from Odern practically worshiped the ground the Great Ones used to live on. No matter what they said about the Rof Golani, they never said the Rof Golani hated the Great Ones, either. But they do." She looked at the sprawled corpses, shuddered, and looked away. "And the Great Ones hate them, too. Otherwise, they wouldn't be doing—this." She spread her hands in an all-encompassing gesture.

"Tell me about it," he said. He looked away from the carnage, too. "From what we've seen of the way Foitani treat other races, I'm glad they didn't just shoot us down without asking questions first."

One of the Great Ones swung his head around to glare at the two humans. By the way he hefted his weapon, he wasn't far from doing what Greenberg had feared. He wrapped a hand around his muzzle so it closed his mouth, pointed first at Jennifer, then at Greenberg. *Shut up,* she figured out, and obeyed. Greenberg didn't say anything more, either.

The old-time Foitani—by now a couple of dozen of them might have been outside the tower—spread out into what looked like a skirmish line. One of them pointed west, toward the sound of fighting . . . and toward the research base of the Foitani from Odern. The whole band started moving in that direction.

By the way they set out, fifteen kilometers was a stroll in the park for them. Jennifer looked longingly toward her sledge. The Foitan who'd warned her to be quiet gestured with his weapon—*that way.* She sighed and went that way after the Great Ones.

The old-time Foitani strode along at a pace that suited them fine, which meant it was uncomfortably quick for Jennifer. She kept up anyhow, and so did Greenberg. The Great One who was covering them looked as if he'd happily get rid of them if they slowed him down.

She looked around behind her, wondering if more imperial Foitani were issuing from the central tower. They were, but by ones and twos rather than by hundreds and thousands as she'd feared. They were quite bad enough by ones and twos.

By the time the leading Great Ones neared the edge of the radius of insanity, both their human captives were panting and footsore. Another few kilometers like that, Jennifer thought, and she'd look forward to being shot. Her coveralls were soaked with sweat; it ran stinging into her eyes and dripped from her chin.

Unlike the Foitani from Rof Golan, the Great Ones seemed immune to sweat. They tramped down the processionway as if on parade. Jennifer's uneasy vision of old-time Foitani leading defeated aliens in triumph came back to her. All that made this seem different from a small-scale version of it was that they were walking away from the tower, not toward it.

Even after the processionway ended, the imperial Foitani strode grandly along. A gnarled shrub grew by their line of march. Jennifer thought nothing of that at first. Then she realized it meant they were out of the precinct of the Great Unknown, for no plants lived within it.

Ahead, the firelight between the Rof Golani and the Foitani from Odern continued. Both sides had to be going crazy, wondering what had happened to their fliers. Jennifer thought the Great Ones were crazy too. She turned her head toward Greenberg and muttered, "Do they think they're bulletproof, or what?"

"I don't know," Greenberg muttered back, soft enough so as not to earn the wrath of their watchdog. "I know I'm not, though."

Just then, the communicator in his pocket spoke up in loud, clear, translated Spanglish. "Humans Bernard and Jennifer, this is Thegun Thegun Nug. You will tell me immediately who those strange Foitani with you are. You will also tell me whether they are in any way responsible for the difficulties our aircraft have encountered over the last few minutes."

That was Thegun Thegun Nug all the way, Jennifer thought: whatever he wanted, he ordered the humans to deliver *immediately*. He also had a gift for opening his mouth at just the wrong time.

The Great One who'd kept Jennifer and Greenberg from talking with each other snarled at them and held out his hand for the communicator. Greenberg gave it to him. He held it close to his face for a moment, as if figuring out how it worked. Then he spoke into it in sharp, abrupt tones.

Silence stretched. Jennifer wondered how a Foitani translator system that was geared to handling Spanglish would deal with suddenly getting its own tongue back. After a moment, she also wondered how close the language the Foitani from Odern used really was to the speech of the Great Ones.

Evidently it was close enough, for Thegun Thegun Nug seemed to understand it. The first part of his reply came back in Spanglish. "We greet you, Great Ones, returned to the world at last after so long. We shall serve you to the best of our ability and obey you in all regards, for we—"

The translator program suddenly went out of the circuit. Thegun Thegun Nug's own voice came over the communicator. Even speaking for themselves, Foitani from Odern seldom sounded excited. Thegun Thegun Nug was no exception. "If I witnessed the Second Coming, I think I'd show a little more feeling than that," Jennifer complained to Greenberg.

"The Foitani have been waiting ten times as long as Christians," he answered. "Maybe after twenty-eight thousand years, some of the rush has gone out of it."

"Maybe," Jennifer said. But her own reference to the Second Coming rang a bell in the scholarly part of her mind. What rough beasts were these old-time Foitani, slouching out of the Great Unknown to be reborn? She looked up to the sky, which still had no fliers in it. She shivered. The old-time Foitani might be very rough indeed.

Somewhere much too close, a Rof Golani hand weapon barked. Bullets shouted past. Jennifer went flat and tried to claw holes in the ground with her nails. She couldn't call this combat, because she had nothing with which to shoot back. But by now she knew what to do when somebody started shooting at her. So did Greenberg, who might have hit the dirt a split second before she did.

One of the Great Ones was down, too, down and shrieking. His blood was even redder than Jennifer's. His comrades cried out. A couple of them stooped beside him to give what help they could. It wasn't much. His screams went on and on.

The rest of the imperial Foitani did as Jennifer and Greenberg had—they dove to the ground. But they were armed, and armed with weapons more terrible than any mere firearms. With dreadful thoroughness, they turned those weapons on one possible spot of cover after another, as far as the eye could see.

A few more bullets came their way, but only a few. They stopped all at once. The silence that settled round the Great Ones was punctuated only by the cries of their wounded comrade.

Jennifer didn't yet dare to raise her head, but she did turn to face Bernard Greenberg. "Looks like it's going to be the old-time Foitani and the ones from Odern against the Rof Golani," she said.

"I'd say the Rof Golani are in big trouble," he answered. He lowered his voice. "I'd say we are, too. I don't mean just you and me, I mean everybody."

"I know what you mean," she answered as quietly. "I've already decided I'm going to tell Pawasar Pawasar Ras that I'm sorry." But she suspected that by then, Pawasar Pawasar Ras would be happy to see the Great Ones out and loose, not afraid of them any more. Thegun Thegun Nug had all but groveled to them on the communicator, at least in the brief part of that conversation that had been in Spanglish.

The wounded Great One's shrieks shrank to gurgles. He had an amazing amount of blood in his body; the spreading puddle was a couple of meters wide. One of the other imperial Foitani spoke to him. He gasped out an answer. The second Great One touched his weapon to the wounded one's head. The wounded one jerked and lay still.

"What are they doing?" Jennifer said, more than a little sickened. "He just killed him. The old-time Foitani have to have the medical technology to save him. Otherwise, they wouldn't still be here after so long in cold sleep, if they use cold sleep. So why did he kill him instead of helping him or getting him back to the tower where he could be worked on properly?"

"Maybe he only stunned him," Greenberg said. "We don't know what all their weapons can do."

"That's true, we don't." Jennifer mentally kicked herself for jumping to a conclusion. Just because the Great Ones had done their level best to exterminate every Rof Golani Foitan within range of their weapons, that didn't have to mean they were as callous among themselves.

But everything she'd learned about the imperial Foitani argued that they might well be. Races with gentle, tender dispositions didn't make a habit—maybe even a sport—of genocide. They didn't fight

Suicide Wars, either, for that matter. And the way the Great Ones tramped on and left behind the one who'd been shot argued that they had no further use for him. They were, as Jennifer had long since concluded, not nice people.

The communicator spoke up again. Jennifer caught Pawasar Pawasar Ras's name in the middle of a lot of unintelligible Foitani chatter. Her spirits rose slightly. Maybe the administrator's good sense would warn him not to trust the Great Ones too completely.

"Maybe," Greenberg said when she spoke that thought aloud; their keeper seemed more willing now to let the two humans talk. He didn't sound as if he believed it, though. He kept looking back toward where the one old-time Foitan had been shot. He obviously didn't believe the Foitan was just stunned any more either.

The sun set when the imperial Foitani were still a couple of kilometers from the research base. By the way they glared at the western horizon, they looked about ready to order it to come back up and keep lighting their way. Jennifer knew a moment's fear it might obey them, too.

But however great they were, the Great Ones had no Joshua among them. They did the next best thing: they surrounded themselves with glowing globes that filled their camp with a light about as bright as daylight.

"That's all very well if they don't have any enemies left out there," Greenberg observed, "but if they do, the only way I can think of to make themselves more conspicuous would be to paint 'shoot me' on their backs in big fluorescent letters."

In spite of everything that had happened through a long, exhausting, terrifying day, Jennifer found herself giggling. She dug out a plastic pouch of Foitani kibbles and crunched a handful between her teeth. "These things had better have all the nutrients humans need in them," she said, "because I've used up just about everything that used to be in me."

"You and me both." Greenberg pulled off his shoes and stared at his feet. "I keep waiting for them to swell up right before my eyes."

"Me, too," Jennifer said. She shed her shoes, too, and sighed in exquisite relief as she wiggled her toes. "I didn't come out here set up to hike." She swigged from her canteen. She would have killed for a cold glass of beer; warm, rather stale water was at the moment a more than adequate substitute.

Greenberg also ate some Foitani people chow. He washed it down with his own water. "Better—a little better," he said. "If they're going to the research base tomorrow, at least they won't walk our legs off, Jennifer . . . Jennifer?"

Jennifer didn't answer him. She hadn't heard him. She lay sprawled on her side in the dirt, fast asleep.

The old imperial Foitani must have eliminated or at least intimidated the Rof Golani on the ground, for Jennifer woke up the next morning. At first, she wasn't sure she liked the idea; she felt almost as bad as she had after Thegun Thegun Nug stunned her.

She grimly went through a stretching routine she hadn't used since she was in the field on her last trading run. By the time she started to sweat, some of the kinks in her legs and back began to come loose. The Great Ones watched her with impassive curiosity.

Greenberg also needed limbering up after a rugged day and a night on the ground. When he was done stretching, he looked around for a bush to go behind. But when he started to go behind it, one of the old-time Foitani growled and lifted his weapon. Greenberg sighed. "Sorry about this, but I can't wait any longer," he said to Jennifer as he turned his back on her. She heard him open his fly.

"Don't turn around," she warned him. "In coveralls, this is a lot more inconvenient for me than it is for you." As she unfastened herself and squatted, she thought again that this was a problem Middle English science-fiction writers had ignored, especially for women. She wished she could ignore it herself. She also wished she could ignore the Foitani. As they had while she was exercising, they studied her now.

Relieved—and also relieved of her dignity—she got to her feet. "It's all right now," she told Greenberg.

"All right," he said, and turned around. "Shall we have a lovely breakfast of dry dog food?"

"Since our other choice is leaves and whatever Gilver uses for bugs, I suppose we might as well."

They crunched for a while. Jennifer watched the Great Ones while they watched her. They might have been sleeping on featherbeds instead of hard dirt; not a single tuft of fur seemed out of place. Some of them wore belts with pouches. They took what looked like slabs of raw meat out of the pouches, shared them around, and devoured them.

After a cautious pull at his canteen—who could guess when he'd get a chance to refill it?—Greenberg said, "I meant what I told you yesterday, you know."

"What did you tell me yesterday?" she asked, a little testily—far, far too much had happened yesterday. When his face fell, she remembered all at once what he'd told her. She felt herself turn red. "I'm sorry, Bernard. I know you did."

"And so?" he said.

It was a good question. Over the years, a lot of men had said they loved her, a lot more than she wanted to hear it from. To many of them, it meant nothing more than that they wanted to go to bed with her. She was already going to bed with Bernard, and it had been her idea as much as his. She knew that said something. But living with Ali Bakhtiar, in the beginning, had been as much her idea as his, too.

She shook her head. "Bernard, right now I just don't know what to say to you. I think maybe the only thing I ought to say right now is that this isn't really the time or place to say much of anything. You know I'm fond of you—or if you don't, I've been doing something wrong." She smiled wryly. "But love? I'm not even sure what love is. Let's talk about it later, when we can think straight and feel something besides being scared out of our minds."

"Fair enough," he said, his voice unreadable.

They had no further chance to talk about it, anyhow. The imperial Foitani, with the gift for timing all Foitani races seemed to share, chose that moment to break camp and start for the research base of the Foitani from Odern. They still didn't want the humans talking while they marched. A warning growl made that quite clear.

The Great One who had Greenberg's communicator used it to call the base. Jennifer heard Pawasar Pawasar Ras's name. That was all she understood of the conversation. She wished for some of the tricks to enhance recall that science-fiction writers had invented: memory-RNA pills and who knew what else, all guaranteed to let somebody learn a language in twenty-four hours flat or your money back. Trouble was, nobody'd bothered with such things after effective translator programs came along. Trouble with that was, as she'd found more times among the Foitani than she cared to remember, take away the translator program and she was helpless without it.

Far off to the south, gunfire crackled. From several kilometers away, it sounded cheery rather than terrifying. The Great Ones grew alert when they heard it, but it wasn't close enough even for folk as aggressive as they to hose down the area with their hand weapons.

The breeze, a fickle thing, played with the marching Great Ones and wearily trudging humans, blowing sometimes from behind them but more often into their faces. The old-time Foitani ignored it; like their descendants from Odern, they were good at ignoring anything they didn't care for. Jennifer rubbed grit from her eyes as she tramped along. Stopping didn't seem like a good idea, not with that Foitan and his weapon right beside her.

She walked past a couple of emplacements the Foitani from Odern had built to protect the way to the Great Unknown. No one came out to greet the returning imperial Foitani. She looked down into one gun pit close by the side of the road. A blue Foitan lay inside, sprawled and dead.

"I hope Pawasar Pawasar Ras knows what he's doing, treating with the Great Ones," she whispered to Greenberg. She got another growl from the armed Great One for that, but no more, for it was the first thing she'd said since the day's journey began.

When the party of Great Ones came within a few hundred meters of the research base, Foitani from Odern emerged to meet them. Jennifer watched the old-time Foitani watching the blue successor race. She wondered what the Great Ones thought of them as compared to the insanely aggressive Foitani who'd developed on Rof Golan.

She still had trouble telling one Foitan from another, but thought she recognized Pawasar Pawasar Ras and Thegun Thegun Nug among the Foitani from Odern in the group that had come out of the base. All the Foitani from Odern bowed low and chanted at the Great Ones. Without the translator, Jennifer couldn't be sure, but she thought the chant was the same as the one her kidnappers had intoned when they bowed to the ancient ruins on Odern after they'd brought her there: here were the Great Ones, freed from earthgrip at last.

The gesture of submission seemed to have meaning to the imperial Foitani. They came out of the skirmish line in which they'd advanced and formed up into a single compact group. Once they were all together, they bowed, too, though not nearly so low as the Foitani from Odern had.

After that recognition ceremony, ancient and modern Foitani walked toward one another. The two groups were only a few meters apart when the breeze stopped blowing into Jennifer's face. She knew a moment's relief—*no more grit in my eyes,* she thought.

The Foitani from Odern had been moving forward with every sign of the reverence they gave to anything that pertained to the

Great Ones. All at once, they stopped short. They bared their teeth. Pawasar Pawasar Ras—Jennifer was sure now it was the project leader—growled something deep in his throat.

Without any more preamble than that, the Foitani from Odern roared and charged at the Great Ones.

For an incredulous half a second, Jennifer gaped at the onrushing blue Foitani. Then Bernard Greenberg tackled her. A couple of Great Ones managed to get their weapons up before the Foitani from Odern crashed into them, but only a couple. Most had their deadly small arms torn or kicked from their hands before they could use them.

Even without weapons, the Great Ones were a match for the suddenly berserk Foitani from Odern. They smashed them to the ground with a savage skill for which battleball scouts would have paid millions. All Jennifer and Greenberg tried to do was roll out of the way of the battling behemoths.

A Great One who hadn't been disarmed slew a pair of Foitani from Odern. Then, all at once, he ceased to be. Jennifer closed her eyes against a terrible glare that had already struck and vanished—an antiship laser, fired now at a ground target. Another old-time Foitan sizzled into nonexistence. A voice from the research base, amplified to a volume that approximated divine wrath, bellowed a command.

The imperial Foitani seemed better at giving orders than taking them. Another Great One fired in the direction from which the laser had come. Jennifer didn't know whether he took it out. Another laser, from a different position, cut him down. That bolt flew much too close to her. She felt a blast of heat and smelled ozone as if lightning had struck nearby. Only a few meters away, sandy ground bubbled into glass.

The amplified voice roared again, louder than ever. This time, the Great Ones, those few left on their feet, spread their arms wide. The ones with weapons dropped them. Only a couple of Foitani from Odern were in any shape to keep fighting. Regardless of whether their foes had quit, they started to attack again. The voice from the base cried out once more, this time with different words. Reluctantly, the Foitani from Odern held back. One—Jennifer thought it was Pawasar Pawasar Ras—shouted what was plainly a protest. The voice from inside the base shouted him down.

More Foitani from Odern emerged. All of this group were heavily armed, with rifles similar to the ones the Rof Golani carried. An armored fighting vehicle also came forth from some concealed entrance and clanked toward the Great Ones. It carried a fat laser tube and a cannon whose muzzle seemed to Jennifer's frightened eyes to be about as wide as her head.

The armed modern Foitani advanced on the imperials who had come out of the Great Unknown. They were more than cautious but less than the bloodthirsty maniacs into which Pawasar Pawasar Ras's party had turned. Greenberg noticed that at once. "How come they don't want to tear the Great Ones limb from limb?" he said.

"The breeze is blowing from the base to us again," Jennifer answered. "Maybe they can't smell them any more."

"Maybe the Great Ones haven't had a bath in the last twenty-eight thousand years," he said.

Jennifer made a face at him. Taking advantage of the fact that nobody was going to point a gun at her for talking, she said, "Maybe they—"

The voice from the base boomed forth once more, this time in Spanglish. "Humans Bernard and Jennifer, this is Aissur Aissur Rus. I suggest you come into the base through the passage from which our soldiers have just debouched. They are ordered to let you pass through them. We would not want you to come to harm through staying too close to the *kwopillot* from the Great Unknown."

"The who?" Jennifer said at the same time as Greenberg said, "The what?" The translator program had missed a word. Maybe it didn't have a Spanglish equivalent, even an approximate one. That happened now and again with translator programs. Trouble was, when it did, the word that refused to translate was almost always vitally important.

Aissur Aissur Rus didn't answer either Greenberg or Jennifer. Neither of them felt like asking again—whatever *kwopillot* were, he'd made it clear it wasn't safe to be anywhere around them. The behavior of Pawasar Pawasar Ras had done a pretty good job of that, too. Both humans hurried to pass through the ranks of the Foitani from Odern. The big, blue aliens ignored them, keeping eyes, attention, and weapons on the Great Ones.

The fickle breeze shifted again just as Jennifer was about to go down into the underground research base. Behind her, the Foitani from Odern bellowed in rage. A rifle began to bark, then another and another. Aissur Aissur Rus was screaming for the soldiers to stop shooting, but they wouldn't stop. The Great Ones went down like ninepins. When they were all dead, the soldiers rushed forward to kick and beat at their shattered bodies.

Sickened, Jennifer turned away. The kibbles she'd eaten sat like a ball of lead in her stomach. She hoped they'd stay down. "Back inside the radius of doom, the old-time Foitani treated the ones from Rof Golan the same way," Greenberg said.

"I know," Jennifer said. That had been only yesterday. She shook her head in disbelief. "I didn't like that, either."

"Neither did I. Let's get away from the Foitani with guns before they decide we might make good targets, too."

She let Greenberg take her by the elbow and lead her down the passageway. As soon as they were at the bottom, Aissur Aissur Rus spoke to them in Spanglish once more. "Come immediately to the command center. The ceiling light will direct you."

Following the moving light like a will-o'-the-wisp, they soon came to the screen-filled chamber from which Aissur Aissur Rus had spoken. He said, "I congratulate you on penetrating the tower at the center of the Great Unknown, humans. But had I known it was filled with *kwopillot,* I would have agreed with Pawasar Pawasar Ras that it remain sealed forever. I thought them merely the stuff of legend and modern depravity. Would I had been right."

"What *are kwopillot*?" Jennifer demanded. Bernard Greenberg opened his mouth, then closed it again. He'd evidently been about to ask the same question.

But before Aissur Aissur Rus could answer, Pawasar Pawasar Ras and Thegun Thegun Nug limped into the chamber. They were dirty and bloody and looked more like beasts of prey than intelligent beings. "*Kwopillot!*" Pawasar Pawasar Ras exclaimed. Had she not thought he'd tear her limb from limb, Jennifer would have kicked him.

Thegun Thegun Nug said something. Aissur Aissur Rus's translator turned it into Spanglish. "Filthy, reeking perverts! If the Suicide Wars were fought against them, suppressing them was worth the price."

"Aye, so it was," Pawasar Pawasar Ras declared. Aissur Aissur Rus didn't say anything, but he didn't look as if he disagreed, either.

"What are *kwopillot*?" Greenberg got the question out this time.

Word by word, the translator turned it into the Foitani language. That seemed to remind Aissur Aissur Rus and his colleagues that the humans were there. His answer, though, was less than helpful. "Never mind, human Bernard. They are practically extinct, and it is as well."

"No, they aren't," Greenberg said loudly. "Whatever they are, you may have murdered as many of them as came out of the tower in the middle of the Great Unknown, but how many do you think are still left in there? It's a big tower, you know, and it's awake or active or whatever you want to call it, thanks to us. What do you want to bet that more *kwopillot* will pop out of it soon?"

Aissur Aissur Rus, Pawasar Pawasar Ras, and Thegun Thegun Nug all bared their teeth at him. Thegun Thegun Nug growled something. Aissur Aissur Rus's translator turned it into, "What a terrible thing to say." Jennifer suspected the original had been rather more pungent.

Aissur Aissur Rus said, "Unfortunately, the human may well be right. We should make preparations on that assumption, at any rate. Those who came forth may have been *kwopillot*, but they were also Great Ones, with all the powers we have long believed the Great Ones held. If the *kwopillot* truly hold all the resources contained within the Great Unknown, how are we to resist them?"

"Better to ally with the Rof Golani than to risk such filth spreading through our sphere," Pawasar Pawasar Ras said.

Maybe he had just been indulging in rhetoric, but Aissur Aissur Rus took him up on it. "An excellent suggestion, honored kin-group leader. Call them at once; we have already observed that they too know the proper response to this menace."

"As you say, Aissur Aissur Rus." Pawasar Pawasar Ras went over to a communications panel and started talking into it. Before long, the image of a gray-blue Foitan from Rof Golan appeared on the screen on front of him.

"What are *kwopillot*?" Jennifer asked. It was the third time the humans had tried that question, and they were still without an answer.

"They are disgusting," Thegun Thegun Nug said. "I go to wash their reek from my fur." He stalked off.

Jennifer turned to Aissur Aissur Rus. "Will you please explain what's going on, and why you've all started killing each other on sight?"

Aissur Aissur Rus made a noise that might have come straight from a wolf's throat. The translator rendered it with a sigh. Jennifer had some qualms about the translation; nothing that sounded so . . . carnivorous . . . had any business being merely a sigh. Aissur Aissur Rus said, "This subject is not easy for us to discuss, human Jennifer. It is also one we never thought could arise—as the Great Ones were believed to be extinct, surely the degenerate *kwopillot* had to be gone. Sadly, this now appears not to be the case."

"So what are *kwopillot,* and why do you keep calling them such nasty names?"

"Wait a minute," Bernard Greenberg put in, his eyes lighting up. "This has to do with sex, doesn't it? Otherwise you wouldn't mind so much talking about it."

"You are, as usual, astute, human Bernard," Aissur Aissur Rus said with another of those bloodthirsty-sounding sighs. "Indeed, the matter of the *kwopillot* does turn on sex, or more precisely on gender."

He paused, plainly not eager to go on without being prodded further. Jennifer looked at Greenberg in open-mouthed admiration. His shot in the dark had struck home—had it ever! If the Foitani were anything like most other species, they'd find sex worth fighting about no matter how technologically advanced they were. All at once, the Suicide Wars had a rationale that made some kind of sense.

Aissur Aissur Rus still stood silent. He looked big and blue and unhappy. Jennifer said, "May I ask, solely for the purpose of remedying my own ignorance, and with no desire to cause offense, what *kwopillot* do that other Foitani disapprove of?"

The variant of the trader's standard question paid off. Aissur Aissur Rus said, "You know that my race is unusual among intelligent species, in that we are born female and become male after our thirtieth year, more or less."

"You said so, once, yes," Jennifer agreed. "I didn't think much of it. We humans have found that intelligent races vary widely. Also—again I speak without intending to cause offense—Foitani are not sexually interesting to humans."

"The converse also holds, I assure you," Aissur Aissur Rus replied at once. He waggled his ears. "I thank you, human Jennifer. You have given me an idea so vile to contemplate that beside it the depravities of the *kwopillot* fade almost—not altogether, but almost—into insignificance."

Aissur Aissur Rus was the only Foitan Jennifer had ever suspected of owning a sense of humor. If he did, it was a nasty one, and he didn't bother with trying to speak inoffensively. She tried to match him irony for irony: "*I'm* glad I've given you something new and revolting to think about. Meanwhile, though, you'd started to explain what *kwopillot* were."

"I had not started yet," Aissur Aissur Rus said. "Indeed, I approach the task with considerable reluctance. You may perhaps have observed that we Foitani are somewhat reticent in discussing matters which pertain to the reproductive process. The Middle English term for such affectation of reticence, I believe, is *Victorian,* is it not?"

Jennifer stared at him. "That is exactly the word, Aissur Aissur Rus. I've thought it of your people myself. Now I have another reason for wishing you hadn't kidnapped me—I'd love to have seen the research paper you would have turned in. If you didn't outdo all the humans in my class, I'd be amazed."

"As may be," Aissur Aissur Rus said. "That, however, is at present irrelevant. Rather more to the point, one of the reasons we are as reticent as we are concerning reproductive matters is that they are relatively simple to disrupt among us."

"And *kwopillot* choose to disrupt them?" Greenberg pounced.

"Exactly so, human Bernard. For unnatural reasons of their own, they choose through hormonal intervention in the egg"—this was the first Jennifer had heard of Foitani coming from eggs—"to produce creatures . . . monsters might be a better word . . . male from birth. Even more outrageously, those born properly female, again by means of hormones, opt to retain their initial gender. That is what it is to be a *kwopil*—to be or to have been of the wrong gender for one's age."

"Why would anybody want to do that?" Jennifer asked, though she doubted she would get a rational answer. When it came to sex and gender, few intelligent races were rational.

Sure enough, Aissur Aissur Rus said, "*Kwopillot* act as they do because, being afflicted with perversity themselves, they wish to have others with whom to share it."

"Wait a minute," Greenberg said. "Suppose you have a male, uh, *kwopil.* What happens after he gets older than the age at which he was supposed to turn male anyway? Isn't he pretty much normal from then on?"

"No," Aissur Aissur Rus said. "For one thing, the hormone treatments which made him a *kwopil* leave their mark: he never smells as a proper Foitan should. For another, how could he be normal even were that not so, when he has spent all his previous life in a gender unnatural to that phase?"

"I see your point," Greenberg said slowly. So did Jennifer. No matter how refined the surgical techniques that changed them had become, transsexual humans were often pretty strange people. That might be an even greater problem for the Foitani, where the alteration was made before an individual ever saw the light of day, and where there was no natural equivalent of, say, a ten-year-old male.

She asked, "How do you know these things, Aissur Aissur Rus? Are there still *kwopillot* among you? You said they were extinct."

"Sadly, I overstated," Aissur Aissur Rus admitted. "Every starfaring Foitani world knows them, and many of those still sunk in planet-bound barbarism. The modification techniques, as I said, are far from difficult. Depraved and wealthy individuals, anxious only for their own degenerate gratification, generally create the first ones on a world. But once there are *kwopillot* on a world, they make more like themselves. In a way, it is understandable—who else but others of their kind would care to associate with them?"

Jennifer and Greenberg looked at each other. They both nodded. Humans made genetically engineered sex slaves every now and again, too. A year didn't go by without a holovid drama showing that kind of lurid story. Jennifer didn't know whether to be relieved or depressed that another race could act the same way.

Pawasar Pawasar Ras was talking to the gray-blue Rof Golani officer. He spoke too softly for Aissur Aissur Rus's translator to pick up what he was saying, but Jennifer heard one word she understood: *kwopillot.* When Pawasar Pawasar Ras said it, the Rof Golani Foitan's red eyes opened wide. So did his mouth, displaying his large, sharp teeth. *The better to eat you, my dear,* Jennifer thought. But where before the Rof Golani had wanted only to attack the Foitani from Odern, now this one listened attentively to everything Pawasar Pawasar Ras had to say.

"They both hate these *kwopillot* worse than they hate each other," Greenberg said.

Jennifer quoted the title of a Middle English novel: "The enemy of my enemy—"

Greenberg knew the saying from which it had come. "Is my friend. Yes." He turned to Aissur Aissur Rus. "Obviously the Great Ones knew of *kwopillot,* too. Did they feel the same way about them as you do?"

"There can be no doubt of it," Aissur Aissur Rus said. "Because we normally find it distasteful in the extreme to discuss such reproductive issues, the speculation is not published, but many, I think, privately believe the *kwopillot* problem to have been a possible cause of the Suicide Wars. I am one of those, and not the only one here at the base."

"What's the point of thinking if you don't publish?" Jennifer said. What she was thinking of was her fruitless search through the Foitani records on Odern. She'd never so much as heard the word *kwopillot* there, not even from Dargnil Dargnil Lin, who was supposed to be helping her learn about the Great Ones. She made a mental note to give him a good swift kick the next time she saw him.

Before Aissur Aissur Rus could answer her—if he was going to—Pawasar Pawasar Ras broke his connection with the Foitan from Rof Golan. When he turned and spoke directly to Aissur Aissur Rus, the latter's translator caught his words and turned them into Spanglish: "The barbarians have agreed to parley with us. Even they know the extent of the *kwopillot* menace."

"Excellent," Aissur Aissur Rus said. "All the resources we and they both can bring together will be important in eliminating revenge-minded *kwopillot* backed by the technological power of the Great Ones."

"You have stated my precise concern." Pawasar Pawasar Ras went on, "Humans Bernard and Jennifer, your presence will be required at this parley. You had the greatest and most significant contact with the denizens of the tower."

"May we go back to my ship first so we can rest and wash?" Greenberg asked.

"Rest and wash here," Pawasar Pawasar Ras said. "If further trouble erupts from the Great Unknown, this base is the most secure place on the planet. We would not want you to be lost before you have provided us with the information we need."

"What about afterward?" Jennifer said. Pawasar Pawasar Ras did not deign to reply, from which she drew her own dark conclusions. Reluctantly, though, she admitted to herself that the Foitan administrator had a point. She wished the *Harold Meeker* were an armed and armored dreadnought instead of a thoroughly ordinary trading ship.

By Foitani standards, the chamber to which Aissur Aissur Rus led her and Greenberg was luxuriously appointed, which is to say that it had its own plumbing fixtures and a foam pad twice as thick as the one she'd enjoyed—or rather, not enjoyed—on her journey from Saugus to Odern. Aissur Aissur Rus took the door with him when he left, but Jennifer was sure the room was bugged.

Sighing, she walked over to what the Foitani used for a toilet. "Turn your back," she told Greenberg. "I hate this miserable excuse for plumbing."

"I know what you mean," he answered. "Still, given the choice between this and what the Great Ones had us do earlier today, I'll take this."

"Not my idea of a pleasant choice," she answered.

A little later, they both got out of their clothes and washed in the lukewarm washbasin water that was the only water they had. Greenberg shook his head as he examined his tattered coverall. "I should have insisted on going back to the *Harold Meeker,* for fresh clothes if nothing else."

"Too late to worry about it now." Jennifer scrubbed and scrubbed until most of the dirt came off her hide. She looked down at herself. Even clean, she was several different colors, most of them unappetizing. "With all these scratches and bruises and scrapes, I look more like a road map than a human being."

"A relief map, maybe. The terrain is lovely," Greenberg said. Jennifer snorted, not quite comfortably; even foolish compliments made her uneasy. Greenberg went on, "What do you think we ought to do now?"

She chose to think he was talking about the situation generally rather than the two of them in particular. She was too tired to worry about the two of them in particular. "Given the chance, I'd just as soon sleep," she said. "If we're going to be talking to the Rof Golani, we shouldn't be punchy while we're at it."

If he'd had anything else in mind, he didn't show it. He got dressed and lay down on the pad. Jennifer joined him a moment later. No sooner was she horizontal than exhaustion bludgeoned her.

"Wake up, humans!" The flat Spanglish from the translator was loud and abrupt enough to make sure they did just that. Jennifer found she'd snuggled against Greenberg while she slept, whether for warmth, protection, or no particular reason she couldn't say. The voice from overhead went on, "The delegation from Rof Golan has arrived. Your immediate presence at the deliberations is necessary."

"Yes, Thegun Thegun Nug," Jennifer said around a yawn.

A brief pause, then. "How do you know to whom you speak? The translator eliminates the timbre of individual voices."

"It doesn't eliminate personalities," she answered; let the order-giving pest make of that what he would. Whatever he made of it, he said nothing more. She asked Greenberg, "How long were we out?"

"A couple of hours," he answered after a glance at his watch. "Better than nothing, less than enough."

"Enough of your chatter," Thegun Thegun Nug said. "As I told you, your presence is required immediately."

Jennifer was fed up enough with his arrogance to tell him to take a flying leap, but a door opened in the wall just then. Behind it stood a Foitan with one of their nasty stunners. He gestured imperiously. "Charming as always," she said to the ceiling as she stood up. Thegun Thegun Nug did not bother answering.

The Foitan gestured again: *out.* He stepped back to make sure Jennifer and Greenberg could not get behind him. They followed a glowing ceiling light. He followed them. After a while, he rapped on a hallway wall. When the rap produced a door, he pointed through it. The two humans went in. The door vanished behind them.

Pawasar Pawasar Ras, Aissur Aissur Rus, and several other Foitani from Odern stood against one wall of the room. A smaller number of blue-gray Foitani from Rof Golan stood against the opposite wall. No one carried any weapons. From the way the two groups kept empty space between them, Jennifer got the feeling they'd fight with bare hands if they got too close together.

The Rof Golani turned their red eyes on the humans. Pawasar Pawasar Ras spoke; his translator passed his words to Jennifer and Greenberg. "Warleader, these are the aliens of whom I spoke. Humans, know that you face the Rof Golani warleader Voskop W Wurd and his staff."

Voskop W Wurd took half a step forward to identify himself. He looked like a warleader, especially if the war was to be fought with claws and fangs. When he spoke, his words had the howling quality Jennifer had heard before from Rof Golani. Pawasar Pawasar Ras's translator abraded emotion from them. "You are the creatures who effected entry into the Great Unknown?"

"So we are," Greenberg said. "Your soldiers did their level best to kill us while we were in there, too."

Several Foitani from Rof Golan snarled as that was translated. Jennifer was glad they were unarmed. Voskop W Wurd spoke to Pawasar Pawasar Ras. "You are soft, blue one. You allow the vermin more license than even a person deserves."

Aissur Aissur Rus answered for his boss. "And because of it, Rof Golani, we have learned more than we would have with our usual straightforward approach to non-Foitani intelligences."

Voskop W Wurd's wordless snarl told what he thought of that. But in his own way he too was an officer and leader. "This is a parley, to seek information," he said, as if reminding himself. "Very well, creatures, inform me."

Having met Enfram Enfram Marf, Jennifer knew what the typical "straightforward" Foitani attitude toward other intelligent races was like. The Great Ones had shown it, too, so Voskop W Wurd's version was less irritating than it might have been otherwise. She merely wished him into me hottest fire-pit in hell before she began telling what had happened over the previous couple of days. She and Greenberg took turns with the story. They must have been interesting, for Voskop W Wurd eventually settled down and listened just as if they had been Foitani.

At one point, he asked, "What is the mechanism that creates a ring of insanity around the Great Unknown?"

"We do not know that," Pawasar Pawasar Ras answered. "We have been trying to learn for many years."

Again, a little later, "How is it that you creatures were able to enter the central tower and we True Folk not only failed but also failed to perceive the existence of an opening?"

"I don't know how that happened, either," Jennifer said. "The Foitani from Odern also couldn't see the opening; I do know that."

"It is so," Pawasar Pawasar Ras admitted. "Voskop W Wurd, when the humans went inside the central tower, our visual observations and the readings of our instruments reported that they were penetrating a wall which remained solid. Indeed, it did remain solid for your soldiers close by. The Great Ones seem to have mastered selective permeability of solid matter. How they did this, I cannot say."

"Selective is right," Greenberg said. "When we wanted to get out of the tower later on, the wall was solid for, or rather against, us, too."

"Tell mc of the Great Ones," Voskop W Wurd said. As best they could, Jennifer and Greenberg did. When they finished, the Foitan from Rof Golan made a ripping-cloth noise the translator rendered as a thoughtful grunt. "To think they truly have survived, to think their knowledge is available for hunting down."

"I see two problems with that," Jennifer said.

"You are not a Foitan. Who cares what you see?" Voskop W Wurd said.

"If you don't, why are you asking me questions?" Jennifer asked. Voskop W Wurd's lips skinned back from his teeth. Jennifer ignored him and went on, "First, now that the Great Ones are awake again, they may be interested in hunting down what you know, too. And second, they're *kwopillot,* so how do you propose to deal with them?"

Voskop W Wurd turned to Pawasar Pawasar Ras. "There can be no doubt they are *kwopillot*?"

"None." Pawasar Pawasar Ras spoke to the air. "Bring in the

evidence." A door opened in the wall opposite the one by which Jennifer and Greenberg stood. Two Foitani from Odern dragged in the torn corpse of a Great One. Pawasar Pawasar Ras addressed Voskop W Wurd, "Judge for yourself."

Voskop W Wurd's nostrils flared. The snarl he had given Jennifer was as nothing next to the one he unleashed now. The gray-blue Foitani from Rof Golan who were with him echoed the cry. He said, "Aye, that is the harshest *kwopil* reek I've ever had the misfortune to encounter. They were all thus?"

"Every one we encountered," Pawasar Pawasar Ras answered.

"Then every one needs to be tied down in the hot sun and disemboweled. That's how we keep the menace of *kwopillot* from spreading among us," Voskop W Wurd declared.

Jennifer gulped. She hoped the Foitani from Odern would denounce Voskop W Wurd for the bloodthirsty barbarian he was. But Aissur Aissur Rus said only, "We use lethal injections ourselves. Still, the principle remains the same."

Greenberg whispered, "I wonder what *kwopillot* do to ordinary Foitani when they're the ones in power."

"Nothing good, I'd bet," Jennifer whispered back.

"You Oderna are too soft with your aliens," Voskop W Wurd said to Pawasar Pawasar Ras. "There they go, plotting who knows what between themselves."

"Repeat yourselves, humans Jennifer and Bernard, loud enough for the translator to pick up your words," Pawasar Pawasar Ras said.

Before Jennifer could repeat herself, a Foitani voice started shouting from a ceiling speaker. The translator brought her the gist of the announcement. "Honored kin-group leader, radar reports the central tower of the Great Unknown has lifted off from the surface of Gilver and is performing as a spacecraft. We have visual confirmation as well. Please advise."

VIII

"A spacecraft?" Pawasar Pawasar Ras, Aissur Aissur Rus, and Voskop W Wurd said it in the Foitani language, Jennifer and Greenberg in Spanglish.

Voskop W Wurd recovered first. He shouted in the Foitani language. "Shoot the foul-smelling thing down," the translator said. "Your ships and mine together, Oderna. We can kill each other any time we choose. The *kwopillot* will not wait."

"That is a reasonable assessment of the situation," Pawasar Pawasar Ras said after a moment's pause for thought. He spoke to the ceiling. "All ships from Odern are directed to destroy the spacecraft which has arisen from the Great Unknown. Warleader Voskop W Wurd instructs Rof Golani ships to cooperate in this effort."

"Missiles launching," the ceiling speaker reported.

Voskop W Wurd bared his teeth. "This is not a proper headquarters, Pawasar Pawasar Ras. If I cannot bite the foe in person, at least let me see how my fellows' fangs sink in."

"As you wish," Pawasar Pawasar Ras said after another pause. "I do not think you or your followers would be in a good position to betray us." He rapped on the wall behind him, then hurried through the door he had called into being. Aissur Aissur Rus and his other aides followed. The Foitani from Rof Golan were right behind.

The Rof Golani did not bother making the doorway close after themselves. "Come on," Jennifer said to Greenberg. "If we follow them, we may get some idea of what's going on."

"We may get our heads bitten off, too—literally, if the Rof Golani have anything to say about it," he answered. All the same, he went after the Foitani. So did Jennifer.

They had to trot to catch up with the bigger aliens, then to keep up with them. A couple of Rof Golani snarled at them, but otherwise left them alone. They hurried into the command post hard on Voskop W Wurd's heels.

The plan had been chaotic enough before the Rof Golani came in. Foitani from Odern ran here and there, shouted at one another and into headsets, pointed at screens and holovid radar plots. A couple of the dark blue Foitani turned in threatening fashion toward the gray-blue interlopers from Rof Golan. Pawasar Pawasar Ras said, "They are become our cobelligerents against the flying tower. Furnish Voskop W Wurd with communications gear, that he may command his spacecraft to cooperate with us against the common foe, for *kwopillot* cannot be other than the enemies of all proper Foitani."

One of the Foitani from Odern gave Voskop W Wurd a headset. He screamed into it. Watching one of the radar tanks, Jennifer saw red sparks begin to move in unison with blue ones as both colors converged on a bigger white point of light.

Greenberg was watching the tank, too. He said, "The Rof Golani came here intending to smash up Gilver. They ought to be able to blow the tower into the middle of next week, no matter how big it is."

"Do we want them to?" Jennifer asked. "I know they say the old-time Foitani are evil and vicious, but as far as I can see, they're just acting the same way the modern ones do. And since when are aliens' sex lives any of our business?"

"I'd feel better about being neutral if we still had a way home in case the Great Ones wrecked the *Harold Meeker,*" he answered. "As long as it's sitting outside this base, I'm for the Foitani from Odern and Rof Golan."

"Something to that," Jennifer had to admit

She and Greenberg did their best to stay out from underfoot as Foitani hurried this way and that. Jumping clear was all up to them, for the Foitani would not change directions for their sake. Jennifer wondered if that was because humans were too small for Foitani to bother noticing, or just because they were non-Foitani and therefore not worth dodging. Whichever way it was—she suspected the latter—she quickly learned to grow eyes in the back of her head to keep from getting trampled.

A Rof Golani ship abruptly vanished from the radar tank. Voskop W Wurd screamed something that the translator rendered as, "How extremely unfortunate." A good deal of juice seemed to have been squeezed out somewhere.

More ships started disappearing. No matter what sort of Foitani perverts crewed it, no matter that it had been grounded for twenty-eight thousand years, the ship that had been a tower was a formidable killing machine. Voskop W Wurd made noises suggesting a wild animal with a leg caught in a trap. Pawasar Pawasar Ras sounded calmer—that seemed the way on Odern—but no happier.

After a dismayingly short while, the course of the battle grew clear: the Great Ones were mopping up everything the modern Foitani could throw at them. Pawasar Pawasar Ras ordered one of his few surviving ships to break off and head back to Odern.

Voskop W Wurd yowled a phrase that sounded as if it would have made a pretty good operations order for the end of the world. "A cowardly act," the translator reported bloodlessly.

"By no means," Pawasar Pawasar Ras said. "Suppose we are defeated and destroyed here. That will leave the *kwopillot* free to rampage through the Foitani sphere, with no one to know what they are until they come within smelling range. Our homeworlds must be warned. What I do is wisdom. Deny it if you may."

The Rof Golani warleader did not reply directly, but spoke into his headset. Before long, one of the red blips in the radar tank turned tail and boosted toward hyperdrive kick-in. Voskop W Wurd said no more about it. No Foitan Jennifer had ever seen was any good at admitting he was wrong.

"I just hope the Foitani sphere is all these revived Great Ones worry about for a while," Greenberg said. "If they have records of humans, they know where Earth is."

"They'd find out soon enough anyway, from dealing with the Foitani from Odern," Jennifer answered. It was not much consolation. One way or another, trouble was coming.

Trouble was, in fact, already here. The ship that had spent a geological epoch being a tower was still dreadfully efficient in its own role. Gallant to the end, the Foitani from Odern and Rof Golan kept attacking long after they must have known they were doomed. Back on Earth, a long time ago, tribesmen had shown insane courage by charging straight at machine-gun nests. But for making them end up dead in gruesomely large numbers, their courage hadn't got them anything. Similar bravery served the Foitani no better now.

"Attack from space imminent," Pawasar Pawasar Ras called. "Prepare to resist to the end."

Jennifer was certain the Foitani would do just that. She was also certain the end had become quite imminent. She squeezed Bernard Greenberg's hand, hard. "I love you, too," she said. When the end comes, some words should not be left unspoken.

He hugged her. She hugged him, too. She did not care what the Foitani thought, not now. The only good thing she saw about being here was that the end would probably be quick. The Great Ones up there had overwhelming weapons and could hardly miss.

Voskop W Wurd said, "Get me a hand weapon, Oderna, that I may shoot at my slayers as they destroy me."

Jennifer watched the tower-ship in the radar tank. It hung overhead, an outsized sword of Damocles. Suddenly one of the communications screens lit up. A green-blue Foitani face peered out of it: a Great One. A technician spoke to Pawasar Pawasar Ras. "Honored kin-group leader, the, ah, Foitan Solut Mek Kem would address you."

Jennifer's heart leaped. Surely one did not seek to address a person one was on the very point of destroying.

Pawasar Pawasar Ras saw things in a different light. He said, "So you have called to gloat, have you, *kwopil*?" Jennifer's hopes plunged as far and as fast as they had risen. Pawasar Pawasar Ras could not help knowing his own species, knowing what its members did and did not do.

The Great One called Solut Mek Kem said, "By your murderousness, I gather your kind still exists, *vodran*." Jennifer felt like screaming at the translator program for falling asleep on the words that really mattered. Meanwhile, Solut Mek Kem went on, "We all hoped earthgrip would have taken you by the time we returned to the sphere at large."

But for once, the problem was not the translator's fault. Pawasar Pawasar Ras said, "*Vodran?* I do not know this word, Solut Mek Kem."

Voskop W Wurd echoed him, less politely: "Trust the stinking *kwopillot* to come up with a foul-smelling name for proper people."

"You've grown old in depravity, to think it the proper state for Foitani," Solut Mek Kem said. "I see the race has had time to degenerate physically as well as morally, else our sphere would not be plagued with such hideous specimens as you."

Voskop W Wurd told the Great One what he—or was it she this time?—could do to himself, in explicit anatomical detail. Jennifer did not think any of the suggestions sounded like much fun and did not think many were physically possible. Those limitations didn't bother humans in a temper, and they didn't bother Voskop W Wurd, either.

When the Rof Golani warleader ran down, Pawasar Pawasar Ras added, "You tax us with murderousness, yet outside this tower which is now a ship, you *kwopillot* wantonly slaughtered a great many Foitani, many of them unarmed and all of them mentally disabled by whatever means you employed to keep us from your precinct on Gilver."

"You are *vodranet,*" Solut Mek Kem said. "You deserve no better. As I said, we had hoped our fellows would have exterminated you from the galaxy by the time we reawakened. Though I see it is not so, we shall join with the worlds of our kind and finish the job once and for all."

"What worlds of your own kind?" Pawasar Pawasar Ras said. "*Kwopillot* have no worlds. They merely plague true Foitani whenever a nest of them appears. This is so on every world where our kind survives, and has been so ever since the Suicide Wars cast our sphere down into barbarism."

"Lie all you like, *vodran,*" the old-time Foitan said. "We could not have been destroyed in a few centuries."

Jennifer hurried over to Pawasar Pawasar Ras and tugged on the fur of his flank. "May I speak to the Great One?" she asked urgently.

Pawasar Pawasar Ras brushed her away, or tried to. She hung onto his massive arm. "Are you stricken mad?" he said. "Get away. This is not your concern."

Unexpectedly, Voskop W Wurd came to her rescue. "Why not let the creature talk to the stinking *kwopillot*?" he demanded. "Do *kwopillot* deserve any better?"

"There is some truth in what you say, warleader," Pawasar Pawasar Ras admitted. Under other circumstances, Jennifer would have been furious at the denigration inherent in what the Rof Golani Foitan said and in Pawasar Pawasar Ras's agreement with it. Now all she cared about was having this Solut Mek Kem hear her. After a pause for thought that seemed endless, Pawasar Pawasar Ras said, "Very well, human Jennifer, you may speak. Here." He overturned a plastic container for her. "Stand on this, so you will be tall enough for the vision pickup to notice you. I shall stand close by, that my translator may render your words into the speech of the Great Ones."

"Thank you, honored kin-group leader." Jennifer clambered onto the container. She could tell Solut Mek Kem saw her; the old-time Foitan's teeth came out. She said, "Honored Foitan—"

"So you *vodranet* consort with sub-Foitani, do you?" Solut Mek Kem interrupted. "We might have expected it of you."

"*Will* you listen to me?" Jennifer said. "Your tower hasn't been sitting on Gilver for a few centuries. You've been there twenty-eight thousand of your years."

"It is amusing, *vodran.*" Solut Mek Kem still refused to speak directly to Jennifer. "But why should I listen to its lies any more than yours?"

"I presume your tower or spaceship or whatever it really is recorded Bernard and me when we went inside," Jennifer said. "Check those records, why don't you? For one thing, you'll see we have stunners that aren't like yours. For another, you'll see one of your people comparing us to—I don't know whether they're specimens or records of my kind back when we were savages. You figure out how long it might take for a race to go from savages to star travelers. And if I'm lying, then you can go right on ignoring me."

The screen that had shown Solut Mek Kem went blank. Aissur Aissur Rus said, "Well done, human Jennifer. You have made the wicked pervert pause and examine assumptions, something we did not succeed in accomplishing."

Bernard Greenberg said, "You ought to think about examining your own assumptions, Aissur Aissur Rus. Since when is someone who differs sexually from you necessarily a pervert—or necessarily wicked, for that matter?"

"*Kwopillot are* wicked perverts," Aissur Aissur Rus said.

Jennifer felt like banging her head against a wall; Aissur Aissur Rus not only wasn't examining his assumptions, he hadn't even noticed them. She asked, "What's a *vodran*?"

"We do not know this word, either," Pawasar Pawasar Ras said. "It is a piece of offal the *kwopillot* have appended to the pure and beautiful speech of the Great Ones, nothing more."

Just then, Solut Mek Kem reappeared in the holovid screen. "I will converse with the sub-Foitani creature," he announced.

"We call ourselves humans," Jennifer said pointedly.

The Great Ones, whether perverted or not, had all the arrogance of their descendants and then some. Solut Mek Kem said, "I care nothing for what you call yourself, creature. I have some concern, however, over your statements. It appears true that Foitani encountered your kind in the past. You were noted as being uncommonly brutish and scheduled for extermination. Why this failed to take place is a matter of some puzzlement to me."

Jennifer opened her mouth, then closed it again. Hearing that her species was going to have been killed off was not something she could take in at once. Into her silence, Aissur Aissur Rus said,

"No doubt the Suicide Wars intervened and prevented the Foitani of that distant time from completing the protocol they envisioned."

"Suicide Wars?" It was Solut Mek Kem's turn to pause. Not even a Foitan could care for the sound of that.

"Suicide Wars," Aissur Aissur Rus repeated. He spoke to the command center's computer system. A holovid star map appeared in front of him. "This is the area the Foitani once inhabited, not so?"

"No. Wait. Yes, it appears to be," Solut Mek Kem said. "We customarily oriented our maps with the other direction to the top, thus my brief confusion."

"One more thing about the Great Ones of which we were ignorant," Aissur Aissur Rus observed before returning to the business at hand. "These are the known Foitani worlds now." The few points of light Dargnil Dargnil Lin had shown Jennifer back on Odern now sparkled in front of her. Aissur Aissur Rus said, "All other worlds within the sphere are devoid of our kind, or even of intelligent sub-Foitani life forms."

"More *vodran* lies, fabrications to confuse me," Solut Mek Kem said.

"If you will arrange a data link with us, we will supply you with documentation sufficient to change your mind," Aissur Aissur Rus said. "We could not have prepared this volume of information in advance to trick you, you will realize, because we had no idea we would discover you alive in the tower, and still less that you would prove to be *kwopillot.*" More flexible than most of his kind, Aissur Aissur Rus managed not to affix a malodorous epithet to the term.

"Send your data," Solut Mek Kem said. "The *Vengeance* will refrain from destroying you until they are evaluated—you are no spacecraft, and cannot run. But woe betide you if we detect falsehood. It will only make your fate the harsher."

How could any fate be worse than destruction? Jennifer wondered. She did not speak her thought aloud. The Foitani might have answers to questions like that.

"Did you notice the name of the ship?" Bernard Greenberg said. "The old-time Foitani who set up the Great Unknown must have figured their side might not win the war. I wonder if they figured no one would win it."

Jennifer thought about the map Aissur Aissur Rus had shown to Solut Mek Kem. She thought about the sphere the Foitani had once ruled, about the handful of worlds they still inhabited. She thought about how many other species the imperial Foitani must have destroyed, about the calm way Solut Mek Kem remarked that humanity was on their list. Softly, she said, "Maybe that's just as well."

"Maybe it is," Greenberg agreed.

The Foitani in the command center seemed to have forgotten about the humans again, now that Jennifer had bought them some time. That was typical of them, she thought, but she could not make herself angry. She only wished they'd never heard of her in the first place.

Solut Mek Kem came back on the screen after perhaps half an hour. He said, "Our computers have been analyzing and summarizing the information you are presenting to us. The problem does seem rather more complex than we may have envisioned."

From a Foitan, even so small an admission had to spring from profound shock. Jennifer realized that at once. She wondered if Pawasar Pawasar Ras or Voskop W Wurd would see it. To them, it might be taken as only a sign of weakness. Before either of them could speak, she climbed on the plastic box and said loudly, "Then you agree it's wiser to talk, Solut Mek Kem, than to try to fight off every starship from every Foitani world that still knows about spaceflight?"

Pawasar Pawasar Ras growled at her. Voskop W Wurd snarled at her and took a step in her direction. His clawed hands stretched greedily toward her. She felt like Miles Vorkosigan—much too small and extremely breakable. How would the Middle English SF hero have handled this particular mess? Audacity, that was his only way. She went on quickly, not giving any Foitan a chance to talk: "A peace conference seems the appropriate solution, don't you all think? None of the modern Foitani are likely to get any of the technology of the Great Ones without peace, unless the *Vengeance* shoots it at them. And you Foitani from long ago will only be hounded all through this sphere unless you come to some kind of terms with your modern relatives."

"Peace with *vodranet*? Never," Solut Mek Kem said.

"Talk with *kwopillot*? I'd sooner claw my own belly open," Voskop W Wurd said.

Jennifer glumly waited for whatever bellicose ranting Pawasar Pawasar Ras chose. But before the honored kin-group leader could get a rant in edgewise, Aissur Aissur Rus said, "Save over communicators, how can we talk with those on board the *Vengeance*?" Again, he had sense enough to keep to himself the slurs he was no doubt thinking. "If we and they come into the same room, their smell will make us want only to kill, and ours no doubt the same with them."

Jennifer felt like kissing him, no matter how repugnant he might find it. *How* could be solved; *never* left little room for negotiation. She said, "If you wanted to meet face-to-face, as I can see you might, do you have nose filters to keep your two sides from smelling each other?"

"We would still know they were *kwopillot*," Pawasar Pawasar Ras said.

Voskop W Wurd put it more pungently. "I'd smell that perverts' reek if you cut off my nose."

Solut Mek Kem seemed no more enthusiastic. The *kwopil* said, "Better to exterminate all *vodranet* and begin to populate the sphere anew with Foitani who have not been altered to the point of degeneracy and decay."

"You are the altered ones, you *kwopillot*," Pawasar Pawasar Ras said.

Jennifer filed that away for further consideration; she had more pressing business now. She said, "Don't you think, *kwopillot* and *vodranet*, both sides have done enough exterminating here? Aissur Aissur Rus, call up those maps of how your sphere looked in the days of the Great Ones and how it is now."

Aissur Aissur Rus did as she asked. The few points of light that still glowed in what had been a great shining globe told their own story. Another round of war at that intensity might leave no Foitani of any sexual persuasion alive anywhere. The projection was plain enough for even the big aliens to get outside their ideologies and notice it.

Pawasar Pawasar Ras saw. He said, "You can destroy us here on Gilver, *kwopillot*, but I doubt you can destroy all our worlds without being slain yourselves in the attempt."

"Let's fight them now," Voskop W Wurd said. "The more damage we do to them, the easier a time the attackers who come after us will have." Some people, Jennifer thought, did not want to get the message. But even one of Voskop W Wurd's subordinates took the warleader aside and spoke urgently to him.

Solut Mek Kem said, "What a dolorous choice: the galaxy without Foitani or full of accursed *vodranet*. We shall have to consult among ourselves as to which alternative appears preferable." He disappeared from the screen.

"Talking with *kwopillot*!" Pawasar Pawasar Ras shook his head in a very human gesture of bewilderment and dismay. "Who would have supposed it would come to that?"

"You know, one of the things Foitani really need to learn, if you'll forgive my telling you, is diplomacy," Bernard Greenberg said. "The Great Ones never seemed to have used it—they were always one people themselves, and other races were just there to be exploited or massacred. Then when they had this split into *kwopillot* and *vodranet,* the only thing they knew how to do with beings who were different was kill them. There are other choices. You Foitani from Odern and Rof Golan—and I suppose your other starfaring races—are starting to get the idea, because you have to deal with each other, and I suppose also because you have the old-time Suicide Wars as a horrible example. But none of you is what you'd call good at dealing with anybody from outside your own immediate group."

"He's right," Jennifer said. "Now you're all in a place where you can see that a big war isn't the right answer, but you don't have any other weapons—you should pardon the expression—handy with which to attack the problem."

"War is simple and direct. Its answers are clear-cut," Voskop W Wurd said.

"A writer of my species once said that, for any problem, there is always a solution that is simple, obvious—and wrong," Jennifer answered. Voskop W Wurd started to snarl at her, then stopped, looking as thoughtful as any Rof Golani Foitan she'd ever seen. She suddenly laughed. Here she was, doing exactly what the Foitani from Odern had kidnapped her to do—using her knowledge of human literature—even if not science fiction this time—to help them deal with the problem of the Great Ones.

Solut Mek Kem, who personified the problem of the Great Ones, came back onto the screen in front of Pawasar Pawasar Ras. The *kwopil* said, "We will speak with you, unless you would rather fight." By the way that came out in the Spanglish, and by the way he let his teeth show, Jennifer guessed he was half hoping for a battle.

"We will talk with you," Pawasar Pawasar Ras said. "War is the obvious solution; but for every question, there is an answer that is obvious, simple, and wrong."

"An interesting point of view," Solut Mek Kem said. Jennifer didn't know whether to be angry at Pawasar Pawasar Ras for taking her thought without giving her credit or glad he had listened to her. She got little time to think it over, for Solut Mek Kem went on, "In any case, we will also talk, I suppose. Do you possess nose filters such as the yellow-haired creature suggested? They might keep our two sides from fighting whether we so intend or not. The odor of *vodranet* cannot help but inflame us."

"I will put our technical staff to work fabricating filters," Pawasar Pawasar Ras answered. "We are similarly aroused—and not in any sexual sense, I assure you—by the way *kwopillot* smell. As for these non-Foitani, they are without a doubt ugly, but they have their uses."

From a Foitan, Jennifer knew, that was about as good a recommendation as she was likely to get.

Just when all seemed sweetness and light—or as close to sweetness and light as was practicable after ground and space combat between two groups each of which wished extinction upon the other—Voskop W Wurd reminded everyone that there were in fact not two groups involved, but three: "Nose filters? I don't give a putrescent fart about nose filters. I don't have to smell *kwopillot* to know they stink, either. Let them come after Rof Golan if they've the stomachs for it. We'll blast them into incandescent gas, and better than they deserve, too."

"Oh, shut up, you hotheaded fool," Aissur Aissur Rus said—hardly diplomatic language, but the most direct statement Jennifer had yet heard out of a Foitan from Odern.

Greenberg added, "Voskop W Wurd, think about this: Suppose they blast your people on Rof Golan into incandescent gas instead? That sort of thing happened all the time during the Suicide Wars. Wouldn't you rather talk first and then fight, given the chance? Think of it in terms of tactics if you don't understand diplomacy. Before you start a war, you ought to learn about your enemies."

"I know they are *kwopillot.* What more do I need?"

"You might remember they're also Great Ones," Jennifer said. "And remember how many ships you just lost. You might even remember that if the Foitani from Odern do talk with them and you don't, they might make common cause and leave you out in the cold."

"We would not do that," Pawasar Pawasar Ras and Aissur Aissur Rus protested in the same breath, so perfectly in chorus that the translator turned the two sets of identical words into a single sentence. Were less riding on this ticklish situation, it might have been funny.

However pious their protest, the two Foitani from Odern failed to convince Voskop W Wurd. "Of course you would, if you saw any advantage to it," he said. "You Oderna are like that, and what's more, you know it perfectly well. But if you think you'll make a deal with the perverts behind my back, think again. This creature has given me a good reason to enter into these talks: to keep you as honest as may be."

"Congratulations," Greenberg told Jennifer. "You've just made this a problem with three sides instead of two. Now the Rof Golani are ready to take on the Foitani from Odern again."

"Maybe there are three sides, but they're all going to talk," Jennifer answered. "When there were just two, they weren't talking. Sometimes even going backward is progress."

"I'm sure the Foitani from Odern would have agreed with you, the way they blindly loved the Great Ones till they found this batch of *kwopillot.*"

Before Jennifer could answer, Solut Mek Kem said, "If we are to enter into these distasteful discussions, *vodranet,* let us begin. We will send down a flier to bring your representatives back here to the *Vengeance.*"

"Come up into your lair?" Voskop W Wurd exclaimed. "Do you take me for a male altogether bereft of his senses? Treating with the Oderna is quite bad enough. Why should I tamely walk in and let you do as you would with me?"

"The wiser course would be for your envoys to come down to this research station," Pawasar Pawasar Ras said.

"That will not happen," Solut Mek Kem said at once. "We have already seen how you treat our kind when we approach this research base of yours. You merely seek the opportunity to dispose of our representatives quietly."

"Your behavior toward the Rof Golani in the precinct of the Great Unknown and toward the fliers of both sides in our recent dispute naturally leaves us suspicious of your good intentions," Aissur Aissur Rus said.

"We will not meet with you inside your station," Solut Mek Kem said.

"We will not meet with you inside your spaceship," Pawasar Pawasar Ras said.

"I wouldn't want to meet you *kwopillot* squatting over a waste-disposal hole," Voskop W Wurd added.

"These talks aren't off to what the diplomats call a constructive start," Greenberg observed.

Jennifer could only reply with a mournful shake of her head. If the parties allegedly negotiating couldn't even agree on where they would allegedly negotiate, the alleged negotiations looked anything but promising.

Then she said, "If the one side won't come down here and the other won't go up there, why don't you all come to the human ship, the *Harold Meeker*?"

"Yes, why not?" Greenberg chimed in. Under his breath, he added for her ears alone, "Anything to start this moving and give us a chance to get out of here." Jennifer let out a small, silent sigh of relief; it was his ship, after all, that she'd just proposed as a negotiation site.

"Come aboard the human ship for these discussions?" Pawasar Pawasar Ras said. "I would almost prefer bearding the *kwopillot* in their den." Jennifer blinked and wondered what the literal Foitani version was of the phrase the translator had rendered in that fashion.

"Go aboard a ship constructed by creatures?" Solut Mek Kem said. "We do not treat with creatures; we destroy them."

"You wouldn't be treating with us. You'd be treating with Pawasar Pawasar Ras and Voskop W Wurd," Greenberg said. "I might add, just so you know, we humans range across as much space as you Foitani did when your empire was at its height."

"You are telling me you are widespread and dangerous vermin," Solut Mek Kem said.

"I'm telling you we're widespread and dangerous, yes," Greenberg answered, "But to us, you are the vermin. You'd better bear it in mind."

Solut Mek Kem snarled at that. So did Voskop W Wurd. So did Pawasar Pawasar Ras, but not as loudly. Aissur Aissur Rus said, "Unlike others here, I have been into human space. They lack our race's straightforward character, but are not to be taken lightly. Success is the best measure of a species' true attributes; by that standard, their attributes are formidable indeed."

"They are small and weak and ugly." This time Solut Mek Kem and Voskop W Wurd said the same thing together. Neither looked happy at agreeing with the other.

Well, you Foitani are big and fuzzy and vicious, Jennifer thought. She kept it to herself. Studied insult of the sort Greenberg had given was one way of breaking through the arrogant contempt with which the Foitani viewed those who were not of their kind. Indulged in too often, though, it degenerated into name-calling of the sort five-year-olds used when they argued over toys.

"Just remember, the *Harold Meeker* is neutral ground," Greenberg said. Now he sounded calm and reasonable and persuasive: downright diplomatic, Jennifer thought—too bad the translator would wash all tone from his words. He went on, "Neither of you trusts the other's stronghold. If you can't trust my ship, at least all of you can distrust it equally."

"You are in the company of *vodranet,* creature," Solut Mek Kem said. "Before we would hazard ourselves, we demand the right to examine the proposed chamber for booby traps. *Vodran* treachery is notorious and despicable."

"Inspect all you like," Greenberg agreed cheerfully.

"We will have monitors present when the putative inspectors board your ship, human Bernard," Pawasar Pawasar Ras said. "Who knows what *kwopillot* might install under the pretext of removal?"

"That's fine, too," Greenberg said. "If both kinds of Foitani are going to be on the *Harold Meeker* at the same time, though, everything had better wait until you get those nose filters designed. I don't want anybody blowing holes in my cargo bay because he doesn't like the way someone else smells."

"One other thing," Jennifer added. "Everyone should remember that ships from Gilver are on their way to Odern and to Rof Golan. They'll probably bring big warfleets back with them. It would be nice to have some sort of agreement by the time those fleets get here. If we don't, I think another round of Suicide Wars starts right here. Is this fight worth your whole species?"

After she asked the question, she realized all flavors of Foitani could be intransigent enough to answer *yes.* When no one—not even Voskop W Wurd—said anything, she counted that a victory. The modern Foitani still lived in the long horrid shadow of the Suicide Wars; they knew too well what another round of such insensate frenzy would do to their surviving worlds. As for the newly revived Great Ones, perhaps they were still in shock from learning what the rest of their race had done to itself while they lay dormant through the millennia.

Greenberg prodded everyone along. "Have we decided, then, to meet in the cargo hold of the *Harold Meeker* as soon as nose filters make it possible?"

Again, none of the Foitani said anything. Again, Jennifer counted that a victory.

Being back in the *Harold Meeker* was almost as good as being home on Saugus, at least when the alternative was the Foitani research base. The lighting felt right to human eyes, the plumbing fixtures were as they should be, the chairs were made for human fundaments—and, best of all, the Foitani kept out of the crew compartment.

They were and stayed busy down in the cargo bay. They moved

around boxes and bales to create a clear space on the floor where they installed their own furniture and computer gear. The Great Ones cleared out bugs set by the Foitani from Odern. The Foitani from Odern, in turn, cleared bugs set by the Great Ones. The Foitani from Rof Golan took a turn clearing everyone else's bugs, and, presumably, planting a few of their own.

All the Foitani of whatever race who entered the cargo bay wore a little silvery button in each nostril—"The better not to smell you, my dear," as Jennifer said to Greenberg. The nose filters seemed to work; at least, no fights broke out between *kwopillot* and *vodranet.* Greenberg manufactured a little silvery button of his own and left it on an out-of-the-way box. A suspicious Foitan from Rof Golan found it and took it away, either to destroy it or to glean from it what he could of human electronics.

"Good luck to him," Greenberg said when he discovered his little bait had been taken. "It's filled with talcum powder."

He and Jennifer got Foitani electronics to study: they persuaded Aissur Aissur Rus to give them each a translator. "I'm bloody tired of having Foitani talking all around me without the slightest idea of what they're saying," she said.

"True enough," Greenberg said, "but now that we are supposed to understand them all the time, they'll ask more from us. You'll see."

That hardly struck Jennifer as requiring the mantic gift to predict. Greenberg was proved right soon enough, too. All Foitani factions distrusted the humans and affected to despise the *Harold Meeker.* All of them, however, distrusted their furry fellows even more and actively feared the headquarters of those fellows. Thus Jennifer and Greenberg spent a good deal of their time keeping the Foitani from one another's throats. When the actual discussions started, all factions insisted that the two of them sit in as mediators.

To keep potential carnage to a minimum, only two representatives from each group went inside the trading ship's cargo bay. Pawasar Pawasar Ras and Aissur Aissur Rus spoke for the Foitani from Odern, Solut Mek Kem and a colleague named Nogal Ryn Nyr for the Great Ones, and Voskop W Wurd and his chief aide Yulvot L Reat for the Foitani from Rof Golan.

At the first uneasy meeting, all three sets of purported diplomats spent the first several minutes standing around and glaring. Voskop W Wurd let out a series of ostentatious sniffs. His nose filters must have been working, though, or he would not have been so restrained. Since the Great Ones and the Foitani from Odern seemed willing to ignore him, Jennifer did the same.

She said, "Let's start this off with an issue that I hope we can easily deal with. It doesn't involve any quarrel between the newly revived Foitani and their modern relatives. In fact, it concerns us humans. Solut Mek Kem, do you really have specimen humans aboard your ship"—she almost said, *your tower*—"or are they just images in your data storage system?"

"The distinction is not as clear as you made it, ignorant alien creature," Solut Mek Kem answered. "They are at present potential, but could be realized in actuality. Do you seek live copies?"

Jennifer gulped. She looked at Greenberg. He seemed shaken, too. Taking a pair of genuine Paleolithic people back to human space would set every anthropologist's pulse racing, and likely would be worth millions. But would it be fair to the poor CroMagnons themselves? Could they ever be anything more than specimens? How could they possibly adjust to twenty-eight millennia of changes?

"Do you seek live copies?" Solut Mek Kem repeated.

"Let us think about that. It's not something we have to decide right now," Jennifer answered. If the cave humans had been frozen so long in Foitani data storage, a little longer wouldn't hurt anything. She went on, "Tell me the meaning of a term you use, one our translator does not interpret: *vodran.*"

"These are *vodranet.*" Solut Mek Kem pointed to the Foitani delegations from Odern and Rof Golan. "They are depraved and disgusting."

"They call you *kwopillot,* and say you're perverted and revolting," Greenberg said. "We needed a good deal of work, but we finally got them to explain what *kwopillot* were. I'm not of your species; I make no judgments about what's right or wrong as far as your sexual habits go. But right or wrong, they're an important issue here, one the human Jennifer and I need to understand. Could you please explain to me what makes these Foitani *vodranet*?"

"Explain to us as well," Aissur Aissur Rus added. "This is not a word my people comprehend."

"Nor mine," Voskop W Wurd said. "What could be vile enough for a stinking *kwopil* to despise?"

"You could," Nogal Ryn Nyr told him. Aissur Aissur Rus at least grasped the concept of diplomacy, even if he didn't always use it very well. Voskop W Wurd hadn't a clue, and infuriated other people with his own aggressive lack of tact.

"Stay calm, everyone," Jennifer said, wondering how she and Greenberg could make the Foitani stay calm if they didn't feel like it when they were about the size and disposition of a like number of bears. She went on, "We're here to discuss your disagreements rationally, after all." She wished disagreements about sexual habits more readily lent themselves to rational discussion.

"Let's try again," Greenberg said. "Foitani from what is now the ship *Vengeance,* what are *vodranet*? We can't have any kind of discussion if we don't all understand what our terms mean."

"Discussing matters pertaining to reproduction is not our custom under most circumstances," Solut Mek Kem said—a view he had in common with Pawasar Pawasar Ras, though he didn't know it. "It is doubly unappetizing when attempting to evaluate manufactured monstrosities such as *vodranet.*"

The Great One obviously bought tact from the same store that had sold it to Voskop W Wurd. The Rof Golani Foitan yelled, "You're the monster, *kwopil*!"

Greenberg yelled, too. "Enough!" Trying to outshout a Foitan was like trying to hold back a spaceship with bare hands, but he gave it a good game go. "Let Solut Mek Kem finish, will you? You can say whatever you want when he's done."

Fortunately, Aissur Aissur Rus supported him. "Yes, calm yourself, Voskop W Wurd. Gather intelligence before commencing operations." Advice set in a military context seemed to get through to the warleader. He snarled a couple of more times, but subsided.

"Solut Mek Kem?" Jennifer said.

But Solut Mek Kem, again like Pawasar Pawasar Ras, refused to go on. He gestured toward Nogal Ryn Nyr. *Let the flunky do the dirty work,* Jennifer thought—some attitudes crossed species lines. After a couple of false starts, Nogal Ryn Nyr said, "An unfortunate discovery made long ago is that the sexual physiology of Foitani is all too easy to alter."

"That is true enough," Aissur Aissur Rus said. "The problem of *kwopillot* would not exist were it otherwise."

"We, obviously, perceive it as the problem of *vodranet,*" Nogal Ryn Nyr said. "And with greater justice, for, after all, *vodranet* represent a distortion of the original Foitani pattern, which is to say, ourselves."

Jennifer needed a second to grasp the implications of that. The Foitani from Odern and Rof Golan caught on quicker. The bellows of outrage they emitted, however, were so loud and so nearly simultaneous that they overloaded her translator, which produced a noise rather like an asthmatic warning siren.

Finally Voskop W Wurd outroared everyone else. "You lie as bad as you smell! We are the true Foitani, the true descendants of the Great Ones, not you wrongsex badstink perverts."

"Were you there in those days, *vodran*?" Nogal Ryn Nyr shot back. "How do you know whereof you speak? We can prove what we say, just as, regrettably, you appear to have proved to us the existence of the Suicide Wars and their long and painful aftermath."

"Who would believe proof from a *kwopil*?" Yulvot L Reat said. By all signs, his charm easily matched that of Voskop W Wurd.

"The suggestion is implausible on the face of it," Aissur Aissur Rus said, more politely but just as certainly. "How is it that all modern Foitani worlds are populated by normal Foitani—Foitani I would judge normal, at any rate—and *kwopillot* are universally reckoned aberrations?"

"The reason is painful to me but nonetheless obvious," Nogal Ryn Nyr said. "It appears that, insofar as the Suicide Wars had winners, those winners are *vodranet*. No doubt massacres on planets reduced to barbarism completed the overthrow of normality by—your type."

In her mind, Jennifer saw mobs of big, green-blue aliens rampaging through bombed-out cities, sniffing like bloodhounds for the hated scent of those different from themselves. Would there have been massacres at a time like that? By all she knew, the Foitani were appallingly good at massacres; they almost seemed the chief sport of the species, as battleball was for humans. The picture Nogal Ryn Nyr painted had an air of verisimilitude that worried her.

It convinced Voskop W Wurd, too; he said, "You deserve being massacred."

"We thought the same of *vodranet*, I assure you," Nogal Ryn Nyr said. "Our chief mistake appears to have been waiting too long before attempting to stamp you out."

"I will believe none of this without proof," Pawasar Pawasar Ras said. "Nothing impedes you from making any claim you like, simply for the purpose of improving your own position at these discussions."

Solut Mek Kem tossed a silvery wafer onto the table, then, after some hesitation, another one, the latter in the direction of Voskop W Wurd and Yulvot L Real. "Here are the data," he said. "Shall we adjourn until you have put them in your computers and had the opportunity to evaluate them?"

"Let's wait one Gilver day—no more," Greenberg said. "Remember, fleets are on the way. You can start the fighting all over again, if you like."

Jennifer waited for Voskop W Wurd to say that was a good idea. But even the Rof Golani warleader kept quiet. He picked up the little data storage device as if it were a bomb. In a way, it was, for it seemed likely to blow away his misconceptions of his species' past. The four modern Foitani were quiet and thoughtful as they left the *Harold Meeker*'s cargo bay. When they were gone, the Great Ones left, too.

"Whew!" Jennifer sagged against a box which Greenberg had neatly labeled FOITANI ELECTRONIC WIDGETS. "Far as I'm concerned, the diplomats are welcome to diplomacy. Give me a simple trading run any day."

"You said it, especially when the people we're supposed to keep from each other's throats are as all-around charming as the Foitani," Greenberg said. "Right now, I would kill for a beer; Foitani kibbles and water aren't my idea of a way to unwind."

Jennifer quoted Heinlein. "One more balanced ration will unbalance me."

"I second that," Greenberg said, approving of the sentiment without recognizing the source. He went on, "The other thing is, I don't know whether we ought to be encouraging the Foitani to make peace with each other or to slug it out. If they do band together and have the technology of the Great Ones to use, they could turn into a real handful for the human worlds to deal with. But I can't say I'm eager to think of myself as the fellow who touched off the second round of the Suicide Wars."

"I know." Jennifer turned and thumped her head against the box of widgets, "The trouble with the Foitani is, they have no notion of moderation whatever. Whatever they think, whatever they do, they think it or do it all out, and they're sure anybody who thinks or acts differently deserves nothing better than to have her world blown up. Still, setting them at each other's throats—"

"How could we look at ourselves in a mirror afterward?" Greenberg walked over next to Jennifer and thumped his head, too. "The thing is, as best I can tell, getting them to slaughter each other will be a lot easier than making any sort of peace. And if they do have peace among themselves, how do we keep them from attacking all their neighbors? That seems to be the way they use peace among themselves."

"From time to time, when I remember, I think I'd like to live through this, no matter how it turns out," Jennifer said.

"Me, too." Greenberg made the hair-pulling gesture he must have started using when he had more hair to pull. He said, "I'm going up to the living quarters and take a shower. Maybe once I soak my head, all this will make better sense. Somehow I doubt it, though."

Jennifer rode up the lift with him. As usual, just being in an area designed by humans for humans cheered her up. Even the noise of the plumbing in the refresher chamber as Greenberg washed himself reminded her of other trading ships and of planets where she'd lived. The sound of Foitani plumbing reminded her of nothing but kidnapping and fear.

Greenberg came out with a towel around his middle. "You want a turn?"

"At what?" With a mischievous smile, she pulled down the towel. When Greenberg reached for her, she skipped back. "There, you'll see, the communicator will buzz just as we get started." Her words didn't stop her from undoing the straps of her coveralls.

Just as they got started, the communicator buzzed. Jennifer said something rude. Greenberg said, "You might as well have had that shower." He sounded more resigned than martyred.

Voice replaced the insistent chiming. "Humans Bernard and Jennifer, this is Aissur Aissur Rus. I would like to consult with you concerning the new information presented by the—" He hesitated, plainly not wanting to call them either Great Ones or *kwopillot*. "—by the recently revived Foitani from the Great Unknown."

"Go ahead," Jennifer said, knowing perfectly well that he would go ahead whether she invited him to or not.

"Although analysis can at this stage be only preliminary, the data appear to possess validity."

"Do they?" Jennifer wasn't surprised. Solut Mek Kem and Nogal Ryn Nyr had seemed very sure of themselves. But if the Great Ones had originally been *kwopillot,* that made a hash of everything the successor races believed about themselves and their past. In an abstract way, she admired Aissur Aissur Rus for being able to acknowledge that. He had a lot of integrity, but he couldn't be very happy right now.

He said, "As I stated, they appear to." He wasn't going to concede anything he didn't have to, integrity or no. Jennifer supposed she couldn't blame him.

"If they were *kwopillot,* how did you get to be *vodranet*?" Greenberg asked. "Did a mutation spread through the species?"

"In a manner of speaking, yes," Aissur Aissur Rus said, and said no more.

Having dealt with Foitani for some time, Jennifer suspected that abrupt silence meant he knew something he didn't care to let out. She tried to figure out what might make him reticent, and asked, "Was it by any chance an artificial mutation?"

More silence from the communicator. Greenberg drew his own conclusions from that and made silent clapping motions. Finally, Aissur Aissur Rus said, "If the records of the *kwopillot* are to be trusted, it was, yes." The translator was emotionless and Foitani from Odern didn't sound upset even when they were, but Jennifer knew he was anything but happy. He went on, "If they can be believed, our variety of Foitan was—engineered—for no better purpose than increasing the variety of sexual pleasure available to every individual."

"What's wrong with that?" Greenberg said, in spite of Jennifer's frantic shushing motions. With the Foitani attitude about sex, anything that had to do with sensual pleasure was automatically suspect.

Aissur Aissur Rus said, "I can conceive of no greater humiliation. How would you like it if your entire species had been deliberately redesigned, merely to allow a greater number of sexual opportunities to its members?"

Put that way, Jennifer thought, it didn't sound appetizing. It had to be all the more galling for the Foitani, who had spent the millennia since the Suicide Wars thinking their original configuration a horrible perversion.

"No wonder it is so easy to produce *kwopillot*," Aissur Aissur Rus went on. "They are, after all, merely a reversion to our former evolutionary pattern. If the Great Ones are to be believed, the origins of *vodranet*—our origins—sprang from the desire of some Foitani at the time to experience both male and female sexual pleasure, which are for us quite different in sensation. Others resisted the introduction of such a radical change into the germ plasm of the race, and the result—the result appears to have been the Suicide Wars."

Jennifer said, "Aissur Aissur Rus, of all the Foitani I've met, regardless of race, you strike me as the most adaptable. The new data from the Great Ones seem to have crushed you. What do the rest of your people think about what you've found out today?"

"Pawasar Pawasar Ras has gone into his quarters. He has spoken to no one. He has forbidden me to discuss this with any person. I have chosen to interpret that to include only Foitani. Our sexual difficulties and conflicts must be of merely academic interest to you humans."

"Not if we end up getting killed on account of them," Greenberg said.

"Yes, that might affect your thinking to some degree," Aissur Aissur Rus admitted. "Nevertheless, although I have always been one to favor the expansion of knowledge by whatever means become available—as witness my recruiting the two of you to help enter the Great Unknown—I would, for the sake of my species' future, be willing, indeed eager, to see that no mention of what we have learned here ever reached Odern."

"The only way to make sure of that would be to destroy the *Vengeance,*" Jennifer said.

"Were it in my power, I would cheerfully do so," Aissur Aissur Rus said. "Unfortunately, however, the *kwopillot* are much more likely to destroy me. Perhaps the soundest course would be merely to string these discussions along until the fleets from Odern and Rof Golan arrive, and hope they can rid us of the *Vengeance*—and our problem—once and for all."

"If it is, you've just given the game away," Greenberg pointed out. "Or don't you think the Great Ones are monitoring your radio traffic?"

"I say nothing they could not reason out for themselves," Aissur Aissur Rus answered. "They are depraved and perverse; they are not foolish." That was a distinction most humans would have had trouble drawing; Aissur Aissur Rus was able to be dispassionate even over matters that involved his passions.

"The other thing is, you don't think even full warfleets could beat the Great Ones, so you'd better talk with them," Jennifer said.

"You overstate the case," Aissur Aissur Rus said. "I am in doubt as to the likely outcome. The same must hold true for the *kwopillot,* else they would feel no need to continue discussions with us."

"You may well be right about that," Jennifer said.

"You humans have sexual deviants; I read of them in some of the materials in your course, human Jennifer. How is it that you have failed to destroy yourselves as a result of this fact?"

"That's a good question," Jennifer said slowly. Aissur Aissur Rus had a knack for asking good questions. That was probably how he'd come to be a leader of the team investigating the Great Unknown. He'd even gotten answers to his questions there, though by now he wished he hadn't.

Greenberg said, "One difference between Foitani and humans is that humans who differ sexually don't stand out in any obvious way like smell. When we fight, we fight about things like religion or politics or race, not sex."

Jennifer had what she thought for a moment was a brilliant idea. Then she realized that if it were all that brilliant, the Foitani would have thought of it for themselves. She threw it out anyway, to let Aissur Aissur Rus shoot it down if he wanted to: "Is there any chance that you and the *kwopillot* could put on perfumes that would keep you from going berserk at each other's odors?"

"There are no records of this succeeding," he answered. "The pheromones are most distinctive and most different. In any case, we need to be able to perceive these pheromones if we are to function sexually."

"Just a thought," Jennifer said, remembering that she had been about to function sexually before Aissur Aissur Rus called. She wasn't even angry at the Foitan; by now, she was used to getting interrupted.

For a miracle, Aissur Aissur Rus gave up about then and broke the connection. Grinning—he must have been thinking along with her—Greenberg stepped close. "Shall we try again, and see who calls next?"

"Sure, why not?" Then she asked, "What all do you have in the cargo bay, anyhow? A proper science fiction hero—or even heroine—would be able to improvise his way out of trouble with something that had been sitting there all along, just waiting to be used."

"You're welcome to look," Greenberg answered. "If you think you can improvise a way out of this mess with a bunch of trade junk, go right ahead and try."

"Maybe another time," Jennifer said. "Thing was, SF writers had the habit of putting things that would really help into cargo bays. I've got the feeling that real life isn't so considerate."

"The only thing real life has been considerate about is giving me the chance to fall in love with you. Even then, the damned Foitani keep calling at the wrong time."

"They aren't calling right now," Jennifer said softly.

"So they're not. Let's enjoy it while we can."

"What are you doing, human Jennifer?"

"Just examining cargo," she answered. Since the Foitan on the communicator had known her name, it was probably someone from Odern. Whoever it was, he had to have been monitoring her through some of the spy gear aboard the *Harold Meeker.* If she and Greenberg could sell that alone to one of the more paranoid human intelligence services, they would show a profit for the trip. The only problem there was getting the goods to the marketplace.

Armed with Greenberg's labels, with the computer to give her more details about what was in each crate or box or plastic bag, and with a pry bar, she wandered through the cargo bay, opening packages that looked interesting. A lot of them were interesting: pelts and spices and books and works of art and electronics. She knew she would have had trouble assembling such a rich variety of goods while keeping everything of high quality, as Greenberg had. He deserved his master rating. Somebody back in human space would be sure to want everything the *Harold Meeker* carried, and want it enough to pay highly for it.

Whether any of it would be of any use in keeping the next round of the Suicide Wars from breaking out was another matter. Maybe the Great Ones would admire some of the sculptures produced by a planet-bound Foitani race with which Odern traded, but that would not keep them from hating the artists as so many *vodranet.* Maybe the Foitani from Odern made marvelously compact and clever holovid scanners, but that would not keep them from loathing *kwopillot* or, if the claims of the old imperial Foitani got loose among them—as was very likely—from despising themselves as altered versions of the original Foitani plan they had been trying for so long to emulate.

Frustrated by her complete inability to find anything that might stop big, bluish aliens from massacring one another, Jennifer gave up and went back to the crew compartment. "Any luck?" Greenberg asked when she came out of the lift.

"None. Maybe a little less." She ran her hands through her hair, making tugging motions at it the way Greenberg did. "I should have known better. We don't have a writer stowing away a *deus ex machina* for us. We're going to have to do this ourselves, with our brains."

"Which haven't done us a whole lot of good so far."

"Isn't that the sad and sorry truth?"

Negotiations resumed the next day. The representatives of the Great Ones started things off by declaring in unison, "We have the solution to this problem."

"You and all your perverts are going to go and commit suicide so you don't bother decent Foitani any more?" Voskop W Wurd asked. From a human or an alien of different character, that would have been sarcasm. Jennifer thought the odds favored Voskop W Wurd's meaning every word of what he said.

Pawasar Pawasar Ras said, "Despite contemplation, I have not come upon anything that so much as approaches such a solution. I would be willing to hear one from any source, even a source as unreliable as *kwopillot.*"

"Yes, tell us," Greenberg urged. "Jennifer and I haven't found anything that looks like an answer, either."

"Very well." Solut Mek Kem spoke for the old-time Foitani now. "The solution is classic in its simplicity. You have seen that *vodranet* are an unnatural alteration of the true Foitani way of being. Is this so, or not?"

"We see that the Great Ones appear to have been *kwopillot,* yes," Aissur Aissur Rus said. "Nevertheless, since the Suicide Wars we have built our own reality."

"What you say, though, *kwopil,* appears to remain in essence true, if bitter," Pawasar Pawasar Ras said. "If we are to have emulation of the Great Ones as our goal, we must bear this unpalatable fact in mind."

"Excellent," Solut Mek Kem said. "Then to solve the problem of strife between *vodranet* and proper Foitani, all modern Foitani must abandon their present distorted way of life and become as we are. As you have seen for yourselves, turning a *vodran* into a proper Foitan is easy—and no wonder, given that you are poor modifications of the true form. In a generation's time, the race can be whole again, and as it always should have been."

"I like the way I am just fine, and if any stinking *kwopil* has the brass to tell me my get or I would do better as perverts, we'll see how well he does radioactive," Voskop W Wurd said. Great Ones, Foitani from Odern, and Rof Golani had all installed weapons checks outside the *Harold Meeker.* Had it been otherwise, Jennifer was sure the blue-gray Foitan would have blazed away with everything he had.

Pawasar Pawasar Ras, as was the way of the Oderna, was more restrained but no less certain. "I fail to see how this proposal in any way benefits the Foitani now living within our sphere. We gain nothing from it save the commitment of the *kwopillot* not to attack. Buying safety with capitulation is always a poor bargain."

"On the contrary: you *vodranet* gain a great deal. Being as you are, you have lost the possibility for lifelong relationships between the sexes, the cornerstone of Foitani society since time immemorial," Solut Mek Kem said.

"He has something there," Jennifer whispered to Greenberg. Greenberg nodded. Maybe stable home life would be more likely to lead to a stable existence for the species than the serial relationships in which modern Foitani perforce engaged. On the other hand, the Great Ones, while stable among themselves, had wreaked unmitigated havoc on every other race they met. Human notions of right and wrong were anything but universal outside humanity.

Aissur Aissur Rus said, "Perhaps, *kwopil,* we lack the characteristic you extol. Yet can your kind claim to understand our race's whole nature, as we do? We give birth and sire, nurture and conquer, all of us together. Why should we give that up? If you put the proposition to our species on any surviving world of the sphere, few would choose it."

"Then as I believed from the outset, there is no point to these talks," Solut Mek Kem said. "We will have war."

IX

For all his ringing proclamation, for all his departing from the *Harold Meeker* and flying up to the *Vengeance,* Solut Mek Kem did not commence battle at once. Jennifer took that for a hopeful sign—with how much justification, she did not know. Trying to provide more justification, for herself and everyone else, she called the Great One. There was, she knew, a real chance the Foitan would not deign to speak to her, she being, after all, a mere alien. In that case, though, she—and everyone else—would be no worse off than if she had not called.

As far as she could interpret Foitani expressions—which wasn't far—Solut Mek Kem was anything but delighted to get on the screen with her. But the Great One did not refuse. Again, she took that for a hopeful sign. "Thank you for being willing to listen to me," she said, wanting him to know she realized the concession was unusual.

"It is no inherent merit on your part, let me assure you." Like most Foitani, Solut Mek Kem did not waste politeness on beings outside his kin-group. "My willingness, as you call it, is purely pragmatic. I am forced to recognize that the situation in which I find myself is not that which I anticipated on returning to awareness. You are part of this new situation. I will learn what I can, then act."

From a Foitan, that was a miracle of moderation; had Jennifer had to devise a motto for the Foitani, she would have come up with something like, *Shoot first, then question the corpse.* She said, "I have two things I want to discuss with you. One, obviously, is the prospect of a second round of Suicide Wars."

"This, again obviously, has my interest, though many aboard *Vengeance* feel it would be worthwhile if it meant exterminating all *vodranet.*"

"But isn't it as likely to result in getting rid of all you *kwopillot,* or maybe all of your species?"

"This prospect is all that has stayed our hands thus far."

"Wonderful." The Great Ones used little in the way of subterfuge. They'd had scant need of it; whatever they wanted, they'd simply taken. Jennifer could have done with more socially lubricating hypocrisy—facing up to such straightforward self-interest was daunting. She said, "The other matter has to do with the humans you hold in your data storage system."

"Here we may have room for discussion, assuming it can be completed before fighting commences. As I told you before, I am indifferent to their fate," Solut Mek Kem said. "I asked you once if you wanted live copies produced for you."

"I don't think of them as copies. I think of them as humans," Jennifer answered. "I don't like the idea of their being in your hands; they aren't experimental animals."

Bernard Greenberg came up beside her. "That's right. What would you do if some other race held Foitani just to find out how they worked?"

"Destroy that race," Solut Mek Kem answered at once, his own voice as flat as the Spanglish words that came from the translator. "It has happened before. With the contemptible popguns in your vessel, however, you do not enjoy that option. You exist here on sufferance, not through strength. Remember it."

"We're here because Foitani thought we could solve a problem that baffled them, and the *Harold Meeker* is only a trading vessel, not a warship. I suggest you remember that, if you ever go into human space. We're better able to protect ourselves now than when you kidnapped those primitive ancestors of ours," Greenberg said.

Jennifer clapped her hands. From all she'd seen, matching the Foitani arrogance for arrogance was the best way to make them act in a humanly reasonable fashion. They could be made to respect power. Weakness they simply trampled.

Solut Mek Kem said, "I repeat, this matter is subject to discussion."

"Then let us come up to *Vengeance* and discuss it," Greenberg said. "I might point out that if it hadn't been for us, your ship would still be a tower and you would still be sleeping and impotent inside it." *And the war on Gilver would have only two sides, not a good potential for three,* Jennifer thought.

"A race that relies on the gratitude of others to cause them to act on its behalf is well on the way to extinction," Solut Mek Kem observed. "Nevertheless, you may come—in your own ship, not one furnished by either race of *vodranet* with which we have had the misfortune to become acquainted. Make note that I do this from considerations of my own advantage, not out of sentimentality." The screen blanked.

Greenberg called the research base. "I presume you were monitoring our call to the Great Ones' ship. They've given us permission. If you start shooting at us, it might annoy them. You don't want that, do you?" To Jennifer, he muttered under his breath, "I know damn well I don't."

The Foitani needed a couple of minutes to reply. Finally, a translated voice came back to the *Harold Meeker*. "You have our consent to undertake this mission, but you shall not under any circumstances enter into agreements binding up Odern in any way."

"We won't, Thegun Thegun Nug," Greenberg promised.

Another pause. "One day I must learn how I am so readily identifiable."

"It's your charming personality, Thegun Thegun Nug," Greenberg said. "What else could it possibly be?"

"Undoubtedly you are correct," Thegun Thegun Nug said. "Out." Jennifer and Greenberg tried to hold it in, but they both started laughing at the same time.

Greenberg began talking with the *Harold Meeker*'s computer, making sure the ship was ready for space. Jennifer waited for a furious call from Voskop W Wurd. The Rof Golani knew how to delegate authority, however, for the furious call that came was from his aide Yulvot L Real, accusing her and Greenberg of selling out to the perfidious *kwopillot* and threatening to shoot them down if they took off.

"If you do that, you risk starting the war with the Great Ones again," Jennifer pointed out. "Not only that, you might antagonize the Foitani from Odern. Besides, we're just humans, remember? Do you expect any self-respecting Foitani to take seriously anything we say?"

"Probably not," Yulvot L Reat admitted, "nor do you deserve serious regard."

"Thank you so much, Yulvot L Reat," Jennifer said. "Out."

"You're getting to be able to handle them pretty well," Greenberg said.

"Bernard, I don't think that's necessarily a compliment. I just want to get into space again."

"Me, too. Stuck on the surface of Gilver like this, I've felt like a bug with a shoe poised over it. Once I'm flying on my own power, at least I'll have the illusion of being a free agent again, even if I'll still be under the guns of *Vengeance*."

The *Harold Meeker* lifted off a few minutes later. Jennifer watched the Foitani research base fall away. The screen's view expanded to pick up the Great Unknown. The precinct looked strange and incomplete without the central tower, as if all roads led, not to Rome, but to nowhere.

The sky quickly darkened toward black. Stars came out. Jennifer looked at the radar pickup. On the way in to Gilver, it had shown a hideously jumbled swarm of ships and missiles, their tracks and signals jammed to provide them the greatest possible protection. Now only one artificial object swung in space near Gilver: the *Vengeance*. On radar, it was only the palest of flickering ghosts.

"I'm just glad to see it at all," Greenberg said when Jennifer remarked on that. "If we couldn't pick it up, that would be bad news for human space."

A Great One sent a peremptory signal. "Approach slowly and directly, or you will be destroyed without further warning."

Jennifer acknowledged, then shut down the communicator and sighed. "They're such a charming race. I don't know what those CroMagnon people will do once we get them back, but we have to do it. The more I think, the more it looks like I couldn't live with myself if I just left them there in that Foitani database."

"I know what you mean," Greenberg answered. "At first, I didn't worry too much about it—they were in storage and weren't aware of anything that happened around them. But if the Foitani can call them up again and again, do what they want with them every time—test them to destruction if they've a mind to, which they probably do—I think we have to get a live copy back, and get the Great Ones to wipe the files so they can't make any more."

"Sounds good to me," Jennifer agreed. She didn't know what sort of deal they would have to make with the Great Ones to accomplish that. Whatever it was, that price needed paying. Sometimes profit didn't count for everything.

The *Vengeance* might have been more or less invisible to radar, but before long it showed up visually in the *Harold Meeker*'s forward screen. It looked even bigger alone in space than attached to a planet . . . and no wonder. It wasn't the size of a spacecraft. It was the size of a baby asteroid—maybe even a toddler asteroid. It also bristled with weapons emplacements that hadn't been visible while it slept away the centuries on Gilver.

What worried Jennifer most was that the *Vengeance* was an artifact from the side that had lost the Suicide Wars. What sort of craft had the winners used? Whatever the answer, those ships were gone now, either destroyed in the war or turned on one another afterward. The *Vengeance* remained, huge and deadly and all alone, as if a last *Tyrannosaurus rex* had somehow been raised from the grave and turned loose in the jungle parks of modern Earth.

The abrupt voice came out of the speaker again. "Berth your vessel at the lock with the flashing amber light, non-Foitani."

Jennifer looked in the screen. The flashing amber light seemed bright enough to be visible down on Gilver, let alone from just a couple of kilometers away. She said, "They aren't crediting us with a whole lot of brains."

"We aren't Foitani. How could we have brains?" Greenberg answered. "They're giving us more credit than they think we deserve just by talking with us. For that matter, how smart are we? Here we are, going to dicker for specimens from our own race and for a way to keep the Suicide Wars from starting over, and what can we offer? What do we have that the Great Ones might want?"

It was a good question. As with a good many others lately, Jennifer would have admired it more had she had a good answer for it. She rocked back and forth in her seat, not so much concentrating as trying to relax and let her subconscious come up with one. In SF novels, inspiration was usually enough to let the hero make the story come out right.

Inspiration did not come. In any case, inspiration looked puny when set in the balance against the kilometers of deadliness of the *Vengeance*. A mammal in the jungle park might be more inspired than any *Tyrannosaurus rex* ever hatched, but that wouldn't keep it from getting eaten if the dinosaur decided to open his mouth and gulp.

A human in the jungle park, of course, would think about a weapon to use against a monster dinosaur. Put a character from a Don A. Stuart novel in that park and he would think of a weapon one day, build it the next, and eat *Tyrannosaurus* steak the day after that. The spacegoing *Tyrannosaurus* engulfing the *Harold Meeker*, unfortunately, had already thought of more weapons than any Don A. Stuart character ever born. The Foitani, whether ancient or modern, put a lot of effort into destructive capacity. If only they'd expended even a little more on learning how to get along with one another, they would have been much nicer people . . . and Jennifer wouldn't be coming aboard a spacecraft called *Vengeance*.

"If only . . ." Jennifer sighed. That was one of the ways old-time SF writers had gone about building a story. She wished it had more bearing in the real world.

The communicator spoke. "You may now exit your ship. You will find atmospheric pressure and temperature maintained at a level suitable for your species; at least, the specimens of your kind in our data store take no harm of it."

Jennifer's hands curled into fists. Those poor cave people were getting the guinea-pig treatment again, and then being—what? Killed? Just erased? She thought of the explorer in *Rogue Moon*, who died again and again as he worked his way through the alien artifact on the moon. She wondered if, like him, the CroMagnons in the Foitani data banks remembered each brief incarnation, each death. She hoped not.

"Atmospheric analysis," Greenberg told the *Harold Meeker*'s computer. It, too, reported that the air was good. Greenberg said, "I don't trust the Foitani any further than I have to." He cocked a wry eyebrow. "If they do want to kill us, I guess they could manage it a lot more directly than lying about the air outside."

"I don't blame you for not trusting them," Jennifer said. "I don't, either. And they have something we want, too. I only wish we had something they needed."

"A way for them to live in peace no matter whom they go to bed with would be nice. You don't happen to have one anywhere concealed about your person, do you?"

"Let me look." Jennifer checked a pocket in her coveralls, then mournfully shook her head. Greenberg snorted. Jennifer said, "Shall we go see if we can get our own remote ancestors out of their clutches—and maybe even ourselves, too?"

"That would be nice," Greenberg said. He and Jennifer went through the air lock one after the other. They peered around. The *Vengeance* was so big that Jennifer didn't feel as if she were on a spacecraft; it was more as if the *Harold Meeker* had inadvertently landed in the middle of a good-sized town.

A green-blue Foitan with a hand weapon stood waiting for them. Jennifer was tired of aliens ordering her around with jerks of a gun barrel. It didn't stop happening just because she was tired of it. The Great One led her and Greenberg to a blank metal wall. He rapped on it. A door into a small chamber opened. He chivvied the two humans inside, then rapped on the wall again. The door disappeared, in the way Foitani doors had a habit of doing.

The guard spoke to the air. "The offices of Solut Mek Kem," the translator said. Jennifer felt no motion, but when the Foitan opened the doorway again, the small chamber was not where it had been.

Solut Mek Kem stood waiting. "Well, creatures, shall we get to the dickering?" he said. "What can you offer that might persuade us to give you copies of these other creatures of your kind, now maintained in our data store?"

"That's not all we want," Jennifer said. "Once we have these—copies—we also want you to erase the archetypes of the humans you have in your data bank, as long as you can do that without causing them any pain. Can you do that?"

"Yes, we can, but why should we?" Solut Mek Kem said. "I repeat, what will you give in exchange for this service? Be quick. I am not in the habit of bargaining with creatures. Were it not for the service you rendered in slowing the outbreak of a combat whose result is uncertain, I would not waste my time here, I assure you."

"Oh, I believe it," Jennifer said. "Your whole species is like that. If only you were a little bit more easygoing—"

"What exactly do you want from us?" Greenberg demanded. "I can provide trade goods from Odern, and others of human manufacture. I can also give you information about what this part of the galaxy is like these days. Just how much, of course, is what makes a dicker."

"These things may perhaps buy you copies of your fellow creatures," Solut Mek Kem said. "They will in no way persuade me to clear our patterns in the matrices. Your kind, evidently, is a part of the galaxy about which we shall require a good deal of information. If you expect us to forgo it, you will have to do better."

"I've told you what we have," Greenberg said slowly.

Jennifer felt her face twist into a scowl. She didn't want to leave any vestiges of the CroMagnons in Foitani hands. "What would it take?" she said. "Do you want us to tell you how to live in peace with all the modern Foitani, who'd like nothing more than seeing every last one of you dead?"

"If you can tell us how to live in peace with *vodranet,* creature, you will have earned what you seek."

Jennifer looked down at her shoes. If only she were a Middle English SF hero, the answer to that question would have been on the tip of her tongue. Would Miles Vorkosigan or Dominic Flandry just have stood there with nothing to say? "If only . . ." she said softly, and then, a moment later, more than a little surprised, "Well, maybe I can."

"Go ahead, then, creature," Solut Mek Kem said. "Tell me how

I shall live in peace with beings for whom I have an instinctive antipathy. Instruct me. I shall be fascinated to imbibe of your wisdom." The *kwopil* used irony like a bludgeon.

"Actually, I can't specifically tell you how," Jennifer said. "But maybe, just maybe, I can tell you a way to go about finding the answer for yourselves, if you really want to." That was the rub, and she knew it. If *kwopillot* and *vodranet* wanted to fight, they would, and good intentions would only get in the way.

"Say on," Solut Mek Kem said, not revealing his thoughts.

"All right. You know by now that the Foitani from Odern brought humans—my people—to Odern because by themselves they couldn't safely enter what they called the Great Unknown—the area around your ship."

"We made sure prying *vodranet* would not be able to disturb us, yes."

"Fine," Jennifer said. "The reason the Foitani from Odern got me in particular is that I'm an expert in an old form of literature among my people, a form called science fiction. This was a literature that, in its purest form, extrapolated either from possible events deliberately taken to extremes or from premises known to be impossible, and speculated on what might happen if those impossible premises were in fact true."

Solut Mek Kem's ears twitched. "Why should I care if creatures choose to spend their lives deliberately speculating on the impossible? It strikes me as a waste of time, but with sub-Foitani creatures, the waste is minimal."

"It's not the way you're making it sound," Jennifer said. "Look—you know about military contingency plans, don't you?"

"Certainly," Solut Mek Kem said.

"I thought you would. If you're like humans at all, you make those plans even for cases you don't expect to happen. Sometimes you can learn things from those improbable plans, too, even if you don't directly use them. Am I right or wrong?"

"You are correct. How could you not be, in this instance? Of course data may be relevant in configurations other than the ones in which they are first envisioned. Any race with the minimal intelligence necessary to devise data base software learns the truth of this."

"Whatever you say, Solut Mek Kem. Do me one more favor, if you would: give me the connotations of the word this translator program uses to translate the term *fiction.*"

The Great One paused before answering, "It means something

like, *tales for nestlings' ears.* Another synonym might be, *nonsense stories.*"

Jennifer nodded. A lot of races thought that way. With some, the only translation for *fiction* was *lying.* She said, "We use fiction for more things than the Foitani do, Solut Mek Kem. We use tales that we know to be false to entertain, yes, but also to cast light on true aspects of our characters and to help us gain insight into ourselves."

"And so?" Solut Mek Kem said. "What possible relevance does a creature's insight into itself have to the truly serious issue of *vodranet*?"

"Bear with me," Jennifer said. "More than a thousand years ago, back when humans were just starting to develop a technological society, they also developed the subform of fiction called science fiction."

"This strikes me as a contradiction in terms," Solut Mek Kem observed. "How can one have a nonsense story based on science?"

"Science fiction doesn't produce nonsense stories," Jennifer said, reflecting that Solut Mek Kem sounded like some of the contemporary critics of the genre. "It's sort of a fictional analogue of what you do when you develop a contingency plan. Conceive of it as a method for making thought experiments and projections when you don't have hard data, but need to substitute imagination instead. You *kwopillot* don't have hard data about living with *vodranet,* for instance; all you know is how to go about killing each other. You need all the imagination you can find, and you need a way to focus it. If imagination is light, think of the techniques of science fiction as a lens."

"I think of this entire line of talk as a waste of time," Solut Mek Kem said.

"Let me tell you this, then," Jennifer said quickly, before he could irrevocably reject her: "The Foitani from Odern sought me out and brought me here specifically because I'm an expert in this kind of fiction."

"The foibles of *vodranet* are not a recommendation," Solut Mek Kem said, and she was sure she had lost.

But Bernard Greenberg said, "Consider results, Solut Mek Kem. Before Jennifer got here, you had been dormant for twenty-eight thousand years. The Foitani from Odern weren't close to getting into the Great Unknown, let alone into the *Vengeance* by themselves. Look at all that's happened since Jennifer came to Gilver."

Jennifer put her hand on Greenberg's arm. It was completely

in character for him to minimize his own role in everything that had happened so the deal could go forward.

Solut Mek Kem opened his mouth, then closed it again. Greenberg had managed to make him thoughtful, at any rate. At last the Great One said, "An argument from results is always the most difficult to confute. Very well; let me examine some samples of this alleged science fiction. If I think expertise in it might prove of some value to the present situation, I shall meet the terms you have set: copies of the creatures of your kind in our data stores, with the originals to be deleted."

Jennifer clenched her teeth. *Put up or shut up,* she thought. While she tried to decide which stories Solut Mek Kem ought to judge, she said, "May I please call Aissur Aissur Rus at the research base of the Foitani from Odern? He has a program that translates between your language and the one in which the stories were composed, one which we humans no longer speak."

"First scientific nonsense or nonsense science, I know not which. Now you haul in the *vodranet,*" Solut Mek Kem grumbled. "Do what you think necessary, creature. Having stooped so low as to negotiate with sub-Foitani, how could *vodranet* befoul me further? Speak—your words are being transmitted as you require."

"Aissur Aissur Rus?" Jennifer said. "Are you there?"

The reply came from nowhere. "That is a translator's voice, so you must be a human. Which are you, and what do you need?"

"I'm Jennifer," Jennifer said. "Can you transmit to the *Vengeance* the program you used back on Saugus to read Middle English science fiction? You thought someone who knew it might be able to give you insights on the Great Unknown. Now the Great Ones hope its techniques may help them figure out how not to fight the next round of the Suicide Wars." She knew she was exaggerating the Great Ones' expectations, but no more than she would have in arranging a deal of much smaller magnitude.

"I will send the program," Aissur Aissur Rus said. "I would be intrigued to learn the Great Ones' opinion of this curious human discipline."

"You aren't the only one," Jennifer said.

Solut Mek Kem turned to glance at something—evidently a telltale, for after a moment he said, "Very well. We have received this program. On what material shall we make use of it?"

"I've been thinking about that," Jennifer said. "I'm going to give you three pieces. You know or can learn that humans are of two sexes, which we keep throughout life, just as you do. *The Left Hand of Darkness* speculates on the consequences of discovering a world of humans genetically engineered to be hermaphrodites."

"That is not precisely similar to our case, but I can see how it might be relevant," Solut Mek Kem said. "It is not the sort of topic about which we would produce fiction."

"Species differ," Jennifer said. Mentally, she added, *You might know more about that if you hadn't gone around slaughtering all the aliens you came across.*

"You spoke of three works," Solut Mek Kem said. "What are the other two?"

"One is 'The Marching Morons,' which looks at the possible genetic consequences of some of the social policies in vogue in the author's day. The events it describes did not happen. Kornbluth—the author—didn't expect them to, I'm certain. He was using them to comment on his own society's customs, which is something science fiction did very effectively."

She waited for Solut Mek Kem to say something, but he just looked at her with those dark blue-green eyes. She went on, "The third story is called 'Hawk Among the Sparrows.' It warns of the problems someone used to a high technology may encounter in a place where that technology cannot be reproduced."

"Yes, that is relevant to us," Solut Mek Kem said. "Again, it is not a topic we would choose for fiction. I will consider these works. I will consider also the mind-set which informs them, which I gather to be the essence of what you seek to offer me."

"Exactly," Jennifer said, more than a little relieved the Great One understood what she was selling.

"Enough, then. You are dismissed. I shall communicate with you again when I have weighed these documents. You would be well advised to remain in your ship until that time, lest you be destroyed by one of my fellows who has less patience with vermin than I do. The guard here will escort you."

Jennifer fumed all the way back to the *Harold Meeker.* The worst of it was that she knew Solut Mek Kem had been trying to help. The Great Ones simply had no idea how to deal with any beings unlike themselves. No wonder they had started fighting when the split between *kwopillot* and *vodranet* developed among them, and no wonder they kept fighting until they could fight no more.

The only glimpses she got of *Vengeance* were of the open area around the *Harold Meeker,* which she'd already seen. Just a couple of Foitani beside her guard saw her, which she soon decided was just as well. By the way they automatically took a couple of steps toward her, she was sure they would have attacked if the guard had not been with her. They probably assumed she and Greenberg were prisoners. By the way the guard acted, that was what he thought. She didn't care to find out what would happen if she tried going in the wrong direction.

The quiet hiss of the air-lock gaskets sealing made her sag with relief. Logically, it shouldn't have mattered. She was just as much in the power of the Great Ones inside the *Harold Meeker* as she had been outside. But logic had little to do with it. The barrier looked and felt strong, no matter how flimsy it was in fact.

"I have a question for you," Greenberg said. "Suppose you do manage to convince the old-time Foitani you've given them a way to work out how to exist alongside their modern cousins? The modern Foitani don't have that way. You need two sides to have peace, but one is plenty to start a war."

"You're right." She paced back and forth, as best she could in the cramped crew compartment. "I'll call Aissur Aissur Rus. He's had some actual experience working with the concepts I'm selling. If anyone can interest the others in them, he's the one."

"Not Voskop W Wurd?" Greenberg asked slyly.

She rolled her eyes. "No, thanks."

As it happened, Aissur Aissur Rus called her first. She explained to him the deal she had put to the Great Ones, knowing all the while that Solut Mek Kem or one of his aides was surely listening in. She finished, "You were the one among your people who thought someone used to the ideas of science fiction would be able to help you on Gilver, and you turned out to be right. Do you think that you modern Foitani can apply this same sort of creative extrapolation to the problem of living with *kwopillot*?"

"That is—an intriguing question," Aissur Aissur Rus said slowly. "If the answer proves to be affirmative, its originator would surely derive much credit therefrom." *You would derive that credit, you mean,* Jennifer thought. Aissur Aissur Rus continued, "If on the other hand the answer is in the negative, the Suicide Wars begin again shortly afterward, at which point no blame is likely to accrue, for who would survive to lay blame?"

"Then shall I send you the same materials I gave to Solut Mek Kem?" Jennifer asked. "Maybe you can use them, if not to change Pawasar Pawasar Ras's mind, then at least to open it a little bit."

"What materials did you furnish to the Great One?" Aissur Aissur Ras asked. Jennifer told him. He said, "I presently have all of those, I believe, save 'Hawk Among the Sparrows.' We kidnapped you before you gained the opportunity to discuss the literary pitfalls of overreliance upon advanced technology. Though alien, I find them most intriguing documents. 'The Marching Morons' presents a quite Foitani-like view of what constitutes proper behavior under difficult circumstances—not that we would ever have permitted culls to breed as they did to establish that story's background."

"Aissur Aissur Rus, I'm convinced you would have gotten an *A* in my course," Jennifer said.

"So you have said, human Jennifer. I shall take this for a compliment. My people have said repeatedly, in talks you have heard and in many more conversations where you were not present, that they could not imagine how they were to live with *kwopillot.* I still cannot imagine how we are to accomplish this. Nevertheless, perhaps you have furnished us a tool wherewith to focus our imagination more sharply on the problem. If this be so, all Foitani will be in your debt."

"That's not something you ought to tell a trader, you know," Jennifer said.

"Possibly not. Nevertheless, you are at present in no position to exploit my words. Will you send 'Hawk Among the Sparrows' to me now?"

Jennifer fed the piece into the computer for transmission to Gilver. She remarked, "You know, Aissur Aissur Rus, you may end up as Odern's ambassador to the Great Ones if you do manage not to fight. You're better with strange peoples than any other Foitan I've met. Thegun Thegun Nug, for instance, would have ordered me to send him that story just now, instead of asking for it."

"He is an able male," Aissur Aissur Rus said stoutly.

"Have it your way," Jennifer said. "Out." She turned to Greenberg. "Now we wait to see what the Great Ones have to say."

"I hope we don't wait too long," he answered. "I'd be willing to bet Odern's fleet is already heading this way, and I have no idea how for from Gilver Rof Golan is. For once, I wouldn't mind if the communicator interrupted us."

"Is that a hint?"

"You know a better way to pass the time?" Greenberg asked.

"Now that you mention it, no," Jennifer said.

The communicator did not interrupt them. Like Greenberg, Jennifer almost wished it would have.

"You will report to me at once," Solut Mek Kem said, as abrupt as if he'd been Thegun Thegun Nug. Jennifer and Greenberg traded worried glances as they hurried out through the air lock. The communicator had been silent for thirty-six hours before that sharp order. Solut Mek Kem knew what he thought of the works Jennifer had given him. Whatever it was, he wasn't letting on.

A Foitani guard waited outside the *Harold Meeker.* Jennifer could not tell if it was the same one who had escorted her to Solut Mek Kem before. The guard said nothing and gave no clues, merely gesturing *come along* with his hand weapon. One of the nice things about human worlds, she thought, was that sometimes whole weeks went by without anyone pointing a gun at you.

She also could not tell if she and Greenberg went by way of the same moving chamber as they had the last time; one blank room looked much like another. Solut Mek Kem was definitely in the same office he had occupied before. The company he kept there, however, was a good deal different.

Some sort of invisible screen—possibly material, possibly not—kept the CroMagnon man and woman from either running away or attacking the Foitan. The two human specimens turned fierce, frightened faces on Jennifer and Greenberg as the guard led them into the chamber. They shouted something in a tongue as dead as the woolly mammoth.

"You have won your wager," Solut Mek Kem said. "The concept of extrapolation mixed with entertainment is not one we developed for ourselves, yet its uses quickly become obvious as we grow acquainted with it. I wonder how many other interesting concepts we have exterminated along with the races that created them." Jennifer had not imagined a Foitan could feel guilt. A moment later, Solut Mek Kem disabused her of her anthropocentrism, for he said, "Well, no matter. They are gone, and I shall not worry about them. The masters of these creatures—" He stuck out his tongue at the CroMagnon couple, "—are also now gone from our data store; I keep my bargains. The copies are yours to do with as you will."

Jennifer started to ask if there was any way for her to check that, then held her tongue. If the Great Ones wanted to cheat, they could; how was she supposed to thread her way through their data storage system? Besides, questioning Solut Mek Kem was liable to make him angry, and at the moment he was about as well disposed as a Foitan could be toward members of another species.

Instead of complaining to him, she turned to Greenberg. "I suppose the kindest thing we can do for these poor people is stun them and put them out of their sensory overload before they scare themselves to death." She wasn't sure she was exaggerating; half-remembered tales of primitive humans said they might do just that.

The translator carried her words to Solut Mek Kem. "I will take care of it for you," the Great One said. He rapped on the wall behind him to expose a cavity. From it he took a weapon smaller than the one the Foitani guard carried. He started to point it at the two reconstituted humans.

"Wait," Jennifer said quickly. She didn't know whether the Great Ones used the same stun beam as modern Foitani, but if they did, the CroMagnons wouldn't like waking up from it. She drew her own stunner from a coverall pocket, turned it on the man and woman from out of time. They slumped bonelessly to the floor.

"Let's take them back to the ship and get them into cold sleep," Greenberg said. "I don't want them awake in there and bouncing off the walls."

"Sounds good to me," Jennifer said. She spoke for the first time to the guard. "Honored Great One, could you please carry these humans to our ship? With your great size and strength, you can easily take them both at once."

Flattery got her nowhere. The guard said one word: "No."

She appealed to Solut Mek Kem. She got four words from him: "No. Carry your own."

She and Greenberg went over to the CroMagnon couple. Whatever had kept them in their corner of the room didn't keep the traders out. Greenberg grabbed the unconscious man by his shoulders. Jennifer took hold of his ankles. He was hairy, scarred, flea-bitten, and smelly. He seemed to weigh a ton, and Jennifer was sure he would only get heavier as she toted him.

"Let's go," Greenberg grunted. Neither of them had much practice at hauling what was in essence deadweight. Having the Foitani guard alongside watching did nothing to make matters easier. Getting the limp CroMagnon into and through the cramped air lock of the *Harold Meeker* was a separate wrestling match in itself. Breathing hard, Greenberg said, "Give him another dose, Jennifer. We want to make sure he's out until we can bring his mate back."

"Right," Jennifer said. Thinking of all the trouble a primitive who woke up too soon could get into on a starship was enough to make her blood run cold and then some.

After the man was sent into deeper unconsciousness, she and Greenberg went back for the woman. She was just as dirty and smelly and flea-bitten as her companion, but, fortunately, a good deal lighter. Greenberg once again handled the head end. "You know," he said, looking down at his burden, "clean her up a little—well, a lot—and she might be pretty."

"Maybe," Jennifer said. "So what?"

"It makes life easier." After a few steps, Greenberg noticed Jennifer hadn't answered. "Doesn't it?" he asked.

"A lot of the time, all it does is make things more complicated," she said. She thought about it for a few more steps, then added, "This one, though, will need all the help she can get. For her, I suppose, being pretty really is going to be an asset instead of a nuisance."

The woman was starting to wiggle and moan by the time they got to the *Harold Meeker.* Greenberg stunned her again before he and Jennifer hauled her through the air lock. He said, "Let's put them into cold sleep as fast as we can, before they start getting frisky again."

The cold-sleep process was designed to go fast, so it could be activated in case of sudden emergency aboard ship. As Jennifer hooked the male of the pair up to the system, she said, "What *are* they going to do when we get them back to human space? Nobody's had to deal with human primitives for hundreds of years; it must be a lost art."

"I haven't the slightest idea what they'll do," Greenberg answered. "I'm not going to worry about it, either. Whatever it is, it has to be better than life as experimental animals for the Foitani."

"You're right about that," Jennifer said. Just as she was connecting the nerve-retarder net, the communicator buzzed. "No, damn it, not now," she shouted at it. "We're not even screwing!"

The communicator ignored her. The words that came from it were more like snarls than speech. The translator turned them into flat Spanglish. "Answer me, you pestilential sub-Foitani creatures. When Voskop W Wurd deigns to speak with you, you are to take it as a privilege."

"Oh, shut up for a minute," Jennifer said, enjoying the license given her by a good many thousand kilometers of empty space between herself and the Rof Golani warleader. When the CroMagnons' pod retreated into its storage bay, she decided to notice the communicator again. "Now, what is it you want, Voskop W Wurd?"

"Whatever documents you have passed on to the Oderna and the *kwopillot,*" Voskop W Wurd answered.

"Oh," Jennifer said. "Yes, I can do that. I would have done it sooner, but it never occurred to me that you might want them, Voskop W Wurd. You hadn't shown much use for humans, you know." *You haven't shown much use for anything, you know,* she added mentally.

The warleader said, "If my potential allies and my enemies have these data, I should be privy to them as well. Explain to me why the Oderna and *kwopillot* are interested in these long effusions by sub-Foitani."

"I love you, too, Voskop W Wurd," Jennifer said sweetly. But the more minds trying to find avoid a new round of Suicide Wars, the better, so she did explain to the warleader the concept of science fiction and its potential application here. Voskop W Wurd was vicious, but not stupid. Jennifer finished, "The books and stories are examples intended to turn your thinking in the appropriate direction."

Voskop W Wurd remained silent for some time after she was through. At last, he said, "This new concept will have to be analyzed. We on Rof Golan write and declaim sagas of great warriors of the past, but have nothing to do with the set of organized lies you term fiction, still less with using it as if it were fact."

"Let me know what you think when you've looked at the documents," Jennifer said. "You might also want to talk to Aissur Aissur Rus. He comes fairly close to being able to grasp another race's point of view."

Voskop W Wurd switched off without replying—typical Foitani manners, Jennifer thought. But she remained more cheerful than otherwise. The Rof Golani hadn't dismissed the concept of trying SF techniques to extrapolate ways in which *kwopillot* and *vodranet* could live together in the same galaxy. From him, that was an excellent sign.

Greenberg said, "The primitives are down and freezing. Assuming we ever get to leave—and assuming we don't run into any more leftover weapons from the Suicide Wars—we shouldn't have any trouble getting them back to Saugus."

"Saugus? Why Saugus?" Jennifer said.

"For one thing, it's the planet you live on these days. For another, I assume the university where you're teaching is a good one." He waited for her to nod, then went on, "It ought to have some good anthropologists, then. I can't think of any people better suited to helping show our unwilling passengers how the world has changed since they were last around to look at it."

"Makes sense," Jennifer said.

"Saugus also ought to have a merchants' guild hall." Again, Greenberg waited for a nod before continuing. "In that case, I can do a couple of things. First, I can recommend you for master status." He held up a hand to forestall whatever she might say. "You've earned it, you ought to have it, and you're going to get it. If we do manage to get out of this mess, it'll be thanks to your expertise. And we'll show a profit, and a good-sized one. You qualify."

"All right." The only thing Jennifer really wanted was to get back to teaching and research, but she'd learned that having something else to fell back on could come in handy. She said, "That's one thing. What turns it into a couple?"

Greenberg hesitated before he answered. "The other thing I was thinking of was transferring my base of operations to Saugus. That is, if you want to turn us into a couple once we're back."

"Oh." She felt her face twist into a new expression as the implications of that sank in. The expression was an enormous grin. "Sure!" She hugged him.

"I don't want you to leap into this, you know," he said seriously. "I'm not going to stop trading, which means we may be apart big stretches of time. And I know you'd sooner stay at the university."

She shrugged. "We'll do the best we can for as long as we can. That's all we can do—that's all anyone can do. Right now, I don't want to worry about complications, except the ones that are keeping us stuck in Foitani space."

"Sounds sensible to me," he said. "People who borrow trouble usually end up repaying it at high interest." He yawned. "I wouldn't mind going into cold sleep myself. I'm far enough behind on the regular sort that I guess that's the only way I'm likely to catch up. Shall we try to gain on what we can?"

"When going to sleep sounds like a better idea than going to bed, does that mean the romance is starting to fade?" Jennifer asked. Greenberg had just pulled his shirt off over his head. He bunched it up and threw it at her. She tossed it aside, undressed, and settled down on her foam pad. She didn't care about romance right this second, only about how tired she was. Greenberg told the computer to turn down the lights. Sleep hit her like a club.

The communicator hauled Jennifer and Greenberg back to life after about five hours of sleep—just enough to leave them both painfully aware they needed more. A Foitani voice roared from the speaker. "Answer, humans," the translator supplied.

"What is it now, Voskop W Wurd?" Jennifer asked, rubbing her eyes and thinking wistfully of coffee.

"This is not Voskop W Wurd. This is Yulvot L Reat. The warleader ordered me to evaluate your concept of scientific lying."

Jennifer wondered whether the translator was hiccuping or whether Voskop W Wurd had given that name to the Middle English literature as he assigned it to his subordinate. That didn't really matter. "What do you think of it, Yulvot W Reat?"

"To my surprise, I find myself quite impressed," the Rof Golani Foitan answered. "It serves to make extrapolation palatable, and by extension even speculates logically about the consequences of propositions known to be false, something I had not imagined possible."

""Then you think it might let you find a way to live with the *kwopillot* aboard the *Vengeance?*" Jennifer asked hopefully.

"It might let us look for a way," Yulvot L Reat said. "I take that for progress. So will the warleader Voskop W Wurd, since we never imagined—"

Yulvot L Reat's voice vanished from the speaker. A moment later, that of a different Foitan replaced it. "Humans, this is Solut Mek Kem. We have detected ships emerging from hyperdrive in this system. Your presence compromises *Vengeance*'s defenses, to say nothing of the fact that your drive energies could be used as a suicide weapon against us. You will leave immediately."

"Of course, Solut Mek Kem," Greenberg said. "I'll order the computer to—"

"Look in the viewscreen," Jennifer said. Greenberg did. His eyes got wide. There was the *Vengeance,* some kilometers away and visibly shrinking. When Solut Mek Kem said *immediately,* he didn't fool around.

"One of these days, I'll see if our instruments picked up any clue of how they just did that," Greenberg said. "Right now, though, I think the smartest thing to do is put as much distance between us and the *Vengeance* as we can."

Jennifer did not argue with him. The *Vengeance,* at the moment, was the biggest target in the Gilver system. No, the second biggest—Gilver itself was still down there. "Can we monitor traffic between the ship and the ground?" she asked.

"Good idea," Greenberg said.

The first signal the *Harold Meeker* picked up was almost strong enough to overload its receiver. "Solut Mek Kem aboard *Vengeance,* calling the base on Gilver. We will act for our own defense only for a period of two rotations of Gilver, in which time you are to persuade your newly arrived ships to break off combat so that we and your leaders may extrapolate ways in which we need not destroy each other. If they continue to attack thereafter, we shall fight as we see fit. Be informed and be warned."

"We did it!" Jennifer exclaimed.

"We may have done it," Greenberg said, less optimistically. "Let's see what Pawasar Pawasar Ras thinks of the offer."

The answer was not long in coming. "Incoming Foitani fleet, hold your fire," Pawasar Pawasar Ras said. "This is Pawasar Pawasar Ras on Gilver. I speak without coercion of any sort. Know that the Suicide Wars arose out of conflict between our sort of Foitani and *kwopillot.* Know also that if we and they fail to come to terms now, the Suicide Wars will return; earthgrip will hold sway over us all, and it shall be as if our race had never existed. Let us talk and explore other ways before we fight."

A louder, shriller voice followed that of Pawasar Pawasar Ras. "I, Voskop W Wurd, Warleader of Rof Golan, declare the time for fighting is not yet—and who would dare coerce a warleader? Hear me and obey, my brethren of Rof Golan!"

"Do you think they'll listen?" Jennifer asked.

"I don't know." Greenberg glanced toward the radar. So did Jennifer. The screen was full of ships. All of them were headed straight toward Gilver, or rather toward the *Vengeance,* which hung above the planet in a synchronous orbit that held it right above the precinct of the Great Unknown—and the Foitani research station. He looked at the radar plot again and shook his head. "I don't intend to wait around and find out, either. Computer, initiate hyperdrive acceleration sequence, vector exactly opposite that of those approaching ships."

"Initiating," the computer said.

If Greenberg had hoped to sneak out of the brewing fight while no one was paying attention to the *Harold Meeker,* that hope lasted less than a minute. A Foitani voice came from the communicator. "Human ship, this is Solut Mek Kem. Why are you abandoning this solar system? Answer immediately or face the consequences."

When a Foitan said *face the consequences,* he meant *dig your grave and jump in.* Greenberg said, "When you pushed us away from your ship, Solut Mek Kem, you left us sitting right next door to you as the modern Foitani head in on an attack run. We can't defend ourselves; this is a trader, not a warship. This isn't our war, anyhow. If you were in our position, what would you do?"

"Extrapolate, please," Jennifer added, knowing the only way

Foitani usually put on other people's shoes was after those other people had no further use for them.

No answer came from Solut Mek Kem. Jennifer found she was grinding her teeth, made herself stop, then found she was grinding them again. *Vengeance* could swat the *Harold Meeker* out of the sky like a man swatting a gnat.

"Weapon homing!" the computer shrieked.

"It's not the *Vengeance,*" Greenberg said after a quick look at the radar tank. "It's from one of the ships that just came into the system."

"Can we get into hyperdrive before it catches us?" Jennifer asked:

"No," he and the computer replied at the same time.

Jennifer went over to the radar tank and watched the missile close. Others trailed it, but they did not count; the *Harold Meeker* would hit hyperdrive kick-in velocity before they reached it. That first one, though . . . some Foitani pilot, not knowing what the fleeing ship was, had been fast on the trigger—too fast.

Then, without warning, the missile ceased to be. Greenberg shouted and pounded his fist against his thigh. "Human ship *Harold Meeker* to *Vengeance,*" Jennifer said. "Thank you." Still no answer came. Less than half a minute later, the *Harold Meeker* flashed into hyperdrive.

Snow clung to the ground wherever there was shadow. The distant mountains were cloaked in white halfway down from their peaks; a glacier came forth from them onto the nearer plains like a frozen tongue sticking out. Musk oxen and the larger dots that were mammoths moved slowly across those plains.

Jennifer shivered. The synthetic furs and hides she was wearing were not as warm as the real things. Her arms were bare; gooseflesh prickled up on them as she watched. Her breath came smoky from her nostrils. "They'd better hurry up, before I freeze to death," she said, making a miniature fogbank around her head with the words.

"Maybe there's such a thing as too much realism," Greenberg agreed through chattering teeth.

On the ground a few paces away from them lay the two humans they had brought back from the Foitani sphere. The CroMagnons were just on the point of coming out of cold sleep. The anthropologists at Saugus Central University had gone to a good deal of effort to make them as homelike an environment as possible in which to awaken. Putting the temperature somewhere below freezing struck

Jennifer as excessive. Still, in trying to bridge the gap between Pleistocene and starship, who could say what detail might prove crucial?

The woman stirred. A few seconds later, so did the man. "Here we go," one of the anthropologists radioed into the little ear speakers Jennifer and Greenberg were wearing. "Remember, you people are the link between this familiar—we hope—place and what they've gone through. When they see you here, they ought to get the idea that they aren't really home, or not exactly, anyway."

"We'll see soon," Jennifer answered. Getting through to the primitives was going to be as hard as any first contact with an alien race. They'd have to learn a new language from scratch; not even theoretically reconstructed *Ur*-Indo-European went back even as far as a quarter of the way to their time.

The man sat up first. His eyes, at first, were only on the woman. When she opened her eyes and also managed to sit, his face glowed with relief. Then he noticed Jennifer and Greenberg. He rattled off something in his extinct speech.

"Hello. We're peaceful. We hope you are, too," Greenberg said in Spanglish. He held his hands out before him, palms up, to show they were empty. That was about as old a pacific gesture as humanity knew. Nobody could be sure, though, whether it went back to the Paleolithic. Everything the CroMagnons did taught researchers something.

The man didn't return the gesture, but he seemed to understand what it meant. He stood up and took a couple of steps forward to put himself between the woman and Greenberg and Jennifer. Then he spoke again, this time in a questioning tone. Jennifer made what she thought was a pretty fair guess at what he was saying. *You were there in that strange place with those monsters. Now you're here. What's going on?*

"Time for that special effect we were talking about," she whispered, for the benefit of the anthropologists outside.

Without warning, a holovid projection of a Foitan sprang into being, a few meters away from the primitives. The woman let out a piercing shriek. The man shouted, too, fear and fury mingling in his voice. He looked around wildly for a stone to throw.

"You!" Greenberg said in a commanding tone, stabbing out his forefinger at the alarmingly perfect image. "Go away and never come back!" He struck a pose that proclaimed he had every right to order the big, blue alien around so.

The projection winked out as if it had never been. The man

and woman shouted again, this time in amazement. Then they both hurried over to Greenberg, embraced him, and pounded him on the back. He staggered under the joyful blows. "They're stronger than they think," he wheezed, trying to stay upright.

"Congratulations," the anthropologist said into his and Jennifer's ears. "You are now a powerful wizard."

"Good." Greenberg turned his head. "Ah, I see the second part of the demonstration is on its way."

Four plates floated toward the humans. Each one carried a thick steak, a couple of apples, and some ripe strawberries. The primitives needed another few seconds to spot them. Then they started exclaiming all over again.

Jennifer intercepted two of the plates, Greenberg the other two. She passed one to each Cro-Magnon, then unhooked a couple of knives from her belt and handed them to the primitives, too. She drew one more for herself. Greenberg had his own. She cut a chunk from her steak, stabbed it, and lifted it to her mouth. Fancy manners could come later.

Neither of the humans just out of cold sleep had recognized the metal knife for what it was—they were used to tools of bone and stone. But they caught on quickly. The man grunted in wonder as the keen blade slid through the meat. He grunted again, this time happily, when the first bite went into his mouth. Jennifer knew just how he felt. After so long on Foitani kibbles, every meal of honest food was a special treat.

The primitives made the steaks vanish in short order. They inhaled the strawberries and ate the apples cores, stems and all. When they saw that Greenberg and Jennifer didn't want their cores, they made questioning noises and reached out for them. Getting no rebuff, they ate them, too.

"Hunter-gatherers can't afford to waste any amount of food, no matter how small," the anthropologist said.

The man kept trying the edge of the knife with his thumb. The woman said something to him, rather sharply. With obvious reluctance, he held out the knife to Jennifer. The woman held out hers.

Jennifer shook her head as she made pushing noises. "No, they're yours to keep," she said.

When the primitives realized what she meant, they whooped with glee and pummeled her as they had Greenberg. The man also reached under her synthetic fur and squeezed her left breast. She knocked his hand away. He didn't try twice. She gave him points for getting the idea in a hurry.

She pointed to herself. "Jennifer," she said.

"Bernard." Greenberg did the same thing.

The man's eyes lit up. He thumped his own chest. "Nangar," he declared.

He spoke to the woman. "Loto," she said, touching herself.

"I wonder if those are names or if they just mean 'man' and 'woman,'" an anthropologist radioed to Jennifer and Greenberg. "Well, we'll find out soon enough."

Language lessons went on from there, with parts of the body and the names of things close by. Nangar seemed to have an easier time picking up Spanglish words than *Loto* did.

"Maybe the tribe next door spoke a different language," the anthropologist suggested. "We think men traveled more widely through a tribal range than women, so he could be more used to using different words than she is."

After a while, Nangar pointed to the distant herds, which were actually holovid projections on a not-so-distant wall. With his own speech and many gestures, he got across the idea of hunting and then feasting. He gazed confidently at Greenberg all the while. Jennifer said, "After you got rid of that Foitan, Bernard, he figures you can do anything."

Greenberg grinned wryly. "No matter how big a wizard I am, I don't think I can put much nourishment into a projection. Maybe it's time to distract him again." He spoke as much to the waiting anthropologists as to Jennifer.

A few seconds later, a couple of the scientists came out from behind a boulder. They wore modern cold-weather gear. Nangar and Loto drew back in alarm. "Friends," Jennifer said reassuringly. She went over and smiled at the newcomers, patting them on the back. So did Greenberg.

The primitives remained dubious until one of the anthropologists reached into her backpack and took out several pieces of roasted chicken. When she passed them to Loto and Nangar, she found that the way to their hearts lay through their stomachs. Although they'd eaten a good-sized meal not long before, they devoured the chicken and gnawed clean the bones the anthropologists discarded.

The woman who'd given them the treat looked faintly appalled. "The way they eat, it's a wonder they aren't two hundred kilos each."

"The fact that they aren't tells you how often—or rather, how seldom—they get the chance to eat like this," her male companion answered. She thought it over and nodded.

Seeing that friendly relations had been established between the primitives and the people whose job it would be to guide them into the modern worlds, Greenberg and Jennifer strolled casually toward the boulder from in back of which the anthropologists had emerged. Several more anthropologists waited in the doorway the boulder concealed. They greeted the two traders with almost as much enthusiasm as Nangar and Loto had shown. One of them—in the crowd, Jennifer couldn't tell which one—let his hands wander more than they might have. Whoever he was, he didn't have Nangar's excuse for bad manners—he was supposed to be civilized.

Jennifer changed back into proper clothes with more than a little relief. Greenberg was waiting in the hall outside her cubicle when she emerged. "Do you want to hang around for a while and watch them work with the CroMagnons?" he asked.

She shook her head. "Do you?"

"No, not really," he said. "They do want us to stay on call for a few days, though, in case they run into trouble and need our familiar faces."

"I suppose that's fair enough." Jennifer sighed. "Still, what I'd like most would be just to start picking up the threads of my normal life again."

"Normal life? What's that? I gave it up when I decided to become a trader. But I will say that the time I spent in the Foitani sphere turned out to be even farther from normal than I was quite braced for myself." Greenberg smiled and set his hand on her waist. "Not that all of it was bad, not by a long shot."

Her hand covered his. "No, not all of it was bad. We wouldn't have ended up together if they hadn't kidnapped me, and I'm glad we did. But I'm a whole lot gladder to be back on a human world again and to feel fairly sure no one's going to shoot at me or fire a missile at my ship in the next twenty minutes."

"Amen to that," he said. "All the same, I can't help wondering whether the *kwopillot* and the *vodranet* decided to talk things over or just slug it out."

"I wonder, too," Jennifer said. "Still, you did the right thing when you got us out of there. We never would have found a better chance. But I would like to know what the Foitani ended up doing. I wonder if we'll ever find out."

"Hello, dear," Ella Metchnikova said as her path crossed Jennifer's on the edge of the university campus. "You must come over to my place before long. I have a marvelous new—well, old, I should say—drink that everyone loves. It's called a Black Russian, and you simply would not believe what drinking two or three of them will do to you."

"Set you up for a liver transplant?" Jennifer asked, not altogether in jest—some of Ella's concoctions seemed to have been invented by ancient temperance workers intent on demonstrating the evils of ethanol poisoning by horrible example.

Ella laughed heartily. Despite mixological experiments too numerous to remember, her liver was still intact—unless, of course, this was her second or third by now. She said, "They're not as bad as all that. And bring your Bernard by. Perhaps he'd be interested in the recipe as something he could trade to, ah, aliens."

To unsuspecting aliens, Jennifer thought, inserting a likely word into Ella's hesitation. Her friend meant well, though, so she said, "Maybe he would be—you never can tell. Still, I can't bring him by for a while; he set out on a trading run last week and he won't be back for a few months."

"Really? What an—interesting—arrangement. Do you plan on, ah, consoling yourself with someone else while he's off being primitive?" Ella's eyes went big and round.

"No," Jennifer said shortly. Ella Metchnikova wanted everything to be melodramatic. Jennifer had been in the middle of enough melodrama to last her a lifetime. But however volatile Ella was, she came through in a pinch. Jennifer said, "Thanks again for putting my stuff into storage when I disappeared."

"It was only my duty, dear," Ella said grandly. "Unlike some I could name but won't—Ali Bakhtiar, for instance—I was always sure you would come back."

"There were a lot of times when I wasn't," Jennifer said. Her kidnapping and spectacular return with Nangar and Loto had given her brief media fame on Saugus; she wasn't the least bit sorry it had finally started to wear off. She and Greenberg hadn't given the snoops all the lurid details of their adventures; that would only have made getting back to the ordinary course of day to day life harder.

Ella looked down at her watch. "Oh, dear, I'm late; I must fly. Call me soon, Jennifer—promise you will."

"I promise," Jennifer said. She was late, too, not a good thing to be on the first day of a new semester. Ella went on her way. Jennifer hurried across the campus. Out of the corner of her eye, she saw people stop and look at her. That had happened before the Foitani kidnapped her, too, but now about as many were women as men—a legacy of having had her face in the holovid tank a lot. She hoped that sort of attention would die down soon. She wanted no part of it. Aside from Bernard, all she wanted was to get back to work.

Even that wouldn't be easy. Almost in a trot, she went past the building where she'd lectured before notoriety came her way. No hall in that building was big enough to hold a class the size of the one she'd be teaching today. The enrollment was three times as big as she'd ever had before, which angered her more than it pleased her. She wanted students who would be interested in the material she presented, not in her as a curiosity.

She checked the time and swore. Five minutes late—that was disgraceful. But there at last ahead of her lay the second biggest lecture hall Saugus Central University boasted. The rear double doors were closed, which meant all the students were already inside. She swore again. They had to be thinking unkind thoughts about her. She fairly ran toward the special faculty entrance, which let her in right behind the podium.

She dashed up the steps onto the lecturer's platform. "I'm sorry, class," she began as she got her first look at this year's crop of students. "I—"

She stopped dead. She knew she shouldn't, but she couldn't help it. Better than three-quarters of the seats in the huge chamber were occupied by Foitani—blue Foitani from Odern, gray-blue Foitani from Rof Golan, green-blue Great Ones, purple and brown and gray and even pink Foitani from worlds she'd never heard of. Hundreds of pairs of round, attentive, deeply colored eyes bored into hers.

They didn't kill each other off, she thought. *Good—I think.* She took a deep breath and started her lecture. Translators droned to turn her words into ones Foitani could understand. Somehow she got through it. "I'm sorry; I can't take questions today," she said when she was through.

She hurried out of the lecture hall, found a public phone, fed her access card into it, and checked the listings. Then she made a call. A man's face appeared on the screen. "Universal Protective Services," he said. "We're the best on Saugus."

"You'd better be," she told him.